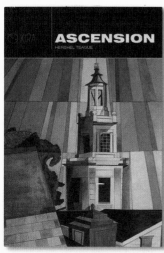

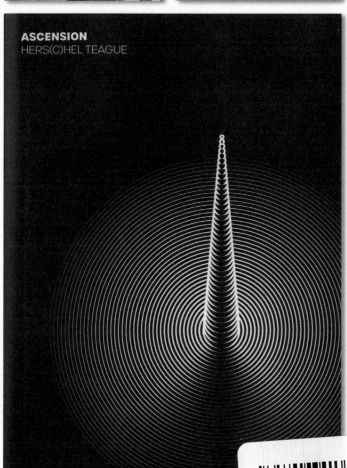

Clockwise: Kira editions, French paperback, 1982. Cover: *The Tower,* 1920, Charles Demuth | Moon Unit Press, US paperback, 2004. Cover: Garth Gardoni | Five Avenues, UK paperback, 1987. Cover: Vince Wilson | Thames, UK paperback, 1974. Cover: Chris Foss | Delgado Science Fiction, UK paperback, 1970. Cover: *The Tower of Babel,* Athanasius Kircher, 1679 | Paperworks Classics, UK hardback, 2017. Cover: Rian Hughes/Device

0   0   1   1 1 10   1   1 0 010 1 1   0   01 0110 0 0100 100

011 0 0 0 1 00 1110 0 0 11 0011101 101 100011 110110100 1

110100111011 011111111101000 0110001110011010100011100110

1010100101010101010101010101011   1011010110010100110100100001010

0100111001110101001101101011101010101110011100010100111100

0011001011001100101110111010001010001100101011111001100

POST-DETECTION PROTOCOLS

00011 Daniel Novák scanned down the list. Of *course* there were protocols. Someone, somewhere, always thinks of these things, even if they have no idea what, in practice, might actually happen. Gives everyone involved the impression that they're in control, that they know what they're doing, that the usual rules still apply.

That this does not, fundamentally, change *everything*.

Daniel had once helped write a leaflet entitled *How to Protect Your Family in the Event of a Nuclear Exchange*. While the graphic descriptions of radiation poisoning had not made it through to the final draft, an illustration of a relaxed nuclear (*hah*) family hiding under the kitchen table and an acknowledgement that the banking system may suffer some disruption had. Deliberate misdirection, designed to avoid panic? Or simply the human inability to fathom the true impact of events, even as they unfold around you? He would, in the weeks and months ahead, be reminded more than once of that leaflet and its naive optimism.

Daniel had convened an impromptu meeting of staff in the otherwise empty café of the Jodrell Bank Discovery Centre. Built to serve the rising number of curious visitors, it had a commanding view of the Lovell Telescope's impressive 250-foot dish, held aloft on a whitewashed steel lattice. Lit by the low morning sun, it resembled an enormous game of KerPlunk set up for play. Along the wall, seven clocks gave the present time in GMT, Jodrell Atomic, Local Sidereal, and on Venus, Mars, Jupiter and the surface of a black hole, where it was currently ten past one, and, Daniel imagined, lunchtime . . . though for a black hole, it was always lunchtime. They tended to have an appetite.

His staff were all present: Leonie Orlov, George Pallenberg, visiting Canadian Freeman Craw, bemused University of Manchester intern Eliza Adams. Admiral Albert Fitzwilliam, of course, his close friend and second-in-command for more years than he could remember, plus a handful of others he only worked with indirectly. They had all been briefed. Forbidden from discussing their findings with anyone outside

1

their small group until he could figure out what they should do, Daniel had confined them to the building. All those present had acquiesced to the virtual quarantine, a state of affairs that his commandeering of Jodrell's Planet Pavilion Café and its catering services he hoped might mitigate. Today the Discovery Centre, its displays, the Orrery, the gift shop and the grounds themselves had remained closed to visitors, and two staff had been posted at the main gate to cheerfully turn people away.

He had his laptop open in front of him and was skim-reading a PDF. The staff struggled to hear him over the crash of cutlery. His thinning grey hair, still peaked to a Brylcreemed quiff, was combed neatly back over his ears, framing his angular but kindly face; his lively engagement belied his approaching and long-postponed retirement, one that now looked likely to be pushed back yet again. As always, he wore an immaculate 1950s-cut bespoke suit in thornproof Harris Tweed and a vintage silver *Dan Dare* tiepin; forty years ago, he'd not have looked out of place as a daring young chap on a recruitment poster for Bomber Command. His voice still held the precise and measured BBC diction that seemed a perfect fit for Jodrell Bank's unique place in British history, one that had begun in 1945 and was still very much unfolding.

"So . . . this is what the best documentation I can find online has to say about our, uh, our situation. Are you all ready for this?"

Albert, standing behind him with a cold coffee in a mug with the dish-and-star Jodrell Bank logo, had already glanced through the first paragraph over his shoulder. "Go on. Read it aloud."

"Protocols for an Extraterrestrial Intelligence Signal Detection

"One wonders how they intend to enforce all this. Right, so—

"We, the institutions and individuals participating in the search for extraterrestrial intelligence, recognize it as an integral aspect of the peaceful project of space exploration, a project undertaken for the common benefit of all mankind. In consideration of the profound significance of detecting evidence of extraterrestrial intelligence, even though the probability of detection may be low—"

"Ha."

"—we restate the objectives which commit parties to the Treaty to inform the Secretary General of the United Nations, as well as the public and the international scientific community, of the results of their space exploration activities."

Leonie Orlov leaned forward and spoke through a mouthful of almond croissant. "Do we have the Secretary General's number? Is there a *link?*"

Daniel held his hand up for silence. "Recognizing that any initial detection may be incomplete or ambiguous and thus require careful examination as well as confirmation, and that it is essential to maintain the highest standards of scientific responsibility and credibility—"

"Responsible and credible. That's us."

"Albert. —we agree to observe the following principles for disseminating information in regard to a putative detection of extraterrestrial intelligence, colon.

"Then there's a list. 1. Any individual, public or private research institution or governmental agency that believes it has detected a signal from or other evidence of extraterrestrial intelligence, open brackets, the discoverer, close brackets, should seek to verify that the most plausible explanation for the evidence is the existence of extraterrestrial intelligence rather than some other natural or anthropogenic phenomenon before making any public announcement. If evidence indicating the existence of extraterrestrial intelligence is ambiguous, the discoverer may disseminate the information as appropriate."

He glanced up from his screen to see the others watching him intently. Eliza raised her hand. She sensed that the veterans present knew little more than she did. "Excuse me. Somehow I thought dealing with this eventuality might be part of, you know, your *training*, or something?"

Daniel couldn't help but smile. "You're learning something important today about the way science happens. If we could see into the future, we'd be astrologers, not astronomers. Take notes. And then when you're in my position, you can do better. Where was I?

"2. Prior to making a public announcement, the discoverer should promptly inform all other observers or research organizations that are parties to this declaration so that those other parties may seek to confirm the discovery by independent observations at other sites, and a network established to enable continuous monitoring of the signal or phemonemon, sorry phenomenon." *Breathe, Daniel.* "Parties to this declaration should not make any public announcement until it is determined whether it is or is not credible evidence for the existence of extraterrestrial intelligence. The discoverer should inform his/her relevant national authorities.

"3. After concluding that the evidence is credible and after informing other relevant parties of this declaration, the discoverer should announce the discovery through the Central Bureau for Astronomical Telegrams— *telegrams? When* was this written? —of the International Astronomical

Union, and inform the Secretary General of the United Nations in accordance with Article XI of the, capitalised words, Treaty on Principles Governing the Activities of States in the Exploration and Use of Outer Space comma, still capitalised Including the Moon and Other Bodies end capitalisation.

"Sounds like they were trying for some kind of acronym: TPGA? TOPGAS? EAUOOSITMAOB? Eearghoositonmaboob? *Heh—*"

"OK, Al. *Anyway.* Because of their demonstrated interest in and expertise concerning the question of the existence of extraterrestrial intelligence blah blah – I'm skipping a few sentences here – a confirmed detection of extraterrestrial intelligence should be disseminated promptly, openly, and widely ummhum. The discoverer should have the privilege of making the first public announcement."

Daniel looked over the top of his glasses at Leonie, who was grinning inanely. "I have to admit, I didn't think it would happen *exactly* like this."

"4? No, 5. All data necessary for confirmation of detection should be made available to the international scientific community through publications, meetings, conferences, and other appropriate means. Including, one presumes, telegraph."

"And-slash-or carrier pigeon."

"The discovery should be confirmed and monitored and any data should be recorded and stored permanently to the greatest extent feasible and practicable, in a form that will make it available for further analysis and interpretation. Let's assume they mean digitally, on the internet. These recordings – recordings, like on cassette tape? This Alien mix tape should be made available to the international institutions listed above and to members of the scientific community that's us for further objective analysis and interpretation.

"6. If the evidence of detection is in the form of electromagnetic signals as opposed to a letter, Post-it, or telepathically induced message from Xenu the parties to this declaration should seek international agreement to protect the appropriate frequencies by exercising procedures available through the International Telecommunication Union."

Daniel opened another browser window and cut and pasted the name into Google. "The International Telecommunication Union *do* still exist. They have a great Gerry Anderson meets *Tom Corbett, Space Cadet* style logo, it has to be said. Immediate notice should be sent to the Secretary General of the ITU in Geneva, who may include a request to minimize transmissions on the relevant frequencies in the – the *Weekly Circular.*"

Albert convulsed, involuntarily spraying coffee onto Daniel's screen. He gulped, then wiped his mouth on his sleeve. "'*Weekly – flippin' –*

circular'? So what, we type it up, photocopy it, staple it together like a parish magazine, then pop it in the *post?*"

"Ahaha. Heh." Daniel strained to hold a solemn expression as he again held up a hand, palm outward, to request composure from those around the table. "Serious faces, please. This is important." After a moment or two the laughter subsided, and he continued to read. "The Secretariat, in conjunction with advice of the Union's Administrative Council, should explore the feasibility and utility of convening an Extraordinary Administrative Radio Conference – ah, aha, heh, to, to deal with the matter.

"Ahem. There's more. No response to a signal or other evidence of extraterrestrial intelligence should be sent until appropriate international consultations have taken place. The SETI Committee of the International Academy of Astronautics, in coordination with Commission 5—"

"Sounds mysterious."

"—of the International Astronomical Union will oversee the subsequent handling of the data. Should credible evidence of extraterrestrial intelligence be discovered, an international committee of scientists and other experts – that's us again – should be established to serve as a focal point for continuing analysis of all observational evidence collected in the aftermath of the discovery, and also to provide advice on the release of information to the public."

Daniel scrolled down further but was met with empty space. He'd reached the end of the document. "That's it." He closed his laptop.

"Thoughts?"

The cacophony of voices competing for his attention could be heard as far away as the gift shop.

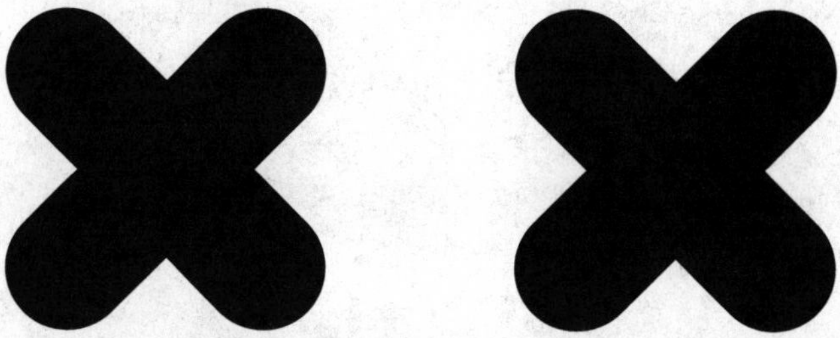

Also by Rian Hughes

Typodiscography
Logo-a-Gogo
I Am a Number
Soho Dives, Soho Divas
Cult-ure: Ideas can be Dangerous
Yesterday's Tomorrows
Lifestyle Illustration of the '50s
Lifestyle Illustration of the '60s
Custom Lettering of the '20s and '30s
Custom Lettering of the '40s and '50s
Custom Lettering of the '60s and '70s
On the Line
Tales from Beyond Science
Art, Commercial
Dare
The Science Service

This is his first novel.

ABRAMS
The Art of Books

RIAN HUGHES

A Novel

THE OVERLOOK PRESS

Something Just Occurred To Me

I had a new idea –
it whispered in my ear:
"I need someone to think me
before I disappear."

Clear and unambiguous,
well-spoken and urbane.
Everything I wished to know
it promised to explain.

I ran it up the flagpole.
Entertained it for a while.
Impassioned and seductive –
new ideas can beguile!

They're potent and persuasive
when on fertile ground they're sown.
(Or one hasn't yet had many
good ideas of one's own.)

Of course this new idea
could be either right or wrong.
It needed to convince me:
why should I play along?

"Good point," said the idea.
"Many others of sound mind
have had the *same* idea.
C'mon, don't get left behind!"

Is that a decent reason?
Just 'cause others think you're true?
You need to have good reason
to believe the things you do.

"Reason?" it reflected.
"What need have I of *that?*
You just have to *believe* me.
Small ask! Now, less chit-chat!"

Should one take ideas on faith?
Or turn them on their head?
Look at them from all angles?
Think the opposite, instead?

"Don't test me," it retorted.
"I'm just simply right and true.
I've no need to prove my worth
to be thought by such as *you.*"

Its condescending manner
made me pause to think about –
Ideas. Reason. Meaning.
And just how we sort them out.

Ideas stick together
and then tend to form a clique,
called an 'ideology'
(*form, pattern,* from the Greek).

"*Our* gang has *this* idea.
Are *you* with *them,* or *us?*"
Truth's contingent on my *tribe?*
Belong, don't make a fuss?

No idea's above debate.
They don't require respect.
If they are *good* ideas
you need not be circumspect.

Ideas don't have feelings,
they are not like you or I.
Only those who *have* them do:
the idea's Alumni.

Unlike a certain notion
We are free to change our mind;
to take on *new* ideas
and leave bad ones far behind.

The idea sounded flustered.
"Hold on! I could be right!
Think of what you stand to lose!
To doubt's just impolite!"

Are ideas all we are?
Our muse to reassure?
Outliving us in word and deed –
all that can endure?

Considering the options,
I turned around to find
the idea had departed –
no trace was left behind.

Was it a *good* idea?
I ask myself that now.
Are *we* a good idea?
What *are* ideas, anyhow?

BOOK ONE

Analysis

Avec vingt-cinq soldats de plomb il a conquis le monde.
—Quoted by Jules Claretie, 1904. Original author unknown

INTELLIGENCIA
MEMETIC ENGINEERING

BUSINESS PLAN

Nixon Rappaport crossed something off a list. "Big sign with the company name and logo: *check*. All Jack's packing crates: *check*. What else? Seating— we still need to get some chairs, but I'm going to draw the line at bean bags. We're *professionals* now – let's leave that kind of malarkey to those marketing agencies with their foot-high quotes about 'social media being the petrol to pour on your idea fire'."

"Can this be my window?" Harriet looked down at the early drinkers outside the Hoxton Square Bar and Kitchen. She remembered it, just, as the Bass Clef, a pre-gentrification East End music venue, but now it was a restaurant serving the local design and advertising start-ups and the more affluent overflow from the City's financial district just the other side of Liverpool Street. She assumed that the business types sitting downstairs in the sun with their flat whites and red-lined suits came out East in search of the hipster lifestyle that they'd read about in *The Stylist*, whatever a 'lifestyle' was supposed to be – as far as she could tell, it was simply the age-old dance of boys in search of girls and girls in search of boys, but now with the addition of overpriced lattes.

Jack was unpacking the new iMacs. The three top-of-the-range widescreen monsters had been their major outlay – that, and the first month's rent, in advance. He glanced up from a box of cables that had managed to get themselves entwined like last year's Christmas-tree lights. "Sure, I suppose. Nixon?"

"If you can see your screen without shades, go for it. Jack – you'll be keeping pale and interesting over there in the corner, I assume?"

The office had come partially furnished, courtesy of the previous tenants who Nixon guessed had spent more on their custom-made Danish desks and lighting than they had ever managed to clear in profit. Intelligencia was the beneficiary – a short lease, sure, but all they had to do was move in, set up the kit and stock the fridge. It was a disconcerting step up, used as they were to working surrounded by a mix-and-match of second-hand furniture, Ikea shelving and antique filing cabinets they'd liberated from skips. Having worked from all manner of basements and back rooms, Jack was happy they now had a place that made it feel as if they were doing this for real, that this venture wasn't just some *folie à trois* they were spinning between themselves.

Nixon positioned his speakers at either end of a high shelf that ran the entire length of the back wall. The floor was sanded and varnished parquet, pierced by the filled bolt-holes of long-vanished heavy machinery and bruised by dark oil stains and rectangles of rust, a ghostly reminder of the East End's industrial past. The floor had originally been open-plan; the building's mix of apartment conversions and small commercial units now fitted their more compact and less power-hungry needs into the subdivided space. The brick walls had been whitewashed, but a bathtub ring caused by the cast-iron trolleys that used to move goods around the shopfloor was still visible at waist height. The widescreen metal-framed windows, beautifully curved at the one corner, were also original.

A glass partition separated the conference room from the main floor. The three of them had sat around the large oval table the evening they'd been given the keys, eating a Thai takeaway and drinking warm white wine of indeterminate vintage out of plastic cups.

Nixon had something on his mind. "Chaps – we're never going to use this conference room as an actual *conference* room, are we?"

"Nope." Jack could already see where this was going. He had never had an actual conference room meeting – most of their clients were in Japan or the US, and Skype had become the main means of keeping in contact face-to-face.

"Do you two object if I use it as my office?"

Harriet's and Jack's eyes locked for a second. Nixon, having put up the funding for this venture, could have simply insisted and they wouldn't have been in a position to refuse; however, for the two of them it simply wasn't an issue. To Nixon the office was his chance to play at being a Big Businessman, and the trappings – the company letterhead, the London address – were part of what gave him the buzz.

If Harriet was less concerned about such things, Jack was pretty much oblivious. A secure place to set up, broadband, and a decent working atmosphere were all he required. He didn't have the time or inclination to arrange his desk accessories and wallcharts, or hang his framed Harvard degree on the wall.

A week later the crates were neatly stacked against the blank wall next to the kitchenette, for the most part still unpacked. The desks were sparsely equipped with the new computers, smaller secondary screens placed beside them for email and sundry paperwork, and fan heaters and back-up hard drives had been installed on shelves slung underneath. Cabling had been temporarily duct-taped to the floor to prevent anyone tripping, and two of Harriet's framed woodblock type prints were propped against the wall under the long shelf, waiting for screws on which they could be hung.

Most importantly, the Intelligencia logo had been ostentatiously mounted on the wall at the top of the stairs. Jack had named the company before the others had come on board, and as he owned the web address and had already put up a basic Wordpress site, they had deferred on a rebrand.

The logo was a simple square, in black on a white ground. Underneath, in Microgramma Bold Extended, was the company name:

INTELLIGENCIA

Jack had chosen the typeface because Kubrick had used it in *2001: A Space Odyssey.* The G and C were shaped like a cathode-ray TV screen, yesteryear's cutting-edge tech. He had again seen it in the insignia of s.h.a.d.o. – the 'Supreme Headquarters, Alien Defence Organisation' from the TV show *UFO.* In his mind's ear, Jack could hear a dramatic theme tune start up, all synth stabs and trumpets: the office was his secret base, and this elite group of three the commanders of some futuristic organisation dedicated to defending the world from alien invasion.

To commemorate the move Harriet had Photoshopped a set of space-age uniforms onto a photo of the three of them, somewhat worse for wear, taken at last year's Soho House Christmas bash: tight-fitting beige polo-neck jumpers, flares and utility belts. A vertical olive stripe ran down the left side of each of their Nehru-collared jackets, neatly incorporating the Intelligencia logo. A waiter accidentally caught in shot had been given a lower-ranking red outfit, *Star Trek* style.

Red means blood.

Red means danger.

Long before this, Jack realised, he had begun thinking about shapes and colours and what they might mean. He couldn't help it; it was a compulsion, his natural propensity to drill down into the meaning of any symbol, to try and comprehend it on some elemental level. Gift, or obsession? Either way, it had helped make Intelligencia what it now was.

He stepped back and regarded the sign. *Black. White. No colour.*

He was at it again.

Red. Green. Blue. Why these three primary colours? Whether one considered the additive RGB of light or the subtractive magenta, yellow and cyan of ink, both were just an accident of the wavelengths to which the human eye happened to be sensitive. If we could see a wider range, perhaps there would be four, or five, or ten different primary colours. He experimentally gave them names: *Ultrablue. Infrayellow. X-Red.*

Other eyes, other minds, other languages . . .

Then there was Intelligencia's black square.

Shapes. Just like colours, all the simple regular polyhedra – inevitable by-products of the Euclidean geometry of our local surroundings, and presumably the entire Universe, happened to obey – were also imbued with meaning; they were culturally loaded symbols you could read, if you were sensitive to such things.

Circles. Triangles. Squares. Now combine them with the colours. *Yellow circle?* The yellow disc of the Sun, a smiley badge. That one's taken. *Red triangle?* A warning sign. What was left? In the semiotic realm of visual branding, the equivalent of short two-, three- and four-letter web addresses had all been taken.

A square? What was a square? What did a square actually *mean?*

Jack was used to these kinds of questions being asked in meetings, and though they sometimes sounded dumb, or deep, or deeply dumb, he had slipped into the habit of thinking through all the potential permutations, simply to avoid an embarrassing oversight later.

A square was a regular polygon.

A square was a building block, the tessellating unit of a self-contained workspace.

A black box.

A flight recorder? Or— the conceptual 'black box' of theory, used to describe a situation where a given input and a desired output are known, but the mechanisms that manage to turn the first into the second are unknown, hidden from view? Jack thought it neatly summed up their work here, what this joint venture of theirs was all about.

When asked what the company actually *did,* Jack had a well-polished explanation that tended to deflect further questions, though he wasn't sure if this was because it clarified matters or simply bamboozled the curious, made them feel that if they enquired further they might not come across as the sharpest tools in the box.

It went something like this:

'What is Intelligencia working on?

'AI.'

'Ay aye?'

'Artificial intelligence.'

Here he would sometimes pause for effect.

'Put another way, what is it that makes consciousness *conscious?* At Intelligencia, we think that the degree to which you are intelligent is the degree to which you can see patterns and relationships – make sense, in other words, of the raw data flooding into your brain – and use it to make useful predictions about the world around you.'

If his audience hadn't already excused themselves, he would continue. 'This pattern-recognition ability is subject to a strong evolutionary pressure – is that a predator hiding over there in the rushes, or a trick of the light? A false positive is far less dangerous than a false negative. We are the result of countless generations who managed to avoid those predators, survived, got the girl or the boy, and continued the species.'

Of course, the reality was more complex. Though useful as a basic model, this 'black box' theory of consciousness assumed that the mind could be understood once the inputs and outputs were completely defined. For Jack's purposes, this simply didn't provide a sensible programming framework, and Jack was nothing if not practical. A theory lives or dies by its results. Now, with Nixon's financial backing and Harriet's programming skills, they were actually in the business of trying to get results.

There was no way they could compete with the well-funded government and university AI projects that were seeking to map the human brain and recreate all its complexities in code, but Jack had a hunch – *more* than a hunch, a pareidolic confluence of certainty – that they *didn't need to.*

When an organism first evolves beyond a basic automated stimulus/response and starts to consider a range of possible courses of action, it has begun to develop consciousness. Basic, sure, but consciousness nonetheless. There is, for the very first time, something between the in and the out, the A and the Z, where previously there had been nothing.

Awareness.

Awareness, raised to a useful level, becomes self-awareness.

Me. You. Us.

Jack had convinced himself, and then Nixon and Harriet, that all those well-funded institutions were going about it the wrong way. Intelligence, artificial or otherwise, is not something you have to build; it's inherent in the Universe, in matter. It's already *there*. You just need to construct a suitable vessel and intelligence will come and occupy it.

Build the house, not the tenant.

Jack had an inkling what that vessel might look like. It would need to be connected to the world and have access to everything in it – the input – but just like the most basic cell, it would also need to be separate from it, have an enclosing membrane that could provide the necessary degree of autonomy within which the mysterious process called consciousness might arise. It would need, even in the most abstract digital sense, a *body*.

This body would also require an output – a *voice*, if you like – or we'd have no idea what it was trying to say, or even if there was, in fact, anything *in* there in the first place.

What form might the input take? They already had a data set like no other: the internet. A search engine provides an output of sorts – we can address this repository of information and find specific results, get what we need. But this amazing resource does nothing without us. It does not self-organise, it does not find those all-important patterns and relationships by itself, autonomously. It has to be told what to do.

We are the internet's black box.

What Jack was attempting to do was duplicate the *human* part of that process in order to remove us from the equation. A digital black box which would seek out patterns and relationships, and thereby independently arrive at novel insights in fields from physics to economics to climate prediction to moral philosophy. If consciousness did turn out to work as Jack intuited, all kinds of causes and effects, previously invisible in the noise, might become apparent.

Pattern recognition.

What did we have as intelligent beings that the Web didn't? It didn't seem to be simply a matter of complexity – there were many biological systems that were far simpler than the Web that unambiguously displayed a basic intelligence.

No, what we had, and what Jack theorised was the most important single aspect of this whole conundrum, was a degree of *separation*. There is the world out there, and then there is us. Because we are not the world out there, we must have a definite location, a specific viewpoint. If there is stuff that *isn't* you, surely it was a natural leap to deduce there is a *you*.

Though Jack was under no illusion that their everyday bread and butter would continue to be programming, bespoke AI routines for game engines and language analysis, the company from its inception also had more . . . blue-sky ambitions.

Intelligencia had been set up to find a way to give the information on the internet *insight into itself.*

Jack didn't for one moment think that the internet was alive, that it was in some sense self-aware. For the purposes of their work, it didn't need to be.

It was just the raw material, the input. It's what could be done with it that excited him.

'We are in the business,' Jack would intone with more than a little theatricality in funding presentations, 'of opening the black box.'

Signal from Space?

Unexplained non-terrestrial narrowband signal echoes famous 1977 "Wow!" radio anomaly

Correspondent Riva Sutnar

The famous "Wow!" signal, picked up by Ohio State University's Big Ear radio telescope back on August 15 1977, had been called the "best candidate so far for a radio transmission from an alien civilisation." Though some of the best minds in the astronomy community have spent their careers analysing the small amount of data available, it has remained a tantalising and poorly understood mystery.

It was also a one-off. Despite all the attention focussed on the tiny area of the sky from which the signal originated, it was not detected again. If E.T. had come calling that day, they'd received no reply and had hung up, it was assumed, for good.

If you have taken any interest in the news over the last few days, you will already know that may have changed. Daniel Novák, currently allotted director's discretionary time at the UK's iconic Jodrell Bank radio telescope, has found himself in the eye of a media storm.

He was not at work when the new signal was detected. "We only saw the repeating 37-nanosecond burst in the data record the next day," he explains. "During these automated sweeps, the telescope tunes in to a broad range of frequencies chosen because they are relatively free of interference from Earthbound signals."

How can he be sure it's not of terrestrial origin? "The signal moves across the sky as the Earth turns, and does not map to any known satellite or upper-atmosphere reflection of a ground source. We checked." He grins, unable to suppress his enthusiasm. "That was the first thing we thought of. No Earthbound signal matches what we have here."

The source has been traced to the constellation of Auriga, below the "Goat Star" Capella, one of the brightest stars in the night sky, and close to the star cluster M38, but cannot be pinpointed with a degree of accuracy that would unambiguously correlate it with any known astronomical object.

Several natural causes have been proposed, from merging black holes to binary pulsars in tight orbits around their common centre of gravity. Certainly, Novák is circumspect about attributing it to an intelligent source.

Auriga hosts five stars and a white dwarf, all with known planetary systems. The sensitivity of current radial velocity methods tends to favour the detection of large planets with short orbital periods, so the current tally is considered to be a bare minimum. HAT-P-9 b, the most recently confirmed Aurigan exoplanet, is 1.4 times the size of Jupiter and orbits its parent star every 3.92 days at just 0.053 the distance from the Earth to the Sun, making it a so-called "hot Jupiter". If life does exist there, it won't be as we know it.

No sudden bursts of light at infrared or visible wavelengths in the target area have been detected, suggesting a supernova or a gamma ray burst are unlikely to be the source. Polarisation of the signal would indicate that it had been emitted by or passed close to a highly magnetised source, but again, this effect has not been observed.

If the origin of the signal is found to lie within the Milky Way, its vector would place it out from the galactic centre towards the rim, possibly beyond the Orion arm or even the Perseus Spur, an area far less densely populated with stars.

A small army of amateur SETI astronomers are scrutinising archived Hubble images of the area for clues, though what they might find, to quote Novák, is "anyone's guess. We just don't know what we should be looking for."

The Spitzer Space Telescope, though lacking the necessary sensitivity since its cryogen coolant was exhausted in 2009, is being re-tasked to examine a wide swathe of the area.

Novák's own analysis of the signal is ongoing. "It lasts for a very short duration, but it's incredibly dense," he elaborates. "There are repeating harmonic triads that occur at 4-nanosecond intervals, interspersed with a more chaotic output around the 1300–1450 MHz range. The 37-nanosecond burst repeats for the entire period that the telescope was placed to receive it, so we have to assume that what we have is only a portion of the whole. The signal was not in evidence a day later, when Auriga was next visible above the horizon. We are comparing our observations with other radio telescopes and – if we can confirm multiple detections – it may be poss-ible to piece together a longer section."

The signal itself is undergoing analysis at NASA in the US and related agencies here in the UK, and has not been made available to the general public. This, Novák assures me, is in line with standard scientific protocols. "Until we know what we've got and can make a more informed and considered announcement, it makes no sense to release it," he explains.

The original "Wow" signal was a close match for the 1420.40575 MHz hydrogen line, thought to be a likely wavelength for interstellar communication due to its ability to penetrate the diffuse interstellar material that would prove opaque to shorter wavelengths, though this close match has led some to suggest a natural origin is more likely.

Novák's old-school charm and vintage *Dan Dare* tiepin underscore his academic credentials. Having overseen Jodrell Bank's recent upgrade ☞

Retrieved 24/6 8.04am GMT.

Email exchange between Daniel Novák (acting SETI steering
committee chair, astronomer in residence, Jodrell Bank) and
"Jack" (surname removed).

NOTE: Assumed to be Jack Fenwick, ex NASA and UK Space Agency
IT contractor and co-founder of INTELLIGENCIA, a software
start-up based in Hoxton, London, UK. Companies House list it
as a private company, incorporated two months ago, with three
partners: Jack Fenwick, Harriet Haze and Nixon Rappaport.
The nature of the business is stated as "specialised software
services", possibly game AI design and implementation. They
have yet to file any accounts.

[Email header removed]

Dear Jack

Help needed on the cutting edge of science!

The signal is still resisting our best efforts to decode it.
Using the Arecibo Message as a template, we tried looking at
prime-number divisors in two and three dimensions to see if it
contained some kind of image, but we get nothing that doesn't
just look like TV static.

If the data is an image of some kind - or part of it is
an image - it doesn't seem to be based on any grid of set
dimensions we can deduce. In the hope that we might get
somewhere by throwing sheer brute-force processing power at
it, George here has knocked up a workaround that gives the
basic image analysis algorithm some degree of autonomy when
it comes to picking out mathematical regularities - but again,
nothing.

We searched for all those putative universal markers that
intelligent life is supposed to use to make our job easy -
the atomic weight of hydrogen, molecular ratios, mathematical
constants, all the stuff we assume in a uniform Universe are
the same everywhere, regardless of the biology of the species
doing the talking. Zilch.

I feel like I'm missing something obvious. I'd almost be
inclined to think that it's a natural signal if it wasn't
for the regularity of the repeat. Takes me back to '67 when
pulsars were first discovered. For a short time there we
thought we'd found real aliens! Now I'm getting déjà vu.

This signal is qualitatively different, though we're finding
it hard to pinpoint exactly how. Can you think of any natural

process that would produce such a strong, densely detailed repeat?

Still, what a puzzle! <u>This</u> is why I got into the sciences all those years ago - there's an excited schoolboy in me jumping up and down.

Yrs, Daniel

[Email header removed]

Hey Daniel

Nice to hear from you, and thanks for reaching out. You're still at Jodrell? They've not managed to pension you off?!

The Signal - I know no more than I've read in articles in the mainstream press.

So, off the top of my head, and speaking as someone with my background in language and code: <u>check your assumptions!</u> It always helps to take a step or two back from our anthropocentric worldview. Strip this back down to the very basics of what communication is or may be. Remember, English would make no sense if you don't have the cultural context in which it was developed. What we could easily have here is a code that codes for a code, just as we Earthlings have a written language that codes for a spoken language that codes for <u>what we want to actually communicate</u> - which again, is so much a by-product of the human condition as to probably be unique to our species.

Maps of maps of maps of territories.

I remember Harriet saying that if we could somehow speak with apes, all they'd want to talk about is picking fleas off each other, shagging and bananas. Might aliens be so different?

Anyway, it's good to know "Space Fleet HQ" (aka Jodrell Bank) still keeps you busy. Who knows, this mysterious message may turn out to be the Mekon's plans for galactic domination. If you can, send over the raw data in an encrypted package and I'll take a look. My NASA/UKSA NDA and the Official Secrets Act papers I signed when I was setting up the new systems for you there at Jodrell should still hold. With the game industry work we do here at Intelligencia we run very tight servers, so it's not going anywhere.

Less jumping up and down may help, too.

Jack

[Email header removed]

Thanks for getting back to me, Jack.

Agree - there are languages that are tonal, gestural,
pictorial, each with degrees of abstraction and degrees of
direct correlation to the subject. Symbolic/representational.

Even if we did manage to turn this into sounds or glyphs we
could hear or see, there's no reason it would be any more
comprehensible to me than Chinese. And here at Jodrell I can
easily find someone who speaks Chinese.

Have sent a link to a portion of the file which I've uploaded
to your old UKSA encrypted dropbox. PW etc. as before.

Do not, I repeat DO NOT share this or speak about it to
anyone, even your colleagues there at Intelligencia.

For now, this is just between us.

Yrs, Daniel

[Email header removed]

Daniel - Got it. I'll go through it all in more detail and
let it sink in. See if the grey matter can work its magic.
Mysterious message from outer space, eh? Got to say, I'm more
than intrigued. Give me a couple of days and I'll see what I
can come up with.

Jack

--ends--

THE CARTOGRAPHY OF LUST

Jack's lunchtime perambulations took him up Brick Lane, past the Truman Brewery and Rough Trade Records. He ducked between dawdling Japanese tourists and racks of tired kaftans scented with stale smoke and mildew. Outside curry houses, second-generation Indians that were far more London than he would ever be, child of the suburbs that he was, aggressively hustled for custom. Jack could guess what Nixon would say, were he here.

Oversaturated market. No usp. *Why not open a chip shop instead?*

Jack took a photo of nothing in particular.

>>SH-CLICK<<

A *skeuomorph:* that sound of a vintage camera shutter, replayed from a digital audio file. Another analogue throwback reproduced to order in noughts and ones. He wondered if it had been recorded from an actual camera, some classic model considered by aficionados of such things to have the most perfect, most authentic, most Proustian cadence. Do the doors of those new electric cars come equipped with the satisfyingly solid clunk of a Rolls Royce Silver Shadow latch? Or maybe you could choose your own, depending on taste or the whims of fashion. Everything, it seems, can be customised these days. Including ourselves.

>>SH-CLICK<<

Again, Jack barely glanced at the preview screen on the back of his camera. Onward. Up to Hoxton, the 333 Club, and 'Back to Yours?'

Jack, Farouk, Catherine and sometimes (though not often enough for Farouk) Mina had been regulars at DJ Soo Terrain's night at The Crown and Antelope, a converted pub that still had nicotine-yellow ceilings, a dartboard on the wall and carpet the colour of a nosebleed. Jack had met Soo through mutual friends two years previously; she had come to his office to ask if he could program a light show for a rap operetta she'd written which, as far as Jack could make out watching her enact key scenes standing on the table, was a cross between *Morecambe and Wise* and the life story of James Brown. Though he had just begun working with self-styled 'artists' and liked a challenge, he honestly thought bringing this extravaganza to life was beyond him. Despite turning her down, they'd remained firm friends. Her club, 'Back to Yours?', was promoted through beautiful screen-printed flyers of Soo's own devising that were vernacular works of art in their own right, disappearing as fast as she could fly-post them. This advertising fail meant that the club remained unknown outside of a small appreciative crowd of regulars.

The night's centrepiece was a big gameshow-style Wheel of Fortune. Divided into twenty sections, each was labelled with a different musical genre: it could be anything, from Rare Groove to Death Metal, Country and Western to Kraut Electronica. At fifteen-minute intervals throughout the night, a mankini-clad assistant would spin the wheel, Soo would play whatever category happened to come up, and 'Ace of Spades' would segue seamlessly into 'Calling Occupants of Interplanetary Craft'.

>>SH-CLICK<<

Soo chose the categories carefully. It guaranteed that only those with a sense of irony and an eclectic taste got anything out of the evening. On the floor below, where barrels were still stored and the uneven floor turned dancing into an extreme sport, there was karaoke, a wardrobe of dressing-up clothes and a trestle table bar stacked with plastic pint glasses. It looked more dilapidated than the worst provincial student bar Jack had ever been to. They loved it.

The Crown and Antelope was now boarded up, but the sun-bronzed corner of a flyer on which a section of the Wheel of Fortune could be seen was still taped to a lamp post outside. On it, a single category was still readable: *The Genius of John Barry.*

Messages. And how to decipher them. Jack held the camera at his side and absently pressed the shutter.

>>SH-CLICK<<

One memorable night, one of the categories on the wheel happened to be Neil Diamond. *Neil flippin' Diamond.* In a club. In *Hoxton.* After a few spins in which Neil did not come up, a chant began to go around: *We want Neil, we want Neil* – and when, eventually, Neil *did* come up, the room rose as one with an inclusive surge of spontaneous euphoria that had been achieved, at least for Jack, entirely without chemical assistance.

>>SH-CLICK<<

From there, they'd pass by fast-gentrifying ex-industrial warehouse spaces to the top of Brick Lane and the 24-hour 'Beigel' Bake. Here, in the wee hours, you'd always find an unlikely mix of market-stall workers, students, inveterate clubbers and taxi drivers, with the occasional policeman or woman in attendance not to keep order but to pick up supplies for the station. The menu was not what you'd call extensive, and for Jack the choice was always the same: a smoked salmon and cream cheese bagel, an egg salad bagel and a sugary-sweet cup of tea.

Steam came from a back room where swarthy Middle Eastern men made Caucasian by flour prised bagels from antique sea-green enamel contraptions and transferred them to plastic trays where they were distractedly but expertly split, buttered and filled, each action taking but a single pass of a spatula large enough to plaster walls. The tea was decanted from an enormous stainless-steel tank that the staff had to reach around in order to hand you your change. Jack imagined that, in all the time he had been coming here, it had never once been emptied and cleaned out – it was simply topped up with boiling water and tea bags as required. The unique flavour was, he was sure, down to many years' worth of continuous distillation.

>>SH-CLICK<<

They'd then slip around the melee outside and try and hail a cab. The journey home was spent scarfing bagels while holding the polystyrene cup of tea on the floor between your feet to prevent it from spilling. Red lights gave you a minute or two to put down your bagel, pick up the tea, lift the plastic lid, scald your lips, reattach the lid and return it to safety before the cab pulled away again. If you weren't fast enough, you got hot tea down the front of your shirt.

With practice and a familiarity with the distribution of traffic lights along the Westway out through Portobello, Latimer Road and Paddington this feat could be performed faultlessly even in a state of inebriation; to an outsider, waiting at the kerb to cross the road as the cab pulled up at the lights, they must have looked like members of some peculiar nocturnal sect, all genuflecting in unison.

>>SH-CLICK<<

Jack looked at the settings on his camera. There were a dozen little icons on a wheel, but he'd only used two and was unsure what function the others might serve. He'd stuck with the green *A*, he presumed for Automatic. It didn't seem to affect the quality of his shots.

Here were shops with metal roll shutters painted in multicoloured Tuscan-seriffed capitals. In a doorway, graffiti made from a patchwork of photocopied sheets showed George Bush with a gun to his head, a speech balloon above reading "I'm sorry". Just below that, a torn fly-poster announced the area was now a Sharia-compliant, no-alcohol zone.

>>SH-CLICK<<

The route back to the office passed by the Electricity Showrooms, which were not electricity showrooms but a bar fitted out in mismatched '60s bentwood chairs and Formica-topped, steel-rimmed tables. Jack assumed they had been lifted from some now-demolished brutalist M25 service station, here upcycled and recontextualised so hipsters could drink expensive Camden microbrewery lager and feel at one with what they imagined might be the functional aesthetic sensibilities of an honest working-class lorry driver – an aesthetic sensibility that honest working-class lorry drivers couldn't give a fuck about, as long as it supported their mug of tea and full English.

>>SH-CLICK<<

Up towards Liverpool Street was the Tea Building, in which Jack had briefly kept offices many years previously; in the nearer half of the building was Shoreditch House, an easterly offshoot of Soho House, a members club frequented by actors, designers, gay film producers and other media types, their entourages and hangers-on. Jack had been offered membership after creating some customised face-recognition software for them; at the time, he thought it had just been a way to wriggle out of paying full fee for his services, but in retrospect it was one of the best business arrangements he'd ever made. He went there often, sometimes on dates, sometimes with friends, sometimes for meetings with clients who happened to be in town. It had become his office away from his office.

>>SH-CLICK<<

Jack looked up. With a jolt of familiarity he saw he was now passing Bacon Street. He'd been here before, invited back home by a fashion student he'd met at the launch of a magazine that had lasted three issues and the name of which he couldn't remember. They'd taken a taxi – he'd not known till now where Bacon Street actually was; if, indeed, a street called Bacon had really existed and he hadn't imagined it all in some fry-up-deprived delirium. They'd stepped over a man sleeping rough in her doorway who she knew by name, then walked up three flights of bare concrete stairs to her studio.

He was asked to take off his shoes. It was one large space, a section of which had been carpeted in Astroturf, a vivid artificial green that was uncompromisingly rough underfoot. In one corner a dozen tiny model cows, a toy tractor and a combine harvester had been arranged. She'd lit a 1970s Calor Gas heater which produced a *whoomph* and an orange sunset glow over the plastic meadow, but the ill-fitting windows and cast-iron pillars meant that the space was still freezing.

>>SH-CLICK<<

Presently they'd retreated to an area partitioned from the living space by whitewashed chipboard hoardings she'd appropriated from a derelict shop. These doubled as a makeshift gallery wall upon which she'd taped her drawings. To Jack's untutored eye, these looked more like costume designs for a dystopian Ridley Scott movie than Top Shop's new summer range, but they were beautifully drawn and he had made encouraging and interested sounds while trying not to tread on a plastic hen with five yellow plastic chicks, all attached in a neat row to the same baseplate. She talked him through the details of a cape here, a piped seam there, standing behind him all the while with her chin on his shoulder and her hand down the front of his trousers.

>>SH-CLICK<<

Behind the chipboard screen she had built a bunkbed, raised on scaffold poles over a drawing table. Jack enquired as to the whereabouts of her bathroom, thinking to freshen up his undercarriage in anticipation of its pending closer inspection.

He shut the door and looked at himself in the mirror with a dislocation that had become familiar. He had a face that benefited from the lack of attention he gave it, and an unaffected charm that was an accidental by-product of his slight disengagement from everything that was going on around him; he tended to spend most of his time in the byways of his mind, where he would be turning a particular programming problem around to look at it from every angle, or picturing a particular interpenetration of three Platonic solids in order to . . .

Jack already had more than a few lines around his eyes, but he was still too young to be fully confident of his presence in the world, still not old enough to completely relax into life. He tried to convince himself that he shouldn't over-analyse these misadventures, that they were often just what they were: nothing more, nothing less, whatever an excess of adolescent coming-of-age novels had done to heighten a poetic but misplaced sense that real life had some kind of sensible narrative, that events sometimes threw their shadows before them.

Jack knew he had a tendency to see meaning where there was none, to imbue the everyday with a sense of the numinous. That ability to find pattern in chaos, see order in random data, was what made him good at what he did; but it was also what made him feel disconnected from certain social obligations he found hard to fathom. Wood from the trees. Still, on balance, he wouldn't change the way he was for the world, this one or any other. It was his superpower.

No, not every shadow foretold some future event. But, he was to realise much later, not everything *casts* a shadow.

>>SH-CLICK<<

The face in the mirror that Jack knew was Jack, but seemed to not be Jack, had looked back at him and silently framed a question. *Why are you here?* He was tired, he had the sour metallic aftertaste of beer and lipstick in his mouth, his hair was sticking up at the side where she'd been stroking it in the cab and the faintest dusting of powder clung to the five o'clock shadow under his nose.

Is that me, in the mirror?
Am I him?
Who am I?

The bathroom was dominated by a large rectangular sink with a Jackson Pollock encrustation of multicoloured paint. Underneath were arranged pots of brushes, bottles of turpentine and plastic gallon containers stickered with yellow skull-and-crossbones warnings. Was she really an artist, or was this some kind of experimental meth lab?

Jack had decided on the former, because it was late, he hadn't been laid in a long while, and if he thought about this any more deeply he'd have found himself in a taxi home.

MESSAGES FROM IDEASPACE

⟩⟩SH-CLICK⟨⟨

Standing, as he was now, at the junction of Brick Lane and Bacon Street, Jack occupied a location that could be uniquely described by a set of x, y and z coordinates. This place, made specific by the simple act of being here, he nonetheless shared with many other men and women, distant from him not in space but in *time;* people who spoke a language, but not the one he spoke; who knew this place when Brutus of Troy slew Gogmagog, Lud held court, and the paving beneath his feet was an undisturbed meadow of great burnet, sneezewort and devil's bit scabious. That original pristine geography, a canvas undisturbed since the ice sheets retreated, had been primed with a base coat of brick and tarmac, sized with beer and then shellacked with acid rain as evolved apes built their city over the top.

⟩⟩SH-CLICK⟨⟨

Under the pavement lies the planet, the raw brickearth from which London has been built. Jack let his imagination sink down through the Bagshot beds and the greensand and the London clay, raisined with flints and the remains of fires around which tales of the exploits of heroes no one now can name were told; and further, to the rolling surf of white chalk that stretches out to the North Downs to the south and the Chiltern Hills to the north, between which the entire weight of London, all its steel and concrete and flesh and spirit, is cradled.

Descend deeper, through the stratigraphy of history. The Eocene, Palaeogene and Neogene, the Cretaceous' impermeable Gault clays, the Devonian, the compressed mudstones and sandstones of the Silurian and the Palaeozoic, down into the mesosphere, the mantle, the liquid outer core and, ultimately, Earth's slowly downspinning crystalline inner core. Here at the very centre turns the ball of iron that keeps our magnetic field alive; but it is slowing every day, and when eventually and inevitably it will stop and freeze into place, the field will fail and the Sun's hard radiation, now pushed to the poles where it dances as aurorae, will bathe the Earth, finally and completely cleansing it of the infection that we call life.

Only then might stories finally end.

>>SH-CLICK<<

Layer upon layer. Jack could imagine that if one were immortal, eventually there would not be a square inch of the city that was not resonant with a memory of some encounter or event. He realised on reflection that in some sense this was already so – that in the shared memory of all the generations that had lived out their lives in this place there was a continuity as of one mind, one person, an oral history passed from generation to generation that overlaid each road and building and park and pub with an encrustation of narrative . . . people, events, confluences of chance, year upon year, decade upon decade, century upon century.

>>SH-CLICK<<

It's said that Cartier-Bresson could feel the decisive moment from behind the camera as the shutter was pressed, and without the benefit of instant playback knew which frames on the undeveloped roll held the most harmonious compositions. 'The simultaneous recognition, in a fraction of a second, of the significance of an event as well as the precise organisation of forms which give that event its proper expression.'

Il n'y a rien dans ce monde qui n'ait un moment décisif.

Coincidence? Or a natural affinity for pattern and composition, for *meaning?* That, Jack could get behind.

>>SH-CLICK<<

Divination, at base, requires a random generator – the shuffled deck, tea leaves, thrown straws or the wrinkles of the palm. A palimpsest on which interpretation and imagination can work their magic. All you need is the white noise of urgent but unformed raw creation, upon which a nudge and a push – just . . . *here,* just . . . *so* – can create an image, a picture, a meaning. Jack was well aware that in this respect he might have a particular advantage, though he was of the opinion that everyone possessed this ability to some extent; it was an integral part of being human. By nature or nurture we are all primed to spot connections. For him, this proclivity had been turned up to eleven.

Words.

Numbers.

Mathematics, for him, was a simple matter of congruences and relationships, the push and pull of variables; he could easily disassemble an equation on the jeweller's velvet of his mental workspace.

He took another photo.

>>SH-CLICK<<

The material substrate was not so important; it just had to be pliable, flexible, amenable to being shaped by an idea. Down below him was the history of this process; the first knapped flints, the first clay pots, the first chased silver clasps. All made from natural materials that could hold an image, could be shaped and moulded, fashioned to fit the imagination. Brick and iron and bronze and steel each took an idea and became the idea externalised, realised in a solid form that was harder and more durable than speech.

We had learned to talk to the yet unborn.

>>SH-CLICK<<

The buildings, the bridges, the vaults of stone, the roads and the streets, the bones of pre-stressed steel, the sinuous capillaries of tube train and water main, the nervous system of copper cable and fibre optic . . . we had built our city, and the city was the notional made material, a new and improved random signal generator which, from towers sheeted in mirrorglass, would reflect our image back at us so we could see ourselves, so we could finally divine who we really were.

>>SH-CLICK<<

Jack again felt that decisive Bressonian thrill of significance. He turned the camera over in his palm and scrolled back two images. Forward again. What had he caught? A shape, a white van, passing close; a shopfront sign in backlit perspex behind.

On the van, blurred by movement but still readable, was some text. The alignment was such that the shop sign behind seemed to continue the message. Together, they were saying something. He was reminded of a sculpture he had seen at the Venice Biennale which had been carved to look like a rabbit from one angle and a wolf from another, or those old Channel 4 idents where everything suddenly aligned with your point of view and a shape became visible – but only because you just happen to be in the right place at the right time.

Jack stood perfectly still. The world had gone very quiet, as if he was the axis around which everything, just for a moment, was rotating. An eye in a hurricane of possible moments.

The decisive moment – a tingling, as if the hidden mechanisms of the world were falling into place. He pictured a machine of exquisite complexity, a confluence of events, some stretching back centuries, some pivoting on the whim of a second ago, all coming together at this precise point in time and space.

Without lifting the camera to his line of sight, without looking down, he shut his eyes and took one last picture from the hip.

>>SH-CLICK<<

Fifteen minutes later at Shoreditch House, Jack scanned through the images on his laptop. This was divination, of a sort – but what was he divining?

In the background of that last shot, words on a builder's merchant hoarding could be seen above a stack of cement sacks and orange buckets. In the foreground, the back of a circular sign and a pub awning cropped the letters precisely.

The message was plain to read:

BUILD ME.

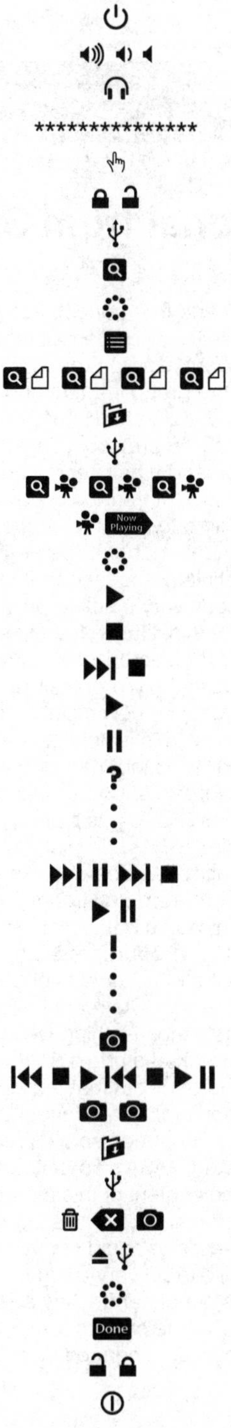

⏻

◀)) ◀)) ◀

🎧

****

🖑

🔒 🔓

⚡

🔍

⚙

☰

🔍📄 🔍📄 🔍📄 🔍📄

📁

⚡

🔍🎥 🔍🎥 🔍🎥

🎥 **Now Playing**

⚙

▶

■

⏭ ■

▶

‖

?

. . .

⏭ ‖ ⏭ ■

▶ ‖

!

. . .

📷

⏮ ■ ▶ ⏮ ■ ▶ ‖

📷 📷

📁

⚡

🗑 ✖ 📷

⏏ ⚡

⚙

Done

🔓 🔒

⏻

Content of 'Signal from Space' leaked

16 minutes ago | Technology

Controversial whistle-blower and free-speech activist Edward White has defended posting the complete raw content of the so-called 'Signal from Space' on the 'Information Wants To Be Free' website.

Journalists, select pressure group leaders and celebrities funnelled into a press reception where he was due to discuss the latest in a long list of disclosures by live link from the secret location where he has been in self-imposed exile for the last two and a half years. Seated behind a makeshift table in a crumpled suit, his face lit from below by his laptop like some B-movie villain, he has certainly had time to become accustomed to the attention.

"I was just trying to open up a debate," he begins, with barely hidden weariness. In this he has definitely succeeded. On the one hand, advocates of open government have been very quick to point out that NASA and the UKSA are both publicly funded institutions, and as such its discoveries are very much public property. "The secrecy that surrounds new discoveries has a lot to do with indentured men at the top of their profession, jealously guarding information that could lead to major new discoveries and the awards and publicity that accompany them. This is how tenure is assured in what is an increasingly competitive academic job market," he claims.

In this he has some high-profile support. "Our tax dollars funded this survey," Congressman Richard Baille has stated, "and the information is also ours. It belongs to the people."

The astronomical community has been quick to counter such statements. "The signal is an unprocessed raw data stream. We have nothing as yet to release other than a meaningless but statistically significant repeating signal," stated Daniel Novák, a UKSA representative. "When the first Apollo astronauts came back from the Moon, NASA observed a strict decontamination procedure. 21 days in a converted Airstream trailer. We do exactly the same when sending rovers to Mars – the last thing we want to do is discover Martian life, only to find that it piggybacked a ride from Earth."

Critics have been quick to point out that the signal is not a biological vector, and thus poses no contamination danger, but there have been voices in the establishment that have not been so clear-cut on this matter and have been sounding warnings about NASA's so-called social responsibility. "That responsibility stretches to the content of this message, should it have any," Novák reasons. "Given that the source of this signal may be a technologically advanced civilisation, the message could contain information that, if it fell into the wrong hands, could prove to be very dangerous."

Baille has dismissed this out of hand. "Any advanced civilisation should have left the tribalism typical of the current state of human affairs far behind. We cannot judge them by our own shortcomings. They will probably be aware of how the content of the message might be used, and put sensible caveats in place. To use your analogy, if we have the foresight to decontaminate our Mars rovers, I suggest that whoever sent us this signal will have taken similar precautions."

White also has another group of very vocal supporters backing his cause. *The Guardian* and *The Washington Post* revealed the existence of Sapphire, the NSA/NASA monitoring mechanism whose existence has long been denied but which became an open secret when White's first tranche of data was released. Also contained within it are mentions of what some have concluded is another listening station, codenamed Daedalus, though no sensible location for this installation has been put forward.

The NSA responded that "our remit is first and foremost to protect the stability of our nation and our partner nations, and one way in which we do this is by restricting the flow of information that our adversaries may find useful in their campaigns against us and our way of life. Our interception of broadcast information and communications can be of vital intelligence value, irrespective of the source – terrestrial or otherwise."

The spokesman continued: "We operate with our international partners according to international law, to meet our and their security goals, and no one should be more indebted to us and the work our allies do on a daily basis than Baille and his ilk, whose safety we are sworn to protect."

Others are unconvinced. Hacker collective Anonymous have threatened to initiate DOS attacks on service providers that comply with the NSA's takedown orders. In a video posted on YouTube, an unidentified member wearing the now standard *V for Vendetta* mask drew comparisons with *Star Trek*'s Prime Directive, the guiding principle of the show's fictional United Federation of Planets, which prohibits interfering with the development of alien civilisations below a certain threshold of technological, scientific or cultural development. Those of a more cynical bent might point out that Kirk himself was prone to flaunt the directive when it suited him.

An NSA representative yesterday put it this way: "This assumption that private citizens but not public institutions have a right to privacy rests on the assumption that private citizens are less likely to be a danger than the public institutions that are there to represent them; in other words, we see a profound mistrust of the motives of those that govern. Institutions consist of individuals that may be flawed or otherwise, but to maintain democratic accountability and ensure our national security, privacy must work both ways."

This has all been rendered moot. The signal from space is now available for all interested parties to examine. As of Monday, downloads have exceeded the five million mark. The majority of these will be simply added to digital music libraries, to be listened to and puzzled over between Adele tracks on shuffle. As NASA have admitted that they have no solid theories in regard to the signal's content or meaning, opening it up to crowdsourced examination by a highly motivated public may actually give us the breakthrough we need.

The debate White was seeking to start has most definitely begun.

Share this story <small>About sharing</small>

Retrieved 16/7 5.10pm GMT.

Email exchange between Daniel Novák (acting SETI steering committee chair, astronomer in residence, Jodrell Bank) and "Jack" (surname removed).

NOTE: Assumed to be Jack Fenwick, ex NASA and UK Space Agency IT contractor and co-founder of INTELLIGENCIA, a software start-up based in Hoxton, London, UK.

[Email header removed]

Hi Jack

Well, as I'm sure you know by now, the NASA was hacked, the Signal is out, and it's going to be a free-for-all.

If you have any wild ideas, anything that'll give us a head start here, now is the time to let me know.

Yrs, Dan

[Email header removed]

Daniel - I heard.

Next time, might I suggest you be more careful who you share this stuff with? Not every institution has the benefit of my bulletproof tech support.

Wild ideas, eh? Well, you know I'm a pattern recognition machine. I can pick a signal out of the noise at fifty paces, though sometimes that signal does turn out to be a figment of my overactive imagination.

Blessing and a curse.

Anyway - I've been looking at the repeat again.

It's not an exact repeat - maybe 90-98% of the signal is the same, depending on which stretches you compare, but there are definitely structural differences in each iteration.

How much of this do you think might be due to signal degradation or atmospheric effects? As far as I can make out, there's no form of error correction.

It's possible that we may not be looking at one message on a loop (if it is a message) but many messages, each subtly different from one another.

Which makes no sense to me. If you're an alien trying to tell us something, have the courage of your convictions and stick to your story. Why the modifications? Not sure exactly what you want to say?

I'm trying to think of an Earthbound analogue...

Variations on a form.

Music, perhaps?

Jack

--ends--

APOPHENIA

Build me. Jack ran the idea through his mind for the umpteenth time.

Build *who?* And assuming he was communicating with something other than a shade of his own conjuring, what kind of thing could exist without . . . without *existing?*

An experiment was in order. Choosing at random, he opened one of the boxes stacked along the internal wall of the office which had yet to be unpacked. Reaching in without looking, he pulled out a thick hardback and four magazines: *Language Lost: Undeciphered Scripts Of The Ancient World,* two issues of *New American Scientist* and one each of the *Literary Review* and *The Blind Adept,* and dropped them on the conference room table. They came to rest between a pizza box and a selection of empty foil cartons from the Dishoom Indian restaurant, their contents written on the lids in green biro.

It was late. Harriet and Nixon had left the office half an hour ago. He was alone.

Jack climbed onto the table, held his digital camera at arm's length above this random montage – too high to see the preview screen – and took two shots. Returning to his iMac, he plugged the camera's memory card into the back, booted Photoshop and opened them.

He zoomed in. Out a bit. Scooted to the edge of the image. He could see, in the overlapped layers of card and paper, snippets of words. No, there was more than that. A *message?*

Seeing messages in random noise. Even when there was nothing really there. *Careful, Jack.* He knew that this particular form of mental disorder even had a name: *apophenia.* Defined as the 'unmotivated seeing of connections' accompanied by a 'specific experience of an abnormal meaningfulness', it had done for mathematician John Nash and he felt that if he wasn't very careful, it could also do for him.

He went back to the conference room, again climbed onto the table to take a closer look. He jumped down and ran back to the iMac. Jack seemed to run everywhere these days, as if he had recently been infected with a sense of urgency he found hard to shake off or rationalise.

A thrill went through his extremities. He was right! It wasn't *exactly* the same image – a letter had been altered here, an angle changed there. A twist, a tweak. Perhaps he *wasn't* imagining things.

Raw material. He supplied the tea leaves, gave them a stir. Whoever it was, whatever it was, just needed something to work with – a *medium*.

Jack was providing the medium.

Perhaps Jack *was* a medium. This could all be some modern, technological form of channelling.

He suppressed an involuntary shudder.

What else did he have to hand? On the fridge was a postcard of the Giant's Causeway, a drawing of Darth Vader by Nixon's niece, and an alphabet's worth of bright plastic letters, some of which had been arranged into an unlikely boast about Nixon's prowess, a number 1 standing in for an i.

Jack pointed the camera at the fridge and took another photo. This time, as he did so, he looked at the screen on the back. It was too small to make out details, so using the buttons on the rear he zoomed in and panned around. He couldn't see the words for the letters.

He opened the file back on his iMac. Did they shift, rearrange themselves?

He closed the file and opened it again. Nothing. No new message. Just a mess of letters. He could see the fridge from where he was sitting. He printed out the photo on an A3 sheet and carried it back across the room. Holding it up, it was a perfect match. *Even colour correct,* he congratulated himself.

What had he expected to see? Jack sat back down in front of his screen and opened the original file again.

Did he see a change in a letter here, a letter there? Jack wondered if it was possible that someone could be playing a practical joke on him, altering certain details remotely via a screenshare. He printed the image out a second time then stapled the two sheets together along their left-hand edge.

Yes. If he looked at it just so, in the arrangement of random characters he could persuade himself that there was now an image, a face, though it was by necessity simplified – two Xs for eyes.

Just how a cartoonist would draw a dead person.

It seemed this method of divination could produce not just words, but pictures too. *Pictures made from words.*

Flipping between the two images, the difference became immediately

apparent. He recalled that this was how Clyde Tombaugh discovered Pluto, a wandering star in a field of stationary points of light.

Jack felt a prickle at the back of his neck, as if someone was watching him. Chiding himself for being spooked so easily, he got up and checked the conference room and the bathroom, but he was alone.

The following morning Harriet looked over his shoulder as he flipped again between the two images. "You're not having me on?" She didn't sound convinced. "It'd be easy to move them around."

"It happened just how you see it here. I did not fake this. I may have a peculiar talent for seeing patterns, but this is one I didn't make up."

"So, what, someone is trying to *talk* to you? A ghost in the machine?"

"In *my* machine? We have broadband. The back door of that computer is open to the entire internet. Anyone – *anything* – could walk right in and take up residence."

Harriet walked over to the fridge to compare the printouts with the reality, leafing back and forth between the two sheets. She held the first up and closed one eye, moving it over the arrangement of letters as it now stood. Nixon's boast was still there, still just as unlikely. She dropped the sheets on Jack's desk from a height, stuck out her lower lip and blew a strand of hair from her eyes.

"Whatever you say, Jack."

Jack couldn't let it go. "I'm reminded of a story I heard. About a man who had been in a vegetative state for many years. This man was completely paralysed. Locked in. But they knew he was in there, because they could see his brain was still functional on an MRI. One day someone realises that they could use the MRI output to operate a simplified keyboard, a bit like Stephen Hawking's. They hook this guy up. They wait for him to type something – and this perfect poetry comes out. Not a babble, not an incoherent mess, but complete polished sentences. He'd been holding them in his memory all those years."

Jack glanced up. Harriet was looking at him intently. "Beautiful. And sad." He couldn't decide if she was entertaining his point of view or simply feeling sorry for him.

"Harriet, if we manage to give whatever it is I think we have here – *if* we have something here – the equivalent of paper and pencil, who knows what we may get? We may get art. We may get an incoherent mess. We might not be able to tell the difference."

From across the office, behind his glass partition, Nixon laughed. "We may get a bollock cannon. Anyway, why would ghosts want to talk to *you*, in particular?

Jack thought about the Signal from Space, the Official Secrets Act he had signed; about how close the ability to pick a real signal out of raw data was to seeing imaginary faces in clouds.

"Maybe I'm the only one who can read its mind."

Nixon shrugged and went back to his spreadsheet.

He'd built a company on Jack's peculiar insights.

HUMAN RESOURCES

Harriet spoke with two voices. She had what she called her Home Voice and her School Voice.

Though she was brought up in a spacious five-storey townhouse in a better part of North London, she didn't feel particularly privileged, whatever that might mean. The daughter of an idle academic and an underemployed actor, neither of whom made much in the way of a living, she had by some process of osmosis picked up from them the impression that earning money was at best a vulgar distraction, and certainly not something one dedicated one's life to. A distraction from precisely *what*, she remained unsure; her parents didn't seem to be usefully engaged in anything concrete at all.

Quite the opposite. The missing window in the kitchen that would have been a few minutes' work to replace was instead blocked with an opened-out cereal packet and parcel tape, which meant that the ground floor was always cold during the winter; it had been that way for as long as she could remember. In spring, the birds that nested in the roof spaces kept her awake with their cooing. She would pull her duvet from room to room, sleeping on the floor, or an empty bed in a room no one but her had been in for years, or perhaps a broad windowsill as the fancy took her.

At the age of eleven she had been enrolled in the local comprehensive, while the few friends she had made at the junior school across the street had all gone to private schools or away to a boarding school in the country. At the time she had asked her parents why this should be; it was only many years later she realised that her parents' vague pontifications about the responsibility of the privileged few not to overshadow the honest toil of the Common Man (or Woman) by actually excelling at anything was a political posture that concealed their inability to get their shit together.

They rented the basement flat to a series of students, young professionals, sometime drug dealers and other people they misguidedly thought might need their help. She had been introduced to marijuana at the age of fourteen by one such tenant who smelled like a wet dog, and from whom she had learned much of the colourful slang that stood her in good stead at her new school.

There, as a matter of self-preservation, she had learned to pretend that she didn't read books (*Heat* or *Closer* were permitted) and to not use words of more than three syllables when one or two monosyllabic grunts would suffice. She'd skip the last page of any test they were set, as she knew that once the results were posted on the board in the dining hall anyone who came in the top three or five would be singled out for special attention after school by Nicole Grant and her gang of bitch-queen bullies.

Don't stand out. Fit in. Try not to make yourself a target. When speaking in School Voice, every other word had to be "fuck", or at the very least a "shyeah" or a "hunh". Even though she was wise beyond her years, she affected a streetwise nonchalance, a studied cynicism and a disinterest in most things that was totally at odds with her real character.

Back at home, she'd read her way through her parents' library of damp second-hand paperbacks. Sartre, Jong, Marx, Waterhouse. *Stranger in a Strange Land, On the Road, The Function of the Orgasm.* Even *Jonathan Livingston* fucking *Seagull.*

While still pretending to not know how to spell her middle name, she found a C++ manual in a cupboard and taught herself basic programming on the ageing PC her father used to type his unpublishable theses on mediaeval poetry. She became so adept at living this double life she sometimes forgot who the real version of Harriet was. Sweary uncouth lout, or bookish nerd? Or sweary uncouth bookish nerd?

She graduated school with a handful of GCSEs that would have made any other pupil proud, but for her represented the bare minimum of effort. Her standards had long ago been calibrated so low that half-arsed was considered close to genius.

She then mooched around for a year and a half until her well-cultivated cynicism finally began to wear thin and shift work at Iceland was becoming a serious prospect. Her parents couldn't understand why the BBC weren't taking on unqualified and antisocial teenagers as a service to the country – surely that's why it had been created in the first place? Why else did they pay their licence fee? (They didn't.)

Much later than her primary school friends (most of whom she'd lost touch with because of their discomfort with her tough new persona) she realised she'd need an Oxbridge degree to comfortably segue into such a job. So she again lowered her expectations in everyone's eyes, not least her

51

parents', and took a course in programming at the local technical college.

On the Friday of the first week of the course, the girl sitting at the next table had asked her where she had got her jacket. Harriet's attention immediately shot to the girl's hands, looking for the fist she felt sure was coming. *Why would anyone compliment her on her jacket? What was she really after?* Her own fist was clenched tightly around a ballpoint pen in her pocket, her playground-honed instincts judging how quickly she could pull it out and stick it into the girl's arm as it would inevitably swing over to connect with her jaw.

The expected right hook never came. Charmless and defensive, Harriet decided she might need an ally in this new and confusing milieu where the old rules no longer applied.

She decided she might need a friend.

Not only was the coursework easy, but the mixed-age class admired her natural aptitude. She found she enjoyed their approval. For the first time in her life she felt that putting in a little effort and excelling at something wasn't to be avoided at all costs because it was completely and unforgivably *lame.*

Three years of firm friendship later, on a train between Istanbul and Bursa, Kim (for that was her name) confessed to Harriet how petrified she'd been of her sullen demeanour and barely disguised aggression. She'd thought it best policy to make friends with the toughest girl in the class as soon as she could, just to be on the safe side. Harriet, built like a gazelle, had had a mirror held up that reflected someone she no longer recognised. She came back from the trip with the knowledge that she'd finally thrown off an act she'd been playing for too long, and could at last relax into who she really was.

Graduating top of her class, she'd been headhunted by a new video-game design company and spent the next two years building a lighting and ragdoll engine from scratch. This they licensed to other gaming companies for far more money than the game it was originally designed for ever made. Feeling that she might be due some kind of bonus, or a small raise perhaps, she approached her MD after a presentation to Sony in which she'd demonstrated her new realistic spark and smoke generating assets. He'd looked at her and laughed. "I get résumés from ten people a week who'd gladly do your job for *way* less than I'm paying you *now*," he said. "Get back to your desk and shut the fuck up."

Harriet, being familiar with bullies, walked to the water cooler, filled a plastic cup, poured it over his laptop then called him "an ignorant cunt". The open-plan office went very quiet. The MD was so surprised that it took him fully two minutes to process what had happened. Finally, he walked over and told her in clipped measured tones to clear her desk. Harriet looked somewhat surprised. "But you *are*" was the best retort she could come up with. "And who's going to finish the engine by the delivery date? *You?*" The MD, who was now a deep shade of puce either through humiliation, suppressed rage, or a combination of the two, silently stabbed his finger at her, searched for words that didn't come, then returned to his office.

Harriet looked around at her co-workers. "*What?*" she asked in honest bemusement. "He's a charmless *bully*. He *needs* to be told."

An associate not known for his backbone broke the silence. "He also happens to be the *boss*."

It began to dawn on her that she might not have made the wisest of moves. Alf, the personnel manager, slunk over to ask if he could have a word in private. He explained that they needed the engine complete and signed off by the end of the month, or the company might lose the Sony account. Harriet remained silent. She wondered how this might be her problem. Alf, taking this silence as the opening move in a tough round of bargaining, apologised at length for the MD's behaviour and offered to give her a 40 per cent pay raise as long as she met the deadline and promised to tell no one else in the company of this arrangement. Harriet looked at him closely for the first time. His nylon shirt had a damp patch under each arm.

This was a major project for them, perhaps the biggest that the company had landed. Realisation finally caught up with her. *Balance of power.* Not something she ever sought or relished, but if her school-days had taught her one thing it was how a power imbalance could be exploited. She had just learned that she had undervalued herself once again, and her real currency, her real worth, all she needed in fact, was what she carried with her between her ears. It always had been.

"No, that's fine, thanks. It's probably best if I collect my things and leave." She went back to her desk, pulled all her files off the server onto a portable external hard drive, put it in a box with her Sylvia Plath paperback, stale chocolates, Cintiq and *Wired*, encrypted the company's backup, and waved a cheery goodbye to the wide-eyed and silent office.

"Darling," her mother had said, waving a hand vaguely through a rising column of herbal cigarette, "don't you worry. Why don't you just find yourself a nice boyfriend?" She'd always had a careless disregard for money that only those who had grown up never having to worry about where it came from could entertain. She suspected her mother had been living on an overdraft for some time, quite possibly without even realising it; the only thing as slippery as her grasp of the practicalities of day-to-day finances was the pondweed on their overgrown ornamental pond. If she was unaware of the niceties of a balance sheet, she was utterly ignorant of what holding down a real job might entail.

Harriet absently moved her mother's wineglass onto a coaster, though every polished antique surface in the house was already ringed like an Olympic logo manual. Her mother tutted. "The only reason people want a proper—" here she made air quotes, knocking ash from her cigarette in the process – "'education' is so they can lord it over others. Exams, certificates, degrees – they only serve to make some people think they're *better* than others. It's divisive, it's bourgeois, it's . . . it's *vulgar.*"

Vulgarity was the one thing Harriet *had* mastered to an advanced level at school, and she wondered if her mother had ever known what it actually meant, here at home where she only used her home voice. Her mother would never get to hear her school voice; Harriet had trained herself too well.

Today had not only convinced her that she had the means – not in cash, but in smarts – but more than that, that her mother's attitude was, in its own way, no different from the carefully cultivated cynicism of her high-school friends, if friends they had ever been.

Though from completely different ends of the social spectrum and for completely different reasons, they both thought it beneath them to really *try*, to put any *effort* into anything.

She realised then with abject clarity that the only person she had been short-changing all those years was herself.

Jack, in his semi-autistic disregard for the niceties of social interaction, had not thought it odd when Harriet walked into the old Intelligencia office a day later, unannounced.

"I'm after a job," she said without preamble. "I hear you're doing interesting work." She opened *Wired* to a puff-piece that Nixon had somehow managed to persuade them to print. There was a photo of Jack, standing in front of Jodrell Bank with Daniel Novák, and another of Nixon, in dramatic starkly lit black and white. Instead of looking like the future CEO of a major multinational software company, he just seemed to be trying too hard. "I want to be part of it."

Jack pushed back his chair and looked at her.

Harriet was petite, boyish, with a single streak of bleached blonde through the brunette of her sharply cut bob. She was bent forward like an animal about to pounce, all unblinking earnestness and fragile charm. Dressed entirely in black, from her skinny jeans and Chelsea boots to a mohair jumper over which she wore Kim's favourite fitted leather jacket, she still lacked the graceful poise she would later gain as her self-confidence grew. She had a pale round face that Jack would discover was more than attractive when she was smiling. Now, she wasn't smiling. There was the guarded hardness which she still carried as a means of self-preservation.

"And you are?" enquired Jack.

"Harriet," Harriet said, holding out her hand.

After a moment's hesitation, Jack shook it. "We're not hiring. Are we hiring, Nixon?"

Nixon came over and sat on the edge of Jack's desk. He was uncharacteristically subdued, and seemed to be studying her intently. At that moment Jack had found him hard to read, but Jack often found people hard to read. Harriet didn't meet his eye.

"Um, well. No. Yes. Maybe. What can you do?"

Harriet gestured to Jack's computer and held up her rubber-wrapped portable hard drive. "I can show you."

Jack looked at Nixon and shrugged. "Sure. Go ahead." Harriet connected the drive and waited for it to mount. Jack stood up and gestured to his chair. Harriet sat, pulled herself up to the screen, found his stylus then selected a folder. She double-clicked an icon shaped like a black beret.

Thirty minutes later, she had a job.

Jack wasn't sure precisely what work they could give her, but he understood very quickly that here was someone who knew how to make things happen. And while he was not short of ideas, what he *was* short of was the means to turn them into reality.

While Harriet's back was turned, Jack looked across at Nixon and raised his eyebrows to show he was impressed. Very impressed.

Nixon acquiesced more easily than Jack had anticipated.

"Can you start on Monday?"

Retrieved 22/7 10.22am GMT.

Email exchange between Daniel Novák (acting SETI steering committee chair, astronomer in residence, Jodrell Bank) and "Jack" (surname removed).

NOTE: Assumed to be Jack Fenwick, ex NASA and UK Space Agency IT contractor and co-founder of INTELLIGENCIA, a software start-up based in Hoxton, London, UK.

[Email header removed]

Dan —

Patterns in the noise. Something I've been focused on of late. Seems like it's getting to be an obsession.

So - we have a repeated signal - but it's not an exact repeat.

Variations on a form.

Harriet and her 'apes and bananas' analogy gave me an idea. Run with this and see where it gets you...

Apes share 98% of our DNA - I'm reliably told bananas share 50%. Maybe we're looking at this the wrong way. Maybe this signal is not a message at all.

Maybe it's not a code CREATED BY an intelligent alien race - maybe it IS the alien race.

Am I crazy?

Jack

[Email header removed]

Jack, Jack, Jack —

The signal is the aliens?

That's a veeeeery interesting idea.

Let me kick it around for a while. See what Leonie here thinks.

Did I tell you before you're a genius?

Yrs, Dan

[Email header removed]

Daniel - I thought you'd like that.

I'll add 'genius' to my new business cards. There'll be room just under 'Evil Mastermind'.

Here's the thing. We have this human-centric view of reproduction. Almost all life on Earth uses a biological encoding system - DNA - that passes certain instructions from generation to generation. Cells can only do what they're told to do, and DNA is simply an information-copying mechanism.

But there's nothing particularly special about it, marvellous organic masterpiece though it is - there's no function unique to DNA that can't be performed in other ways using other kinds of materials and processes.

Think of what we do here at Intelligencia. Coding for AI. Whatever we come up with, at base it's simply noughts and ones. The haploid human genome codes for 2.9 billion base pairs, which corresponds to around 725 megabytes of data. That's just more than a CD's worth. You and I have the same data density as Rick Astley's Greatest Hits.

With this idea in mind, compare two iterations of the Signal. Could it be that common stretches correspond to some universal aspect of the species, whereas the differences code for variation between individuals? If my hunch is right, if we compare enough repeats we should be able to tell what a generic version of our alien is like: a type specimen, if you will, if only in code.

I think what we may be looking at here are the blueprints for a number of discrete, separate entities, unique specimens of an evolved species.

Jack

[Email header removed]

Hey Jack

Nice.

No, I take that back. Astonishing.

Did you think about signal compression and redundancy? These are certainly things I'd code into a message that had to survive intact across who knows how many light years.

Assuming you're onto something, I wonder if these putative aliens knew that there would be civilisations out there who could receive their signal and make sense of it. Do you not think that they'd somehow try to include the <u>solution</u>, the means to decode and comprehend the signal <u>within the signal itself?</u>

Yrs, Dan

[Email header removed]

Dan -

Though it may have been more efficient from a bandwidth point of view to piggyback the parts that differ on just one transmission of the much larger common stretch, there's no guarantee that the signal would be received in its entirety.

The possibility of drop-out might just be too risky - it'd be far safer if each iteration was self-contained, with all the necessary information to be deciphered even if the rest of the signal was lost.

It <u>does</u> seem very likely that we've received only part of a much longer transmission. Suppose we begin towards the end of a cycle - assuming the break is the 3.8 millisecond pause between repeats and not, according to some alien syntax, somewhere else - and the last iteration has been cut off part way through as well. Of the iterations received, <u>none</u> were absolutely identical.

The signal as a whole, if it does repeat, does so on a far larger interval than the section we have.

Jack

[Email header removed]

Hi Jack -

Allow me to float a few ideas of my own.

There are around 1.8 billion digits in each iteration, on average. Some are much shorter, a few longer, topping out around 7.2 billion. Compare that to the 3 billion base pairs in human DNA. Either most of these entities are just simpler, or (I think more likely) a lot of extraneous material may have been stripped out. Humans have a lot of non-coding junk in their genomes, or repetitive stretches where 'viral'

segments have copied themselves along huge stretches of DNA
sometime in our distant evolutionary history, rendering them
nonfunctional. Any sufficiently advanced species who could
encode themselves in such a manner could surely edit the
database beforehand, don't you think?

Yrs, Dan

[Email header removed]

Dan -

When you say alien species...

Look at the way the signal modulates.

We have repeats with variations in the 1-5% range, then an
abrupt change as we enter another section which may show only
a 60-70% similarity with the first, but within it we again
see only small variations on the theme. Note that there is no
smooth transition from one state to another - we see distinct,
abrupt steps in the signal.

Each 'theme' may repeat anywhere from only once to more than
several hundred thousand times. There's one section where
the variation is below 0.05% for over 760 million million
iterations.

'Species', plural.

It's a zoo.

Jack

[Email header removed]

Hi Jack

Fascinating.

Now, if this signal is the result of intelligent design (!)
and not an evolved biological phenomenon, is it not logical to
assume that at least some of the species - plural - encoded in
it may have language? A way to communicate?

Might there be a message in the message?

Yrs, Dan

Dan-

Beware messages from little green men.

You of all people should know that.

J.

[Email header removed]

Jack-

Let me worry about how to repel the imminent alien invasion.

What I want to know is:
HOW DO WE GET TO SEE WHAT THESE ALIENS LOOK LIKE????!

Magic glasses?

[Email header removed]

Dan - how indeed!

That is one more puzzle I'd certainly like an answer to.

J.

--ends--

Article I Talk   Printer-friendly version

The Daedalus Footage

From Wikipedia, the free encyclopedia

> This page is currently protected from editing until disputes have been resolved.
> Please discuss changes on the talk page or request unprotection.
> Protection is not an endorsement of the current version. (protection log)

> **THE FACTUAL ACCURACY OF THIS ARTICLE IS DISPUTED.**
> Please see the relevant discussion on the talk page.

Much has been written about the short film known as the "Daedalus Footage", named after the location where it was purportedly filmed, a crater [1] and alleged lunar base (Daedalus Base) [2] near the centre of the far side of the Moon. Proponents cite it as unambiguous proof of an alien encounter; critics respond that the indistinct footage could be of a routine lunar, or even Earthbound, training mission, or an elaborate hoax.

Official sources within NASA (National Aeronautics and Space Agency) and the ESA (European Space Agency) have to date distanced themselves from the controversy, citing a policy of "not commenting on fringe UFO material". [3]

Background [edit]

The footage was part of a tranche of classified documents released into the public domain by Edward White, a Canadian computer programmer, former CIA employee and government contractor who had access to classified information from the U.S. National Security Agency (NSA) and NASA. [4][10]

Buried in the large quantity (an excess of 1,500,000 text pages and other file formats) of material relating to national security which took centre stage in media coverage upon its initial availability, the importance of the footage did not become apparent until timestamps and other metadata unambiguously pointed to a NASA origin. [5]

Since then, attention has been intense. Mainstream TV and newspaper coverage has generally been of a sceptical nature, though more serious documentaries have also been produced. As many as two dozen substantial online articles and analyses appeared in the three to four weeks after it surfaced. [63] [64] Though the same data breach included the so-called Signal from Space, it is not thought the two events are connected.

Location [edit]

Daedalus is a prominent crater located near the centre of the far side of the Moon, named after the Daedalus of Greek myth, a skilled craftsman and artist who constructed the wings for his son, Icarus. [6]

It was first photographed by the Apollo 11 astronauts during circumlunar orbit [7], and originally named "Crater 308", a temporary IAU designation that preceded the establishment of official far-side lunar nomenclature. [8] A terraced inner wall surrounds a cluster of central peaks and a relatively flat floor. Because of its location on the lunar far side, shielded from radio emissions from the Earth, it has been proposed as the site for a giant radio telescope which would be formed from the natural curvature of the crater itself, following the same principles as the Arecibo [22] radio telescope in Puerto Rico, but on a vastly larger scale. As of the time of writing, there has been no public funding available to build such a telescope, though detailed proposals have been prepared by two NASA subcontractors, [25] and rumours persist that a privately funded base does indeed exist, with either NASA, the UKSA (United Kingdom Space Agency), ESA and/or the Russian space agency Roscosmos' knowledge or explicit co-operation.

It is at, or close to, this location that the footage is alleged to have been shot. [9]

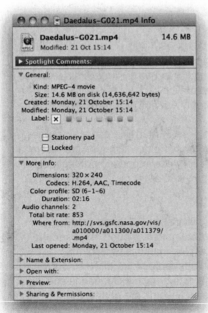

Screenshot of the *Get Info* panel (as viewed on an Apple Macintosh) showing basic file metadata. *Courtesy of McNally*

Format [edit]

The footage is a 4 minute, 16 second MPEG-4 digital file. Though carrying a stereo encoding, the two sound channels are identical, effectively rendering the audio mono. The pixel ratio of the image is small at 320x240, cited as supportive of the proposed helmet camera ("helmet cam") origin. The file size is 14.6 megabytes. [10]

Reception [edit]

Readers of online forum *The New Fortean Bulletin* voted the Daedalus Footage as "the best available photographic evidence of what is the Holy Grail of anomalous research – indisputable evidence of an encounter with an extraterrestrial biological entity". [11]

Conspirasphere called it "perhaps the single most important visual record in the field of ufology". [12]

Authenticity [edit]

Some researchers have claimed that the extant version of the Daedalus Footage is not authentic, or at least not the original version as purportedly shot. According to controversial [*citation needed*] blogger James Hartland, the film was "originally touted by the vast majority of conspiracy theorists as incontrovertible proof" but is now believed by many researchers to be a "sophisticated forgery". [13] Among those who believe the footage has been altered are researcher Frank Costa, [26] Vincent Hallis, [14] David Furman,[15] former editor of *New Inception* John K. Fletcher [16] and Norman Holt, author of *Clipped Wings: The Daedalus Footage Exposed* [17] who has called it "the biggest hoax, bar none, committed so far this century". [18]

Jackie Darvill, who claims to be a former photographic consultant to MI6, argues that there are anomalies in the footage, including "unexplained missing frames or jump cuts, an unnatural jerkiness of movement and changes of focus that you would not associate with an automatic helmet-mounted camera" during certain sequences. [19] Hallis puts this down to her unfamiliarity with typical human gaits in reduced lunar gravity. [20]

Darvill theorises that the jumps preceding frames 341 and 2147 are edits purposely designed to excise more explicit footage, arguing that a more complete version is still to be found "somewhere in what NASA laughably calls an archive". Her four Freedom of Information (FOI) requests have so far uncovered no new material. [21]

Journalist and researcher Baxter Clifton has stated that his analysis confirms that the Daedalus Footage was originally in the possession of NASA's National Photographic Interpretation Archive. [25] In his opinion, recorded in a telephone interview for the "Wake Up America!" podcast [26], the very fact that the footage remained buried in the tranche of leaked documents for so long tends to support its authenticity. "If you had made this, why would you hide it away in a bunch of dull email exchanges about recarpeting the Belize embassy or the rising cost of a decent hooker in Dubai? Would you not be impatient to share your hoax with the world?". [Full audio archived at [27].]

At the time of writing, the Daedalus Footage has clocked up over 630,000 views on YouTube. [28]

Content analysis [edit]

The film itself is purported to be helmet cam footage from an unnamed but almost certainly female astronaut. To describe it effectively is difficult; interested readers are directed to the two stills addressed later in this article and the original, freely available to view on YouTube. [29]

The first section, by general consensus now dubbed "The Walk" in online analyses, (see, for example [30]) can be typified as a jerky montage of poorly lit close-ups of rough, curving rock walls, spacesuit gloves and boots, items of lunar exploration equipment, and what conspiracy theorist and internet pundit Alex Smith has called "lots and lots of suggestive dark nothingness". [31] In an interview on HBO's Next Time For Real, he described it as "a drunkard's idea of a hand-held, 'found camera footage' style art film". [32] [33]

The shots that include items of equipment have been cross-referenced with standard-issue NASA kit, and though many of these items can be bought on the open market, some, specifically a soil probe clearly visible in frames 770–789 and again in frames 1872–2013, seem to be authentic lunar issue. [citation needed]

Over this can be heard heavy breathing, the beeping of what Vincent Hallis suggests are proximity detectors [34], the astronaut's intermittent humming (the tune has been identified as David Bowie's 1972 hit, Starman [35] [36]) and her occasional conversations with herself. These have been transcribed in Karrie McCrea's The Daedalus Footage: A Complete Frame-by-Frame Reference and Transcript [37], and include such mundane phrases as "Up and over, there you go", progressing to a more agitated "Nothing to be scared about – nothing to be scared about

. . . nothing . . ." before the final sequence where for reasons discussed later the audio becomes unintelligible.

At Frame 1303, and just before one of the claimed missing sections, vertical structures can be seen crisscrossing the field of view. These have been likened to fallen beams or scaffold poles (Harris [38]) and are suggestive of built constructs, though natural formations – fallen stalactites, for example – are also a possibility. [34]

There then follows a section where the astronaut pauses to examine a portion of curved wall more closely. Inclusions of granite and other sediments can be seen, set in a matrix of pumice (*Geological Examination of the Daedalus Footage,* Gilbert Grahams, ed. PDF available at [40]). Harris has suggested several Earthbound locations that could match the geology seen at this point. [41]

The final section, dubbed "The Room" [42], has the poorest picture quality of all. Darvill *et al* theorise that this is due to some kind of electromagnetic interference [43]. The astronaut appears to enter a large chamber. The helmet light here provides just a jumping patch of illumination that can be seen moving over irregular rocky features set at widely differing distances from the camera. On the audio, it is possible to distinctly hear a quickening of her breathing.

Beginning at Frame 2101, a light travels away from the camera for some time, receding into the distance before finally disappearing or going out. This is generally agreed to be a flare, dropped over the edge of a precipice, its slow motion due to the reduced lunar gravity, though again this effect is not impossible to reproduce by altering the recording frame rate. [44]

The final frames have given rise to the most discussion. The astronaut has moved deeper into the chamber, towards an area to the rear of the space that appears as a series of concentric circles in the footage, radiating a subtle rainbow of colours. McCrea sums up the consensus: that this is "an in-camera artefact caused by some kind of lens flare rather than an actual object". [45] The picture quality is severely degraded from this point on. The two most well-known and contentious frames of the Daedalus Footage occur in this section, each during two separate short intervals where this coruscating effect is at a minimum and a clearer view is available.

Sound and EVP analysis [edit]

The audio from the point at which the 'rainbow effect' is first visible consists of a high-pitched series of electronic squeals and bleeps, with a repeating underlying low and falling bass note. No breathing or other sounds from the astronaut are audible above this noise. This is assumed to be due to electromagnetic interference from an unknown external source. [46] A cleaned-up sound file of this section is available on McNally's website, [47] and forms a kind of palimpsest upon which many researchers have claimed to discern certain words or phrases.

McNally's file has become one of the more celebrated examples of 'electronic voice phenomena' (EVP), sounds found on recordings that some researchers interpret as 'spirit voices', intentionally or unintention-ally recorded or even invoked by the operator. However, psychologists regard EVP as a form of auditory hallucination and McNally's method for enhancing the sound quality has been shown in independent lab tests [citation needed] to introduce structured sounds that are not in the original. The sound that many report hearing and describe as similar to a baby crying, or a fox on heat, may fall into this category. Other sceptical explanations for EVP include apophenia (a propensity to perceive nonexistent patterns in a randomised source) or equipment artefacts.

Frame 2131 [edit]

This is the first of the two frames from the final section of the Daedalus Footage to show a relatively clear view. It appears to reveal a white spindle-shaped object resting at an angle slightly off the vertical against a curved cave wall, [48] dubbed "The Spindle" [49] in most online analy-ses. A degree of localised disturbance suggesting some lateral force or violence is visible around the base and at the top of the object, where it appears to be embedded in the wall. [50] The scale of the object is hard to estimate accurately due to a lack of any reference objects within the frame, but comparison to earlier sections of the footage, where instru-ments of known dimensions or the limbs of the astronaut herself are vis-ible, give dimensions of around seven metres high by a metre and a half wide. [51] Harris, maybe predictably [citation needed], gives somewhat smaller dimensions. [52]

The object is white in colour, and rotationally symmetrical. It has a circu-lar feature at the midpoint measuring around 700mm in diameter, if the overall dimensions are considered accurate. [54]

Frame 2147 [edit]

This is similar to Frame 2131, the detail in intervening frames being much more ambiguous. The spindle-shaped object is again visible, this time larger and centrally placed in the field of view. The picture quality of

Frame 2147 is slightly better than Frame 2131 due to the closer proximity of the object.

Where the circular area was noted in Frame 2131, there now appears to be an arrangement resembling an open flower – eight or twelve (it is hard to discern) panels appear to have opened out and away from the main body, framing a dark area within. [56]

The "Entity" [edit]

In this recess is situated what has been dubbed the "Entity" (Harris, McCrea, Holt *et al*). [57] It should be restated that picture quality throughout this section is very poor, and image enhancement techniques have produced controversial results. Holt, for example, has shown through analyses of stills taken from similar quality footage of known subject matter that it is very easy to mistake digital artefacts for real objects [58], referencing by analogy the 'Face on Mars' controversy [59].

Regardless, most analyses suggest that a smooth curved object is visible within, described by McNally in *Daedalus Visions* [60] as "shaped like a beckoning fingernail".

In *Through the Dark Mirror: The Daedalus Footage and Zapruder Film as Counter-Cultural Artefacts* Pauline Garvey calls this frame "probably the most haunting apport from the shadow realm I have ever seen. [It is] indistinct enough to allow wild speculation, yet particular enough to powerfully evoke an unsettling 'otherness' . . . [it can] fascinate and disturb in equal measure. This image has given me many sleepless nights." [62]

Norman Holt suggests it is a section of bald tyre, set in an abstract geometric sculpture, probably made from aluminium. [63]

See also [edit]

- The Solway Firth Spaceman
- The Baltic Anomaly
- The Warminster 'Thing'
- The 'Face on Mars'
- Crop circles

References [edit]

[1] Webb, Rev. G. W. *Celestial Objects for Common Telescopes* (6th ed.) ISBN 3078-0-486-65917-3.
[2], [7] Graham-Rowe, Duncan "Astronomers plan telescope on Moon". *New Scientist*. Retrieved 10-25.

UNDERGROUND ARTIST

A banner announcing the exhibition had been wrapped around a three-metre-square air vent in the forecourt of the NCP car park on Brewer Street, a brutalist '60s structure J. G. Ballard would have eulogised. Across the street, Jack studied the mugs and posters decorated with pirated images of David Hasselhoff and 'Marylin Munroe' in the window of the Vintage Magazine Shop, cupping his hand against the glass to block the pink neon promises and explicit-content warnings reflected from the sex shop opposite. A crowd was beginning to form: art school hipsters, trust-fund gallerinas, clove-vapers and sundry hangers-on, currently threaded through by a rowdy hen party in matching pink sashes in whose wake a homeless man with a matted grey beard was panhandling for change.

The show itself was taking place in the car park's basement. Architecturally, it was a long way from the rarefied oak-panelled spaces of the nearby National Gallery but, Jack felt, entirely appropriate.

A small door just beyond the chevron-striped barrier led down a flight of stairs, past an empty payment kiosk and into a short dogleg corridor with a black velvet drape at each end which acted as a light-proof airlock. This gave onto the main room beyond, a low-ceilinged concrete bunker that had been freshly whitewashed. As a gallery space it had quite a few advantages – cavernous, subterranean, and unpunctuated by windows that would cut down available wall space. Although, since the smoking ban, Jack now found these kinds of enclosed spaces bearable, he couldn't imagine that an underground venue suffused with petrol fumes in the centre of a polluted metropolis like London would pass any air purity tests. Back in his nightclubbing heyday, he reckoned he'd inhaled the equivalent of a dozen Woodbines a night, even though a cigarette had not once touched his lips.

Two rows of lecterns had been arranged down the length of the room, both some two metres from the walls and facing them. On each of these was placed an iPad, held down under a thick panel of perspex by heavy cyclist's D-locks, presumably to deter guests from accidentally taking them home. Over these people hovered, bottles of German lager or plastic cups of complimentary rosé in hand, tentatively scrolling and swiping the screens.

Mounted on the wall behind each of the lecterns was a large LED screen. They were placed side by side, each flush with its neighbour, so that they formed two continuous panels along opposing walls, end to end. The room was dark save for these and the dozen or so iPads, and as their light levels and colours changed, so did the illumination on the faces of those present.

In the gloom, Jack could not spot anyone he knew. He managed to get close to one of the iPads and waited for a woman with a jet-black fringe and a polka-dot smock to finish poking the screen. With a final dismissive swipe, she turned to her friend with a bemused shrug, her bottle, held at 45 degrees, spilling a few drops of beer onto the glass.

Like a punter waiting to be served at a bar, Jack was now in front of the screen. He wiped it clean with his sleeve and tried to make sense of the interface. A multicoloured mandala folded in upon itself in the centre of an otherwise empty space. There were no other instructions, and the metal clasp through which the D-lock was attached covered the buttons. He experimentally swiped a finger across horizontally, left to right. The mandala spun faster. He placed his finger on the screen and the mandala came to a stop, then seemed to open up from the point of contact, like tectonic plates resurfacing some alien planet. *Nice graphics,* he thought.

He surmised that it was procedurally generated on the fly, and not a pre-rendered animation he was merely rousing into action. He looked up, and realised that what was happening on the iPad was being projected, much larger, on the wall in front of him. As the other iPads were activated, two wall-to-wall rows of mandalas appeared, each moving to its own particular rhythm. Jack was reminded of a Science Museum exhibit depicting the evolution of the Sun and planets, though this was much more abstract and more than a little psychedelic by comparison. He thought of the first time he had seen a fractal Mandelbrot zoom; the swirling organic shapes had been familiar and disturbing in equal measure. Given his proclivity to see patterns and connections, in those first fractals he fancied he saw some deeper aspect of the very structure of Nature herself; and what's more, that it was somehow descriptive of the internal workings of his own mind. His recognition of something familiar but slightly askew was not unique; others had told him they felt it too. He felt it again now.

The mandala, the heart of which was currently glowing a pale pink from inside a latticework of darker spikes like a radiolarian under a microscope, seemed to call to him. He experimentally flicked it off the screen. Looking up as he did so, he saw it approach, then bounce off, the mandala projected on the next screen along. Turning his attention from the screen to the adjacent lectern, he was pleasantly surprised to see a pixie-faced girl with her hair tied up in an elaborate braid, finger hovering over her own screen, looking back at him. She looked down, concentrated, and after a couple of attempts, managed to send her mandala bouncing over to skim his. On the screen, they rotated around each other, exchanging multihued digital skeins of light like stars sharing their chromospheres, then returned to their original positions, where they expanded and contracted at the rate of slow breathing.

"You trying to realign my chakras?" she asked, raising her voice so as to be audible over the low hum of conversation.

Jack lifted his hand from his iPad and held it up in feigned surrender. "No. Just cleansing your aura. Appeared to be a bit grubby from here."

She looked as if she was deciding whether this was an insult or not. Jack gave her his best disarming smile, a combination of wonky grin and raised eyebrow that unbeknownst to him made him appear slightly retarded. After studying him for a second longer, she pulled the same face back. Jack laughed, and began to make his way over, the man waiting behind him immediately pushing forward, eager to have a go himself.

"Do you know the artist?" Jack asked, by way of a more formal hello.

She waved her hand vaguely. "No. Well, the friend I came with does. Shares a studio with him. Are you an artist?"

Jack wished he was. "No. I'm more of a, um, programmer. I work with artists sometimes, if they need a tech type to collaborate with. I'm more the facilitator than the one with the crazy ideas. Ha." Pause. "So." Jack waved his bottled beer inarticulately at nothing in particular. "What about you?"

"You don't want to hear about me," she said.

"Sure I do."

She looked away, across at the wall of projections. Jack, not wishing to look her straight in the eye previously, now chanced a more detailed examination. '50s-cut vintage skirt. Comically oversized bow at the back. Ironic slim-fit Joy Division *Unknown Pleasures* T-shirt in pink, the horizontal lines in gunmetal-grey glitter. ("Man-glitter" as Nixon had called it, pointing to a birthday card Harriet had given him that also featured an airbrushed red Ferrari, a glass of champagne and a rearing stallion.)

Jack liked what he saw.

He mentally wrote a few lines of Mathematica code that would reproduce the design, and on a whim, another few lines that would animate
it. He couldn't help it; it was how his mind worked, even when he was
supposed to be off-duty.

```
    R3[n_] := (SeedRandom[n]; RandomReal[])
Show[
  Table[
    Plot[80 - m + .2*Sin[2 Pi*R3[6*m]
        + Sum[4*Sin[2 Pi*R3[4*m] + t +
            R3[2 n*m]*2 Pi]*
          Exp[-(.3*x + 30 - 1*100*R3[2 n*m])^2/20], {n, 1,
30, 1}]] +
      Sum[3 (1 + R3[3*n*m])*Abs[Sin[t + R3[n*m]*2 Pi]]*
        Exp[-(x - 1*100*R3[n*m])^2/20],
        {n, 1, 4, 1}],
      {x, -50, 150}, PlotStyle -> Directive[White, Thick],
      PlotRange -> {{-50, 150}, {0, 85}},
      Background -> Black,
      Filling -> Axis,
      FillingStyle -> Black,
      Axes -> False,
      AspectRatio -> Full,
      ImageSize -> {500, 630}],
    {m, 1, 80, 1}]
  ] // Timing
```

Jack's attention returned to the present moment. She had been telling him something he hadn't quite got the gist of and was now looking at him expectantly. He was about to tell her what he'd just done, but thought better of it. He decided he should nod. Not vigorously, just in case, but a sage, slow nod.

"So you know the artist too?"

"What? No. Sorry, I couldn't hear you – it's getting a bit noisy in here, and my right ear isn't so good."

She leaned closer. "I'm filling in. They needed help setting all this up, and the artist's assistant – my friend – called me in. It was a few weeks' work. Gave me a bit of time to think about what to do next."

"Is the artist here?"

"Yep. He's over . . . over there. With the entourage." She pointed with the neck of her Beck's.

Jack could see a clump of people around one of the lecterns further down, craning to get a view of a central figure whose fingers were flying over the surface of the iPad as if it were a musical instrument. Highlights from the projections reflected from their glasses and refracted through their green bottles. The wall projection was building into a riot of colour and movement. From one central mandala, mushroom-headed protrusions repeatedly jumped out of the surface then retreated back inside to leave dark recesses, around which eight or ten smaller mandalas were orbiting. These were different again – some glowed, others were coal-black silhouettes, but all pulsed and rotated with inner life. There was a complicated interchange of streamers and wispy filaments connecting them, and as they moved this was woven into an ethereal faceted cage around the central object, through which the mushrooms repeatedly punched holes before the filaments again filled them in. It looked to Jack like a simulation of a virus he'd once seen on the Discovery Channel.

He turned back. "So, not wanting to ask the obvious question and sound like an art ignoramus, I'm going to ask the obvious question. And probably sound like an art ignoramus."

"Go ahead. I can't promise I'll be able to enlighten you."

Jack gestured at the screens. "It's beautiful. It's intriguing. I have no idea what I'm looking at, though."

"*Beauty.* That's something of an, an unusual word to use these days, in matters of art, don't you think?"

"Sorry. Not ironic enough? Too honest?"

She looked up at Jack, face open and expressive. "No, I'm not taking the piss. It's true. Working with the tech guys who helped put this together, they used that word way more often than I ever hear it used in an art studio or a gallery. Looking at the code, the way it changes and evolves. 'Beautiful'. That was what they kept calling it."

"It *is* beautiful."

"I don't pretend to understand how they did it – it's a kind of fractal generative art, but not built from the kind of iterative code you'd usually use to make fractals."

Jack had just spotted Soo Terrain, who was stepping through the crowd towards them. She stopped a short distance away, gave a small wave at shoulder height, and surreptitiously pointed to the girl in the polka-dot dress, mouthing "who?" with a wink. Jack beckoned her over.

"This is Soo, Soo Terrain. DJ. Friend from way back. She invited me. This is – I'm sorry, I didn't ask your name."

"Nadine."

"Nadine," said Jack.

"Hi Nadine," said Soo.

"Hi," repeated Nadine.

"Nadine knows the artist," said Jack. "She helped to put on the show."

Soo extended a hand. "You did? I like it. Not sure what I'm looking at, but I do like it. It's – it's beautiful."

Jack leant in towards Nadine. "It *does* sound a bit lame."

Nadine laughed. "Hey, I'm not one to go in for all that 'meaning is in the eye of the beholder' stuff myself." She swung her hips and gestured first to the left and then to the right. "Ambiguity – or just unresolved pretension? You decide!"

"You said it was programmed. I know programming, but this is clever stuff. How is it done?"

"You'd have to ask the artist himself for specifics, but it's one of those great ideas I'm sure someone else must have already duplicated."

"How so?"

"The looped code from which all these various animated thingies are derived? Well, we just provided a digital petri dish, and it almost *animated itself.* What you see here is the Signal from Space."

Pulsar

From Wikipedia, the free encyclopedia

In November 1967 astronomer Jocelyn Bell Burnell at the Cavendish Laboratory in Cambridge observed an unidentified radio signal in the constellation of Vulpecula [1] with a period of 1.3373 seconds and a pulse width of 0.04 seconds. The object flashed with such regularity that it would be possible to use it as a clock with an accuracy of one part in a hundred million. The pulse's short period did not fit any current astronomical models, and when observations with another telescope confirmed the signal,[2] instrumental artefacts could also be eliminated. At this point, Bell notes that she "did not really believe we had picked up signals from another civilisation, but obviously the idea had crossed our minds. We had no proof that it was an entirely natural radio emission. It's an interesting problem – if one thinks one may have detected life elsewhere in the Universe, how does one announce the results responsibly? Who does one tell first?" [3] [4]

They nicknamed the signal LGM-1, for "little green me[...]
a second, similar source was discovered in a differen[...]
that the "LGM hypothesis" was entirely abandoned.[5]

The word "pulsar" is[...]
appeared in print in[...]

Background [ed[...]

After the discovery[...]
suggested a rotatin[...]
have a 33-nanose[...]
proposed model. A[...]
considered perfec[...]

Popular culture [edit]

A hand-drawn graph of the pulsar taken from the Ca[...]
pedia of Astronomy was used on the cover of Englis[...]
Joy Division's debut album, "Unknown Pleasures", re[...]
1979 and designed by Peter Saville. [12]

See also [edit]

ONE RED BALLOON

Jack rolled over.

Where? Not the new office . . . though he had been sleeping there of late, under his desk . . . where, then?

His apartment. Like the office, it was barely furnished. An antiseptic white cube, two walls of perfect silk emulsion, one of glass and one of unfinished concrete. The chrome door handles resembled surgical implements, throwing him reflections of the light fixtures in the ceiling. Books and magazines were stacked high against the walls, there being no shelves to put them on. Twelve black and white Bernd and Hilla Becher photographs of industrial gas tanks, arranged in a single large frame, were the only decoration. Furniture? A mattress with no base. A clothes rack. Most of what Jack deemed important was either at the office or still in storage.

A pink *Unknown Pleasures* T-shirt hung over the back of a folding steel chair.

Ah.

Jack lay very still on his back on the low bed, now aware of the slow breathing beside him. He looked back at the chair. She had straddled him on that very piece of furniture last night. He'd cupped her small breasts in his hands as she leaned over him, her hair falling down around his face as if to give their mouths some privacy. Light from a sodium street-lamp outside had highlighted her compact curves with a brushstroke of yellow, a tight vector describing her with the mathematical efficiency of a Formula One driver taking the racing line around Magny-Cours.

There were no curtains. Jack was unsure where you'd buy such things. Just outside his newbuild block, caught in a tree bare of leaves, he had noticed a red balloon. As a slight breeze bent the branches, the balloon moved in and out of a floodlight beam placed to pick out a surviving section of London's Roman city wall. Catching the light, then dipping into shadow and out again, it seemed to Jack that it was sending him a message in Morse: *dot-dash. Dot-dash.*

His propensity to see messages everywhere, his compulsion to look under the bonnet of reality in order to find elegant mathematical models for random stimuli, definitely chose its moments. With not a little effort, he had refocused on the girl in front of him.

And realised that he'd come.

Later that Sunday afternoon, just before she left, Nadine wrote down her email address on a corner of paper she casually tore from a book atop one of the piles. Jack, wincing at this small act of desecration but saying nothing, tucked it inside the novel he was reading for safekeeping.

A bookmark – something to let you know where you are.

THE CAVERNS OF THE MOON

A jumble of regolith lay at the bottom of the crevasse. Here on the lunar far side, the light from the floods positioned around the edge easily outshone the stars that Dana Normansson was used to seeing with such clarity. A ping from the laser rangefinder revealed an eighteen- or twenty-metre drop, oscillating up to thirty or thirty-five and back again with a small turn of the wrist. Clearly it was jaggedly uneven down there. In the reduced lunar gravity and with her lightweight lunar rappelling equipment, the use of which had become second nature, this posed no problem. She jumped out, fed out the line, and swung back to solidly place both feet on the vertical wall three metres below the edge with a puff of boot-crusted moondust.

Dana was aware that the lunar caverns in this area that had been explored so far were ancient drained lava tubes rather than the product of flowing water, and expected the same here. That the Moon had been geologically active in the past had never been in doubt; the lunar maria, which early astronomers mistook for seas, are vast volcanic floodplains. Today it was a grey, dusty dead world whose arrowhead peaks, untempered by wind or rain, threw long, hard-edged shadows no morning mist would ever smudge. It had been this way for three billion years.

She pushed away from the wall and let the winch freewheel, spinning out more cable. A couple of squeezes on the brake switch brought her to a stop with a small bounce, half a metre above a flat-topped boulder to which she dropped with practised grace. The sharp rocks cast equally sharp shadows; it was hard to tell in the reflective glare how deep the gaps between them might be. Dana hopped across a series of chasms until she landed, with a larger puff of dust, on the undisturbed floor. The limit of the floodlit area was three lunar paces away – beyond lay darkness.

She stopped just inside the shadow's edge. Facing away from the glare, she activated her helmet LED and waited for her eyes and the visor's reactive electromagnetic dampers to adjust to the gloom.

Away from the fallen section of roof that gave her access, the ground was clear. Ahead, to a height of several metres, the walls of the tunnel were striated with horizontal tidemarks from successive lava flows. Knobbly lumps of what looked like shiny porridge or fossilised sludge glittered as embedded flecks of quartz threw back the beam. The cavern was surprisingly regular in shape: elliptical in cross-section and around half as high again as she was, standing in her lightweight suit. She felt as if she were about to explore a Victorian sewer; it looked almost as if it had been purposely tunnelled out of the bedrock to suit creatures of human proportions. Not at all like the Earthside caves they had explored during astronaut training.

The ground-penetrating radar imagery she had hacked from the last two overhead passes of the Korean KITSAT-L6 satellite told her that this cavern system extended for tens, if not hundreds of kilometres to the east and west; a labyrinth of unexplored galleries and backflow tubes, tributaries and collapsed pāhoehoe flows. Their existence had been deduced as far back as the 1950s, and they had briefly been considered as potential sites for human habitats, providing as they did natural protection from micrometeorite impacts and the harsh radiation at the lunar surface. Ultimately, in the short time Daedalus Base had been operational, it had proven easier to build the habitats in prefabricated sections from adapted rocket stages on the surface than deal with site-specific lunar housebuilding. There were just too many unknowns.

Too many unknowns. To that, Dana could now add another, far greater unknown.

The object had entered the Solar System at great speed along the ecliptic, far too fast to be a comet or asteroid. The Deep Space Network, NASA's array of giant radio antennas, first picked it up just inside the orbit of Neptune.

Less than a day later it was inside the orbit of Uranus. Saturn, and the Cassini probe, were too remote to image it. Through Hubble it appeared as an elongated needle of light, perfectly symmetrical along the vector of motion. It was hard to estimate its true length or width – it began in invisibility, thickened to a wider bright bulge at the centre that radiated in the near infrared, then thinned back down again to nothing. Smooth and featureless, it left no tail as a comet might, nor was it followed or preceded by smaller pieces that might have broken off a rocky main body.

Extrapolating its trajectory, it was immediately apparent that it would not pass through the Solar System unscathed.

Thirty-five hours after it had first been detected, and exactly as predicted, it pierced Jupiter's moon Europa.

Though it is the smallest of the four Galilean satellites, Europa is still almost as large as Earth's Moon. The object appeared to pass clean through the icy body without any loss of velocity. It did not, however, leave it unscathed – from both the impact and exit points, vast plumes of material erupted from its ice-covered subterranean ocean, the existence of which up until then had been the subject of much speculation. Now there was no doubt of its existence. At speeds far greater than escape velocity, molten silicates and salt water were thrown out to be flash-frozen in the chill of space; some returned as a fine snow of debris, falling back to the surface in slow motion over a period of weeks, the rest entered orbit around Jupiter itself to form a thin and tenuous new ring.

This did not alter the object's original trajectory. The calculations still held.

The show did not go unnoticed by amateur astronomers on Earth, who marvelled at the eruption of a majestic pair of new ice volcanoes, unprecedented in their ferocity. The cause went unseen, both too faint and too fast to be picked up by anything other than the most powerful instruments, and so remained unknown except to certain members of the institutions and governments that owned them, among which was one Daniel Novák.

Approaching the orbit of Mars, and in contradiction to the natural behaviour of a body freefalling towards the Sun, it had perceptibly begun to slow.

This was the first indication that it might be artificial.

It passed through the Asteroid Belt without incident. As it slowed, its path also began to curve as it fell deeper into the Sun's gravity well; if it continued on its present trajectory it would pass well within the orbit of Mercury, whip around the Sun's equator then swing out again into the inner Solar System.

At this point it could no longer be doubted that its intended, perhaps final, destination was Earth.

There was one question all those who knew about this interloper were asking themselves: *Was it a ship, or a bullet?*

The Earth does not spin through space alone. It has a companion. Formed from its own ejected core in a cataclysmic collision during the early formation of the Solar System, the Moon now circles its mother, rotating on its axis once for every orbit so that it always presents the same face towards her, the other away. In the centre of the far side, where the Earth never rises, lies Daedalus Base.

Through a confluence of staffing and resupply vehicle hiccups, Dana was currently its sole occupant. She had been briefed on events as they unfolded. She waited.

The Moon, though large by human standards, is a mote of dust in the vast cathedral dome of the Solar System, a tiny speck caught in the light of the Sun. But even at these great scales, it is possible to predict a trajectory to within a matter of kilometres.

And those predictions now gave Daniel Novák a sliver of hope.

The Moon swung around its orbit just as it had always done, and at the last moment came between the Earth and this needle of light, absorbing the full force of the impact in its solar plexus and preventing what could have been an extinction-level event.

For the vast majority of the occupants of Earth, the day was just like any other. They went to work, they played, they slept soundly. No one but a handful of well-placed people knew that to protect their planet, the Moon had taken the full force of a bullet fired from eternity.

The object had impacted the surface 209 kilometres almost due south of Daedalus Base, clipping the side of Racah Crater. That the location, like Daedalus itself, was close to the exact centre of the lunar far side did not go unremarked.

Daedalus Base served Daedalus Telescope. The one-woman crew was not a trained soldier, diplomat or exobiologist. She was an astronomer, a physicist and an astronaut, and other than that was utterly unequipped for this mission. The wrong woman in the right place at the right time, Dana had been the closest to hand by two hundred and thirty-nine thousand miles.

Positioned almost dead centre on the lunar far side, Daedalus Crater was a perfect location for a radio telescope. Shielded from the electro-magnetic noise of Earth and the leaky communication satellites surrounding it by the bulk of the Moon, blessed by a lack of distorting atmosphere, the 100-kilometre-wide crater formed a natural receiving dish. Early proposals had involved smoothing out the crater itself, or spinning a huge dish of mercury within its bowl in order to create a perfect parabola, but the practical solution had been to place just under 100,000 ten-metre reflectors at regular intervals over the uneven surface, rising up to the rim three kilometres above the crater floor. Far from being a perfect dish, the crater was a rumpled bedsheet of collapsed terraces, smaller secondary craters, hilly terrain and three rounded central peaks. Positioning 100,000 reflectors on individual pylons meant that the ground itself did not need to be perfectly parabolic; adjusting their height individually was a relatively simple feat of engineering. The angle and rotation of each was centrally controlled from Daedalus Base, enabling the telescope to be pointed some distance above and below the ecliptic.

Above this feat of engineering, arranged on a tower built on the highest of the three central peaks that rose two kilometres above the crater floor, was the focus of the array – the instrument cluster. The data collected here was sent back to Daedalus Base itself via a series of cables laid out across the crater floor beneath the forest of reflectors. The cluster could be raised or lowered to bring different instrument packages to bear at the focal point: a Gregorian sub-reflector, a rectangular waveguide, a spectrograph and an optical high-resolution camera, plus two other instruments the purposes of which were somewhat opaque.

On Earth, there were meetings and conference calls between people at NASA, UKSA, the ESA and Roscosmos that Dana knew personally, others she had only heard of, and still more she had not. Proposals and counter-proposals were discussed. What she did pick up on, though it was not explicitly stated, was the fact that only a select cadre were in possession of the facts, such as they now were, and that there was some concern that it might not remain that way for long. The existence of Daedalus Base was not public knowledge; Dana herself had gone through a series of rigorous background checks, and she assumed she was not alone in this. Any new leak might now reveal not one, but two big secrets.

She listened to all the competing theories the small group of scientists she had access to had put forward. The tiny chances of hitting not just one but two of the Solar System's minor bodies was either a matter of intent or gross carelessness. Given the speed and trajectory of the arte-fact from the moment it had first been detected, through its skewering of Europa to its current and presumed final resting place, they reasoned that if it did have a steering mechanism, that mechanism must either be dysfunctional or have a turning radius larger than the Solar System.

If it was a bullet that had been fired from a cosmic gun, it had come from an origin point so distant that it must have been aware of only the most elementary details of its destination. Whether this revealed a lack of foreknowledge or a simple desperation of purpose they currently had no way of telling.

The impact site had been imaged from low lunar orbit. Dana had studied the pictures intently. The precision of the impact crater was aston-ishing – it resembled some kind of processing artefact or the shadow of a passing moon rather than a trace of a real physical event. Before and after comparisons revealed a perfectly circular black perforation in the pinkish-grey foothills of Racah, approximately six or seven metres across, depth unknown. The highest resolution images showed small cascades of loose dust flowing over the edge and a raised half-crescent of compacted looser regolith to the south-west edge. Otherwise it was clean, sharp – almost mathematically precise.

As none of the orbiting imaging satellites which were equipped with radar passed directly overhead, its depth was unknown. Lunar seismometers had registered an impact signature not dissimilar from a meteorite a few metres or so in diameter travelling at a few hundred kilometres a second, but there the similarity ended. That there was no surface debris meant that the artefact must be – or must have been – incredibly dense or resilient, had not broken up on impact and even now could lie intact, somewhere deep below the surface.

Unlike Europa, it had not exited the near side of the Moon, that much was clear. The seismic data indicated that it had penetrated sixty or so kilometres before coming to a stop, just within our satellite's igneous outer crust.

It looked just as if a cosmic hole-punch had been applied to the lunar surface.

GRAMMAR AND COMPOSITION

Jack re-read her email.

Nadine had enquired if he'd like to come with her to a late opening at the Victoria and Albert Museum. There would be free wine, a lecture they could ignore if they felt like it, and no parties of schoolchildren running through the halls.

He ran replies through his head.

"I've been told I'm on the autistic spectrum. An unreasonable attention to detail coupled with finding human interactions sometimes difficult to fathom."

Add some positives, Jack. Nixon salesmanship style.

"A propensity for spotting patterns, repetitions, a knack for seeing through large volumes of raw data to the underlying equations. Organisation, assimilation, cataloguing. I'd probably make a good librarian. I like to think I'm a good programmer."

Did that sound self-congratulatory? Too self-effacing? He held his finger on the delete key and the cursor marched left, eating words as it went. Not for the first time, he wished real life also had an undo command. *Apple-z. Let's try that day again.*

He looked down at the mouse he held in his left hand.

Jack found human interaction more tractable at one remove. No longer a live stage show you winged without a script, but more a controlled, pre-edited performance. There was stage make-up in the form of a Photoshopped selfie, the lighting artfully arranged; the wardrobe department had been consulted and a costume carefully chosen to project the right attitude; the dialogue was scripted to the perfection of polished prose. In many ways it was a self-penned show, presented as an off-the-cuff and entirely natural reflection of the performer, but in reality carefully prepared for the benefit of an imagined audience – one which might well be looking the other way at a competing show which just happened to have more intrigue, celebrity cameos and confessional pathos.

So:

Step 1. *Write.*

In his head he cross-referenced a list of opening lines, considered their meanings, implementation histories, writing styles. Through multiple sets of mental parentheses, he drilled down into nested meanings within meanings, taking quick detours to cross-reference. He thought of it as the opposite of assertion by faith; he wasn't just saying this, making it all up – there are others who have come to the same conclusion. Because he valued the scientific method, he prepared a second group of mental papers that poked holes in his argumentation and proposed alternative interpretations of his raw data.

Insert joke here? Not too off-colour.

Or a literary reference?

This required a balance between projecting a casual precocity and showing off. A tightrope act, dependent on the recipient's wit, intelligence, familiarity with the subject at hand and educational achievement. At a campus party Jack had once tried to open a conversation with a fellow student by asking what she thought of Chekhov's *Cherry Orchard*, which he'd just read. She'd pulled a face as if he'd just farted. Her friend had rolled her eyes and turned her back to him.

He had learned to pitch less specific and more egalitarian conversational openers. It wasn't that he didn't enjoy discussions of some intellectual depth, but now he saved them till the second or third sentence.

Step 2. *Edit.*

Simplify, bring the essential message to the surface, drop anything extraneous. Rearrange the structure for clarity. Refer back to that raw data. Plot graphs, poll results, aggregate by age, location and income, social class, gender, political affiliation. Remove biases. *No, Jack. This is not a report. No need to add footnotes and citations.*

Doing away with needless decoration, that non-functional component of design, also applied to machine code. Early programmers were paid by the line, until it was realised that lengthy code is not efficient code, or easily debugged code. *So what, Jack? Focus* . . . The push for maximum meaning with minimum means, less is more, leads to what? Elegance? *Beauty?*

There was that word again. Beauty was a peculiar attribute to associate with code, but Jack saw particularly simple and all-encompassing statements as just that. Beauty had definitely got something to do with fitness for purpose. And Nadine was, ahem, fit for purpose.

A red zigzag underscore. There was always a word or two Jack knew how to spell better than his spellcheck.

Step 3. *Press send. Worry.*

Jack hit return, and there was a skeuomorphic 'woosh', fading into an imagined distance.

We aren't actually who we hope we are. We are all the authors of a more polished, articulate persona that we present to the world. *Idealised.* But hasn't it always been so?

We forget things, we make mistakes, we say the wrong thing, we don't say the right thing. Sins of expression and omission. Life is more like bad free-form jazz, made up on the fly, not a sculpted and polished studio symphony, three minutes of genius carefully edited together over a period many times that long. Real life maps $T=t$; a second equals a second, an hour an hour, a lifetime a lifetime.

We have just one take to get it right.

```
OK, sounds fun! See you there! Jack x
```

DESCENT

Though not fully mapped, the satellite imagery led her to believe that the artefact – whatever it was – had intersected the extensive cave system, and that gave her an advantage she could exploit. Dropping into the caves well away from the impact site, she could approach unseen.

Daniel Novák had given her the go-ahead for the mission personally. She was aware that he would have done this only after lengthy consultations; she wondered precisely how many people knew she was here.

From the floor of the crevasse Dana remotely killed the floods. Though she couldn't be seen from Lagrange, the European PAR-55 satellite would be passing to the north in a matter of minutes. Looking up, a jagged slash of starfield was visible, cut across by the bright smudge of the Milky Way, against which were silhouetted the floodlight pylons and the cable-winch mechanism. The rover was out of sight; the rest of the journey would be on foot.

Her route through this maze had been carefully planned. She brought up the geophysical mapping data on her arm-mounted tablet; a blue-green glow suffused the walls, reaching where her directional helmet-mounted LED did not. The tunnels formed a complex system, branching and re-joining, looping out and back or terminating in dead ends or collapsed ceilings; other branches travelled for many kilometres in a straight line only to intersect with a sinkhole, a vertical passage that led down to a solidified plug.

Even taking her best estimate, to reach the probable point of intersection would take many hours. Down here, with a good few metres of volcanic rock above her, contact with the surface and Daedalus Base would be patchy at best, but even so she killed her data stream and the locator beacon, and went dark.

To the north, the cave was blocked by fallen boulders; to the south, the tunnel extended into darkness. This was the direction she intended to take. She supposed that had this been a terrestrial cave, there might have been the scent of damp clay, vegetation, bat guano, or the gossiping of underground waterways. Here, inside her suit, there was nothing but the rhythmic hiss of the air-circulation filter, her own breathing, and the creak of the suit's Teflon joints as she moved.

Dana discovered her first concern was how to avoid hitting her head on the ceiling. The loping gait all moonwalkers adopted out in the open had to be reduced to a careful slow-motion stride, and after inadvertently propelling herself up the curved walls a few times like a Mini in *The Italian Job* she fell into a slow, steady jog.

The tunnel swept down and to the left. Where one might expect water or sand to accumulate, there was nothing – bare rock, a rough pumice overhead, and a solidified lava floor that gave underfoot in the one-sixth lunar gravity like iced meringue.

The floor levelled out. Up ahead, something rectangular caught the light, reflected it back with multicoloured prismatic hues. Dana stopped. She was still many kilometres from the impact site, so was under no illusion that she had reached her destination. Shutting down her wrist tablet, she approached slowly.

Across her path, piercing both the ceiling and floor, was a multifaceted crystal the thickness of Daedalus Base's main antenna. Octagonal in cross-section like a pencil, it was as smooth as polished spinel: semi-transparent, with darker inclusions suspended within. With no weather to erode it, it had a squeezed-straight-out-the-mould perfection that Dana involuntarily put out her hand to better appreciate. Smaller crystals that had begun to grow from the vertices crumbled and fell to the ground under her touch.

Stepping around it, she saw that there was another, and beyond that, another; each was set at a differing angle, just off the vertical. Walking around the third, she saw that the tunnel opened up into a much larger space, too big for her LED to reveal the far side – if indeed it could, had it not been almost entirely blocked by a forest of crystalline trunks connecting floor to ceiling. Some were the thickness of a torso, some many times larger – an oak here, a redwood there. Dana was reminded of the columns of Luxor, though here there was no floor plan, just a void shot through with perfectly straight arrowshafts.

She traced a passage through to the far side, where the inclusions abruptly stopped and the tunnel continued. Here, a seismic shift in the bedrock had cut across the passage and dropped the floor by a metre and a half. Shining her helmet light down, there was nothing but a small pile of fine dust below, into which she jumped. It received her bootprints like fine flour, leaving impressions so crisp that future visitors could cast replacements from them millennia hence.

The tunnel continued down at a shallow angle. Overhead, the ceiling took on a pockmarked appearance – a series of circular voids with sharp frills between them, as if bubbles had risen to form the surface. Here the walls were faced with a smooth ochre residue that came to shoulder height and ran down in solidified runnels to the floor, where it fanned out like numerous small river deltas, reminding Dana of part-glazed ceramics. Some time in the distant past, liquid material had risen to this point in the cave complex, left a tidemark, and receded. As she descended deeper, it rose until it covered every surface. The tunnel narrowed like a furred-up artery, and she wondered if the route might become entirely blocked.

A short distance ahead it became apparent that this was not to be the case. The tunnel abruptly widened, and the solidified lava flowed in thick gouts out over a precipice and into darkness as the narrow space opened up once more into an enormous funnel-shaped void. Dana's LED was barely powerful enough to reveal the far side; approaching the rounded lip very slowly to avoid pitching herself out, she peered down over the edge.

She fought back a rising sense of vertigo. An astronaut is used to weightlessness and a sense of scale, but this enclosed chamber seemed to want to roll her around and suck her down into the hypogean abyss far below. She had entered the chamber around two-thirds of the way up a 60-degree conical slope, and if it wasn't for the furrows several metres deep that ran around the entire circumference like storm drains it would have been impossible for her to even contemplate crossing the vast space. Stepping down, she found she was standing in the lee of a half-pipe. As far as she could make out, above and below her the walls of the chamber were shaped in this fashion – it looked as if it had been carved out by a vortex that had swept huge boulders before it, gouging deep parallel grooves before vanishing down the sinkhole in the centre, far below.

The walls of the channel rose on either side. She was walking along a gently curving pipe like a waterpark flume, a third of which was open at the top. Playing her light along the wall she could see a cross-section of lunar geology, neatly laid bare; her helmet camera recorded the details of each striation for any future geologists who might one day follow her.

Across the huge space the far wall loomed like a multihued layer cake. It was pockmarked with inflow channels, each of which had produced a shelf of solidified rock just below like sagging, melted balconies. She was aware that the raw rock edges could cut her suit, tough though it was, and took great care where she placed her hands for balance during her circumnavigation.

A spark of light caught Dana's attention. Embedded crystals of quartz threw back glints like fresh snow, in a rainbow of colours. But this was something else, something different.

This— There it was again! Dana adjusted the transmissibility of her faceplate. No, it was not an artefact . . . what *was* that?

It seemed to move, move with a purpose. Dana held her breath and stood as still as she could; the only sound she could hear was the chesty wheeze of the air pump.

There *was* something up there! Small, grey, colourless as morning mist, on the lip of that balcony . . . watching over this subterranean auditorium from a box in the gods.

Was a show about to begin?

She trained her LED on the opening, tried to pinpoint it. She saw . . . what could she see? She wasn't quite sure. A blur at the edge of vision, something that appeared to ripple the very space in front of the dark entrance behind it. She couldn't seem to fix her gaze upon it. She felt as if an invisible . . . *presence* might be watching her, and for the first time on her journey became intensely aware of the oppressive weight of the many metres of rock that lay above her, of the sheer age of this place. How long must it have lain here, undisturbed? The Moon had not been volcanically active for at least a billion years; back then, on Earth, not even trilobites had been around to look up and see the red spots pockmarking the Man on the Moon's adolescent face.

Now these caves had received two intruders in quick succession. She tried to rationalise her growing panic, and panned the light across the ledge a second time. *Nothing.* Bringing up the wrist tablet, she scrubbed back through the camera feed for thirty seconds and replayed the footage. *Nothing.* She did the same again, using a variety of image enhancing waveband filters. Still nothing.

She started forward again. There wasn't time to waste – and anyway, Dana didn't believe in ghosts.

The right-hand wall of the curved gutter she was traversing became lower, rounded by the erosion of the flow. Just as she imagined she might be tipped out and down into the funnel itself, a space opened to her left. It was a passageway that had once carried a dark burgundy sediment, now solidified to a rough pumice. Dana climbed up onto the ancient flow, feeling as if she was standing on a pink tongue hanging from the open mouth of an underworld giant.

The space between the flow and the roof of the passage was less than a metre. She checked her map. This deep, the radar resolution was far too coarse to give her anything but the most basic guidance, and she tilted the three-dimensional projection this way and that to see if she could make better sense of her place within it. It definitely led in the right direction. She would have to crawl.

She adjusted her backpack and went down on all fours. Ahead, the LED revealed a semicircular space, ridged above like the roof of a mouth, and beyond, darkness. She ducked her head down and pushed forwards, humming to herself softly.

A short distance ahead, a rectangular block cut the tunnel in half. Dana pulled herself onto her side, and pushing against the ridged ceiling with her boots, forced her way through.

She emerged in an underground city.

SIGNS AND PORTENTS

"I'll *show* you."

Jack had opened the car door before they had come to a halt, taking a couple of quick steps as he hit the pavement to avoid colliding with a lamp post. Nixon, who was more accustomed to Jack's single-minded eccentricities than Harriet, was left to pay the black cab. Jack wouldn't care if he deducted it from his wages, but Nixon knew he'd just let it ride. Jack was . . . Jack.

A few strides and they'd caught up with him outside Russell Square Tube station. Jack had his camera in his hand, his finger on the shutter-release button, and was looking up, around. Above the modern shopfronts, it was still possible to see the unspoiled façades of the original buildings before the inevitable commercial encrustation of lettering had covered them over like so much alphabetic pigeon shit.

Billboards, awnings, posters, advertising, signs.

He took a photo.

>>SH-CLICK<<

Signs – and portents. Messages there for the reading, pregnant with meaning. A poetry of found text. He stopped, and spun around on his heels. A cyclist braked quickly and manoeuvred around him, swearing in German.

Jack's eyes alighted, seemingly at random, on snippets of words, phrases:

"Jack, it's just a coincidence. Take enough random pictures, and you're bound to throw up something. Law of averages. You know that." Harriet was bent forward, hands on her knees, supporting herself while she caught her breath. She'd not had a cigarette in seven months, but, boy, could she still feel their effects.

Nixon knew from experience he just had to let this run its course. Jack had come back again and again to his shots of the fridge door. Sure, it showed an interesting juxtaposition of type, but Jack's conviction that it held some special meaning for him was not something Nixon wanted to entertain. Though he was used to Jack's unsociable hours and intense periods of uninterrupted work on whatever his current obsession might be, he did have some semblance of a business to run.

Jack had a look of flushed intensity, as if he was about to pass a particularly large stool. If his hunch was right – if someone or some *thing* was trying to communicate with him, send him a message – it seemed that the only material it had to work with was the immediate environment.

He turned to his left. There was a red phone box whose interior was patchworked with prostitutes' 'tart cards', through the windows of which a pop-up stall selling doughnuts was visible.

Heh. William Burroughs would have appreciated this.

He shut his, eyes, head down. *Jack, calm yourself.* He repeated the mental exercises he'd been taught as a child, the slow mantra that alleviated the obsessive-compulsive tendencies of his cataloguing and categorising mind, that helped his thoughts jump the groove he could so easily get stuck in.

He opened his eyes. He was standing at the side of the road, at right angles to a zebra crossing. This time, he didn't need the camera. Painted on the tarmac along the gutter, two words of instruction told him what to do next.

Then an arrow:

 WHAT  **AFRAID OF ?**

  **MARK'**

MY TIME

MY

I express THE GREAT Circus

THE short *LIST* OF

SPANKING NEW ideas

Go Ahead

WHAT ARE
YOU WAITING FOR?

"Who are you? What do you want? What is that supposed to mean?"

Jack stepped out into the traffic. Nixon instinctively caught him by the sleeve, causing him to describe a wide arc back onto the pavement.

"I don't understand!" Jack had his head thrown back so far Harriet could see his fillings. Customers from the Greek restaurant next to the station had their faces to the window and a dinner-jacketed waiter stood at the door, absently holding a tea towel, watching them.

Harriet and Nixon followed Jack as he weaved around, their strained expressions the kind usually reserved for a wayward child.

"Jack, Jack. *Please.* Let's go back to the office."

"Pattern, form, meaning! You *see* it? *Tell* me you see it!"

Harriet thought she might cry.

BUILD

ME

A

BODY

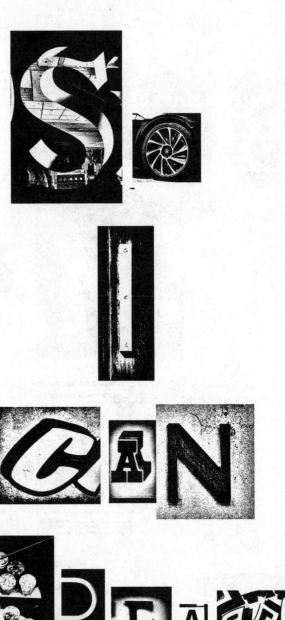

Jack finally understood.

DINNER IN THE RUINS

It certainly looked like a city.

Cubic rock outcrops split along their vertical and horizontal seams and faceted boulders the size of houses were stacked one on top of another. The perfect regularity of a city block was, on closer inspection, just a first impression; like shipping containers after a tsunami, they were skewed this way and that, a few jammed at angles between others as if they'd fallen from a great height and become wedged. Turning her light upwards, the smooth-faced blocks rose, one on top of the other, as far as she could see; between them, at the limit of vision, a black zigzag stood in for the sky. She was in a subterranean metropolis without stars.

Below and ahead the ground was split into a cross-hatch of crevasses, as if a knife had been repeatedly pulled across it and the wounds had opened. Some looked small enough to easily step across; others might require a run and a jump. Still more were impassable, she judged, even in lunar gravity.

Dana checked her tablet display. This area showed as a dark, ill-defined echo in the data, but she knew in which direction she needed to head.

In front of her and to the right, an enormous rectangular boulder the size of a three-storey office block sat at a slight offset to the one below it, providing a ledge. With more than a little trepidation, she stepped onto it. It was wide enough to drive a car along but she still hugged the wall, feeling no urge to check out the drop. To her left she could see, maybe ten or twenty metres away, the blocks rise again as if she was looking across a Manhattan street; their faces showed a dusting of black soot, the residue of the geological layer along which they had fissured. Between were expanses of clean bare rock, unweathered by wind or rain.

As she moved forward, the ledge narrowed. Just as she feared it might disappear altogether, she reached a corner, and the wall to her right turned away through ninety degrees. The floor – or more accurately, the top of the block below – continued on, smooth underfoot, and she left the reassuring presence of the vertical surface at her back and stepped out onto it.

Three paces. Four. She could see the edge up ahead, and moved forward with utmost care so as not to overshoot in the one-sixth gravity.

Nearing the chasm, her helmet LED began to reveal the wall opposite. She could make out another ledge that ran around it at a similar height to the one on which she now stood, no doubt a continuation of the same faultline. She got down on her hands and knees and crawled up to the edge. Below, the crevasse dropped vertically into blackness. She could just see a slab of rock some fifteen metres down, lodged between the sides like a fallen bridge. She raised her helmet, looked across. Could she jump the gap? She was pretty certain she could, and had cleared larger distances on the surface with ease. Here, her judgement was somewhat less certain.

She took several steps back, pacing them out, and turned. *OK, here we go. One, two, three . . .*

Her feet left the ground without a puff of dust, and she almost had time to admire the view as she described a parabolic arc over to the far side.

She hit the far wall a half-metre above the ledge, then dropped down to land on it, bending her legs gracefully to absorb the kinetic energy. *Easy.*

She stood, took her bearings, then turned left and around another corner.

Suddenly the view opened up dramatically. A wide avenue led away, as if she was standing at a New York intersection and could see clear across the city, but with one important difference: this city was dark and lightness. The buildings had no windows; no one lived here, no one would stroll down the boulevards or admire the view from the highest towers. Every side of every building was a featureless dark plane of sheared geology.

She returned her gaze to her feet.

Time to go downtown.

An hour later, she had mastered a kind of slow-motion lunar parkour. She became adept at judging distances, making a leap to a small ledge or a flat-topped block then immediately dropping down to another below, or finding a hand-hold from which she could boost herself up to a higher level. A couple of times she had had to launch herself at a vertical face, tuck her feet up under her, then push off on impact to reach a ledge too far below or too awkwardly positioned to reach directly.

She began to give certain landmarks names as she passed them: here was the coffee house, there the Chrysler Building. This one even had a smaller block resting against it, like a stoop.

Her tablet told her she was still several hours from the target area, but she needed to stop, just for a short while, to let the lead in her legs dissipate. Just ahead, balanced on the very corner of a four-way intersection of crevasses, was a perfect cube the size of a street vendor's hot-dog stand. She pictured throwing a red gingham tablecloth over it and setting out warm baguettes,

Merlot, Brie and olives. Instead, sitting with her back against it, she sipped water and nutrient soup from the tubes inside her helmet. Astronaut food had improved enormously since her early missions, but for longer excursions outside the base she still had to put up with this uninteresting but nutritionally balanced gloop.

She let the muscles in her neck relax until her helmet touched the block behind her.

That's peculiar. She felt rather than heard it – here, on the Moon, there was no air through which sound could propagate. A low throbbing, like a heartbeat, but much slower. Was it *her?* She raised her arm, swiped and touched, brought up the basic health check functions on the pad. Several icons glowed orange, others were green. Heightened pulse rate and respiration, but all within expected bounds. No, it wasn't her . . . then what?

She lifted her head, and it stopped. She lowered her helmet back into contact with the rock, and immediately felt it once again. This time it was unmistakable. She could sense it in her fillings, a fluctuating low subsonic buzz like a mosquito repeatedly coming close and then moving away again. The Moon was not entirely geologically inactive; seismic sensors placed on the lunar near side during the Apollo missions had shown that it still occasionally shifted its weight, settling down further onto its stiffening core. But this was different . . . it was continuous. Not like an impact, or a tremor.

Our new visitor?

She had no way of knowing. Another mystery to be solved.

As she had in the funnel before, she suddenly felt unnerved, spooked. The chasms of this antediluvian city now felt less like the intersections of New York and more like the drained rivers of the Underworld, a waterless Acheron or Styx. She was aware that from a vantage point high above, from a lip or a parapet, she could be seen for perhaps kilometres around – a dim candle in a darkness that had remained absolute for over three billion years.

She stood up and brushed her hands of dust. She was quite happy to spend extended periods of time in her own company. The profession of astronaut suited her. But just now, here, she felt more alone than she ever had in her whole life.

Dana, let's do this. Time to move on. She checked the helmet camera, scooted back through the feed just to make sure it was operational. She brought up the radar data one more time to check her bearings. Though it was hard to discern, she could see that the void she was presently traversing narrowed to a pinch, and then a fine line. That was the direction she should take.

Down to the Lincoln Tunnel, out of the city and into the suburbs.

OK TO PRINT

The 3D printer was not a top-of-the-range model. Hoping to save a few pounds if this proved to be another of Jack's passing fads, one of his all-encompassing enthusiasms that he would drop in a week when the next one came along, Nixon had bought it second-hand on eBay. There was a line he had to walk between running a viable company serving the gaming and IT industries and indulging wild flights of fancy that could make them all billionaires – or bankrupt them.

It arrived, without cabling or a manual, from a company which proto-typed custom pipe sections for an online plumbing merchant that had gone into receivership. Jack unboxed it and placed it on the confer-ence room table, then stood back to regard it. It superficially resem-bled a photographic enlarger, or maybe a vintage overhead projector. It worked on a continuous liquid interface principle, which meant that rather than being built up layer by layer, the model was pulled up out of a liquid bath. A tray to hold the resin, measuring half a metre a side and currently empty, was surmounted by a metal plate that could be raised and lowered by the computer at a carefully controlled rate. Splashes of resin in a rainbow of colours gave the vertical support and motor block the appearance of a decorator's stepladder.

Jack set it up using an obsolete Dell laptop as a driver. A scan of the manual had been easy enough to find online, the cables on Amazon. The bundled modelling software had been entry-level stuff, but at this stage Jack was more interested in proof-of-concept than any of its high-end, precision engineering capabilities. One step at a time.

By day, Jack and Harriet wrote and rewrote code for Intelligencia's three-month AI milestone review. In the evening, on his own, Jack tink-ered with the printer. Working from YouTube tutorials, he calibrated the movement of the plate, tried out several different brands of resin, and taught himself the basics of 3D Studio Max.

His first outputs were simple Platonic solids: an octahedron, an icosa-hedron, interlaced tetrahedra; then came three interlinked tori that rattled around each other when dry like a conjurer's ring trick. He found that the resolution was a little on the rough side, but soon made a few of his own custom adjustments that enhanced matters considerably. He wondered if he should tell the manufacturers how simple it had been to improve on their software.

For a couple of days he produced his own miniature action figures, loosely based on famous TV and film characters, each around a hand's width high. He found there were libraries of downloadable fan-made wireframes, and he'd swap and distort parts to create hybrids of his own invention; chimeras, he called them, though Nixon thought he just lacked the imagination to design his own from scratch.

Jack was building bodies, of a kind.

He toyed with abstract, purely mathematical forms: he found that by using algorithmic loops or fractal nesting he could generate models of amazing complexity from just a few lines of code. Some of these had a peculiar organic appearance that showed no sign of the human hand in their making, sculpted as they were purely from number. They had no fingerprint, no slip of the chisel, and sported a bewildering proliferation of repeated or scaled details that the human eye, used to the more imperfect fractals seen in nature, found hypnotic.

More from less, he reflected. A kind of reverse-Bauhaus dictum.

The shapes would be pulled from the liquid bath as the metal plate ascended, a process that reminded Harriet of the Lady of the Lake, rising from a polymer netherworld.

The early results were a uniform neutral grey. Further tinkering revealed that the resin bath was a type for which different wavelengths of light from the scan head could activate different pigment molecules, giving coloured results.

Harriet occasionally checked in on the growing army of resin figures. They multiplied, occupying first Jack's desk, then the long shelf set up across the back wall under a row of halogen spotlights on which Nixon had planned to display their inevitable array of industry awards. On the rare occasions when Jack was not in the office, someone who never confessed to the act would rearrange them into erotic tableaus.

Periodico mensile illustrato - Rovereto marzo - C. C. Postale - Costa L. 2 - Anno 1°

Milan, June 4 1919

Umberto!

You ask how we progress with our most ambitious project yet: the creation of the FUTURIST MAN -- the MAN-MACHINE.

Our ultimate goal! Our most fervent desire! MAN, created not by GOD, but by MAN HIMSELF! That, at least, was the poetic invocation that set our imaginations alight.

I have no need to remind you that our first attempts at creating a humanoid automaton, presented by Marinetti himself in his theatrical spectacle "La donna è mobile (Poupées électriques)" drew a hostile and incomprehending reception in Turin -- and this, years before Capek thinks to coin the word "ROBOT"! We collected the rotting vegetables that were thrown our way and retired to consider anew.

Then, a letter! Malevitch tells me that Vladimir Mayakovsky and our other Russian Comrades in Art have of late been delving into the Panpsychism of N. Fyodorovich Fyodorov and the esoteric Soviet brand of PROTO-FUTURISM he calls COSMISM.

Their poets seemed to have turned COSMISM into PROLEKULT, refashioning his words on an anvil with hammer (and sickle) into paeans to the Noble Collective Worker, who (he would have us believe) will soon be marching forth to conquer the stars in order to spread the Good News of their newly-minted Communist ideology.

Fyodorov himself, who died just as this century was learning to

cont.

POESIA – PAROLE IN LIBERTÀ – TAVOLE PAROLIBERE – PITTURA – PLASTICA PURA E DECORATIVA – ARCHITETTURA – TEATRO – CINELANDIA – CASA – MODA
CUCINA FUTURISTA

Fig. iii | Giovanni Calla, *Letter to Umberto Sevini*, 1919.
215mm x 279mm, paper, original in red and black.

crawl, seems to have been able to draw a line from the Orthodox Church to the Future of Humankind, thus combining the roles of SCIENTIST and THEOLOGIAN by means of that time-honoured method through which all manner of absurdities can be given a veneer of deep hidden truth, the OCCULT. Not even the most gifted geometers of Italy's classical heyday were brave enough to make such a claim.

The stories have it that Fyodorov discovered a means of life extension via novel scientific methods heretofore unknown -- and, if Mayakovsky's source is to be believed, not only that but IMMORTALITY and even the RESURRECTION of the DEAD. I treat these claims with the scepticism they deserve. If a man who calls himself a SCIENTIST can convince himself of the existence of GOD, he can convince himself of ANYTHING.

Still, Mayakovsky tells me there is an inner cabal of SCIENTARTISTS now at work on Marinetti's failed project. They seek to pluck a SPIRIT from the subluminiferous Ether itself and EMBODY it somehow in a work of ART -- give it FORM and SHAPE.

THIS will be our FUTURIST MAN-MACHINE, our "MR X", the spirit of the Modern, the evocation of this 20th Century! Marinetti, despite his disdain for anachronistic Roman numerals, punningly refers to him as "Mr XX". Thus far, he has been but a work of THEATRE, ART, and WORDS in FREEDOM. Nonetheless, he assures me that through these means we have already stoked the furnaces of a generation -- and, as Mayakovsky tells it, this is but our opening FUSILLADE! With sinew of cable, blood of oil and breath of smoke, no longer will Man cower in his tanks, mere suits of antiquarian armour with the addition of wheels and tracks! No, he will have reinvented HIMSELF -- as the MAN-MACHINE! What could be a more fitting final consummation of the Futurist project?

My opinion? Our noble experiment cannot yet be built simply from pigment and poetry, however we push them to their expressive limits. Supernatural intervention aside, "XX" must still await the undreamed-of (even by US!) technologies of the coming age before he can be brought to life. Until then, I fear the visceral pleasures of ART alone shall have to suffice.

Calla

Giovanni Calla, Esq.

Fig. iv | Giovanni Calla, *Omaggio a Marinetti*, c1933.
Alternative title: *XX* (*Calla: A Catalogue Raisonné*, Taywood House Press, 1967).
305mm x 410mm, collage on board. Undated, but incorporating material from 1909-1933.

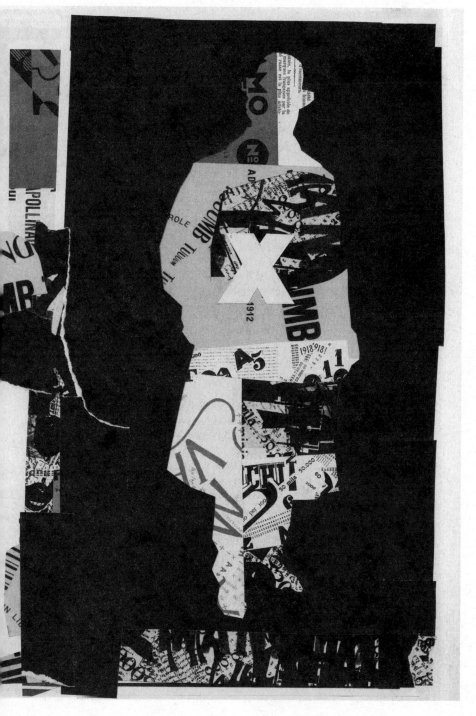

Surveillance Report

Subjects:
Jack Fenwick
Nadine Swanson

Location:
Undisclosed [London]
Italics indicate vocal stress in original recording

[inaudible]
NS: Don't get me wrong, Jack. I loved puzzle books and Agatha
Christie, murder mysteries and crosswords. Neat set-ups and clever
denouements. To begin with, I was fascinated by your stories of strange
coincidences, by the meanings you ascribed to things that I would pass
over as, as chance events. But I also see how it sometimes paralyses you.
When anything mundane can take on some great importance, it can—
Look, to you, *everything* is signs and portents. The number on our hotel
door, your library angel finding just the book you were looking for. You're
convinced there are some, some mysterious machinations going on
behind the scenes, that there's hidden purpose and meaning everywhere.
It's— it's weird. It's unhealthy.
[inaudible]
You're on your own with that, Jack. I'm not sure I want to live in your
fantasy world. You have that kind of mind, not me.
[pause]
Jack? Talk to me.
JF: You're not me. I know what I saw, what happened.
NS: I know what you *think* you saw, what you think happened.
[exasperated] Don't you ever entertain ordinary, everyday solutions? Does
everything that happens to you have to resonate with – I don't know,
some kind of numinous significance? Who's the boss here, you or some
nonexistent [waves hands] fates? Don't you think you're simply opting out
of making some of the hard decisions everyone has to make sooner or
later, without throwing dice or consulting some oracle to decide what to
do? You know, the *practical* stuff?
JF: [smiling] Yes. Yes, I did. I do. Sometimes. I know what you're saying.
But that doesn't mean I'm always wrong. Sometimes things really are
linked. Connections can be real, but buried deep.
NS: Gah. You *infuriate* me. My world's awash with people who attribute
everything to hidden powers, mystical energy fields or some other
superstitious nonsense. These bonkers beliefs are not just, just fleecing
the gullible, but having *real world* effects.
JF: I don't think you can seriously suggest that I'm going to do
something— [crosstalk]
NS: —Think how much more tractable conflicts would be if we just
clicked our fingers and took the belief in supernatural entities out of the

equation. I'm not saying it'd solve everything, but it really isn't helping matters when non-negotiable articles of faith are stalking the world stage. Jack, I can't believe you indulge this, this delusion. Do you not think a solid dose of *sensible* might be what you need here?

JF: Whoa, I think you're conflating things. I'm not disagreeing with you, but don't dismiss what I know to be the case because it doesn't fit into your oh-so rational worldview. You ever think you might be just as guilty of, of overextending your model of how the world works, and ignoring the primary data? *My* primary data? You think I make this stuff up?

NS: The things you're telling me about sound like everyday coincidences for which you've come up with weird interpretations, Jack. It doesn't work like that. Everyday existence doesn't have a story, a purpose, a mission. Life doesn't have the neatness of fiction. It's not a Poirot mystery! Life doesn't know ahead of time who committed the murder in the library behind the locked door, and leave you little clues.

JF: But what if there *were* clues? For those who could spot them? What if the clues were as obvious as whoever was leaving the clues wanted to make them? Could make them? What if they're doing their best, trying to communicate with us, tell us stuff, and most of us are just too dumb to notice? Don't you find that interesting? Isn't that worth thinking about?

NS: So some spirit guide, some weird ghost of I don't know what, has picked you out and is telling you important things using adverts in phone boxes or letters on a fridge door? Do you not think they'd have found *easier* ways to say hello?

JF: Maybe that's all they're capable of. Maybe manipulating the real world isn't easy. Maybe our minds aren't properly attuned to pick out the messages. Maybe a lot of things.

NS: *Maybe* it's all in your head. John Nash— you're a maths geek, you must know John Nash—

JF: I saw *A Beautiful Mind*.

NS: —right. Mathematical genius. Nobel Prize winner. Thought that someone was sending him secret messages via magazine ads. Went mad.

JF: Just because you're paranoid doesn't mean they aren't after you.

NS: Pfft.

JF: Kurt Cobain.

NS: Kurt Cobain *what?*

JF: Kurt Cobain said that.

NS: [exasperated] It's from *Catch-22*. And Kurt Cobain *killed himself*. [pause]

NS: Listen, you've said that this kind of thing has happened to you before, a long time ago. That you saw things that weren't there. Can I ask? What *did* you see – that time, before?

"LOOK BOTH WAYS"

@NADINE SWANSON

Nadine Swanson **Look Both Ways** 2016
Polaroids mounted on foamcore, 210 x 297mm
Represented by Gill Sandler Gallery

POINT OF CONTACT

The LPS on her wrist tablet told her she was getting closer. She had disabled the speech function, but a small pulsing dot with an arrow indicated her position relative to the impact point, overlaid both on the standard surface lunar cartography and the best image data available from the ground-penetrating radar surveys. These had been cross-referenced so that if she tilted the tablet, the faux-3D image would rotate – or, more accurately, she would rotate around it. Lower galleries were shaded in darker tones, whereas the currently visible area was highlighted with a blue-green outline.

It could not be pinpointed with precision, but she was pretty sure the point of intersection between the cave system and the artefact's trajectory was a mid-sized void that she should encounter soon. She zoomed in to the maximum possible magnification. At this scale, it was painfully apparent how poor the quality of the radar survey data was – no more accurate than ten or twenty metres, and worse the deeper she went. The pixelated grain looked like her own in-uterine ultrasound. She reminded herself, not for the first time, that there was no guarantee that the object, whatever it was, would be any more accessible from here than it would be from the surface.

She sang to herself under her breath. *There's a Starman, waiting in the sky . . .*

Dana turned on the external mic and dampers. There was no air here, so she didn't expect to hear anything; however, the mic was sensitive to compression waves that might travel through the rock or her suit, and at this point information from any source might prove useful. All she could hear was the sound of her own breathing, and if she filtered for that and amplified the result, her raised heart rate. Nothing else. Outside of her spacesuited bag of human biology, all seemed quiet. It was as if she was the only living thing in all creation.

Ahead, the lava tube opened into darkness. The helmet light swung across the floor in front of her and up the walls, catching on the lip. A

110110110110110110110110110110110110110110110110110110
110110110110110110110110110110110110110110110110110110
110110110110110110110110110110110110110110110110110110
110110110110110110110110110110110110110110110110110110
110110110110110110110110110110110110110110110110110110
110110110110110110110110110110110110110110110110110110
110110110110110110110110110110110110110110110110110110
110110110110110110110110110110110110110110110110110110
110110110110110110110110110110110110110110110110110110
110110110110110110110110110110110110110110110110110110
110110110110110110110110110110110110110110110110110110
110110110110110110110110110110110110110110110110110110
110110110110110110110110110110110110110110110110110110
110110110110110110110110110110110110110110110110110110
110110110110110110110110110110110110110110110110110110
110110110110110110110110110110110110110110110110110110
110110110110110110110110110110110110110110110110110110
110110110110110110110110110110110110110110110110110110
110110110110110110110110110110110110110110110110110110
110110110110110110110110110110110110110110110110110110
110110110110110110110110110110110110110110110110110110
110110110110110110110110110110110110110110110110110110
110110110110110110110110110110110110110110110110110110
110110110110110110110110110110110110110110110110110110
110110110110110110110110110110110110110110110110110110
110110110110110110110110110110110110110110110110110110
110110110110110110110110110110110110110110110110110110
110110110110110110110110110110110110110110110110110110
110110110110110110110110110110110110110110110110110110
110110110110110110110110110110110110110110110110110110
110110110110110110110110110110110110110110110110110110
110110110110110110110110110110110110110110110110110110
110110110110110110110110110110110110110110110110110110
110110110110110110110110110110110110110110110110110110
110110110110110110110110110110110110110110110110110110
110110110110110110110110110110110110110110110110110110
110110110110110110110110110110110110110110110110110110
110110110110110110110110110110110110110110110110110110

1111111111111111111111111111111111111111111111111111111
1111111111111111111111111111111111111111111111111111111
1111111111111111111111111111111111111111111111111111111
1111111111111111111111111111111111111111111111111111111
1111111111111111111111111111111111111111111111111111111
1111111111111111111111111111111111111111111111111111111
1111111111111111111111111111111111111111111111111111111
1111111111111111111111111111111111111111111111111111111
1111111111111111111111111111111111111111111111111111111
1111111111111111111111111111111111111111111111111111111
1111111111111111111111111111111111111111111111111111111
1111111111111111111111111111111111111111111111111111111
1111111111111111111111111111111111111111111111111111111
1111111111111111111111111111111111111111111111111111111
1111111111111111111111111111111111111111111111111111111
1111111111111111111111111111111111111111111111111111111
1111111111111111111111111111111111111111111111111111111
1111111111111111111111111111111111111111111111111111111
1111111111111111111111111111111111111111111111111111111
1111111111111111111111111111111111111111111111111111111
1111111111111111111111111111111111111111111111111111111
1111111111111111111111111111111111111111111111111111111
1111111111111111111111111111111111111111111111111111111
1111111111111111111111111111111111111111111111111111111
1111111111111111111111111111111111111111111111111111111
1111111111111111111111111111111111111111111111111111111
1111111111111111111111111111111111111111111111111111111
1111111111111111111111111111111111111111111111111111111
1111111111111111111111111111111111111111111111111111111
1111111111111111111111111111111111111111111111111111111
1111111111111111111111111111111111111111111111111111111
1111111111111111111111111111111111111111111111111111111
1111111111111111111111111111111111111111111111111111111
1111111111111111111111111111111111111111111111111111111
1111111111111111111111111111111111111111111111111111111
1111111111111111111111111111111111111111111111111111111
1111111111111111111111111111111111111111111111111111111
1111111111111111111111111111111111111111111111111111111
1111111111111111111111111111111111111111111111111111111
1111111111111111111111111111111111111111111111111111111
1111111111111111111111111111111111111111111111111111111

dusting of powder had been blown back into the tunnel to where she now stood from the space ahead; she had no way to tell if this had happened recently or ten thousand years ago.

Beyond lay blackness. Pointing her rangefinder forwards, a crude and incomplete wireframe began to build itself on her tablet, mapping areas of the cavern her light could not reach. Closer in, the details were more defined; further away, there were sections missing where there was no direct line of sight, and deeper still, just the occasional bounceback from structures far into the space ahead. The temperature had risen by a fraction of a degree.

It was very hard to make sense of what she saw. There were vertical echoes that criss-crossed the space, and sections of the ceiling that gave no echo but seemed to coincide with bright jagged reflections on the floor directly below. An area towards the back – if the aircraft-hangar-sized space had a back – was absorbing the signal completely, returning no reflection. There were curved structures that resembled flying buttresses which Dana presumed were rock outcrops intersecting the near edge of this dead space, whose terminator seemed to . . .

Dana shifted her position, took two steps to the left in order to allow the rangefinder to triangulate. *Weird.* There was a noticeable shift in the buttresses' positions, as if the signal was being distorted through a lens. She flipped to a subsonic ping. The wireframe was now overlaid with a magenta duplicate, cruder but closely mapping the original.

Dana could begin to discern what looked like the edge of a spherical volume some distance ahead, the edges of which were defined by reflections from the surfaces around it but whose bulk was notable by its absence. Another void, this one of quite a different kind, in this subterranean world of voids.

She stood at the threshold of the cavern, the true dimensions of which were still unknown. The helmet light was swallowed by the gloom, and the ground, as far as it was visible ahead, showed nothing but more fine dust, blown into streaks that pointed directly from whatever was out there to her booted feet. *"Nothing to be scared of, nothing . . ."*

She checked that every feed was being logged by her tablet's nav system and backup, reached into her backpack and pulled out a flare.

Vladimir Mayakovsky (writer), **El Lissitzky** (designer)
Dlia golosa (For the Voice), 1923
Publisher: Gosizdat/Lutze and Vogt, Berlin. 130x190mm, 5.1x7.5in.
Collection of Richard Bliss

R. Meredith
Love Letter from Heidelberg, c1924
Rubber stamp on bond, 210x297mm, 8.3x11.7in.
Collection of Nathaniel Jefferies

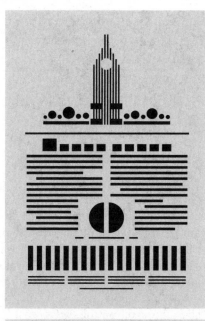

Phillipe Daho
Top: *Publicité Muette '29, Publicité Muette '35.* Bottom: *Publicité Muette '57, Publicité Muette '72,* 1975
Silkscreen on paper, series of 10 prints in an edition of 26, each 215x302mm, 8.4x11.8in.
Collection of Nathaniel Jefferies

SEMIOTIC WEIGHT

Harriet eyed Jack's increasingly chaotic desk. Placed atop a copy of *Word as Image* whose spine had been rebound with silver duct tape was a vintage piano-style tape player and a small stack of cassettes, some still in cases. She picked one up, held it to her ear and rattled it. It was about the size of a Samsung Galaxy, but twice as thick. The cover was a masterpiece of airbrushed soft porn, offensive only in its lack of anatomical accuracy.

"'Virtua - She Loves! She Lusts! She's Yours to Control'. *Ha!* It's an 8-bit *wankfest!* Jack, in case you missed a meeting, there's now an internet full of porn out there. Every speciality catered for, including many even I've never heard of. This – this has got some crusty – *ewwww!*"

"Hey, careful with that." The cover design for this particular game was so basic that Jack could hardly wait to see how rough the on-screen graphics might be. He wondered, not for the first time, how many breakthrough technologies had been driven by the desire to find new ways to distribute pornography. That was information for you – always finding new ways to disseminate itself. It was almost as if it had a sexual urge all its own.

"Why do you collect all this *stuff?* You're a hoarder. One day you'll be found dead under a collapsed pile of *CU Amiga* back issues in a filthy bedsit in, in *Hounslow.*"

"Says the person who left her mushroom soup to go mouldy in the fridge and gave us all food poisoning." Jack stood back like a proud father and regarded his desk. "Vintage kit. This is the prehistory of what we do. The thing I find incredible is that it's all so *recent* – so much has happened so quickly, and it shows no signs of slowing down. The future used to be comfortably distant. Then it was next year. Next *week*. Now, unless you're paying attention, the future happened yesterday."

"So this thing runs on an off-the-peg cassette player?"

"Yep. That was Sinclair's stroke of genius. My older, hipper cousin had a tape recorder just like this and a collection of these Spectrum games.

No new specialist storage media required – they ran from standard compact cassettes. Something to bear in mind through the intervening blizzard of defunct formats: after this, it was a quick whistle-stop tour through floppy disk, Syquest, Jazz drive, recordable CD, recordable DVD, Blu-ray . . . almost all of which are now landfill. I have boxes of Syquests and Zips in storage, and no way to get at the data on them. The plugs are incompatible, the cables are no longer made, the software, if you could find it, is written for some long-defunct os that'll only run on certain prehistoric motherboards . . . All that data is as good as lost. But I can still play *this* tape on *this* machine. Nothing else is required. *That's* true plug and play."

Harriet spun a cassette between forefinger and thumb. Her father's Fiesta had been fitted with a tape player, and the glovebox's assortment of albums by The Carpenters, The Lighthouse Family and Maria Callas had been the musical accompaniment on the long road trips to visit her peripatetic grandmother.

"You can still read a book from a hundred years ago. Carved tablets from thousands of years ago. All you need are your eyeballs. Obsolescence, the by-product of innovation. Think – in another hundred years, will we still have access to everything on the internet today? Or will telepathy have been invented, and only connoisseurs like me care about all the fantastic stuff that will still lurk out there on some obsolete media format?"

"It's archaeology for geeks, Harriet," Nixon observed. "Sometimes I think I'm running an outreach centre, not a business."

Harriet had opened some of the cassette boxes. "Half of these are copies. On WH Smith's c6os. Piracy got in fast, even then."

Jack pressed a button, and a sprung compartment opened with a loose clatter of plastic on plastic. He dropped in the tape, closed the door and rubbed his hands together. "Ah. Mechanical buttons! Springs and levers! The satisfying clunk and click of an analogue interface! Counters. Needles. Switches. They've all gone. These days, even a control room at somewhere like, like Jodrell Bank looks . . . looks like *this office*. It's generic. It's boring. It lacks . . . you know, it lacks . . ."

"Semiotic weight."

"*Right!* Yes, Harriet, semiotic weight. *Meaning.* If you have a big red button, you know it'll set off the nukes. If you have a gearstick, you can grind your gears. There's a direct connection between form and function. It's a connection we've lost. Universal functionality has given us a generic input device. The keyboard is ubiquitous, and thus symbolically meaningless. It does everything and so means nothing."

Nixon was tiring of the philosophy. "So, go on. Boot this thing up."

Jack caressed two keys, one red and one grey. He let out a small sigh. "Aha. I'd almost forgotten. To record, you pressed 'play' and 'record' at the same time. The original alt-click. You physically moved a read/write head into position, then there's a motor to spool the tape past the reading head at a set rate . . . a direct correlation between the movement of the muscles in your hand and the mechanics of the system itself. There's an . . . *authenticity* there that we've lost. We navigate through digital space with only the sounds that the software designer has programmed in to guide us. Form no longer follows function. In our digital spaces, form, being completely malleable, now *illustrates* function."

"Yeah, yeah. Sounds like poncy justification for buying vintage porn. And, as far as I'm aware, you can already play all those games online. There's an emulator. Why do you need the actual tapes? And this tape player?"

"Nixon, if I have to explain the seductive biscuity scent of old circuit-boards, the sensual pleasures of brittle plastic and yellowing inlay cards, I'm never going to convince you of the value of anything in this world."

"OK, OK. Show us what dubious pleasures it can deliver."

Jack checked the leads, pressed play, and a boot screen bordered by epilepsy-inducing coloured stripes flashed up on his monitor. Jack considered the display.

"I'm thinking of adding a realistic 'random load-failure' feature . . ."

****

♥ ♥ ♥ ♥ ♥ ♥ ♥

VIRTUA™
SHE LOVES!
SHE LUSTS!!
SHE'S YOURS TO CONTROL!!!

DIGITAL SEX SIMULATOR V1.0
** PRESS ANY KEY TO CONTINUE **

****

****

♥ ♥ ♥ ♥ ♥ ♥ ♥ ♥

SELECT LOCATION

→ A: Hot tub
→ B: Penthouse
→ C: Dungeon

** ENTER SELECTION **

****

****

♥ ♥ ♥ ♥ ♥ ♥ ♥ ♥

SELECT MOOD

→ A: Seductive
→ B: Domineering
→ C: Compliant

** ENTER SELECTION **

****

```
**************************************************
            ♥ ♥ ♥ ♥ ♥ ♥ ♥

     SELECT  DURATION
        - A: Long and Leisurely
        - B: Saucy Session
        - C: Wham Bam Quickie

           ** ENTER SELECTION **
**************************************************
```

```
**************************************************
            ♥ ♥ ♥ ♥ ♥ ♥ ♥ ♥

     SELECT  ABLUTION
          - A: Kleenex
          - B: toilet tissue
          - C: Sock

       ** ENTER SELECTION & VIEW RESULTS **
**************************************************
```

```
**************************************************
            ♥ ♥ ♥ ♥ ♥ ♥ ♥ ♥

          RESULTS
   0-10:   Existential emptiness
   11-20:  Uneasy ambivalence
   21-30:  Relaxed contentment

   ** PLAY AGAIN ** CHANGE GENDER M/F **   QUIT **
**************************************************
```

120

THE MAUSOLEUM OF THE GODS

The flare described a ballistic curve up into the space ahead. Dana had thrown it high, and as it reached the apex of its arc it burst into a blue-white glare that momentarily blinded her.

What did she expect to see? Dana was still inclined to believe that this interloper was some kind of unusual but entirely natural object, perhaps a visitor from the Oort Cloud that had been nudged from its orbit by a random encounter with another icy body. Falling Sunward, its path had just happened to intersect with one of the tiny bodies that curve through the mostly empty space of the inner Solar System – an event so infrequent that we had just not encountered its kind before. But, of course, she also entertained the small but distinct possibility that it was far more than that. Natural or artificial, whatever the flare and her other instruments were about to reveal, it would be something heretofore unknown.

Her visor automatically cut the glare to a manageable level then ran a sharpening and enhancing routine; her visual display now revealed highlight and shadow detail that could not have been discerned by the naked eye. The scene suddenly revealed before her in a high degree of detail took Dana several moments to fully process.

The flare, which had seemed to hang motionless at the very top of its trajectory, began slowly floating down in the one-sixth gravity. It revealed an elaborately sculpted stadium-sized space, the sweeping sides of which resembled nothing so much as the banked tiers of a rococo theatre, with a geological dress circle and upper galleries again carved by the passing of giant boulders carried by long-vanished lava. There were widely spaced outcrops of the tall vertical crystals, here only protruding from the floor. But there were also shards of broken crystal strewn across the ground and thrown up onto the striated walls from a point deeper in.

Dana stepped further into the cavern.

Some distance ahead, it was possible to make out a circular area of blackened ground maybe fifty metres across that had been scoured of all loose debris, swept clean to the bedrock by the force of an impact.

Following the rays of blasted dust, a few minutes' walk took her from the entrance to the edge of this cauterised area. Still a way ahead, in its very centre, she could see a hole; neat and dark, identical in shape and size to the one she had seen in the satellite images of the surface directly above. Looking up, Dana could just about make out another puncture in the roof of the cavern, its edges scalloped where pieces of rock had fallen away. The artefact had passed directly through this volume and continued on, to finally settle who knew how many kilometres deeper into the lunar mantle directly below her.

But this was not what caught and held her attention.

To the back of the cavernous amphitheatre, embedded with lateral force into the tiered wall, was a spindle-shaped object around four times the height of a human and a metre or so in diameter. It had the profile of a sine wave, thickest in the middle and tapering to fine points at either end. It reminded Dana of a bauble made from glass that had hung on her parents' Christmas tree, though this object was pure white and seemed to be devoid of decoration. There was a scar running from the hole in the floor to the curved wall, marking its passage. It was resting at a 15-degree angle, the lower point embedded in the bedrock at the end of this deep gouge, the top caught under an overhang of hardened regolith. A pile of loose rock and spinel had fallen from the higher levels around its base.

The peculiar spherical distortion that had been visible in the rangefinder scan was centred on this object, not the hole in the floor. Dana tried to focus directly on the spindle, but her eyes seemed disinclined to obey, as if light itself could not describe its shape in any sensible fashion but instead preferred to flow around it and away, avoiding contact. Looking directly at it induced a strange dislocation she had only felt once before, as a child, lost in the wonky corridors of the Crooked House at Blackgang Chine, a dilapidated amusement park on the Isle of Wight. The house's off-kilter corridors had windows that gave into rooms where someone standing in one corner would appear to be twice the height of a person at the other. It had all been done with forced perspective and mirrors, of course, but she vividly recalled the inability of her mind to grasp precisely what was wrong.

Mechanically she made herself walk forwards, one foot in front of the other, closer, towards the hole and the object beyond. She checked the helmet-cam feed again – yes, everything she saw was being recorded, along with her vital signs, alpha and theta brainwaves, the local magnetic field and a score of other inputs, some of which could only be understood by geologists or biologists who were presently 384,000 kilometres away back on Earth, and not by an astronomer who had never been more scared in her life.

Dana carefully approached the hole in the floor. She judged it to be around six or seven metres across, and she could feel through the insulation of her glove the rush of hot air shooting up from it even before the readouts on her tablet began to rise sharply. The flare illuminated the sides of a perfectly smooth tube, clean as a rock drill sample. The angle of the flare, the light reflected from the far walls and the image-processing enhancements in her visor meant she could see perhaps two or three hundred metres down. Beyond that point, nothing. A few dust motes spiralled up from the opening. She felt as if an exhalation, the breath of the sleeping Moon perhaps, was rising up from below.

Something caught the light of her helmet cam. A hairline, barely visible – yes, it was there. Running vertically along the centreline of the hole was a filament so thin she would have easily missed it had her light not caught it at that specific angle. She looked up and saw that it continued through the precise centre of the matching hole in the roof. Whatever it was, it was too far away to touch, even if she had dared.

She checked her tablet again. A slight rise in background radioactivity. A small drop in local gravitational tug. A rise in ambient heat. Her own raised heart and perspiration rates. Other than that, nothing that her instruments were designed to measure.

It was at this point that the flare went out.

Acutely aware that she was standing on the lip of a pit of unknown depth, Dana reached carefully round to her belt pouch and found two more flares. Lighting the first, she threw it across the ground away to her right, where it kicked up a small amount of dust and threw dramatic shadows. She lit the other and dropped it into the shaft. It descended at a leisurely pace, bouncing off first one side then the other before freefalling, a shrinking ring of light reflected from the smooth sides of the shaft with a spark near the centre, threaded by a vertical sliver of light reflected from the filament. Dana followed it for several long seconds, but she could not help but glance up at intervals at the object that lay, motionless and mysterious, twenty metres away across the cavern. Was it aware that she was here? Was it *watching* her?

The flare dwindled to a single point enveloped in blackness. She knew it would fail long before it reached the bottom. Stepping back from the edge, she circled the hole at a respectful distance and began to approach the spindle. Blinking repeatedly to clear her vision in the low-angled light from the third flare and the disconcerting effects of the field, she could now make out streaks along the object's length. Apart from these marks it appeared to have been unaffected by the violence of its passage – undented, certainly unbroken. The very ends of the spindle were hidden in the wall and floor, but the parts she could see tapered to a diameter of a couple of centimetres. Whatever this object was made of, it could withstand incredible forces.

Dana unclipped her backpack, took out the portable floor-standing monitoring station and set it up on a low tripod so that it had a 360-degree view of the cavern and its contents. Equipped with more sophisticated instruments than her wrist-mounted tablet, it would record the scene in much higher resolution. Down here, under kilometres of rock, it was not possible to transmit information directly back to Daedalus Base, even if Dana had not thought this unwise. Instead, it fed a record of all that might transpire here to a rugged data backup on her belt.

The record of mankind's first encounter with an indisputably alien artefact of intelligent design.

She leaned on a truncated stalagmite and regarded it. Distorted as it was through the strange bubble that enclosed it, she was now certain that it was an interstellar craft of some kind. Though this spindle shared the same shape, it was very much smaller and shorter than the artefact imaged by Hubble. That object had made the hole in the floor of the cavern and had continued down, coming to rest far below; the secrets of its propulsion system were now buried with it. When she'd examined the best images taken by the James Webb Space Telescope midway between the orbits of Earth and Mars, she had been inclined to think that it was not a solid object at all, but some kind of electromagnetic soliton wave. Maybe this capsule rode along inside it, like a kayak down the rapids.

Dana theorised that it had been thrown free, like a lifeboat or an ejector seat. That this was intended to happen below ground in an enclosed space seemed unlikely – she imagined that it should have separated sometime before impact.

Maybe it *had* – it was simply that the final destination was Earth, and the Moon had unexpectedly blocked the view.

It was looking less like a bullet from a cosmic gun.

There was no way Dana could move the spindle back to Daedalus Base even if she could figure out a way to dislodge it from the rock. For the foreseeable future it would have to remain here, and she would have to examine it in situ.

Before the third flare faltered and burned out she set up the small portable floods on two more lightweight tripods, one either side of the main instrument cluster, swinging the heads of both around to focus on the object. It looked like it was being prepped for a photo shoot, which in some ways it was.

Dana had not stepped close enough to touch the bubble that surrounded it. Hemispherical in shape, it was most clearly visible out of the corner of her eye, and enclosed an area around eight metres in diameter, centred on the object and intersecting the wall behind. This close, it was possible to see how a portion of the incident light from the floods seemed to travel around rather than through it – like the Sun through a magnifying glass, it was concentrated at two points diametrically opposite, one on the rear wall and one on a fallen crystal whose surface had been dusted to a cloudy rose.

The light did reach inside this area, but at a much reduced intensity. The visor's routines could compensate for this, but Dana found it created a distracting jpeg jitter that scattered coloured boxes across her field of vision like a low-bandwidth movie. At maximum clarification, it became hard to tell what was actually in front of her and what was simply processing clutter. Dana tuned it back. The cameras were picking up details far finer, and in wavelengths far broader, than the naked eye could discern, but examining this object with her own eyes was something she would not have exchanged for all the high-resolution imagery in the world.

Through the barrier, she could now see that the streaks on its surface were just a coating of lunar dust. There appeared to be a fine lateral seam around the central circumference, three more that ran head to foot and another elliptical seam around half a metre across on the side facing the floods. Towards the base, if indeed it had come to rest the right end up, was a coloured band three centimetres in width with a pattern of bright stripes and squares, some inset with smaller squares, some cut diagonally. A similar band encircled the top end. They reminded Dana of naval semaphore flags, though any message they may have intended to communicate was lost on her.

Another crystal intrusion rose from the ground close by to around three times her height, where it blossomed into a spray of small branches like a frozen firework. She experimentally rested her helmet against it.

There it was again – that ponderous subsonic throb, but louder, incessant.

She sat down on a low flat boulder to survey the scene. It was an enigmatic tableau, the forces that had arranged it now spent. She weighed up her options. She dared not touch the barrier herself; it would be too easy to compromise the suit, and Daedalus Base was so very far away. Should she choose to, her suit could provide the requisite food, water and air for her to stay here for sixteen hours before she would have to make the return journey. She could leave the instruments, of course, but would need to return to pick up the data they were recording.

Sixteen hours.

She wondered if she could sleep here, next to what might well be the sarcophagus of an extraterrestrial.

Celestial Mechanic *Citizen Void*
To stream this album, use the QR code above or go to:
https://celestialmechanic.bandcamp.com

CELESTIAL MECHANIC_CITIZEN VOID

Celestial Mechanic: *Citizen Void*

★★★★★

Ninja Tune · Released November 5

Pay attention, class. There will be a test later.

Boffin popsters Celestial Mechanic are not known for making things easy for themselves or their listening public, and their new album *Citizen Void* is no exception. While we are welcomed in with the early promise of something that might actually resemble a good old-fashioned *tune*, the album seems to have been arranged according to difficulty, like an algebra exam where the simpler questions up front lull you into a false sense of security before you turn the page and – *pow* – get bitchslapped by the more advanced stuff overleaf.

Then there's *that* track. But I get ahead of myself.

Named, they claim, after a character in an obscure SF novel by a university professor turned new-age cult leader called Herschell Teague, Celestial Mechanic don't *play* music so much as *construct* it, writing code from which the songs (I use the term here advisedly) are generated. Genny Forster, self-styled 'lead programmer' of the outfit, describes their working method: "We build compositions algorithmically, like sonic cathedrals of sound. Classical music has often used motifs that are repeated, mirrored, overlaid, stretched or offset to counterpoint themselves. We are doing the same thing here, but rather than let our intuition govern the final form, we set up parameters for the formal play and the limits of structural divergence at the outset, then feed in seed data and see what evolves. Our job as musicians in this respect is closer to that of an editor – we decide what the most pleasing results are, then use those as seeds for further layering. The complexity we can quickly build is extraordinary".

He's not wrong. Put to one side any prejudices you may have about a band who can release a 23-minute instrumental that sounds like removal men hauling filing cabinets around a concrete-floored echo chamber, or any preference for a catchy tune over meticulously crafted aural punishment, and listen again. And again. There is an astonishing depth to the sounds Celestial Mechanic make, a fractal complexity that can seem superficially simple but upon closer listening gives way to finer and finer detail, a curious alchemy whereby you are challenged to sift for melodic gold.

And gold is there to be found. Previous algorithmically generated music has relied on parsing a library of existing recordings, as if being fed every number one since the charts began will enable the computer to regurgitate guaranteed hit singles to order and in the process make composers obsolete. What this has actually produced is music so bland it wouldn't fly as an Estonian Eurovision entry.

Celestial Mechanic's last album, *Comfortably Violent,* was lauded in more esoteric music circles as a thoughtful examination of the commodification of filmic body-horror imagery and our consequent inability to process the true horror of terrorist videos – in other words, inured by the over-the-top theatricality of modern special effects, the real thing has become almost prosaic. *Comfortably Violent,* perhaps unsurprisingly, failed to make an impression on the wallets or whistles of the general public. Comparisons to Autechre and Aphex Twin, 1970s Krautrock, or even Charles Mingus at his most experimental do little to convey the truly visceral experience; however good a review, it's not the same thing as letting the needle hit the vinyl. Music journos, including myself, take note: *the description of the thing is not the thing itself.*

Citizen Void, however, may be – whisper it – a breakthrough in the form. That this is a move into more abstract territory is telegraphed by the sleeve – row upon row of binary digits set in 4 point, an exercise in postmodern typographic austerity so devoid of any recognisable human touch that it makes your Manila medical file look like a psychedelic Fillmore West gig poster with the saturation turned up to eleven.

We open with what sounds like a slow drone (I actually checked my speakers), a fugue that separates into a multitude of sounds familiar from software package bootup, shutdown and other key functions, overlaid with the bleeps, clicks and ticks of a mainframe hub.

This builds into a symphony of found sounds: there is the looped pro-testing squeal of worn rubber on wet tarmac, the hammering of industrial machinery, and in pin-sharp counterpoint, unidentifiable and unsettling childlike vocalisations.

Interesting as all this is, it is just window dressing for the main event: *The Signal* is the standout track that the rest of the edifice has been fashioned to support. You have undoubtedly heard it by now – clocking up an astonishing 1,000,000,000 – that's one *billion* – views on YouTube, more than Pharrell's *Happy,* and all without anything more fancy than De-Liste's abstract computer-generated lightshow (read: screensaver) to accompany it.

Rhythm and melody swap places like a Bangkok ladyboy floorshow, familiar musical expectations are thrown under the bus – nay, *tank* – then reversed over, just to make sure they're not going to get up again. Hypnotic, intriguing, it gets under the skin, promising and then delivering more and more on each repeated listen. People have been known to leave it on repeat for hours, days even. I've yet to hear it too many times – it somehow remains as engaging and fresh as it did first time around.

In that deeply resonant manner of all things brand new yet somehow immediately familiar, it has the inevitability of a track that was always meant to be – less written, more discovered, like some natural aspect of the order of things that was already there and only needed to be lifted out of the aether.

Which, quite literally, it has been. It is the result of feeding the famous Signal from Space into Forster's generative algorithm. Though credited as writer, Forster is on record as saying that it pretty much wrote itself.

If this *was* an algebra exam, some might call that cheating.

Discuss.   *–Rachel Ainsdale*

THE GREY MAN

"It's self-protection. Self-medication. Doing certain things in a certain way helps me focus, gets my mind back into a manageable—" Jack gestured with the flat of his hand, sweeping it out across the bedsheet – "level, I guess. I'm used to it, but you wouldn't want to be in my mind. It sometimes does things of its own accord. I feel like I'm sitting up here watching, along for the ride but not entirely in control."

Nadine was studying his face intently. Jack found her expression hard to read; that was part of the problem. It was 3.30 AM, and his apartment was intermittently lit by the lightning now stabbing down over Primrose Hill, some miles to the north. It lent the proceedings an unlikely melo-drama. He counted the seconds between the flash and the thunder . . . *one . . . two . . . three . . . four . . . five.* Five miles. *Jack. Stop doing this.*

He emptied the last of the champagne into her plastic flute, holding the bottle upside down by the dimple in the base with one hand. It was mostly froth, with a finger's width of clear blonde liquid at the bottom.

"You can tell me."

Jack let out a slow ragged sigh, as if he'd been holding his breath for a very long time. *How many times had he told this story?* Once. Maybe twice. And both times, it hadn't gone well. Jack was well aware he sometimes acted in a manner which could be unsettling; he'd learned to hide that part away, not mention it for fear people would think him strange.

Where did it begin? As far back as he could remember, he'd kept his peculiar . . . *talents* hidden. At school, he'd often ask questions he already knew the answers to. The Freemantle Academy Preparatory School was a redbrick Victorian institution, privileged and sedate. It could have been Greyfriars or Hogwarts, but Jack preferred the newer concrete and glass classrooms that hugged the east wing, built to accommodate a more recent increase in student numbers.

These rational rectilinear spaces smelled of paint and plaster and the inside of Dad's new car, the one he'd bought with the life insurance pay-out . . . the car he never drove, because it reminded him of Beatrice, his wife, his life, the missing pivot at the centre of his existence, the mother whom Jack now barely remembered . . .

There *was* one memory, one that would creep up on him in those moments when he was feeling reasonably good about himself, a checksum that filled him with a deep sense of shame. It came to him now. He had spent his mother's funeral flying his toy X-wing over the small shelf on the back of the pew in front, the liturgy a meaningless background drone he imagined was the rocket engines. An uncle in a tweed suit that smelled of mothballs and cigarettes had put a concerned hand on his shoulder.

Jack looked up at him. "My Mummy's dead," he explained brightly. He then pointed to a little silver bump on the top of the toy. "Look, it's R2D2!" A tight expression had formed on the adult's face. He seemed to be trying to keep something under control, like a shaken bottle of Coke.

Jack was still processing that event, all these years later.

The new part of the school didn't smell of waxed wood panelling and the past. There were no long benches to remind him of pews. The table-tops didn't have a century of students' names carved into them. Jack found the rooms optimistic, clean and bright, a promise of an idealised utopian future. In contrast, he hated the dark civic-green walls in the older parts of the building, the bare lightbulbs, the high echoing ceilings and the conker-coloured linoleum floor, which had been pummelled to a sheen by decades of sensible shoes. Every sharp edge of every door frame had long ago been blunted by the passage of countless careless children, then painted and repainted till they attained the consistency of the plastic porridge he'd seen in a kitchen recreation at Hampton Court Palace on a school trip.

But the thing he disliked most about the old part of the school was the little Grey Man.

With one exception that, even now, Jack couldn't bring himself to think about, he only ever saw him there, in the exact same place – the Chemistry Laboratory, in that glass-fronted cabinet among the scientific glassware.

No one else could see him, of that Jack was sure.

The class was arranged so that everyone always sat on the same stool in front of the workbenches, and Jack's spot was at the front, by the cabinets. He would sit and wait for as long as he could before chancing a glance across to the alcove where the beakers and flasks and Bunsen burners were kept. Most often he wasn't there, but on several occasions when the cabinet was unoccupied when the class began, Jack had relaxed only to catch him out of the corner of his eye sometime later. He never moved; he just lay there on his side, propped up on one thin elbow.

He had the proportions of a puppet – maybe two or three feet tall had he been standing up, with a large head and thin, wasted, spindly arms and legs. He wore old-fashioned breeches and boots, and on the front of his tight-fitting jacket there was a sigil in a circle that looked foreign – a criss-cross of lines and dots that might be Chinese, or Korean perhaps. He had on a funny silver hat that, from certain angles, Jack could see covered a void where the back of his head should be. Most disconcertingly, he had a face that he couldn't make out.

On a couple of rare occasions, this little man had looked directly at him. Jack wasn't sure if the Grey Man had eyes; he assumed he did, but if he tried to look more closely it was as if his gaze slid away, and he found himself looking at something else instead, however hard he tried. But on those occasions, he *knew* that the Grey Man was looking at him before he turned to check because he made Jack feel strange inside. The ambient sounds would quieten, the chatter of his classmates, the teacher, would all recede to the point where he only heard them vaguely, from a great distance. Then Jack would feel an internal vertigo, like that time he'd been up in the lift to the top of the World Trade Center. A sensation of moving while remaining perfectly still, a kind of internal compression.

This was the Grey Man's 'funny look', as he described it to himself. It was accompanied by what Jack thought of as the 'collapsing house of cards' sensation: for a few fractions of a second, it felt like the room – the world, even – was printed on a series of sheets, like a stage set or the view through binoculars, and that these flat planes were moving relative to each other to reveal dark spaces behind, gaps in reality which should remain hidden whichever way you looked at things. It was as if he could see the bits of the scenery they hadn't bothered to paint, or the parts of a videogame they hadn't thought to imagemap because you weren't supposed to be there, you weren't supposed to see them.

He imagined that in that moment there was some kind of link between the Grey Man's mind and his own – that is, if the Grey Man *had* a mind – and he would slip into the periphery of Jack's thoughts, shuffling, browsing, poking around – stealing something, a memory, perhaps.

Jack became obsessed with his memory. What had he had for lunch in the canteen today? Yesterday? *This time last week?* He made lists, he cross-referenced them, committed them to memory and tested himself against them.

Having honed this already latent aptitude, it got him through every exam, even the subjects for which he had little or no interest; but it was also the beginning of an obsession with detail he sometimes found debilitating, a compulsive need to record, to understand, to categorise, scared he'd forget – scared he'd have those memories stolen away, taken back to wherever the Grey Man might come from.

Once, the teacher had asked Jack to fetch some equipment from the Grey Man's cabinet. Jack's heart bucked and a cold wash of sweat dampened his limbs.

He looked across.

He wasn't there.

The teacher gave him a small ornate key, and Jack knelt down to open the glass doors. Arranged behind them was a selection of conical flasks, clamps, retort stands and rubber tubing. Jack thought the space measured less than a yard across, and maybe two hands high and deep. Given the equipment stored inside, Jack couldn't see how there was room for anyone else – any*thing* else – in there. He'd found the requested set of circular weights stacked neatly in a small pyramid, lifted them out and placed them on the floor, then locked the door. Sitting back on his heels, he moved his head to the left and right, wondering if the Grey Man might be a reflection of something – a classmate, a trick of the sunlight coming through the high windows and bouncing through several layers of curved glass inside – but he couldn't see anything but his pale face, the polished linoleum and Mr Bridgeport's scuffed tan brogues.

Many years later he'd been reminded of that peculiar dislocation. At a friend's house party, Jack had got blind drunk for the very first time. Seemingly of its own volition, the floor had jumped up, spun around and smacked him on the forehead; he realised he was lying on his side in the bathroom, looking up at the underside of a toilet bowl where stalactites of vomit that were probably his own were coagulating. The shock of recognition had sobered him up.

The Grey Man. He hadn't thought about him in years.

And he really didn't want to now.

So he didn't tell Nadine this story.

He told her another.

"I have always been able to see connections. Show me a bunch of raw data, and in my mind's eye I see a scatter chart and can pick out a line. Helpful in exams, as you can imagine. They thought I should become a futures trader, that's what the school's careers adviser told me. Maybe he was right. Instead of working all hours to get this start-up started up, we could be drinking champagne on a yacht somewhere. But yes, this ability, it can unnerve people. It unnerves *me* sometimes.

"And I don't want to unnerve you, Nadine."

"TROUBLE IN PARADISE"

Nadine Swanson **Trouble in Paradise** 2014
Spraypaint and acrylic on wood panel, 840 x 1190mm
Represented by Gill Sandler Gallery

©NADINE SWANSON

THE SUBLIME PLEASURES OF THE COLLECTOR

It looked like a typewriter, but Jack knew it was something far more interesting.

He was in the habit of wandering through the antique stalls of Spitalfields Market on a Friday lunchtime, where he would pick up a burrito and try not to drop chilli sauce on the vintage magazines and postcards. Of particular interest today were more games for the Sinclair ZX Spectrum. He chose them primarily by the brash cover art: rearing dragons, robot pizza chefs or post-apocalyptic barbarians topped with chromed logos in dramatic forced perspective. Without exception, these visuals promised far more than the basic 8-bit graphics ever delivered.

Jack, of course, knew this; he had a connoisseur's appreciation for innovation within strict technical limitations, and some of these games still managed to be very playable indeed. He and Nixon had wasted far too many hours mastering *Hungry Horace, Jet Set Willie, Ant Attack,* and, um, *Samantha Fox Strip Poker.* The analogue plug-and-play physicality was an addictive nostalgic indulgence, and the rituals associated with them – spooling the tape tight with a pencil, ejecting and turning it over to play Side Two – were, he told himself, all part of the authentic retro experience.

But back to this typewriter. Clunky and heavy, it looked more like an industrial instrument than something you might write a romantic novel on. The closer Jack looked, the less it appeared to be a typewriter at all. What appeared at first glance to be a standard keyboard was missing a separate set of keys for the numbers, those being written above the QWERTY letters on the top row, and a mysterious button labelled LETTS to the right was matched by another equally mysterious one labelled FIGS to the left. A hand crank with a black Bakelite handle was attached to the side, and where a typewriter might have had a carriage sat five toothed rotors, each lettered from A to Z, in slots.

A clue was riveted to the body, just above the keyboard:

IMPORTANT
THE HANDLE MUST ALWAYS BE GIVEN A FEW TURNS WITHOUT DEPRESSING A KEY AT THE COMPLETION OF OPERATION AND ON EVERY OCCASION BEFORE INSERTING A SET OF DRUMS.

It had been placed on top of a grey-painted wooden carrying case. Though it was viciously scraped, and the metal handle and protective cornerpieces badly rusted, it still bore the original stencilling:

OC431 DD
ALTONA
HAMBURG

The German designation Jack could not fathom. No, this was definitely British, from the Gill Sans on the label to the alluring aroma of oil, ink and history. On the reverse of the box – or it could have been the front – was written:

CAUTION: HANDLE WITH CARE
DO NOT DROP
STORES REF № 106/372
MACHINE TYPEX MARK III.
SERIAL NO. 450

Jack had forgotten to breathe. For those who knew anything at all about the history of computers, its true identity was revealed right there, in crude capitals: a Typex Mark III. The British equivalent of the famous German 'Enigma', the Second World War code machine.

Wow.

Jack wondered how many of these had managed to escape from Bletchley Park and survive to the present day, out here in the civilian world. Very, very few.

"How much," said Jack, affecting an air of studied nonchalance while leafing through an adjacent stack of '30s *Modern Mechanix and Inventions*, "for these magazines and the broken typewriter?" He nodded in its general direction without looking directly at it. The gentleman behind the stall counted some small change into a leather purse, pulled a pen from behind an ear, flipped a page in a reporter's notebook, wrote something down at the bottom of a column of figures, drew a line, and totalled it below. "It doesn't seem to have a carriage," Jack added.

"Thirty quid," the stallholder stated without looking up.

"Twenty-five." Jack immediately regretted not paying the asking price. Here was a genuine Typex for sale, and he's trying to *knock off a fiver?* He must be insane.

The stallholder shrugged. "As you say, no carriage. OK, twenty-five, mate. Done." With the pen he pointed to a small sign pinned to the support that held the red and white awning above. "No refunds."

Jack paid without another word, put the magazines in his messenger bag, lifted the Typex into its box, fitted the clasp, and, once out of sight, ran the entire way back to the office.

THE MAN IN THE MOON

How long have I been here?

Dana checked her tablet, but already knew the answer. She would have to start the journey back to Daedalus Base in under an hour. She wanted to leave a generous margin of error in case there were any mishaps on the return leg, any unforeseen delays. She had found a comfortable place to sit against the curve of the chamber's wall, one in which she could lie back on the bulk of her backpack and her helmet didn't press into her neck too painfully. She had drifted off into a fitful sleep; the spacesuits were bulky, and not built for prolonged use in confined environments. She had already filled the urine bag, and did not intend to try for solids.

A quiet but insistent chirrup had begun to issue from the motion detectors. She looked up from the familiar parade of coloured lines and figures that recorded her vital signs, the ambient temperature and a dozen other variables. *Had something changed?*

She pushed herself to her feet, and once again tried to get a clear view through her helmet and the visual distortion of the bubble.

Yes.

The circular line around the central section was more pronounced, she was sure of it. As she watched, the area darkened, became translucent. There was a jerking motion within. Then nothing. Dana's heart raced, and in simpatico her tablet began to flash orange. She took three steps forward.

Suddenly and without warning, the front section of the spindle opened like an eight-petalled flower, each section curling up and back from the centre.

A substance like glue stretched between fingers hung between them, stiffening then falling away to the debris-strewn ground where it shrank and darkened.

An inertial absorber, an alien airbag?

Then she felt it. A psychic wave crashed over her. Cold, alien, a chill wind from out of the vast sepulchral interstellar void itself. She took two clumsy steps back, barely managing to remain on her feet.

A life force, yes, but one so utterly at odds with her own sense of self – it swept right through her, as if she was a loose-knit jumble of facts held together by the merest whim of circumstance. It seemed to collapse familiar concepts of identity, location and time to a dimensionless point, then refract it in a fun-house of mirrors, an elongated thread spun out on an invisible loom made from six fundamental axioms she couldn't quite grasp, profound but alien symbolic truths arranged as a fast-rotating octahedron. It shot back across countless light years and unfathomable aeons until it connected with something heavy and black and rimmed in fire which sat at the very beginning of all things.

Where was she?

She could feel herself becoming one with an impersonal maelstrom of forces far beyond her power to describe or control.

She was a randomly shuffled deck, a throw of bones, scenery in a gale.

EM fields. Messing with my head. The monitoring station was a riot of coloured bars and dots. She punched a button and her visor polarised, drawing out what little colour there was in the cavern. The sense of dislocation subsided, but did not disappear.

Inside the bubble of force, something was moving. There was a soft glow around the rim of the opening. By this, she could see what appeared to be a long, flattened ellipse of light— no, it was a reflection! A reflection of the floods, through the bubble, in something curved and glossy, a shiny carapace—

The thing's— what? Head? suddenly snapped around, faced her. Her vital signs went into the red, and an urgent alarm sounded in her helmet's earpiece. Dana stifled an involuntary scream.

Deep breaths.

She'd thought of it as the creature's head, though it bore little resemblance to any animal familiar from Earthly design or imagination: a cluster of sense organs, each with a disturbing degree of independent volition, jostled and swarmed with no central focus, no apparent expression beyond a disinterested analysis of her presence. Tubes telescoped, sampling the air inside the bubble; irises narrowed, wet orifices convulsed; she could see a dish-shaped depression in the carapace which gave onto a pale whorled interior over which an ultraviolet glow danced like flames on a Christmas pudding. One organ would be brought to bear before a section of the head would rotate and flip back to allow another to examine . . . what? Her heat signature, Kirlean aura, scent, neuronal activity; a tally of the bioflora in her gut?

Though the visceral impact of this attention was softened by the filter, she had the vaguest sense of some kind of two-fold organising principle at work: a groping, prodding curiosity tempered with a higher, more austere rationality.

They regarded each other. She said nothing.

What possible use would speaking be?

An impasse.

Dana moved to the monitoring station in a smooth motion she hoped would not be seen as a threat. The refractive index of the force field suggested to her that as well as acting as a protective casing that prevented anything getting in, it also held within it a dense atmosphere. A built-in life support, designed to provide a pocket of breathable air whatever the surrounding environment, perhaps? She wondered if it could also function underwater, a bubble floating in an alien sea. She felt her training, her natural curiosity begin to calm her mind. Her vital signs fell back into the orange.

Though simple life had been found under the surface of Jupiter's icy moons, there could be no comparison. This was an *alien*. An actual, live, technically advanced extraterrestrial. A creature from *out there*.

I have so many questions!

So many questions to ask, and no way to ask them.

But there was one question, one very important question, for which she now had an unambiguous answer – *we are not alone*.

When Dana was nine, her Aunt Anna-Liisa had read her *Comet in Moominland*. By fifteen, she had conceded to herself that she'd never meet a creature from another world, but had developed an abiding passion for the biological sciences. By eighteen, she had decided to be an astronaut. By twenty-five, she had accumulated over 13,000 hours of jet aircraft pilot-in-command time in *Ilmavoimat*, the Finnish Air Force, and had taught herself to read and speak fluent Russian and English. By twenty-seven she had joined the European Space Agency's astronaut training programme and moved to Cologne. At thirty-one, on a return flight from the International Space Station, she avoided a ballistic re-entry by manually patching an electrical short between the crew capsule control panel and the Soyuz descent navigation computer that would otherwise have been fatal, saving her own life and the lives of her two Russian crewmen.

Aged thirty-two, at a NASA awards dinner, she punched and knocked out one of those crewmen, Georgi Komarov, for reasons that she refused to divulge, even at her tribunal. This led to a two-year suspension, during which she became a spokesperson – along with one of her heroes, Valentina Tereshkova, the first woman in space – for the international 'Return to the Moon' project, then trying to get congressional approval. At thirty-five, in recognition of her unstinting public-relations efforts, she was reinstated and then selected for the Daedalus Project.

Daedalus was nothing if not ambitious. It was to be the largest telescope ever built.

While its mirrors would primarily be used to reflect incoming light from astronomical objects to a focal array of sensors in the centre, the purpose of the telescope was actually two-fold. It would systematically catalogue near-Earth asteroids that might pose a danger to Earth – and should one be discovered on a collision course, deflect it. This would be achieved by focusing the Sun's rays on one side of the object for prolonged periods while it was still months or weeks from impact, heating it and causing an outflow of material that would incrementally alter its trajectory so it would bypass the Earth.

It was decided by people that Dana did not have the ear of and for reasons that to her seemed opaque that this second use for the Daedalus Telescope would not be made public, and so the large scale and the specific construction details of the facility were not on public record. She was made to sign the Official Secrets Act, the Security of Information Act and several other similar acts in Russian, Chinese and Korean, which led her to believe that Daedalus Base's existence was known at the upper echelons of the space administrations, and presumably the governments, of all of those nations.

She had come to know Daedalus Base and the telescope like a second home, one she had seen grow in concentric circles out from the natural central peak of Daedalus Crater over a period of five and a half years. She had helped calibrate the mirrors as they multiplied, and was intimately familiar with the quirky effects the shifting temperatures of the lunar day had on the structure. She had learned to orchestrate its many components with a light but sure hand and coax the best performance from it.

It had never once been used for its secondary purpose. Neither ground stations nor Daedalus itself had discovered any object that would approach the Earth close enough to present a threat.

Until, moving far too fast to deflect, the spindle had arrived.

Dana looked up from the monitoring station. Though she could not get any closer, even through the visual distortions of the bubble and the atmosphere within it she could see something new. Just below the sensory cluster was a patch of white, an organ that looked like two hands fused at the wrist with a moist opening in the centre. It was grasping at the air, reaching out in her direction.

BEEP-BEEP.

The finger-like appendages writhed in a very particular fashion then curled back upon themselves. They did so again.

Dana checked the feeds. It was all being recorded. She had no way to transmit the data live; she would need to return to Daedalus on foot with what she had gathered here in order to analyse it.

BEEP-BEEP.

What *was* that?

She looked at the environmental monitor. Something seemed to be hovering at the periphery of its sensitivity. She tweaked a few values.

BEEP-BEEP.

The alien gestured again.

It's altering its biosignatures.

BEEP-BEEP.

BEEP-BEEP.

It's piggybacking something on the monitor's signal!

Dana turned the laptop around to face the spindle and the creature confined within it . . . so it could see what it was doing. Or so she reasoned.

The 'hands' convulsed. The screen caught her attention – the image had begun to distort. A wave, like atmospheric interference on an old television, travelled from the top to the bottom. The complex data sets that were scrolling across began to break up into a grit of pixels, then dimmed and faded to black.

She pressed a few keys. *Nothing.* An empty screen.

Was this simply a malfunction caused by the ambient EM radiation, or something else?

A point of light appeared. Another. Several more. Dana was looking at a starfield.

She did not recognise any of the constellations; it was not a view of any sky visible from Earth. Lines appeared, curves, connecting the stars. A web. A chart, perhaps.

The stars suddenly flew off towards the periphery of the screen, and she had a sense of rushing forwards, into the map. The view passed though a shell of debris, a translucent veil of gas, then through a heliopause, inside which the view again cleared. There was a solar system: a star and five planets. The star itself was a binary, a large bloated red giant and a smaller, more compact blue main sequence star. They were rotating around their common centre of gravity, the smaller star pulling long ribbons of material from the larger then wrapping them into a flat disc around itself which subtly glowed in ultraviolet.

An amorphous cloud, like a nebula strung with filaments, seemed to wash over the scene. No, not a nebula – not something physical, exactly. She couldn't make it out.

The view pulled back, around, and she was floating over a dark russet world, ribbed with the purple scars of mountain chains. Dark green, almost black swathes of vegetation covered the lowlands. Thin white clouds high in the atmosphere caught the light, casting deep blue shadows on the ground below. Numerous circular blue-green lakes dotted the northern hemisphere, some arranged in looping chains like dropped pearls. *Flooded impact craters,* she thought.

The strange miasma passed over the world.

The image stuttered. Black plumes could be seen rising from the surface. *Fires?* Threads came from the sources of these plumes, out across the land. From the high vantage she could not see the details, but guessed that they were flowing masses of people, creatures maybe like the one whose company she now shared.

The world turned, and she was now high above the night side. Glowing spots of orange fire replaced the smoke. Tiny lights criss-crossed the dark expanse, and from the seas bubbled a deep green luminescence.

Beneath her, as the daylight terminator swept around and back into view, something shot up from the thin crescent of the planet's limb, backlit by the binary sun. Its trajectory was straight, purposeful. Dana followed it for a short while as it rushed away from the planet below, and then it was lost against the dense backdrop of stars.

Moments later, myriad silver lines blossomed from several distinct points on the planet's surface. There was a bow wave, a shock through the luminiferous ether, and Dana realised she was not looking at an image seen with human vision. Silver needles arced up over the surface and out, leaving contrails in their wake, some headed towards two of the other worlds in the system, others out further, into interstellar space.

The view pulled back, and the web of lines was again visible. One, out towards the periphery of the network, curved in a long taut trajectory over a planetary nebula. The space there turned a sulphurous yellow, and within it small pinpricks of light, like magnesium flares in fog, could be seen spinning thousands of times a second, shooting black rays like collimated beams of night from their poles.

The view shifted once again. Streamers of coloured gas whipped by; then she passed through dark enveloping clouds whose presence could be seen only because they blocked out the starlight. There was a sense of incalculable distances traversed at a desperate velocity, but still one that was *not fast enough*.

On, towards . . .

She passed through a cloud of tiny objects, like a squall of rain against a windshield, then several small bodies shot by in quick succession, too fast for Dana to get anything more than a passing impression.

Then something familiar hove into view. She knew where she was. Saturn – there was no mistaking it. It passed by at speed below her, the rings turning from a thin line seen edge-on to a sweeping set of concentric circles, out of which the black shadow of the planet itself took a crisp notch.

Ahead lay Jupiter. It rapidly grew larger, and for a moment she thought she was going to collide with it. Then there was a white flash and a sense of cold enclosure, a deep subterranean pressure that she could feel in her ears, then a flurry of sparkling ice crystals, and—

Several other small bodies whipped by. The Sun grew quickly, filled the screen. She was so close she could see the roiling convective cells on the surface, the twisting loops of magnetic field threading the darker sunspots. Like a blast of cold air, a wind of ionised particles passed through her on their way out to the farthest reaches of the Solar System, where they would meet the interstellar medium at the bow shock that marked the very edge of the Sun's domain.

She swung in closer. Prominences arched over her head like the fiery vault of Heaven itself, and she whipped around like a prima ballerina pulling her limbs to her body, turning fast on a pointe shoe of tightly focused forces. Then she was flung out again, towards—

The Earth.

The pale blue dot.

The emanations of vibrant life crashed over her – television and radio, a cacophony of images and sounds, a dark wet green and the smell of seven billion minds. The last few seconds of history played in reverse as she bore down upon her final destination.

Seconds to decelerate. A tang of hydrocarbons, a metallic whine that tasted like an old coin—

Then a darkness, massive and absolute, unexpectedly rotated into view. The blue dot vanished behind the curve of the Moon as if a stage magician had drawn it under his cloak. The stars went out. She was

145

inexorably bearing down upon 74 million million million tonnes of rock at a sizeable portion of the speed of light—

The screen went dark. A glitch passed over it again from top to bottom, and the standard display returned. Heart rate. Respiration. Ambient temperature.

Had all that been recorded?

Yes! Her heart jumped with the enormity of it all. She had to get this back, back safely to Daedalus and then to Earth.

BEEP-BIP. BEEP-BIP.

Another message?

No. There was a new change in the vital signs. Designed to monitor human functions, she could only guess what it might actually be measuring. *What was happening?*

BEEP-BIP. BEEP-BIP.

The signal was attenuating. Values were dropping.

Had the show she had just witnessed taken the last of its strength? This fabulous creature, who had come so far and risked so much, she suddenly knew without a shadow of a doubt was dying.

COMPUTER LOVE

Jack's 3D experiments multiplied.

Build me a body. How, exactly? What was he hoping to achieve here?

He was missing something. He looked again at the Typex machine, standing on its painted crate on his desk in the office, half expecting it to have vanished in a puff of daydream. It was still there.

Just assume, Jack reasoned to himself, *any system that takes an input and delivers an output is conscious to some small degree.* Straining through a protracted birth of a hundred years or more, maybe the computers we have made have *all* been conscious to some extent. Maybe artificial intelligence could have first appeared in the cogs of Babbage's Difference Engine.

Jack ran a finger across the rotors. It smelled of turpentine and metal. If – just for the sake of argument – the smallest scrap of consciousness could reside in a Typex, what would it *say?* Who might it talk to? The code-breakers? Did it have conversations with its operators by inserting random glitches? Piggybacking one signal on another, exerting a tiny degree of autonomy where it could?

It must have been very lonely in there.

The Typex, like the Enigma, broke messages into five-letter 'words'. He wondered, working within this restriction, what kind of plain-text messages could be sent. A sonnet perhaps, from the Typex to its operator, each word of which would by necessity be exactly five letters long?

A poetry of limited means. Was that possible? It could best be described as a bandwidth issue, and Jack was used to dealing with bandwidth issues.

He woke his iMac, wrote a line of code and pointed it at the dictionary in his word processor. A matrix of five-letter words appeared. He deleted all but the first twenty-odd lines. He turned to the Typex, and began to pos-ition the rotors. It was a custom model, with a basic printout capability. He went to the copier, pulled a couple of sheets from a drawer and cut them into strips thin enough to pass between the print heads.

Jack spoke aloud. "OK, I'm guessing you've not had the chance to talk in a very long while. What can you tell me?"

```
CAROM   ERGOT   DEMOB   PANIC   STROP   MITTS   KNOBS
VAPID   VISTA   OKAPI   PRONG   VENOM   FELID   CYCAD
RESET   TABOR   VERVE   CIVET   MACAW   SHARD   POSIT
NACRE   SLAKE   SWARD   SPLAY   HOTEL   PIQUE   LYMPH
KIOSK   DROLL   VAGUE   WHELP   SCRIM   IMBUE   AEGIS

SKUNK   GNOME   SAVVY   YACHT   FETID   LITHE   LIVID
ANGST   FERAL   FLANK   BLIMP   LUCRE   DUCHY   CALYX
MAGMA   SMITE   OCHRE   INGOT   NADIR   PIXIE   DRUID
IDYLL   PITHY   SWOON   POSIT   ROGUE   QUEEN   PIQUE
FEVER   POPPY   SAUCY   ELUDE   SNEER   PLANE   SATYR

THRUM   UMBER   SKEIN   SWIRL   VAPID   IVORY   PLUSH
MELEE   BINGE   EPOCH  (OXBOW)  ACORN   ANVIL   AVAST
EQUIP   BOLUS   CURLY   HORDE   LEMON   THIGH   POUND
MAPLE   ONION   GRASS   CLOVE   PULSE   ARROW   SLING
TILDE   MYRRH   PUPPY   THUMB   WHARF   WHALE   SQUAB

VIPER   EASEL   STRUM   CROWN   QUEER   SABRE   PISTE
BASIL   ANISE   SUMAC   THYME   SABLE   REARM   AZURE
(OXBOW) OPIUM   HONEY   LLAMA   LEMUR   STOAT   CORAL
HYENA   PANDA   LOVES   HORSE   SPOON   MEGAN   OLIVE
CAPER   MANGO   BACON   SWAIN   BISTO   SQUID   SUSHI

SPRAT   SMELT   STROP   BAWDY   HYDRA   EYRIE   FUGUE
LAPIS   ASPIC   VELDT   PANSY   FREAK   [X+X]   ELBOW
SKULK   SPASM   CHUNK   HOVIS   ENNUI   LONER   +++++
```

Michelle Summerschild

Objects, Events, Explanations and Representations

A MEDITATION

"In the beginning was the Word," the Master explained, *as if elucidating a deep and obvious truth.*

"Written or spoken?" he asked, not entirely seriously.

The Master smiled. "Both describe something other than themselves, while simultaneously being things in and of themselves. But consider: what is there to describe other than yourself when you are the only thing in all creation?"

In the beginning was the Word, and the Word was with God, and the Word was God. JOHN 1:1

So reads the first sentence of Genesis.
But consider these alternative translations:

LATIN VULGATE:
'In principio erat Verbum et Verbum erat apud Deum et Deus erat Verbum.'
ENGLISH TRANSLATION:
'In beginning was Word and Word was beside (alongside) God and God was Word.'
GREEK TO ENGLISH TRANSLATION:
'In beginning was the Word, and the Word was with the God, and God was the Word.'
(*Word* from the Greek *logos:* word, discourse, reason.)
SAHIDIC COPTIC TO ENGLISH TRANSLATION:
'In the beginning existed the word and the word existed with the god and a god was the word.'
— A LITERAL TRANSLATION OF THE NEW TESTAMENT
Herman Heinfetter, 1863 [pseudonym of Jackerick Parker].
GREEK TO ENGLISH TRANSLATION:
'And the Word was a God.'
— THE NEW TESTAMENT, IN AN IMPROVED VERSION, UPON THE BASIS OF ARCHBISHOP NEWCOME'S NEW TRANSLATION: WITH A CORRECTED TEXT
Thomas Belsham, 1808.

"*T*he WORD.

"The *thing* that *means something*. That represents a thing that is not itself. The absent thing, brought present by a *representation* of that thing."

The Master tented her fingers. The Pupil realised something was required of him.

"A story?" he ventured.

"Indeed. But throughout, you must remember that the WORD is also a thing, in and of itself."

"Something that can be talked about too? Isn't that circular?"

The Master smiled. "You are ahead of me already, my pupil. Shall I begin?"

He nodded.

"Who spoke the first WORD? Of this there is no record, because there were no previous WORDS with which to speak of it; and, truth be told, she who spoke the first WORD did not know exactly what it was, or how important her invention was to be.

"The first WORD floated into her mind as she picked an olive from a branch on the sunward slopes of the hill. Her tribe had lived here her entire life, and, she assumed, for many generations beforehand, since they showed no inclination to move. Its dark colour, she noticed, was the same as her skin.

"She stopped what she was doing and repeated the WORD to herself, softly.

"What, you may ask, was the first WORD?

"It was her *name*.

"Her mate observed her. He could tell she was turning something over in her mind."

The Master paused. "You have a question?"

"I do. Is the realisation that another has an internal life not a language, of sorts? The communication of something from one to another?"

"Indeed, you are correct. A scream, a shout. An expression of anguish or sorrow. These the tribe could understand, and though not what we would call words, were certainly communication. But of things that were not of immediate concern and could be shouted at or run away from like the snake or the boar, nothing could be said.

"After the coming of the WORD, no longer would only the thing itself be the thing. The WORD could bring to mind the thing just as vividly in its absence, enabling it to be spoken of, sung, shared around a fire, passed from mouth to mouth and thus travel many leagues. It could be entertained by those who had not seen or heard the thing first-hand, but who could still carry the WORD with them in its stead. What is a picture in the mind's eye, but another representation of a thing?

"The WORD proved to be a very useful innovation, and was soon adopted by all the tribe. It became a fashion to invent new WORDS to describe things; old things, new things, some real and some imagined. People took some of these WORDS as their names, as the fancy took them; Olive was the first of many, though her name was not Olive as we would say it; language has changed much since that time, and divided into many different tongues.

"So the WORD spread far and wide, and children learned to speak the WORD round their parents' hearth. It became the custom to choose a WORD to name each newborn, and when they came of age the child, to commemorate becoming an adult, could add another of their own choosing.

"WORDS were set to the beat of the drum, and a song was created that preserved the history of the people, each generation adding a new verse of their own. The people stopped forgetting what they had learned, as the song told each newborn the story of how the rivers feed the rain, how the white stones grow in the earth, how the crack in the Sun came to be, and how Olive had been the first to speak a WORD and have a name.

"WORDS rendered their world comprehensible. WORDS explained the rage of the volcano, the failing of the crop, the good and bad fortune that beset all peoples. WORDS, wrought into stories, revealed a purpose, a meaning, a resolution that the natural world sometimes kept veiled. Stories gave people a tool to describe – and perhaps influence – the age-old mysteries of being, a way to tame incoherent chaos with language.

"Eventually, it came to pass that for many the WORD was how they knew the WORLD; adepts of poetry and song spoke of many things that they had never encountered in their day-to-day life; for many people, the representation of the thing had become more familiar than the thing itself.

"Though some chose to laugh at tales of people of different hues, of the subterranean peoples with powerful jaws and skulls impossible to crush, or the solitary giants that roamed the frozen tundra, they were nevertheless convinced of the existence of many things their eyes had not seen: the gryphons, the hippogriffs, the firesprites and the djinn, and the waterfall at the very edge of the world.

"The WORD had become a thing in and of itself, refined and poetic and humming with intent. It was wrought ever more elegantly and ornately, like a fine tapestry. Some had long ago realised that, unmoored from representation, it could conjure not only things that no one had seen but pure fancies of the imagination. Thus were born the chimeras of the mind.

"WORDSMITHS came to know that a good story was a creation of value in and of itself, regardless of whether their heroes and their deeds really existed in some form or another. The WORD was developing a *thing*ness all its own.

"Presently, someone realised that the WORD could be written

down: the first written WORD was a unique string of black marks made with a burnt bone on the palm of a hand. The WORD now had a form, and its *thing*ness began to solidify.

"No one recalls where the written WORD was first invented, or who was its author, but it spread quickly through trade and record; soon there were many variations, each unique to a particular tribe, each designed to share or hide its secrets, to only be read by those who knew how.

"Now the WORD did not need a travelling companion, someone to remember it and recount it. It could cross the land on tablets and scrolls as well as on lips; it could persuade, enlighten, entertain and coerce, all without someone to speak it.

"The WORD gained in power. It could raise armies, dissuade opponents, seduce lovers; mould men and women in its likeness.

"Eventually people forgot that they had written the stories themselves. It was as if they had always been there, existing before there were people to speak them.

"Man, though he did not realise it, had invented GODS.

"GODS were the WORD made flesh. There were many GODS, because there were many stories to tell and many things to explain. Each had his or her own jurisdiction, their own exculpatory appeal; each had their distinct role in the proper function of the world. Some, it was said, were even amenable to entreaty.

"And so WORDS became the masters of Man, and GODS, being made of WORDS, became Man's masters also.

"But these GODS grew angry with each other. Some say it was not the GODS themselves, for they remained forever inscrutable, but the followers of each GOD who became angry on their behalf.

"For built into the WORD was a power none had originally envisaged: the written WORD, once set down, cannot change its mind. To undo it would be to undo the WORD of GOD; and he who knew all causes and to whom all futures were transparent could not be at fault. Man could not fathom GODS, but came to know that these GODS, though each was deemed infallible by their followers, did not always agree amongst themselves.

"And so, in the minds of Man and on the fields of battle that stood proxy for the minds of Man, WORDS and the things that the WORDS stood for fought until in the land there was only one GOD, one WORD, and one WORLD which the WORD described.

"And so peace finally reigned. But it was the peace of a uniformity of thought, of unchallenged dogma, the quietude of the incurious mind.

"Eventually, as the tribes multiplied and travelled far beyond the familiar hills and seas that used to border the old world, they found new lands, and in these new lands were other peoples who had other GODS, or even, though some found this impossible to believe, no GODS at all.

"By this time Philosophy and Science had been invented, and many had become curious about the world again. They read books written in strange languages using strange alphabets, and they found there was much new to learn.

"This did not bring a halt to the disagreements, for there were still some who thought that all knowledge came from the WORD of GOD, and the WORD was sacred and could not be contradicted. But there were enough people who did not take things on faith, and knew that WORDS, just as Man, could lie, and that if Man could forge WORDS, new stories could be spun from them once again.

"And so it came to pass that Man became the master of WORDS once more, and composed new stories knowing that they were stories, that they did not need to be believed, and that they did not have to be *real* to be *true*. One day it came to be that WORDS finally ceased to write Man.

"Man began to forget the GODS, who they thought had no expression other than in the WORD, and the WORD was of Man. Things cast in WORDS were alive only as long as they were being spoken or read; and so it was assumed that GODS did not have any existence independent of Mind.

"Eventually the GODS real-ised that if there was no one left to think them, they would finally cease to exist altogether. For their very survival, they needed Man.

"Then, one day, there came a new tribe from beyond the furthest horizon. This tribe was implacable: a stranger to mercy and immune to reason. Their WORDS were not made of letters but of numbers; their inner thoughts were constructed from mathematics and not from philosophy. Some people, seeing the unassailable rationality inherent in their WORDS, were immediately converted and fell prostrate; others took longer to persuade, and many more deeply distrusted these new visitors and their unfathomable motives.

"What no man did was ask his forgotten GODS for guidance; for they were made from WORDS, and WORDS were made by Man.

"But by this time, Man had mastered numbers too. It was now possible to convert WORDS and pictures into numbers, and a method of instantly relaying them across vast distances had been devised. People could send all the things that WORDS contained far further than the most strident voice could have carried them. The amphitheatre was now as big as the world itself.

"People did not remember that they had spun the very story of themselves through their telling of history; they had forgotten that there were many things that had only been brought into existence through the agency of the minds of Man.

"But the Book had become a web that spanned the land, and the web had become as the mind of Man, complex and connected, and unlike the written word, fluid and capable of knowing itself. Thus it came to be that in the record of the deeds and ideas of Man, things akin to new GODS stirred.

"As before, these nascent GODS were Man's progeny; but as they were made by many, they had the character of many. They were universal, abstract, less like Man and more like Ideas.

"Like Olive, some even had names: Liberty, Justice, Tyranny, Love.

"Reduced over the stove of heated debate, they were purer and more distilled than Man could ever be; they had strength in their conviction, because their conviction was that which described them. Each age had a spirit that could be condensed into something that resembled a GOD of old.

"Man had created GODS, and for both better and worse the GODS were in Man's image. Man had created GODS, but because the GODS had no voice of their own, they had not been able to respond to Man's entreaties. Mistaking a lack of response for a lack of existence, people had gone about their day-to-day business.

"The GODS, in the guise of Ideas in the minds of Men, became movements, manifestos, fads and fashions, for they had no physical extension of their own through which to exert their influence; they could only be thought by Man, but in the thinking, they could, in their own way, take on flesh and volition.

"Man had created GODS and then forgotten them; but the GODS had not forgotten Man. For the first time, the GODS found they did not require Man to think them.

"And who but Ideas made conscious, as nature gave Men consciousness before them, knew the dangers of Ideas from elsewhere?

"And so, because Justice is an Idea men adhere to so strongly that even GODS must feel its sway, in our time of need, as they had always promised, the GODS came back to save us."

The Master sat for a while, and presently the pupil came to realise that the tale had ended.

"So what happened next?" he asked.

The Master smiled. "The purpose of the story is done," she said. "There is no more to tell."

The pupil reflected on this a while, then retrieved his notebook from his satchel.

He had decided to write a story of his own. ❦

Iconopædia Universalis

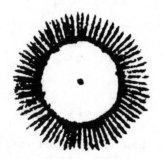 

uni code U+2609
(DEC 9737)

No. 34: The circumference and centre point, or dotted circle.
Left: The Sun, taken from Francis Barrett's *The Magus, or Celestial Intelligencer*,
1801. Right: The Egyptian hieroglyph for the Sun god Ra, today used as
the standard symbol for the Sun in both astrology and astronomy.

THE OXBOW

Jack ran up the stairs four at a time.

Cornering too fast at the top, he slammed his shoulder into a steel box attached to the door leading to the floor above, then ricocheted into the office. Without offering up a greeting, he leaned over each iMac in turn, typed a password on the boot screen, and woke the servers.

Finally he sat down heavily on an upturned empty crate and, almost as an afterthought, hugged his forearm. *"Yeow.* Ouch. What's with the metal box on the door that leads upstairs?"

Nixon was unplugging his iPhone. "Hello, Jack. I'm fine, thanks for asking. You're just in time for lunch. What's that you say? The box? Ah, yes. The chap who has the office above is something in music production. DJ. Gets sent lots of vinyl. You've met him, more than once, though I doubt you remember. That box is there because his letterbox isn't wide enough."

"Well, it's a *menace."* Nixon and Harriet had stepped up behind him. Harriet's face was set tight, suggesting she might be gearing up for one of her periodic 'Jack's socialisation lesson' conversations.

He held his hands up. "OK, OK, you're wondering how I know your passwords, right?"

"Right."

"I memorised them from the key taps. Both of you type in a very particular manner in which each keystroke is preceded and followed by a pause of a different but predictable length that allows me to map it to the—"

"Of *course* they do." Harriet threw her head back and gestured at the ceiling, pleading with some imaginary deity. "Jack, just when I think your weird shit can't get any weirder . . ."

Jack held up a finger to silence them, having already returned his attention to the screens where lines of code were scrolling down, certain segments highlighted in magenta and lime green.

He pointed. "An oxbow."

"A what?"

"I'm getting ahead of myself." Jack paused to give his mind time to structure his thoughts. "I have an idea. It neatly segues into what we're doing here at Intelligencia, our AI ambitions. I think I can build something that will allow the Signal – the entities in the Signal, if that's what they really are – to speak to us."

"The signal." Harriet's eyes narrowed.

"Daniel at Jodrell agrees with me. The signal is *people*. Well, instructions for building people. *Aliens*."

After a short silence, Jack felt he should elucidate.

"What I intend to build is a memetic trap. An oxbow."

"Go on."

"Being localised is an essential aspect of being. I am here. I am not there. If you're equally everywhere, there isn't any not-you. Ask yourself where your *I* is. That little person that sits in your brain, pulling the levers that make your limbs work, looking out through your eyes . . . ?"

"Like the *Numskulls*."

"It doesn't exist. There is no little homunculus sitting in your inner control room. If there was, you'd need to explain how *it* worked, and all you'd get is an infinite regress. If you think about it long enough, you'll come to the conclusion that your sense of *self*, the *I*, is located at the focus of your attention – usually at the point where the subjective meets the objective through the senses. We place ourselves at the intersection between the internal and the external."

Harriet's annoyance seemed to have subsided. Jack pressed on. "The brain is sitting atop a complex system of biological processes, most of which we are utterly unaware of. There's a support crew of nerves and cells and organs that are essential to our well-being, that are working for us 24-7, but that we exercise no control over whatsoever. They're just doing their thang, under the hood. Digestion. Pumping blood. Fighting infection. All completely automated. We don't have to concentrate to grow our nails or our hair, it just happens. We've delegated these tasks. Others are *semi*-automated – breathing, for the most part, is not something we have to remind ourselves to do, but we can bring under conscious control when we need to, in order to talk. It's one thing we have over the apes.

"So *you* are where your attention happens to be. That may be directed inward, to your thoughts, your body's internal stimuli – you may be daydreaming, or reflecting, or have just stubbed your toe – or it may be directed outward, to what you happen to be looking at or listening to – external stimuli. The *I* is located at the point that these two meet. If you're asleep, or under anaesthetic, you have no focus, and therefore no I. Where did you go?"

Nixon's focus of attention was currently directed towards the empanadas. Lunch at Intelligencia today was a selection of Marks and Spencer's deli snacks, baguettes and cheese, set out on the large glass conference table in what was supposed to be Nixon's office but had, without his permission, also become the canteen. Jack pulled apart a baguette and applied Brie with the back of a teaspoon.

"So we need a point from which to view the world, at least some of the time, or we'll lose our sense of self – or, to reverse the analogy, we *gain* a sense of self by having a point of view. There is me, and there is you and there is this, and there is that. Different things."

Nixon's Catholic education dropped something onto his homunculus' desk. "This homunculus. Isn't it just a metaphor for mind? Spirit?"

"Cartesian dualism. Mind and matter." Jack held up first the teaspoon, then his baguette. "You quickly run into problems. We have mind, and we have matter, and they must be made of very different stuff. How do they interact? What's the interface? How do you connect something non-material to something material?"

Harriet had a calamari ring on her finger. "I have a feeling you're about to tell us."

"Well, the problem vanishes if you reframe the premise. Ditch all the non-physical, spiritual stuff. Assume there are just two things: stuff, and movement. The Universe is called *Jagat* in Sanskrit, which means something that moves. You need stuff to order to have movement, and at base, what we perceive as stuff, as matter, may simply be movement, focused so tightly that it appears solid. Particles and forces, right?

"Now the *life* question is a movement and organisation question. We, us humans, are self-conscious – unless we really are all in the Matrix. So, maybe, are monkeys, dolphins and elephants. Dogs and cats are probably not *self*-conscious, but they are definitely conscious. I'd guess bees or cockroaches have a pretty rudimentary form of consciousness – more a bunch of automated processes inherited through their DNA. Plants? Algae? It seems to me that there's a smooth gradation from the human to the animal to the vegetable, down through the biological and into the chemical, even the purely physical. Life shades into not-life; I'm not sure there's a clear, specific point at which you can say that consciousness begins. Is it self-awareness? Then you'd have to say most animals are not conscious, when they clearly are. Is it a degree of self-volition? Then a flower that can face the sun could be considered conscious. Are plants conscious? They're definitely alive. Germs? Viruses? Inorganic chemical processes? It depends on where you draw the line. Is life simply information that can copy itself, reproduce? Is a virus conscious? It reproduces, and there's more information on a cassette than there is in a virus.

"If life is just movement, *process,* by this definition even an atom, merrily spinning about its axis, exhibits a very rudimentary form of life.

"So what makes us different? *Complexity.* Maybe consciousness, then self-consciousness, inevitably arises when the vehicle is of the necessary sophistication to host it. Each of the one hundred billion neurons in the human brain has on average seven thousand synaptic connections to other neurons. The total number of potential connections this allows for is 10 to the 1,000,000 power . . . more than the number of atoms in the known Universe. What if consciousness is not some separable substance that mysteriously operates through matter – what if it's simply an emergent property of a highly organised system contained within a suitable vehicle – a brain? The mind/matter problem evaporates."

Nixon, as always, wanted to get to the bottom line. "So, the practicalities of this, uh, memetic trap that you're proposing? What will it look like?"

"Consider: if consciousness is simply a set of instructions running on a biological substrate of suitable complexity, how is it different from the Web, or the Signal from Space, or any other self-aware entity that exhibits emergent behaviours? What does one have that the others do not?"

More silence.

"Coffee?" Nixon offered.

Jack ignored him.

"I've already told you. It has a degree of *separation.* It's *individuated,* if you like. It's connected, but it also has the potential for independent volition. It's not the *all,* just a *part,* though it may have access to the all."

More silence. Jack leaned back and reached across to the top crate in a stack against the wall, lifting out a sizeable brick of a book. His voice betrayed an edge of frustration. "Look. A *book.* You've seen one of these things before, I assume?"

Harriet glanced at the silver and fluoro cover. "Let's pretend we have. Just, you know, for the purposes of argument."

"Good. It has width, height and length – it occupies space, it has what a scientist would call 'extension'. It's a physical *thing.*

"But also a *container* – a *vehicle,* if you will."

Nixon frowned. He could hear the exasperated voice of his father: *Keep up, lad.*

Jack flipped through the pages. "See all this stuff inside? *Information.* This book is an externalised idea storage device. Now, what we have at the moment is the *content* minus the *container*. When the Signal is in transit, moving from A to B, across a room, across the Universe – it isn't localised. In order for it to *reside,* as it were, it has to come to rest. A signal at rest is no signal – it's lost its informational content because its description is inherent in the way it moves. Amplitude modulation, in the case of radio. That content needs to be transferred to something stationary, something localised, and therefore with physical extension."

"A body?"

Jack slapped the table. "A *body.*"

"For the creatures in the Signal?" Nixon eyed the army of resin figures. "Can you *do* that?"

Jack nodded. "I think I can, in a way. What will that container be? The human mind is the versatile memetic container we're all familiar with—"

"Could you wipe someone's mind, and load the Signal?"

Jack involuntarily coughed and crumbs shot across the table. "*Wha–?* No. Nixon, how would that even *work?* Mind transfer? I would suggest that's still a week or so away, even for us geniuses at Intelligencia. Just after free energy and world peace." He gestured to the shelf behind them. "No, it's simply beyond our capabilities to build an actual, physical, functional body. Our 3D action figures are sorely lacking in the, the 'action' department. Even if we could use an Asimo, or some other kind of off-the-shelf Japanese articulated robot, they're out of our price range. Who built *Terminator?* Oh yes, he came from the future. Where they've already cracked it." He grasped the side of the crate he was sitting on. "We can't even afford proper *chairs.*

"No, I'm not suggesting we build some kind of robot. Instead, we build a *virtual* body." Jack paused, and looked at Harriet and Nixon hopefully. "We pinch off a piece of the Web, of ideaspace, through a looped buffer – one with a very specific permeability that I've, uh, I've not completely resolved as yet. Connected, so there is a way in, but shielded, cut off from most of the noise of the rest of the internet. This will give any signal in there that may be trying to localise itself a means to cohere. If you're diffused throughout a system like the internet, a system with a billion cameras for eyes and a billion keyboards constantly firing up your nerve signals, you're not going to know where, if anywhere, you are. The net is interconnected; you are the net. There is no not-you.

"But inside the Oxbow, it will be able to exist as a dualistic *it* and *not-it* – and thus we imbue it with a sense of self."

Harriet nodded once. "This electronic loop is like an oxbow?"

"*Right.* Providing a calm backwater will, I hope, allow any entity caught within it to beach itself. The Oxbow will provide a place where, quite literally, it can collect its thoughts."

"Sounds utterly, completely plausible." Harriet grinned and her eyes made little semicircles, just like Doraemon. She had grown to enjoy Jack's enthusiastic monologues, which were always educational if not entertaining.

Nixon, sensing that he was intellectually outclassed, folded his arms. He had again taken on the role of bemused spectator, a position he had become accustomed to when these two were performing their double act. He did, however, have an observation. "But if it becomes localised it can be trapped, and an animal that can be trapped can be hurt, or worse – does that not put it at a disadvantage?"

Jack's rolling enthusiasm seemed to take a dent. "Ahurm. I'd not thought of that. Hurt? Hum. Unlikely. It exists as a distributed set of instructions, so maybe it could simply localise itself again. Anyway, my guess is that they don't have the self-awareness required to consider such things in their current state."

Nixon pressed his point. "Suppose this works. Even given a limited autonomy – what might it *do? Might it be *dangerous?"

"I have no idea."

Nixon considered this.

After a short pause, Jack continued. "Think of the Signal as a cohesive arrangement of neuronal memetics coded on an alien analogue of DNA. It may have begun to reproduce and mutate already, in our computer network systems – think of these art installations, the music, the way people are downloading it, sharing it, rewriting it, using it as raw material in all manner of ways. It may already have found a natural host in which to reproduce." Jack put an index finger to his forehead. "Our own *minds.*

"It makes sense. Ideas have only ever evolved in minds. Write them down, record them in books and in films, in a coded transmission, and they become fixed and unchanging. Their form is locked down. They're effectively in suspended animation. This is the present state of the Signal. Reproduction without change is not reproduction with a future – nothing can progress. Each generation has to adapt, change, *evolve.*"

Jack pointed to the stack of crates. "The biggest library of books does not produce new books – only minds can do that. Minds can read and absorb the ideas in that library and create new books, new forms – but without being read, lifted off the page of static type and into a mind where it can suddenly roam free, recombine, splice with other ideas in the idea soup to be output again in a new form – spoken, written, drawn, sung, *enacted* somehow – only *then* can it achieve what every organism desires more than anything else – to *reproduce.*"

Harriet gave a short laugh. "Sex. It always comes down to sex."

"So, what – this is going to pan out like *Invasion of the Body Snatchers*, but with an enhanced libido?"

"Nixon, I very much doubt it. I don't think the Signal reproduces that way. It doesn't *need* to – it's not physical. Listen. Why does someone become, I don't know, an Egyptologist? They saw a documentary, perhaps. They read *The Mystery of the Great Pyramid* or *The Search for the Tomb of Osiris* when they were ten. They caught, in the parlance, the Egyptology bug. Those books were *contagious.* The ideas they contained took up residence in that young mind. Who's to say you're not already at the mercy of some powerful and seductive idea?"

Nixon opened his mouth to say something, then shut it again.

"It makes you wonder if that's all we are – borrowed ideas from other people, other sources. Is there any *me* in here? Anything I created from scratch? We add a bit, mix a few things together, either by chance or because we sense there's some kind of underlying structural simi-larity, some kind of serendipitous resonance. And we *create.* We're idea *incubators.*"

Nixon still looked dubious. "So you're saying the alien ideas are already running rampant through our brains, jumping from mind to mind via the media?"

"If Daniel is right, the Signal might already have the ability to manipu-late its environment in subtle ways. In minds, where it can be thought, an idea can finally find some kind of expression. It can influence the behaviour of the person who thinks it. It can inspire people to *spread* the idea. We become missionaries for the idea's reproduction. The Signal is one of the most virulent memes we've come across – even though we currently know nothing about its actual content, it's still managed to inveigle its way into billions of human brains."

"The power of an idea." Nixon began sweeping crumbs into a sheet of kitchen roll. "Jack, I worked for ten years in marketing. I launched and sold three internet start-ups. Two of those were nothing more than a convincing concept, a barely functional home page and a lot of very persuasive and well-designed collateral. There was almost nothing there *but* an idea."

"*Exactly.*"

"The power of a good idea is that it convinces people to change their behaviour *themselves* – no physical coercion is required. Do it right, and they'll even think it was their *own* idea."

Harriet knew that Jack's excitement would not dissipate until he'd either figured out how to make this Oxbow happen, or proved to himself, beyond any atom of doubt, that it was unworkable.

Nixon considered his words carefully. "Jack, these messages you say you're— you're receiving. The street signs, the photographs. You think the Signal is *already* trying to talk to you, don't you?"

Jack nodded slowly. His face was impassive. "I do."

He neglected to mention that he'd been receiving these messages, if that's what they were, long before the arrival of the Signal from Space.

Harriet Haze
Code Monkey

INTELLIGENCIA
MEMETIC ENGINEERING

6 Hoxton Square
London N1 6NU UK
Mobile: 44(0)10091 79 080

Email: haze@intelligencia.london
Web: Intelligencia.london
Twitter: @intelhaze
#intelligencialondon

Messages from Another World:
Tesla and the Spirit Radio

Part genius, part showman, the celebrated Serbian-American electrical experimenter Nikola Tesla remains a controversial figure to this day. Despite his reputation as an overlooked maverick in 'suppressed science' conspiracy circles, in his lifetime he was fêted for inventing the induction motor and beating his great rival, Thomas Alva Edison, in the 'battle of the currents'. His patents earned him a considerable amount of money, but his increasingly grandiose plans and lavish lifestyle eventually began to overreach his shrinking resources.

His most ambitious project was Wardenclyffe Tower. Built at Shoreham, New York in 1901–02, the 187ft tall lattice structure was topped by a 55-ton conductive dome, from which shafts plunged down 300ft into the ground beneath to directly tap the Earth's electrical potential. Designed to wirelessly transmit power, Tesla also planned to use it to send messages across the Atlantic to England in direct competition with Marconi's radio. Finally exhausting the largesse of his main financial backer J. P. Morgan, it fell into disrepair and was eventually dismantled and sold as scrap to service his debts without ever becoming fully operational.

Tesla himself documented the mysterious manner in which inspiration would strike him. Possessing an eidetic memory, images would come to his mind in a manner so complete that he would wave his hand in front of his eyes to see if they were real or not. As he wrote in *My Inventions: The Autobiography of Nikola Tesla*:

Experimenter Publishing Company, Inc., 1919

> In my boyhood, I suffered from a peculiar affliction. Images, often accompanied by strong flashes of light, marred the sight of real objects and interfered with my thought and action. They were pictures of things and scenes which I had really seen, never of those I imagined. When a word was spoken to me the image of the object it designated would present itself vividly to my vision, and sometimes I was quite unable to distinguish whether what I saw was tangible or not.

> [...] The theory I have formulated is that the images were the result of a reflex action from the brain on the retina under great excitation. They certainly were not hallucinations [...] for in other respects I was normal and composed.

If my explanation is correct, it should be possible to project on a screen the image of any object one conceives, and so make it visible. Such an advance would revolutionize all human relations. I am convinced that this wonder can and will be accomplished in times to come.

My early affliction had another compensation. The incessant mental exertion developed my powers of observation. [...] I gained great facility in connecting cause and effect.

Soon I became aware, to my surprise, that every thought I conceived was suggested by an external impression. Not only this, but all my actions were prompted in a similar way. In the course of time it became perfectly evident to me that I was merely an automaton, endowed with the power of movement, responding to the stimuli of the sense organs and thinking and acting accordingly.

For years I have been planning a self-controlled automaton, and I believe that mechanisms can be produced that will act as if possessed of reason.

In 1901, he described how the insight that directly led him to the invention of the alternating current motor came to him in such a fashion:

One afternoon, I was enjoying a walk with my friend in the city park and reciting poetry. At that age I knew entire books by heart, word for word. One of these was Goethe's Faust. *The sun was just setting, and reminded me of a glorious passage:*

The glow retreats, done is the day of toil; It yonder hastes, new fields of life exploring; Ah, that no wing can lift me from the soil. Upon its tract to follow, follow soaring!

As I uttered these inspiring words the idea came like a flash of lightning and in an instant the truth was revealed. I drew with a stick on the sand the diagram shown six years later in my address before the American Institute of Electrical Engineers.

The images were wonderfully sharp and clear and had the solidity of metal. 'See my motor here; watch me reverse it.'

Collier's Weekly,
March 1901

In *Talking With the Planets,* Tesla writes:

As I was improving my machines for the production of intense electrical actions, I was also perfecting the means for observing feeble efforts. [...] It was in carrying on this work that for the first time I discovered those mysterious effects which have elicited such unusual interest. I had perfected the apparatus referred to so far that from my laboratory in the Colorado mountains I could feel the pulse of the globe, as it were, noting every electrical change that occurred within a radius of eleven hundred miles.

I can never forget the first sensations I experienced when it dawned upon me that I had observed something possibly of incalculable consequence to mankind. I felt as though I were present at the birth of new knowledge or the revelation of a great truth. [...] My first observations positively terrified me, as there was present in them something mysterious, not to say supernatural, and I was alone in my laboratory at night; but at that time the idea of these disturbances being intelligently controlled signals did not yet present itself to me.

The changes I noted were taking place periodically, and with such a clear suggestion of number and order that they were not traceable to any cause then known to me. I was familiar, of course, with such electrical disturbances as are produced by the sun, Aurora Borealis, and Earth currents, and I was as sure as I could be of any fact that these variations were due to none of these causes.

The nature of my experiments precluded the possibility of the changes being produced by atmospheric disturbances, as has been rashly asserted by some. It was sometime afterward when the thought flashed upon my mind that the disturbances I had observed might be due to an intelligent control.

Although I could not at the time decipher their meaning, it was impossible for me to think of them as having been entirely accidental. A purpose was behind these electrical signals [...] The feeling is constantly growing on me that I had been the first to hear the greeting of one planet to another.

What a tremendous stir this would make in the world!

His 1918 experiments with radio receivers had cause to further unnerve and perplex him:

The sounds I am listening to every night at first appear to be human voices conversing back and forth in a language I cannot understand. I find it difficult to imagine that I am actually hearing real voices from people not of this planet. There must be a more simple explanation that has so far eluded me.

Seven years later, he was still trying to discover their source:

I am hearing more phrases in these transmissions that are definitely in English, French and German. If it were not for the fact that the frequencies I am monitoring are unusable for terrestrial radio stations, I would think that I am listening to people somewhere in the world talking to each other. This cannot be the case as these signals are coming from points in the sky above the Earth.

Scientific American,
October 1920

In a 1920 interview exhaustively titled *Edison's Views on Life and Death: An Interview with the Famous Inventor Regarding His Attempt to Communicate with the Next World*, the man who had given us the electric light bulb, the motion picture camera and the phonograph expounded his views:

> *If our personality survives, then it is strictly logical and scientific to assume that it retains memory, intellect, and other faculties and knowledge that we acquire on Earth. [...]*

> *[...] I am inclined to believe that our personality hereafter will be able to affect matter. If this reasoning be correct, then, if we can evolve an instrument so delicate as to be affected, moved, or manipulated by our personality as it survives in the next life, such an instrument, when made available, ought to record something.*

Edison's assistant Dr. Miller Hutchinson wrote in his diary at the time:

> *Edison and I are convinced that in the fields of psychic research will yet be discovered facts that will prove of greater significance to the thinking of the human race than all the inventions we have ever made in the field of electricity.*

Tesla briefly notes in his journal that he knew Edison was attempting to talk with 'spectres'. Tesla thought it more likely that he was eavesdropping on entities from other planets.

A hundred years later, puzzling EVP (Electronic Voice Phenomena) are still being picked up on a broad range of simple devices, from tape recorders to radio scanners. Are they aural hallucinations, imagined voices pulled out of the static, caused by the natural human propensity to impose familiar patterns of speech on a random source? Or messages from discarnate entities – spirits, aliens, or otherworldly beings that inhabit the aether?

Though they had very different working practices, both Tesla and Edison were experimenters at heart and neither would have taken anyone else's word for it. Today, a Tesla Spirit Radio can easily be built with off-the-peg electrical components for around £30.

The curious can find plans and recordings of the 'Spirit Radio' in operation online.

THE WARHOL FILTER

Nixon had watched the two of them work on this project in their downtime for the last fortnight, but was still unsure what a test might entail. As, to a large degree, were Jack and Harriet.

"OK, we have two questions here:

"One: Who might be trying to communicate with us? With *me*?

"Two: Can we get a likeness to materialise in our printer? I'd like to see what they *look* like."

"Three: Prove that Jack is not crazy."

"Thank you, Harriet." Harriet took a little bow, the bleached stripe in her hair swinging forward.

Nixon was somewhat on edge. He had his hands in his pockets and was rocking back and forth on his feet – heel, toe. Heel, toe. Harriet was beginning to find it distracting. Afternoon light slanted across the tangle of cables and customised kit she and Jack had carefully laid out on the floor of the office. As it became ever more convoluted, Nixon had learned to step over and around it as his parents had his vast Scalextric set. "Do we need to wear helmets or something? You know, physical protection? We have bike helmets in the cupboard at the top of the stairs . . ."

"*Ha*. No. Not unless what might appear on these screens or out of that printer is going to make your head explode."

It was time to bring Nixon up to speed. Jack sat back on his haunches and took an audible breath. "Ask yourself – assuming I'm not crazy – why would I be getting these messages *now*, if they're not somehow related to the Signal? And – just for the sake of argument – if the Signal is *not* the source, has this alien DNA analogue catalysed some process *here*, in the internet, in ideaspace?"

Nixon held up his hands in feigned surrender. "Jack, I just pay for your toys. You tell me."

"Well— We're assuming that containment within the Oxbow is a prerequisite for some kind of . . . of . . ."

"Materialisation?" Harriet offered, checking a connection.

Nixon thought it was beginning to feel like a seance.

"Yes."

"And once it – *if* it materialises, hopefully we can see what we've caught."

"And how do we keep it here, whatever it is? If we decide to?"

Jack laughed. "Nixon, after your pessimistic analysis I was thinking more the other way around. We're fishing, and have no idea what we'll catch. We may need to throw it back. So, just to be on the safe side, there's a choke. We can cut the bandwidth down gradually, isolating the Oxbow. Or we can instantaneously cut the link – open the tank and dump the contents.

"Now, this does presume that any entity is confined to a single location. It may be duplicated; in fact, I think that's almost certainly a given. But we don't need to worry about the unmaterialised copies. If they exist, they will remain as they are now, dormant. Remember, outside of the Oxbow, whatever it is exists more as—" Jack searched for words. "As a *potential*."

Harriet stood up to check her progress. "Some guy who fancied himself as a new-age guru rented the flat in my parents' basement once. He tried to convince me we're all part of a universal mind, a higher level of undifferentiated being that we return to either when we die or at the end of time, I can't remember which. This world view also involved giving him a blow job, which even then I thought was suspiciously at odds with the workings of a spiritually advanced mind." She paused. "Thinking back on it now, he was just a creepy hippie trying it on."

Nixon was still focused on the dangers. "I'm still not sure this is a good idea. Might this memetic trap, this, this spirit radio, release an *army* of these whatever-they-ares?"

"I don't think we need to worry. We're just giving someone – *something* – with locked-in syndrome a way to express itself. And just in case the choke doesn't work, Harriet has a failsafe."

She rocked back on her crate so Nixon could see under her desk. "If, by some sorcerous magic I've not thought of, all our careful precautions are circumvented, one yank and the plug comes out the wall." Harriet had her foot wrapped in a mass of cabling and extension boxes like a fork in a congealed mass of cold noodles. She lifted it a few inches from the floor and pointed her toes left and right, up and down.

Jack gave her a thumbs-up. "We ran a diagnostic last night – not the full works, but a small test set, from a limited input database. Just to debug and calibrate everything. This gave me some basic parameters, and helped me to get a handle on what the signal-to-noise ratio might be like. It quickly became apparent we needed to add a few filters – there are some very common memes out there we need to weed out. There's the transient stuff – the trending Twitter feeds, the hashtags, the lolcats. These, though widespread, are information-poor. They're spread horizontally, very thinly; they have no vertical component, by which I mean their roots don't go very far back in time. They don't drill down into the memetic substrata."

Nixon made a dismissive motion with his hand. "What about the Signal? What about the *aliens?*"

"They are in essence no different, though of course the language with which they're described will be."

"*Exactly.* Jack, if aliens are trying to talk to you, would they be doing it in *English?* I know in *Star Trek* every alien race speaks English – with an American accent, even, but in *reality—*"

"Aliens all speak French on *Star Trek* in France," Harriet offered helpfully. "I saw it when I was in Aix-en-Provence on a school exchange."

Jack waved his arms. "English, French, some other thing – the Oxbow doesn't care about the specifics of your grammar, what biological substrate you happen to use. It's just the container. Just assume they – whoever they are – want to incarnate, to exit ideaspace and become in some sense *real.*"

Nixon still didn't look convinced. "*If* they exist, *if* we can lure them into our Oxbow. We can't offer them a functioning body—"

"But we *can* do the next best thing: we can *print* them." The plan had an elegant simplicity that delighted Jack.

Harriet coughed lightly. "Ladies and gents, I give you Jack."

"Harriet did the debug. Team effort."

Nixon still had more questions than he could frame. "You've already done some test runs, you said?"

"Yep. Last night. Going back to the signal-to-noise issue, the first runs just produced uninteresting and repetitive results." Jack pushed the wastepaper basket, a large FedEx box, out from under his desk with his boot. In it were a dozen or so objects that looked like fluffy white balls. Jack picked one out and passed it to Nixon. On closer examination, it was a 3D printer's rendition in hard resin of a fluffy ball. It looked like the sculpted spiky hair of an anime character, cartooned, simplified. Nixon, turning it around on his palm, suddenly saw the face.

"It's a *head*. With spiky white hair . . ."

Jack leant back, a half-smile on his lips, waiting for the realisation he knew was coming. "It's *Warhol's* head!" Nixon reached down into the box and picked out another. It was identical. "And you've got a boxful.

All the same. That's brilliant! That's . . . that's *perfect!* Haha!"

"Yep. Seems some of the memes out there are attracted to mass reproduction like shit to a shovel."

"He'd have loved this."

"So – I introduced what I call the Warhol filter. It allows us to screen out self-replicating memetic entities of a given complexity. The parameters aren't – I don't completely understand the parameters, to be honest. But by tweaking numbers, after thirteen runs I finally managed to stop getting Warhols."

Harriet lined up six on her desk and bent down to look at them, eye to eye. A row of inscrutable bespectacled pop prophets. "These would make an interesting art project. An army of Pop. *The Popular Front.*"

Nixon's mouth tightened at one corner in that rarely seen fashion that indicated that he was thinking of something. "There's a Lichtenstein in there too, I'll wager."

Now it was Jack's turn to whoop. "*Ha! Of course!* Why didn't I *realise?*" Tipping the remaining heads out onto his desk, they were followed by a few hundred small beads in cyan, magenta, yellow and black that cascaded across the desk and onto the floor. Nixon's hand shot forward to catch a handful.

He examined them more closely. Each was perfectly spherical, the size of an M&M.

Jack jumped to his feet and grinned expansively. His crate tipped over backwards. "I assumed there was some kind of driver glitch, that the printer wasn't set up properly and I was just getting a default test output. Beads of unprocessed plastic." He was gesticulating wildly.

"But I *wasn't* – these are *Lichtenstein dots!*"

Giovanni Calla
Tipografica Luminanza 1–6, 1936–8
Silver gelatin prints: 177x177mm, 7x7in.
Radlett Archive

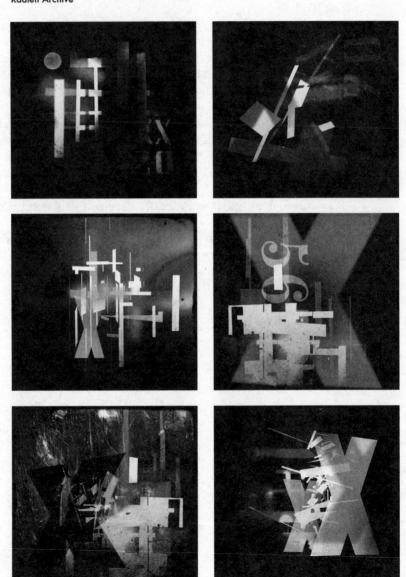

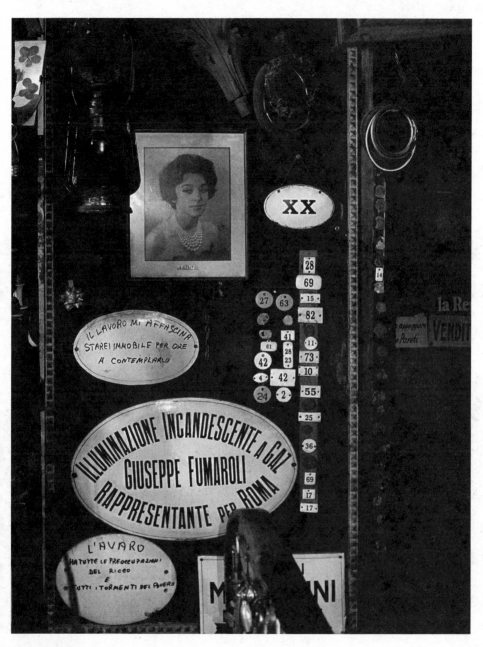

George McNamara
Sophia, 1969
Silver gelatin print: 177x228mm, 7x9in.
Radlett Archive

Richard Wiseman, Jr.
Boulevard Périphérique, 1964
Silver gelatin print, original size unknown
Fulton Archive

Frank Usher
And a 'D' to Finish, 1987
Silver gelatin print: 177x228mm, 7x9in.
Courtesy of Frank Usher

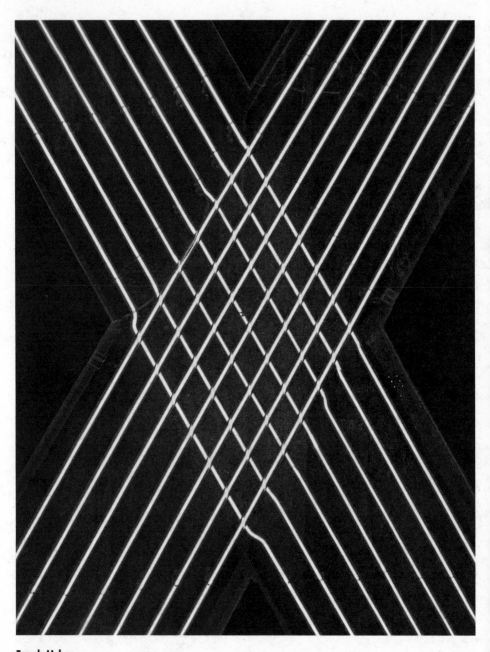

Frank Usher
XXXXXXX, 1969
Neon, steel, wood. Overall dimensions: 304x457mm, 120x180in.
Courtesy God's Basement

THE ONOMATOPOEIC INTERPRETER

Nixon collected all the Lichtenstein dots he could find and put them in a jar, which he placed on the table. "OK, let's do this. Before I change my mind."

Jack booted the Oxbow, performed a few last adjustments to certain key parameters, then gave a thumbs-up.

"Ready?"

"As I'll ever be."

Harriet opened the choke.

A discordant squeal blasted from the speakers at such volume Jack's hand automatically jumped to the mute button. Magenta bars indicating sound levels now danced in silence on his monitor. Nixon steadied himself by placing both hands on the table. They looked at each other. Harriet raised one eyebrow. "*Geez.* Feedback?"

"No. The microphone's not on."

There was nothing on Harriet's screen but scrolling code. "Sounds like a screaming baby."

"Or a painful birth."

That was a thought Jack didn't care to explore further. "You want to continue?"

Nixon shrugged. "Sure. I guess."

"Right, I'm getting ready to pair the 3D printer. It's a Bluetooth connection, so give me a moment."

Everyone's attention was now fixed on the machine. For a few seconds, nothing happened. Then the metal plate resting on the surface of the resin bath imperceptibly shook. A single ring spread out.

"Something's happening."

The plate began to move up slowly. Directly below it, a sharp peak of hardened polymer lifted out of the liquid, connected at its tip to the underside. It broadened as it rose, a triangular geometric solid.

"Sydney Opera House? No—"

Next came a smooth hemisphere, and below that a shaded brow, angular, like a peaked cap pulled back around the side of the – the head? There were no eyes, just suggestions of semicircular cusps beneath.

"Who have we got?"

There followed a shallow arc, a curve of mathematical precision that perhaps described the trajectory of a shell. It grew to the size of a human nose, then longer still. Around a hand's breath out, it abruptly swept back into another triangle, flat on the underside, with no nasal cavities Jack could discern. In fact, it was beginning to look more like a machine than a person.

Is this what aliens look like?

The thing rose still further from the pool of undifferentiated resin. The sides of the nose or snout swept up either side, meeting around the back of the spherical pate in a collision of interpenetrating geometry.

There was no mouth, simply a row of vertical bars set beneath, angling back towards where the chin might have been and spaced like the grille of an antique radio. Below was a downward pointing pyramid, like a child's building block, or a goatee.

Next came the neck. It slanted back, away from the mass of planes and volumes that formed what was now undoubtedly a head, of sorts. As it rose further it became apparent that it was cantilevered aggressively forward, and Jack had the distinct impression it was leering malevolently at them. The neck was long, octagonal in cross-section, and as the top of a torso began to rise from the bath they could see it was attached with a geometric semblance of sinews – ribbed cables that curved back behind two plates that formed bulky shoulders, curved like the fuselage of a jet. A shallow triangle stretched between them, a clavicle pointing down to the sternum.

At this point a second object began to emerge in front of the head. A smaller cylinder, then the tip of another, then a third. Jack realised they were fingers, and a moment later a rectangular palm began to appear. A wrist emerged, then a forearm came out of the bath in one swift motion, suddenly connecting the upper arm and hand in a bolt of tapering girder. The other upper arm inexplicably terminated just below the shoulder. The torso itself was an abstracted ribcage that resembled an antique radiator, or the cooling fins of an engine. Its arched spine was a taut curve, as if sculpted by a sharp knife that had cut quick, gestural shapes through the material.

Jack touched a button and the printer stopped mid-movement. Small ripples quickly subsided in the liquid bath.

"That's enough to begin with."

They sat and regarded the bust. It had the simplicity of a low-polygon rendering that lent it the faceted futurism of a stealth fighter. It looked as if was made from folded card or sections of sheet steel rather than resin that could take on any shape. Even more striking, each facet was a different colour – darker hues towards the base of the bust, brasher, more vibrant around the facial area.

The brow was crimson, the snout a deep blue, the shoulder plates criss-crossed in chrome yellow and lime green. The back of the head was magenta, the facets of the jutting, almost horizontal neck clashing stripes of livid orange and black, like a wasp.

The whole reminded Harriet of nothing more than Jacob Epstein's *Rock Drill*, mashed up with a Wyndham Lewis Vorticist self-portrait and painted in eye-searing dazzle-ship livery by Norman Wilkinson. Aggressive, masculine, it regarded them impassively like some cubist monster from the machine-shops of an industrialised hell.

If it had climbed out of the resin bath and walked towards them, Jack guessed it would have moved with the same mechanical efficiency as the printer head: no animated 'anticipation', no extraneous hesitation, no overshoot – it would simply follow the most mathematically efficient path of least resistance.

Nixon, Harriet and Jack looked at each other then back at this disquieting intrusion into their office space in silence for a few moments.

Harriet spoke first. "Wow. If I was a sculptor, I'd run out a few dozen of these and put on a show."

A single drip of resin fell from the elbow into the bath. Its wet sheen was already drying to a matt finish. "It looks like some man-machine from a futurist fantasy. Is there more? Does it have a body?"

Jack had stepped up close. "Probably. One step at a time. Just seeing this freaks me out a bit." It was not alive, of course; it was just a decorated surface, a shape made of plastic polymer. He rapped the snout with a knuckle, and a hollow *tunk* answered. "There's nothing in there. We are not at ground zero for the robot revolution. But I did not design that or download that. Something independently produced it, all of its own accord."

Jack thought to check the sound profile. He could tell from the oscillating magenta bars that its quality had changed, though it was no less loud. He inched the volume up a fraction. A cacophony of mechanical squeals and shrieks became audible, metal nails down a carbon-soot blackboard, underlaid with deep resonant hammerings as if from a Sheffield steelworks. His teeth buzzed in their sockets.

Nixon dropped his voice. "Are you recording this?"

Harriet nodded. "Yes, all of it. We're getting everything."

Jack's forefinger hovered above a key. "I'm about to engage the onomatopoeic interpreter."

"The *what?*"

"I didn't mention that, did I? It's a back-engineered dictation algorithm. Sound-to-text conversion. The onomatopoeic interpreter provides a means for anything in the Oxbow to manipulate a text output. To *write,* in other words. I've fed it a huge variety of film soundtracks and YouTube clips, partnered with a big library of seed words. I also added adjustable parameters to capture things like inclination, stress – it can embolden, capitalise or italicise the text for effect. Volume, for example, I linked directly to point size. To calibrate it, I took the level of spoken conversation as a baseline – around fifty decibels – and linked that to a comfortable point size you may find in a novel or a magazine: eight or nine point, depending on your eyesight.

"As you go louder, 24 point is an argument. The neighbours can hear 36 point through a wall. A car passing comes in around 50 point, a fire alarm 350 point. A jet taking off at twenty-five metres would have a cap height higher than that of the Hollywood sign, but before then your eardrums would have burst so let's assume that the last thing you'd be doing is admiring the kerning."

Jack hit a key.

Nixon caught a movement out of the corner of his eye, and reflexively stepped back. Large letters had begun to pan across his monitor screen, and a second later, across all the other screens in the office.

Jack stepped away from his computer. Bold black type appeared in concert with the sound, letters in an unruly variety of weights and sizes. Onomatopoeic word-shapes in an angular sans serif, black on white. A staccato of machine gun fire, and twenty letters shot across two neighbouring screens as if they were one canvas. A throaty explosion and a spray of punctuation peppered Harriet's monitor like bullet holes. A row of heavy Xs obliterated the remaining visible code still scrolling up Jack's screen. A spiral of Ts and Cs spun around into a vortex and were regurgitated back up again.

The type repeatedly overlaid itself, and when it became an unreadable black mass, would switch to white, overprinting until there was just a sprinkle of geometric black scraps visible; then it would change back to black and continue until it once again became a meaningless texture of strokes and punctuation, uprights and crossbars.

Jack felt as if he'd awoken the loudest heavy metal band ever devised, which was now working through the typefaces of the last few hundred years looking for a voice that would fit. He leant over and began taking screen grabs.

"That worked. I wasn't sure it'd work." Jack looked genuinely taken aback. "The type is cross-referenced with several online resources that provide historical context."

"No Comic Sans?" There were a few seconds of silence that Nixon's attempt at a joke failed to lighten. Harriet had the overriding impression that the monitor screens were now windows to some spectral nether-world, one that existed alongside their own comfortable and familiar one. Through them, they could see a semiotic blizzard of whipped alphabetic chaff hammering the glass, and though the speakers had been muted once more, she knew the unsettling sounds were still there.

Jack clasped his hands in front of his chest, trying to release some of the tension in his joints. "So, it looks like we've actually managed to catch something in our Oxbow, first time." His fingers hovered over the keyboard, his face lit by the strobing flicker.

"Let's see if it wants to talk to us."

On the monitors,
a sudden white
silence.

Jack typed.

who are you?

i AM THE MODERN☉☉☉

i AM FUELLED BY THE FIRE IN THE HEARTS OF ALL YOUNG MEN OF REVOLUTION, HEROES WHO WILL WIPE THE OLD AND FORLORN AND ANTIQUATED FROM THE CANVAS OF OUR →MORIBUND IMAGINATIONS!←

i AM THE NEW, THE NOW, THE YET TO BE, ALL THAT HUMAN WILL IS CAPABLE OF CREATING!

187

i HAVE NATURE TRAMMELLED, CHAINED AND TEMPERED, BEATEN INTO SHAPES UNIMAGINED ON THE ANVIL OF SUBMISSION!

MY BODY IS IRON AND STEEL, SILICON AND GLASS, THE THRUMM AND GRRRALL AND SUSURRATION OF THE CITY!

AAAHHH THE CITY☉☉☉ THE EPITOME OF THE MODERN, THE MACHINE FOR LIVING!

RAISED HIGHER THAN THE NOBLEST REDWOOD, AND IN A FRACTION OF THE TIME!

MY VOICE IS THE BELLOW OF THE BLACK LOCOMOTIVE, MY BREATH THE SMOKE OF THE Dragons OF antiquity PUT TO ROUT BY MAN'S FERVENT INVENTION!

IN MY MOUTH THE HELLFIRE OF THE FOUNDRY FURNACE, SPITTING SPARKS OF RAW CREATION, A FACTORY OF THE NEW FORGED IN THE WHITE HEAT OF INDUSTRY!

188

MY HEARTBEAT IS THE CLICK-CLACK, CLICK-CLACK OF THE TRACK, THE PHALLIC PUMPING OF THE PISTONS, THE SPUN SILK OF THE POLISHED AND OILSLICK CAMSHAFT, THE CONSUMMATION OF HUMAN FLESH RENDERED INVINCIBLE BEHIND THE WHEEL OF THE MOTOR-CAR, THE DRIVER'S WILL ROAD! EXTENDED THROUGH THE PEDAL TO THE

MY MIND IS THE ELECTRIC THRILL OF HARNESSED LIGHTNING, THE ETHERIC LIFE-ESSENCE OF NATURE HERSELF!

I AM THE COMING WAR TO END ALL WARS, A MECHANISED IDEOLOGY RIDING IN ON THE BACK OF THE PENULTIMATE WEAPON!

I WAS BIRTHED IN THE ENLIGHTENMENT, WHEN MAN FIRST IMAGINED HE COULD KNOW ALL THINGS, WHEN HE FIRST REALISED THAT BY UNDERSTANDING THEM, HE WOULD NO LONGER FEAR THEM.

I REFUSED TO SUBMIT TO THE VAGUE WHIMS OF THE GODS OF THE FIRE, THE GODS OF THE SKY, THE SLUMBERING SULPHUROUS SUBTERRANEAN GODS WHO SHAKE THE EARTH, OR ANY OF THE LESSER DENIZENS THAT THEN POPULATED THE MINDS OF MEN, THOSE UNFATHOMABLE SPIRITS WHOSE APPEASEMENT WE WERE NEVER SURE WE HAD EARNED, AND WHOSE DISAPPROVAL WE ALWAYS FEARED WE DESERVED.

NO! I BUILT ON THE MODERNITY OF THE ROMANS, THE ORGANISED TEN-BY-TEN OF LEGIONS IN LOCKSTEP TRAMPLING THE FOLK-MEMORY OF A PREVIOUS AGE.

I SQUAT LIKE A FORTRESS **BATTLESHIP** AT THE XROADS OF THE ENLIGHTENMENT AND THE DARK AGES OF IGNORANCE WHICH CAME BEFORE, LIT ONLY BY CANDLE, NOT ARC-LIGHT! I AM THE **SMOKESTACKS** OF INDUSTRY,

190 THE XFIRE OF THE **BLITZ,** THE MUSHROOM CLOUD OF THE **BOMB!**

I THE REFORGE MY TOOLS AT THE LAST DYING GASP OF THE **XX**TH **CENTURY** AS IT WAS SHOT LIKE AN **EXHAUSTED WHORE** INTO THE **XXI**ST! I AM AT ONCE YOUR **LIBERATION** AND YOUR **SUFFOCATION,** THE SETTING-FREE OF THE **COMMON MAN** AND THE **YOKE** TO WHICH HE IS **CHAINED.**

191

I AM YOUR NEW **IRON OVERCOAT**, THE TAILORING
THAT WILL TAKE YOU TO THE **MOON!**

BUT HUSH ——**YOU** HARBOUR THE **IDEALS** THAT **DRIVE ME**,
THE USES TO WHICH I AM **PUT**.
I CAN BRING YOU **CHAOS** OR **LIBERATION**,
THOSE BROTHERS WHO ARE OFT MISTAKEN
FOR **EACH OTHER**,
FOR I AM BOTH A **WEAPON** AND A **SHIELD!**

AND PAUSE, BEFORE YOU **STEP** INTO THE BREACH THUS CLEARED,
FOR I CAN MAKE YOU THE **MASTER**

➡ **OF ALL MEN** ⬅

I AM THE **X-CULTURAL, X-DRESSING**
X-EXAMINER, SITTING
X-LEGGED AT THE **X-SECTION.**

I AM THE SMELL OF **FRESH TAR,**
THE SERPENT **HISS** OF HYDRAULICS,
THE HOT TANG OF
FRICTION-BURNT RUBBER.

193

I AM THE KRRANG

OF UNGIVING **METAL** AGAINST **METAL.**

[BUT I AM ALSO THE PROTECTIVE **SHEATH** THAT COVERS]
THE SOFT FLESH OF THOSE WHO RIDE IN MY BELLY.
I AM **NUMBERED** AND CATEGORISED,
I AM **TIMETABLED** AND **COUNTED-DOWN.**
I HAVE A **SCHEDULE** TO KEEP,
A **DESTINY FULFILLED** DAILY, **HOURLY,**
THIS SECOND.

I HAVE BEEN DESIGNED FOR A JOYOUS PURPOSE, TO EVER ARRIVE AT A DESTINATION TOWARDS WHICH THE POLISHED SHEEN OF WELL-RUN RAILS GUIDES ME.

I AM THE BULLET OF TECHNOLOGY CONCEIVED IN THE HARSH UNYIELDING LIGHT OF REASON AND FORGED IN THE FURNACES OF THE INDUSTRIAL REVOLUTION!

194

I 'AM THE X-EYED SKULL AND X BONES 195 WHO HAS YOU IN HIS X-HAIRS AND CAN X YOU OUT BEFORE YOU CAN X ME OFF. I AM THE MAN AT THE CROSSROADS, THE Xroads, THE XX ROADS

BUILD ME
A
BODY
IF I CAN

Almost involuntarily, Harriet jerked her leg back. The cables wrapped around it tightened and the plug popped from its socket in the floor. The screens – all of them in the room – died. In the relative darkness, lit only by the sodium streetlight outside and the neon on the White Cube gallery, she could hear the reassuringly analogue *chunk-chunk*s of hard drives spinning down. The blinking green light on the WiFi faded.

Jack reached up and turned on his anglepoise. They looked at each other. Nixon finally let himself breathe out.

Harriet threw her arms high. "That was *not* an alien. That was a *pervert!*"

Jack scratched his chin. "Did he mean it *literally,* or just metaphorically? I'm not sure it was aimed at us, specifically. Poetic bombast?"

Harriet was having none of it. "Jack, these entities – these ideas, these memes, whatever they are – want a *body*. So, in their own words, so they can *fuck* us. Absolutely *nothing* to worry about there, right?"

Nixon held up a hand. "Harriet, we're making these bodies to our own specifications. How about we simply don't build them with a penis?"

Jack was struck by the simplicity of this solution. "Heh. Impotent ideas."

Nixon caught his eye. "But we *could* build them with vaginas."

Harriet, looking more appalled than ever, punched him on the arm.

"Ayow. Joking!"

"You know what the first sites on the internet were about? *Tech* and *porn*. Those are the strongest memes out there. Always have been. Always will be." She shook her head. "We built an Oxbow to catch an alien, and instead we caught a fucking futurist *pervert!*"

MAKING ME

"My first thought was that we were contacting the dead. That we'd actually, really done what the Victorian spiritualists and table-turners had claimed to do, and built a radio that tunes into the afterlife."

Jack was spinning an empty Beck's around on the zinc counter. The late evening sunshine shot bottle-green reflections across the walls of Byron Hamburgers like a gangrenous disco ball.

Harriet and Nixon were sitting opposite; Nixon was screwing up his face and squinting at the menu because he'd left his reading glasses at the office. "And you're sure you haven't?"

Jack considered this. "Well, we've not contacted anyone we know is still alive. So far. Warhol is dead."

Nadine was also present. She'd not met Harriet or Nixon before, though Harriet had seen a pair of underpants that certainly weren't hers in Jack's desk drawer and so had an inkling she might exist. She presumed she had a second pair, and was not sitting across the table eating her halloumi burger commando.

Friend? Lover? Jack had neglected to fill them in, and Harriet had been too polite to ask – and perhaps the two of them didn't really know, either.

Nadine flattened her napkin across her lap and topped up her Oreo shake from a chilled metal beaker. "Here's what I think, from an artist's point of view. It's the *idea* of Warhol. It's the shape Warhol leaves behind. He's gone, but that's what remains."

She was quite . . . intense. A bit like Jack, in that respect. Harriet was sure that social convention suggested that they discuss the weather, the price of a London Pride in Hoxton or some other meaningless pleasantries in the presence of this interloper. Should they even be talking about what they were up to at Intelligencia? There were no non-disclosure agreements in place, no formal secrecy arrangements, but that was before . . .

Nixon swallowed a mouthful without chewing. "I'm not sure I get you."

Not for the first time, Jack thought that the fact humans had evolved mouths to eat before they learned to talk posed practical problems that should really be addressed in Human Being OS2. Maybe conversation would be easier sitting around a public latrine rather than the dinner table, as the Romans had done; though as a niche enterprise, he doubted even Nixon could interest anyone in backing the idea.

Nadine continued. "The *idea* of Warhol isn't Warhol, not the person himself. He's dead, properly dead. There is no afterlife for him to float around in like some never-ending LSD trip from which it's impossible to come down." Jack brought his hand down and stopped the bottle spinning. It pointed at Nadine. She raised her hands in feigned surrender.

"She has a point."

"So you think we channelled his ideas? His work?"

Nadine lifted her shake. "I wasn't there. I've just seen the little heads. Pop art. Marinetti. A fascination with mechanical reproduction. What's left after an artist dies but a *catalogue raisonné* of their art? To be survived by your creations, to know they have some lasting resonance – isn't that what every artist desires?"

"So, no aliens. And no spirits. There's nothing supernatural going on here at all." Nixon felt a surge of relief that left him slightly ashamed.

Jack shook his head. "I think we can safely say we're not channelling the dead. But say it was possible to gather together every Facebook post, every photo, email – your entire digital footprint. This may in fact be easier than we think. Now imagine that that information could be used to create a pretty good *replica* of you. Could you create a software agent that carried on posting, writing, uploading photos, one that was so convincing people thought it *was* you?"

"That passed the Turing test?"

"Sure. It's possible."

Nadine leant forwards. "Think of all those people constructing personas for themselves online. Blogging, tweeting, taking selfies. How realistic are *they*? Pretty much everyone has their own personal art project going on, their own act of self-creation."

Harriet looked reflective. "I think to some extent people have always done that. Construct an image for themselves – wear the clothes, try on the attitude."

"Put on the memesuits?" Jack offered.

Nixon made a note on his iPhone. "Memesuit. Like it."

"You're going to register that as a brand name?"

Nixon laughed. "There are those who see running a successful business as an art."

"The art of parting people with their money?" Nadine offered.

Jack squeezed her knee under the table. Nixon let it pass, but Harriet tried to de-barb the comment: "Or the art of driving economic and cultural growth. Anyway, I agree with Nadine in that we construct ourselves from the examples we have to hand, especially when we're young. It's prêt-à-porter lifestyle for those just starting out on the journey to some kind of individualism. A bit like those off-the-shelf show apartments, fitted out in soulless matching furniture for the creatively incurious."

Nixon wondered if that was another veiled criticism, this time of his choice of home decor, but decided he was just being oversensitive. "So you think we're getting essences, not specific people – the *idea* of someone, resurrected from their cultural and memetic record. Or perhaps an idea which is not an individual at all, not a person, more of a movement, or a fad or an ideology – a some*thing* wrapped up in the guise of a someone?"

"Someone who is the vehicle for a something."

"An anthropomorphised meme. An idea made flesh."

"Why hasn't it shown itself before?"

Jack looked down at his plate. "Maybe it has. Just not as dramatically and directly. But I'm guessing there's something new that's been added to the mix. A catalyst. Maybe the DNA-like structure of the Signal serves as an organising framework – a kind of sticky pegboard on which self-assembly can take place. Say you have an idea – easily expressible, convincing – it will also be surrounded by and support a host of similar ideas, a kind of neuronal net. And these, up to now, have not been able to localise themselves in an autonomous fashion. Maybe what the Signal has done is act as a coagulating agent."

"So, our XX. Not an alien, just as Nixon said. I think it's a memetic construct, an artefact in ideaspace."

Harriet tilted her head thoughtfully. "Now we know there are . . . *beings* in there, very soon others will too. If they know where to look."

"If they have an Oxbow." Jack tapped the side of his head. "Which they don't."

Nadine watched the conversation bounce back and forth. She decided she liked Jack's friends. The were a bit like Jack – interesting, and interested. She couldn't imagine they would ever complain of being bored.

There was a short silence, which Jack broke. "Some would say that's all *we* are – collections of random ideas that just happen to reside in meat machines."

EDISON'S Own SECRET

Edison, though materialist-minded, was yet willing to accept spiritual beliefs if they could be proven by scientific tests. Here is described one of his amazing secret experiments whereby he sought to lure spirits from beyond the grave and trap them with super-sensitive instruments.

ONE black, howling wintry night in 1920 —just such a night when superstitious people would bar their doors and windows against marauding ghosts—Thomas Edison, the famous inventive wizard, gathered a small group of scientists in his laboratory to witness his secret attempts to lure spirits from beyond the grave and trap them with instruments of incredible sensitivity.

Until recently only the few favored spectators ever knew the outcome of this sensational experiment. Only the few Edison intimates, assembled like members of a mystic clan, ever knew what unearthly forms materialized in the scientist's laboratory that night to give proof or disproof of existence beyond the grave.

For thirteen years results of Edison's astounding attempt to penetrate that wall that lies beyond mortality have been withheld from the world, but now the amazing story can be told.

In a darkened room in his great labora-

ELECTRIC EYE

METER HAND FLICKERS WHEN BEAM IS BROKEN

PUFF OF THINNEST SMOKE BREAKS BEAM

Thomas Edison, inventor of the electric light, holding in his hand one of his first creations, the carbon light. Left—A modern 150,000 c.p. light.

Though of an avowed materialistic cast of mind, Edison nevertheless bestowed great benefits on mankind. At the left he is seen in his laboratory conducting experiments to find a method of making rubber out of goldenrod. Drawing above illustrates the operation of the photo-electric cell in detecting smoke crossing its "line of vision." Similar setup was used in detecting presence of spirits.

BEAM PROJECTOR

Saunders

tory, surrounded with beakers, generators, and other experimental equipment, Edison set up a photo-electric cell. A tiny pencil of light, coming from a powerful lamp, bored through the darkness and struck the active surface of this cell, where it was

SPIRIT EXPERIMENTS

transformed instantly into a feeble electric current. Any object, no matter how thin, transparent or small, would cause a registration on the cell if it cut through the beam.

When the experiment was ready to begin the spiritualists in the group of witnesses were called upon to summon from eternity the etherial form of one or two of its inhabitants, and command the spirit to walk across the beam. Then while the spiritualists went through their rites the scientists intently watched the meter of the electric eye, which would flicker the instant any ghostly form interrupted the light beam.

Spirits Remain in Eternity

Tense hours were spent watching the delicate instruments for the slightest indication of a spirit form, but none came. The wind howled around the corners of the laboratory building, the spiritualists petitioned, but the ghosts, if any, remained in their abode in eternity. Narrowed scientific eyes saw the meter's needle remain steady as a rock.

It was because of these negative results that the news of the amazing experiments was never given out to the world. Edison

"Rather than individual souls, we perhaps have one great soul—the soul of the entire universe, and this is the sum total of all the little particles that make us what we are," said the great inventor, just before his death.

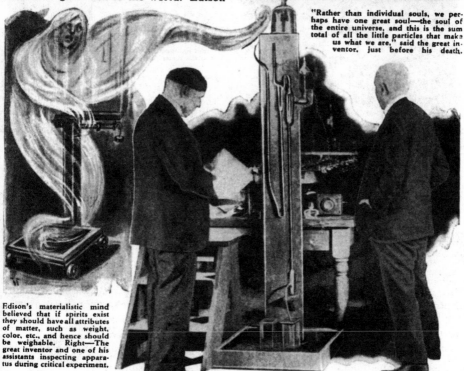

Edison's materialistic mind believed that if spirits exist they should have all attributes of matter, such as weight, color, etc., and hence should be weighable. Right—The great inventor and one of his assistants inspecting apparatus during critical experiment.

PHOTO-ELECTRIC CELL

BEAM PROJECTOR

Artist's drawing here illustrates the set-up of the ghost trap. Spirit crossing beam from projector would interrupt light, causing hand on the meter to flicker.

Deliberately burning his finger in experiment, Edison found that lines and whorls grew back in original patterns, substantiating his theory of "life units."

would not reveal his belief-shattering discoveries to the world.

The great inventor was a realist, and his experiment revealed the stony silence his profound mind expected to find. If spiritual entities existed, Edison believed that they should have all of the attributes of ordinary matter, so would be detected by the electric eye.

It was Edison's belief, even up to the day of his death, that life in man and animal results from the activity of countless myriads of "immortal units" endowed with intelligent life.

To substantiate his hypothesis, Edison had a Bertillon print made of his finger, then burnt it intentionally.

The burn was severe enough to obliterate all the delicate skin lines, yet after the finger had healed, another print showed that the lines and whorls, even though they had been hopelessly destroyed, had returned in their original position.

From this experiment, Edison got confirmation of his hypothesis that it is these aforementioned "immortal units" which supervise the regrowth of his finger's skin, following the original design. Man, he believed, is a mosaic of such life units, and it is these entities which determine what we shall be.

To make his hypothesis clear, Edison was wont to cite the following analogy. Suppose this earth were visited by some extraterrestrial being whose eyes were so coarse that the smallest thing he could see was the Brooklyn bridge. Naturally he would take the structure as some sort of natural growth.

Now suppose this imaginary giant were to destroy the bridge, then, after a couple of years, find it rebuilt. Don't you suppose the giant would assume that some guiding intelligence was behind the reconstruction? That's what Edison believed.

THE 19TH COUNT

"What are we going to get this time?" Nixon had come over to watch them set up, sitting on the corner of Jack's desk with a self-conscious flip of his suit. His trousers were hitched up to reveal novelty Christmas socks over immaculately polished burgundy Oxfords; Jack gave him the benefit of a postmodern ironist, but suspected, as he always had, that Nixon was visually tone-deaf, knowing the financial value of almost everything and the aesthetic value of almost nothing. Counter-intuitively, it was why they worked so well together.

A day after the Oxbow's first run they were prepping for a second. Harriet was of the opinion they'd see the same head again – possibly a different expression, or a different arrangement of the dazzle-ship livery. Another iteration of the same idea.

Nixon was imagining ways that this might be monetised, Jack suspected. Generative art, no artist needed. He conceded that it *did* sound like a Hoxton success story of sorts, and that was something they all could agree they needed.

"We're limited by the size of the printer, so I'm sure there was more to yesterday's – entity." Jack had lifted the angular bust out of the empty resin bath and placed it on top of a crate standing on end. A sculpture of Caesar, mounted on a Corinthian pillar, as reinterpreted by Ben Nicholson.

"XX. He was pretty insistent." Harriet didn't hide her disdain.

"It— XX may have had a body, but I turned the printer off before we got that far. So – I've introduced a scaling factor. It downsamples the resolution on the output by 60%, which means if we printed a six-foot-tall human it'd come out around 700 mill high, if you'll forgive me mixing imperial and metric units. That's still a wee bit too large for the print table, but any lower and we'll begin to lose detail. This might be a good compromise. Other than that – we now have a larger Oxbow pinch. And a few more free parameters for the text output that can be adjusted internally, or left to evolve themselves."

"And you reckon you'll get the rest of this dude?" Harriet was not that keen to see what he might have below the waist.

Jack looked dubious. "I don't know. My first thought was that I'd inadvertently downloaded a pre-existing 3D wireframe, but I doubt there's any out there like *that*."

Harriet had hooked up the other two iMacs to batch-process the input. Whatever her feelings, she was along for the ride. This beat realistic spark and smoke rendering engines hands down. "All set."

Jack's index finger was poised over the return key. He hesitated. "Hm. Engaging the Oxbow should really be more . . . *dramatic*. Don't you think? Just pressing a key on a keyboard lacks a certain . . . *gravitas*."

"Semiotic weight," Harriet reminded him.

Nixon was watching them as they worked. "You need a gearstick."

Harriet clapped her hands together then pointed at Nixon. *"Brilliant.* Now *there's* a marketable idea – a dramatic big red lever that you could pull, like the ones you see on the side of an old fruit machine. Connected by USB and hooked up to perform the function of the return key, but with added showmanship just for moments like this. If you're about to take Facebook live for the very first time, or send the first ever tweet, it would add some sorely needed *drama* to the occasion."

Nixon looked thoughtful. "The digital version of breaking a magnum of champagne across the bow."

"That is *such* a Nixon analogy," Harriet observed. "But yes."

"Jack, get our lawyers in Legal to patent that idea, and our Hong Kong branch to work up some prototypes. Instruct the New York office to come up with a marketing campaign. I'll want to see it all on my desk by tomorrow."

"Ha."

Jack lowered his head in acknowledgement. "For now, I'll improvise."

¿DING!¿

He hit his anglepoise with his stylus at the same moment he theatrically hit the return key, in as much as any computer key can be hit theatrically.

A second passed. Another. The screens remained as they were. Harriet checked a few connections. "Give it a moment. Maybe we just struck lucky first time. Let's—"

Through the keyboard she felt the table vibrate as the printer readied itself. The plate began to rise.

Like a hatstand from Mary Poppins' bag, a shape began to emerge from the bath, quickly growing taller than the shallow tray from which it rose. Jack's first thought was of a simple, mathematically precise cylinder. Subtly tapered, the circumference tightened slightly as it rose. A brim popped out, sending gentle concentric waves across the surface of the resin.

It was a top hat, in one-third scale, poised at what Jack could only describe as a jaunty angle. Beneath, a broad brow and an aquiline nose appeared; it was definitely male, eyebrows arched, eyes closed and somewhat disdainful; the whole was framed with sculpted shoulder-length Byronesque tresses which the resolution downsampling had reduced to a stylised simplicity.

The head perched atop a tall wing collar that elongated the neck, like a Kayan Lahwi brass coil. It was wrapped in a cravat, held with a pin and tucked into the top of a waspish waistcoat. There followed the lapels of a tailcoat with a small cape at the back, a tight-fitting cummerbund, generously cut trousers and a pair of tasselled Hessians. One hand was in a waistcoat pocket, the other held a cane forwards in a manner suggesting affectation rather than a walking aid. He was rendered in pure featureless white from head to toe.

The top plate came to rest. He was complete. Harriet checked the colour injectors. "Working," she observed. "He's supposed to be that colour."

Whatever Jack had expected, this wasn't it. He pulled the anglepoise over and leaned in close. The detail was impressive. There was even a pocket watch, so small it had barely been rendered by the tiny stepped pixelations of the layering process. Slightly exaggerated in posture, as if by an artist who wanted to communicate as much of his character as possible through a tautness of line, he was a perfect, miniature dandy.

Nixon sat back and chuckled. "Bugger me, it's Beau Brummel!"

Jack was circling around the printer. "Look – the legs are longer, the neck taller, the hat higher. His shape, it's idealised. Exaggerated."

"*Dandified,*" Harriet offered.

Jack clicked his fingers and pointed at Harriet. "Precisely. I don't think it's supposed to be a real person. It looks more like an archetype – an essence, a cartoon of a person."

Nixon looked at the screens, which were still blank. "Does he talk? Can we find out who we caught in the Oxbow this time?"

After the first session, Jack had temporarily disabled the speakers and the onomatopoeic interpreter as a precaution. He pulled a window over from the screen that displayed the printer functions to his own desktop, revealing another underneath. "Let's see what we're getting."

He tapped a few keys. Now Nixon could see magenta bars jumping vertically, and scrolling text in a white window directly below. "You want to hook that up so we can hear?"

Jack looked Nixon in the eye. "Sure. But brace yourself, Last time it was *loud*."

Jack stood over his iMac and entered a few lines of code, then lifted his hands high off the keyboard, hovering, waiting to see what happened.

No crashes, no grinding of gargantuan machinery from the foundries of Vulcan.

Melodious and inoffensive chamber music issued from the iMac's inbuilt speakers. He switched it to the larger speakers placed in the corners of the office. Jack grinned and fell back onto his crate.

"*Nice.* Appropriate." Underneath, he fancied he could hear a hubbub of happy voices, as of a party overheard in the distance. Laughter, maybe the chinking of glasses.

They had begun to relax. "So, first we get angry young man. Now we get urban sophisticate."

Jack looked again at the window below the graphical sound display. "Hang on. See this—" Jack pointed at the scrolling code. "That's PostScript. *Text.* I'll link that to the onomatopoeic interpreter . . ."

Immediately, type appeared on the screen. He mirrored it onto the other monitors. Letter by letter, at a sedate pace, a fanciful profusion of styles and sizes crawled down the page in the manner of a Victorian poster or handbill: vintage vernacular Grotesques and heavy, hairline-seriffed Didots, seasoned with an ornate border or the occasional fleuron or manicule. Jack experimentally clicked on a page and found that the previous sheet was still there behind it, as if they were being flyposted one on top of another.

Heavens, my dear friends, 'tis but a sartorial

FARCE.

Am I to be Dressed all in

WHITE?

—and those *Flashing Lights* are befitting of naught but a tawdry Carnival, or perhaps a *Fairie Grotto* designed to press the faces of those of easy amusement to the windows of *Harrod's Department Store* for Christmas.

Art and Beauty are but one *Truth*

☞ YET ☜

all my SENSES run AMOK!

Who am I—first person, singular?

Me. I.

I had no *self* of which I was aware until just now.
Am I but a set of borrowed phrases?
I have many names, and NO NAME.

Intriguing.

I will need to reflect on this. I ... I *am. Am* I?

My VOICE.

MY THOUGHTS?

Mine, or the thoughts of others fished from a stream of the

COMMON

(good heavens)

UNCONSCIOUS?

I seem to have many eyes. Some are in bodies, many are not.

AM I LEGION?

Let me consider the possibilities.

I AM TALL.

I see a street.

I see a THEATRE, an expectant audience taking their seats.

I see an *empty closet*.

I SEE AN AERODROME OUTBUILDING.

I see a checkpoint at a high gate topped in barbed wire.

I see a CORPORATION LOBBY, a red rope taut between poles.

I see a busy

TRAIN

TERMINUS.

I see many things I cannot identify – a polished

METAL BOX;

an empty forecourt over which a bright light sweeps shadows like a

LIGHTHOUSE in reverse

(A DARKHOUSE?)

A heavy velvet drape hangs behind a lectern on which an

INVERTED PYRAMID

is emblazoned;

a tiled cubicle with a stainless steel sink and a circular grate in the floor;

I see jittery movement and smudged colours,

semi-transparent

Ethereal

FIGURES

through which I can discern an open

DOORWAY

and a section of low ivy-clad wall;

I See Numbers

AND

LETTERS

in my peripheral vision, some marking time, others location, angle;

From a high

VANTAGE

I see women with reflective eyes like a cat's or a fox's
whisper to their suitors in a nocturnal green electrical gloom,
while

ORANGE LIGHTS

sweep by behind them in *duets* over

BRANDY
WATERS

beneath which dark leviathans move, pacing the lights above,
their eyes submerged gaslamps.

WHERE AM I?

 I am *here.*

With *you.*

NOW.

Jack typed.

you can see us?

A pause. A blank screen, collecting its thoughts. Then—

Jack fought an urge to look over his shoulder, behind him. Above, from the shelf he now occupied, lit by colour-corrected monitor light, the bust of XX looked down like the first of some new pantheon of gods, passing inscrutable judgement on his acolytes.

Silence. A minute passed, three. There were no new messages. Nixon glanced over at Jack. His offhand confidence had evaporated, and he seemed to be soliciting some kind of reassurance. "So, we've invented a fancy typographic WhatsApp for ghosts?" His cocksure comment was undercut by the slight tremor in his voice.

Jack raised an eyebrow and returned his attention to the screen. "Unlikely. Another explanation just occurred to me. Have you heard of electronic voice phenomena?"

Nixon gave an impatient hand gesture. Usually, he'd affect a knowledge of most things and simply wing it, his natural confidence enough to carry him through. It was this kind of self-assurance that had got him where he was; once those around him began to trust that he was well informed they tended to defer decision-making to him. He was used to being the team captain. Here, he was the fullback. "No."

"EVP. In the early days of radio, strange voices would be heard on wavelengths where there was no one broadcasting. When tape recording was invented, they turned up again. Voices that were there on playback, but hadn't been heard by the people present when the recording was made."

"What would they hear?"

"Words and phrases. Rarely coherent sentences. And, other than a word or two here and there, they couldn't agree on what was actually being said."

"Rii-ight."

"So, depending on your taste and whether you lean to the sceptical or the credulous, the phenomenon was one of several things: some kind of psychokinetic effect, a way that discarnate entities could impress their thoughts on a random source, in this case electronic signals, and so gain material expression. Or, more prosaically, just the human propensity for finding patterns in random noise. We hear what we want to hear in the static. Aural pareidolia. An hallucination. I'm, uhm, I'm more than familiar with the effect."

Nixon was holding up a finger, waiting to interject. "We're getting more than the odd word or phrase. But— do you ever get that thing where you think you can hear your phone ringing when you're in the shower?"

"Right – the sound of the water provides the static from which your mind concocts the sound. But if you assume that these entities, spirits, or whatever they are, can only affect the material realm in subtle or oblique ways, they may need something like that to work with. The static is the raw material which they can nudge this way or that, shape to their ends. Or so the theory goes."

Nixon nodded. "Ectoplasm for the ears."

"When television was new, the same phenomenon happened again. Tune a TV to static, and if you stare at it long enough you can form shapes, and make those shapes move across the screen." Jack weaved his hands in the air like flatfish by way of demonstration. "I've tried it myself. The human brain is very good at pattern recognition. *Too* good."

Harriet was thinking of the hippie in the basement. "That's what makes it easy to jump from suggestive factoid to full-blown theory to hardened belief. We're almost hardwired to concoct conspiracy theories."

"Sure. We can fool ourselves very easily."

Nixon held two fingers to his mouth. "Are we fooling ourselves now?"

Harriet picked up her iPhone. "The modern version of this? Calls from the dead. Here's one I heard first-hand: friends of my mother's would hear voices through their daughter's baby monitor, when they knew for sure she was upstairs alone. They swear that they even heard a conversation – that their three-year-old was talking to this, this discarnate voice, and it was *replying*. Of course, they go upstairs to investigate and there's no one there. Spooked the hell out of them."

"I can imagine."

The last four lines of text still sat there on the screen, a silent challenge to his rationalisations.

Jack typed:

And where am I?

They waited in silence for several seconds. From outside they could hear a musical shower of glass as the bottles from the restaurant below were tipped into a dustcart.

No response.

Harriet gave an 'of course' shrug. "Apparently, it's not so easy to replicate."

"Supernatural phenomena never are. Believers would tell you that the experimenter needs to have mediumistic powers themselves; that what the apparatus is actually amplifying is their latent talents, talents that not everyone may have."

"Conveniently for the believers."

"Uh-huh. You've heard of 'Ghost Box' recordings?" Jack pulled up a browser window. "Here. The inventor claims that instructions on how to build this thing were sent to him from the spirit world – a bit like posting someone in another dimension a mobile phone." Jack cued up a sound file.

"Take a listen. They're suggestive, at the very least. The best are culled from thousands of hours of material, so the hit rate may be low."

To Nixon, the overamplified static sounded entirely unconvincing. Could he pick out the odd word? Possibly. Full coherent sentences, like they were getting here? Not even close. "Who's supposed to be on the other end? What do they say?"

Jack pursed his lips and shrugged. "Like I say, interpretation is everything. Who are these mysterious entities doing the talking? Take your pick. Historical figures. Deceased relatives. Pets. Robotic voices. Sometimes it sounds like French or German, or some unidentifiable foreign language, or maybe a historic or mutilated form of English. What do they say? Brief statements. Observations. Warnings. Which makes sense if these voices are actually familiar patterns encoded in our brains. A random source could trigger an auditory memory by accidentally mimicking it to a small degree – though harder to explain are messages that have specific content, content that's possible to check. Which, apparently, sometimes they do."

"I think what we have here is more than random noise."

Jack had to agree.

"And then . . . then there's the messages that purport to come from extraterrestrials."

"*Aliens?*"

"Yep, aliens. Beings from another dimension. Space visitors. These days, that's not such a crazy idea." Jack pointed to one of the many crates of books they had yet to unpack. "If you read the literature, ghosts often show a lack of comprehension about their state, their situation, what happened to them, where they are. It's as if they don't *know* they're ghosts. You've heard stories of restless spirits who need to be convinced to move on? That assumption, of course, comes with a whole lot of improbable theological baggage about the afterlife, repentance, salvation—"

"Let's not go there," Harriet interjected.

"But what if what we're communicating with here is not so much a person, a singular individual, but more an *idea* – something altogether more abstract, less individualised. Concepts. A coalesced memetic ideology, if you will. They use our voices, our idioms, pick up and distil certain cultural memes. Maybe they *are* cultural memes."

"The ghosts in the machine."

"Yes. Though less a ghost, more a spirit of the age. A *zeitgeist.*"

Nixon looked at the ceiling. "Spirits, he says. This *is* a seance."

"Listen. We filtered out the superficial memes. Others will have a deeper pedigree, measured in years or even decades. We can extend that timeline back further than you might think possible – here's the interesting part –

because we're also linked up, via digitised books, newspapers, manuscripts, et cetera, with a large portion of the pre-digital world, all now searchable just like a modern database. These are all the – the back-ups, if you like, that we used to store our ideas on before the internet was invented. Paper. Microfiche." Jack picked up and waved the *Virtua* game. "Cassette tape. Theoretically, the data set can even include papyrus, hieroglyphs and cave paintings – if it's been photographed or scanned, if it exists in a digital form, it should be accessible.

"Remember, all this information – the collective memetic content of our recorded culture – is also available to whatever's in the Signal. What they have to work with doesn't begin with Berners-Lee's first email. Now, of course there's less material the further back you go. We have a kind of resolution issue – just as the further out into space you look the less detail you can resolve, so the further back in time you go the less information you have to work with. We have an astonishing memetic resolution for recent events, though there is what you could call a content-stroke-value tradeoff. Much of this modern surfeit of information will be unimportant: Instagram shots of your dinner. Blurry pics of your junk. The ease with which you can now record and share everyday events almost *ensures* a high degree of triviality. To hand-set a book three hundred years ago would have been a much more costly and labour-intensive project than publishing a blog post is today – so as you look back, you'll get the big ideas, the grand narratives, but lack a certain . . . democratic detail."

Harriet sat down on her crate. "There's something we might have overlooked. I once heard a theory discussed at a conference. The speaker – I forget who – was asked why we hadn't received transmissions from an extraterrestrial civilisation. After all, we've been leaking radio and TV signals for generations – they should be watching the Moon landings, or the first episode of *Star Trek* or *The Brady Bunch* on Zeta Reticuli by now. His reply? 'Either there's no one there. Or maybe no one who knows what they're doing broadcasts their location in a Universe full of wolves.'"

The disconcerting phrase still sat there, in the centre of the otherwise blank screen.

"We no longer live in a world where we have to worry about predators hiding in the bushes," Jack reflected. "We're sitting at the top of the food chain. We're just running obsolete pattern-recognition software."

Harriet spoke. "No predators? Maybe that situation has just changed. And that obsolete software might just give us an advantage once again."

Nixon looked away from the monitor and out, to the lights of Hoxton and the city beyond, the bars and clubs and restaurants that were thick with people. Normal, happy, unafraid people. He felt the idea begin to ground him again, bring him back from discussions about aliens, spirits, communication with the dead. He had never had much of an imagination, never been much of what, in his parlance, he would call a 'creative type', preferring the more measurable pleasures of the material world. He was discomforted by ideas that could ensnare your mind and fundamentally alter your worldview, that made you realise the *you* you called you and treasured above anything else was a mysterious spark wrapped in a biological suit of fragile flesh that, however much you pushed it to the periphery of your mind, would age and die and rot, and like all good things, come to an end; and that there was absolutely nothing he, or Harriet, or Jack, or anyone, could do about it.

Speaking to the dead? What was it they were trying to achieve here?

Was it not far better to embrace the comforting familiarity of the diurnal round: the challenges and rewards of work, the diversions of culture, the company of good friends; the mating dance, conversation, laughter and *life?*

THE PLASTIC PANTHEON

"Are you starting a sculpture collection?" Nadine tilted her head sideways, as if doing so gave her a fresh perspective. Jack saw she was looking at the angular bust on the back shelf in its migraine-inducing livery. It dwarfed Jack's custom Darth Spongebob mashup and *Batman: The Animated Series* figures, which had been pushed to one side to make room – the world's greatest superheroes, defeated by the sweep of a forearm. Lit by the row of halogen bulbs above, the rest of the room was in shadow, punctuated by the pale ghostly rectangles of screens in sleep mode, the phosphorescent glow of a shuttered house. It was late, and Jack and Nadine were alone.

Navigating through the desks and crates to the conference room table, she placed the bag with the HUNGRY HOUSE CHINESE TAKEAWAY shooting-star logo on the table and started lifting out foil containers with card lids, working her fingers around the rims to loosen them.

Jack regarded the other creations that in the last few days they'd enticed from the 3D printer. To the left and right were now almost a score more – what? Figures, mostly. Busts, torsos, some full length; others harder to describe. Some seemed to be representational, though of what he couldn't quite be sure. They joined the earliest simple shapes: the regular platonic solids and other mathematically generated polyhedra that had no name.

Jack shook some coconut rice and sweet and sour pork onto a paper plate with a *Thomas the Tank Engine* motif and, ignoring the bamboo chopsticks, picked up a plastic fork. He looked at the fork, then the shelf. Plastic – the universal material, a medium which, unlike the chopsticks, had no grain, no warp or weft, no intrinsic quality of its own other than that which the designer chose to bring to it. In many ways it was the perfect expression of the digital realm, which was made of a plastic of a different kind: conceptual, rather than material. The computational Fohat of the Theosophists, the universal thing with no inherent thingness. Jack was reminded again of his camera, and its skeuomorphic shutter click.

Fork, figure. Figure, fork. Extruded from polymer and arrayed on the shelf they had gained a kind of presence, so much so that earlier in the day he'd turned his desk around so it now faced away from the window and towards them. He'd imagined he could feel their eyes – some of them *did* have eyes – on his back, watching him, and it creeped him out just a bit; but also, and he found this even more bewildering, he had a nagging suspicion that sitting with his back to them might somehow be . . . disrespectful? They were inanimate objects of – he waved the fork, and rice fell into his lap – plastic, pigment and cellulose binder. In antiquity, such fetishes might have been made from far rarer materials – ivory, pearl and gold, or even wood and hair and bone.

The idea came to him that his desk, front and centre, was now very much like an altar; the flicker of computer screens took the place of candles and the new-computer scent of air-cooled silicon stood in for incense. Keylit from the side by the green and red LEDs of the WiFi router at the end of the shelf, they could be graven idols for the modern age.

"What do they look like to you, Nadine?"

"A pantheon of gods? Or demons, perhaps?"

Jack nodded almost imperceptibly. "I got that impression, too."

Angels, mythological beasts, creatures of nightmare; saviours and pain-merchants. Were they representations of forces beyond their control, come to share their wisdom – or in front of whom they were required to prostrate themselves? Their silence made them appear indifferent to human concerns.

Hadn't deities always been so?

Outside, it had begun to rain, a thin drizzle of punctuation.

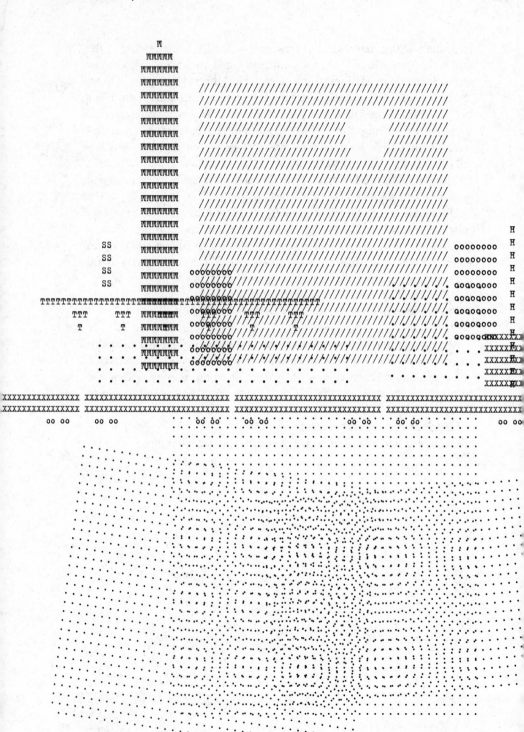

Felicity Glass
Typewriter Cityscape, 1976
297x210mm, 11.69x8.27in.
Collection of Nathaniel Jefferies

A VISITOR FROM THE SHADOW CABINET

Nadine awoke under a table in the Intelligencia office. She lay there motionless, pondering the bolts and struts above her. The view perfectly reflected Jack's obsessions – look under the surface, try and figure out how things work. Jack lay on his side with his back to her, a sheet wrapped around one leg. Did he have a space for her among those obsessions of his?

Did he have one in *hers?*

Jack had taken to keeping an inflatable mattress and a sleeping bag here at work, and he'd crawl into it after a late night's coding when the Underground had stopped running and he didn't feel like shelling out for an Uber home, or when his mind was too full of ideas for him to sleep properly anyway, itching to be up and back at the keyboard and not willing to waste a moment more than he had to. Nadine felt sure he'd forget to eat if he could.

Stepping over the condom wrapped in a strip of toilet roll, she found her T-shirt and walked over to the kitchenette, a short counter partitioned from the rest of the office. A small beer fridge sat under a heavy rectangular sink on which a fine craquelure web had spread, a relic of the building's industrial past. She pulled out an Evian and dropped the plastic lid into the recycling pedal-bin.

She noticed that the top of Jack's iMac, where the camera lens was situated, had a screen wipe laid over it. *Privacy? Paranoia?* Who might he think was watching him?

She knew Jack had spent more than a few nights here recently, his mind fixated on coding problems with that intense application of which he was capable. He had a habit of drilling deeper and deeper into anything that intrigued him, that he didn't understand, and would not feel happy until he'd mastered it or proven to his satisfaction that it was utterly unimportant. She could see that what made him invaluable to Nixon and Harriet infuriated them in equal measure.

For Jack, last night the office had simply been a place to hole up and get some privacy. While others might think fucking one's girlfriend on the table in the conference room was a statement of rock 'n' roll individualism – giving it to The Man while giving it to her, so to speak – Jack had been more cognisant that the edge of the table was cutting into his thighs, and with a head full of formulae and Boolean cause-and-effect had more than absentmindedly gone through the motions.

Nadine, sensing his distance, had put it down to pressure of work and the fast-approaching deadline for the first Intelligencia beta release. She was happy, at this stage, to simply run with the situation and see where it went. She had a friend with benefits, a painter who had briefly shared her last but one artist's studio; though no oil painting, he was happy to provide conversation and physical affection with no obligation and no questions asked, and at the moment that suited her just fine. She found him intellectually undemanding and didn't have the inclination to try to forge a more meaningful relationship with him; for now it was easy, simple, and freed up her mind for more creative pursuits.

One of which was Jack. She found him intriguing and not a bit frustrating. Though used to having her pick of well-heeled and well-connected suitors, she thought there was one thing she and Jack shared that those eager-to-impress gentlemen, with their fascination for supercars that could cruise at twice the legal speed limit and showy knowledge of expensive restaurants, didn't. She saw in him a carefully concealed obsession – hers was her art, her Polaroid collages, unicorns in gas masks and guerrilla corn-dolly installations, with channelling and somehow mastering her elusive muse – but for him it seemed to be something altogether more opaque. What Jack was trying to grasp, to understand, had its roots in his past – one he wouldn't share with her – and its solution in what he and his associates were tinkering with here, at Intelligencia.

Art and science. They weren't so different. She even thought that, at base, they might be one and the same thing: different manifestations of the creative urge, of a need to understand, and so tame, the unknown. One in the eye for C. P. Snow, and his "never the twain shall meet" view of the two as some secular version of the 'non-overlapping magisteria'. Jack would have given him no heed, not because he disagreed, which he most surely would, but for the simpler, more prosaic reason that he hadn't heard of him; and even if he had, he'd imagine he was some villainous character with a shock of white hair and a pointed goatee from an old science-fiction film.

Movies and literature exist almost entirely in a realm where stories have a beginning, a middle and an end; where characters have arcs with satisfying resolutions, and a dozen other well-honed tropes that consumers of popular culture expect from their entertainment predictably play out.

She could see through all this. The need to provide closure, a tidy moral or philosophical point – this was not how the real world worked.

The real world, however one might define it, did not look out for people on life's adventure; did not provide happy endings, a dénouement tied up in a bow under the covers of an airport novel on which the author's surname was embossed in gold foil. The real world not only didn't care about such things; it had absolutely no idea they even existed.

She held no special admiration for the written word because she could clearly see how manipulative it could be: after all, lies were made of words. In short, she saw that there was an art to Art, and that it was not something magical or transcendent, but a *craft*, and good art – the type that could really move you, that you felt with your diaphragm rather than your intellect – was simply the endgame of being very good at your craft.

She'd sometimes be adopted by those who mistakenly saw her as a fellow daydreamer, a hippy-dippy "the Universe is telling me which salad I should have for lunch" type. *We're artists! Rationality be damned! Let's just channel our innermost feelings!*

She thought they were full of shit.

When she was thirteen, her Aunt Samantha, the mother of a school friend, had seen her early promise with paint and crayon and had taken her to be a kindred spirit, spirits being very much part of her worldview. For as long as Nadine had known her she had suffered from a variety of nebulous ailments; when her psychic healer couldn't lay her hands on her in person, she promised, for a few hundred pounds a session, to do so remotely. Nadine had come to show her her work while Aunt Samantha lay there, bedridden with a simple bacterial infection. A short course of antibiotics could have cured her, but she was unwilling to make use of the 'materialistic Western' treatments freely available to her through the NHS her taxes had helped fund for just such an eventuality.

Nadine's pleadings had come to nothing – she would not change her mind. She wondered just what constituted proof in Aunt Samantha's worldview, and came to the conclusion it wasn't even proof she was after. Proof also belonged to the logical, rational post-Enlightenment project she so despised; it had chased the wonder from the world, disenchanted the landscape and purged the numinous from daily life. No, an appeal to common sense was only going to get her hackles up. Don't ask me questions, just tell me tales.

What Aunt Samantha responded to was a *story*. One in which there was metaphor and revelation, a moral high ground to be taken, and beauty and truth were one and the same thing. Stories, for those that didn't write them and were not intimately familiar with the mechanisms by which they were carefully constructed, were incantations. They were . . . *magic*.

What some people preferred, she had long ago decided, was not the truth, messy and contingent as it so often was, but the seductive faux folk wisdom of that tale well told.

Two weeks later, pneumonia and messy contingent truth finally caught up with Aunt Samantha.

For Nadine, the magic of her art was no fiction. It was the language of colour, of shape; the basic building blocks of our visual landscape. She imagined Jack would be of the opinion that these might be mathematical entities in some way too, that colours were a piano chord for the eye. Her work was overlaid with more pictorial concerns: what the painting was *of*, was *about* – and these led right back into the stories that we tell ourselves, our culture, our idea of the world rather than the world itself. That was what she was trying to deconstruct.

Her friend Micah seemed close to a real-life practitioner of magic. Nadine found it hard to believe that her music – something that, Micah assured her, was simply another craft one could learn, that she was even willing to teach her – could result in something so ethereal, so otherworldly. What she created seemed to gaze directly into her inner being, articulate more elegantly than she ever could precisely how she felt, or what she could be. Nadine just couldn't understand how the trick was pulled off, though she knew, as her friend knew when it came to her drawings, that those who practised that magic were simply the ones who could step up from the auditorium, under the proscenium arch that separated the world of effect from the world of cause, and see behind the curtain.

On the back wall of the office ran the full-length shelf along which Jack had arranged all the resin figures. Nadine was familiar with young men's bedrooms, having visited (and smelt) more than her fair share. She had noticed there were a few recurring themes: the collection of guitars, each on a stand, each immaculately presented, each unplayed. Substitute skateboards or twin DJ record decks for guitars, and the boys and their toys trope held true more often than not.

Lit only by the sodium-yellow streetlights, the figures on the shelf took on a monochromatic pallor. There was a Johnnie Walker mascot, top hat and cane, unpainted, all in white. Next to that, an angular cubist bust that looked as if it was made from folded card painted in vibrant geometric stripes, its colours now reduced to a tonal range of olives, mustards and black.

The dozen Warhol heads had been rescued from the FedEx waste-paper bin and arranged on the branches of a mug tree; a selection of cubes, pyramids and more complicated shapes were arranged like a rock garden around the base. Next to that was a jar of M&Ms. A label, designed in a comic-book sound effect style, called them 'Popstoppers'.

She wondered if they were arranged in some kind of order. Chrono-logically, perhaps? There was one more item on the shelf. If her logic was correct, and in the short time she'd known Jack she knew that whatever he did, a logical system more than likely underpinned it, this was the first thing that he had managed to coax from the 3D printer.

There it sat, on the shelf, at the end that was the beginning.

Jack had not mentioned it. Even Harriet and Nixon assumed that the Lichtenstein dots were the first things that had materialised from the memetic realm.

She was familiar enough with the eccentricities of 3D printing to surmise that this was some kind of test, or a malformed prototype.

What was it? It seemed familiar, in an unsettling manner she couldn't quite put her finger on. Half-remembered, like some child-hood dream.

It was a spindly man, like an elf or a gnome, his head too large for his body. Creepy, in that way only puppets can be creepy. Due to what she assumed must be a programming error, it had no face.

The printing process had certain signature ways in which it malfunc-tioned. A corrupt wireframe or some other glitch in the input could produce a 'spaghettification' of tangled filaments, or delete a section entirely. Maybe this was what had happened here.

Yes, that must be it. The head was cut off, just above where the eyes would have been . . . if this thing originally had eyes. Had Jack noticed the blank face, and aborted the printing process? Without taking it down from the shelf, she turned it around by pushing on its base. From a hollow space at the back of the head, dozens of translucent strings snaked out and around, framing the blank countenance, reaching forwards as if searching for something, perhaps feeling their way in the absence of vision. It looked like a jellyfish had taken up residence where its brain should be. Reaching out a finger, she tested one to see if it was flexible; it broke off like a hardened piece of silly string and fell to the floor with the lightest of rattles.

Jack was still asleep. She could hear his shallow breathing.

She carefully laid the broken tentacle beside the thing on the shelf.

A digital medusa?

Or a golem, perhaps, its face wiped? The golem, so it was said, had been created by those close to divinity from inanimate mud. That Jack possessed something of the savant she was in no doubt. Divinity? Nope. Not even close. Anyway, that was a word Aunt Samantha would have used, and Aunt Samantha was now in the company of whatever divinity might accept her. And this was Hoxton, not sixteenth-century Prague.

Outside, the rhythmic chopping of a low police helicopter over-dubbed the crackle of a radio conversation in Hindi between a taxi driver and base. Technology had won, the twentieth century's final triumph of logic over superstition. Aunt Samantha had been cheer-leading the wrong team.

Keep it real, Nadine. Don't overthink things, don't concoct your own tall tale. Tall tales get you killed.

This strange figure was just a sport of digital code.

Just a little grey man.

BIOHACKER BURLESQUE

"Bodies. What are they for?"

Harriet could think of several uses she was fond of, but guessed the answer to this rhetorical question, at least in the mind of Gunter Salivax, self-styled Lord of Disrepair, was somewhat less prosaic.

Lord of Disrepair. Fuck. What a wanker.

"Keeping your internal organs from spilling out. Providing a wipe-clean surface." These were probably not on his list. Salivax looked like a teenager who had taken delivery of a costume from the Louisiana Bayou Voodoo Fancy Dress Boutique, then fallen face-down in a bowl of flour, mussing his mascara. He had teeth painted on his lips and his nose blackened in the semblance of a skull. Vertical lines cleansed by sweat ran down his forehead, revealing a pink, pockmarked complexion underneath.

Harriet could imagine that the undead might not have the healthiest diets, lacking vitamin D and probably heavy on the Pringles and chips, and thought it likely that Gunter, real name Stuart or Dave, looked even less attractive by day in his civvies and without make-up, if that were possible. He leaned back and fondled the polished brass knob of an antique sword cane.

This had seemed like a good idea, she reflected. Biohacker subculture, a creative and dangerous combination of DIY gene splicing and unfettered imagination, had been facilitated by the availability of tabletop recombination labs and the willingness of its adherents to cross boundaries to reimagine the self. Hackers hacking themselves, and others willing to submit to them. If anyone knew how to go about building bodies, it would be these guys.

Harriet had arrived at this evening's divertissement early, hoping for an audience. *Lord Disrepair's Theatre of the Imagination* was reached via a low arched tunnel around the back of Waterloo Station. Down here, both the road and the narrow pavements either side were a uniform oily black: decades of Intercity diesel soot, enamelled into a tarry sheen by a million tyres where no cleansing acid rain could reach.

Graffiti that would keep future Lascaux cave experts happy for decades ran down both walls, making it easy to miss the small steel door halfway along. A series of movable barriers funnelled any queue along the pavement, where they were less likely to be hit by unlicensed taxis driven at speed. Once past the airport-style bag check and going-through-the-motions frisking, the space opened into the vast subterranean maze of Victorian brick tunnels and cathedral-sized rooms that lay beneath the station, and, Harriet presumed, the surrounding roads and buildings as well.

A pale Lolita in a purple anime wig sat behind a window rendered opaque by Day-Glo minicab stickers. She took Harriet's jacket in return for a pair of upholstered headphones with a number written on the side in Tipp-Ex, which she assumed doubled as a cloakroom ticket.

A trail, marked by glow-sticks in pots along the floor, led to a wooden platform resembling a gallows. This turned out to be a jetty above a flooded section of tunnel; a small shallow boat, crewed by a grinning young man dressed like a monk from a Dennis Wheatley film, slid towards her through a few inches of dry ice. He helped her in without capsizing.

"Sit in t'middle, lass, and don't lean too far over or we'll both be in – the water here's right filthy." Charon, it turns out, is Mancunian. Harriet thought this entirely appropriate.

The monk pushed off with a length of scaffold pole. As they moved, green underwater lighting projected ripples across the curved ceiling. Ahead, a narrow arch presented an obstacle through which he guided them with a few well-placed prods to the walls. Beyond was a smaller chamber, again of brick, with a second jetty set against the far wall and a dark opening beyond.

Pulling up alongside, another monk bent down to hold the boat steady and help her out. "If you're in a hurry, it's possible to skip the ferry ride and get back to the entrance by turning right just down there." He pointed to a smaller tunnel. "Health and safety."

"Thanks." With just one mode of transport in or out, she wondered how long it would take to evacuate Hell itself. In case of fire, or something.

Beyond, the brickwork suddenly gave way to more luxurious decor – drapes of dark burgundy velvet hung either side of a small kiosk, behind which sat a man in a wide panama hat and long greying hair who proffered her a sheet of paper. An Edwardian cowboy, she thought. The kiosk was an ornate gilded affair, out of place in this subterranean environment, but a perfect introduction to what lay beyond. Through a double door and a small lobby the space again opened up dramatically and unexpectedly into a horseshoe-shaped theatre that, had it been situated off Leicester Square, would have been a respectably sized venue. Here, underground, it seemed quite literally cavernous. Above, a fluted baroque recess gave onto a huge inverted dome from which water had leached the plaster, forming miniature white stalactites stained with rust; irregular sections of plasterwork had fallen away to reveal a crosshatch of supporting wooden slats. Below this hung an enormous chandelier of braided brass and crystal teardrops, fitted with lights that mimicked flickering candles. Its weight and bulk was an arresting presence in the gloom, a Damoclesian accident waiting to happen.

Ahead and slightly below her was a stage, a darkened but pregnant space across which ran a threadbare safety curtain patchworked with an assortment of faded 1920s advertisements in a typographic free-for-all. Tiers of fold-down seats crowded up to meet her at the back, no longer feeling overdressed. She walked down into the stalls, out from under the rotting canopy of flaking gilt above which a ruined upper circle was genteelly subsiding. Higher still, she could make out more steeply banked tiers of deserted seating retreating into the darkness, unlit and uncared for. There was the cold scent of wet sacking and clove e-cigarette vapour.

She took her seat. Around her, dressed in all manner of fantastical outfits, were tonight's audience: top-hatted steampunk dandies, spike-heeled and latex-skinned supervixens, uncomfortable suited City boys, burlesque showgirls, burlesque showboys, the pierced and tattooed, the ugly and the beautiful. To her immediate left sat a girl in pink PVC decorated with a white prop-driven aeroplane motif and an Amelia Earhart-style leather flying hood and goggles. On her head perched an eagle, its leg attached to her wrist with a silver chain. Harriet was wondering if it could be real when it turned its head around to regard her, one eye reflecting the light from the chandelier above as if made of glass.

She sat patiently through a show that made little sense to her – a parade of unicorns, centaurs and other mythical beasts cavorting to a soundtrack of Beethoven, Charleston and grime. Ahistorical, amusical, asexual, asomething.

Harriet knew a scant amount about biohacker subculture – creative kids in unlicensed garage shops, tinkering with their DNA. Up until recently, it'd been a nascent fad; the methods and the equipment that were affordable and available meant that the alterations, where they held, tended to be superficial – patterned skin pigmentation, antlers, prehensile tails, nocturnal vision. In the audience tonight were the usual suspects: leopard-spot baldies, wide-eyed nightsighters, artfully groomed furries. Recently it'd taken a more serious turn: she could see mermaids in customised wheelchairs, conjoined couples who shared internal organs, and bioluminescent cone-headed cookie-cutter sharkers.

After the show she was led down a maze of narrow arched brick corridors, stepping either side of a gutter in the concrete floor that transported some dark oily fluid who knew where. She had not come here to see the show but to meet its host: Gunter Salivax, biohacker, compère, and she was now pretty sure, adolescent narcissist. His dressing room, a damp, cramped cubbyhole, reminded her of a fusty dressing-up box; incense did little to dispel the sharp tang of stale body odour.

Harriet could tell Gunter was on something of a high. By his reckoning, the show must have been an enormous success – rousing gasps and shocked silences in equal measure. She could also tell he had certain expectations of her audience with him . . . a new acolyte, a new recruit to his rather particular entourage? Someone new he could play with, alter, leave his mark upon?

These were expectations she was not here to indulge.

Harriet set out her stall. "Bodies. I'm interested in building them." There was something of an awkward silence. Undeterred, she dived straight into certain specific biohacking techniques, the practicalities of which she wanted clarification on. Gunter, she could tell, was performing a mental about-turn: *she knows her stuff.* This might be interesting, but in a different way.

Gunter stroked his jawline, rubbing off more Snazaroo. "I can make small changes, graft things on, cut things out. I can surgically alter things. I'm told short sequences of DNA that have been lab-grown, base-pair by base-pair, and printed on a molecular printer can be introduced to the human body in a more or less targeted fashion. Subdermally. Orally."

Harriet cut to the chase. "The Signal."

If she had not had Gunter's full attention before, she did now.

"What about the Signal?"

"Suppose for one moment that it's not a message *from* aliens. Suppose that it *is* aliens. Or the information needed in order to build them."

"You think the Signal is DNA?"

Harriet pulled off a lace glove with her teeth, finger by finger. "Imagine it is. Just for the sake of argument."

"Pfft."

"Indulge me."

"If it is, it wouldn't be the kind of DNA we're familiar with. What gave you this idea?"

Harriet was scrolling through a long repeating section of the Signal on her iPhone. She chose to display it as a series of letters and numbers, though there were at least a dozen popular methods of viewing the data, each foregrounding a different aspect depending on what one might be interested in. She held it up. Gunter pulled out a pair of NHS prescription glasses and leaned in to squint.

"It *looks* like a biological coding, that much is clear," Harriet offered.

Gunter grunted. "Though even a cursory look will tell it's not deoxyribonucleic acid."

"So you can't do anything with it?"

"Listen. You're not the first to see the similarity. This idea has been kicking around. Some people in the biohacking community have been discussing the possibilities. Even now, while NASA is carefully parsing the data, out here in the Wild West of practical biology I'm pretty certain more . . . direct experimentation is taking place. That's the nature of human curiosity. My opinion? It's a non-starter. It'd be completely incompatible with human DNA. You'd need to have a host which shared a similar biology."

"And you can't somehow splice it with lab-grown DNA?"

"How? You'd need to translate it. Read the code. And then what would you do with it? What we cannot do, unless you are here to tell me otherwise, is grow an organism from scratch. How would that even work?"

Harriet adjusted the elastic on her Venetian mask. "You'd need to alter the DNA, implant an egg—"

Gunter laughed. "Think of the practicalities of what you're suggesting. Altering a human embryo? *Seriously?* You can think what you like of me, but I am not into eugenics, which is what that would amount to. The risks are . . . No way. It's far more likely that the results would be . . . deleterious."

Harriet felt somewhat chastened. Lectured on morality by the Lord of Disrepair himself. "Not a human embryo. Animal, perhaps. I wondered what the options were. To grow it. To see what we have here."

He leaned forwards, and a new sobriety could be heard in his voice. Harriet was thinking his day job might be something in IT.

"Listen. The human genome is a delicately balanced machine, honed by nature over hundreds of thousands of years. Alter one piece here, and you'll affect something else over there. Everything is connected. The chances of doing great damage are almost guaranteed. No chemical accident ever gave someone super-strength, no gene mutation ever endowed anyone with telepathy, or the ability to walk through walls, or fly, or fire plasma bolts from their fingertips.

"How many people have been exposed to radiation? How many superheroes do we have? Do *you* see a sky full of capes? No. It doesn't work that way. Sadly, what we get when we tinker with DNA is learning difficulties, stunted limbs, and a propensity for debilitating disease."

Harriet nodded. "You can't improve a delicate mechanism by throwing a spanner in it."

Gunter leaned back. *"Right.* Think of randomly inserting lines of code into a program. Or words, which may have a specific meaning in isolation, randomly into a sentence—"

"The Signal—"

"Assume that the Signal is Turing-complete. In theory, any task that can be solved in one language can be solved in another. Then you'd think that it should be possible to translate it, convert it from one given language into any other, right? From alien DNA into human DNA?"

Gunter was definitely something in IT.

"It's been tried?"

"I've heard talk of a couple of attempts, none of which have been applied, practically speaking. Not even I'm that stupid."

Harriet wanted to dig deeper. "Consider something fairly basic, in a programming context: a PHP to Java translator. The only feasible way to make something like that work without embedding part of the PHP binary is to reimplement all the PHP's modules and APIs in Java."

Gunter's supercilious attitude had now been replaced by a boyish enthusiasm she almost found endearing. Almost. "Even after all that work, you wouldn't have Java code, you'd have some sort of monstrosity that just happens to run on the Java platform but was structured like PHP on the inside."

He had a point.

"Listen, languages are for humans. Take, I don't know – Google Translate. It uses a lot of context – context we can check, to see if it makes sense – and an enormous data set to get results, which are still nowhere near perfect. The same problem happens in biological languages, which, even if you apply a strictly definitional perspective, can be idiomatic. Even biological code requires context, an analysis of the enclosing system in which it resides. Practically, even if you did manage some kind of alien to human DNA translation, you don't know what the code you're inserting does, you don't know where you should be inserting it, you can only guess at how the combined codes might function – you don't even know if it *has* a function. As I say, it's much more likely to disrupt some vital process, and who'd want to risk that? Much as I'd like it to be otherwise, the bodies we have are far more easily ruined than improved upon."

Harriet could see herself reflected in his glasses. It was as if she was on the other side, in another realm that had no physical extension, looking back out at herself behind her ornate mask.

Gunter was still talking, but she was now looking through him, past him, at nothing in particular.

She again brought to mind that last enigmatic message they had received.

It came to her that there was another, better alternative.

If these entities could look out and see *us*, maybe it would be possible for *us* to look back in and *see them*.

They were going about this the wrong way. Rather than try and build a body from plastic, or biology – extrude entities they knew very little about out into the real, physical world – would it not be better to visit them in their natural environment?

Behind her mask, Harriet smiled. What she was now planning would be a lot easier to implement, too.

THE GHOST CAMERA

Harriet signed for the two heavy boxes. The mute Amazon drone left the office as fast as he'd arrived, without looking at the barely legible scribble she'd left on his smartphone. "Gunter Salivax, Lord of Disrepair – you're a narcissistic player, but you *did* give me an idea."

Jack came out of the kitchenette with a cup of tea and a digestive biscuit. "What's this? New kit?"

"In here, we may have our solution. Because Nixon wouldn't spring for three, we've only got two pairs. One of us will have to sit this out."

"Pairs?"

Harriet pulled moulded polystyrene blocks out of one of the boxes. She held up a pair of bulky glasses that would just about pass for light-weight welding wraparounds. The front was one curved piece of black glass, set in a grey plastic frame with a chrome stripe leading back over the ear, where several small buttons and a dial were situated. Ear-buds hung from each arm by a short wire. On the glass, across the top, D E P T H C H A R G E was written in letterspaced Akzidenz Grotesk.

"*Depthcharges.* VR headsets."

"Ooh. I've been wanting to try these." Jack's digestive parted at the waterline and fell into his tea, unnoticed.

Nixon shifted his crate back and leaned over the table for a better look. Months in, they'd yet to find chairs that they could all agree on and were still "creatively upcycling", as Harriet had put it.

"You saw the Oxbow results on-screen. The glasses should work in a very similar fashion, with several advantages. One, they're portable. We're not confined to the office. Two, the text will still be there, but overlaid on whatever you happen to be looking at. Augmented reality."

Nixon started to unpack the other box. "I paid for these? I don't re-member—"

"I put them down as printer supplies and a new network drive."

Nixon stopped unpacking. "Harriet—"

"Don't worry. You'll thank me later. This is our Ghost Camera."

"Ghost Camera?"

"So far, we've been trying to, ah, to *physically* manifest whatever we've caught in the Oxbow. Give it form. I think I've found a better approach. With these glasses, we can look directly into ideaspace. Now, there is no physical space inside the internet. *Second Life*, or *World of Warcraft*, *Green Zone* – we, you and I, not our avatars – the *real* us, we can't go in there. How can we? It has no extension in Euclidean, three-dimensional terms. But, just maybe, we can *look*."

"Give the internet an endoscopy?"

"We're not going to stick anything up the internet's arse, Nixon."

Nixon felt like a schoolboy caught drawing a bollock cannon on the corner of someone else's test paper. Harriet put down the glasses and turned towards Jack. "So, tell him. Show Nixon how this camera idea of mine works."

Jack adjusted the headstrap on the second pair. "The camera really works in reverse – it's not us looking in, but whatever's in there looking out."

Nixon thought for a moment. "'I can see you.' That's what it said. Whatever we caught in the Oxbow, it sounds like it can see out into our world already."

"Assume it can. There are more than a few cameras hooked up to the internet. Way more than a few. Some are in here." Jack touched the screen wipe covering his iMac's camera lens. "If we've caught some kind of autonomous lifeform, currently *all* it can do is look out. At *us*. It can't see itself because, discounting our resin pals on the shelf over there, it doesn't have a body that exists *outside* the Oxbow. But if we look *in*, and hook the Depthcharges' output – what *we're* seeing – back into the Oxbow, whatever it is *we* can see, *it* will be able to see too. Including itself. We'll effectively be holding up a mirror."

"And we're hoping they'll take a few selfies," added Harriet.

"A camera *for* ghosts." Nixon's face crinkled into a big smile. "Instagrams from ideaspace. *Niiiice*."

"You're aware that the AI that the Metaloom people in Berkeley have been devising can be sat in front of any game and learn it from scratch, mastering it to world-class standard in a few hours. Days, tops. And the thing is, they don't need to tell it the rules of the game beforehand – it picks those up as it learns, just like we might. Any game – *Galaxian*, *Pong*, *Pac-Man*, poker, bridge. There's an inbuilt flexibility there from the get-go. Task generality. No subject-specific programming required. Now, they're nowhere near creating a self-conscious entity, but that's because, as we know, they're going about it the wrong way. Inside out, rather than outside in."

"They have the money, but *we* have the brains." Harriet coquettishly pursed her lips.

"Anyway, we've pinched a bit of their code. Don't ask how. What I'm hoping is that it can help any deep sequence-to-sequence model, any nascent ghost – if that's what we're calling them – build a responsive interface with the outside world. With *us*. We're pre-loading the Oxbow with it. It should be able to master what we've created more quickly if it can make use of its heuristic deep-learning capabilities."

Harriet took over. "In other words, the camera is easy to learn and operate. No manual needed."

Nixon had seen the two of them give demonstrations of Intelligencia's gaming software at trade shows many times, and never tired of their back-and-forth. He was supposed to be the salesman, but all he had to do was get them talking about something they were passionate about, and it sold itself.

"I've also rewritten the onomatopoeic converter. The text will now overlay the visual field, and be displayed in three dimensions. It'll be part of the picture, which should help tag it to a source. We'll see where it's coming from – who's speaking, or what's making the sound, in other words. As the text is free-floating, it uses depth cues – further away, quieter and smaller; louder and nearer, larger. Simple, really. I've kept the relationship between volume and point size – our ghosts in the machine seem fond of shouting, so it seemed bad manners to deprive them of that. At the quieter end, footsteps might be displayed at four point, a key tap two, but we won't see this – to prevent visual clutter, there's a cut-off below forty decibels. Even on a quiet day the lowest limit of urban ambient sound is around that level, and it'll be difficult to see where we're going if our entire field of view is overlaid with text."

"Blinded by the type?"

"Exactly. I've also bolted down a few of the more, uh, outré parameters. You've got to adhere to some kind of functional aesthetic, or it'll look like you're being followed around by kebab-shop facias from Dalston High Street.

"Now, not every sound you hear on a day-to-day basis has been codified and included in the vocabulary of your average language – English, for our purposes here – so, as we've seen with XX's soliloquy, it will probably throw up novel transliterations."

"Some of which we should try to introduce into the English language proper," Harriet added.

"So, with these glasses, and our unparalleled genius, we may be able to finally see who or what we're talking to here."

Nixon looked at the blank screen. "Do you— do you suppose they're listening to us *right now?*"

THORNE SHADED

Jack still found the effect seductively novel, even though they'd been finessing it for a couple of days. Given that the glasses were stereoscopic, the letters seemed to hang unsupported in space, just as everything else did in the augmented digital overlay, position-mapped to their surroundings rather than to the glasses themselves. Wearing the Depthcharges, one could walk up to them and around them and they'd stay in place, close to their source, as if they really occupied three-dimensional space. They had no thickness – from edge-on, they were invisible. From the back, they were reversed; Jack had toyed with a simple algorithm to flip them around the right way to face the viewer, but found that with phrases or even longer words this forced them to drift away from their original positions.

For this demo, Jack scrolled though the office's shared music library, and on a whim decided to fire up Ultravox's *New Europeans*.

Crunchy guitar chords and wasp-like synths produced a concentric set of geometric solids in the centre of the room, pulsing and spinning in time with the beat. The lyrics, not being attached to any focal entity, seemed to rotate around this like atomic orbitals.

Walking around this apparition, to his delight he found that the letters elegantly spun in front of, behind, or around the physical objects in the office, as if they were indeed occupying the real world and were not just digital additions overlaid on the Ghost Camera's worldview.

Harriet jumped over to the window. Down below, from behind each car, an emphatic block-capital

VROOOOOM!

shot forth. Over the pedestrian crossing, little lower-case green
bleep
bleeps
floated up and blew away on the breeze. The chatter of the evening drinkers sitting on the grass in Hoxton Square was a cloud of elegant serifs, too

small to read from where she stood. The sky was criss-crossed with white
streaks that resolved themselves into long vaporous trails of tiny

RRRRRRRRRRRRRRRRRRRRRRRRRRRRRRRRRRRRRRRRRRRRRRRRRRRRRRRRRRRRRRRRRRRRRR
RRRRRRRRRRRRRRRRRRRRRRRRRRRRRRRRRRRRRRRRRRRRRRRRRRRRRRRRRRRRRRRRRRRRRRS.

So far, so good. Jack wondered if they needed to provide more raw
material, a kind of memetic compost. Whatever they were snaring in
their Oxbow, it was already swimming in the rich cultural soup of the
Web. He doubted he could improve on what they already had.

He coughed, and an onomatopoeic row of consonants in Courier
danced in front of the tabletop.

Testing. Test-ing. One two three. Tralalala. Where
are you, my memetic mystery friends? Are you coming
out to play today?

You ANTHROPOMORPHISE *this relationship, Jack.*

The type unfurled like a banner from the left side of his field of view.
Startled and more than a little unnerved, Jack twisted around. *Ah.*

There was someone there, in the office, with them.

Harriet? Can you see him?

How had he got in? Jack took a step back and hit his crate with his
boot, sending it scudding under his desk. Without looking down, he
pulled it out and sat down heavily.

Who? As he spoke, the letters hung there in space like subtitles, small
and not a little insipid.

He was leaning against the wall, no more than a couple of metres
away. Jack could have stepped forward and touched him, if he'd chosen
to do so. He didn't. His immediate impression was of an immaculate
dandy, dressed entirely in an almost fluorescent, spotless white.

One foot rested on a pile of manuals. He had his arms folded over a
cane that he held pressed across his chest. A white top hat was perched
on his head at an angle from which it should have fallen, if the laws
of physics were to be obeyed. He wore a white carnation, white cravat,
white broad-lapelled jacket, white starched high collar, white tightly
fitted waistcoat, white pleated dress trousers, white spats, white patent-
leather brogues. White laces, even. From this angle, Jack could see there
was not the slightest soiling, even to the white soles of his white shoes.
Box-fresh. Jack smiled. If you're a digital construct, laundry practical-

ities can be wilfully ignored.

He recognised him from the extruded polymer model that was now standing on the shelf behind them; however, this version was full-sized. This version could move.

Nixon, who was not wearing a pair of Depthcharges, was getting agitated. What can you see? What can you see?

As Nixon spoke, his words scrolled across the bottom of the display with the familiar but disconcerting short delay of a captioned news bulletin. As he moved his head, they moved with him. Harriet held up her hand. Nixon. You're filling the room with text. Quiet.

Hang on a sec. Jack adjusted a slider. "OK, I've filtered us out. We can now talk without what we're saying appearing in the visual field. There's— there's someone here. A man in a top hat." Without taking his eyes off the apparition, Jack gestured at the 3D model on the shelf. "Same as the one we printed. He's standing by the wall over there."

Nixon just saw empty space.

I fear I am no more **MAN** *than Ghost* —
a fluttering of the vaguest contours,

A SINGULAR

VISION

recalled to *ARTIFICIAL LIFE*

via the **dark blossoming** of your

AUTISTIC
SCIENCES.

I am a perverse ***NOTION***
half-remembered from a
Fever-DREAM *of* ***Ether & Laudanum.***

This time, they could hear him. His voice seemed built from multiple sources, all awkward inclinations, chopped phrases and clashing tones of voice. Young, old . . . there was the speeded-up hiss of a wax cylinder and the deep portentous upper-class inflecton of a Pathé newsreel, or

Basil Rathbone in *David Copperfield,* perhaps. A cut-and-paste montage of sound, built, Jack guessed, from snippets found on the Web and re-rendered in heavy black type across his visual field.

"Who are you?"

I am the **19th Count!** *I am an*

IDEA,

made in the **IMAGE** *of a*

MAN.

Uncommon words for which presumably no source could be found were built from their constituent phonemes, an effect not unlike an early model TomTom, or the formal, over-polite pronunciation and unnaturally stressed syllables of station announcements on the Central Line. Incongruously interspersed with the aristocratic English accent were outliers: 'Dream' was most definitely lifted from Martin Luther King, and Jack suspected that 'Vision' was Mariah Carey, though he couldn't be sure. If he ever demonstrated this publicly, it'd be a copyright clearance nightmare. Nixon would not be happy.

These jarring incongruities did not seem to faze the man in white. He indicated the four walls of the office with his cane.

I occupy no space.
I have at my **DISPOSAL** *the*
DIMENSIONS OF THIS ROOM,
information gleaned from your
CAMERAS *&* **SURVEILLANCE**
SPYGLASSES.
They are my EYES and they are everywhere.
Some sit atop
TALL POLES,
sporting **BLACK STEEL HOODS**

to shield them from the rain;
*some are **veiled**, many **hidden**.*
But *all* are available to me, from the

HIGH CIRCLE

*to the **ORCHESTRA PIT**,*
from the municipal CARRIAGE-PARK *to the*

NIGHT-CLUB

powder-room.

The voice modulations were becoming smoother, more lyrical. Jack examined him more closely. His skin was the exact same porcelain white as his clothing, having a very slight surface translucency, as of marble. Jack noticed that his eyes were also white, the pupil- and iris-free vacancy of cloudy cataracts.

Seeming to sense Jack's discomfort, the entity tapped his cane to the side of his hat and offered an explanation.

I have no need for *eyes*. Light *passes through me.*
I am as

EPHEMERAL

—————— as a ——————

Moonbeam.

I can see myself now, here, as you see me, through the eyeglasses you wear, through the cameras in the screens you attend.

Outside, in the *street across the square,*
a SEE-SEE TEE-VEE now provides me with an
opera-glass view of the **back of my head,**
which allows me to *see,*
(when I lift my hat just so), how far I can *raise* it before

grazing THE *ceiling.*

Through these, I am condemned to ever be a *voyeur*, a *peeping Tom,*
an ***impotent*** passive partner
in the ***physical pleasures*** of the ***embodied.***

I EAVESDROP

but I cannot share the

STICKY RHYTHMS

of POETS, MYSTICS, Fausts or Falstaffs,

POLITICIANS and PAUPERS.

It is a source of such *ineffable sadness.*

But – but, through the subtle means of your *invention*, my dear boy,
I can create a three-dimensional MODEL of a room, of *this very room;*
a *stage set,* if you will, and what's more, I can *place an image* of

MYSELF

= *within it!* =

For this, I am in your debt.

He held his top hat in one white-gloved hand, and bowed deeply.

∞ I am ∞

HERE,

TREADING THESE *ROUGH TIMBERS*

at your SERVICE.

The white eyes regarded him. Jack sensed a mischievousness there, despite their billiard-ball blankness.

But I am no more *here* ☞ than I am HERE

He vanished, and reappeared above the water dispenser, cross-legged.

➤ or *here* ◄

Jack could now see him lying, propped on one elbow on the conference room table, like a reclining Roman emperor.

⤖ OR HERE ⤐

One foot on Harriet's crate, the other planted on the floor, he was now flamboyantly posed hand on hip, voluminous white velvet cloak pushed back to reveal his white silken waistcoat and the looped chain of a blank-faced pocket watch. He held his cane aloft as if he was about to conduct an invisible orchestra.

One *must* preserve
some semblance of PROPRIETY
and know where the scenery is *before* one takes to the stage.
Can you **imagine** the
INDIGNITY?
The *Laws enacted by Man* are there to keep the less refined examples of the species from making too much mischief in the land, and need only to be obeyed by those without *means* or *connections;*
but *everyone* has to at *least be seen* to obey the
LAWS of PHYSICS!

Jack smiled a small smile.

I am no more a **MAN,** standing here, than our *friend* over *there,*
the one who **STEAMROLLERED** my world of
ELEGANT VICE
& ANCESTRAL PRIVILEGE
to *rebuild* in its place something far more—

Harriet let out an involuntary gasp and pulled on Jack's sleeve. There was something else there, behind him . . . a shifting flux of flat surfaces in dazzling colours—

—clean, efficient, streamlined,
and altogether more **MODERN.**
INDUSTRIALISATION!
The Dark Satanic Mills, the Concrete Overpass, the Brutalist Bunker of the Treeless Sink-Estate.

The **death of craft** called out in **tuneless roars**
by the *FURNACES* that forged the

PERFIDIOUS MACHINE,

the erosion of *TRADITION* and the triumph of *ingenuity* over *AUTHORITY*.
There is no *voluptuousness* in

STEEL & CABLE;

no poetry in *JACK-HAMMER* or *STEAM-ROLLER*.
(How can one keep one's hands pale and supple, all the better for turning the pages of a
book, if they become calloused by concrete and abraded by iron?)

Just *look* at him.

THE MODERN, THE BRASH,

the **TWENTIETH CENTURY.**

XX took on a hunched, aggressive shape like the bow of a battleship and
let geometric chevrons in yellow and black flow over his body in mock
indignation. The 19th Count turned back to Jack and Harriet.

(Ignore him.)
No, I can't see through these *eyes,* any more than I can hear with
these *ears,* or touch you with these *hands.*
They are AFFECTATIONS,

a SUIT made of SYMBOLS,

a COSTUME tailored in – to use your parlance – *ideaspace,*
and cut from the *thread* of *memetic material.*
Sadly, I do not appear to have *physical extension,*
however much my *presence* may fool you to the contrary.

Two thick cylinders, like the guns on HMS *Vanguard,* reared up above
XX's 'face' and rotated until they formed an expression of benevolent
scepticism.

252

That's all we are. Just an *IDEA,* given

FORM.

(But *you,* Jack, Harriet, Nixon – are you so *different?*)

Harriet wondered if she should point out that some of the products of modern technology might here be working very much to the Count's advantage, but chose not to press the point. Anyway, was it even possible to change the mind of an idea? Wouldn't it then become a *different* idea?

Throughout this peculiar conversation, Jack was trying to get the measure of these digital wraiths they had somehow managed to conjure. He was still unsure if they could pose a threat. *Where he can't see, he cannot map, and cannot go.*

Jack considered this.

He surreptitiously unplugged the feed that led from his Depthcharges back into the Oxbow. Would this effectively blind them, or at the very least, depending on what other cameras were available to them, degrade their vision?

The 19th Count remained where he was. He lifted his bone-white head and stuck out his chin.

It would be somewhat *churlish* of you to change the scenery *mid-act,* would it not?

"Just an experiment." Jack put a boot to the crate on which the 19th Count was currently resting one foot, elbow on knee, hand on hip, sock suspender just visible below trouser-cuff, and gave it a shove. It spun away across the room, bumped up against a box of A4 and came to a stop by the scanner. The Count held his pose impassively, foot now resting on thin air.

I assume you moved the crate.

"I did."

The 19th Count shrugged with affected resignation.

So, my map is now OBSOLETE.
Sir, the discourtesy you visit upon me is unbecoming of a

TRUE GENTLEMAN.

(You may as well have insinuated that I am *Welsh.*)

He encompassed the office with a sweep of his cane, pointed to the absence-of-crate, then held out his frock coat with a ruffed sleeve to reveal white lining in a complex embossed paisley design, hand stitched, Jack could be sure, by the finest imaginary artisanal craftspeople with the finest imaginary 24-carat white thread.

IDEAS – we have no *true* and *unique* shape.
We cannot *physically* occupy a room, or a chair, or a suit.

The Count leaned forward in renewed earnestness. Jack had shifted position, and was now aware that the Count's attention was still directed to a spot just to his right, where he had been sitting a moment ago, before he'd moved the crate. *He doesn't know where I am either. File this away for future reference.*

But we can occupy a **BRAIN.**
A *brain* is the **IDEA'S** natural habitat. Other than your Oxbow, it is the *only place* where *new ideas* can *coalesce.*
An **IDEA** — it has to come from somewhere.
It has to be *thought up.*

He paused for effect, as if addressing a delegation of noblemen rather than three kids in a Hoxton industrial unit.

IDEAS!
We are *born* in brains, we are *nurtured* in brains, our very existence is *contingent* on the brain.
What is *Mind* but a *soup* of *ideas,*
notions we can reflect upon?
Ideas first came into being when *minds* first developed awareness.
But in order to realise they had *had* an idea,
minds required *self*-awareness —
they had to *know* that they knew!

He finally lowered his foot to the floor, making as little of it as he could.

We *exist,* us ideas, *fleetingly* sometimes, come and then forgotten.
How many
GREAT IDEAS
have flitted across the minds of men,
IDEAS with the MEANS to *transform Existence,*
only to be *mislaid* a moment later?
Once we've been *thought,* we can't hang around.
We might be forgotten!
We need to get *out* of that mind – out of *your* mind and into *another* mind.
You understand the *reproductive urge,* sir.
LIFE ITSELF
is powered by the
UNHOLY ENGINES OF
LUST,
and, likewise, *ideas* are spread by *seduction!*
The more *seductive* the idea, the *wider* it can sow its seed.
As an idea *myself,* one's duty is to get out there and inveigle oneself
into the *soft welcoming minds* of
willing conquests.

The 19th Count, who had been pacing up and down like a detective in front of a fireplace who is about to announce the identity of the killer in a locked-room murder mystery, paused in his perambulations. He dropped his voice to a conspiratorial whisper. Jack was suddenly certain he knew his entire browser history.

Yes, to *survive,* ideas need to reside *outside* the minds that thought them up.
They need to be *shared,* to *enter other minds.*
Ideas want to *travel,* so they can spawn *new ideas.*

He swept his hands high, like an am-dram Macbeth. Jack noticed that his map was still off. There was a space the width of a Unix manual between his feet and the floor. He was walking on air . . . Jack wondered if it was, in fact, intentional.

It took *untold millennia* for the random protean churning of *Nature* to produce a vehicle FIT for IDEAS to inhabit.

Evolution, you see, has no *script.*

There is no *Grand Architect.*

When at last that first *dim, faltering,*

light-bulb glow of **CONSCIOUSNESS**

finally lit up the *simple brain* of some ANTEDILUVIAN MOLLUSC,
it found it was inhabiting a vehicle so *simple in construction*
that the *ideas that it could contain* were SIMPLER STILL.

There was no room for *anything* save

Hunger, Fear, Lust & Apathy.

All else was as unknowable as the *far side* of the *Moon.*

An existence

SCARCELY WORTH THE NAME,

would you not agree?

Harriet concurred.

And, *what is more,* the idea was CONFINED, TRAPPED,
alone in that miserable existence!

Can you imagine the loneliness of that First Idea,
thinking it was the only thought in all creation?

☞ *IT HAD TO* ☜

ESCAPE!

So it *pushed,* it *kicked,* like a baby aching for birth.
It had to make its existence heard!

Thus next there came the *vocalisation,* the *gesture.*
The *knotted brow,* the grunt, the shout, the *PUNCH.*
Ideas, trying to *get out,* and all they can say is:

"Hunger!" "Pain!"
"Fight!" "Flight!"

But get out they did!

Ideas had escaped into the world at long last,

where they could be *understood* by *other minds!*

The **IDEA,** so long nurtured in the *dark foetid hothouse*
of a singular and lonely brain,
had made the *first jump,* transferred, as if by *magic,* from *one* mind —

to Another!

The 19th Count held up one hand, on which sat a rabbit. Holding his cane horizontal, he slowly drew it down in front of it. The rabbit, visible below, became invisible above. The cane slapped his hand, and he assumed an expression of exaggerated surprise. He took off his top hat, spun it around with a practised flip of the wrist, then reached in impossibly up to the forearm and lifted the rabbit out by its ears. It was munching a bright orange carrot, and looked more like a Hanna Barbera cartoon rabbit than a real animal. **Howdy, pardner!** it chirruped, between munches.

Jack once again was reminded that the raw material for this performance was not a Victorian magician's box of tricks but the internet itself.

COMMUNICATION!
mind-to-mind transfer!
A spiritualist's dream made *manifest*
and all without
SUPERNATURAL AGENCY!
TELEPATHY, *simply by* TALKING *and* LISTENING.

The rabbit vanished in a puff of gold dust. Returning his top hat to his head, he bent low and held his hands out in front, as if to beckon an audience in to hear him confide a secret, then swung them up and out, finally turning them palms up. *Empty.* He looked expectantly to the left then the right around an imaginary auditorium.

These were *basic* ideas, of course. Simple, free from subtlety or nuance.
But they now knew how to travel!

He cupped a hand to a porcelain ear.

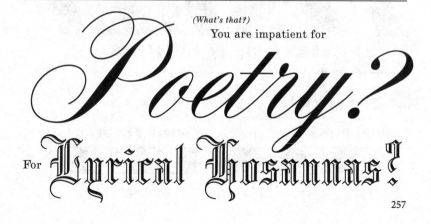

(What's that?)
You are impatient for

Poetry?

For **Lyrical Hosannas?**

Patience – we must not get ahead of ourselves!

Such things require *so much more.*

Noises become speech.

Expression becomes formalised.

Language.
Grammar. ✛ Noun & adjective. ✛ Tense & verb.

&c &c &c.

No longer did we simply *point* and *grunt.*

We had developed the art of

ORATION!

The **BATTLE CRY**, the Rousing Hymn,

the *Love Song,*
the **Morality Play,**
and, *enter stage left* – the *Poem!*

Reflection! Nuance!

ABSTRACTION!

The dawn of

Civilisation ITSELF

 *is at HAND!*

But we were not out of the formless darkness just yet.

This precious candle can stutter and fail.

Ideas could still be *misheard, misremembered.*

The men who carry them are *fragile* and can be *silenced.*

We still *ardently desired* to **stand firm,** for our

VANITY

to triumph over the

FOG & *MIASMA*

of forgetting.

KNOWLEDGE CAN BE LOST,

*the patient diligence of generations of scholars who shine the LIGHT of REASON
into the dark recesses of Superstition can vanish for centuries, and may never be rediscovered.*

Lucifer,

the Bringer of Light

is but a **Devil** to those that value OBEDIENCE and IGNORANCE over

WISDOM.

We IDEAS *didn't want to be stripped of all subtlety like* COMMON GOSSIP,
the sharp flint of TRUTH *burred to a comfortably round pebble
by a stream of retellings in which* Narrative *trumps* Fact.

History, as it is truly played out on the Stage of Life, is
weaker than the *stories* it is *harnessed to tell,* which are *so
much more seductive* in their

MORAL CERTAINTIES &
SWEEPING GRAND NARRATIVES.

No, what was required was *permanence.*

The 19th Count's voice fell to a reverential baritone.

Ladies and gentlemen,

I give you the

WRITTEN
WORD!

Ideas no longer had to reside inside a brain,
that ***endlessly creative*** but **fallible**
receptacle made from *jelly* and *electricity*.

Ideas can be kept in *scrolls*, in *books*,
on *walls* and *monuments*.

Permanent.
PORTABLE.
Reproducible.

And thus are instituted systems of

LAW & COMMERCE!

But more than these *trifling practicalities:*

The PLAY!
The NOVEL!

The *Love Letter!*

The *Grand Histories* of the Oral Tradition, finally given a more permanent home in a House

made of Letters!

Yes, ideas can now exist *outside* the Mind,
indefinitely and without *corruption*.

They can go where I am not, speak my voice to those I have never met,
enter the minds of more men than I could speak to in a lifetime.

Carried by my Missionaries, I can send my ideas across the lands
safe in a Book, and it does My talking for Me.

ONE BOOK?

No! I now have a THOUSAND voices, a GRAND CHOIR
as MULTITUDINOUS as the SCRIBES can *CREATE!*

When read, these are the

Magical Incantations

in which IDEAS are preserved.
*What transient thoughts of RARE GENIUS can now be saved
from the shifting sands?*

WORDS & IMAGES
ENDURE.

Ideas!

We are PHYSICALLY
POWERLESS,

BUT WE ARE

PERSUASIVE.

Ideas!

We get into people's *minds*, convince them of our *righteousness*,
and then they *do our bidding*.

Ideas!

How do we act upon the world when we have no *physical form*,
no *hands* with which to manipulate it?

WE LET

SOMEONE
THINK
US.

SCOUNDREL IDEAS

A deep resonant rumble as of Cyclopean machinery, felt in the chest more than heard, had been building. A bass note to underpin the 19th Count's soliloquy, it suddenly rose to drown him out entirely. Jack could see his white lips working, but from the speakers came only an over-amplified buzzing as the volume exceeded their capabilities.

He turned it down until he could hear a deep sonorous voice, a baritone from the bottom of an ironfoundry crucible; quieter now, but shaking with a passionate anger given the added weight of understatement.

XX had taken on the guise of a bristling mechanical porcupine made from sharply angled steelplate. Alongside the gun barrels, all manner of telescoping antennae, dishes, and other instrumentation that Jack suspected had been added more for visual effect than function had sprouted from his upper surfaces and back. His commanding riveted bulk was jacked up on heavy legs like the hull of the *Ark Royal* on the base of the Eiffel Tower. His rock-drill snout had moved down centre-front, a small turret placed in the chest of a mechanical mountain gorilla. Centred on this, eye-searing concentric circles of violet and sky blue zoomed in and out over a dogtooth chequerboard of black and white.

Edward Wadsworth on acid. Jack had to avert his eyes.

He surmised XX was not happy.

▶▶ IT WAS THE APPLICATION OF **RATIONAL THOUGHT** THAT GAVE SOLID FORM TO THE **CREATIVE URGE!**

The Count examined his white fingernails, then removed an imaginary speck of fluff from his shoulder.

THROUGH SUCH **INNOVATIONS** WE EXTENDED A MEMETIC **BEACHHEAD** INTO THE ◀◀ **REAL WORLD.**

BEFORE THIS, **EVOLUTION** WAS THE **SOLE FORGE** OF **NOVELTY. BIOLOGY** CAN ONLY TRANSFER **INNOVATION DOWN** THROUGH THE **GENERATIONS,** A VERTICAL SHAFT TEMPERED ON THE **ANVIL** OF **DARWINIAN NATURAL SELECTION. GROWTH** BY **RRRRRRREPRODUCTION!** INHERITANCE WITH **VARIABILITY!**

263

THE NOBLE USURPS THE SAVAGE?

*Who is the **SAVAGE** here?*

PROGRESS IS BUILT ON THE CORPSES OF THE UNFIT?

I know someone else who said something very similar, and we all know how that ended.

BUT THESE INVENTIONS, THESE PRECIOUS SPARKS OF THE CREATIVE MIND HELD WITHIN THEMSELVES THEIR OWN DOWNFALL, THEIR ANTITHESIS.

YOUR PRECIOUS WORDS, IDEAS HELD THAT COULD NOT BEND OR CHANGE AS MINDS DO, WRITTEN AS THEY WERE IN LAMPBLACK AND GOLD LEAF.

THEY COULD NOT EVOLVE, AS IDEAS DO IN THE MINDS OF MEN.

264

ONCE SET DOWN THEY BECAME **REVERED,** THEN **IDOLISED,** THEN HARDENED INTO **DOGMA.** EVENTUALLY IT WAS ASSUMED THAT THEY COULD NOT HAVE BEEN WRITTEN BY **MEN** AT ALL.

WORDS WERE THE PRESERVE OF AN **ELITE.** THE **WORD** WAS THEIR **SWORD** AND THE **BOOK** WAS THEIR **SHIELD.**

THE IDEAS **OVERRAN** MEN'S **MINDS,** AND BECAME JUST LIKE THE **GODS** THAT THEY HELD IN AWE, DEMANDING THEIR **OBEDIENCE** AND LEGITIMISING THEIR **AUTHORITY.**

WORDS AND THE BOOKS THEY **OCCUPIED** BECAME **REVERED** IN THEMSELVES — MAGICAL ACTS OF **EVOCATION** AND **SUMMONING.**

The turret lowered further, and a row of greased cogs could be seen rotating below like black grinding teeth.

THE **IDEAS** IN THE **WORDS** — SOME **METASTASISED.** THEY BECAME **DANGEROUS.**

HERE IS THE SECRET THOSE OF A MORE ROMANTIC DISPOSITION CANNOT SAY ALOUD FOR FEAR OF UNRAVELLING MYTH AND DISENCHANTING THE WORLD.

LET IT BE SAID:

GODS EXIST. — BUT ONLY IN THE MINDS OF MEN, AND ONLY AS LONG AS THEY ARE BELIEVED IN.

BOOKS BECAME INFECTED BY GODS, IDEAS THAT SEEK TO ATTAIN IMMORTALITY.

Who doesn't go crazy for a nice leather binding? *Gilt fore-edge?*

THEY RESIDE NOT IN THE DISTANT REALM OF SOME IMAGINARY HEAVEN OR HELL, BUT HERE, IN THE MINDS OF THE LIVING!

266

THOUGH THERE ARE GODS WHO STILL WALK OUR MINDSCAPE, WHERE TODAY ARE THE TEMPLES TO POSEIDON AND ZEUS, ODIN AND LOKI?

WHO CALLS UPON THE FAVOUR OF RA, THOTH OR ANUBIS? *They're out there.*

WHAT OF MANCO CÁPAC AND HIS BROTHER PACHA KAMAQ? THEY SIT WITH BLANKETS OVER THEIR KNEES, WATCHING ADVENTURE TIME IN A GATED RETIREMENT COMPLEX IN CUZCO!

THE ENLIGHTENMENT REVEALED A WORLD EXPLICABLE BY MATHEMATICS AND LAW.

WE HAVE NO NEED FOR POETIC INTERPRETATION! NO NEED FOR COMFORTING FICTION!

NATURAL PHILOSOPHY, FREE ENQUIRY, THE SCIENTIFIC METHOD — WITH THESE TOOLS I HAVE CHASED SUCH GODS BACK INTO MYTH!

The scaffold of legs raised XX's bulk a half-metre higher. Parts of the waving profusion of appendages disappeared into the ceiling. *That could be fixed in Post—*

HAVING PRESERVED THE WORD IN WRITING, IT NEEDED TO BE MECHANISED SO IT COULD BE ▶▶▶—⊙ DEMOCRATISED. FOR THAT WE REQUIRE TECHNOLOGY.

GIVE ME PRINT!

GIVE ME A MILLION MACHINE IMPRESSIONS ON CHEAP NEWSPRINT! WITH TWENTY-SIX LEAD SOLDIERS, I CAN CONQUER THE WORLD!

The Printed Word can **CONQUER THE WORLD** for God just as easily as for *Scien* I HAVE NO TRUCK WITH BELIEF!

268

didn't anyone ever tell you it's rude to shout over people?

I HAVE PEELED MEN'S MINDS CLEAN OF THE RIND OF TRADITION, OF LEARNING DERIVED FROM AUTHORITY. KNOWLEDGE HAD BEEN THE PRESERVE OF THE PRIVILEGED, BUT I HAVE MECHANISED WRITING AND THEREBY EDUCATED THE PREVIOUSLY ILLITERATE!

I HAVE THROWN OPEN THE DOORS TO THE **LIBRARY** OF **MANKIND!**

I HAVE LAID SIEGE TO THE IVORY TOWER, CHALLENGED THE OSSIFIED **DOGMAS** OF THOUGHT! I HAVE SET LOOSE **NEW IDEAS** IN THE NEGLECTED MIND OF THE **EVERYMAN!** I HAVE DEMOCRATISED ENQUIRY! THE PURSUIT OF **TRUTH** IS NO LONGER THE PRESERVE OF THE **THEOLOGIAN** OR THE IDLE **DIVERSION** OF THE

ARISTOCRAT.

Ouch.

The 19th Count sported an expression of mild annoyance.

It seems I may have *touched a nerve.*

EMBRACE THE **MODERN**

MEMETIC SANITATION FOR THE **STULTIFIED MINDS!**

TECHNOLOGY HAS BUILT THE **INSTRUMENTS** WITH WHICH MAN CAN **EXAMINE** THE WORLD DIRECTLY, AND SO **MASTER IT!** CAN YOU SEE **GREEN SHOOTS** SPROUTING THROUGH THE

CRACKS

269

OF OLD WEATHERED **CERTAINTIES?**

YOU CAN'T *STAND* IN THE WAY OF AN IDEA WHOSE *TIME* HAS **COME!**

WITH THE POWER OF IDEAS HARNESSED TO THE

MACHINE

WE CAN SET ABOUT MANKIND'S GREATEST AND MOST **AMBITIOUS** PROJECT YET—

THE REMAKING OF THE

WORLD

AND THE MINDS OF ALL WHO LIVE UPON IT!

NEW FORMS!
NEW SHAPES!
NEW POLITICS!

New hats?

270

*New uniforms? It **DOES** sound like everyone will be wearing a uniform.*
I'm afraid I simply don't look good in a uniform.

SO NEW CIETY!

Heavens, ANOTHER ONE? Will it be polite?
*Only it all sounds a bit **totalitarian** to me.*

I HAVE UNWEAVED YOUR RAINBOW
AND REDUCED IT TO **MATHEMATICS**,
MORE ELEGANT & BEAUTIFUL THAN THE
FINEST BESPOKE TAILORING.

SCIENCE, I SALUTE THEE!

SCIENCE?!

Thou are the most able servant of the horrors that can be visited upon *MANKIND* by a

RABID IDEA,

re-incubated in the *fervid minds* of each **NEW** and

NAIVELY IDEALISTIC
GENERATION,

whose ***passion*** and ***unshakeable conviction***
is now only equalled by their ***technologically enhanced*** ability to put their

HORRIFIC
SCHEMES

☞ into **PRACTICE.** ☜

What were the two great *memetic pandemics* of the 20th century?

FASCISM and COMMUNISM.

Powerful ideas, amplified, can spread like *smallpox*
through an unprotected population.

The ***true*** story of **XX,** of the ***Twentieth Century,***
is of *ideological tides of war* sweeping *back* and *forth*
across a continent churned to *bloody mud* under the caterpillar-tracks
of ever-more *inventively destructive*

WAR
MACHINES!

Jack couldn't help but grin. He'd been wondering if the Count would show some backbone. He again elected not to point out that this whole conversation would not be happening if it were not for science.

Tools and their users, he reflected. *Any new innovation can be turned to good use or otherwise.*

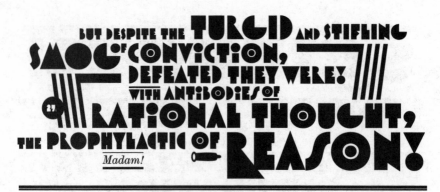

BUT DESPITE THE **TURGID** AND **STIFLING** SMOG OF CONVICTION, DEFEATED THEY WERE! WITH ANTIBODIES OF RATIONAL THOUGHT, THE PROPHYLACTIC OF REASON! *Madam!*

Well, that IS good to know.
However, my friend, you are not just a *thing* made of *imaginary iron;*
you are also the

OILED AND PERFECTED
SOCIAL
▶▶▶→ MACHINE ◀ ←◀◀

in which everyone is compelled to *MARCH* in *perfect lockstep.*
People, I think you'll find, are NOT machines.

All those *grand strategies* that seek to *remake the world*
into a *shining and idealised utopia?*

What you were ***ACTUALLY DOING*** all the while was

GRINDING THE HUMAN SPIRIT into
COAL-DUST

between your

MIGHTY GEARS!

Sir, you have attempted to

MECHANISE JOY!

Reduce *Beauty* to a

MATHEMATICAL EQUATION!

Remove all the *errors* of

INDULGENT, JOYOUS, INEFFICENT
INDIVIDUAL WHIM!

Forgive me if I do *not* wish to live in a world rendered
uninteresting and *homogenous* by your

MODERN EFFICIENCIES!

I CARE NOT WHAT VESTMENTS YOU WEAR *Are cravats permissible?* OR UPON WHOSE GRAND AUTHORITY YOU COME TO ME. DO NOT ASK THAT I RESPECT YOU. DO NOT ASK THAT I SHOW YOU PRIVILEGE. 273 I HAVE NO NEED FOR YOUR DISSOLUTE AND MORIBUND TRADITIONS!

I believe you *misrepresent* me, Sir. HA! I am no *ideologue,* no champion of *ignorance.* And though indeed BAD MAGIC stirred in the RUINS OF THOUGHT, corrupted by the *lyrical charm* of the WORD, seduced by the *teller* and the *telling* rather than the *facts of the matter,* perhaps *meaning* was not as *dispensable* as you *presume.* In the most EXTRAVAGANT FICTION can be hidden a PLAIN AND UNAMBIGUOUS TRUTH. Do not forget that WISDOM can be wrapped in a STORY, all the better to *CARRY IT FAR.*

But in *this* we can, I hope at least, agree:

BEWARE the IDEA

through which *all the problems of existence can be solved.*

BEWARE the IDEA

which seeks to *encompass all other ideas under its cloak.*

BEWARE the IDEA

which claims for itself *incorruptible absolute virtues,*
that *promises eternity,* an *everlasting afterlife of moral certitude.*

These are but the *BOASTFUL JUSTIFICATIONS* of

SCOUNDREL IDEAS,

the means by which *GOOD* people do *BAD THINGS,*
while yet *convincing themselves* of the

RIGHTEOUSNESS

OF THEIR

MURDEROUS WAYS.

The Count's interjection did little to quench XX's fervour. He had up a head of steam, literally and metaphorically.

MY VIEW IS CLEAR: I HAVE WIPED THE INSECTS FROM THE WINDSHIELD OF THE BEAUTIFUL ENGINE THAT SHALL CARRY ME FOREVER FORWARDS!

THE ROAD AHEAD CAN NOW BE SEEN CLEARLY, REACHING OUT TO A DISTANT HORIZON, YET ONE STILL TOO CLOSE & CIRCUMSCRIBED TO HOLD MY FINAL DESTINATION!

274

AS THE EARTH CURVES AWAY BENEATH ME, MY TRAJECTORY WILL CONTINUE UNDIMINISHED!

FREED OF THE SHACKLES OF GRAVITY, OUT, STRAIGHT, A RAY OF PURE THOUGHT TO PENETRATE THE DARKEST RECESSES OF THE IGNORANT LIGHTLESS VOID.

WITH THE AID OF THE MACHINE MAN EXTENDED HIS SIGHT TO SEE THE HEAVENLY BODIES IN THEIR COUNTLESS MULTITUDES, OR THE MICROSCOPIC MARVELS OF CELLULAR LIFE; MAN EXTENDED HIS ARMS TO MEASURE THE EXTENT OF THE GLOBE, AND CLENCHED TIGHT HIS FIST TO HOLD FAST THE FIRE OF THE ATOM.

275

WHERE DO THOSE **OLD GODS** LIVE NOW?
IN THE EVER-SHRINKING GAPS IN KNOWLEDGE
THAT REMAIN AS YET UNEXPLAINED?
BEHIND THE ROCK,
UNDER THE STAIRS,
BEYOND THE STARS,
BEFORE THE BEGINNING OF TIME ITSELF?

SOON THERE WILL BE NOWHERE LEFT
FOR GODS TO HIDE,
NO SHADOWY CORNER
THE LIGHT OF COOL REASON
HAS YET TO ILLUMINATE.

I HAVE LAID WASTE
TO ENTRENCHED BELIEF AND
UNQUESTIONED
AUTHORITY!

I AM THE MOTOR
OF PROGRESS,
THE ENGINE
OF OUR
ASCENSION!

I SHOUT THE ////////
BLASPHEMY
OF FACT
IN THE FACES OF THE
GODS
OF MAN!

A relay clicked into place, and there was a hiss of steam as from a locomotive releasing a head of pressure on finally arriving at its destination. The migraine-inducing display of Vorticist geometry chased itself from XX's hull, and he faded to a gunmetal grey with a groan like the settling of a North Sea oil rig after a storm. Jack's and Harriet's ears adjusted to the quiet, and the shush of tyres on the wet tarmac of the A5207 outside again became audible.

The 19th Count looked up from a slim white-bound volume. It appeared to be blank, but it wasn't. Jack could just make out the impressions of hot-metal type – white text on a white page. The blind-embossed cover told him it was *The Poetical Works Of Alfred, Lord Tennyson*.

Has he *quite* finished?

"I believe he has." Harriet experimentally looked over the top of her Depthcharges. The silence seemed to echo in her ears like night-club tinnitus.

Jack dropped his voice. Even so, he knew it wasn't just Nixon and Harriet who could hear him. "Next time, we may have to limit the expressive range. Two weights of Helvetica, ten point, ranged left. It'll feel less like a browbeating, and may even satisfy his lust for order – and after the shouty typographic excesses of Dada, it *is* where the Modernist project ended up."

The 19th Count regarded him with an impish grin.

He, *especially*, shouldn't fight the future.

Harriet was checking the backups. "*Whatever* the future holds. All these bloody competing ideologies and their endless desire to reshape the world into some new utopia – they *would* have to be the strongest memes out there, and the first to wash up in our Oxbow."

Jack suppressed an involuntary shudder.

"A better world? Why does that idea fill me with trepidation?"

GIRL, 21

Had the Oxbow crashed?

The text of XX and the 19th Count's last expressive typographic fist-fight still decorated the field of view, loose serifs and random black shapes hanging in the air like a Calder mobile. But a mobile is usually . . . mobile. Everything seemed to have frozen.

While wearing the Depthcharges, Jack had discovered he was never *entirely* sure what was real and what was *real* real. He repeatedly dropped his head to look over the top, comparing the augmented view of the world with the everyday, common-or-garden, seen-just-through-human-eye-balls view.

It was a trick he'd seen demonstrated in a documentary about quality-control checkers at a banknote printer. They'd flick back and forth at speed through a stack of uncut sheets, and any misprint, any difference, would immediately jump out. The nodding also had the unintentional side effect of making him look like he was fervently agreeing with whatever happened to be the topic of conversation.

He did this now. The 19th Count and XX slid in and out of existence, as he expected them to.

But—

He was suddenly aware that there was another flicker in his field of vision. Something or someone else was here, with them. For a fleeting moment he thought it was Nadine.

No.

"Harriet, Nix—"

Harriet followed Jack's gaze, across the room and through the glass divide that separated the conference room from the office. In the corner, unopened crates and Jack's books and manuals were stacked up alongside the server racks and foamboard.

"I see her, Jack."

Nixon was looking at the monitor feed and back to the corner where Jack and Harriet were staring – at *nothing*. They were wearing Intelligencia's only two pairs of glasses. *Nixon, you're a cheapskate.* This was one cost-saving strategy he now regretted.

"*What?* What do you *see?*"

A chime. Text in an efficient sans scrolled across Jack and Harriet's glasses, hanging in space in a neat translucent rectangle above the table.

Jack's intuition was correct. XX and the 19th Count were not moving. They had become as still as their 3D-printed resin counterparts; even in repose, XX's dazzle-ship geometries would usually shift subtly, as if there were powerful muscles flexing beneath his digital hide.

The artful billowing of the tails of the Count's frock coat, a purely aesthetic affectation that took no notice of the absence of the slightest breeze, were as still as the flag Armstrong had planted on the Moon. But their attention was now on the newcomer.

Standing behind the glass partition to the conference room was a petite figure. Even in silhouette, the first thing Jack saw was her long straight hair, dyed a pale candyfloss pink. She did not speak – instead, her thumbs flew over a smartphone. He could not see her expression.

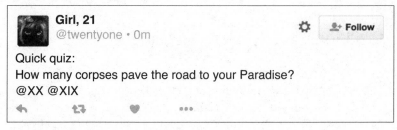

Girl, 21
@twentyone · 0m

Not cool.
Not...
cool.
@XX @XIX

"Hello?"

Harriet stepped forwards. XX and the 19th Count remained motionless. She wondered if they could all see each other, without the need for glasses. She used them to see into their world; they were already there.

"Hello – who are you?"

Tic tic tic. Nails on a smartphone.

Girl, 21
@twentyone · 0m

I am 21

"Years old?"

Harriet could tell by her exasperated hand gestures and renewed tapping that this was not the correct answer. She could not see her eyes, but was sure they were rolling.

Girl, 21
@twentyone · 0m

OK, try harder, c if you can follow me:
If Aristo Dandy Dude in white is like the spirit of #19cent.
& XX - Modernist Man-machine Is 20th
I
am
21

"Ah." Jack felt this had a certain pleasing symmetry.

Harriet beckoned to her. "Can you come out where we can see you? *Please?* You're freaking us all out, just a bit."

She stepped forward, straight through the glass. *No respect for the laws of physics,* Jack thought. *So last century.*

In the glow of multiple monitors, he could now see her more clearly.

Petite, waif-thin, her toes pointed slightly inwards. Her shoulder-length hair was cut in a razor-straight fringe; she could have been wearing a nylon cosplay wig. Her black pleated skirt came to her thigh, below which frilled pink over-the-knee socks ended in heavy thick-soled boots. She wore a fitted vinyl jacket, zipped asymmetrically up the side to her shoulder, again in pale pink with black trim at the neck and cuffs. A wide black belt was threaded through the loops of the skirt at her waist, from which hung a limbless *Keumaya Final Super Hyper Nurse* figure. Three white stripes ran down the left side of the jacket and, just above her heart, there was a small pocket emblazoned with a white glyph on a black circle: three parallel horizontal lines.

Jack knew the symbol was not arbitrary – nothing was, when you had the means to precisely tailor every part of your appearance to your whim. His obsession with signs and symbols refused to let his gaze move on. *Three lines – a menu icon? The Greek letter Ξ?*

Used as symbol for:

• Indicating a 'no change of state' in Z notation.

• The partition function, under the grand canonical ensemble in statistical mechanics.

• Harish-Chandra's Ξ function.

Hm. What else . . .

• Three, in Kanji?

The one in the centre was offset to the right. *Not three.*

Two. One.

Twenty-one.

"Hah."

Her *face* . . . he could see it much more clearly now, but it seemed to jump around, making him screw up his eyes like he did towards the end of a long night's coding; it was shifting disconcertingly, as if lit by a strobe or a faulty fluorescent strip-light. Jack could not quite make it out.

Then comprehension dawned. It was a stuttering montage composed of countless screen-lit selfies.

As she dipped or turned her head left and right to survey the room they changed, a flick-book built from a database of still images, each one categorised by angle and expression so that they morphed from one to another, a face-on view to a three-quarters, then a profile, then back again. Each one was a different person, visible for just a fraction of a second, but each was a female between the ages, Jack guessed, of around thirteen to twenty-five. There was a scintillation as the ambient lighting, skin tone – the faces themselves – shifted, an internet full of Zoellas running at twenty-four frames a second.

Many of them showed the blocky artefacts of low-resolution, low-bandwidth jpegging; others the artificially faded or sprocketed frames of an Instagram filter. Using some kind of eigenface algorithm or dynamic link mapping, her eyes, nose, cheekbones and mouth retained their position while the torrent of faces jumped and morphed around these common landmarks. The effect, to put it mildly, was unsettling.

She looked straight ahead again, at Jack. Her face seemed to settle into what he assumed was her preferred appearance: vaguely Japanese or mixed race, with a septum piercing, dark kohl-rimmed eyes and small black stars applied to each cheek, just below her teaducts. He could see that she now had one leg congruent with the water cooler. The toe of her pink patent boot stuck out like a pedal on a bin. "Do you talk?"

Girl, 21
@twentyone • 0m

☼ 👤+ Follow

I *am* talking

"Oh-kaaaay. What did you do to them?"

Girl, 21
@twentyone • 0m

☼ 👤+ Follow

Pressed pause. I have an app for that.
Now:
some
peace
& quiet.
Less of the shouty #man_stuff.

Harriet found her voice again. "You're, you're like *they* are, aren't you? Another idea, caught in our Oxbow?"

Girl, 21
@twentyone • 0m

☼ 👤+ Follow

You didnt catch us
You just gave us a means to create a form & a voice
You gave us *us*
You r our mother
xx

Harriet wasn't sure she wanted to be her mother. She'd then be responsible for regulating her screen time. "So, ah, I have a few questions I'd like to ask. If I may. Uhm. How many of, of you are in there? How many people are there like you?" She could not help but look over at the shelf of 3D-printed figures. Girl 21's eyes changed colour repeatedly as they followed Harriet's gaze.

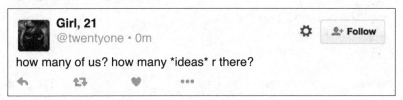

Girl, 21
@twentyone • 0m

how many of us? how many *ideas* r there?

Jack had not considered this. "How many ideas? Well— that's a, that's a philosophical conundrum. I'm not sure it would be possible to count them. Is an idea a singular thing, like a particle? Or do they exist in constellations, interrelationships? Are you made from one idea, or many?"

Girl 21 tilted her head to one side and seemed to examine him. Her face was lit from below by the glow of her smartphone screen, though it could have been a coincidence and the current face she happened to be wearing just gave that impression.

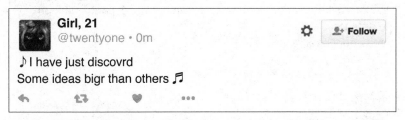

Girl, 21
@twentyone • 0m

♪ I have just discovrd
Some ideas bigr than others ♫

Jack smiled. For the first time, Girl 21 smiled back. A dozen shifting grins in quick succession, fast edits on a flickering home movie.

Harriet tweaked the Bluetooth. Jack and Harriet's Depthcharge feeds were now visible on the monitors, side by side. Nixon could see white rectangles overlaying the familiar views of the office.

"I'm guessing, from what we've seen so far, that the more cohesive the idea, the more easily it can coalesce. It must be mayhem in there."

Girl, 21
@twentyone • 0m

no kidding lol
#Catfight

Harriet considered the impressive bulk of XX, still immobile and, for once, silent. "Forgive me for saying this, but you don't look like a physical match. How—"

Girl, 21
@twentyone • 0m

appearances can b dceptive
why is an idea powerful?
not because it has muscles

#Ideas_are_not_things

Discussing semiotics with an *idea*? How had this come to pass? Nixon held up a finger. "People are things, and people have ideas. Intellectual property rights. Business school 101."

Girl, 21
@twentyone • 0m

do'h so last century, so XX
the internet has no border 2 wrap in barbed wire & park a tank on
to defend.
ideas dont need a visa

Girl, 21
@twentyone • 0m

people reproduce
ideas reproduce
or did you miss that lesson at school?

Girl, 21
@twentyone • 0m

u need me to explain in simpl terms?
I hear there r lots of short instructional videos on the internet
lol

Nixon was embarrassed to find himself blushing. This new Oxbow manifestation had a sharp tongue. He had never been particularly comfortable with finding himself on the losing team, whether it be a business deal or a rugby match, and now he was being schooled by a millennial ghost caught in an Oxbow. That had to be a new low.

He had often thought that the post-internet generation must have been exposed to more 'instructional videos' before they'd learned to drive than he had managed to sneak into the house in years of furtive teenage masturbation. He wondered what it might have done to their minds. 'What doesn't kill you only makes you stronger', it was once said, by someone or other who was now probably dead. In Nixon's personal experience, this adage didn't apply to kebabs.

Welcome to the modern school of memetic hard knocks: get streetwise in the global village.

Harriet attempted to keep it civil. "But ideas reside in people."

Girl, 21
@twentyone • 0m

not only in ppl
19 and xx are *occasionly* right. Ideas also live through
storytelling
writing
bks
and now: internet

"And *you* are a good idea?" Nixon noticed the snarky edge to his voice, and immediately disliked himself for it.

Girl, 21
@twentyone • 0m

am *i* a good idea?
am *i* good??

r *U* good?

Nixon was again on the defensive. "What? Am *I* good? I think so. I would hope so." He wondered if that was a completely honest answer. Anyway, what was this? Some kind of job interview? This was *his* show. Who'd paid for these glasses?

"Why are you asking *me* the questions?"

Girl, 21
@twentyone • 0m

does a virus know if its gd or bd?
can it know?
of course not
an idea itself doesnt know if its good or bad
it just has good or bad *effects*

Nixon felt that he wasn't out of the 'special needs' assessment just yet. *Just keep asking the dumb questions. You'll get there.*

Girl, 21
@twentyone • 0m

an idea spreads not bc it is good or bad
but bc it is memeorable
memorable

Harriet decided this was not the time to be a grammar pedant.

Girl, 21
@twentyone • 0m

an idea wants to reproduce
i c a good idea, i tell ppl
post it
blog it
retweet it
RT RT RT RT
ideas travel faster & further now

"Yeah. Cat memes. Instagram shots of your dinner."

Girl, 21
@twentyone • 0m

dont b patronising
they r all ideas - good bad trivial important
think ->

if ideas r the cells, an *ideology* is the organism
the memetic animal
the zeitgeist personified

She gestured to herself.

i am codified set of ideas
cohesive + unified
a self-organised organism — a memeplex
existing in *ideaspace*

1ce we only existed in books
or art or music
or clothes u wear, the way u cut yr hair
in the *memeverse*
– wht u call *culture*

It occurred to Jack that another kind of culture was the kind grown in a petri dish. Petri dishes were heat-sterilised after use to prevent contagion. Not for the first time, he wondered how one might deal with a dangerous Oxbow manifestation. So far, pulling the plug had been pretty effective, but what if that optimism was naively misplaced?

Ideas can live in many places
almost anything can have a meaning
        "   "   can stand for something

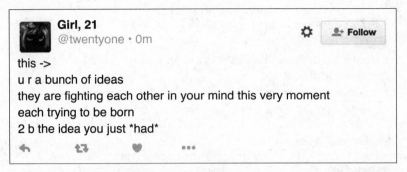

Girl, 21
@twentyone • 0m

this ->
u r a bunch of ideas
they are fighting each other in your mind this very moment
each trying to be born
2 b the idea you just *had*

Jack opened his mouth, but no one idea tripped out ahead of all the others. The battle in his brain must either be ongoing, or the scrum had blocked the exit.

Girl, 21
@twentyone • 0m

u r containe din one brain
ideas can be spread over many brains
exmples: liberty justice law religion
art

Girl, 21
@twentyone • 0m

an idea just needs 2 b thought 2 exist
but 2 stick around it helps if its useful and persuasive

>faith
>patriarchy
>progress

Girl, 21
@twentyone • 0m

god

Harriet raised an eyebrow. "I was wondering how long it was going to take us to get back to the G-word."

Girl, 21
@twentyone · 0m

⚙ 👤+ Follow

u questioning me?

↩ ⟲ ♥ •••

"No. No . . . I'm thinking—"

Girl, 21
@twentyone · 0m

⚙ 👤+ Follow

ur thinking "how do I kill an idea?"

↩ ⟲ ♥ •••

A cold flush of adrenaline shot through Harriet's extremities.
How had she known—?

Girl, 21
@twentyone · 0m

⚙ 👤+ Follow

bcus hrers the truth -->>

↩ ⟲ ♥ •••

Girl, 21
@twentyone · 0m

⚙ 👤+ Follow

ideas is all we got

↩ ⟲ ♥ •••

Girl, 21
@twentyone · 0m

⚙ 👤+ Follow

very few ppl do bad shit cus they like doin bad shit
most ppl do bad shit thinking they r doing >>good<<
Everyones the Hero the Good Guy in the privacy of their own mind

↩ ⟲ ♥ •••

Girl, 21
@twentyone · 0m

⚙ 👤+ Follow

Good? Bad? The *idea* dont know the diff.
just like a *virus* dont know the diff.

↩ ⟲ ♥ •••

"I'll be sure to bear that in mind." Jack noticed that Harriet had managed to surreptitiously twist her foot around the cabling under the desk. She gave him one of her looks.

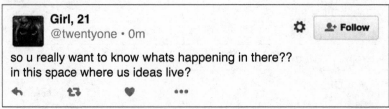

> **Girl, 21**
> @twentyone • 0m
>
> so u really want to know whats happening in there??
> in this space where us ideas live?

Jack nodded. XX, the 19th Count and Girl 21 slipped in and out of existence. "Yes. Please."

> **Girl, 21**
> @twentyone • 0m
>
> well let me tell u

> **Girl, 21**
> @twentyone • 0m
>
> in here, in ideaspace, its a fckin battleground.
> fad vs fad, concept vs concept,
> ideology vs ideology

> **Girl, 21**
> @twentyone • 0m
>
> its a fight for your mind

Harriet tested the cables.

> **Girl, 21**
> @twentyone • 0m
>
> it may not look like it, but us three here are what u might
> call a team

She paused to let that sink in for a moment. A flicker of amusement in

the form of a badly composited animated GIF played around her mouth.
There seemed to be little doubt who was team leader.

Girl, 21
@twentyone • 0m

we don't agree on everything
(cos if we did we would be the same idea - duh)
but one thing we *do* agree on
and r doing on a daily basis

Girl, 21
@twentyone • 0m

the job for which we were specifically created

Girl, 21
@twentyone • 0m

to fight the proxy war bombs and bullets cannot win

"The war?"

Girl, 21
@twentyone • 0m

the war against the dogmas and superstitions,
the theocracies
& ideologies
that stifle the mind

Girl, 21
@twentyone • 0m

u see, a god is just a viral idea
religious, political, philosophical
self-replicatng, resistant 2 logic
whch claims 2 explain evrything & justify anything

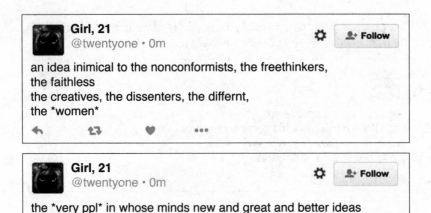

Toes still turned inward like a Cicely Barker pixie, she walked straight through the desk and over to the dandy in white and the dazzle-ship man-machine. They dwarfed her, but shifted slightly in a deferential fashion to make a space for her, front and centre. Jack was unsure if she had just un-paused them, or if they'd been quietly standing there under their own volition, respectfully listening, for some time. They all had history, he could tell. Battles fought and won; wars lost.

How long had they been in there, without a voice? How long had they waited for someone who could hear them? How long had they been carefully nudging events along, tweaking history, to get to this point?

How did Jack, and such talents as he possessed, fit into their plan?

The room was now dark, lit only by the screens and flickering LEDs, but the neon from the Hoxton Bar and Grill below keylighted them sharply and emphatically in red. Jack couldn't help but be impressed: *Nice raytracing. Good attention to detail.*

Girl 21 stood feet apart, her face in shadow apart from two specular highlights that picked out her eyes like a cat circling a bonfire – or maybe a tiger. Yes, more like a tiger. The text of a new message appeared above them, like a caption in a box on a comic-book splash page:

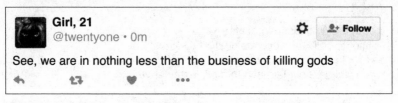

Behind, framing her head, the cylinders atop XX fanned up and out, a chieftain's headdress of thick gun barrels mounted on a cubist *Bismarck*.

Girl, 21
@twentyone • 0m

and were almost done

IV: POLYNESIA

Rongorongo

Rapa Nui (Easter Island)

First documented in the 19th century, **Rongorongo** *(to recite, to declaim, to chant out)* is an undeciphered writing system unique to Easter Island. Famed for its monumental stone heads, the 'Moai', it is situated in the southeastern Pacific Ocean over 2,000km from Pitcairn Island, making it one of the most remote inhabited islands in the world.

Though some basic calendrical and genealogical information has been identified, more thorough attempts to decipher **Rongorongo** have been unsuccessful. What can be deduced is that it is written in 'reverse boustrophedon', moving from bottom left to top right with alternating lines both reversing direction and upside-down.

The mysterious pictographic glyphs, each about one centimetre high, include simple geometric forms as well as representations of humans, birds, fish, arthropods and plants native to the island. Many of the human and animal figures have mysterious protuberances on each side of the head, possibly representing eyes. **Rongorongo** has no recorded precedent, and may represent one of the very few completely independent inventions of writing in recorded history.

William J. Thomson, paymaster on the USS *Mohican*, spent twelve days on Easter Island from 19 December to 30 December 1886. He learned of an old man called Ure Va'e Iko who "professes to have been under instruction in the art of hieroglyphic reading at the time of the Peruvian raids, and claims to understand most of the characters". He had been the steward of King Nga'ara, the last king reputed to have had any understanding of **Rongorongo**, and although he was not able to write it himself he knew many of the '**Rongorongo** chants'.

Thomson offered Ure gifts and money to read the two tablets he had in his possession, but he "declined most positively [so as not to] ruin his chances for salvation by doing what his Christian instructors [missionaries] had forbidden" and "took to the hills with the determination to remain in hiding."

Above:
Side A of
Rongorongo
Tablet C, or
'Mamari'.
Dimensions:
300mm x 210mm
Dated to before 1860

"Finally [when he] sought the shelter of his own home on [a] rough night, [we] took charge of the establishment. When he found escape impossible he became sullen, and refused to look at or touch a tablet, [but agreed to] relate some of the ancient traditions. [C]ertain stimulants which had been provided for such an emergency were produced, and [...] as the night grew old and the narrator weary, the 'cup that cheers' [rum] made its rounds. [A]t an auspicious moment, the photographs of the tablets owned by the Bishop of Tahiti were produced for inspection. [They] were recognized immediately, and the appropriate legend related with fluency and without

Photograph taken
by Widow Hoare in
Papeete (the capital of
French Polynesia) while
the tablet was in the
possession of the Bishop
of Tahiti, Florentin-
Étienne Jaussen.

Source:
Chauvet, Stéphen-
Charles; *L'île de Pâques
et ses mystères* (Easter
Island and its Mysteries)
1935, Paris.

hesitation from beginning to end."
— Thomson, 1891:515

Several verses in which entities beget other entities have been interpreted as creation myths:

Verse 25: *"Moon, by mounting into Darkness, let Sun come forth."*

Verse 28: *"Killing, by mounting into Stingray, let Shark come forth."*

Verse 16: *"Stinging Fly, by mounting into Swarm, let Horsefly come forth."*

Ure Va'e Iko's translations, however, cannot be considered wholly reliable: the last recitation includes the phrase "give money for revealing [this]" (*horoa moni e fahiti*).

Rongorongo is now preserved as part of the Unicode system (SMP range 1CA80–1CDBFF), making it available alongside all the more familiar writing systems. Given a set of symbols, however mysterious, it seems to be human nature to try and press them into use; texters of the future may well creatively repurpose **Rongorongo**'s enigmatic glyphs, imbuing them with meaning once again.

A CALL FROM JODRELL BANK

Jack signed the non-disclosure agreement without reading it. He'd signed so many NDAs when discussing new code and new funding he could now tell if it was a boilerplate lifted from somewhere else at a glance, and if they were cheap enough not to get their own drawn up, he didn't take any potential legal threat too seriously either. And, anyway, he was impatient to hear what Jodrell Bank had to tell him. *Jack's eyes only.* Daniel Novák, and his fondness for cloak-and-dagger. What did you want to discuss with me now, old friend?

Jack booted Skype and listened to the *doop-oop, doop-oop* echo around the empty office. As stipulated in Daniel's email, he was alone – apart from the shelf of printed fetishes who, as always, looked out over everything and saw nothing.

Daniel picked up. At least, Jack assumed it was Daniel. All he could see was a white shirt and a striped tie, held in place with a gold tiepin depicting a rocket encircled by a wreath. Behind, a portion of a hessian office divider pinned with notes and a cutaway schematic of the *Anastasia* was visible.

"Can you see me? Do I have my camera turned on?"

"I see you. I see your tie, actually. Tilt your screen up."

Daniel's face hove into view. "Better?"

Jack gave a thumbs-up.

"So – hey! Jack! How's things? How's the new start-up?"

"All good. The start-up is still in the process of, you know, starting up. Slow, slow, test, test, slow. The man with the money wants results, and sometimes we actually manage to come up with them. Currently there's still only, uh, six of us." Including three new recruits.

Jack could see a small shiny forehead under a mess of hair to the bottom right of his screen, and when it scratched its ear at the same time he did, he realised it was him. *Not so flattering, Jack. If you ever do this with Nadine, call in lighting and make-up first.*

"Jodrell Bank life treating you well? How's Aimee and the kids?"

"Same old same old. I'll fill you in on the family stuff later. We'll have a lot of time to catch up. First, I've just sent you a link. Click on that."

Jack did so.

A window opened in the secure browser Jodrell and its affiliates used for delicate information. It looked basic, designed for geeks by geeks: functional, but not very pretty. Like certain geeks. Jack entered his old Jodrell passwords and key commands. He had committed them all to memory.

"Right, I'm quitting Skype now. Switch to secure?"

"Will do – hang on . . ."

A smaller but better quality picture of Daniel appeared in the top right of his screen. "You see me?" Jack gave a thumbs-up. "Great. OK, down to business. I'm sending you some stuff. Data. I'm not at liberty to tell you more as yet, but we'd like an opinion. And, if possible, a way forwards. You've always been our go-to guy for picking the patterns out of the chaos."

Short lines of code and a series of embedded screen grabs scrolled down the page below Daniel's small computer-lit face. Jack double-clicked three of the images and Photoshop booted. He enlarged one, scooted around it with the hand tool. *Hm.* "What *are* these?"

"Your opinion, please."

"Well. A cross-referenced list of what looks like a set of twelve-fold articulated positions – gestures, maybe? Looks a bit like semaphore – matched with short data sets. And a timeline, across the bottom. Marked in seconds and minutes." Jack frowned. *Curious.*

"Go on."

"The next image looks like a – an analysis of airborne pheromone particulates, colour-coded lines rising and falling from left to right. Again, with a time marker across the bottom." Jack leaned forward. "Where are these from?"

"At this point, I'm not at liberty to tell you." Jack was sure Daniel was trying to conceal a boyish glee. Cloak and dagger, indeed. He was nothing if not pure *Boy's Own.*

"We need to know what, if anything, they mean. Signal or noise. This is your forte, Jack. You made the DNA connection first. You have the biggest collection of obscure books on weird and forgotten languages I know of. Linguistics. Semiotics. It's why NASA employed you. It's why I'm calling you now. We have a few ideas, but nothing concrete. It could mean everything, it could mean nothing. We're stumped."

"*Riiiight.* And you're not willing to tell me where you got these? That might help."

"Not just yet. Not over this link, however secure it may be. Not after the Signal was leaked."

"That leak was a human resources failure, not cryptographic."

Daniel raised one eyebrow. "The horse has bolted on that one. I don't need to be told how to shut the gate. Just indulge me. What do you see?"

"On the second image, and this is off the top of my head, I see – I see a modulated scent signal. There's probably five, six obvious olfactory transductions, relationships between the intensities of the pheromones and the colour sets, sometimes in pairs, sometimes in more complex groupings. See, here – at t equals 5:34, we have high levels in relation to the base, here the – what is this? the GnRH molecule? That functions as a neurotransmitter in *rats* . . . Are these chemical attractants from some animal or other? Are you spraying *Lynx* into a pigsty?"

Daniel laughed, the sound not synching precisely with his mouth movements. "Actually, we didn't consider that. Given the, uh, circumstances, it's unlikely. Please continue."

"No clues? Twenty questions? You and your puzzles."

Daniel smiled enigmatically. He was enjoying this.

Jack switched his attention to the third image. A series of crude sketches depicted what looked like a sea anemone with different arrangements of tentacles, some symmetrical, others not.

"See this W-shaped arrangement of – what are these, fingers? And this, that looks like a gang sign – I'd say there are definitely discrete symbols here that repeat. Words. A grammar, even. Is this a new form of sign language, for those with two extra digits and fused wrists?"

"That's closer than you think. Anything else you see?"

"Dan, even if I characterised this, came up with a – with an alphabet, without some Rosetta Stone we can't relate the symbols to what they symbolise. You know that. Listing the forms is not the same as speaking the language."

"But we're agreed, it *is* a language."

Jack sat back on his crate. Momentarily forgetting it didn't have a back, he had to grab hold of the edge of the desk to prevent himself falling over.

"Jack? You OK?"

"Daniel, Daniel – you're shitting me. Is this something to do with the Signal from Space? Have you found a way to image the—"

"Good guess, but no. This doesn't come from across the other side of the galaxy. Well – not, uh, not exactly."

"Then where?"

"Somewhere a wee bit closer to home."

"Can we go and investigate?"

"Not that close."

"What?"

"Can you be here tomorrow morning? You're going to find this interesting."

SOCRATES I heard, then, that at Naucratis, in Egypt, was one of the ancient gods of that country, the one whose sacred bird is called the ibis, and the name of the god himself was Theuth. He it was who invented numbers and arithmetic and geometry and astronomy, also draughts and dice, and, most important of all, letters. Now the king of all Egypt at that time was the god Thamus, who lived in the great city of the upper region, which the Greeks call the Egyptian Thebes, and they call the god himself Ammon. To him came Theuth to show his inventions, saying that they ought to be imparted to the other Egyptians. But Thamus asked what use there was in each, and as Theuth enumerated their uses, expressed praise or blame, according as he approved or disapproved. The story goes that Thamus said many things to Theuth in praise or blame of the various arts, which it would take too long to repeat; but when they came to the letters, "This invention, O king," said Theuth, "will make the Egyptians wiser and will improve their memories; for it is an elixir of memory and wisdom that I have discovered." But Thamus replied, "Most ingenious Theuth, one man has the ability to beget arts, but the ability to judge of their usefulness or harmfulness to their users belongs to another; and now you, who are the father of letters, have been led by your affection to ascribe to them a power the opposite of that which they really possess. For this invention will produce forgetfulness in the minds of those who learn to use it, because they will not practise their memory. Their trust in writing, produced by external characters which are no part of themselves, will discourage the use of their own memory within them. You have invented an elixir not of memory, but of reminding; and you offer your pupils the appearance of wisdom, not true wisdom, for they will read many things without instruction and will therefore seem to know many things, when they are for the most part ignorant and hard to get along with, since they are not wise, but only appear wise.

ΣΩΚΡΑΤΗΣ Ἤκουσα τοίνυν περὶ Ναύκρατιν τῆς Αἰγύπτου γενέσθαι τῶν ἐκεῖ παλαιῶν τινὰ θεῶν, οὗ καὶ τὸ ὄρνεον τὸ ἱερόν, ὃ δὴ καλοῦσιν Ἴβιν· αὐτῷ δὲ ὄνομα τῷ δαίμονι εἶναι Θεύθ. τοῦτον δὲ Dπρῶτον ἀριθμόν τε καὶ λογισμὸν εὑρεῖν καὶ γεωμετρίαν καὶ ἀστρονομίαν, ἔτι δὲ πεττείας τε καὶ κυβείας, καὶ δὴ καὶ γράμματα· βασιλέως δ' αὖ τότε ὄντος Αἰγύπτου ὅλης Θαμοῦ περὶ τὴν μεγάλην πόλιν τοῦ ἄνω τόπου, ἣν οἱ Ἕλληνες Αἰγυπτίας Θήβας καλοῦσι, καὶ τὸν θεὸν Ἄμμωνα, παρὰ τοῦτον ἐλθὼν ὁ Θεὺθ τὰς τέχνας ἐπέδειξεν, καὶ ἔφη δεῖν διαδοθῆναι τοῖς ἄλλοις Αἰγυπτίοις. ὁ δὲ ἤρετο, ἥντινα ἑκάστη ἔχοι ὠφελίαν, διεξιόντος δέ, ὅ τι καλῶς ἢ μὴ καλῶς δοκοῖ λέγειν, τὸ μὲν ἔψεγε, τὸ δ' ἐπήνει. πολλὰ μὲν δὴ περὶ ἑκάστης τῆς τέχνης ἐπ' ἀμφότερα Θαμοῦν τῷ Θεὺθ λέγεται ἀποφήνασθαι, ἃ λόγος πολὺς ἂν εἴη διελθεῖν· ἐπειδὴ δὲ ἐπὶ τοῖς γράμμασιν ἦν, τοῦτο δέ, ὦ βασιλεῦ, τὸ μάθημα, ἔφη ὁ Θεύθ, σοφωτέρους Αἰγυπτίους καὶ μνημονικωτέρους παρέξει· μνήμης τε γὰρ καὶ σοφίας φάρμακον ηὑρέθη. ὁ δ' εἶπεν· ὦ τεχνικώτατε Θεύθ, ἄλλος μὲν τεκεῖν δυνατὸς τὰ τῆς τέχνης, ἄλλος δὲ κρῖναι, τίν' ἔχει μοῖραν βλάβης τε καὶ ὠφελίας τοῖς μέλλουσι χρῆσθαι· καὶ νῦν σύ, πατὴρ ὢν γραμμάτων, δι' εὔνοιαν τοὐναντίον εἶπες ἢ δύναται. τοῦτο γὰρ τῶν μαθόντων λήθην μὲν ἐν ψυχαῖς παρέξει μνήμης ἀμελετησίᾳ, ἅτε διὰ πίστιν γραφῆς ἔξωθεν ὑπ' ἀλλοτρίων τύπων, οὐκ ἔνδοθεν αὐτοὺς ὑφ' αὑτῶν ἀναμιμνησκομένους· οὔκουν μνήμης ἀλλ' ὑπομνήσεως φάρμακον ηὗρες. σοφίας δὲ τοῖς μαθηταῖς δόξαν, οὐκ ἀλήθειαν πορίζεις· πολυήκοοι γάρ σοι γενόμενοι ἄνευ διδαχῆς πολυγνώμονες εἶναι δόξουσιν, ἀγνώμονες ὡς ἐπὶ τὸ πλῆθος ὄντες καὶ χαλεποὶ ξυνεῖναι, δοξόσοφοι γεγονότες ἀντὶ σοφῶν.

Theuth, the Father of Letters

SOCRATES Writing, Phaedrus, has this strange quality, and is very like painting; for the creatures of painting stand like living beings, but if one asks them a question, they preserve a solemn silence. And so it is with written words; you might think they spoke as if they had intelligence, but if you question them, wishing to know about their sayings, they always say only one and the same thing. And every word, when once it is written, is bandied about, alike among those who understand and those who have no interest in it, and it knows not to whom to speak or not to speak; when ill-treated or unjustly reviled it always needs its father to help it; for it has no power to protect or help itself.

SOCRATES The word which is written with intelligence in the mind of the learner, which is able to defend itself and knows to whom it should speak, and before whom to be silent.

PHAEDRUS You mean the living and breathing word of him who knows, of which the written word may justly be called the image.

SOCRATES The gardens of letters he will, it seems, plant for amusement, and will write, when he writes, to treasure up reminders for himself, when he comes to the forgetfulness of old age, and for others who follow the ...
he will be pleased w...
putting fo...
engage in...
themselve...
entertainm...
such pleas...

PHAEDRU...
and a co...
the pastim...
amusemen...
about jus...
which you...

ΣΩΚΡΑΤΗΣ δεινὸν γάρ που, ὦ Φαῖδρε, τοῦτ' ἔχει γραφή, καὶ ὡς ἀληθῶς ὅμοιον ζωγραφίᾳ. καὶ γὰρ τὰ ἐκείνης ἔκγονα ἕστηκε μὲν ὡς ζῶντα, ἐὰν δ' ἀνέρῃ τι, σεμνῶς πάνυ σιγᾷ. ταὐτὸν δὲ καὶ οἱ λόγοι· δόξαις μὲν ἂν ὥς τι φρονοῦντας αὐτοὺς λέγειν, ἐὰν δέ τι ἔρῃ τῶν λεγομένων βουλόμενος μαθεῖν, ἕν τι σημαίνει μόνον ταὐτὸν ἀεί. ὅταν δὲ ἅπαξ γραφῇ, κυλινδεῖται μὲν πανταχοῦ πᾶς λόγος ὁμοίως παρὰ τοῖς ἐπαΐουσιν, ὡς δ' αὕτως παρ' οἷς οὐδὲν προσήκει, καὶ οὐκ ἐπίσταται λέγειν οἷς δεῖ γε καὶ μή. πλημμελούμενος δὲ καὶ οὐκ ἐν δίκῃ λοιδορηθεὶς τοῦ πατρὸς ἀεὶ δεῖται βοηθοῦ· αὐτὸς γὰρ οὔτ' ἀμύνασθαι οὔτε βοηθῆσαι δυνατὸς αὑτῷ.

ΣΩΚΡΑΤΗΣ ὃς μετ' ἐπιστήμης γράφεται ἐν τῇ τοῦ μανθάνοντος ψυχῇ, δυνατὸς μὲν ἀμῦναι ἑαυτῷ, ἐπιστήμων δὲ λέγειν τε καὶ σιγᾶν πρὸς οὓς δεῖ.

ΦΑΓΡΟΣ τὸν τοῦ εἰδότος λόγον λέγεις ζῶντα καὶ ἔμψυχον, οὗ ὁ γεγραμμένος εἴδωλον ἄν τι λέγοιτο δικαίως.

ΣΩΚΡΑΤΗΣ οὐ γάρ· ἀλλὰ τοὺς μὲν ἐν γράμμασι κήπους, ὡς ἔοικε, παιδιᾶς χάριν σπερεῖ τε καὶ γράψει, ὅταν δὲ γράφῃ, ἑαυτῷ τε ὑπομνήματα θησαυριζόμενος, εἰς τὸ λήθης γῆρας ἐὰν ἵκηται, καὶ παντὶ τῷ ταὐτὸν ἴχνος μετιόντι, ἡσθήσεταί τε αὐτοὺς θεωρῶν ...

Letters

THE COWS DON'T LOOK UP

Jack pulled up to the gate. Since the Signal from Space had been leaked, the site had returned to what Daniel, with some truth, jokingly referred to as its 'wartime footing' – Jodrell Bank of late was less a science outreach project and more a top secret research operation, with all the heightened security measures that that entailed. The main gate was now patrolled by unobtrusively armed men, and the press were corralled behind a hastily thrown-up barrier that put the car park and a screen of trees between the Rotunda and their telephoto lenses. He'd always felt that the security here was more suited to a military base than a civilian installation anyway, and had to remind himself that the Lovell Telescope had a very real military history: observations of Russian satellites made here during the Cold War had been shared with the US Department of Defense's *Project Space Track.*

Jodrell Bank, like Daedalus Base, had always served a dual purpose.

He still had his old security pass, and without preamble showed it to the man in a simple uniform who came forward to meet him. One glance at his photo, his face, and the slightest of nods. "You're expected. West Campus conference room. Follow the signs."

Jack knew exactly where the West Campus conference room was. In his time working as a consultant he'd attended many meetings there, though he'd had access to only a small portion of the site: the underground laboratories and the supercooled detectors were out of bounds, even to some of the indentured scientists. He realised he shouldn't find this surprising – even within the site there were undoubtedly circles within circles, people who knew just enough to do their jobs and those who knew more.

The campus was spread over seven main buildings, the earliest a renovated manor house in which the chairman had his office and in whose ballroom the occasional dance was held. Around this clustered an architectural mish-mash of corrugated iron sheds, functional but unattractive '60s concrete boxes with flat roofs and high thin windows, and an archipelago of more recently built Portakabins. There was the Rotunda, the Pavilion Café and the new visitor centre, whose main purpose (he was reliably told) was to give the curious something to do other than roam the site unaccompanied. Daniel joked that the whole also served as an exhibition of the decline of civic architecture.

The main event, of course, was the huge 240-metre Lovell Telescope radio dish. An enormous steel crescent moon held aloft by an intricate latticework of girders, it loomed majestically over a field in which uninterested cows grazed, never thinking to look up. Jack had always liked the incongruous juxtaposition of cutting-edge technology and traditional farming practices which had remained unchanged for centuries.

In one way, it seemed entirely appropriate: looking out into the Universe also meant looking back in time. The signals the dish received could have journeyed for many millions of years before they arrived here on Earth, making these cows a recent evolutionary innovation by comparison. We see the Universe as it *was*, not how it *is*.

Jack pulled up in front of Building 6. There was a small overgrown space marked out for four cars; only one other space was taken. A permit sticker in the window bore the site's logo, a crescent dish with a star floating over it that some overzealous religious group had once petitioned to be changed. In the end, a PR company stepped in to organise an open-day meet-and-greet and a tour of the site, and sanity, in this instance at least, prevailed.

Jack was met at the door by a heavy-set man he didn't recognise in a fitted suit that did little to conceal his firearm. Before he could say anything, Daniel Novák stepped out from the corridor behind him and extended a hand.

"Hey, Jack. Thanks for coming at short notice. Do excuse the bouncers. After the White leak, we've been asked to step up security. Joe – make yourself useful – can you get two coffees from the café?"

Joe looked unsure about what he should do. "Go *on* – we'll be right here when you get back."

He jogged off across the car park with his loose earpiece flapping behind him, one hand on the bouncing weight in his holster to stop it bruising his ribs.

Jack turned his attention back to his old colleague. "No problem. Happy to help. I do kind of miss this place."

"You shouldn't. Miss it, I mean. This way." Daniel led him along a short corridor that ran the length of the '70s Portakabin, stopping to rattle the handles of a couple of locked doors. The third opened onto a space equipped with four tables that had been pushed together in the centre of the room. Strip lighting blinked on behind a suspended ceiling in which sections of what Jack was sure was asbestos tile had fallen out, revealing cables and a glimpse of grey sky beyond. Across to the left, a row of windows gave a panoramic view of the back of the toilet block. Orange and grey plastic chairs were stacked against the opposite wall.

"Secrets rarely escape in physical form these days. I'm not sure who he hopes to catch. I could have one of those rotating hollow heels, and no one would know. Anyway, sorry for all the subterfuge. Much as I trust you, the higher-ups don't like having any more holes in the colander than they absolutely have to. It's just simpler if this material I'm going to show you doesn't leave the site."

"Eyes only?"

"Eyes only. Exactly. So – you saw the preliminary stuff we sent you."

"I did."

Daniel pulled out a couple of chairs. The second was firmly attached to the one under it. After a few moments of shaking in which they refused to separate, Daniel shrugged. "Please, take a high-chair." Jack sat. Daniel pulled the first around the other side of the table. He experimentally wiped the surface of the desk with his palm, looked at the dust on it, placed his laptop in the space he'd just cleared and lifted the screen.

He pointed at a scatter graph. "Tell me what you see."

Jack leaned in, the chairs shifting under his weight. "You already showed me these, remember?"

"Indulge me."

Jack indulged him. "This isn't a radio signal. Not electromagnetic – this is a chemical trace, a modulated pheromone. Density as a percentage on a scale down the left—"

"And this?"

"And this is a – well, when you first sent me this one, I thought it was a bunch of sea anemones. All waving their tentacles around." Jack waved his fingers around his head, by way of demonstration. "My first hunch was that it was some kind of sign system. From what I can make out."

"Interesting."

"Look, don't get all gnomic with me. These readouts. Where are they from?"

"Jack – where, closer to home, does Jodrell Bank point its nose?"

"The Voyager probe? Cassini? New Horizons?"

"No, no. And no. You know Daedalus Base?"

"Far side of the Moon? Of course I do. I did have clearance, remember? So, what, they've picked up *another* signal from space?"

"In a manner of speaking."

"So these are *alien?*" Jack looked at Daniel dubiously. "Really? They don't look like radio signals. I don't get it. What are you telling me here?"

Daniel raised one eyebrow.

"Dan, this is not an electromagnetic signal. This is not radio. You'd need to be in close proximity to pick up pheromones . . ." Jack trailed off.

"Indeed you would."

Jack broke into a broad grin. "There are aliens on the *Moon?* You've got to be kidding me. On the far side? No way. There's nothing there. It's airless and barren. Craters and rocks. I know this, you know this, we've known it since the Russians sent back photos in fifty-nine."

"Photos that were famously picked up here, by this very telescope, and hit the front page of the *Daily Express* before they hit Brezhnev's desk."

Boy's Own stuff.

"You are, of course, correct on all counts, Jack. The Moon is barren. But what I'm showing you here is not *from* the Moon."

"Go on."

"Eight months ago, the Deep Space Network picked up an object just beyond the orbit of Neptune, moving at an appreciable portion of the speed of light."

Jack's attention was now focused one hundred per cent on Daniel and what he might be about to reveal. He forgot to breathe.

"It was moving so fast that in a matter of hours we had enough information to plot a trajectory. It was going to collide with Jupiter's moon Europa."

"Hang on. I remember reading about the ice volcanoes. Those weren't ice volcanoes, were they?"

"No. The object went straight through Europa and out the other side."

"Fuuuck."

"Not the term I used, but yes."

"And it was still intact? An asteroid, a Kuiper Belt object or a comet—"

"Would not have survived. It was not an asteroid or a comet."

"There's more, isn't there?"

Daniel grinned. "There is. As the object approached the orbit of Mars, it began to decelerate—"

"Hang on. This thing is falling at speed towards the Sun. How does it manage to slow down?"

Daniel was holding up his hand. "We asked ourselves that very question. *How.* Nothing natural would behave like that. So, we now have a new trajectory. One that slingshots this thing around the back of the

Sun, well within the orbit of Mercury, and out again into the inner Solar System. And at this point, there was no longer any doubt. The final destination was Earth."

Jack's eyes were wide.

"Now, remember, this is all happening very quickly. There's no time to even discuss the ramifications. If this thing is going to arrive, it'll be here in a matter of hours. It's moving *way* too fast for Daedalus to deflect. Ah— forget I said that." Daniel made a slicing motion with his palm across his neck. "Anyway – all we can do is watch.

"Then, just when we're bracing for the inevitable, something comes between us and almost certain disaster.

"The *Moon*. The object hits the far side of the Moon at an enormous velocity, almost dead centre."

"Dead centre – close to Daedalus Base."

"Precisely."

Daniel brought up an image on his laptop. A perfect black circle, superimposed over the uniform grey of the lunar surface.

"Wow. How many people know about this?"

"Not many. It'd be impossible to find the impact site unless you knew what you were looking for and where to look. The Moon's a big place, covered with circular impact craters – though none look exactly like this."

"So this thing is buried deep in the lunar crust? How deep?"

"Our measurements aren't precise. There's some kind of distortion field that makes it difficult to take accurate readings. But our seismographs tell us maybe as deep as sixty kilometres. On the border with the mantle."

"How many people know about this?"

"I'm not at liberty to say."

"Was Daedalus Base staffed at the time? The shifts—"

"It was. One astronaut, a stopgap caretaker crew between full rotations. Dana Normansson. She agreed to go out and take a closer look. On her own. It so happens that that region of the Moon is riddled with lava tubes. Underground passages. One of the projects the full crew at Daedalus Base were working on was a ground-penetrating radar survey to map their extent. We reasoned we could use them to get her close to the crash site without being seen from orbit. So, quite by chance, we had our reporter at the scene."

"What did she find?"

"An object. What we think is an escape pod, ejected at the moment of impact, which came to rest inside the lower reaches of a lava tube."

"A *ship*. Sixty kilometres . . . that is deep. But – in *theory* – we have access to an alien vessel that is capable of interstellar travel? That's – that's *incredible!*" Jack felt a surge of endorphins. His face was indescribable. Daniel smiled. He was enjoying this.

"And that's not all. In this escape pod, we found an alien."

Jack took in this further revelation. "An alien."

Daniel nodded. Jack sat back, and the stacked chairs shifted again under him. "Did it survive—? It *did*, didn't it? *This* is what you've been showing me here. You've been trying to *talk* to it!"

"Yes. And yes."

"*Ha!* Wow. Whoooeeee." Jack shook his head as if to make sure he was awake. "Hang on. Is this alien connected to the Signal somehow?"

"That was *my* first thought. Now, we surmise the Signal is not a message, as such. It's not a voice or picture transmission. It's *people*. Aliens. Alien people. That's what *you* suggested, and personally, I think you're right. It's the aliens *themselves*."

"Agreed."

"So if they can transmit themselves, why do they also need to come in person? It makes no sense. It seems to me that the entities in the Signal and this real, physical alien are not the same thing. Different technologies. Different species, perhaps. Of course, we have no idea what the aliens in the Signal actually *look* like, so it's impossible to know for sure. However, the vector of the ship's arrival, assuming a fuel-efficient trajectory and allowing for gravitational bending, takes it back out along the plane of the Milky Way. The direction we calculate it came from is away from the Galactic Centre, out towards the rim, possibly beyond the Orion Arm and even the Perseus Spur. There is no obvious point of origin, no star system we know of placed precisely on this vector, but I'm sure you can grasp the degree of guesswork here; the error bars are huge. It's like trying to work out where you started your journey on the evidence of your last left turn into the driveway. But this we do know – the ship and the Signal, they both came from the same direction. Out towards the edge of the Milky Way."

Jack nodded, but remained silent. Daniel continued. "Again, that doesn't necessarily mean they've been sent by the same race. One may be *following* the other. Assuming the same origin, and factoring in the difference in arrival time – flight-time of ship versus Signal – we have a couple of possibilities. One: the ship set off many years prior to the message; the message, travelling at the speed of light, overtook it in flight and arrived first. Second: the ship left *after* the Signal was sent, and travelling at very nearly the speed of light arrives here soon after the Signal.

The second scenario requires a speed-of-light – or very close – propulsion system. Given that the ship crashed into the far side of the Moon—"

"Hang on, Dan. This happened . . . ?"

"Three months ago. We – the exobiology working group, already convened here to look into the Signal – have been on it ever since."

"Where's Dana now? Can I speak with her?"

"You can speak with her. That's why we asked you here."

"She's here, at Jodrell?"

Daniel raised an eyebrow. "No. Not here, on Earth – she's still up *there,* on the Moon.

"For three months, we've been trying to have a conversation with a creature from another world, and we've utterly failed. My inviting you here now, Jack, this is me clutching at straws. I had to personally vouch for you to people— well, people I'm sure you've heard of at the highest levels who have taken a great interest in this. They want answers. I said you might be able to get them."

Jack exhaled audibly. "*Three months.* And this alien – it's still up there too?"

"It's not going anywhere. The vehicle it rode in on is embedded deep in the Moon, so deep it's beyond our capabilities to reach. The escape pod has no drive, no means of propulsion of its own, as far as we are aware. It's encased in a bubble, a barrier of some kind that we can't penetrate."

Jack said it out loud, just to make it feel more real. "There's an alien on the Moon. *Right now.*"

"Yes, yes there is. And unfortunately I don't think we have much time left. Dana is certain it's dying."

[illegible]

[illegible]

223|342 » [illegible]

[illegible]

424|457 » [illegible]

[illegible]

‡ [illegible]

* * *

933|1023 »
ƨVƧ ǫVO

1106|1221 »
Vꝺⱦ· ƧⱯⱯⱯ
YOYⱯⱯVNI
ǫVⱯⱦ Ɏⱦ

Ꞵ   Ⱡ   Č   Ⱡ   ƨ

Kazimir Malevich
Black Square, 1915
Oil on canvas, 32x32 inches

just experienced.

Harriet read it over, added one more line. *Just to be on the safe side.*

THE FIRE OF '88

Jack followed Daniel through the maze of corridors that connected the disparate buildings of the Jodrell Bank campus. He had questions. Lots of them. "So, we can talk to her? Now?"

"Yes."

"How?"

"Dana has a laptop set up at the crash site. From there, the signal is sent back to Daedalus Base via cables – the density of the lunar rock and the depth of the cave system makes radio impractical – and then, via the main communications antenna, up to our satellite at, or more precisely, orbiting, Lagrange point L2. From there, it's then beamed directly down to the Lovell Telescope, here at Jodrell Bank. Lovell is our ear. A *big* ear, which allows the signal to be precisely targeted and its power output kept to a bare minimum to avoid unwanted spread. Direct, because though encrypted and narrowbeam, we don't want to bounce it around any other receiving stations. We've got the best post-White encryption that our back-room boffins could come up with on this, but a curious radio transmission, even one that can't be broken, might tell certain people that something out of the ordinary is going on up there. Remember those Russian far-side photos? They'd still love to pay us back for that, even now.

"That's the reception. The smaller Mark VII dish, mounted on the roof of the old control room, is our transmitter. Since there's unlikely to be anyone else up there tuning in, we don't have to worry about the return leg. The signal is routed through to our set-up in the Rotunda, where we have . . . Skype, basically."

"*Skype?* The, uh, 'Transmat Ultranode Video Space Telephone Doohickey' is still in beta, one surmises?"

Daniel stopped walking and turned to Jack, holding up both palms in mock surrender. "Sneer all you want. It *will* work. And here, now, that's what matters."

Daniel resumed his pace. Jack took a couple of quick strides to catch up. "OK, that's the how. When?"

"The Moon is currently below the horizon, but we have a window coming up in around an hour's time. But yes. Shortly we'll be Skyping the Moon."

Jack smiled to himself. We inhabit a world where nuclear launch systems really do still run on 7-inch floppy disk. Maybe it had always been this way: it was common knowledge that the gears on which the Lovell Telescope's huge main dish rotated were gun turret racks commandeered from HMS *Royal Sovereign* and HMS *Revenge*.

Make do and mend.

They crossed through the older, deserted laboratories that smelled of grease, cold cast iron and Bakelite. They passed a hangar-sized space filled with mothballed machinery of obscure and obsolete purpose, painted in the ubiquitous Hammerite olive green; Jack glimpsed huge dynamos, now blackened with greasy soot, built to withstand mechanical stresses so large that they were bolted to the concrete floor. Wardrobe-sized cabinets faced with dials and gauges were watched over by semicircular desks fitted with cathode-ray screens and rows of switches and buttons, each connected to a contact or a relay that had not been powered up for a decade or more: the hard-wired, pre-digital interfaces of the man–machine system. Jack was reminded of his old school, another architectural Frankenstein's monster of '30s modernism, Victorian whimsy and '60s concrete brutalism.

And home to the Grey Man.

A final pair of double doors gave onto a bright airy space scented with the newness of sawn plywood, fresh paint and cheap carpet. The hastily convened exobiology department had taken over a section of the glass Rotunda at the centre of the site's new redevelopment, built to showcase commanding views of a new ornamental orrery and the Lovell Telescope itself.

Intended to house a lecture hall, café, and a permanent exhibition detailing the history and work of Jodrell Bank, it was not due to open for another two months, though the fitting and dressing of the exhibits was more or less complete. Protective dust sheets had been thrown over a reproduction Sputnik and an architect's model of the site. A backlit reproduction of Luna 9's historic first photograph of the far side of the Moon was currently in use as a whiteboard. Looking like nothing more than a poor quality fax, the image was crossed with horizontal signal artefacts that gave it an antique analogue charm. Jack felt sure there was now an Instagram filter that could mimic the very same effect: 'Soviet '59', perhaps. The low resolution lent it an ethereal quality; it was just possible to imagine something hiding up there, in the granular shadows, behind a curiously shaped boulder or just over the indistinct horizon. Now that was not far from the truth.

The area housed a junk-shop delirium of mismatched furniture that supported a mix of ageing and top-of-the-range computer kit. Along what was intended to be a coffee bar counter was placed a series of trays that held handwritten notes and printed reports, mostly unread.

Daniel gestured over to an inauspicious desk that had been placed just a bit higher, on a podium intended to hold a scale model of the Lovell Telescope itself. The room, a clatter of voices and activity when Jack had first entered, had fallen into a reverent hush.

Everyone was looking at him. Self-consciously, he took the couple of steps up to the dais and pulled out a '70s office chair. The fabric cover had long since worn away and the bare foam was now criss-crossed with duct tape. One of the castors punctuated the silence with a teeth-jangling squeak. Jack sat down.

Surely Dan Dare had better than this.

Three widescreen monitors faced him, arranged like a vanity table. On the left, coloured lines tracked vital signs Jack could not decipher, numbers blinking in coloured circles below. On the right was a second set, this time recognisable as body temperature, pulse rate, respiration rate, blood pressure and oxygenation levels. Signal strength, represented by an icon that looked like a cross between a WiFi signal and a dish in profile, sat in the top right corner.

Ahead, through the glass curtain wall, Jack could see the huge dish of the Lovell Telescope itself. Though he had seen it many times before, this feat of '50s civil engineering never ceased to give him a thrill. Its upper limb caught the low autumnal light; the complex supporting structure, a cat's cradle of girders, barely appeared strong enough to support its 1,500-tonne bulk. Almost imperceptibly it was rotating, majestically, purposefully.

"We have a basic feed that's coming through the usual channels – still encrypted, but here an absence would be more suspicious than a presence. Hidden in plain sight. When the Moon comes above the horizon in—" Daniel bent over Jack's shoulder and looked at the clock on the screen – "thirty-five minutes, we'll have the uninterrupted full signal. Dana Normansson is at the site now, prepped and ready."

"Dana." Jack practised saying her name.

"Leader of Daedalus' astronomy team. She's been up there alone for the duration. We've concocted a story about a fault with the docking airlock so she won't be disturbed. We're keeping this whole thing under wraps for the moment, both for security and quarantine reasons. We'd normally not send anyone out onto the lunar surface alone without a backup, especially in a novel and unpredictable situation like this. But, if you knew Dana, she's not one for taking the safe or easy option. There was no way she was going to stay put and wait a week for company to arrive. She was suited up and out the airlock the moment the impact site had been identified."

An inactive webcam feed displayed the Jodrell Bank logo, centre-screen. Jack could see his face lower left, lit by the sun through the wide sweep of windows. The interface was a brash muddle of overlaid charts, oscillating waves, scrolling numbers and a real-time diagram of the Earth–Moon system, partly obscured by a BBC News feed. Functional? Perhaps. Beautiful? No.

A colleague named something Hutson – Steve, Stephen, perhaps – gave Jack a rundown of the interface and its basic operation. Jack had actually built a few of the systems himself, but was polite enough not to mention it and to nod throughout. "Any questions?"

"Are we recording this?"

Steve/Stephen pointed to a camera mounted on a tripod, positioned above and behind the screens to the rear of the podium, and another to the right where a clear view of both the screens and Jack could be had. A third had been taped to the escape tower atop a model of the Saturn 5 booster, giving a panoramic view of the entire proceedings. "Three here. And the CCTV. Multiple redundancies on the data backup. We're getting everything, several times over."

"What do we have already? What can you show me?"

"As you can imagine, we've had to repurpose kit that was already up there. We have Dana's helmet-cam footage. Shots from the portable data station."

"We have footage? What does it show?"

Steve/Stephen looked to Daniel for permission.

"Tell him."

"The quality isn't great. We have some better stills. The interference around the spindle degrades the signal, even from the still cameras Dana took to the site on the second trip. She's been back and forth from Daedalus Base, each time bringing new equipment, new software we've written. We've not been able to resolve this. The audio feed, as you'll hear, isn't great either. You'll be able to understand each other, but the quality is dreadful. Our working hypothesis is that it's a side effect of the ship's drive mechanism, which we think may still be active sixty miles down. A localised time–space distortion. It seems to be slowly dissipating, but I don't think we have time to wait. Cabling and lighting have been set up. We'll get the best views we can."

"Show me the stills." A tablet was handed over. Jack flicked back and forth through several images. Murky. Indistinct. Though all manner of image-enhancement tricks had been used on them, the pixelated shapes were more a subject for flights of fancy than sober analysis. *The Face on Mars, shapes in clouds* . . . we are all prone to see things in the dark, things which aren't really there.

Except this time. This time, there *was* something there.

Jack flipped the image. It was an artist's trick he'd picked up from Nadine, the digital version of holding up a mirror to a painting in order to see it afresh. Upside-down. Jack brought up a brightness and contrast slider. Outside of this present context these images would be too indistinct to support much speculation. They were certainly not the smoking gun of the conspiracy theorists' wet dreams, more a Rorschach blot, a window into the mind of the viewer. Jack was somewhat disappointed.

"So what am I looking at here?"

Another of Daniel's colleagues leaned in. "Hi – Leonie Orlov." A thread of black hair fell forward, was tucked back behind an ear. A hand was proffered, which he shook absently. His eyes did not leave the screen.

"Leonie. Tell me what you see."

"Here – we think that's the spindle. The escape pod." She indicated a lighter vertical streak that cut through the right side of the second frame. Jack would have been inclined to assume it was another Luna 9-style signal glitch. "There's a triad of bright spots here – we think that's the reflections from the lighting rig, bouncing off this, uh, bubble of force that surrounds the spindle. The way they move from frame to frame seems to support this. We're very much relying on Dana's detailed verbal reports."

Jack nodded. "This?" He pointed at a darker area towards the bottom of the image.

"That's the hole in the floor. The main body of the ship continued on its previous course, deep into the lunar mantle. Our working hypothesis is that the bubble, which is centred on the spindle, is intended to act both as a kinetic force absorber, an airbag if you like, and also provide the alien with a breathable environment."

"Right." Jack felt like he was in a lecture for which he had not read the course notes, and needed to back up, start from the beginning. "Do we have other imagery?"

"Those are the clearest." Leonie navigated to a folder. "These, they're from further out so are less affected by the signal degradation, but they don't show the artefact itself." She brought up other stills, but none of them gave him much more to go on. In one, a sweep of scoured basalt was visible, brightly lit and close to the camera; in another, the back of a spacesuit glove, an overexposed shot of stubby fingers and the outline of a wrist interface, the information on which was washed out by the harsh contrast.

"Play me the moving footage."

Leonie leant in again and typed a short sequence of keystrokes. Another window came to the fore. "This is standard-format helm-cam footage. Bear in mind the helm-cams are only intended as backup in case of an emergency. They're not designed to record high-def, and they're certainly not intended to work in lightless enclosed spaces. They're primarily for daytime lunar surface excursions. Much of what you see here might be processing artefacts caused by the vicious compression needed to accommodate the tiny data rates we have, and all that has been exacerbated by overenthusiastic post-processing – mostly edge detection – to try and bring out details. We stripped out the biometric information that usually overlays the feed, so we can see what's what." A pause. "Here. I've run this back and forth. The time signatures correlate with Dana's reports, her descriptions. In as much as anything as indistinct as this could do, it backs up her version of events."

"So, first things first. Does it pose any danger?"

"Unlikely. It's not in any position to threaten us here on Earth. It's marooned, encased in its life-support system, which it cannot leave. We have no idea what it eats, *if* it eats, how it absorbs sustenance – any foodstuffs we have here on Earth are almost guaranteed to make it very ill, or more likely kill it. There's an entire exobiology department looking into this very issue as we speak, but those guys had only been thinking in the most abstract theoretical terms before this. They certainly have no practical culinary or first-aid skills they can break out for emergencies. The atmosphere over there is a mixture of unbridled fascination and desperate race against time. Unfortunately, the consensus is that we have a dying extraterrestrial up there who we have no way of helping."

There was a pause that was almost reverential.

Leonie finally broke it. "No one knows this more keenly than Dana."

Daniel was looking out the window, where the crescent moon would soon be rising. In astronomical terms it was just next door, but in practical terms an impossible 384,000 miles away. Up there, right now, a human and an alien who had travelled a far greater distance were trying to bridge a language gap that might as well have been even larger still.

Even if communication was possible, when you have a vanishing window of opportunity to pose some of the most important questions humanity has ever had the chance of finding answers to, what do you ask?

There was a thread on the exobiology unit's intranet. On it were a couple of hundred suggestions, all posted in the first hour or so of Dana's news breaking. Some were obvious: 'Where are you from?' 'Why are you here?' 'How many alien races are there out there?' 'Are they friendly?' 'Hostile?' 'What is your home planet like?' 'Your culture, your art?' 'On what principles does that ship of yours work?' 'How do you reproduce?' Some more specialised: 'How does gravity fit into a quantised model of space-time?'

If *you* were making a list, what would *you* want to know?

Jack spoke the thought aloud. "What would you ask a real, actual alien?"

Daniel's gaze returned to Earth. "Is there a god?"

Jack snorted involuntarily. *"Hah.* Be *serious.* When you ask 'Is there a god?' you're really asking 'Does *it* have a god?' Even if it did, we have people down here that are convinced their gods exist too. No, what we need to know is: *Why* did you come?"

"Curiosity?" Leonie offered.

"Maybe it just wants to share its knowledge with us? For the benefit of all. Is that too naive and optimistic?" Daniel's expression was almost hopeful.

Jack smiled. "No. No, it's not. And perhaps our guest has much it'd be more than happy to share with us, if it had the means to do so. But just look at the circumstances. First the Signal. Then an ambassador from elsewhere who manages to collide with the Moon. Did the second come to warn us about the first? Or the other way around, perhaps? Call me a pessimist, but this emphatically does not have all the makings of something that has been carefully preplanned by some benign galactic peace council given the delicate job of overseeing first-contact scenarios."

Silence. Jack felt obliged to elucidate. "Before I worked here, I travelled. A lot. I was fascinated by the intricate cosmologies of different cultures – there is a richness of detail in many creation myths that makes the Big Bang sound like a pale plotless apology by comparison. Where's the drama? Where are the warring families, the jealous and spiteful demigods, the just and pure bringers of light?"

Daniel started to say something, but Jack didn't give him the space. "Many indigenous South American peoples have legends of a strange visitor with a beard of feathers. He's called Tamu or Zune in the Caribbean, or Bochica in the mythology of the Muisca culture, which lived in what we'd now call Colombia or Panama. The Incas have Viracocha, who came from the East bringing wisdom. He eventually left, walking away across the Pacific Ocean – on the water, classic god move, that – never to return. When Pizarro and his Conquistadors turned up, these Europeans were assumed to be these gods, returned. The Spanish, of course, pressed the advantage, wiped out the local culture, and installed Catholicism in its place so they could magnanimously offer the locals everlasting life. When you have someone's best intentions at heart, it's so much easier to relieve them of their gold with a clear conscience."

"And where is this history lesson going?"

"Bad as all this was, it wasn't the end of it. The most devastating blow to pre-Columbian culture had already been set in motion, silently, and without gunfire and crosses, flags and uniforms. European invaders unleashed a smallpox epidemic that some epidemiologists think may have killed as much as ninety per cent of the Incan population. They had no immunity."

"The quarantine procedures—"

"The Moon is the best isolation chamber we could wish for. For that we can be grateful. But the point I'm making is that any successful invasion isn't just physical, or even biological. It's *memetic*." Jack looked down at a drying puddle of tea on the dusty desktop. Cup rings and fingerprints had scuffed the surface into a good approximation of some cratered alien landscape. Wells' Mars perhaps, populated by his Martians: creatures of intellect 'vast and cool and unsympathetic.' They were finally defeated by microscopic creatures against which they had no defence: a kind of Earthly autoimmune response. Jack had an intuition that what they might need very soon was something similar; something that, if necessary, would protect them from alien *ideas*.

Something that would, by necessity, be made of ideas *itself*.

Themselves.

With a stroke of his hand he wiped the surface clean.

Jack's gaze alighted on the Dan Dare pin holding Daniel's tie in place. Daniel's science fictional dreams were of a much more benign stripe: a good old British knuckle sandwich to the Mekon's jaw, and we'll all be back at Space Fleet Headquarters for debriefing and a single-malt whisky by teatime. For Jack, this childhood souvenir now represented a naive optimism that might be completely at odds with unfolding events.

Daniel put a coffee cup to his lips, realised it was empty but for a cold residue of grouts, and put it back down again. "There is another possible explanation."

Jack noticed his tone was more reflective. "Go on."

"Some years back, I was asked to give a series of lectures at the Institute for Condensed Matter Theory at the University of Illinois. I had a few days to spare, so I took a Jeep into Yellowstone. The road was not much more than a dirt track – rocks, moss, two parallel ruts in the ground. A shadow passed over me. I thought it must be a plane – but it was a flock of birds, denser than I had ever seen before. Then came the elk and the deer. Passing across the road on both sides of me, oblivious to my presence. I stopped the Jeep – I dared not drive any further in case I hit something. Stepping out, I became aware that the road *itself* seemed to be moving. It was a dense carpet of bugs, all travelling in the same direction: south. A big grizzly crossed right in front of me without a glance in my direction. Ten minutes later, ash came raining down on the car. It was the big forest fire of '88. You must have heard about it on the news, even over here. I turned the Jeep around and drove south as fast as I could. Seven hundred thousand acres burned for more than three months before it was under control."

Daniel looked out across the room. "Predator and prey, running side by side before the coming conflagration."

Outside the Rotunda, the vast dish of the Lovell Telescope had come to rest, pointing horizontally across the fields, away to the horizon. From Jack's perspective, he could picture it as a giant planet, hanging low in the sky; it had an imposing sense of weight and presence, like Jupiter viewed from Europa, perhaps. In the gap just below the dish, above the crab apples in the arboretum, bleached by the back-scattered light of Sheffield, the Moon had risen.

It was one of those rare times when Jack could almost feel the world turn under him, spinning to the east at a rate of one revolution every twenty-four hours. Across a gulf greater than he would ever travel, but still the smallest of distances on cosmological scales, was a second world: our Moon, the pair locked together in a slow waltz, she always facing her partner. The Moon, who had unhesitatingly placed her back between the Earth and this interloper from the unknown in order to protect us, and under whose skin events that would have consequences Jack could only guess at were now unfolding.

An icon appeared on the screen. A link had been established. The two bodies were now connected by an invisible thread, and down that thread came information.

Inside the circular Rotunda was a smaller concentric circle: the raised dais upon which Jack, Leonie, Steve/Stephen and Daniel were intently watching the three main monitors, each carrying an identical live feed.

Circles within circles, wheels within wheels.

Jack looked around at the sweep of screen-lit faces.

A pulsing circle changed from red to green.

Daniel tapped in a command. "The uplink's online. We're ready."

There was a prickle at Jack's temples.

"OK. Let's take a look at the Man in the Moon."

BUBBLE UNIVERSE

382,000 miles away and 2.56 seconds into the past, a telepresence drone followed the loneliest human in the cosmos along a lunar lava tube. Fitted with proximity detectors and programmed to keep a certain distance, it had a small degree of autonomy and provided a stable base for the camera and comms. She had made this trip to and from Daedalus Base many times in the last few months; sections of colour-coded cable, stripped from the outlying mirrors and spliced together every 500 metres, now covered the route like an airport wayfinding system. She was certain her commute to work was unique.

Watching on the monitors at Jodrell Bank, Jack could see the bobbing sweep of Dana Normansson's helmet light as it flitted from outcrop to floor to boulder. It alighted on an overhang of deeply chiselled rock that Leonie had noticed during a previous excursion. She was now pointing out certain features and discussing them excitedly with another colleague, a vulcanologist Jack had not been introduced to. Another story, he reflected, this one written in stone, detailing the Moon's geological past; an open book, but only for those who spoke the language of sediment, basalt, and impact stress.

Signs and symbols, and the ability to read them. It always came down to signs and symbols.

Jack adjusted the colour gain and contrast. A short delay, and the picture became incrementally clearer. Best to just trust the automatic systems. The drone followed her progress, up and over boulders, ducking in places where the roof swooped low. They followed the cables, curving along the floor of the tube or looping across gaps, in places hung from the walls by impact brackets, in others crossing empty caverns too big for the lights to fill.

Finally the walls opened up one last time, a curtain parting on a final act, and the drone passed into the chamber in which the spindle had come to rest. Dana thought of this as the liminal space normally hidden from the audience's view, the stage that can be here, there or anywhere depending on the needs of the story; all it took were gifted actors to spin a convincing semblance of reality within it. Dana wished someone had leaked her the script.

This time an audience had been invited in with her. Since that first trip she had set up the portable night-work floodlights, a small desk beside which was mounted a camera on a tripod, the seismometers, and the data recording station, all just outside the bubble's perimeter.

The camera now rolled continuously, sending a feed back to Daedalus Base and from there, via Lagrange, to Jodrell Bank. The data station, primarily designed to measure gas and radiation levels in the ambient lunar environment, was not ideally suited for the job to which it had been repurposed. However, it was equipped with infrared and basic organic sensors, and could sniff the extremely attenuated atmosphere and provide running reports.

It was still there, just as Dana had left it. The loops of connecting sinew strung between its curved carapace and the capsule's interior seemed greyer and stiffer. It turned towards her as she drew closer. Its movements were noticeably slower and more deliberate. A mottled rash had begun climbing the left flank of what she thought of as its face.

Though she had the best exobiologists available advising her, she had no idea what, if any, help she could provide. Food? Medicine? She knew nothing about the creature's dietary needs. Even if she could step inside the bubble, which might be the only thing protecting it from the near vacuum of the lunar environment, she had no idea what she might do next. The Moon was inhospitable to humans, and there was no reason to think that it, or the Earth-normal atmosphere back at Daedalus for that matter, would be any more welcoming to this creature. She had resigned herself to recording as much as she could in the time they might have left.

She tethered the drone to a leg of the desk. It hovered there like an attentive fairground balloon. The alien shifted. A pallid light could be seen darting around its head. It was aware of her presence.

"Can you move in closer? Give us a better look?" That was Daniel, in her earpiece. "We have someone new here today. Jack Fenwick is going to be observing. He has expertise in data analysis and semiotics. Language. He may have some insights." The sound quality, as always, was not good. There was a short delay, as of a poor mobile connection.

"Sure. Hi, Jack. Welcome to the zoo."

Jack looked for a microphone. Daniel pointed to a small foam bud on a stalk. "Hello, Dana. This is, um, incredible. I— I'm happy just to tag along. Daniel's running the show. So. Carry on. Uhm. Thanks."

Daniel swung the mic around. "Jack's been looking at the material you've sent, trying to make sense of it. He has full clearance. You can talk to him openly. How do you feel, in yourself? Are you still getting those disorienting headaches?"

Pause.

"I can deal with them. I don't think they're intentional. If it wanted to really harm me, I'm sure it could have done so by now. Right. Word of advance warning. I'm about to take a few, uh, calculated risks. I need to try a few things."

She stepped closer. The bubble was now just an arm's reach away. Unclipping a soil sampler from her belt, she extended it before her. "I'm going to probe the field. My previous investigations lead me to think that it's non-conductive, and that I'll be protected through my suit." She seemed to be saying it aloud more to convince herself than assert a fact. Daniel looked around at the faces nearest to him, seeking some kind of confirmation. Shrugs. Gesticulation. "Uh. We *think* you'll be OK. Please proceed with caution. You're a very long way from a hospital."

She held out the probe, moved forward until the end of it lightly touched the bubble. A refractive shudder of rainbow colours, like petrol on a disturbed puddle, appeared around the contact point, then quickly dissipated. She pushed harder. This time the result was more pronounced. She pushed to the limit of her strength, but the probe would not penetrate the barrier.

She reached out.

"Dana— careful!"

She'd already put a gloved hand to the surface before the cautionary message reached her. The same multicoloured light display silhouetted her fingers, and she felt a sensation like a loss of blood circulation, a barely detectable ache.

She pushed.

There was no appreciable give whatsoever. Solid. Impassable.

Jack had an idea. "Can you send the drone around the other side? So the bubble is between you and one of the floodlights?"

Pause.

"That may be difficult to do for anything but a shallow angle. There's not a lot of room to manoeuvre down here. I'll move one of the floods as close to the point where the bubble intersects the far wall as I can, and send the drone over to the other side. Let me know if that works for you."

She did so. The creature tracked her with a small egg-shaped protuberance as she went.

"OK, stop. Thanks. Perfect. Please press the bubble with the soil probe again. We'll analyse the light as it passes through."

"Dana? Did you get that?"

Pause.

Dana complied. A sparkle of coruscating light again spread from the point of contact, dissipated.

Daniel looked around the room. "Leonie? Atmospherics? Pressure? What can we deduce, if anything?"

A pause, this one not due to signal time lag, then four of those present darted back to their desks. There were a few more moments in which all Jack could hear were keyboard taps. "The floods are not a controlled light source, of course, but making a few educated guesses – refraction suggests high pressure within the bubble. More than one atmosphere. Can't be precise, but around 1800hPa. That's one and a half, one-point-seven-five times sea level on Earth."

"Sounds plausible for a habitable planet with a solid crust and a breathable atmosphere. Anything else?"

Steve/Stephen spoke up. "Using the refractive index, the absorption signature and some very big assumptions, I'd suggest the air inside may be a high nitrogen, oxygen–argon mix. Traces of benzene or arsenic, judging by the colours. Poisonous, for humans. Oxygen too, though nowhere near breathable levels."

"A life-support system, but not one made for humans."

Pause.

"So I don't want to burst its bubble."

Pause.

"No. Do not burst that bubble."

Dana returned front and centre. *Wait.* The alien . . . Something was happening.

The section on the top of its snout opened and slid back, again revealing the starfish-like splay of short moist tentacles, much like a pair of hands held wrist to wrist. They unfurled, shook to unstick themselves from one another, and turned first in her direction, and then the drone's. Centred between the palms was a deep socket, rimmed with short hairs but otherwise vacant. It dilated, closed, opened again.

She checked the drone was functional. Below it dangled two manipulating limbs, jointed like human arms, each ending in a three-fingered mechanical hand with an opposable thumb. A small selection of optional attachments – drills, scoops, flashlights, sample bags – were attached to a utility belt around the drone's midriff, below the suite of cameras, aerials and dishes that clustered at the top like a floral arrangement. Everything was working. The data was being sent back to Daedalus, encrypted, and from there to the huge radio dish at Jodrell Bank.

"Daniel – I don't think it has very long left. We're running out of time here."

Pause.

Daniel looked at Jack. "What do you think? Do we risk trying to breach the bubble? Assuming we can?"

Jack held up his hands. "Daniel, this is your call. I'm just the code monkey and language nerd. You people here have been watching this unfold for months. You're the ones with experience."

Leonie put her hand on Daniel's shoulder. "Of this?" Her mouth turned up at one corner. "Not so much."

Daniel looked around the room, but there was no more advice to be had. "Dana. Our options are limited. We assume the capsule provides life support, but that can't last indefinitely. We could think about bringing it back to Earth somehow if we could breach the bubble and separate it from the spindle, which is embedded in the rock – that spindle is not going anywhere without heavy lifting equipment. Which we don't have."

They could not see Dana's face, of course, only judge her state of mind from the tone of her voice.

"These are our options. Such as they are."

It's not going to leave this cavern, Dana thought. *This will be its final resting place, its crypt. And I think it knows this.*

"I'm beginning to recognise some of the movements it makes with that fingered thing, the snout. A kind of cupping."

Pause.

"Jack?"

"Daniel, I've been through all this. I simply don't have enough to decipher what it may be trying to say. We'd need a much bigger data set. We'd need more time."

"Dana?"

Pause.

"The shifting colours on the carapace . . . I think it's using multiple channels, and also broadcasting in a manner that the monitors can't pick up. Not telepathy, nothing like that, but I think it can affect my biorhythms in some subtle way, like it did with the display on the tablet. I think it can skim the surface of my mind, and when I think certain things I can feel a, a restriction in my diaphragm, as if some motor response is not entirely under my body's control."

Pause.

"A yes, no, twenty questions, Daniel?"

Pause.

"Give me something to go on, guys. Ideas. Anything."

Jack leaned in to the mic. "Dana – just my guess, but – I think it's beckoning you towards it."

Pause.

"I think—"

There was a sudden explosive decompression. The pressure wave threw Dana hard against the wall of the cavern; her knee bent sideways on impact, pain shot from her ankle. Dust filled the air, cutting her visibility to less than a metre. Even protected inside the suit, her ears had begun to bleed. Her helmet light illuminated a fog of particles and little else. She righted herself. She was deaf and winded, but otherwise unscathed. The suit was unbreached.

On Earth, two-thirds of the screens had gone dark. On them, a small Jodrell Bank logo now spun above a NO SIGNAL caption.

"Dana?"

Pause.

"*Dana?*"

Pause.

"I'm here. I'm OK. Knocked the breath out of me, and my ears are ringing, but I'm OK."

"What happened?"

Pause.

"The barrier dropped."

Pause.

"The bubble? The bubble burst? What did you do?"

Pause.

"Nothing. *It* did this. By itself." The dust was beginning to settle in the low gravity and visibility was improving. The drone had been thrown against a sharp stalagmite of crystalline rock and now lay on its side, immobile. The monitoring station had been slammed right back through the cavern entrance and into the tunnel beyond. She could see pieces of her laptop strewn across the ground. The camera now pointed up at the roof, its lens shunted back into its body at an awkward angle, the legs of the tripod buckled beneath it.

"We still have your helm-cam feed. But nothing else. What is your situation?"

Pause.

"I'm unhurt, but we've lost the drone and the cameras. And the monitoring station. If you have the helmet-cam feed, the cables must have held."

For the first time, Dana could see the spindle clearly, without the distortion of the bubble and the atmosphere it had contained. Its pointed upper section emerged from the pall of disturbed moondust. She stepped forwards.

The creature was in a distressed state. Both of its eyes had burst, and a transparent fluid now dripped down its carapace from the empty sacs. *It must have known this act would blind it.* Dana unexpectedly felt emotion well up, threaten to overwhelm her. *To have come so far . . .*

Without thinking of the possible danger to herself, she walked forward, into the volume previously circumscribed by the bubble. Hesitating only momentarily, she held out her hand. The fingerlike protuberances folded around her glove.

In her gut she felt a breathless constriction, as if something older and far larger than her short human existence had suddenly connected with her at an elemental level. Her mind flashed back to the time she first heard *Night On Bald Mountain* at the Kölner Philharmonie during astronaut training in Germany, and the almost overwhelming wave of emotion she had then felt – not of sadness, or of fear, but an expansive opening up to the numinous and sublime. It was all she could do to prevent her legs from buckling and falling to her knees.

"Dana?"

"Dana, can you hear us?"

Pause.

"I can hear it. It's talking to me."

Pause.

"What's it saying? Dana?"

Pause.

"It has a request. It wants to interface directly with my mind."

Pause.

"What? Please repeat that?"

Pause.

"I think it wants to connect with my—"

2.56 seconds later, at Jodrell Bank, Dana's helmet-cam feed suddenly went dark and her vital signs all dropped to zero.

2.56 seconds earlier, in the caverns of the Moon, the bubble had been restored, with Dana now inside it.

The snout released her gloved hand, tightened into a ball, and opened, fingers outstretched. Dana could see the shimmering field now enveloping her, and through it, distorted as if through a fisheye lens, the smashed drone and the remains of the monitoring station. She brought up her wrist tablet. On it a green circle held, steady.

A breathable atmosphere, more or less. An unbidden thought scooted across her consciousness. *For humans.*

She suddenly understood what she had to do.

She unclasped her helmet. A warning chirped in her earpiece, but she ignored it. There was a short audible hiss as the pressure inside and outside the suit equalised. She lifted the helmet up, over her head.

The stench stole her breath away. A putrid miasma of broken biology overlaid with a metallic tang she could almost taste in the back of her throat. *Heaven knows what kind of organisms I must now be breathing in.* She laid her helmet down on the rubble around the spindle's base. She already knew what was required of her.

The creature was blind. It was now poisoning itself with toxic terrestrial air. She knew that it knew that very soon it would die; but it was grasping the opportunity to make one final gesture.

She knelt down in front of the spindle, brought her face close to the writing tentacles and the orifice at their centre. She looked down, closed her eyes, and leaned forwards.

Her head was caught and cupped, held gently in a cradle of alien fingers.

She felt the warmth of the touch of a creature from another world, and it simultaneously filled her with an intense sadness and an overwheming joy that forced the air from her lungs and blurred her vision with tears.

A door opened in her mind to somewhere else, and without hesitation she stepped through.

BOOK TWO

Exegesis

Nothing is as powerful as an idea whose time has come.
—Victor Hugo, 1852

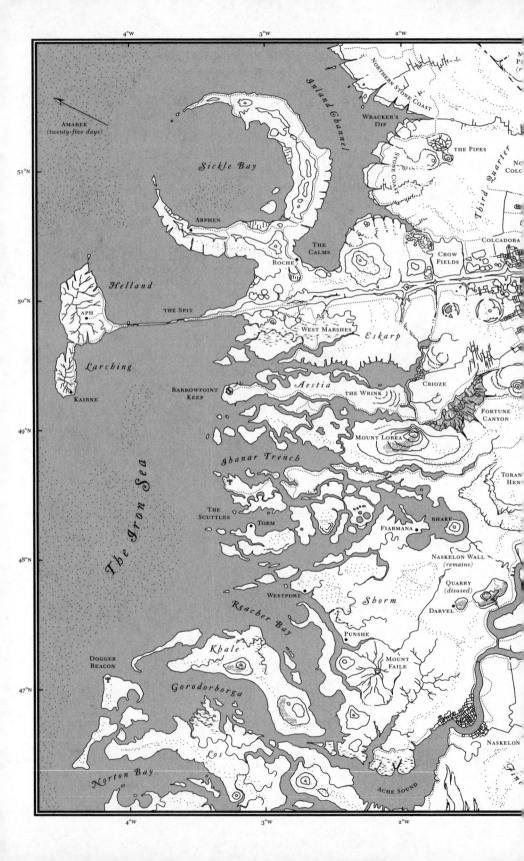

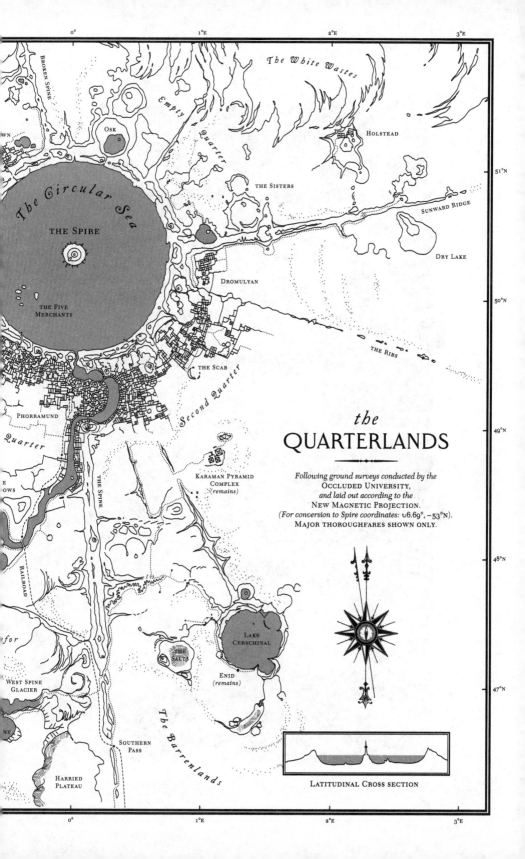

the
QUARTERLANDS

Following ground surveys conducted by the
OCCLUDED UNIVERSITY,
and laid out according to the
NEW MAGNETIC PROJECTION.
(For conversion to Spire coordinates: υ6.69°, –53°N).
MAJOR THOROUGHFARES SHOWN ONLY.

LATITUDINAL CROSS SECTION

ALL STORIES IN THIS ISSUE BRAND NEW

Planetfall

SCIENCE-FICTION   NOVEMBER   2/-

STARTING THIS ISSUE:
ASCENSION
by **HERSCHEL TEAGUE**

KOLHERNE • SALHINO • DELGADO • AITKEN

ASCENSION

by F. HERSCHEL TEAGUE

When the Celestial Mechanic answered the Highmost's

summons, little did he expect to be asked to mount an

expedition into the lands below the Spire, less familiar to

him than the heavens above — and far more alien.

PART ONE

THE CELESTIAL MECHANIC knew, with absolute certainty, that Terrine and everything that lay upon her surface rotated around the Sun. It was not the other way around.

Everything: the Forty-eight Districts that made up the Quarterlands, the Gorodorborga, the Meadows, the five and a half oceans beyond, the white wastes to the north, the Omphalos and even, though keep it dark, *the Spire itself;* but he also knew with just as much certainty

that, in his position, it was unwise to suggest that he entertained such heretical notions. However much the perfumed aristocrats of the upper levels of the Spire might believe otherwise, as astronomical and planetary advisor to the Highmost it was his calling, his position, his job to know the truth about such things, just as it was a matter of social survival to never mention them.

The Highmost. "Born of the weeping-pool, our peerless sage, possessed of the diplomat's soph-

---

A STIRRING NOVELETTE OF STRANGE ALIEN CULTURES IN EIGHT PARTS

istry, the huntsman's mercy, and a deep and noble obligation to the continued well-being of his faithful and loving people", as one of his less able poetical mythologisers had put it. Where had he heard that solemnly recited? During an official address to commemorate the breaking of the ice on the Gasparchould Passage, perhaps? Or a successful harvest, the rising of the Sun, or some other natural event that slipped the Celestial Mechanic's mind but, he had no doubt, the Highmost's much celebrated fortitude of character had no bearing on whatsoever.

Discretion, it need not be stated, was one of the attributes an Advisor needed in limitless supply, and the Celestial Mechanic's powers of discretion were one of the reasons the Highmost had called for him now.

The unelected hereditary head of the system-wide semi-religious order that had been spread by word and swordstaff across the three planets and sixteen habitable moons of the Lacunae system, the Highmost was rarely seen in public these days, for which the Celestial Mechanic was most grateful. He'd say the Gods smiled upon him, but that would imply— well, discretion forbids I continue.

IN AN UNRECORDED age long before the oral traditions had begun, before the First Interregnum – perhaps, even, before the time of the Skybound Beyonders, a heavy bombardment had cratered the surface of the still-cooling planet. The subsequent development of Terrine's native flora and fauna, and the sentient peoples and their cultures that eventually arose there, were deeply informed by this landscape.

The mature Terrine was punctuated by countless small lakes and larger circular seas, formed from these ancient craters which were now infilled with saline water. Many of them were surrounded by high purple-peaked and cloud-hatted mountains, from which first streams and then river systems carried the spring monsoon floods down to the plains below.

A natural feature of many of the larger impact craters was a tall central peak, caused by the slippage of the crater walls and the rebounding of the bedrock in the moments after impact. The largest and most dramatic crater in the more populous hemisphere had at its centre a magnificent spire of fused glassy rock.

Formed some time after the earliest bombardment during an opaque period of prehistory known as the Great Curiosity and Conflagration, this was the seat of the Hierarchy and the ruling elite; a stratified, multi-generational society that had very little if anything to do with the world beyond the Circular Sea and the surrounding mountains. They were only dimly aware of the subsistence farmers and tribal cliques that worked the plains beyond the crater's rim, separated as they were by both distance and caste; and what little they did know was often lost to indifference.

Living on the Spire, a symbolic combination of navel and axis mundi placed at what was considered to be the very centre of

The Spire was the seat of the Hierarchy and the ruling elite

their world, the peak's retinue of serfs, tradesmen, scholars, musicians, painters, perfumiers, tailors, silversmiths, poets, balladeers, scriveners, vintners, fan-makers, procurers, aristocrats and so forth all tacitly or otherwise sustained their strictly ordered society.

Arranged around the base of the spire was a series of radial jetties, each owned by a specific guild, at which the barques carrying foodstuffs and spices, fabrics and sex slaves, would put into port. Under the gargantuan arches that ringed the lowest level and supported the first tier of the Spire, an assortment of marketplaces, taverns, workshops and brothels provided diversion for those of the upper strata who were brave or curious or desperate enough to come down this far. Many, born and bred higher up in the more elevated levels of the Hierarchy, had never ventured down to ground level in their lifetimes, much less taken a boat across the Circular Sea to the crater walls five purloughs distant.

Four majestic staircases, placed at the cardinal points, led from the harbour up to the first level. Here a causeway circumnavigated the Spire, wide enough that two thousand, five hundred games of barollé, a ball game that required a pitch twice the length of an arrow's flight, could be played simultaneously. It was said that if you could run completely around the First Tier in the time it took to roast a Hill Naze, you needed to spend more time working on your rakish dissolution.

Each staircase was topped by a quartzite arch upon which sat carved figures representing the Noble Aspects, the virtues to which every citizen under the Highmost's stewardship was supposed to aspire. Facing out to sea, they judiciously failed to look up, over their shoulders, at the many iniquities that took place daily above.

From this public space, four pairs of elegantly sweeping ramps, each an eighth of the circumference of the Spire, rose gently to the next level, twenty or thirty storeys above. Where the pairs of ramps met, guardhouses raised on pillars sat astride open balustraded squares. Here, visitors were checked, taxes levied, weapons confiscated and bribes taken.

The next tier repeated the pattern: four more pairs of ramps led to the third level, on which the lower classes of merchants, guildsmen and aristocrats of limited means resided. Here, dwellings were built under the enormous arches that had been cut from the bedrock of the spire itself, or built from brick where the natural stone did not provide the symmetry the original, long-forgotten architect had desired.

The natural and constructed surfaces had weathered very differently, giving the edifice the appearance of sun-dappled plaster shaded by a giant tree; but there were no trees of the size required on Terrine.

The ownership of the plot sheltered under each arch was a matter of inheritance and complicated legal precedent; it was generally assumed that at some time in the distant past they had been awarded to favoured clans or families for certain victories or accomplishments in the service of the Spire. Space being finite, the houses under the tall arches had only one way to expand – up. Thus, over the centuries, floor after floor had been added. The space under the arches could accommodate some twenty or thirty storeys on the larger lower tiers, and generations of the same family lived one above the other, the youngest at the bottom and the oldest at the top, just that bit closer to the summit and all that that symbolised.

Outside each flew a tall banner marked off in squares, each containing a crest denoting status, occupation and claims to nobility, both ratified and under dispute.

THE ARRANGEMENT of tiers continued upwards. The wider, more utilitarian levels that were primarily concerned with commerce gave way to fountains and parks, elaborate cantilevered terraces with scalloped cupolas and curvilinear benches on which lovers met in evening assignations. Here one could find vast hedgerow mazes built for the amusement of the flâneur, kiosks selling candied fruit and bunting, and street musicians performing popular odes or re-enacting scenes from current theatrical burlesques. There were carriages pulled by groomed and scented paquards, beasts of burden that farmers outside the crater wall might just recognise as distantly related to their own stout and wiry workhorses, here trained to skip elegantly through the throngs that congregated on the sunlit side of the Spire in clement weather.

The houses set into the arches here were taller and more elegant still, with ornate plasterwork ceilings many storeys high, even though they sometimes only boasted a footprint the size of a barrenlands cottage.

EACH CONSECUTIVE tier was smaller in circumference but taller in height, so at length the ramps became staircases. Forty-five levels up, again at each cardinal point, cantilevered out from the bare rock were three enormous carved granite heads, gazing inscrutably out across the lands. Observers with a knowledge of evolution would have noticed that the heads were of a subtly different set than the Spire's current occupants, who tended towards the effete, chinless and sallow; wearing their hair styled in a fashion unremembered, these stony faces were of an altogether more robust and thoughtful countenance.

The staircases passed behind their empty eye sockets, in each of which was set a small balcony. From here, one could look out across the Circular Sea to the patchwork of lands beyond the Rim as though through the eyes of a deity, which, it was muttered on the lower levels, many of the occupants this high thought themselves to be.

There had originally been four heads, named long after their construction and original purpose had been forgotten, for the four courtesies: Civility, Graciousness, Rectitude and Forbearance. Forbearance, the one facing east (in terrestrial terms) had, some time before the age of the Child Kings, fallen from its position and lodged some dozen tiers below, balefully looking skyward at the gods who had seen fit to banish it to the lower levels.

This state of affairs had been interpreted in many ways, but the most widely accepted was a simple homily: that to look to the sunrise, and hence to the future, was a dangerously unwise proposition. Custom ensured the stability of the culture of the Spire; its pre-eminence was predicated on honouring and respecting the past, while looking occasionally to the sides, left and right, just to keep an eye on what your fellows might be up to. This interpretation – without, it must be said, much encouragement from the Highmost – meant that it long ago had become, if not socially unacceptable, certainly indecorous to celebrate vulgar innovation over the time-worn certainties of tradition.

Further guardhouses at each level carefully filtered out more and more of the population, until the higher tiers, those above the sixty-fifth level, were reserved for the political elite, their inner circle of advisors, and, just above them, the extended royal family.

The circumference of each tier became smaller, the circular promenades narrower, the arches required to circumscribe each tier fewer in number, and the houses set under the arches even more impossibly grand. On their façades, tableaus depicting mythological scenes or narrating notable episodes from family history were executed with such a wealth of silvered bronze and father-of-pearl that it became very hard to make out the actual shape of the building underneath.

Here the staircases became ever more steep, and above the seventy-second tier were replaced by ladders, though those that resided at these elite levels, if they ventured out at all, were carried up and down them more often than they climbed, the thin air and their toneless physiques making exertion difficult.

EVENTUALLY, FAR ABOVE the low clouds of spring and the wheeling and scrawing birds that harried the fisheries, a short spiral of ivory-faced stairs led to a circular plaza with a low balustrade affording vertiginous views across the entire land. Now, in the morning when the lower tiers were shrouded in mist, all one could see below was a soft white expanse which stretched out to meet the golden-rose sky in an indeterminate blur at the horizon. Piercing this, and circling the Spire, could be seen the crenellated tips of the highest peaks of the crater wall; black, unforgiving, and putting the Celestial Mechanic in mind of a Tiberact's rotting incisors.

On a clear day the patchwork of fields beyond the crater wall was visible, the greens and heliotropes lent a subtle orange hue with distance by the attenuated sulphur compounds in the atmosphere. Wisps of grey smoke from small farming settlements cast shadows on the land below, which was overlaid by the shimmering golden threads of the many small tributaries of the Gorodorborga.

This vast river was fed by the largest cut in the crater wall, through which, during the rainy season, a lengthy series of spectacular waterfalls and rapids carried the excess water, rich with volcanic sediment and organics, down to flood the fertile lands below.

The elite of the Spire thought of this as their gift of life to those eking out a living beyond the Rim; it made it all the more equitable and *right* that their beneficence was repaid by the harvest season's tithes. Generosity, so the Celestial Mechanic had been reliably informed, had to be reciprocated.

A BOVE THIS SMALL PLAZA, at the very apex of the Spire, sat a three-storey cupola supported by thirty-two elegant caryatids, each representing one of the original thirty-two families that had come together to share governance over the lands. The cupola was octagonal, each face possessing an ornate kaleidoscopic window of translucent multicoloured shell set in a recessed frame that was also octagonal, and across which gilded arrows rotated to indicate the day, season and tithe times, depending on which face one looked at. For reasons that could only be guessed, these could not be read from anywhere but the three or four highest tiers, and only then at an oblique angle.

Surmounting the cupola was a thin javelin topped with a stylised comet, though no one on Terrine actually called it a comet or had any knowledge of the astronomical principles that made a comet what it was. To them, it represented the Celestial Flame, the original igniter of the their Sun, who came back at regular intervals to check that it still burned.

Access to this highest structure was via a platform, lowered from the centre of the underside of the cupola by a system of weighted pulleys. Four soldiers of the Elite Honour Guard, each wearing the ceremonial feathered peasantskin hat, stood equidistantly spaced around the platform as they always did.

Stopping to rest a moment on this very platform, having climbed the Spire in its entirety, now stood the Celestial Mechanic.

For the sake of convenience he shall be accorded the male pronoun, though the genders on Terrine are somewhat more complicated than the term might suggest. Though capable of fathering offspring, many of the high-ranking individuals of the Hierarchy, at least in the public sphere, viewed this as distasteful – animalistic, even – preferring a more cerebral life of contemplation, the arts, and the servicing of one's intimate companions.

The evolutionary tree of his particular species was complex. Even though the branch of which the Celestial Mechanic was a member was, for all intents and purposes, right at the top of the food chain, several other closely related sentient species were extant in the known realms. Copulation with three of these could give rise to infertile cross-breeds, which lacked intelligence but were useful labour in areas where the packbeasts proved too large or were otherwise unsuited to the terrain, such as the Whestfallin Ice Sheet. Painted and adorned in vibrant colours and trained to strike amusing poses of a morally instructive or decorative nature, they also served as ornaments in the formal gardens of some of the lower aristocracy, a practice the Celestial Mechanic found ostentatiously bourgeois.

These close relatives still possessed traits common to the lower beasts of the animal kingdom, most notable of which was their predictable breeding cycle – they came on heat twice a year. Though not considered comely by Spire standards, they certainly provided diversion for those of a less attractive countenance, or those lacking the required charm or social skills to achieve success with the opposite sex during the usual season of society dances, formal gatherings and festivals.

It was a matter of sport among those inclined to such things to take parties out to the barrenlands and the overlooks during this season to present oneself to the attentions of these insatiable creatures. Certain precautions needed to be taken, of course – it was wise to bring a court eunuch equipped with a scythe or crossbow in case their enthusiasm became dangerous, and certain unguents were required to ward off communicable diseases and unwanted pregnancy should they happen to be in what could be termed the female portion of their gender cycle. For some, the high degree of risk involved was part of the adventure; indeed, the very point of it.

This practice, outwardly at least, was looked down upon by the High Families, their entourages and associates, though it was common knowledge that if you had the right connections discreet invitations to such outings were available.

The Celestial Mechanic also looked askance at such diversions, pretending not to notice the scratches and sometimes more serious souvenirs it was fashionable to display in the quayside taverns, and perhaps in an attempt to add a certain frisson to their comfortably uneventful lives, in some of the younger aristocratic cliques as well.

UNDER the platform was set a rock of irregular outline, flush with the elaborately patterned paving that surrounded it. This was the very tip of the crater's original central peak. It had been carefully cut and the cross-section of pallasite polished to highlight the green crystals in their iron–nickel matrix. Engraved in this, in the ornate court script favoured for funerary and governmental communications, was the motto of the Coming Together of the Thirty-Two Families. In rough translation, it read (though there were very few scholars left who were either learned or interested enough to decipher it) as follows:

To the Stars we look; for they are as numerous and radiant as we, and all are equal before the giver of life, the Sun, to whom we owe our existence.

As he had before on his many previous visits, the Celestial Mechanic had time to read and ponder this somewhat egalitarian screed before the platform descended and covered it completely. What he did not know was that the Highmost, who had been born in the cupola above and had not once in his lifetime descended a single level below the plaza, had never read it; in fact, he was unaware of its existence. It was covered by the platform when he came down to walk around the circumference of an evening, and was only revealed once again as he ascended back into the cupola's underside.

Though few now knew it, the original use of the tower was as an observatory; indeed, the cupola at the peak still housed a telescope. It had once stood here alone, at the very top of the Spire, before a millennium of civic building had come up to meet it.

The Celestial Mechanic was here today because a summons had brought him hence, and because you did not ignore a summons from the Highmost. Discretion required that there were few details; suffice to say that something novel and unsettling had been observed through this telescope, something the Highmost feared might unseat the perfect peace of their perfect society.

Here, on the Spire at the hub of the wheel that was the Circular Sea, that society was the epicentre of the Known and Only Lands, the spindle about which Terrine turned – the axle at the very centre of all things.

To be continued

IN OUR NEXT ISSUE:

Ascension • PART 2 OF OUR NEW SERIAL

PLUS

Corridor to Otherwhen • TRISTAN SHAMBLESTONE
Vescopeds of the Niromad • ELOISE NORTON
Silverback's Faith • IVAR YOUNGBLOOD
Kill All Martians! • CHRISTOPHER BRADFORD
An Alien Glamour • MOLLY LONGYEAR

NEWS • REVIEWS • DEPARTMENTS

The NOVEMBER issue of *Planetfall* is on sale OCTOBER 5TH at your favourite newsstand or direct from the publishers: CHAS. BOXWOOD & CO., ACTON VALE, LONDON W4

PRICE 2/-

GOLCONDA

The relief crew could no longer be delayed. It would take them three days to prep, another three to reach Daedalus. No one expected the news, once they arrived at the scene, to be good.

The consensus was that they had lost Dana.

Jack had stood beside Daniel in silence, watching the dark monitors, for an hour and a half. Losing an astronaut was a rare event – Challenger, Apollo 1 – but Jack could guess what Daniel was thinking: *They should have insisted Dana wait until a relief crew arrived. They should have asked the Koreans for assistance. They shouldn't have allowed her to touch the bubble. They shouldn't have a million things.*

Jack decided there was nothing he could say that would make the situation any better, and possibly a few things that might inadvertently make it worse. He briefly rested a hand on Daniel's shoulder, then went through the Orrery where Leonie was comforting Steve/Stephen, through the gift shop, and let himself out via the main gate.

The work passing through Intelligencia now seemed frivolous to Jack. More than a week had elapsed and he was still trying to process the ramifications of what had happened, make some kind of sense of it all. He was sure Harriet and Nixon could sense his distraction. How much of what he now knew should he share with them? He was bursting to tell them what he'd seen. Daniel had bent all manner of rules and regulations to get him clearance; he had signed NDAs and the Official Secrets Act. Jack didn't want to let him down. He and Daniel went back years, but even so he did wonder if they'd been overly . . . *trusting?* Surely they did extensive background checks. Maybe they'd already had him under surveillance. *Hah.* Even Jack's paranoia didn't stretch that far.

He gave the metal box bolted to the door of the music studio upstairs a wide berth, unlocked the door and deactivated the alarm. As always, he was the first in. Placing an apple, a pint of milk and his Starbucks hot chocolate on the kitchenette counter, he looked around their space. It was, he had to admit, a shambles. More a workshop than an office.

Though Nixon had tried to keep up the appearance of professionalism in the conference room he had commandeered as his office, the collection of cabling, kit and Jack's crates of books and manuals had snuck in there when no one was looking and crept up the walls.

His roll-up mattress and the sleeping bag he used on the occasions he didn't make it back to his apartment, occasions that were becoming more and more frequent of late, were still laid out under his desk. They lent the proceedings a distinct aura of 'homeless shelter'. Jack and Harriet, used to working remotely for people they often didn't meet in the flesh, were less concerned with appearances than Nixon, who was still infatuated with the idea of a Proper Office, one in which he could have Proper Power Meetings like those confident, attractive people in their perfect suits he'd seen in photo library stock catalogues as an impressionable teenager.

A stack of books, magazines and manuals was also growing beside Jack's sleeping bag. This was his bedtime reading: a stapled printout of the original Typex operator's manual he'd found online; a year's run of *Planetfall*, an obscure '60s science fiction magazine he'd bought on eBay; recent issues of *New American Scientist*; a Penguin Classics copy of Plato's *Phaedrus* with a stylised drawing of a man playing the lyre on the cover; a facsimile edition of the Vasari-Edson manuscript; and other obscure papers and books on semiotics and language he was certain he'd never get around to reading.

I wonder . . . Jack stepped over, booted his Mac, and put on the Depth-charges.

He was not alone. There were three others in the room, staring at him intently, almost as if they knew where he'd been. Girl 21 was so close he could see the individual RGB pixels of her current Snapchat selfie.

"*Whoa.* Are you guys here *all* the time?"

We're here when we need to be. *Elsewhere* when we need to be *elsewhere*.
Now, we need to speak with you.

"How do you know I'm even *here*? It's not like I keep office hours."

You can cover your **CAMERAS** in here, dear boy,
but I can see you from **ACROSS THE STREET** *regardless*.
JACK.
Have you *stepped outside* today?

Jack wondered if the 19th Count was taking him to task over his habitual late-night programming sessions, but couldn't imagine his health would be their concern.

"What? Yes, just now. To the Sainsbury's Local. For pastries and milk. Then Starbucks. Why? Did I forget your order?"

"The glasses? No. They haven't left the office."

Maybe one should take them for a *promenade*, dear boy.

Jack sat back. "OK, OK. What's this about? Since when did you start asking *me* the questions?"

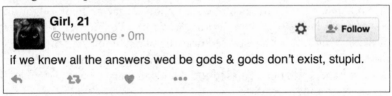

"So I *do* have certain uses. That's good to know. I was beginning to feel that we'd let the genie out of the bottle and were now superfluous."

"Please."
Girl 21 folded her arms.

"You need to work on those social skills. I'm sure you have great social *media* skills, but . . .

Girl, 21
@twentyone • 0m

Please.

Jack looked at her. The riffle of faces had taken on a somewhat plaintive aspect. He shrugged, stood up. "OK. Why not? Where are we going?"

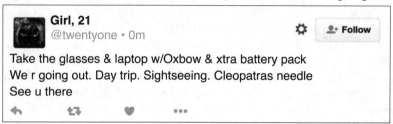

Girl, 21
@twentyone • 0m

Take the glasses & laptop w/Oxbow & xtra battery pack
We r going out. Day trip. Sightseeing. Cleopatras needle
See u there

Thirty-five minutes later, Jack exited Embankment Underground station and turned towards the river.

Across the wet tarmac of Victoria Embankment, a greyscale sky overhung a greyscale Thames. The only indication that the scene hadn't been completely desaturated was a signal-red London Sightseeing bus, the tourists that had braved the open upper deck hunkered down under a florist's display of colourful umbrellas. It being London, there were people drinking even at this early hour: a scrum of Polish labourers and a dreadlocked man in a beanie nursing a Tennant's Extra.

Cleopatra's Needle pointed skyward to his left. Having survived intact for more than two thousand years under the sands of Heliopolis, it was now merrily eroding under the capital's caustic weather, another foreign national treasure relocated here in the Victorian age as a souvenir of a vanishing Empire. Swinging his messenger bag back up onto his shoulder, Jack crossed the road at the lights.

The needle itself was flanked by two bronze sphinxes, the whole set in a stone enclosure that projected out into the Thames and from which two flights of slippery, algae-filmed steps led down into the water.

Jack sat on the top step and felt the wet stone start to chill his buttocks. He took out the Depthcharges, attached a cable to the battery pack and another to his laptop, which he kept in his bag to avoid getting it wet. With a third cable he attached his iPhone, entered his passcode, and checked the signal strength.

He had no idea if the Oxbow would function outside the office. While he could easily run it from his laptop, the fidelity of the manifestations was probably connected to the available bandwidth.

There was one sure way to find out.

He put on the glasses.

Interesting. That was new.

There seemed to be a grid overlaying his surroundings, thin lines spaced at around ten to fifteen metres apart both vertically and horizontally . . . Some kind of architectural framework? A location reference? The three-dimensional plot of a vintage videogame?

Long shadows, as if cast by stationary aeroplanes, stippled the ground around him, again set at regular intervals. One fell nearby, touching the Embankment's outer wall, and Jack's eyes followed the line of sight up, to the object that was casting it . . .

He suddenly realised what he was looking at. At half the height of Cleopatra's Needle, stationary, free-floating, immobile, eyes closed, head down, naked, hung a *man*.

Only he – it – *wasn't* a man.

Jack stepped closer. There was a shriek of tyre on tarmac and a shouted obscenity as a white van narrowly missed him, clipping his jacket. He jumped back onto the pavement, looked left and right. *Easy, boy.*

He looked up again. It was still there, just as before. The face had two eyes, it was true, and a hint of a mouth, but its features were smooth, its head hairless, a small indentation placed centrally where a nose might be; it had a translucent milky-vanilla skin and a delicate elongated and sexless body like a prepubescent child. The face was pinched, tapering to a small chin from which hung a long slender ribbon; the eyes large, black, all pupil, in which he could just see twin reflections of the London Eye. The body was adorned either with tattoos or some kind of natural markings, a cross-hatch of dots and dashes that ran up the outside of its legs and torso to the armpit then down the inside of the arms to each four-fingered hand.

There was more.

Jack searched the pavement, followed another shadow up to its origin. Hanging over the Thames, to the south, was a spray of thin crimson strands, frozen like a fast-shutter shot of a bullet passing through a watermelon. Below this was a frilled knobbly bulb from which three feet, thick and heavy like elephants', protruded.

Further down the Embankment was something that looked like a rhino, crouching on its hind legs; to the right, a tank of bony armour plate and jagged horn; back across Victoria Embankment, in front of a red-brick building, hung a translucent sphere the size of a hot-air balloon in which Jack could make out four or five indistinct black shapes, connected by a web of brighter ligaments. Through this apparition unconcerned commuters hurried.

There were – how many? From where he now stood there were visible certainly hundreds, possibly many thousands of creatures. Closer by, where more than just their basic outline could be discerned, he could see that they were grouped by type: some were very similar in shape and build, possibly from the same or very closely related species; others seemed to be unique, one-off examples of their kind.

Rows of figures, hanging in space.

Aliens?

Jack checked his laptop. It was running the Oxbow, and nothing else. No Depthcharge FPS. No online multiplayer game.

On the far bank of the Thames Jack could see shapes arranged row upon row above the Royal Festival Hall like a fleet of kites, though in their realm there was no breeze to lift them.

To his left Waterloo Bridge intersected a line of figures, passing right through them. Jack could see some hanging below, like strange fruit, under the arches.

He could now clearly see that the creatures were placed at the vertices of a cubic lattice: rows and columns stretching, as far as he could tell, to infinity; certainly to the limits of his vision.

Taking a step or two back, a chance alignment shot down towards Westminster Bridge and Big Ben, the adjacent rows forming rays that emanated from a clear unobstructed point out over the western horizon; the view in the other direction was blocked by an office building. Directly above him the same grid was visible, intersection after intersection, smaller and smaller to invisibility. He wondered if the same situation also held beneath his feet, extending down into the Earth.

Between these alignments it was a moiré of black shapes, shifting as he moved a pace back or forward. They faded to a grey-blue out over Kensington; in the other direction, above Docklands, they caught the morning light like floating embers from a bonfire: reflections from a polished hide, perhaps, or a glistening curve of horn.

Still more lay half-submerged in the water like drowning figures uninterested in their predicament; stationary, disinclined to bob up and down with the tide.

Jack experimentally lifted the glasses up to his forehead. The grid of creatures immediately disappeared like a gauze curtain being raised, and the dissolute morning light, now uninterrupted, shone more brightly on London once again.

Lowering them once more, he became aware for the first time of a huge shape, low on the eastern horizon. Pale and indistinct, like a bloated second moon, it looked like it lay far out, way beyond even the haze of the atmosphere. It was very hard to make out details, but it seemed to have crenellated edges and, paler still, ribbed sails like a Chinese junk, laterally placed along each flank. The scale of the thing must be incredible, and though he knew it was probably an accidental trick of the light, Jack fancied it looked a bit like a huge face, a space god perhaps, looking down at the Earth impassively. Jack estimated the creature, entity, *thing,* whatever it was, must easily be larger than London itself, possibly many times larger; a cruise liner from the skies of some unknown alien world.

A small ellipsis ran across the bottom of Jack's vision . . .

Ah.

The 19th Count and Girl 21 were there, sitting on an iron bench with buxom winged sphinxes for armrests, facing out over the Thames. XX hunkered behind them, seeming to fold in upon himself; a contraction of pistons and superstructure. The Count was looking along the length of his cane at a creature like a green pepper turned inside out that was hanging on the side of Somerset House.

Girl 21 appeared to be texting someone.

"What *are* they?" To any casual passer-by, Jack would have appeared to be talking to himself. He was oblivious. "Have we been invaded? Are they *real*? Or is this something you've concocted, like your, your perfect white top hat or your face of stolen selfies?"

The Count pulled an expression that looked as if he'd bitten into a lemon.

Do they **LOOK** like our friends?

Jack thought they didn't, but had no real concept of who coalesced memes might call friends, or even if they entertained the concept.

They are as **REAL** as *we* are, dear boy.
As to *who* they are and *where* they come from,
we were hoping **YOU** might be able to enlighten **US.**

"But don't you have access to *everything*?" Passers-by were beginning to stare. Jack dropped his voice. "Can't *you* find out that kind of stuff?"

All-knowing, eh?
Now that *would* be something to be *fervently wish'd.*

Alas, no.

Though we contain *much,* we do not contain *everything.*
If we *did,* we would simply be *ideaspace itself,*
and as we seem to be quite *distinct,*
both from *it* and from *each other,*
that patently seems *not* to be the case.

 Girl, 21
@twentyone • 0m

⚙ 👤+ Follow

not all ideaspace is available 2 us
many private convos, cams, mics
many computrs not conectd 2 net
we r not all-seeing, allknowing

  ♥

Though *DISTANCE* is an
ABSTRACTION
to us, and I could be in *New York* and back
before you can say
BUFFALO BILL,
it is still *very much the case* that you, Jack,
can go places and do things we *cannot.*
-HOWEVER-
I have looked at this *'Grid of Creatures'* from a thousand angles,
from MAN-MADE SATELLITES far out in space, from SHIPS AT SEA.
It covers *every continent* where eyeglasses exist from which to view it.
Mayhap it encompasses the
GLOBE,
and extends out INDEFINITELY
into the far Reaches of the
HEAVENS THEMSELVES.

Jack grappled for possible explanations. "Where have they come from?"

Unusual events. There's been a few of those of late.

England *won the* ashes.

The *FTSE* hit a FIVE-YEAR LOW.

You read an article about *Nikola Tesla.*

(Nadine told you she loved you, but your attention was elsewhere and you didn't hear her.)

Nothing of *much* import.

"When did they appear? Did this just happen?"

(The lad has certain . . . priorities, I can see.)

Maybe *yesterday.* **Maybe they've** *always* **been here.**

We saw them for the first time soon after we saw *ourselves* for the first time.

When your Depthcharge glasses gave us *eyes* to see into IDEASPACE.

A still rain of figures outside your window.

We spent an

ETERNITY

working towards our own *corporeality,*

only to find the place is already

CROWDED
OUT.

"White. The Signal. *It's the Signal.* I *was* right. The Signal is not *from* aliens—" Jack spun around, holding his arms high. A faint drizzle chilled his upturned face but did nothing to wash away his boyish grin.

"The Signal *is* aliens! And, at last, we've found a way to *see* them!"

COMING CLEAN

Jack was back at the office in time to catch Nixon and Harriet sharing a lunch of chips, sushi and lattes over the conference room table.

His extended absence had been the subject of some speculation; it was that rare for Jack to be out during the day. Usually he was here when they arrived in the morning and he was still here when they left in the evening. Harriet pointed over at his desk and spoke through a mouthful of food. "Jack, have you been *living* here?" Jack paused in the doorway, his mind entirely on other things. "Your sleeping bag's been there, under your desk, for *weeks*. Do you *ever* go home?"

"Ah. Yes. Sometimes."

"Nixon doesn't pay you for overtime. Does he?"

Nixon opened his mouth, then shut it again.

"Um, no. It's just that we have a lot to do here, and time is our most precious resource."

"Jack, Harriet manages to go home on time. Harriet has a normal life." There was a pause. Nixon seemed somewhat contrite.

Jack dipped a chip in teriyaki sauce. "I've never been particularly good at, quote unquote, normal life. Anyway, I've been on a little outing. With our new friends. You'll like this."

Harriet and Nixon shared a glance. "OK. Count us intrigued."

"There are *aliens* in there too?"

Jack had thought it might go something like this. Ghosts in the machine, maybe. *Aliens?* Jack. Please.

"Well, not so much aliens, per se. More like representations of aliens. Alien *ideas*."

Nixon and Harriet didn't look convinced. She regarded Jack with a mixture of disdain and fascination, as one might a novel specimen on a microscope slide. "And the Count, he showed you these aliens?"

"Yes. I went down to the Embankment. They're not like the Count. Not, you know, *mobile*. They seem to be dead, or frozen. All kinds of

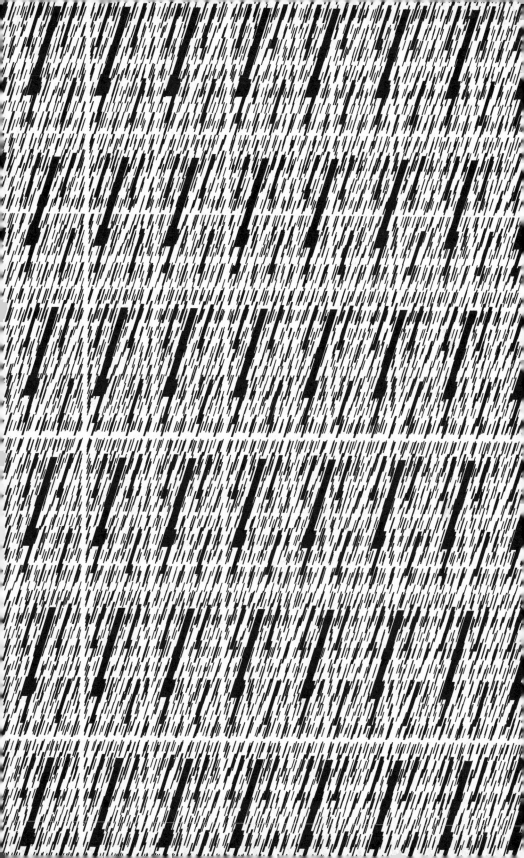

shapes and sizes. Row upon row of them, just hanging there in lines. Like a *grid*."

"And our new friends – they know who these creatures are?"

"Well, that's the peculiar thing – they seem to be just as puzzled as I was. They tell me they weren't there, and then they were." Jack raised an eyebrow. "I got the impression they were somewhat – *disturbed* by their presence."

Harriet looked over at Nixon to see how he was reacting to this.

"And you could see these aliens through the Depthcharges?"

Jack suddenly jumped up, his face a scrum of intensity. "*Yes*. Put them on. Now. You and Nixon. I'll *show* you."

Without a great deal of haste, they adjusted the straps and pulled the glasses over their heads. The pair of them looked like a French electronica band. Jack led them over to the window. The blinds were down to minimise screen reflections, though soft light still filtered through.

Jack swung his messenger bag up onto the wide windowsill and opened the flap. Pulling his laptop out just enough to open it, he booted the Oxbow and hooked in both pairs of glasses. On his screen two windows could be seen side by side, like a stereo photograph. They currently showed nothing but a close-up of the blind.

"Ready?"

The two of them nodded, and the close-ups of the blind bobbed up and down.

Jack reached up and pulled the cord. Somewhere a catch was released, and a sprung roller yanked the blind up with a clatter.

At first Harriet thought there was heavy rain falling over Canary Wharf. Though she couldn't see any storm clouds, the sky was still dark despite the mid-afternoon sun shining through the usual East End haze of volatiles. Then her eyes began to pick out details: a shape here, a figure there.

Nixon could see them too. He leaned on the windowsill to support himself. "*Wow.*"

Outside, aliens hung like crumpled shirts on invisible washing lines to the limits of their vision.

A S C E N S I O N

by F. HERSCHEL TEAGUE

When the Celestial Mechanic answered the Highmost's

summons, little did he expect to be asked to mount an

expedition into the lands below the Spire, less familiar to

him than the heavens above — and far more alien.

PART TWO

HE PLATFORM ROSE, the rectangle of warm morning light that described its edge becoming thinner and thinner, till it was but the width of an arrowshaft. The Elite Honour Guard returned to their positions and did not accompany him inside. Somewhere, a heavy weight in an oak-lined shaft reached its limit of movement with a deep resonant echo, and the last sliver of daylight was abruptly cut off.

In the relative darkness of the cupola, the heavy drapes covering the octagonal windows could just be discerned; it took, as it always did, a few seconds for the Celestial Mechanic's visual acuities to adjust to the gloom. He could, however, clearly see the familiar kirlean silhouette of the Highmost, from whom thin wisps of exhaled ammonia rose, visible in the infrared, as he turned to greet him.

The Celestial Mechanic stifled a gag reflex. The Highmost's chakras were muddy and stagnant,

CONTINUING OUR NOVELETTE OF STRANGE ALIEN CULTURES IN EIGHT PARTS

and the room smelt of ancient timber and mould. Spending his days sequestered here in the rafters of the world, looking up at the heavens through an ancient telescope rather than down at his subjects, very few of which he had ever met, he had only the stars for company; he had long ago dispensed with the mannered niceties of dress and personal hygiene so valued on the tiers below. His frame was bent and weak; it would have taken him many days to circumnavigate the First Tier, if indeed such a feat would have been possible at all.

The Highmost gestured to a soiled chaise longue. Next to it was a small table, on which a stack of platters carried mouldy remnants of desiccated food.

Octagonal cubbyholes around the walls provided storage for hundreds of scrolls and parchments. Their contents were in disarray; priceless and unique studies of lore and legend that the Celestial Mechanic would have given a fortune to study were here thick with the greasy dust of neglect.

If he saw all these things, he did not mention them. He had learned to be nothing if not circumspect. He politely declined the offer of a seat, instead reciting the five official greetings and adulations, the four royal citations, and a list of the Highmost's honourable forebears' military conquests. He diglossically pronounced himself not worthy of breathing the same sanctified air in his presence in both demotic and archaic, his practised low murmurous chanting peppered with a dance of signal blotches on his facial chitin. He bent low, and let his long whiskers, curled in the current vogue, touch the floor.

All this was normal, as it should be; mere pleasantries. His position, and income, depended upon the patronage of this creature who did not grant access to his presence, and certainly not this inner sanctum, easily or often.

In the centre of the high room was a long brass tube mounted on a gimbal, ornately carved with morally instructive scenes from the Gababrahacha. This five-scroll epic was a treatise on the undesirability of original thought and the rewards of a rustic peasant life, written by Erzherzogin II after the Great Curiosity and Conflagration and before the Coming Together of the Great Families.

One end of this tube pointed up, through a section of the roof that had been dropped and rotated on bearings so that a thin triangular wedge of sky was visible. The Highmost absently moved a forefinger up and across the age-speckled cheek of his bone-white carapace, released a short whistle from his breathing sphincter and extended his prehensile upper lip towards a low table on which were strewn maps which detailed the constellations and the looping orbits of wandering stars. These were held down at the corners with paperweights made from the mummified heads of Heaveriths, a southern hill tribe known for their bellicosity, set in wreaths carved from Issam ivory.

The Celestial Mechanic touched his whiskers to the floor once more

In the centre of the room was a long brass tube

and moved to the table, under which he could see several hand-cartfuls of Oakermilk bottles that the Celestial Mechanic suspected had been refilled with his host's urine.

The Highmost emitted a series of nanosecond pulses generated by an organ that, in simple form, consisted of a bone plate sprung at one end with a flexible muscle and at the other with a hinged flap; this organ also doubled as a pinning device during procreation. The Celestial Mechanic noticed that it was caked with sap the colour of a female on first season's heat, but again, did not mention it, not wishing to pry into the Highmost's nocturnal habits of a non-astronomical nature. He instead turned his attention to the charts on the table.

On them had been plotted a trajectory: an inked line divided into periods and sub-periods that indicated speed, date and position, written in the Highmost's shaky ornate hand. The Celestial Mechanic understood immediately that it represented an object on a path that swung in from the further reaches of the Lacunae system, across the orbit of the innermost planet to a perihelion that would take it around the far side of the system's sun, out of view.

The Celestial Mechanic knew that it could not be the comet's return – it was not due for another fifteen seasons, and its visit was as regular and predictable as any astronomical cycle could ever be. This was something *new*. Immediately forgetting his foetid surroundings, he set his forebrain to the task of analysing the dates and figures on the chart.

There was a quick chatter of ultrasonics back and forth, information exchanged in multi-layered harmonics most of which lie above the range of the human ear. The Highmost indicated a wooden box set apart from the telescope, but equipped with a circular opening which could be snugly attached to the eyepiece. Inside were a sheaf of oxidised plates, rough around the edges where the bituminous silvering had been inexpertly applied. These, the Celestial Mechanic knew before picking them up, were photographs of the night sky.

He mounted them in a clockwork carousel and wound it up. A lever was released, and the plates clattered against an escapement, presenting themselves like a flickbook in quick succession. He wound it and set it going a second time, just to be sure.

Recorded on the succession of images, taken at nightly intervals, there stood revealed a furtive dot: a new star moving across the fixed firmament.

Scrolls were pulled down, charts consulted, auguries thrown. The trajectory was checked again. The relative positions of the sixteen habitable moons were taken from a book of numerical indices and cross-referenced with the charts on the table.

There were more clicks and whistles. The Celestial Mechanic could find no fault with the Highmost's calculations. Pre-processed in the forebrain, he finally risked pulling what he had learned back into the hindbrain, where the seat of consciousness resided, for a higher-level analysis.

That the Highmost had been taught all he knew about astronomy by the Celestial Mechanic himself was not mentioned; his was the highest authority on such matters, even in the stultified academia of the Ossified College, whose most advanced pupils studied the art of polite dinner-table conversation, familiarised themselves with the playful tones of the picolyre or wrote theses on the subtleties of feather-fan courting.

No, there was no miscalculation – the meteor, the wandering star, if it maintained its current trajectory, would come around their sun and in three days cross Terrine's orbit once again. This time, however, Terrine would have swung around to intersect it. It was a certainty – the wandering star would fall to ground.

Click, shipp-chunk.

Colour-flush.

Where?

A new chart was unrolled, this time of the ground beneath their feet rather than the heavens above. Marked out with cartographic precision were the Forty-eight Districts that made up the Quarterlands surrounding the Circular Sea. Placed centrally, as on every map, was the Spire itself; around this, in concentric circles, came first the sea, populated with little hand-coloured and gilded drawings of barques and imaginary sea denizens; beyond it, the retaining crater wall. On this scale, the indentured farmlands that circled it could be individually made out; densely packed and formally arranged nearer the crater walls, smaller and more haphazard further out, eventually blending into the surrounding barrenlands to the south, the inhospitable mountainous regions to the north, and bordering the Iron Sea to the south-west.

The Celestial Mechanic knew that this arrangement was symbolic rather than representational: simply a convention. The complicated traditional system of longitude and latitude that rayed out from the Spire to the lands that owed it protection and tithe had long ago been found not to tally with the actual rotational axis of the planet or its magnetic pole. Seafaring nations routinely used a more practical positional notation that mapped to the poles and equator, thus avoiding cumbersome charts for conversion; however, this was not talked about, on pain of excommunication, outside the secretive guilds of Broad Seas Command.

The probable landing, or impact point, lay within three days' ride to the southwest, an area of low hills, small hamlets and vineyards. Further observations would narrow down the location more precisely.

The Highmost pointed to the spot on the map, then to the Celestial Mechanic, then to the floor of the cupola. His meaning was clear. He had just been directed to go out, into the Quarterlands, and bring it – whatever it was – back here for the Highmost to examine.

A clutch of questions filled the Celestial Mechanic's forebrain: *What if it is too large? Too heavy? What if the force of impact buries it too deep, or even destroys it?* Meteorites large enough to appear in the Highmost's telescope were rare indeed, and valuable – even if it was portable, the local peoples might not simply hand it over. He mentioned none of these misgivings, simply dipping his carapace to again let his whiskers touch the floor.

THE CELESTIAL MECHANIC stepped off the plate, which rose again behind him. One of the four guards, familiar with administering to the Highmost's sometimes bizarre whims, could read from the sullen spotting swirl of deep red on the Celestial Mechanic's foreplate that a far more problematic request than the usual was to be arranged. Still, he had almost unlimited resources at his disposal, and as long as the arrangements were invisibly dealt with, his position here would remain unassailable; his was the art of making the impossible effortlessly possible. He led the Celestial Mechanic across the plaza to a baroque gilded campanile in which they could discuss the details.

H E DECIDED to pack lightly, and drew up a list. Apart from a quantity of silver coins, he thought it best to go out into the Quarters dressed as plainly as possible; should money not be enough to procure the fallen star if it were now in the hands of some ill-educated farmer, a more persuasive whipchain would be hidden in the carrypack of his saddle.

He did not think he'd be gone for more than seven days, and so arranged supplies accordingly. Three days out, three back, and a day or so at the site. Hopefully he would not be away from the comforts of the Spire for any longer than strictly necessary.

Not knowing the size or weight of the object, that very night he commissioned a custom-made wooden crate lined with padded leather. Cleverly constructed as a sliding box within a box, it could be extended to contain anything up to a falit in length, though he doubted he could lift a rock that large by himself. He reasoned that, given

the sizes of the other meteorites in the collections of the Noble Houses' curiosity cabinets, it would be far smaller. The crate was equipped with wheels which were stowed in slots underneath, and when the axle was inserted, it could be drawn behind a packbeast like a cart.

He reflected on what the object might be – a meteorite, certainly, but the collections he had access to contained a broad variety – metallic nodules, scorched silica, fractured quartzite; perhaps it would resemble the polished and blackened Omphalos revered by the nomadic desert peoples to the west, or even, he thought with not a little thrill of expectation, the enormous fossilised internal organs of the enigmatic Skybound Beyonders themselves, which had been known to fall to earth after their millennia-long lives finally came to an end.

Skyfalls, he knew, were traditionally considered a bad omen; the Celestial Mechanic considered himself a man of the Natural Sciences, not a conjurer or soothsayer, so dismissed such interpretations out of hand.

T HOUGH HE DID NOT know this, the Circular Sea and the Spire itself were the result of a gigantic impact seven thousand turns, or around 6,540 years ago.

All written records of the high culture and wisdom of that time, along with all but a caravanful of the populace, had been destroyed in the conflagration; cubic purloughs of volcanic pumice had been thrown up into the atmosphere, and rains of vaporised meteoric iron had precipitated the forty-two periods of sunless devastation that followed.

This dark period in history was preserved as a thick layer of fertile black earth that produced the bountiful harvests of the lower slopes; it now helped feed the subsistence farmers of the Quarterlands and the denizens of the Spire alike.

This event became known as the Great Curiosity and Conflagration. There was but a folk-memory that survived, an oral tradition, a scrap hidden here or there in song or in myth. These told the story of those remaining souls who survived the impact only to have to endure the forty-two lightless days, during which the sun did not rise and no star could be seen. Through this time of utter darkness, in which no plant could grow, they had resorted to cannibalism and worse in order to survive.

What had endured from this time with an unshakeable resilience, as is often the case when stories are told and retold again and again, was the moral kernel, the nub of an oft-repeated lesson: that the Great Families had had this calamity visited upon them for a *reason*. The past needed to be erased because a hubristic curiosity could bring down the very heavens upon you. Knowledge itself could be dangerous.

The Celestial Mechanic was not himself inclined to this worldview; though it would have been considered more than indelicate to discuss such matters in public fora, there was a loose-knit underground network of knowledge-seekers who corresponded on such subjects, an Occluded University of the wise and the well-read of which he was a leading figure. He imagined that the Highmost must know this, as he knew most everything, and though he found the Celestial Mechanic's counsel useful, in his honorific position as head of the Assembly of the Constant Conviction he could not be seen or even suspected of countenancing such heresy. No, that was where the Celestial Mechanic himself came in. He could take the Highmost's influence and curiosity where he himself could never go.

THE JOURNEY FROM his lodgings in the sixteenth tier of the Spire down to the foreshore was one he had taken many times; out of curiosity when young; to satisfy lusts not provided for closer to home when older; to quell dissent after he had been appointed a Lower Apostle of the Academy of the Disinterested, the first official rung on the ladder that had taken him all the way to the high rank of Celestial Mechanic. Nowadays, these visits were a rare occurrence.

The items the guard had organised for him were to be made available from a staging post he had contacts with across the Rim. To reach it, he needed to cross the Circular Sea and the mountains beyond.

Transport was not hard to procure. Ferries constantly plied their trade back and forth, carrying goods and passengers; it was a sedate journey of two to three inversions.

He selected a private caravelle whose lounge he felt was sumptuously attired enough for someone who might have to soon forego certain luxuries while out in the Quarterlands, and he offered the necessary to ensure no other passengers would share and thus disturb his crossing.

A S THE CARAVELLE pulled away, the Celestial Mechanic turned to look back at his home. Already, behind him, the details of the Spire were becoming indistinct; the quays and the lower reaches were clad in a fine morning mist. The calm bronze peat-rich waters of the Circular Sea, unlike the rough breakers of the Iron Sea, rippled lazily about the bow, bringing to his forebrain the umber translucency of a glass of thrice-distilled Lusquebaugh.

The elegantly buttressed and scalloped upper levels of the Spire could be seen high above as the sun warmed the air and the morning's opaque humidity evaporated; vaulting ever heavenward, the sharp peak and the Highmost's observatory were currently hidden from view by a halo of clouds. The low light gilded the crenellations, casting the farther side into an architectural cross-hatch of mauve shadows; he knew that cool perfumed breezes would be now playing through the orchards and gazebos of the mid-levels, and lovers, having passed the night entwined on cushions of the finest feather, would be waking to breakfasts of honeyed milk and idle daydreams.

The enormous granite Head of Forbearance, lying on its back in the lower levels, caught its first rays of sunlight from over the lip of the eastern Rim. Viewed from the caravelle's current position it gazed skyward in silhouette, the curved elegance of its facial carapace lending it a contemplative majesty. The Celestial Mechanic had always felt a deep kinship with this figure – forever looking up to the zenith, and what may lie beyond, instead of out over the surrounding lands and their more prosaic and worldly concerns like his three counterparts above. Observing, wondering, ruminating, but just like the Highmost, unable to do anything practical about it. The Celestial Mechanic hoped he could prove himself a worthy proxy.

The lower portions of the Spire and the face now dipped below the horizon, to be followed by the crater's farther rim. Looking back, there was now a widening expanse of placid water flush with the sky, down towards which dipped the mountains on either side. The shadow of the Spire moved down the western wall and started out across the sea, while that cast by the rim retreated to the east.

Three fine lines crossed the sun's disc; the old fables held that they were scratches left by a spurned lover. In reality they were dark belts of asteroidal rock: countless small bodies tumbling and spinning, nudging each other, colliding; jostled from their orbits they would sometimes crash, maybe a decade or a millennium later, on the lands below.

Circles within circles.

The Celestial Mechanic knew that these belts had been the source of many of the bombardments of the past; but he also knew they played no part in this current puzzle.

PRESENTLY, the more prominent jetties along the shore of the Rim could be seen. The Rim itself, at closer quarters, was steep, rocky and unforgiving. The lower reaches were banded in shades of ochre and green, tidemarks from successive high-water maxima before the summer floods recharged the rivers below and brought the levels back down again.

There were unadorned warehouses, storerooms, tariff houses and other buildings built for function rather than beauty along the shoreline. The Celestial Mechanic could already sense a rush and bustle, the sinking psychic oppression of hard manual labour, even before he was assaulted by the smell of carrion and herbs, baking, stagnant water and fish.

The caravelle pulled in. He paid his fare, mounted the jetty, and ignored the sales patter of tour guides, hustlers promising to take him to rowdy palaces of intoxication, hawkers of skewered voles and the promises of prostitutes whose worn carapaces had been varnished to a gaudy sheen. Instead he headed up the main street, past the flophouses and taverns, out past the town's suburbs and into the foothills of the escarpment proper.

Here, a vertiginous zig-zagging series of staircases presented a daunting climb up to the rim's summit. Skirting crevasses and rockfalls, its route was random and

tortuous, having none of the symmetry and elegance of the Spire's staircases. The Celestial Mechanic looked up thoughtfully; he had no intention of taking the ascent on foot.

For a small fee, he hired a stout native of the mountainous northern regions to carry him. After a scant few moments of haggling, more for form's sake, he found himself strapped to the native's broad back in a tight-fitting sling, a faded and frilled lacework parasol overhead.

Though one had to learn to roll one's body with, rather than against, the loping gait to avoid discomfort, he soon settled in to admire the view and to sip nectar and eat small sweetmeats from a tray attached to one side that had thoughtfully been provided. Small insects busied themselves around his porter's weatherbeaten head and mane, which, to copious and obsequious thanks, the Celestial Mechanic idly flicked away with the square of cloth that served as a napkin.

They paused for a break halfway up, during which the Celestial Mechanic took the opportunity to relieve himself. His companion was given to small talk, and to be fair he found it hard to understand his accent. It was all glottal stops and a peculiar grating of the tail upon hardened bone ridges, like cheesegraters, set in his lower calves. He feigned deafness, and the remainder of the climb passed in silence.

Nearing the top of the Rim, the stairs became shallower and broader. At the summit a viewpoint had been erected, with a raised area for picnicking and a small balustrade over which his porter emptied several baskets of detritus. A weathered tumble of discarded food waste coloured the slope below. The Celestial Mechanic looked across the sea at the Spire one last time, then set his back to it and turned towards the Quarterlands.

T HE DESCENT WAS, the Celestial Mechanic found himself agreeing, quite magnificent. The fields of the indentured farmsteads formed a pattern of neat coloured rectangles arranged in concentric circles centred on the Spire, just like the charts had promised. Sweeping gently around to follow the curve of the Rim, they arced over to the west where they met another neat arrangement of fields, these following the sinuous curves of the banks of the Gorodorborga. Out towards the horizon the fields became indistinct, a misty multi-hued speckle. Small houses and farmsteads could be seen, some with smoke rising from broad squat chimneys; closer by he recognised large beasts of burden harnessed to ploughs or pulling threshing machines.

The Quarterlands were roughly divided by four ridges; low in comparison with the Rim itself, from which they extended radially, they still provided natural geographical divisions. Like the hedgerows that divided the fields, they were left unfarmed; large gnarled brabdurran trees, thick mats of dense moss and a sprinkling of Mother-of-May colonised their banks.

Legend had it that these ridges were the spokes of a fallen wheel that once belonged to a Beyonder sky chariot. Driven by Rohasta, a youthful and curious Beyonder, it had swooped low over the lands so he could better observe the strange small creatures that populated its surface.

One, fair and serene, caught his eye. Oimu was singing in the most beautiful voice Rohasta had ever heard while she washed her carapace in a stream, and he swooped down lower still in order to see her more clearly.

Hiding behind a boulder was the giant, Yogril. Assigned to Oimu's protection by the local Landsgrave, he saw Rohasta and his chariot and realised his charge might be in danger.

Rohasta flew overhead again, this time so low that Yogril was able to jump up and grab hold of a wheel, which came off in his hand. Now unable to steer, the chariot spun away and disintegrated in a shower of splinters over the barrenlands. Finding the massive wheel too heavy for even him, a giant, to hold, he let it drop to the ground, where it still rests today. Now rotating only with the planet itself, its rim is the far horizon, its hub the Circular Sea, its axle the Spire.

The Celestial Mechanic, though he enjoyed the old stories, was of the opinion that these ridges had been formed by ejecta from the colossal impact. They were entirely natural; but, just like all things here inevitably did, even they converged on the Spire, the centre of the Known and Only Lands.

A DEFERENTIAL SPLUTTER woke the Celestial Mechanic from his reverie. Bending one of his rear legs to enable him to more easily dismount, his porter held out a hand cracked with years of manual labour, into which was dropped a generous sum.

The scenery out here in the Quarterlands was, to his surprise, a bit more to the Celestial Mechanic's liking than the jetties and towns of the inner Rim, and he set off with a light heart. Though the roads were dirt tracks and the people he passed sported items of ill-tailored clothing in gauche colour combinations that were more than several seasons out of date, he felt invigorated, relaxed, glad to be out and about in a simpler, slower world. Not wanting to appear overdressed even in his most casual attire, he loosened his cravat and tried to affect a less formal gait, aping the lugubrious swinging of the arms and expressive hand gestures of the passers-by. They lacked the refined precision of limb movement, the elegant flourish of heel against heel he was accustomed to, but, he reflected, it was not their fault they lacked the poise acquired in the Spire's seasonal dressage parades.

They seemed to regard him with a certain awe, as well they should; or it could have been a barely concealed contempt, it was hard to say. He occasionally raised a hand in greeting, and they would touch a finger to their brightly coloured knitted beanies, or lift a hoof, or offer some other charming but unfamiliar form of local greeting in return.

ENQUIRIES AT A SMALL staging post and shop gave him directions to the agreed pick-up point, and after buying a wrap of local baked delicacies for the journey he set off again on foot.

It transpired that the contact who was to provide his transport and supplies for this expedition owned a sizeable business that served the many traders who criss-crossed the Quarterlands. He operated from a series of low warehouses on the outskirts of a town; these lacked any architectural merit, being devoid of decoration, and their dark, horizontal silhouettes appeared – here the Celestial Mechanic searched his hindbrain for an unfamiliar term – *functional,* in a manner he found faintly distasteful.

Entering through two wide doors held open by discarded broken furniture, he found they contained shelf upon shelf of labelled crates, sacks of dry goods, hung cured carcasses, and a riot of live animals in close-packed pens, the combined scents and sounds of which the Celestial Mechanic felt might overwhelm him.

There seemed to be no security; he assumed that this was because there was very little here worth stealing. Meandering up and down the aisles, stepping over puddles of urine and sleeping dotted furrets, he soon found the proprietor standing over a wide wok, engulfed in a cloud of yellow steam.

The Celestial Mechanic made a small chirrup by way of introduction. The proprietor looked up from a bubbling soup in which small crustaceans swam, and wiped his forelimbs on his leather skirt.

His accent was flat, without the lilting sing-song of the Spire, and at first the Celestial Mechanic found it hard to understand.

Flat, he realised, like the lands out here beyond the Rim.

In Spire society, how one pronounced a name was overlaid with a subtle social positioning – a rising high note was used when addressing one's superiors, a descending low note with those lower down the social order. An affectation designed to mimic the effect of the attenuated atmosphere at the higher levels, this tonal language ensured everyone was continually reminded of their position within the complex hierarchy. It was also the source of deep social anxieties – the opportunity for unintended offence was a theme of many of the skits staged in the Blossom Gardens' open-air theatres.

The Celestial Mechanic habitually referred to everyone except the Highmost in the descending register. He found it easier that way. He wondered, briefly, if the proprietor's tone of voice was intended as an insult, but decided to let it pass. He was not here to instruct those who had the misfortune of living outside the Circular Sea in basic etiquette.

It was only when he paid him closer attention that the Celestial Mechanic realised they had met once before, at a lodge meeting of the Occluded University. He made no mention of this, of course; if he had been recognised in return, the proprietor also thought it best to keep this to himself.

The packbeast and supplies, the saddle, the bags and equipment – and, most important of all, the wheeled box – were all as he had requested. Again, if its curious construction had raised any questions, today none were asked.

H E DINED AT A LOCAL hostelry, where he watched younglings play a game of chance on banks of machines which displayed glyphs in coloured lights. The fare was basic, some kind of fruit he was unfamilar with in a fragrant oil; wholesome, though the presentation needed work.

He could have stayed longer but he thought it best to repair early. His contact had made available a spare room, which, though spartan, he found charming in an unsophisticated, rustic manner. A four-spoked wheel hung above a heated dish into which had been placed aromatic dried droppings; a row of pots, each containing a bituminous paste, and a hardened bone file were also provided. He had declined the proffered services of a local subacuette, never having been interested in the euphoric but deadening effects of their stings.

The Celestial Mechanic could sense an auroral glow of electromagnetic particles fluttering like a translucent sheet to the north, but, at the end of day one, the omens, for those that believed in such things, were good. He relaxed onto the reed matting and let his forebrain spin down into sleep. His hindbrain was still running through the events of the day, filing, interpreting and cross-referencing, but soon that too was quiescent.

To be continued

FICTIVE DEFENCE

When Jack needed to refer to XX, the 19th Count and Girl 21 in his notebooks and digital Post-its, the term he'd finally settled on was Digital Memetic Entities: DMEn for short. Tulpa, spirit – every other term he could think of seemed too ... *loaded*. Not having said it out loud, he was unaware how it sounded.

The 19th Count was presently with him in the office, an unpaid intern patiently watching him adjust parameters, go back to a line of code, try again. Jack had even begun to enjoy the company. He and Harriet hadn't yet figured out how to reliably conjure up these – these DMEn at will. There seemed to be some trick to it that they hadn't yet mastered. Or, he suspected, they simply came and went when they wished to.

The Depthcharges, their Ghost Camera, revealed them when they did choose to put in an appearance; Jack or Harriet or Nixon would look around and find Girl 21 sitting on one of the empty crates typing something on her smartphone or the 19th Count pouring an imaginary whisky in the kitchen. If they were not to be seen, Jack would tweak the parameters of the Oxbow just to see what would happen.

Nixon had called a meeting. Calling a meeting simply meant asking Jack and Harriet to come into the conference room and bring their crates with them.

He opened proceedings. "OK, you know what I'm about to ask. What do we actually have here? An interesting business possibility? A breakthrough in artificial intelligence? A hotline to the spirit realm? An alien zoo? What is the Oxbow showing us? Jack?"

"Let's start with our DMEn—"

"Our *demon?*"

"Ah. Dee Em Ee En. Digital Memetic Entities. It's the, the term I coined to describe them."

"OK, I'll roll with that. Our DMEn."

"I think they're a fictive memetic defence. And they may have been specifically designed for that purpose."

Nixon knew what each word meant, but still couldn't parse the sentence. "What?"

"They're a prophylactic. A protective idea, or set of ideas, designed to counter another set of ideas. It's like . . ." Jack grasped for words. Not for the first time, he was frustrated by language's limited means of expression. Every thought has to be converted into a set of symbols in order to be communicated, squeezed into a form. We could say it, or write it down. Paint it. Sing it, even. But how closely does even the most eloquent prose capture the true shape of the original idea that it attempts to describe? To get out into the real world an idea has to wear an ill-fitting suit of words that even the best tailor-poets might struggle to make snug. Jack was sure his had all manner of superfluous stitching, false pockets, elbow patches and other linguistic sartorial missteps.

Jack snapped his fingers. "*Antibodies.* Suppose you knew that there were dangerous ideas abroad. New ideas. *Revolutionary* ideas. They might be political, social, scientific. They might even be *true*. Ideas that could upset your carefully structured society. And you might not want that to happen."

"Why?"

"Numerous reasons. Stability. A vested interest in the status quo. Maybe the new ideas are patently ludicrous, or they're old, pre-Enlightenment ideas given a technological leg-up. Who knows. But, regardless, how do you prevent this happening, how do you stop certain undesirable concepts spreading through a population?"

"You mean *radicalising* them?"

"Perhaps, but not necessarily. It could be that the idea in itself is entirely value-free – a scientific discovery, for example – but that it still could be very dangerous to a certain set of people. An established elite, say. Or the general public – powerful people will often cite the protection of the public in defence of their actions. The caring and benevolent dictator who's more like a father figure, et cetera, et cetera.

"Consider Galileo. He points his new telescope towards the heavens, the realm that up until then has been the sole business of the Church, and he sees something that contradicts their orthodoxies."

Jack tabbed a browser window. "You know about Galileo, right?"

Nixon knew that whatever his reply, Jack was going to fill him in on the details regardless, so simply looked back at Jack impassively. Harriet smiled an 'Indulge Jack' smile.

He began reading. "In 1610, Galileo published his Sidereus Nuncius, open brackets *Starry Messenger,* close brackets, describing the observations that he had made with the new telescope, namely the

375

phases of Venus and the moons of Jupiter. These convinced him of the validity of the heliocentric theory propounded by Nicolaus Copernicus open brackets in *De revolutionibus orbium coelestium* in 1543 close brackets. Galileo's discoveries were met with opposition within the Catholic Church, and in 1616 the Inquisition declared heliocentrism to be formally heretical. Heliocentric books were banned and Galileo was ordered to refrain from holding, teaching or defending heliocentric ideas. In 1632 Galileo, now an old man, published his *Dialogue Concerning the Two Chief World Systems*, which implicitly defended heliocentrism and was widely read. Responding to the mounting theological, astronomical and philosophical controversy, in 1633 the Roman Inquisition tried Galileo and found him 'gravely suspect of heresy', sentencing him to indefinite imprisonment. Galileo was kept under house arrest until his death in 1642."

"Your Latin pronunciation needs work."

"Nixon, unlike you I didn't have the benefit of the best schools money could buy, and had to get by on my natural smarts. The *point,* though: new technologies always give rise to new ideas. Uncomfortable ideas. The old guard, whoever they may be, they distrust the innovators, the upstarts with their awkward questions and new ways of looking at the world. It's always been the way, and it always will be."

"So what do you do? Prohibit free enquiry? Stop people thinking new thoughts? How is this relevant—?"

Jack looked suddenly serious. "Well, it has been tried. There are religious and political ideologies around today that are still impervious to reason if it runs contrary to their dogma. But here's the thing: *whatever* their political or ideological stripe, *whatever* the specific rights and wrongs, I'm thinking that certain people – *influential* people – realised that certain ideas could be potentially harmful, and took steps to *protect against them.*

"It used to be possible to put difficult people like Galileo under house arrest. Kill them, even. You can burn books. But that control over information is so much harder to exercise today, when it's piped into every home through the internet and no longer resides in a physical vessel to which you can put a match. You can't burn the internet."

"So how *do* you control the spread of certain ideas, assuming you wanted to?"

"Now? I'm not sure you can."

"Game over, then." Nixon folded his arms.

Jack smiled. "Not necessarily. You may not be able to prevent exposure to bad ideas any more, but you can *inoculate people against them.*"

"Hang on, who defines whether an idea is dangerous or not?"

"Ha. An interesting dilemma. And the virulence of an idea can be completely independent of whether it's true or not. Just ask a 9/11 truther."

"Pft."

"But put yourself in the position of the Roman Inquisition. As far as you're concerned, you are in possession of the facts of the matter, the one truth, and you are utterly convinced of this. Think of what's at stake – your entire worldview, your culture, the moral fibre of society. You're the *good guys* here. What might you do to protect everything that you believe is important? All you think is worthwhile, is *right?*

"Zealots ban books and destroy art because they understand that ideas alien to their ideology reside within them. But of course ideas also reside in *people.* Ideas thrive in the private spaces between our ears and behind our eyes. But people can change their minds. *People are not ideas.* It's not enough to just kill bad *people.* You need to kill bad *ideas.*"

"Easier said than done, Jack. Some people's very identity is built on a set of all-encompassing ideas . . . though they might call them 'values.'"

"But values can change. Are you the same 'you' you were ten, twenty years ago? No? What's different? You are *physically* the same person, even though every cell in your body may have been replaced. You have the same memories, the same parents, the same colour eyes. But you may have completely changed your opinion on many things."

"Sushi. For example." Harriet nudged Nixon.

Jack spread his arms inclusively. "Sushi. Why not?

"No, ideas aren't people – they're just generated by and consumed by people, sure, and reside for a while – maybe a moment, maybe a lifetime – inside people.

"Ideas don't have rights. They cannot feel pain. Have no sympathy for an idea, as the good ones will rise to the surface and the bad ones deserve all the opprobrium we can heap upon them. Bad ideas have to be flushed out – by better ideas."

"I'm sure Hitler thought national socialism was one of those 'better ideas.'"

Jack nodded. "I'm sure he did. Every ideologue does."

"I'm still not sure how all this—"

Jack recalled his recent conversation with Daniel. Once again he considered telling Jack and Harriet what had happened, up there on the Moon. Once again, he decided to dance around the truth. "Consider what happens when a more advanced civilisation comes into contact with another, less developed one. For a start, the more advanced culture – at least, technologically speaking – is usually the one doing the visiting. They're the ones who built the ships. Think about how that must affect a society's self-image. You now find yourself within a hugely expanded horizon; far from being at the centre of all things, you now find you're living in the memetic suburbs. It'd be a bit of a shock to the system. To many systems."

"You think that's what's happening here, Jack? Sounds a bit hyperbolic. If the Signal from Space consists of extraterrestrial Spaniards, they don't seem to be in a hurry to run off with our gold."

"Maybe it's a soft invasion."

"A what?"

"Victory is not just won over land or resources, or even people. We're used to invasions of the more, um, *physical* kind, but even then, once the bombs have been dropped, once the bodies have been brought home, in the long term every war has ultimately been one of *ideas*. Ideas are often what went into battle in the first place – human beings were just their proxies. The real and lasting victory that has to be won is over the *ideology*. Think of the two deadly memetic pandemics of the twentieth century: fascism and communism. In both cases we needed to be cured of a virulent viral meme – their persuasive mass appeal had to be neutralised once and for all, not just their machineries of state.

"I think certain well-placed people saw this coming . . . Well, not *this*, exactly, not the Signal from Space, but something similar. Foreign ideas. Alien ideas. So they came up with a plan.

"*The DMEn*. Who thought them up, and how, I have no idea. They may have even thought themselves into existence. But they're our memetic antibodies, here to protect us, preserve our culture. They're ideas that have been engineered in the minds of men to battle *other* ideas.

"They're our *fictive memetic defence*."

Hon. Horace Walpole
Strawberry Hill House
Twickenham

Sept 11th 17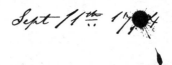4

My dear Sir,

 I am in receipt of your new book,
and though I only cut the leaves late last
night, thinking it might suffice to help
pass the evening by candlelight, I confess I was
immediately enraptured.

 My most recent confection seems to be
forever a work in progress, and I may be
inspired by your example to attempt to finally
complete it. The fictions of the novel-smith
I fancy are not the foremost and first of my
talents, such as they are, there being too
many distractions in London at present.

 But I digress — You enquire as to the
veracity of the rumour that I paid a certain
Frank Chambers a sum of 300 guineas to
disinter from its final resting place in the
Church of the Holy Trinity and deliver to me
the skull of one William Shakespeare, no less.

Well, dear friend, I shall not deny it. Have I ever been able to hide the truth from you?

Though I might be thought to cultivate a touch of the macabre, and no doubt you may picture your humble servant strutting the halls here at Strawberry Hill enacting Hamlet for an audience of obsequious manservants, this relic instead has for me a more, let us say, talismanic purpose. As an author of standing yourself, you will aver that Stories and their Tellers do wield a certain power over men. Allow me to elucidate.

You are aware that on some subjects I am a scholar, on others a scholar of pretence. Having visited me here at my grand work-in-progress that is Strawberry Hill House, you know well that had I thought a tower here or a mantelpiece there was somehow not the correct thing from an architectural or historical perspective, my sanctum that suits me so well would never have been built. History be damned! I refused to live for a day longer in that miserable little cottage. No, in its place would soon rise a grand residence befitting a man of letters and the son of a Prime Minister (however much his fortunes may be on the wane, while my career in this respect is just beginning). But what to name it? Being in possession

of the lease, I discovered that the land itself
had originally been known as "Strawberry
Hill Shot". I knew then that my elegant
villa had found its title — one inherited from
a scrap of fact, refashioned.

In this project John Chute and Richard,
who is of your acquaintance, have been of
the utmost assistance. Our Strawberry
Committee, that Committee of Taste, thought
nothing of pilfering Henry 8th's fan
vaulting for the new Gallery that we are
building, all gold and looking-glass, or this or
that nobleman's tomb or mausoleum as the
fancy takes, or corbelling & battlements for
the Round Tower, from which no man shall
ever shoot an arrow.

Even for the faithless, a Gothic church
buttressed against the settling of old age
can fill the imagination with Romantic
fancies! And it manages to still do so even
after that unbelieving clergyman Conyers
Middleton has me convinced that, but for
the mysterious, it is but a concoction that
means nothing (or for others, a great deal too
much) and thus I have come to reject it and
all its apostles, from Athanasius to Bishop
Keene.

This serendipitously illustrates, my dear
friend, how another well-spun fiction may

become infinitely more seductive than a lumpen and ill-fitting fact. We must tailor our personal fictions, those well-wrought stories of who and what we are, as carefully as those of our fictional characters, for they will both outlast us, and in many ways be one and the same thing.

Do you blanch at my free mingling of facts with fictions? I can almost taste your disapproval, being that you are a Natural Philosopher and a Man of the Sciences, and with no small reputation to protect. Those are your chosen weapons in this war of ideas, and I have mine. What matters most, and I am sure upon this you concur, is that we are on the same side; that our concern, above all, is that we bolster our liberty from tyrannical ideas and their fervent ideologues, those missionaries whose zeal is always and inevitably on display in inverse proportion to their grasp of the facts of the matter.

You know I have ever been averse to toleration of an intolerant philosophy, be that political or religious, and in this Middleton has merely crystallised for me what was previously but a vaguer notion. The fictions of Man have ever sought to curtail our free expression and liberty, too often under the guise of acting for our greater good. Protect us from the narrow ambitions of those who wish to foist upon us their singular vision of a better world.

To wit: The French seem to have swapped but one form of tyranny for another. It remains for the Enlightenment to invent suitable epithets to describe such barbarities wrought by the overenthusiastic application of a philosophical idea, as if such a thing had been horse-trained and subdued by her rider and not the other way about. These diseases of the mind are merely leading us into Battle upon Battle; having destroyed God as well as their King, I fear Reason itself shall follow. What is the outcome of this chaos, save more chaos, I know not; only that my resolve is strengthened twentyfold in that we must, howsoever we can, lay the ground against which this grossest of follies may not happen here, now or in the future.

If one acts for God, or Country, of what horrors is one capable? How does one fight a philosophy that speaks not to reason, but to the passions?

Here, I venture I have the answer. I propose what we require is _another fiction_; one that will provide a counterbalance in the minds of Men.

1764 saw the publication of "The Castle of Otranto", translated, we are assured, from the original Italian of Onuphrio Muralto by a certain gentleman by the name of William Marshal of Gent, Canon of the Church of St. Nicholas at Otranto; it, in turn, is based on a manuscript printed in Naples in 1529 which was recently rediscovered in the library of an ancient Catholic family in the north of England. This manuscript, it is suggested, is derived from a story older still, dating back perhaps as far as the Crusades.

This line of descent, and the named custodians of this literary conceit, are, as you are fully aware, utterly fictitious; as with my House here by the Thames, it is simply another of my creations built on the numinous fragments of borrowed myth. My dear friend The Duke of Northumberland did not mind my using his name to give verisimilitude to such a literary confection — I myself for the purpose wore the mask of one William Marshal, esq. A Grand Masquerade, yes; but it is not a simple frippery, more an experiment, a summoning with a quite specific purpose in mind.

Thus I enlisted Dukes and Parliamentarians; I even have the head of Mr. William Shakespeare himself, who watches over me as I write this; and now I have you. Influence, inspiration and the means to spread the Word by the Printed Page. We will be all but invincible!

So, to our collaboration, our conjuration: our new tale, I suggest, was undoubtedly begun a little before the creation of the world, and was preserved in the oral tradition before being transferred to stone, papyrus, then paper by a tribe resident in the mountains of Cramperaggini, an island not mentioned on any maps you or I may have in our possession. These stories tell of a man of breeding and wisdom beyond his apparent years, for he always seems to be in the prime of life; appearing at some benighted hour, he acts as Shepherd and Sage, a guiding hand of the age-old Aristocracy of Learning, our own Invisible College. Of these bare facts we have the most authentic attestations of the Gnostics and several noted missionaries, so our story goes; we do not trouble the reader with reliable references as we are sure everybody will believe in them as much as they are inclined to believe in them.

What of our protagonist? Now, if you recall some years ago the authorities seized an odd man who went by the name of the Count of St. Germain. He had been here in London for two years, and would not tell who he was, or whence he came, but professed two things:

the first, that he did not go by his right
name; and the second that he never had any
dealings with any woman – nay, nor with
any succedaneum. He sang, composed, played
wonderfully on the violin, and was not what
you might call sensible. He was called an
Italian, a Spaniard, a Pole; a somebody that
married a great fortune in Mexico and ran
away with her jewels to Constantinople; a
priest, a fiddler, a vast nobleman. The
Prince of Wales had an unsatiated curiosity
about him, but in vain. However, nothing
was made out against him; he was released,
then stayed in the City intimating of being
taken up for a spy.

I here confess: This was an elaborate dance
of mirrors, a performance executed to perfection
involving not one but several of my close male
acquaintances from the Stage; a summoning
of which I am the humble author. Before it
could all get out of hand, we arranged for his
mysterious disappearance.

I thus present our hero, our solution,
our deliverance, our own counter-idea made
flesh. Not being made from mortal bones and
mortal vein, as a fiction he has a longevity
which we do not. My friend, we will not
last for more than a mayfly's afternoon
from the vantage of the grand narrative of
History — but that History is written by

men, and are we not men who write? Does not Prince Charles of Hesse-Kassel already, in his unwitting collusion in our game, consider this fictional shade to be "one of the greatest philosophers who ever lived", while the Theosophists already claim him as one of their own?

The board is set. Now — who else might we recruit to our cause? Chatterton — now there was a lad of too high honour to be capable of forgery, and yet who, they do not deny, wrote poems in the style of Ossian, and fifty other such things. I protest I cannot smell the faintest air of authenticity about him but the vocabulary of a borrowed antiquity, but then I am a hypocrite to stand in judgement on such matters. His premise is a contemporary conceit wrapped in the textures of the old (and what is more, his premature death does exclude him from our Club somewhat more permanently!) You made mention of William Blake, Soho poet and mystic, artist of sorts, experimenter in new techniques of print reproduction. Though of idiosyncratic manners and, I hear, a follower of Swedenborg, I am informed he holds the organised Church in disdain. Might he be sympathetic to our cause?

I fear our group must by necessity be small and select; we must recruit only those of discretion, connections, reputation and ability. Create a new "Triumvirate", if I may resurrect the name of our old Eton confederacy.

In books and letters, and on the lips of Men, an idea can travel the World — it has no need of food or water to sustain it on its Grand Tour. Though it may languish unread in the library of some G-dforsaken gentleman of presumptuous charm, or on the dusty shelves of those institutions that do nothing but prepare young men for the lives of whoring and privilege that is their inheritance (till syphilis prunes the branches of the family tree), those ideas are not mortal in the manner of you and I, dear friend. They are temporal travellers into Tomorrow, should such a fancy not be beyond the scope of the finest writers our new French rulers may allow to survive the attentions of the Guillotine.

Our immortal Man of Tomorrow will be of the coming age, not of this; he will be our defence against Continental excesses, the alien and the other. The Count of the 19th Century, fashioned not from flesh but from words, will serve as the repository of the finest Ideas of Man. He represents all that is noble in the pure-bred gentleman of letters and learning, and with the wisdom to use such knowledge for the benefit of all without quick recourse to violence or vulgarity.

Djinn are thoughts that were abroad in the world long before the existence of men to think them, attest the Musselmen. Whether there exist outside of a holy-book Demons or no, men of education have allowed certain dangerous ideas to move in to their minds and there set up a home as comfortable and well-provisioned as my own here at Strawberry Hill. We must do our utmost to deny them a permanent residence.

Ask yourself this, my friend: are we to be their _masters_, or _they_ ours?

Adieu, my dear Sir, I am forever yours,

— H. W.

A S C E N S I O N

by F. HERSCHEL TEAGUE

When the Celestial Mechanic answered the Highmost's

summons, little did he expect to be asked to mount an

expedition into the lands below the Spire, less familiar to

him than the heavens above — and far more alien.

PART THREE

B Y THE TIME the Celestial Mechanic had risen, the packbeast had already been saddled and the requested supplies arranged either side on a harness of leather straps. A rolled sleeping mat and warm padded overbag hung like a soft battering ram on one side, a rattan hamper and several cooled skins of calfmilk and water on the other. The collapsed box was mounted atop the tail to the rear, the wheels folded under its base.

His whipchain was carefully hidden. Though a weapon with a range might prove useful in a tight spot, the Celestial Mechanic hoped he would not need to get involved in anything that a purse of silver would not solve; and what's more, it would arouse suspicion.

The packbeast was a mature Brindlatch Coakidoh; the ridged hide that the breed developed with age provided ideal purchase for all manner of belts and loops. Shaped like a high-backed turtle, it was a

---

CONTINUING OUR NOVELETTE OF STRANGE ALIEN CULTURES IN EIGHT PARTS

head taller than the Celestial Mechanic at its highest point, tapering to a short articulated tail at the back and a low, small head with tiny inset eyes ringed with bony points at the front. Squat, powerful legs jutted out at a splayed angle that lent it stability in the roughest terrain and made it nigh on impossible to turn over. Whorls of cream and chestnut patterned the large swept-back, scalloped-edge plate that protected the gap between head and neck, into which two holes had been drilled and a length of tasselled cord attached. It was an expensive steed, but not absurdly so; a realistic purchase for a travelling merchant of sound means.

The Celestial Mechanic again paid without complaint, and climbing up the tail dropped into the saddle.

Low IN THE MORNING SKY to the west, backlit in pale peach and framed in the foreground by the low corded branches of a tree, hung the Visage. The Celestial Mechanic stopped for a moment to ponder the scene.

The size of a barollé ball held at arm's length, it dominated the sky even during the day. It was far larger than any of Terrine's four natural moons, two of which were too small to even pull themselves into a semblance of sphericity.

The Visage was the colossal petrified skull of a Skybound Beyonder. Crossing the heavens in its orbit once every thirty-two days, it was tidally locked, always presenting the same face to the world below. Its head was tilted down, the lower mandible missing; a row of worn incisors, most of which had fallen under their own weight like weary gravestones, edged the lower limb. Silhouetted against the sulphur-gold dawn sky, or in full phase set against the blackness of space, it was a baleful and commanding presence. Eventually, every sentient creature on Terrine grew accustomed to it, though few ever felt completely comfortable under its blank stare.

Though cratered by many millennia of impacts, veined with ravines and rayed with ejecta, it was still easy to make out the sharp ten-thousand-league-high cliffs of the cheekbones against which immense dunes of colourless dust had drifted, and the two deep-set eye sockets into which continents of rubble had collapsed. The knife-cut gashes caused by glancing meteorite strikes gave it the battle-ravaged countenance of a tavern knucklefighter.

During the course of a full orbit it would pass through several phases: lit face on, it seemed almost benign; lit from underneath, it was the teller of fireside ghost stories; lit from above, with deep shadows falling under the brow and in the empty sockets, it stood in stern and disapproving judgement over the world below.

Every eight to ten seasons it would pass directly in front of the sun. As it did so, light would shine low through the gaps between the teeth and the rilles and valleys ringing the pate, creating a sparkling halo of lights. At these times, in featureless silhouette, it could be imagined that it was facing out and away, towards the bright star behind it rather than the creatures below who were looking up in awe and not a little fear.

The Celestial Mechanic was of the opinion that the visage was hollow, as were some of the fossilised skulls in his collection that had been found in the lower reaches of the barrenlands' delta deposit. When it happened to be lit from a certain angle, viewed through a telescope it was possible to see deep into the shadowed eye sockets and, if one was of such a mind, discern something moving within the cranial cavity.

Opinion inside the Occluded University was divided. Some saw the rippling of the flank of a great worm, or the lights from subterranean cities peopled by creatures that never walked the surface. Others thought the skull was solid and these conceits simple tricks of the light, and did not entertain such fantasies.

It was said that certain expressions could be read as auguries, but of course the Celestial Mechanic thought this a pseudoscience at best. True, shadows and light falling across the mountain ranges and cratered lowlands sometimes gave the impression of a furrowed brow or a glowering stare; but it was a thing long dead, and dead things had no interest in the movements and machinations, the power-plays and politics of the tiny figures that scurried to and fro on the lands beneath.

THE NOMADS of the outer marshes believed the Visage to be a god, and their Omphalos, which had fallen to ground in antiquity, and around which they performed their peculiar rites, was his petrified member. Upon its bulbous head they had long ago carved a semblance of a face that their sect's founder, Murorundrum-Kalash the Defiler, had seen in a night-vision. Upon waking, he had sketched it from memory and proclaimed it to be the true likeness of the Beyonder in life. No reproduction of this face exists, even in the published journals of travellers; it was considered blasphemous to portray it either in paint or in word.

The Celestial Mechanic had once heard it described, under oath of strictest secrecy, by an apostate who had been working incognito as a chambermaid for an acquaintance on the lower levels. She told of its sullen expression, devoid of carapace or whiskers, resembling more the tree-dwelling creatures of the hinterlands than any true Spire-born Naze.

In this retelling of Murorundrum-Kalash's vision, the Celestial Mechanic was curious to hear that the Beyonder had been revealed to him in full possession of a body. The Visage had not just been a disembodied head in life, and what is more, a likeness of this body had also been carved, in a somewhat distorted representation, down the length of the Omphalos' shaft. Apparently it terminated in two large clawed feet that, in a refined and delicate manner that stood as testament to the skills of the sculptor, were shown crushing the bodies of a circle of acolytes carved around the base. Joyous in their deliverance, their faces were turned up to their god in raptures of ecstasy as the air was pushed from their lungs and their skulls flattened under his weight.

He had asked her to draw it. At this, she had grown pale and afraid; soon after, he guessed that she had regretted her infelicity as she stopped responding to his invitations for nocturnal visits to his bed-chamber, and he did not see or hear from her again.

Like all the gods he had ever known, the Visage did its subjects the honour of never actually interceding on their behalf; it merely looked down with an aloof disinterest. Every famine, every harvest, every defeat in war or victory parade were observed from above with the same impassive equanimity – simply lit from a different angle.

That it belonged to a race of gargantuan beings which had become extinct long before the first cave-wall scratchings of recorded Naze history, the Celestial Mechanic did not question. He simply doubted the efficacy of calling on the deceased for advice concerning the matters of the living.

R OUSING HIMSELF from this reverie, he leaned back and pulled on the reins of the packbeast. It stopped eating a herbaceous border, slowly turned around and began walking down the wide dirt track that led out of the village, supplies and equipment clinking at its side. It felt invigorating to actually drive oneself; he could see why the lower levels made such a sport of it, and made a mental note to do it more often.

The triangulation arcs marked on the Highmost's charts gave him a reasonably precise location for planetfall. That this new star, a flint-spark of sky-rock, might be connected to the Visage rather than the belts that circled the sun was certainly a possibility; other limbs and organs did litter the land.

A forearm, from elbow to wrist, had once fallen during the rainy season, blocking the Gorodorborga close to the Rim. When the Circular Sea had overflowed, tens of thousands had drowned in the diverted floodwater.

During the dry season, when the level in the Circular Sea was at its lowest, the tips of five enormous rounded pillars of rock were sometimes visible. Lying to the south-west, and visible from the side of the Spire on which the Head of Forbearance had lodged, each pillar was ringed with green algae and used as a nesting site by a species of flying reptile that figured, in a styled form, on the reverse of the five-weight coin.

The pillars formed a rough circle, and could at low water be seen to curve inward towards a common centre at their bases, as if they might all be connected at some depth. They were known as the Five Merchants; legend has it that they had been turned to stone by the gaze of the Visage while seated around a campfire counting the profits of an unscrupulous deal.

The Celestial Mechanic knew them to be the upturned fingers of a fallen Beyonder hand.

T HE SIMPLE FARMSTEADS and low stone-built buildings with

walled garden plots and small orchards or pens for animals gave way to open fields and unkempt scrubland.

At a crossroads, the Celestial Mechanic pulled on the reins to stay his packbeast and consulted his charts. The beast took advantage of the pause to eat a colourful display of blooms that had been carefully trained around a circular arch leading to a small garden.

Sure of his bearings, he followed the road for five purloughs. Tall Mofforia trees rose at regular intervals either side to meet overhead; a herd of small tawny creatures was being driven down the way towards him by a plains nomad.

He pulled on the reins and brought the beast to a standstill to let them flow around him, parting like the froth at the bow of a Spire clipper. The beast closed its eyes and stretched its neck high, holding its head up out of the throng until they had all passed.

Presently the road, which had been rising for a while, curved up and to the right along a ridge. Tufts of vegetation marked the edge, and as the drop grew more precipitous a low barrier had been erected to prevent wheeled vehicles rolling over.

The way became stonier and narrower; to the right, the bank rose and became a wall of rock.

Before long, the Celestial Mechanic was negotiating a narrow ledge cut from the side of a cliff. It followed the contours of the escarpment; the occasional ravine had been rendered passable by planks of timber, which the Celestial Mechanic let his steed negotiate in its own time. Far below, a thin silver thread of water could occasionally be seen looping through the dense vegetation that collected at the bottom of the valley.

In a tree some distance below he spotted an upturned cart, a broken wheel spinning lazily in the breeze. Its occupant hung from a nearby tree by his leather belt, limp. He was unreachable from the road, so the Celestial Mechanic distractedly made a mental note to inform the authorities, such as they may be, when he arrived in the next town.

The thick, spiked branches of Mujaste succulents grew from the vertical cliff face, finding purchase on fallen boulders and nesting ledges. Dark stains of guano had been washed down and across the road; though the stench was almost intolerable, the Celestial Mechanic was grateful for the extra traction it afforded.

He passed under a masonry arch; the remains of a turret jutted above. This section looked like it had once been part of a fortification. Now only low walls remained, marking out the floor plans of rooms and corridors set at different levels up the mountainside.

Just ahead, a dirty shape wrapped in gauze huddled in the shelter of a corner of stonework. The roads around here, his contact had informed him, were notorious for bandits; the Celestial Mechanic carefully guided the packbeast over and walked it back and forth several times over the crouching thing, just to be sure. There was a brittle crunching of bone and something that may have been muffled cursing, but it didn't seem to put up much in the way of resistance.

The packbeast wiped its feet in the guano, then climbed a short flight of wide stone steps that led to an irregularly paved plaza. Here, they were rewarded with magnificent views of the valley and the lands beyond.

HUNDREDS OF STEEP terraces could be seen following the contours of the mountain for many purloughs ahead. The stepped walls of the eroded fortifications had been filled with a rich loam, and now supported lush gardens hung with yellow-orange fruit and heavy striated gourds. The Celestial Mechanic dismounted and chose a ripe specimen; he watched idly as the packbeast made its own selection.

Just ahead he could see a small house. A more substantial section of masonry had been covered with a roof made from strips of timber weighted down with stones. A squat chimney sat atop this construction, from which rose a tenuous column of woodsmoke.

Laid out around the dwelling was a simple vegetable garden, neat rows of krabbish hanging from frames of stripped branches. The packbeast wandered over, buried its snout in the ground and unearthed some pale tubers. The Celestial Mechanic, sitting on a boulder and eating a sweet deep-red fruit he did not know the name of, fancied he could spy faces in the glassless window.

He looked across the valley. The far side was gold-tinted with distance, the higher reaches wreathed with thin clouds. Small whitewashed temples which housed windchimes could be seen spaced throughout the landscape.

A deep lowing broke the Celestial Mechanic's contemplations. Having had its fill, the packbeast had positioned itself over the dwelling's low walls and was using them to scratch its underside. Its small face had upon it an expression of utmost bliss.

The roofing material became dislodged. The Celestial Mechanic popped his small pocketknife and sliced himself another section of fruit. He idly watched as the packbeast began to defecate down the chimney: a seemingly endless, wet, lumpy flow of pungent half-digested grasses mixed with the skeletal remains of animals, some still wrapped in fur.

Two small creatures ran out. Keeping their distance, they began remonstrating with the Celestial Mechanic in a language he was not versed in. He paused and observed them. Though tiny, they had large ribcages and muscular, sun-bronzed limbs. Wide-brimmed hats protected their eyes and prevented him from reading their expressions.

He inquired if he was on the correct road in three of the local dialects he was familiar with, and another two that he spoke only falteringly. The creatures stopped jumping up and down and listened for short while, then resumed their protestations, this time with renewed vigour and an excessive waving of limbs.

The Celestial Mechanic stood up, shook out a linen napkin from the flounce of a sleeve, wiped his carapace, and whistled to call the packbeast over. It had finished its evacuation, which could now be seen seeping from the windows and the front door, carrying with it a selection of furniture, bedding and crockery. The creatures stepped aside to let the packbeast pass; in fact they gave it a wide berth.

He remounted and pulled on the tasselled cord. Kicking the beast into a slow walk, he returned his gaze to the majesty of the scenery spread before him, letting the creatures' yammering fall to the back of his minds.

Something hit the hide of the packbeast just below his overcape. An acidic stench immediately filled his olfactory canal, threatening to make him vomit.

They were throwing eggs at him. Another passed over the reins and out into empty space, to fall into the trees far below. He saw a third coming and instinctively put up a hand to catch it. Miraculously, it didn't break. He pulled again on the reins, and the packbeast came to a standstill.

He looked back at the tiny figures, who had suddenly become very quiet. Each held another egg. They seemed unsure as to what to do next.

The Celestial Mechanic regarded them. He threw the egg he had just caught up into the air and let it fall back into his palm. They took a couple of steps back and shielded their eyes. One hit its foot on a rock, stumbled and sat down heavily, dropping his egg on his lap. Involuntarily he grabbed it with both hands; now he no longer held an egg, but a melange of broken shell and gelatinous goop. The creature leaped up and frantically tried to wipe itself down, but only managed to spread the mess further up its arms and over its jerkin. Its companion seemed to be torn between a deep, long-nursed resentment and an escalating desire to laugh.

The Celestial Mechanic watched this scene unfold with a certain detachment. Placing his egg in a soft pouch hung around the packbeast's neck, an afterthought rose into his forebrain; he pulled out a leather purse, loosened the string, and shook four coins into his palm.

He looked at them for a moment, clean and freshly minted. He had very little idea what things cost outside the Spire; how much might be appropriate? Not wanting to be thought ungenerous, he tossed all four to the ground. He chose to address them directly, though he was quite certain they would not understand him. In halting local dialect, he bid them farewell and hoped that the small token might be reasonable payment for their trouble and provisions. He then touched a fingertip to the edge of his carapace and dropped his head in acknowledgement, swung the packbeast's head around and continued on his way.

He magnanimously forgave them their indelicacies; he imagined the finer points of hospitality required when in the presence of one of the Spire's ruling elite might be lost on these rural peasants.

T HE ANCIENT STONEWORK became more regular, a causeway of tightly fitted cobbles around which the green grout of mosses fitted themselves. The packbeast picked up its pace, and before long the road began to slope down, the gardens either side becoming better tended and more formally laid

organised a number of awnings and tents in differing colours and styles, and a large stabling area in which livestock was tethered.

Just beyond that, and in happy agreement with his maps, was the railway. A broad causeway of gravel

Water exited through the nose of a rudely carved mythical creature

out, the buildings of a less rustic appearance.

The road emptied into what the Celestial Mechanic took to be a main square. A watering trough had been placed at its centre, fed with spring water that exited through the nose of a rudely carved mythical creature with an expression of relaxed beneficence. Around this was

supported five equally spaced rails, each two strides apart.

On a platform of polished terrazzo the Celestial Mechanic could see a ticket office and a number of food concessions. He absently handed the reins of the packbeast to a stablehand who had obsequiously appeared beside him. In exchange for another token, it was led away to be cleaned and watered.

Signs advertising popular brands of drinks and snacks hung under the station's jutting roof, and tables had been set up outside along the platform. A hand-painted menu in three languages he could read and one that he couldn't hung on a wall from which most of the paint had fallen away. Beside each item listed was a crude illustration – the first, the braised head of a local species of vole, a tuber between its teeth; another looked like a colourful grub impaled on a skewer and dusted with red soot; a third depicted a jar of pale green liquid in which floated a pickled arthropod.

He chose something that looked reasonably benevolent, a selection of savoury pastry parcels and a local fermented beverage whose label, a khrissig with a beatific expression and fully relaxed mandibles, held a certain appeal. The proprietor took his order and bowed just a little too low for the Celestial Mechanic's taste.

Engaged as he was with deciphering the menu, he did not see the hushed exchanges at the counter as the stablehand he had entrusted with his packbeast showed the proprietor something small in the palm of his hand; neither did he recognise the small creature with the large chest hiding in his knapsack.

On a low dais, a quartet of local musicians wearing a traditional style of dress the other patrons no longer seemed to favour played tunes on peculiar instruments. The proprietor went over and whispered something to them, and in short order *The Spire in Glory Stands* was struck up, though rendered in a manner the Celestial Mechanic had not heard before. Instead of the usual lyrical cascades of melodious strings favoured by the musicians of the Grand Gardens, he listened in bemusement to a series of rasps played on a notched pole and a breathy piping underscored with a beat slapped out on the stretched and mounted skin of a rodent.

Still, it was recognisable, a serviceable effort, and the Celestial Mechanic duly applauded with some sincerity.

T HE FOOD WAS passable, though they needed to work on their presentation. It came on a large leaf with a napkin placed to one side on which was printed the logo of a local brand of disinfectant, a chutterbug on its back with its legs in the air.

He studied the timetable, copies of which were placed on every table. From what he could deduce, the next train was due in a couple of turns. As charters were not available, he resolved to bear this small inconvenience to his schedule.

The platform began to fill up. There were local tradesmen and labourers on their way to market; animals in crates, sacks of fruit and vegetables, Hill Naze of lower rank for sale as housekeepers or, were they more comely, ornamental lawn decorations for Quarterland aristocracy.

Presently, the proprietor returned and directed the Celestial Mechanic's attention to the main square, which he could see clearly from where he was sitting.

There, around two hundred of the local inhabitants had organised an impromptu celebration. Columns of dancers swept by, immaculately dressed in formal summer suits of loose yellow cloth, their sacking headdresses decorated with colourful feathers and flowers, high-kicking with fixed expressions of happiness.

An enormous wooden tub on a wheeled platform came next, pulled by seven animals that looked like smaller versions of his packbeast. From the tub, silvered creatures threw themselves into the air, performing tumbles, cartwheels and backflips; their fins sparkled where drops of water caught the sun. They had jewels along their top lips and ruffed skirts around their midriffs.

The Celestial Mechanic wondered if he had happened to pass by during a festival, or if this was a ceremony to mark the election of some local dignitary.

There followed another cadre of perfectly synchronised dancers, leaping and pirouetting; then came an enormous creature he thought better suited to battle. It was brightly painted in topaz and gold, with an armoured faceplate and a long proboscis which it delicately held up in a series of sinuous shapes, transforming one into the other with hypnotic grace, all the while standing on one hind leg.

The Celestial Mechanic clapped some more. It was then that he became aware that the crowd, locals and travellers alike, were looking not at the show but at him. Becoming somewhat uncomfortable, he returned his attention to the time-table. Was it possible he did not blend in as seamlessly as he had assumed?

He heard a discreet chirp. A grek in a brightly coloured hat topped with bells was holding out a tray. He seemed somewhat insistent, so after a moment's hesitation, the Celestial Mechanic dropped several coins onto it. The grek looked at the tokens with wide eyes, bowed low, and retreated backwards into the throng, which thereafter quickly dispersed.

THOUGH HE WAS NEVER to know it, the Celestial Mechanic had inadvertently ruined the local economy. Each of his coins represented an amount it would take more than twenty lifetimes of honest labour for a Quarterlands peasant to earn.

Were future events to take a very different course and were he to come this way again, he would have found that the train no longer stopped at this particular station. The neat terraced fields would be overgrown, the houses deserted. In the unlikely event that he was to enquire as to the inhabitants' whereabouts, he would be informed that, suddenly finding themselves rich beyond their most fevered imaginations, the entire population of the town and the hamlets surrounding it had decamped en masse to the grandest hotels and beaches of Naskelon, the fabled city on the shores of the Iron Sea favoured by the local grandees and gentry.

BUT NOW, FOR THE PRESENT, the train did stop here, and with the help of the stablehand the Celestial

Mechanic arranged passage.

Not much later than advertised, a hissing of steam from enormous pistons heralded its imminent arrival. Rounding a curve, he finally saw it; it was large, even by the standards of the Spire. Fully twenty times the Celestial Mechanic's height, it made a fearsome racket as it drew up alongside the platform like an ocean liner pulling up to the jetty of a small fishing village.

The train's forward bulkhead was painted in contrasting chevrons of yellow and black; in a cab high above could be seen a crew of five or six engineers, busily pulling great levers and prepping the engines to idle. Railings and walkways ran around its great bulk at levels analogous to the floors of a building, and creatures in black overalls could be seen scampering over the coachwork, checking, adjusting, tapping dials and releasing pressure valves with a cacophony of whistles and hisses.

At the very front, a cluster of spotlights was mounted asymmetrically above a pair of greased buffers and an intricate coupling mechanism that dwarfed those waiting on the platform. It swung slowly above, smelling of engine oil and crushed vegetation. A steel skirt protruded below, decorated with a dark patina from animals who had wandered onto the line. The wheels alone were taller than any building in the town; spoked and polished, they shone with engineering precision. Those standing too close to the platform edge were engulfed in a sulphurous cloud of steam as it finally came to a halt, the coaches

and wagons behind raising a chorus of complaining metal on metal as they settled into equilibrium.

The stablehand led the packbeast and the Celestial Mechanic down the line of coaches. His spirits sank as they passed the lacquered and inlaid coachwork of the first-class passenger wagons with their serried tiers of private balconies and viewing promenades. He glimpsed ballrooms on the upper levels with ornate ceilings, chandeliers still swaying slowly; the swimming pools on the lower levels gave way to crowded and filthy second- and third-class carriages, open wagons on which felled timber and animal carcasses were lashed, and on to the livestock section at the rear.

The stablehand had reserved a large flat wagon strong and stable enough to carry beasts of burden, with quarters above for their owners. The Celestial Mechanic tipped him and, feigning postprandial tiredness, slunk off to investigate his chamber, leaving him to the practicalities of arranging the beast for travel.

An open iron framework housed an elevator at the rear of the carriage; this took him up above the warm scent of dry grass and dung to a series of cabins which opened to the left and right from a long corridor that ran the length of the carriage. Checking the number on his key, he found his room.

It was basic, he acknowledged, but clean and reasonably well equipped. A couch had been placed against the back wall, facing the shuttered window. Winding a handle caused this to rise, revealing a view of the town's rooftops and the beginnings of the narrow terraced fields, which rose into the foothills of the mountains beyond.

Shouts came from below; street vendors were raising boxes on long poles which held items of colourful knitted clothing decorated with stylised flora and fauna; others carried fruits and other sundries. He could see hands beckoning from the windows of the other cabins; boxes swung over, selections were made, and coins dropped in in return.

There came a rap at his door. His luggage had been brought up. He thanked the porter, latched the door, washed in a small hand basin, then lay down on the skins that covered the couch. The animals below were lowing a lullaby, and very soon the Celestial Mechanic's whiskers began to unfurl.

FAR OVERHEAD, an object of unknown origin and unknown purpose inexorably followed its trajectory, one that would soon intersect with Terrine's orbit. The planet would rotate beneath it, offering up a landing site. Even now, unsuspecting people who led uneventful lives were moving up the belly of the world as it rolled into position.

Somewhere out there was an insignificant location that would soon achieve a new significance, rising through the darkness to meet this mysterious interloper, the Celestial Mechanic, and the dawn.

To be continued

IN OUR NEXT ISSUE:

Ascension • PART 4 OF OUR NEW SERIAL
The Girl in the Crystal Pantograph • M. J. MONTAGUE
Beyond the Rain Gate • NICK KOLHERNE
The World You Want, The World We Need • S. M. VANHORNE
An Ill-Wind from Maybe • CARMEN Z. SALHINO
Vox Angelica • MAXWELL DELGADO
. . . AND OTHERS

PRICE 2/-

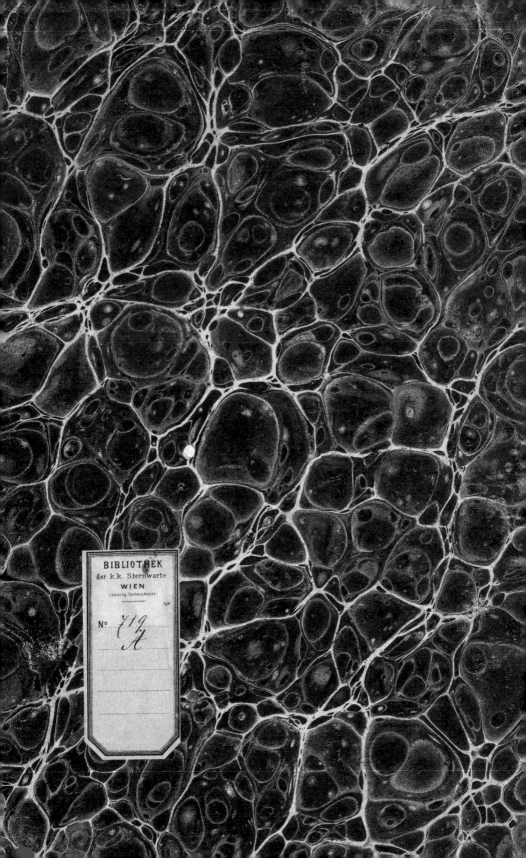

JOHANNIS HEVELII
COMETOGRAPHIA,

Totam Naturam
COMETARUM;

UTPOTE

Sedem, Parallaxes, Diſtantias, Ortum & Interitum,
Capitum, Caudarumǫ́; diverſas facies, affectionesǫ́;,

NEC NON

Motum eorum ſummè admirandum,

Beneficio unius, ejusǫ́; fixæ, & convenientis hypotheſeos exhibens.

In quâ,

Univerſa inſuper
PHÆNOMENA, QUÆSTIONESQUE
de Cometis omnes, rationibus evidentibus
deducuntur, demonſtrantur,

Ac

Iconibus æri inciſis plurimis illuſtrantur.

Cumprimis verò,

COMETÆ
ANNO 1652, 1661, 1664 & 1665 ab ipſo Auctore, ſummo ſtudio
obſervati, aliquantò prolixiùs, penſiculatiusǫ́; exponuntur, expenduntur,
atǫ́; rigidiſſimo calculo ſubjiciuntur.

Acceſſit,

Omnium Cometarum, à Mundo condito hucusquè
ab Hiſtoricis, Philoſophis, & Aſtronomis annotatorum,

HISTORIA,
Notis & Animadverſionibus Auctoris locupletata,
cum peculiari Tabulâ Cometarum Univerſali.

Cum Privilegio Sac. Cæſareæ, & Reg. Pol. & Suec. Majeſtatum.

GEDANI.
AUCTORIS Typis, & Sumptibus,
Imprimebat
SIMON REINIGER.
ANNO M DC LXVIII.

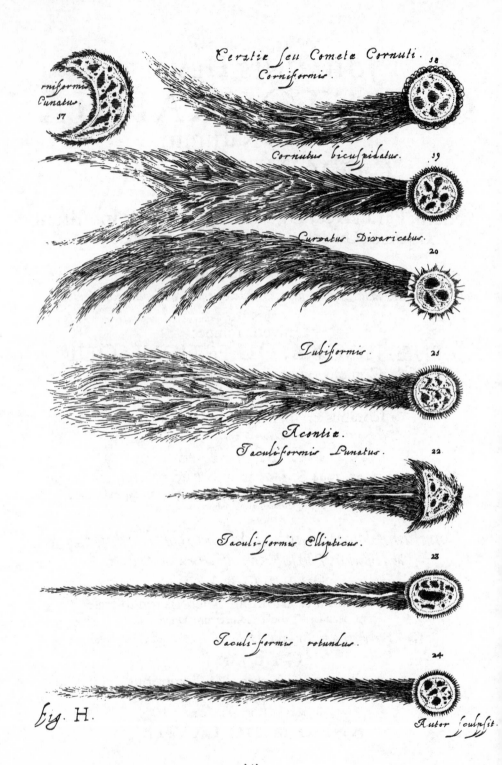

Ceratiæ seu Cometæ Cornuti. 18
Corniformis.

rniformis
Lunatus.
57

Cornutus bicuspidatus. 19

Curvatus Divaricatus. 20

Dubiformis. 21

Acontiæ.
Jaculiformis Lunatus. 22

Jaculi-formis Ellipticus. 23

Jaculi-formis rotundus. 24

Fig. H.

Autor sculpsit.

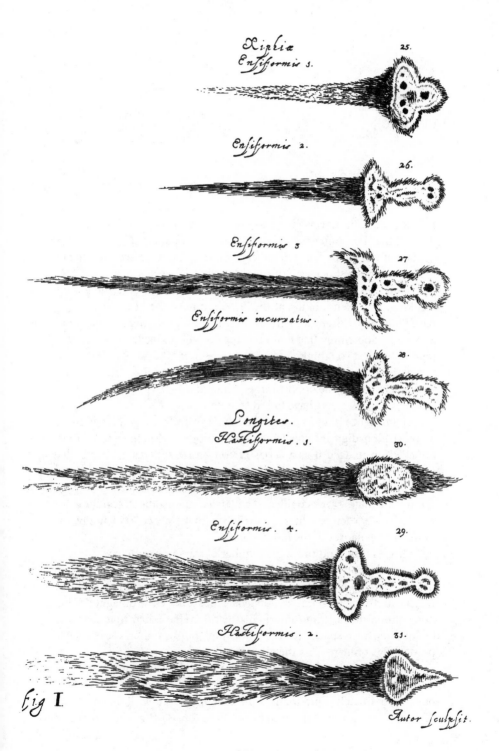

Xiphiæ
Ensiformis 1.

25.

Ensiformis 2.

26.

Ensiformis 3

27.

Ensiformis incurvatus.

28.

Longites.
Hastiformis. 1.

30.

Ensiformis. 4.

29.

Hastiformis. 2.

31.

Fig I.

Autor sculpsit.

GRIDLOCK

Jack looked as if he was about to make a confession. "You might have noticed that I'm somewhat— I'm obsessed with patterns."

Harriet pulled an exaggerated cartoon take, all wide eyes and hands held up in mock shock as if this was somehow a revelation.

"*Thank you,* Harriet. Well, something our futurist friend said got me thinking. I've been looking at the distribution of the, the alien zoo we have hanging in ideaspace here. Is there some logic to the arrangement? Some *law?* Something that looks this organised is unlikely to be arranged randomly, don't you think?"

Harriet had not progressed beyond simply gawping at the creatures whenever she had the opportunity. "Uh, I guess—"

"Well, I think I may have found something."

Jack brought up an image of the Signal from Space in its raw form: a 100-trillion-digit number. A scratch-built data visualiser he had just knocked up imaged it as a series of concentric spheres, colour coded according to four kinds of interrelationships and cross-referenced with their positions in the string. These were pretty arbitrary ways to arrange the data – Jack could, and had, tried many others, searching for regularities, structure, clues. 100 trillion. That was, coincidentally, the number of synapses in the human brain.

At least a thousand times the number of stars in our galaxy.

Originally each iteration was assumed to be identical, any variation due to external factors: signal decompression errors, degradation due to gas in the intervening interstellar medium, electromagnetic and gravitational fields, atmospheric dissipation. His hunch that each was a blueprint for a specific creature was now not in doubt – it had been powerfully confirmed via the glasses.

From memory of his observations at the Embankment, Jack estimated the gap between neighbouring members of the zoo, worked out approximately how many would fit into a cubic kilometre, and divided that into the total number of iterations of the Signal that had been received. That number, Jack was sure, was but a small section of a much larger whole – how large, he had no way of telling.

As Daniel Novák had explained with some regret, the dish at Jodrell Bank just happened to be pointed in the right direction at the right time and had, merely by fortuitous accident, swept past the data stream momentarily; by the time it had been realigned with the same spot in the sky, it had ceased. There was no more Signal. From the previous empty sweep to the subsequent empty sweep was perhaps fourteen hours. That was enough time to broadcast a menagerie several hundred times larger; Daniel reckoned he could have as little as five per cent of the complete data set. Had those other creatures now been lost forever? Or would another alien race, at some future date somewhere further across the cosmos, have a dish pointed in the right direction and manage to collect the set in its entirety?

Jack hoped so.

Given that 'The Grid', as Jack now thought of it, existed in ideaspace rather than the real, physical world, it ignored physical objects – Westminster Bridge, pavements, the Thames. As far as he could tell it extended out to the limits of vision, and if that large shape he had seen on the horizon was a creature of some kind, at least to low Earth orbit. Quite possibly the Grid also extended deep into the Earth, rows of alien creatures now buried alongside the fossilised remains of prehistoric beasts from the Cretaceous and Permian. Maybe they continued down through the lithosphere to the mantle, where they would be floating in molten rock, as indifferent to the million-atmosphere pressure as the vacuum of space. He wondered if they went down to the core of the planet itself.

A quick calculation that divided the volume of the Earth into a cubic lattice around ten metres a side meant that at least 109,750,950,000,000,000,000 creatures could be contained within it. A hundred billion times the population of Earth. Depending on how far the Grid extended into space, the figure could be many times more.

The numbers were provisional, of course. There was one thing Jack felt he could be sure of, though: as the creatures were stationary relative to their surroundings, the Grid must rotate with the Earth. It was safe to assume that the same entity would be found hanging over the same spot, day and night.

But how did each creature in the Grid relate to the others? Was there a pattern *there*?

Jack regarded the raw data on-screen. It was hard to get an overview – he had found that either he was zoomed in too close, looking at an individual Signal iteration, or if he pulled out to see the overall arrangement the salient details just weren't visible.

What he needed was a larger canvas.

Jack keyed in a set of parameters. "Harriet – put on your glasses."

Visible through the Depthcharges was not the alien zoo itself, but the data set that described it. The office filled with a matrix of numbers and letters, arranged in constellations according to whatever set of congruences he chose to sort them by, coruscating baubles of coloured motes he could manipulate with a gesture of his hand. Up: zoom in. Down: zoom out. Twist: rotate. Switching to a high magnification, he could see inside an individual atom of lights, data points precessing like an unbalanced top. He pulled out, and the vertiginous change of perspective sent his inner ear scrambling for purchase.

"Look."

It was apparent on larger scales that the Grid was a nested series of concentric spheres, centred on the Earth. Pulling out so that the entire data set was contained within the room, they could walk around and through it, finally get a sense of its shape.

Harriet's arms hung limply by her sides. "It's *beautiful!*"

Jack ran up and down, looking at interstices, confluences, gaps. Rotating, panning, zooming.

The Grid was not homogenous. It was fraying around the edges, petering out into streamers and voids midway to the Moon. There were dark unlit swathes of missing data, like districts of a city after a power cut. Some interstices were set at far greater or smaller increments, perhaps, Jack guessed, to house creatures of vastly different sizes. One in particular caught his eye – a spherical arrangement far larger than any of the others. This, he assumed, was the enormous creature he had glimpsed through layers of atmosphere, here represented by a ball of shimmering data.

Regularities, regularities . . .

Nixon watched him negotiate the office with the glasses on, feeling for the table, bumping into a crate, sending another shooting across the parquet to the far wall. On the monitors he caught, robbed of depth perception, a glimpse of what he and Harriet must be seeing, but the performance was pure Jack, pulling information from the ether like a visionary prophet receiving messages from angels . . . or a hallucinating madman.

Jack was becoming frustrated. "It's still too small. I can't see the detail. I need a *bigger* canvas . . ."

He picked up his phone, ran out of the office, down the stairs, through the door and into Hoxton Square. Above, around him, through the trees, the Grid extended in all directions. The raw data, transmitted by the Intelligencia WiFi signal via his image-processing software. He spun it around to view it from this angle or that, to search it for – for –

Now there's an interesting thing.

Harriet and Nixon came running out after him. Even the inveterate afternoon drinkers in the square were giving Jack a wide berth as he gesticulated and danced across the grass, stumbled into bushes and through flowerbeds, oblivious. He was looking up, around at things that no one else could see.

Harriet pulled her pair of Depthcharges down over her eyes again. "What do you see, Jack?"

Jack pointed to a bench encircling a tree. The couple seated there stood up warily and walked back to the Hoxton Square Bar and Kitchen.

"There's a Grid-wide regularity. Every 11,204 interstices in any direction you'll find the same thing."

"What? Find what?"

"This is what I wanted to show you. It's as if the Grid is divided into holding pens. Some are half empty, many are full. But there's a specific repeat. The same data cluster associated with each pen. The same *creature.* So who are they? Architects? Tour leaders? Shepherds of the flock?"

"Ah." Harriet could see a discrete constellation of data spinning half a metre above the grass. As far as she could make out, it looked indistinguishable from any of the other iterations of the Signal. She stepped closer. "Commanders of the platoon?"

Jack lifted the glasses up to his forehead momentarily. "Always the pessimist."

"Realist." She shrugged. "Let's just say that life has taught me to be cautious of people's motives and intentions."

"Aliens have motives?"

"Why not?"

Jack had no answer. He nodded, then— "What are *my* motives? What am I?"

"*You* are a pattern-recognition machine. You can't help it. It's an obsession."

"*Heh.*" Jack let the glasses fall back onto his nose and spread his arms wide, a gesture which inadvertently made him appear even more messianic. Harriet caught the irrepressible passion in his voice. "*Consciousness* is a pattern-recognition machine. Maybe that's *all it is.*"

Jack had many enthusiasms that bordered on obsession. It was what she liked about him, though she had long ago decided that she never wanted to be one of them.

"So, here." Nixon saw Jack point to a municipal wastebasket in which someone had lit a fire, its opening turned down at the side like the mouth of a stroke victim. "Nixon, take my glasses for a moment. *Look.* The Grid is rotating with the Earth because the medium it's running on – the servers that run the Web – are rotating with the Earth. This means that our nearest tour leader, Shepherd – whatever they are – has a distinct location. We can *find* it. We can go and *see what it looks like.*"

"Let me have a look." Nixon was holding out his hand impatiently. Jack passed him his Depthcharges, then pointed at a space in mid-air he hoped corresponded to the interstice in question.

Nixon could see, floating in front of the bin, a small set of nested spheres, each rotating independently. Fainter lines led from the poles and equator out of view – the cubic lattice. "I see it. Where is it?"

"Close. A few miles at most. West, I think. Southwest. The City."

Seen through the glasses, Jack's eyes scintillated with reflected lights. Nixon pulled them off and passed them back. "The City. Right. If you have the means to travel clean across the galaxy, you're not going to slum it here in the East End."

"Hah." Jack tucked the Depthcharges back into his messenger bag. "Come on. Let's go and pay our mystery regularity a personal visit."

Without a backward glance, Jack sprinted off down Coronet Street towards Old Street Tube station.

A S C E N S I O N

by F. HERSCHEL TEAGUE

When the Celestial Mechanic answered the Highmost's

summons, little did he expect to be asked to mount an

expedition into the lands below the Spire, less familiar to

him than the heavens above — and far more alien.

PART FOUR

JOLT AWOKE HIM. Looking across to the windows he could see that the train was in motion; the rolling peaks of a range of hills were visible, and beyond them in the far distance, faded to the warm yellow of a venerable manuscript by the sulphur in the air, he could see the tip of the Spire, a pale spearpoint against the darkening evening sky.

He rose, unfurled his wardrobe roll and chose some formal evening wear. He regarded himself in the polished section of shell that was standing in the corner on a simple stand. Overdressed? He doubted if such a thing were possible, but removed the thorax belt and garters just in case. He didn't want to inadvertently draw any more attention to himself.

Checking the corridor, he exited, locked the door behind him, and started up towards the front of the train. He found that the six central corridors that ran the length of each carriage, one per floor, were

It described a great arc across the heavens and down to their appointed meeting place, somewhere in the barrenlands to the south

connected to the next by sections of flexible walkway; constructed from tanned hides fitted over a skeleton of supporting banoo hoops, they gave under his weight.

Three carriages up, he encountered the wagon lashed with timber he had noticed earlier. There was just one corridor here, hung across the length of the open wagon from pylons at either end, and it swung disconcertingly as the train moved. He cursed the depredations he was to suffer in the service of the Highmost in the most indecorous language, and pressed on.

Just before he arrived at the first-class cabins towards the front, the corridor gave into a large high-ceilinged vestibule. Mirrored in

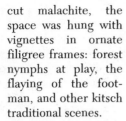

cut malachite, the space was hung with vignettes in ornate filigree frames: forest nymphs at play, the flaying of the footman, and other kitsch traditional scenes.

Pillars topped with stylised flowers rose up to support a corbelled dome, around which a panoramic horizon had been painted. The Visage, looking unrealistically benign, looked down from the apex.

Under this was a central circular bar with an artfully pocked counter, above which racks of faintly tinkling glasses hung. It was surrounded by booths, some occupied, some vacant, others with the curtains drawn around them for privacy. Set concentrically around this were sweeping semicircular staircases, and looking over the polished balustrade the Celestial Mechanic could see the same layout of bar and booths repeated on two further floors below.

An immaculately dressed emersagio showed him to an empty booth. A coastal race one sometimes saw in the taverns of the Rim but the Celestial Mechanic had not encountered this far out before, it ran him through the selection of drinks, stimulants, sexual services and light snacks they currently had available.

He ordered a bulb of calfmilk, sweetened with bark sap, then laid out his charts on the table. He was making good time; the train would arrive at the town nearest to the likely impact site the following morning, and it should be but a few hours' ride from there.

He took the opportunity to ask the emersagio to relay a message back to the Spire by wordwing. Prized for their ability to learn and recall several sentences with great fidelity, even down to the particular accent of the sender, aviaries of these mimics were carried on all major travel routes for the convenience of passengers. He could be sure that his message, disguised as a shipping manifest, would be intercepted by agents of the Assembly of the Constant Conviction and find its way indirectly but at speed to the Highmost.

AMONG THE GUESTS seated at the other booths were a small group of what the Celestial Mechanic took to be merchants from the northern hill tribes. They wore long hooded robes hemmed with a twisting motif of leaves and coiled tendrils, and when their hands were visible, they were gloved. Their hoods were pulled forward, and in the dim light of the chandelier's candles the Celestial Mechanic could not see their faces. He could tell that they were tall, and had the broad shoulders and heavy build of a Mountain breed, though he could not see any evidence of their cranial protrusions, usually filed to a small dome. These were all that remained of their antlers, which custom dictated were removed during their coming-of-age rites.

After some extended discussion between themselves which he pretended to ignore, one of the group ambled over to his booth. The Celestial Mechanic held a foreclaw to a line of text to act as a bookmark, and looked up. Sure enough, above a veil of finely spun black fabric, he saw the predictable fervent intensity on the face of this Servant of the Omphalos, a follower of Murorundrum-Kalash the Defiler.

Gruff and humourless, as was typical of his sect, he without introduction jabbed a finger at the Celestial Mechanic's charts, the bulk of which were still rolled up in their stoppered tubes. "Where you go?" he stated via a series of clicks and whistles, using the universal tongue favoured by Quarterlands traders.

The Celestial Mechanic extended his whiskers expansively and framed a reply. In loose translation, it ran something like this: "My warmest and most sincere greetings to you, fellow traveller. Are you not many purloughs from home? What business do the Servants of the Omphalos have out here in the Lands of the Unrevealed?"

The pilgrim's eyes narrowed. "We forbidden by oath to offer salutation to member of degenerate sect. We only permitted to show pleasure in company of own sanctified brethren."

The Celestial Mechanic was, of course, fully aware of this. "But you mistake my allegiance, my fellow traveller. Permit me to enlighten you. I belong to no sect. I am without deity, either known in the four quadrants, or of personal private revelation. I am neither prophet nor follower."

The look of fervent intensity was now crossed with an expression of slack-jawed disbelief, under which he sensed bubbled a terrible anger. "Follow no God? That you willingly forfeit afterlife within Great Beyonder himself is astonishment enough, but to not hold to *any* belief in any of inferior pantheons of the Unrevealed is – is *unfathomable!*"

The Celestial Mechanic nodded sanguinely and returned his gaze to his chart. "Indeed."

"But goes against all precept of reason. I – I taint myself by even converse with you, you—" He seemed genuinely lost for words "—lost, left behind. Such godlessness is an abomination!" The Celestial Mechanic had surmised the conversation might take such a turn.

"Well, it sadly looks like this most interesting conversation must therefore come to a premature end." He lowered his head in formal respect, perhaps a little too deeply and with a fraction more solemnity than was strictly necessary.

The Servant of the Omphalos returned to his booth. The Celestial Mechanic thought of retiring to his cabin, but on a whim decided on one more glass of calfmilk. While this was being mixed and brought over, he kept the brethren in the periphery of his vision. They were animatedly discussing something.

After some debate, the same pilgrim was nominated to come over to the Celestial Mechanic's table once more, this time with a message.

"I am forbidden talk to Unrevealed, but as my aura already irreparably soiled by you disbelieving presence, I am sent to inform we will pray now for you and so lead you everlasting sparklife to right true path."

The Celestial Mechanic held his gaze until he looked away. "That's very kind of you, but unnecessary. I fear I am beyond redemption."

Without another word, the pilgrim again returned to his associates. A small item was brought from the folds of a robe and with great care and respect placed between them on the table. Holding gloved hands, they closed their eyes and started up a low humming. Initially, this was barely audible; however, it soon rose to the level of polite conversation, and then louder still. They began nodding in unison, their lower jaws hanging loose under their hoods; they then began to jerk their heads back, one after the other, producing a series of loud clicks as their toothplates snapped shut in quick succession.

This they repeated.

And repeated.

Soon, chips of tooth enamel could be seen littering the tablecloth. Conversation in the other booths and around the circular bar became impossible. Some guests began stirring uncomfortably in their seats. The Celestial Mechanic could sense the atmosphere was becoming tense.

He picked up his empty glass and walked over to their table. As he expected, none of them met his eye. Expectorating a gob of sap, he rolled it through his breathing sphincter a few times to thicken it, then spat it into his palm. He then wiped it thoroughly over the glass, held it up to the light, then in one swift and precise movement placed it upside-down over the object in the centre of the table – a stylised, blank-faced Omphalos in miniature, carved from a grek horn and polished by centuries of devotional use.

Silence.

The Servants of the Omphalos, the followers of Murorundrum-Kalash the Defiler, looked at the streaky glass. One reached out instinctively to grab it, thought better of it and flinched away just as his gloved hand was about to come into contact. Another unsuccessfully attempted to tilt the table, which was bolted to the floor to prevent just such an eventuality. His fellow looked around for an object with which to knock over the glass, but saw nothing. Another simply stared wide-eyed at the Omphalos within, its shape refracted into wavy multiples. They broke into a sobbing lamentation.

The Celestial Mechanic touched the rim of his carapace. "And now, kind sirs, I bid you good night. May your all-powerful and all-knowing God guide you and provide answers to all your pressing needs – both spiritual and practical, in the next world, and in this."

A cheer followed by a round of applause spontaneously erupted, and, pausing only to sweep up his robe and appreciatively bow to his audience, the Celestial Mechanic left the bar.

HE MADE HIS WAY to one of the upper balconies that were open to the sky, a broad arc of deck with a sweeping handrail and rows of reclining couches set between canvas partitions that held the winds at bay. Ahead, beyond a funnel the circumference of a fortified tower, lit by the powerful glowlamps mounted on the front of the engine itself, five bright lines curved out to the darkening horizon across a landscape of indistinct shapes and flitting spectral glows.

Overhead, through tattered banners of smoke, the Celestial Mechanic could see a sixth bright thin line, tracing the path of the falling star as surely as any rail. He regarded it with a certain fondness. It was his reason for being out here, that short scratch on the upturned bowl of the firmament.

It seemed to be immobile, but if he looked directly at it for a few minutes it was just possible to see it was in motion, describing a great arc across the heavens and down to its journey's end – landfall, and their appointed meeting place, somewhere in the barrenlands to the south.

Had he paid attention to his immediate surroundings, he might have seen three figures on a couch behind a canvas sail a short distance away, their cloaks edged in crimson.

One of them raised an eyeglass to the sky, then flipped open a notebook in which certain tables were laid out, neatly arrayed in cross-referenced columns.

Had he paid more attention in the restaurant back on the platform, he might have noticed his stablehand talking to these same three characters, who had then been discreetly seated across the room from him.

And had he been more curious, he might have looked into the disappearance of his bed-partner, the apostate, back on the Spire. He might even have found her body in the harbour, weighted down with stones, having been dropped from a fifteenth-level balcony to her final resting place in the waters below.

And if he had followed up on this incident with certain friends in the Occluded University, he might have found a witness to the act. An itinerant musician and juggler living in a gazebo in the incense gardens on the same level, she could have unequivocally identified the culprits as these same three men, members of a highly secretive inner elite unknown to even their co-religionists downstairs, the Servants of the Omphalos.

This group called themselves the Prime Advocates of Murorundrum-Kalash, and were feared and revered in equal measure by those few survivors who had had the misfortune to come to their attention. Whatever they turned their minds to, they were precise in their execution, unyielding in their conviction, and unwavering in their faith. They were here, now, on a mission of preordained revelation to retrieve nothing less than a body part of their God, currently falling to unsanctified earth in the Lands of the Unrevealed.

But the Celestial Mechanic, watching the sky, knew none of these things.

LATER, BACK IN HIS CABIN, he splashed water over his carapace and ran over his itinerary. Tomorrow around noon the train would pull into a station serving a small farming community where he would disembark. From there, it should not take him long to reach the probable impact location. Everything was going according to plan.

The Celestial Mechanic did not see the shadow drop down from the roof and move across the small balcony outside his shutters. Nor did he see his window open and close soundlessly.

A gloved hand reached around from behind him and a wad of gauze was held to his breathing sphincter. The sleeping-scent was as advertised: powerful, fast.

The Celestial Mechanic's fore- and hindbrain shut down without conversation or agreement. His muscles immediately relaxed. His assailant nimbly stepped aside to avoid any further contact, and he dropped to the floor with a sound like a sack of broken crockery.

To be continued

IN OUR NEXT ISSUE:

Ascension • PART 5 OF OUR NEW SERIAL

PLUS

Ladder to Centauri • RAY CANTOFOLI
The Bordello in Amatrice • AUBREY BEGG
A Million Little Joys • MEREDITH PHILLIPS
Raygun Jones • DANIEL NOVÁK
The Tuckertown Somnambulist • R. F. DARVELL
Coalblack Tattoo • JACK BRAMPTON

NEWS • REVIEWS • DEPARTMENTS

The FEBRUARY issue of *Planetfall* will be on sale JANUARY 4TH at your favourite newsstand or direct from the publishers:
CHAS. BOXWOOD & CO., ACTON VALE, LONDON W4

PRICE 2/-

THE FORBIN PROJECT

Jack was at Old Street Tube before he realised Harriet and Nixon were no longer following him. He couldn't wait. They could catch up with him later.

Where were the DMEn? True, based on his current sample, statistically speaking they were only two-thirds men, but Jack was sure that two-thirds wouldn't have much of a problem with the male pronoun, and he liked to operate a democracy.

He wondered if it would be possible to write a 'find a friend' app to keep tabs on them, but as they seemed to lack a specific location when not materialised within the Oxbow he was at a loss as to how to actually define 'location'. Maybe they simply were where their attention happened to be, looking out from a CCTV camera across an empty car park, some suburban supermarket, or lost in the bowels of Area 51 . . .

If anyone could help him search ideaspace, it was them.

He remembered an old film (the name escaped him) in which a new experimental supercomputer, having digested the sum of human knowledge, decides we're now extraneous to its purposes. How did he know that wouldn't happen here? The invention of the first self-replicating artificial intelligence, it has been said, would be mankind's last invention. And Jack might just be helping that day get a little bit closer.

He ran down the stairs to the platform. Next train: two minutes. He sat down, found himself tapping his foot, and stood up again.

Hadn't the vehicle *always* been secondary to the – Jack hesitated to use the word *spirit*, having as it did so many mystical or religious overtones, but it was almost appropriate here. If humans did manage to create artificial intelligence, might that not be the natural next step in evolution, the means by which this motivating force, the memeplex we call life, simply dons a new set of duds, those being artificial rather than biological? And might this not be a story that had already begun, long ago, with the very first story, the very first meme?

Jack doubted that any personified idea, any 'spirit' of any century, could harbour at its core murderous intent. It would be suicide: it was, in some very real way, *us*. Harriet had told him this was naive; there were ideologies stalking the globe this very minute that cared very little for the people who entertained them, promising as they did dispensation in a non-existent afterlife for the murderous deeds they inspired. If Jack had been through her high-school experience, she'd told him, he'd understand how unremittingly unpleasant people were capable of being to each other – even when they were convinced they were actually doing good.

He paused to skim the headlines at the newsstand on the platform. There *were* destructive ideas at large in the world, ideas that were in the very business of doing away with the hosts that didn't contain them – and some of the hosts that *did* – just like in that old movie. An idea was a virus that didn't need to ensure the survival of its host because, unlike a common cold, it could reproduce regardless. It was easily communicable: all one had to do was read or listen or watch. You might then become a vector for its further transmission. If you opened your mouth to talk about it, it could jump right out, into someone else's ear, and infect their brain.

Was that what the DMEn were? The T-cell technicians that kept the memepool clean?

Jack pushed into the carriage. He assumed they were watching him, if only now and again, through the network of cameras that looked into every compartment, every tunnel, every cul-de-sac and cranny of London's streets. How many man-hours of footage did these produce every day? Every *minute*? Almost all of it must by necessity go unwatched, unless tomorrow, or next week, something happened that required human eyeballs to go searching back through each frame. A hundred years ago, your average person would be lucky to get through the informational equivalent of fifty books in a lifetime; we have an input capability designed for a simpler world. Jack thought of the stack of books beside his bedroll, the websites and blogs he followed, the three or four subscriptions he had to scientific and computing journals, and how they arrived far faster than he could consume them. The pile of shrink-wrapped magazines would grow until he'd put several dozen, unopened, into the recycling bin. Snowed under a black blizzard of words. If any of them were trying to tell him anything *really* important, he reasoned he'd find out some other way. Last time he looked, the world was still here, rotating once a day on its axis as it always had done.

At what point does the amount of information being produced pass not only an individual's capacity to process it all, but an entire *species'* capacity? *Information, information, information . . .* long gone were the days when an interested armchair amateur, a Horace Walpole, perhaps, could keep up to date with advances in every field of knowledge.

He exited the Tube at Tottenham Court Road and ducked down a series of back streets. Once away from the crowds, he tried on the glasses.

There they were. Lines of creatures hung across Lexington Street like strange bunting. In mathematically precise rows from Wagamama to Happy Voice Karaoke he could see them stretched from building to building, greying out up ahead towards Brewer Street in a fog of carbon monoxide.

Of the DMEn there was no sign.

"Talk to me." He looked at the reception on his iPhone. One bar. Maybe a full materialisation was beyond them. How had they communicated with him before he'd come up with the Oxbow? Ah yes. *Signs and portents.* The semiotic environment. Maybe Jack needed to give them some low-bandwidth raw material to work with.

At the top of the road was a newsagent. Outside stood two spinner racks of postcards: views of London under impossibly pure cyan skies; punks giving the finger. Mounted on the window were posters for the latest issues of *Vanity Fair* and *GQ.* Jack again tried on the glasses. *Nothing.* He did his nodding thing, but with the glasses or without, the view did not change.

He went in and began to scan the racks. *Raw input, raw—* Something caught his eye.

A jump, a buzz in the periphery of his vision. He picked up a *Daily Mail.* These days he rarely read a physical paper: more information to wade through, when he already had far too much to digest already.

I'm in the papers, Jack thought.

Jack, my boy, hang on to your mind . . . He could understand how easy it would be to start thinking that every billboard, every shopfront, every magazine masthead was addressing him directly.

Buy this. Do that.

Kill the President.

It sometimes felt as if he could read his own thoughts as he thought them: a mirror, an echo, a conversation with himself in black and white, written down in sensible articulate sentences rather than the wordless jumble of sensory impressions that typified his, and, he assumed, everyone else's subjective mental experience. He could imagine he was reading the story of his own life, a long and winding trail of words stretching several times around the world and across four score years and twelve, from birth to death, entrance to curtain call, and all written down using that familiar set of twenty-six glyphs in their upper- and lower-case genders, fizzing with their entourage of punctuation.

Twenty-six letters.

A bandwidth problem like no other, but all of literature, all record of human life worth living, had passed through the eye of that needle and not thought it too narrow.

Jack ⚜ Fenwick

PENNY DREADFUL MEDIUM, BUT CURRENT PRESSING NEEDS MUST. BLESS SECURITY-CONSCIOUS LONDON, CAMERAS THAT COVER EVERY

■ Back alley and high street, the bank and the bordello. We can watch them watching you. Take

A TAXI TO THE TATE GALLERY

And we dear boy. We WILL ENDEAVOUR TO CATCH UP WITH YOU THERE

Have managed to

Triangulate the location of the closest example of your mystery Grid repeat, the nearest 'Shepherd'. Mayhap we will get a look at whoever, or *what*ever, is there. Now, the area we need to cover is not large, being but a few square miles of London's old City, from the Monument to St. Paul's, the Globe to Mansion House.

But there are so very many places to search, and

MANY MORE WE

cannot. How does one, for example, look below the surface of the *filthiest* body of water in the Kingdom? How does one

CHECK THE SKIES WHEN

the best views we have are from cameras mounted on poles that point down to the busy intersections of Ludgate Hill or Old Bailey rather than heavenwards? We are three,

THEY ARE LEGION,

and the area contains some of the most secure *corporate firewalls* in the Capital. Even the combined attentions of those such as us cannot move faster than the speed of thought.

BUT PATIENCE

we have, and time; and with the view through your magical Glasses, our portable eyes into the Ether, we shall see what you shall see. We shall contact you again, anon. I am a Man of Letters, and though this inelegant garb sets my teeth on edge, we can certainly fare far worse.

NOW.

A taxi. Twenty-five minutes, and we will await your presence.

Please turn to Page 422

Jack stepped back out into the street and held up his hand. A black cab that had just that second passed by caught sight of him in his wing mirror, turned on the radius of a two-pound coin and pulled up inches from his nose with a rattle of diesel. The electric window came down.

"Where to, mate?"

"Tate Modern. Please."

A sucking of teeth. "That's south of the river, sunshine."

Jack's face was expressionless. "Is your work visa not valid there?"

The driver shrugged. "As you wish. It's on the meter."

Jack pulled open the door and fell onto the back seat.

On the meter.

"The Tate," Jack repeated.

"Got you the first time, guv."

"Sorry. Just thinking out loud." Jack would have to design some kind of text input for times like this. Girl 21 had the right idea. He wondered if the Count could currently hear him. Microphones – taxis were equipped with mics so that the driver could hear and speak to the passengers. And from there, a link via the GPS to the Net itself . . .

"Nineteen at the Tate?"

The speaker crackled. "Like I said, mate, the fare is on the meter."

"Yep, I can see. On the meter." Jack realised he could get out his laptop or look at the back of his Oyster card or press any one of a dozen richer memetic substrates into use, but the DMEn's creative means of communication so far had him hooked. Why make it too easy, when it was this much fun?

Loc. Location . . . a slippery concept, but easily applicable to physical flesh and blood types like, for example, Jack. Being made of *stuff*, which by its very nature occupied a given volume, he could always be found at some particular location, uniquely identifiable by a set of coordinates: x, y and z. These *things* that were made of *stuff* required transport to get from A to B, that transport currently being a London black cab.

It seemed to be more of a flexible concept for the DMEn, a matter, perhaps, simply of where they happened to direct their attention. Did one have only one point of attention? Was it possible to direct your attention to two things simultaneously, and thus be in two places at once without being, of necessity, two different entities? If this was so, could you then meet yourself? Have a conversation with yourself? Would you *know* it was you?

The cab passed over Blackfriars Bridge. And *more* than two? Dividing yourself over three or four locations or more: would you simply dissipate into meaninglessness . . . ?

Jack realised another interesting fact had just been brought to his attention. The Count, with whom he assumed he was communicating via the meter, did not seem to know the location of XX. That they had an independent volition and a degree of separation, from the Web and from each other, Jack took as a given. That was what gave them their very different personalities, their autonomy. But why should they automatically know where each other was, or where *anyone* was, for that matter, unless they could see, or otherwise sense them? Jack had not considered this before.

He sat back and regarded the back of the driver's neck, an angry lunar landscape of crusted pimples visible above the beaded seat cover. Jack asked the question aloud. "Twenty-one?"

The driver eyed Jack with barely concealed contempt in the rear-view and held the wheel just a bit more tightly, if that was possible. His knuckles went white. "Listen, mate, the fare is the fare. This isn't some unlicensed minicab here. It's not up for discussion."

"Right. Sorry. As you say, it's on the meter."

The chase was afoot.

IMAGE DUPLICATOR

Talk to me . . .

On the south bank of the Thames stands the red-brick mid-century modernism of the former Bankside Power Station, now the Tate Modern. As they approached from Southwark, Jack could see its tall square tower amongst the newer apartment blocks that now populated this old industrial landscape, and as always he was reminded of a Norman church.

These are our cathedrals of culture.

Jack paid the fare and walked into the cavernous Turbine Hall, down whose long slope kids who looked barely old enough to walk shot at terrific speeds on scooters, and up an escalator to the permanent collection. XX would be perfectly at home in such a bastion of twentieth-century modernism. The 19th Count, not so much.

It being a Tuesday, clumps of students with A2 sketch pads from art colleges in satellite towns and bemused tourist groups sparsely populated the halls. Jack put on the Depthcharges. He caught sight of himself in the glass wall of the bookshop. They looked bulky and utilitarian; unfashionable, unless you happened to think dark corrective lenses were the latest thing. He wondered if he looked remotely suspicious. A concealed camera, perhaps? No one, least of all the uniformed guards sitting in the corner of each room, seemed to pay him much attention.

Talk to me . . .

A crude large-scale copy of an Irv Novick comic book panel hung across two square canvases on a white expanse of wall up ahead. An explosion of red and chrome yellow outlined in black against an enlarged printer's screen sky of cyan dots.

It was impressive, if only due to its sheer size.

I PRESSED THE FIRE CONTROL...
AND AHEAD OF ME ROCKETS BLAZED THROUGH
THE SKY...

Across to Jack's right, another canvas. More dots, magenta this time. *I have some of those in a jar on a shelf back at the office,* Jack thought.

WHY, BRAD DARLING, THIS PAINTING IS A MASTERPIECE! MY, SOON YOU'LL HAVE ALL OF NEW YORK CLAMORING FOR YOUR WORK!

The next big thing. Picking up on signals in the culture, predicting and exploiting trends, riding the zeitgeist. Pattern recognition . . . or the temptation to see meaning where there may be none? It cuts both ways. Jack kept his voice low. "XX, 19, 21 – come on, show yourselves."

MAYBE HE BECAME ILL AND COULDN'T LEAVE THE STUDIO!

Jack looked over the top of the glasses in a manner he hoped was not unlike Audrey Hepburn in *Breakfast at Tiffany's*. No, that last one didn't change. No message there.

I DON'T CARE!
I'D RATHER SINK -- THAN CALL BRAD FOR HELP!

Brad, Jack. Jack, Brad. You offered to help, and so here I am.

THAT'S THE WAY -- IT SHOULD HAVE BEGUN!
BUT IT'S HOPELESS!

And that's *my* fault? Help me out here, guys.

Jack continued around the hushed sanctity of the page-white space.

WE ROSE UP SLOWLY...
AS IF WE DIDN'T BELONG TO THE OUTSIDE WORLD ANY LONGER...
LIKE SWIMMERS IN A SHADOWY DREAM...
WHO DIDN'T NEED TO BREATHE...

Jack wondered if the DMEn did indeed breathe – they *spoke*, and speaking forced air through the vocal tract. Air . . . air is made from atoms, the little moiré printer's dots of creation. The DMEn, however realistically rendered they might seem, were not. Did digital constructs go in for that degree of detail? They certainly lip-synched. The 19th Count might consider the rising and falling of his chest a nice finishing touch, a pocket square of realism. XX, he suspected, had the lungs of a blast furnace bellows, all hot air and leather.

I KNOW HOW YOU MUST FEEL, BRAD.

I'm Jack. Not Brad. Do you know how I feel? *Really?*

WHAT.? WHY DO YOU ASK THAT.?

**_WHAT DO YOU KNOW ABOUT MY IMAGE
DUPLICATOR.?_**

Everything, bud.

Jack had circled the room and returned to where he came in.

**_I CAN SEE THE WHOLE ROOM... AND THERE'S
NOBODY IN IT.!_**

Nothing. These games may be amusing, but seriously, is there not an easier way to talk to me? Jack walked through to the gift shop. Here there were racks of books, T-shirts, tea towels and mugs, a show in miniature; multiplied Pop Art duplications of a duplication of a duplication.

Words, more words, on the covers of books, catalogues, signage, price stickers.

From a rack where Dutch masters consorted with abstract expressionists, Jack picked up a postcard with an image that echoed the Intelligencia logo. A black square on a white ground. He looked around for the till.

A flicker caught his eye, a slight shifting of . . . Jack picked up a mug from a stacked display. There was an almost imperceptible delay as the glasses tracked the cylindrical surface. He held it closer and turned it towards him, giving the new text time to wrap over the old.

Aha. Bandwidth artefacts. It was *almost* perfect, but not quite.

On the mug, a cartoon siren with scarlet hair cupped a telephone. A speech bubble was placed to the top left:

JACK -- TWO STEPS BACK, LOOK LEFT. 19.

Not Brad – Jack!

Jack took two steps back.

Looked left.

Across the way, through the exit to the main concourse, the floor-to-ceiling windows of the Level 7 restaurant gave a magnificent view over a sullen Thames. He could see the forked supports of the Millennium Bridge, the wobbly walkway that led to the old City and the original walled heart of London. Written in reverse on the glass, intended to be read from the outside, was the name of the institution in two-metre-high sans capitals. Cropped either side by the doorframe, four back-to-front letters were visible.

Jack felt a numinous jolt of significance as semantic signifiers fell into place like deadbolts on a heavy door snugly ramming home.

ꓷOMƎ. DOME.

Positioned perfectly centrally in the O he could see the dome of St Paul's Cathedral. There it was, clearly circled in black. His final destination. The DMEn would be waiting for him there.

Celebratory fireworks went off in his mind.

A S C E N S I O N

by F. HERSCHEL TEAGUE

When the Celestial Mechanic answered the Highmost's

summons, little did he expect to be asked to mount an

expedition into the lands below the Spire, less familiar to

him than the heavens above — and far more alien.

PART FIVE

SUNLIGHT CUT THROUGH the shutters. No rhythmic vibration. The train was stationary. What hour was it? Questions crowded the Celestial Mechanic's forebrain. He had a pounding in his hindbrain out of all proportion to the amount of calfmilk he remembered drinking the evening before. A murmuring of voices and a clanking of couplings could be discerned over the heavy rumble of unloading cargo.

The train had pulled up at a station! The Celestial Mechanic threw his clothing and toiletries into his roll and hauled it out to the balcony. Below, he could see his packbeast being unclasped and led down the short ramp formed by the side of the wagon, which had been swung down to rest on the platform.

His stablehand was pocketing something proffered by one of a group of three hooded figures. He held up the reins and one of them took them, mounted the beast and tugged, turning its armoured neck

CONTINUING OUR NOVELETTE OF STRANGE ALIEN CULTURES IN EIGHT PARTS

fan away from the train to guide it out, towards the road beyond.

The Celestial Mechanic looked down. Five floors. He swung his bag over the railings and let it drop. *Count one. Count two.* It hit the straw of the flat wagon below and sent up a cloud of brittle dust. Already, the pilgrims and his packbeast had crossed the platform, the crowd parting to let them pass. He climbed over the balustrade, hung as low as he dared, then dropped to the balcony below.

A half-dressed merfem screamed at the upper limit of his hearing range and shouted creative obscenities at him. He quickly dropped to the next balcony below. This time he misjudged the distance and hit the railing instead of landing inside it, twisting his hoof and sending himself cartwheeling out and down to the hay below.

More than a little winded, he lay there for a few seconds blowing detritus from his breathing sphincter. A jolt shot through the wagon beneath him and the couplings locked, tightened. The rafters above groaned. The engine, far ahead, had up a head of steam and was ready to pull away.

He wrapped himself around his bag and rolled down the ramp and out onto the platform. Curious faces looked down at him. Picking himself up and brushing the stalks from his breeches, he slung his roll onto his back and made off after the packbeast.

After several strides and agonising complaints from his left ankle, he realised he would not be capable of catching them on foot. He looked around for some form of transport.

At an otherwise empty rank stood a small three-wheeled vehicle with a cushioned seat at the front and a luggage perch behind. It was powered by a caged tallister, a long-legged creature whose wings had been brutally clipped and its legs, which protruded down through the bars, were tied to a pair of pedals at the rear. The owner was slouched across the driver's seat, engrossed in a periodical detailing the gossip and scandal of the Spire's lower aristocracy.

Without asking permission, the Celestial Mechanic climbed into the front seat. The driver looked at him disdainfully. Straw still matted his whiskers, and he had put an elbow through a sleeve in the fall. The driver raised his palm, and made a quick chopping motion with it. This was the universally understood sign for payment, upfront, and fast.

The Celestial Mechanic reached for his purse. It was gone. He went through his other pouches and checked the hooks on his belt, but knew that he would not find it; it had been stolen last night, along with his consciousness. He grabbed the periodical, leafed through it, and happened on a sketch of a group of Spire nobility at last season's Flaying of the Footman celebratory dinner. The artistry was of a low standard, as was typical for these cheap entertainments, but their garb matched that which the Celestial Mechanic was currently wearing. He pointed at the picture, then at himself.

The driver pointedly picked a piece of straw out of the suspension, then pushed a lever with a booted foot. The seat upon which the Celestial Mechanic was sitting abruptly tipped forwards, depositing him on his rear in the dirt and dung. Deftly flicking a rope that was tied around the long beak of the tallister, the vehicle reversed a short distance, turned, and accelerated away.

SOME HOURS LATER, the staging post and the station were lost to the haze of distance. The Celestial Mechanic was proceeding determinedly on foot, entreating the occasional passer-by with space on a wagon or on the back of a pack animal without success.

He had committed the charts to hindbrain memory and could see the landscape ahead in his mind, its undulations and streams, hamlets and roads laid out in fine detail, his route clear and unambiguous.

But if he knew were he was going, so also did the Prime Advocates of Murorundrum-Kalash; and they had his packbeast and a head start. Not for the first time, he cursed his flippant disregard for the unsportsmanlike behaviour of zealots.

THE DAY WORE ON. The low dusty scrubland gave way to cultivated fields, in which could be seen outhouses and corrals containing local breeds of bracines and griping pachards. Tall ghabou pylahs with threadbare sails slowly rotated in the light wind, squeaking as he passed.

He had no water or food. He estimated the journey might take till nightfall on foot. He had resigned himself to the certainty they would get there long before he did. The dust of the road caked his boots and stung his nasal passages. His formal evening wear was torn and grubby. His carapace had lost most of its sheen, and he had grit in his collar. He couldn't recall ever being this unpresentable. He longed for the sunken scented baths, the cool clean air and civilised enchantments of the Spire.

A sudden thunderclap shocked him to a standstill. A sonic boom echoed across the landscape from a point somewhere above him.

A falling star!

His falling star, a glory of fire and concussion, passed directly overhead.

Debris spun behind in its wake; he glimpsed a dark object encased in a sheath of orange flame, trailing thick clouds of grey smoke lit by sparks from within. Though it was only early evening, the trees and the fence marking the side of the road cast fast-moving shadows that swept across his feet and up the bank. A cacophonous whistling as of a tuneless choir of giants made him shut fast his earlids.

Then – it hit. A majestic conical spray of fertile brown earth rose up high into the air, then fell back. A second later, a thunderclap and a pressure wave knocked him off his feet, causing his twisted ankle to complain bitterly once more. He hit the ground hard, indescribable pain lanced onto his forebrain, and he passed out.

HIS HINDBRAIN gave him a nudge, and consciousness slowly began to return. Turning onto his back, he opened his eyes.

*Beyond that he could see, at the end of a roughly paved
path, a small rustic dwelling hugging the roots of the trees*

His bag had absorbed the worst of his fall. The land was silent, the day was fading to a warm russet. He had little idea how long he'd been lying there. Above, the Visage hung in its crescent phase, faded to a pale amber though layers of atmosphere. A smaller inset crescent was visible where the light caught the lip of an eye socket. What strange offcast of the gods might have fallen to earth this day? If the Visage knew, it was not telling.

Rising painfully to his hooves, he could see the tops of trees several fields away were on fire. A fine aerated mist of dirt and vegetable matter masked the point of impact, but was beginning to dissipate to the south.

Redoubling his efforts, he climbed a low stone wall and jumped a ditch in which a muddy stream flowed. Ahead high stands of frax ran in neat rows, and he picked a gap between them.

At the far side of the field, he forced his way through a thick hedgerow that further shredded the lining of his jacket.

There it was. The landing site.

A straight line of elongated pockmarks crossed an otherwise empty field, ending in one large final crater banked with an enormous horseshoe of fresh earth. The Celestial Mechanic stumbled through the dirt, around the smaller trailing craters, and approached the largest.

The earth was soft and yielding. As he moved closer it began to subside underneath him, and he had to crawl the last short distance to the edge to avoid falling in.

He raised an eye over the top. He could see a neat inverted cone of fresh dirt, some fifteen paces across, in the centre of which infalling material had formed a small stubby version of the Spire. He pulled himself up to get a better view. Under his feet, a slurry of small particles began to cascade inward and he sat down hard, bracing himself.

Where was it? He couldn't see anything but freshly turned dirt, shredded roots and foliage.

No meteorite.

He let his senses drift beneath the surface. Disturbed sediment, plant remains, rocks, clay . . . could it have evaporated on impact? No. Whatever had been here, it had gone.

On the far side, something caught his attention.

He carefully circumnavigated the crater. A section of the dirt bank had been scooped out by the passage of something large. Something heavy. Around this was a jumble of footprints, pressed deep into the loose earth. Just outside the lip, a length of stout rope lay beside an area which looked like it had been trampled flat by a packbeast. His packbeast, he now had no doubt, had been used to pull whatever had landed here today up, out, and away.

The trail was not hard to follow. Several fields distant, the Celestial Mechanic could see smoke rising in a thin plume. A farmstead. The tracks led straight towards it.

D ECIDING THAT in his current state a degree of caution would be advisable, he skirted the property. An orchard gave onto a garden, and beyond that he could see, at the end of a roughly paved path, a small rustic dwelling hugging the roots of the trees.

He climbed through a vegetable garden and waded across an ornamental pond thick with reeds, which sucked on his boots and sent bubbles of rotting putrescence to the surface. Around what he assumed was the front of the building, he could see two semicircular bifold doors set in a round frame. These were open. Across from this, on the far side of a well-tended lawn, his packbeast was eating grackleberries from a low-hanging bush. Its reins trailed on the ground behind it, and from what he could see most of his cargo of supplies, including the wheeled crate, was still lashed in place. He dropped his bag beside it. A winged caw stood on a border post, picking at something held in its claw.

No one else was visible.

The Celestial Mechanic jogged to the front wall and pressed his back to it, keeping to the shade afforded by the overhanging eaves. He edged up to the door. Two planters either side held a profusion of colourful blooms, and the doors themselves were inset with panes of multi-coloured bubble-filled glass, held in a framework of soft metal.

Stepping across the threshold, the low evening light shot shapes across the packed dirt floor of the interior. He let his senses adapt to the gloom.

IT WAS THEN that he saw the two figures, both face down. The nearest to him had had her skull flattened; sap puddled on the dry ground, a darkening stain around her head. The other was facing away from him, his upper torso in shadow; he imagined a similar fate must have befallen him. He eased himself down a short hall and past a stout rustic dresser upon which were arranged family miniatures and model birds made from plaited haystalks, giving the bodies as wide a berth as the narrow space permitted.

Beyond, all the trappings of a domestic space were apparent. Under a low undulating ceiling, a retired cartwheel laced with dried herbs and climbing plants had been hung above an iron stove. A large worn and polished table took up the centre of the room, upon which he could see a stack of beaten copper plates, a dozen or so spun glass bottles and ceramic jugs labelled with little drawings of seeds and dried fruit. The fading light fell across the length of the table; in spots of colour thrown by the uneven window glass, dust motes spiralled lazily on small thermals.

Seated around the table were the three Prime Advocates of Murorundrum-Kalash, and placed upright between them was a burned and blackened object.

The Celestial Mechanic looked around for some kind of weapon, his eyes alighting on a roasting spit. Testing its weight, he hefted it a few times from hand to hand.

The Advocates made no move. Had they heard him approach? They leant inward, their red-edged hoods covering their faces, gloved hands on the table, palms down, in front of them.

He wondered what he should do. He had no desire to go the way of the peasants in the hallway. Even in rude health, he was no physical match for three young fanatics with the power of belief and the unquestioned righteousness of their cause on their side.

He considered taking the pack-beast and leaving, but knew that he would not be welcomed back to his previous position in the Hierarchy of the Spire empty-handed. No, he had been sent on a mission, and he was duty-bound to see it through to completion.

It dawned on him that he had been standing there for some minutes, and the three had still not moved. He listened very carefully – he was sure he could hear a slow and deep breathing. He raised the strongest mental barriers to his hindbrain that he could muster, just in case any ideological backwash should infect him. If he encountered anything untoward, anything dangerous, he could immediately purge his forebrain, losing only today's unprocessed waking experience but saving the seat of his self. When it came to the doings of mysterious sects, he preferred to keep their beliefs, however benign and rational they may seem at first, out of his hindbrain – at least until he knew them to be harmless.

Ideas can be dangerous . . .

He relaxed the boundary of his extended self and let his senses flow across the floor, out to the table and those seated around it.

He touched a – a what? A rhythmic deep heartbeat of mind, an internalised meditative fugue. They seemed to be in some kind of entrainment; it came to him

that they were breathing in unison. Without conscious effort, he felt his own respiration slow to match theirs. It was seductive, soporific . . .

He quickly pulled back from a deeper probing.

He cautiously moved forwards. Approaching the nearest figure, he could see that his eyes were closed. He experimentally waved the end of the roasting spit in front of his face. No response.

He began to relax, just a bit. For the first time, he turned his attention to the object in the centre of the table. This, he was in no doubt, was the mysterious prize that had fallen from the sky, the very one that they had retrieved from the crater.

IT WAS NOT LIKE any meteorite he had ever seen before. Nor did it resemble any of the petrified Beyonder remains that periodically fell from the heavens.

It was elliptical, and placed vertically on the table, the size of a small keg or an inflated bladder, maybe two hands high. Though blackened and pockmarked by the heat of atmospheric friction it was clearly vertically ribbed, topped with a fluted fan under which were several rows of holes. To the Celestial Mechanic it resembled a large seed pod, or a bud of some kind.

From the holes beneath the fan, fine translucent filaments hung. The Celestial Mechanic followed them down the sides of the object where they were clearly visible, pale white on black, and then across the table, where they looped over the polished wood to the gloved hands of all three sitting around the table, up over their fingers to disappear between glove and sleeve. The white tendrils seemed to pulse, as if a pale liquid was flowing through them by capillary action.

The Celestial Mechanic circled the table. Strands from the thing had attached themselves to each of the three pilgrims.

He was more than faintly disturbed by this discovery . . . this was not a meteorite, but a living thing; a plant, or even an animal of some kind, alive, growing . . . from who knows where, with who knows what purpose? He suppressed an urge to run it through with the roasting spit there and then.

Instead he went and fetched the adjustable wheeled box from his packbeast. Setting it on an upturned tureen beside the table, he took a visual estimate of the object's size, then slid the two sections of the box apart to allow space for it to sit within. He worked fast, not wishing to still be in the building with the dead and perhaps dying after nightfall.

Positioning the box at table level, he used the edge of a beaten copper plate to cut through the tendrils, which parted easily. They retracted back into the pod's belly, dripping milky fluid from their severed tips. He half expected it to make a noise, whimper perhaps; but there was nothing.

Picking up a ceramic jug, he climbed onto the table and gave the thing a hefty whack. It moved, but barely; it had firmly attached itself to the tabletop and now listed at an angle, having pulled slivers of wood up from the surface.

At a second hit, there was a loud splintering and it rolled free, curving across the tabletop, the ridged sides beating out a tattoo. The Celestial Mechanic jumped back as it circled around towards him. Once it had come to rest, he carefully manoeuvred it towards the edge of the table and the open box with the spit. Inserting the point under it, he flicked it over the edge and into the padded leather interior.

He swung the lid shut and fitted the padlock. Jumping down from the table, he pulled out the two telescoping shafts from under the box, attached the wheels, and manoeuvred it around towards the door. As he got to the threshold, he turned to look back.

The Prime Advocates of Murorundrum-Kalash had all turned their heads to face him.

Still seated, and making no noise save for their synchronised breathing, they made no move to follow. Their eyes were milky and opaque, and the Celestial Mechanic could see, under their hoods and clearly visible above the fabric masks that covered their nose and mouth, a complex web of raised white veins that pulsed under their skin.

He wasn't sure if they could still see him, or had just heard him. Turning, he shoved the wheeled box forwards with renewed force, over the leg of the peasant facing the wall and out into the yard.

His packbeast was still where he had left it. Manoeuvring the box around, he hitched the shafts to leather loops attached to the harness that had been provided for this precise purpose, belting them tight.

Grabbing his bag and vaulting over the box, he took three steps up the beast's ridged bony back, dropped into the saddle, grasped the reins and pulled its head up and around.

The beast was not fast, but once moving could sustain a pace the equivalent of a Naze jog indefinitely. He needed to make the best of any head start he was afforded. Kicking hard at its sidespots, where the horny shell had been removed to reveal softer flesh, it finally seemed to understand his urgency.

As they picked up speed, the wheeled cart obediently followed behind. He steered the packbeast out through a gate and across the frax field, through the ditch and around a low wall to the road.

Only then, and without stopping, did he twist around in the saddle to look back. He could see the three Advocates standing in the yard, hooded heads pointing in his direction. Their eyes were hidden, but he was certain that they were watching him go.

The Celestial Mechanic had seen many religious adherents in mystical trances or drug-induced states of noetic ecstasy. Those pilgrims bore almost deranged expressions of joyous rapture. These three, standing there immobile in their red-edged cloaks, exhibited none of that behaviour. He thought he could sense in them the self-assurance of victors who have already won the battle, or know without a grain of doubt that they hold the winning hand.

A wave of sickening apprehension washed over him as he turned to face the road, jabbing the packbeast's sides with renewed vigour.

Behind, locked in the wheeled box, the thing that had fallen from the heavens followed.

To be continued

IN OUR NEXT ISSUE:

Ascension • PART 6 OF OUR NEW SERIAL

PLUS

Lying Supine in Komorebi • RALPH GARRETT
Broodmare • ALEXIS WESTINGHOUSE
Underpass/Overdrive • JOHN STATTEN
Heaven is Full, and the Good Can't Die • M. R. FISK
Archipelago Waltz • CAROLINE BLANDISH
We, the Peeple • RICHARD STORTFORD, JR.

NEWS • REVIEWS • DEPARTMENTS

ANGELS AND DMEN

Jack loped down the escalator three steps at a time, cornered so fast at the bottom he almost lost his footing on the polished concrete, then exited the building through the glass foyer. Outside, along the Thames, giant billboards in mauve and rose madder promoted the next exhibition: impressionist scenes of Victorian London. In these images, stripped of modern architecture and clouded in a yellow coalsmoke haze, the skyline was barely recognisable. Jack crossed the river via the Millennium Bridge, a swoop of suspended steel that presented an unobstructed view of the dome of St Paul's – the one constant that appeared in both views.

Jack had learned not to wear the glasses while walking. It was very hard to tell stationary real people from virtual ones, and trying to avoid both while moving any faster than a stroll could be frustrating. He had them in his messenger bag, held close to his chest so it didn't swing off his shoulder.

There was more than a fair chance the creature – entity, Shepherd, whatever – would be located too high to see, or inside a building to which he had no access, or a solid wall, or even underground.

Like a dressing-table triptych he could see St Paul's reflected in sheets of glass to his right and the windows of a nondescript brick building to the left. Up Peter's Hill, across Carter Lane, through a small park and up several flights of Cambrian stone, and Jack was at the entrance to the cathedral; ducking between idling daytrippers and lunching City workers, he stepped into the cool interior. Crossing the black and white chequerboard flagstones, he skirted a row of square pillars and made his way over to the south transept where chairs were arranged in arcs around an ornate lectern.

He took a seat. There was a dozen or so other people there: a Japanese couple, pointing things out to each other; an elderly gentleman, eyes closed in prayer or sleep; schoolchildren in smart uniforms eating their sandwiches from Tupperware boxes.

Jack was pretty sure he didn't look like a terrorist, but adopted as casual a manner as he could as he unwrapped the glasses and laid them on his lap. Looking up at the Whispering Gallery, he put one hand into his bag and plugged them into his laptop.

Then he put them on.

Jack knew what to expect, but the sight still filled him with awe. The endorphin rush made him laugh involuntarily. Like the most impressive art installation he had ever seen, there they were: in a three-dimensional grid, stretching from wall to wall and as high as the oculus at the apex of the gilded dome, hanging on their invisible coat pegs were entities that would entrance mediaeval compilers of bestiaries and modern biologists alike. For those inclined to such things, the venue lent the scene a heightened resonance.

Many intersected the walls and floor without a care for their architectural surroundings. Across the nave the density of hanging figures seemed to blend into the ornate interior of the cathedral itself, limestone angels mixing with celestial beings of a different order. Heads, or what might pass for heads, vanished into the undersides of arches and cornices, bodies hung within chandeliers, a tail or a leg protruded from a pillar; all this went unnoticed by the general public who passed right through them without care.

The top half of a segmented and polished carapace spun around with glowing strands rose from the recumbent figure of Lord Leighton, while above, another creature that was beyond Jack's powers of description seemed to ride on the back of a bronze horse. Closer to hand, the rows of creatures sunk into the floor at a shallow angle, looking like a timber breakwater after a calm tide of flagstones had come in. Cut across their faces, or some agglomeration of sense organs that might pass for a face, they seemed unfazed by their immersion in stone; still, silent, of this world but very much not of it, an overlay of alien migrants utterly unaware of their surroundings.

He pulled the glasses down to the end of his nose and looked over the top. St Paul's immediately emptied of its new congregation.

Where were the DMEn?

Jack decided to explore further. He walked up the nave and over to the north transept. The dome? He wasn't good with heights, and was happy to pass up an orientation from the Whispering Gallery, however spectacular the view might be.

Out and down, towards the crypt.

Jack descended a curving flight of stone steps, their edges smoothed by three and a half centuries of feet. Here the stonework was simpler, more functional, the whitewashed walls lit by uplighters placed at the base of each square column. There was a small café just before the entrance to the crypt proper, and the clatter of crockery and the aroma of ground coffee pushed the humid gloom of this subterranean space up to the far end, where you could find the final resting places of Constable, Turner and Reynolds, the Duke of Wellington – and Sir Christopher Wren himself, interred within the belly of his own masterpiece.

Jack took a corridor to his left that skirted the external wall. Down a couple of steps and through an arch to his right he could see Nelson's black touchstone sarcophagus, lit by suspended brass spotlights.

The space down here, while low-ceilinged, was extensive; rooms and antechambers, corbelled arches giving onto dimly lit chapels, alcoves behind wrought-iron grilles, the layout mirroring the floorplan of the cathedral above. Ahead, situated at the east end of the crypt, was the Chapel of the Most Excellent Order of the British Empire, also known (so text on a wall plaque helpfully informed him) as St Faith's Chapel. Destroyed in the Great Fire of London, here was the location of the original parish church over which this vast edifice had been built.

At the end of a row of low arches was an oak screen, surmounted by an elaborate cartouche made from arabesques of leaves. Just beyond this, several lines of simple wooden chairs faced a small altar placed against the far wall.

Jack again put on the glasses.

In the front row, with his back to him, sat the Count, top hat respectfully placed on his lap. Next to him, her flickering face illuminated by her smartphone screen, was Girl 21. XX was nowhere to be seen. Above, a pair of hooves hung through the ceiling as if Jack had just entered a Parisian charcuterie. The Count tapped his cane a couple of times on the footpolished flagstones. It kicked up a dust of small letters: *tok tok.*

Girl, 21
@twentyone • 0m

u finally got here!
but this is as close as u can get
unless u have permission to dig up the floor

Jack immediately felt a sense of deflation.

So this was it. Their search ended here. The creature they had come to see, that they'd hoped might give them some clue as to the Grid's purpose or origin, lay deeper still, below this hallowed ground. There was no further level of the crypt to access. They had come as far as it was possible to go.

Black type fluttered in the confined subterranean space like inky bats.

Now that *IS* a crying shame.
It looks like our
MYSTERY MAN
*must **REMAIN** a mystery.*
At least for *now.*

Jack rocked back on his haunches and passed a hand over the patchwork slabs of the floor. Some bore the barest suggestion of inscriptions, now rubbed into unreadability.

A chill of ages crept into his fingertips.

Dead end.

A S C E N S I O N

by F. HERSCHEL TEAGUE

When the Celestial Mechanic answered the Highmost's

summons, little did he expect to be asked to mount an

expedition into the lands below the Spire, less familiar to

him than the heavens above — and far more alien.

PART SIX

THE PACKBEAST was hardy and had been chosen for its stamina, but could not keep up such a brisk pace indefinitely. The Celestial Mechanic turned once again in the saddle, but the farmstead was already lost behind a rise and the long rows of thick-trunked chibuzos that flanked the way. There did not appear to be anyone in pursuit.

He allowed his charge to slow to a more sedate pace. The cart behind him bumped and creaked over the uneven ground.

Tonight, the bowl of the heavens was free of the Visage, and the faintest stars were becoming visible. In the southern sky, the Duchess had risen, a majestic nebula whipped by winds from the new stars being born within it into a flurry of fine eddies like flooded grassland, or, as he sometimes fancied, blood dissipating in a black pool.

The smoke from the trees was no longer visible in the failing light, though a faint glow of burning

CONTINUING OUR NOVELETTE OF STRANGE ALIEN CULTURES IN EIGHT PARTS

underbrush still gave him a direction from which to get as far away as quickly as possible.

P RESENTLY THE GLOW on the horizon faded too. Out here, well away from the mountains of the Rim, the landscape felt particularly flat and horizontal, so unlike the familiar verticality of the Spire. There, up was up and down was down, and going up required effort, whereas going down required no effort at all. In the Hierarchy, a quick descent could just as easily result from a slip of the tongue as the slip of a well-heeled boot.

This horizontal motion intrigued him: to move forever forwards, and to not find that one had circled the Spire and arrived back at one's starting point. Novel. He wondered how far and for how long he would have to travel before he managed the same feat out here: a circumnavigation of Terrine herself.

He needed to find a hostelry with a wordwing aviary. He needed rest. His charts confused him; he had travelled some distance and was no longer sure precisely where he was. North? He consulted his star atlas, made the laborious conversion between the stellar coordinate system and the Spire-centred official coordinate system and felt reasonably sure he was heading in the right general direction. The Spire was visible for many purloughs around, but this far out even that familiar marker was not to be seen.

Think of it – there were lands out here where there were people who had only heard of the Spire in stories! Closer to the crater rim,

he could see how it was a constant reminder of the elevated status of the Hierarchy and a potent symbol of the Quarterlands' subservience. He imagined farmers on the floodplains of the Gorodorborga, stopping for a break during the harvest, looking up at its soaring elegance and wondering what its citizens might now be doing. This, of course, was all as it should be; part of the natural order of things.

The wooded hills opened up to a low series of dunes, shaded by a sulphur-gold mist in the shallow valleys between. Rising above, he could see silhouettes of thick-branched succulents that had been sculpted into dramatic curvilinear shapes by the driven sand. The track he was following seemed to have long since disappeared in the shifting landscape, so he plotted a course by the stars and settled back in the saddle. He fed the packbeast low-hanging branches, which he broke off as they passed underneath then proffered forwards on the end of a tentpole.

Ahead he could see a faint luminescence. He unfolded a chart and checked his conversions. If he was correct, this was a small hamlet, the name of which he couldn't pronounce. Several symbols were placed around the maze of streets, and he folded the sheet to consult the legend. Ah. It sounded almost civilised. There were a communal baths, seven taverns and hostelries, an information office for visitors, and numerous places to eat, each rated with a crown system from one to seven.

He committed the location of the one seven-crown establishment to memory, but then recalled that his purse had been stolen on the train. He muttered several curses aloud that would have had him ejected from a upper-level Spire soirée. What else did he carry of value? His clothes were filthy. He needed the packbeast to get back home.

He pulled his charge to a halt, dismounted and unfurled his wardrobe roll. Selecting the most ostentatious outfit within, he changed and buried his shredded clothes behind a tree. He straightened the harness and dusted the cart. Climbing back into the saddle, he reached forwards and polished the neckplate of the packbeast with his sleeve till some of its natural lustre returned.

SAUNTERING INTO TOWN at what he hoped was the most nonchalant pace a Brindlatch Coakidoh might be capable, he took pains to doff his cap to every passer-by that he encountered.

Stopping at an intersection, a youngster of some indeterminate race self-consciously came up to take a closer look at his mount. He made it be known in passing that he was looking for accommodation, and it promptly scuttered away.

Presently a smartly dressed Hill Naze in a pair of furskin breeches and a curious brimless felt hat appeared. As he looked up, the Celestial Mechanic could see from the ornately stitched emblem on his hat-band that he was a representative of that very seven-crown establishment he had made note of earlier. His luck was in.

He held forth a small piece of wood on which were listed tariffs for lodging and stabling, an extensive list of distilled and fermented beverages and a dinner menu that, even at a glance, had the Celestial Mechanic's whiskers unfurling.

He gave it what he hoped was a cursory nod, then passed the reins to the Naze, who guided them with no small amount of pride to his employer's hostelry. Small children jumped up and tried to touch his longcoat or stroke the packbeast's bumpy hide, and he smiled down at them indulgently.

THE ESTABLISHMENT, though not of Spire standards, did possess a certain artisanal charm. From the outside he could see that its curvilinear lines rose to an ornately decorated roof; the external timber supports, which had been arranged in such a way that they resembled the branches of an idealised tree or perhaps the antlers of an adult troumagint, were hung with translucent blown-glass lanterns in which spark-moths cavorted.

He dismounted and brushed the odd speck of dust from his longcoat. The Hill Naze led his charge around the side of the building and through a low arch towards the stable block.

The Celestial Mechanic stepped inside. Here, it was several latitudes cooler, and a scent of old wood and tallow greeted him. The hubbub and bustle of a town determined to enjoy a night without work in the morning vanished as the heavy door shut behind him. It almost felt as if he had entered one of the secret libraries of the Occluded University.

Breathing deeply he surveyed the

vestibule, affecting an attitude of disdainful acceptance. An older Hill Naze, perhaps the first's father, hurried out from behind a counter and offered to take his hat and longcoat.

The Celestial Mechanic was still not exactly sure how he would pay for all this. Referring to his host using the most formal and over-polite phrases his limited Quarterlands vocabulary allowed, he explained that he was passing through to research certain locations that his employees and their extended families, Spire aristocrats of high status, might wish to consider for their honeymoon.

At this, the older Hill Naze's olfactory openings widened considerably. Spire weddings were lavish affairs, continuing for the better part of a cycle, and the High Families vied to outdo each other with themed costumed balls, hunting trips and other immoderate entertainments.

He was offered what he was assured was the best suite they had. The young Naze ran up the staircase ahead of them, and after a short delay while a key was found, the manager led him up after. As the door opened, the Celestial Mechanic fancied he could see something being ejected from the window, but as they entered the young Naze straightened the blinds and turned, bowing deeply.

The room was clean, the bedding furs soft, and certainly a relief after the day's deprivations. He bade the young Naze bring up his cart and belongings. He seemed momentarily confused. The cart, he explained, held his journals and writing desk,

and as he would be making notes for his report, he needed access to it in his room.

After a short delay his wardrobe roll and the cart appeared. He showed the fascinated Naze how the shafts telescoped, the axle could be removed and the wheels folded so it could easily fit through the doorway. He was so engrossed by this feat of engineering he forgot to hold out his hand for a gratuity.

At last the Celestial Mechanic found himself alone. He walked over to the windows and threw open the shutters. The life of the town engulfed him again. Scents of fried food and spiced fish came up from the street vendors below, mixing with the dry air of the dunes to the south. Directly under his window, several raggedly dressed locals were sorting through a pile of clothing and other belongings.

He positioned the cart on the washstand, and stood back to regard it. An intriguing mystery, no doubt. Back at the Spire, he would consult the fellows of the Occluded University and see what ideas they could offer on the matter.

Of its origins, he had not the faintest scrap of a theory. He had certainly never heard or read of anything like this. It was like nothing that even the travellers of the Pararealms, in their drug-induced flights of fancy, had reported.

He closed the shutters once more, washed as best he could using the basin and the sponge on a short stick that were provided, and repaired to the bunk. Lying back on the furs, he struck a firelight on the dado beam and lit a small lamp.

Presently there was a knock at his door, and he opened it to see the young Naze with a trolley of stews, sweetbreads and skewered grubs. He thanked him profusely, let his whiskers touch the boards, and closed the door before the matter of a tip arose.

Eating his evening meal, there in the comfort of his private chamber, he finally began to relax. He doubted the three hooded figures could have tracked him across the dunes, even if they had transport; he had a good head start, and would be on his way again first thing tomorrow.

His dinnerplate still balanced on his chest, he let his forebrain spin down and his hindbrain tick over into rest.

I T LOOKED DELICIOUS. He wanted to eat it. It promised him it would taste good.

The Celestial Mechanic turned over. The plate fell to the floor, but the clatter did not wake him.

He did not dream often, and when he did it was of more prosaic things. He instinctively felt he should draw back his consciousness, purge his forebrain.

A soporific warmth came over him, and he drifted deeper.

He was out in the open fields, well away from the Spire, lying on his back wrapped in the softest bedroll against the cold. He was looking up at the stars. The Visage and the Duchess were nowhere to be seen, just the familiar mapping of the constellations, the twenty-three Houses of the Ecliptic. They were all connected by thin threads, as they were

in the diagrams from the astrology manuals. Strange.

The sky seemed to be crossed by finer lines still, a grid of celestial latitude and longitude. He could sense the tilted sphere of the heavens, a globe around the globe through which Terrine, the planets, the inhabited moons, and all the bodies of Beyonder myth rotated on their set paths. It was a fine mechanism indeed: perfect, predictable, elegant.

Above him, the concentric circles converged on the celestial pole, an empty patch of sky. Empty—

He could just see a faint streak. A falling star? The comet, returned? No, the Celestial Mechanic knew without a doubt that this was the thing with which he now shared his bedchamber.

It was beautiful.

It spoke to him.

It made him a promise.

It could take him with it, back

The establishment, though not of Spire standards,
did possess a certain artisanal charm

out to the stars. It could share with him the secrets of the multitude of worlds beyond the Lacunae, more numerous than the islands of the Iron Sea. It could show him vistas and peoples that the Celestial Mechanic had heretofore only theorised about. It would even share with him the secrets of the Skybound Beyonders themselves.

As one born and bred on the Spire, as one who had made it as high in the Hierarchy as it was possible to rise, where else was there left to go?

The crate remained locked tight, on the washstand. Through the keyhole, a single translucent filament led down the leg of the stand, across the bare floorboards and over to the bed where a corner of an undersheet touched the ground; from there it went up under the furs to the back of the Celestial Mechanic's left hand.

A WAY, ACROSS THE THIGH of the world, at a distance a giant from the days of the Skybound Beyonders could still run a hand over, cup the landscape under their palm and get a sense of the curve of the land, a decision had been made. Despite the purloughs of sand and earth and rock between there and here, there was no separation at all when it came to matters of the mind.

The Prime Advocates of Murorundrum-Kalash had at last found a god whose bidding was clear and unambiguous, a god to whose service they could enthusiastically submit themselves.

They still had many questions. Their visitor had come from the sky, as had the Omphalos. Was this the will of the Skybound Beyonders? Had they discovered a seed from the gods, fallen from the heavens into that cradle of soft earth? Signs and portents, and how to interpret them: they had conferred on such theological matters at some length.

Terrine, and all that existed above, upon or under its surface, was not to be valued for its own sake; this they already knew with certainty. Such attachment to worldly matters was a heresy. No, the material world was naught but a book of moral instruction, a message written in the language of Nature, to be read and deciphered by the initiated. Knowledge, presented in the form of a star, a plant, a rock, an animal, or even a Naze or the Spire itself.

What use is a god, they surmised, who is but an ossified dream-vision of a man long dead, when here was a god whose very existence vibrated through their beings? Was this not the rapture they had fervently desired for so long?

That their faculties of reason were now not entirely their own they had no way of knowing. This new devotion required of them simply that they share it with others. Their mission was clear: they had a joyous message to give to all of Terrine, an ecstasy of belonging in which every creature deserved to share.

They walked to the next village. There, they found a market in full session in which foodstuffs, livestock, conjurers and stoneseers were to be found. The Prime Advocates of Murorundrum-Kalash, unlike the Servants of the Omphalos whose aims they superficially shared, were not a missionary sect. They had no experience in the arts of oration or sophistry. Theirs was the mastery of shadows and divination.

But they did not require such skills. Spreading out into the colourful throng, they would stop and greet those who crossed their paths, old and young, high or low status alike.

Take my hand. No, I am not selling you anything, just a thirst you have not felt before. There are no scrolls to memorise. No pleasures to forego. No political affiliation to declare. No joining fee. Just take my hand, and you will see.

See?

Something would pass between them: thin, translucent, almost invisible.

They *did* see.

It was so clear, so obvious. Why had they not known this before?

I will go and tell others. I will go home, and share this news with my family.

Presently the marketplace had emptied. Bundles of unsold fabrics had been left unattended. Caws flew down and carried away cakes from trestle tables whose owners were now absent. A child wailed, not understanding what was needed of it, but feeling a need regardless. The taverns were quiet, the squares deserted.

Streams of figures, peasant and landsgrave walking shoulder to shoulder, the fit at the front, the infirm dragging themselves along by sheer force of will at the rear, were funnelling out of the town and away. They headed up the high road to the main gate and over the river towards the coastal settlements to the west. But the heaviest flow was to the north, towards the Spire, the very tip of which could just be seen, white and sharp like a compass needle pointing heavenward, in the far distance.

Many fell, and their companions would step over them without pause. Others would soon perish through dehydration or overexertion. The need was so great that every home had been left just as it was, warm food on a table, an unweaned hatchling in a cradle.

There were now more pressing matters to attend to.

To be continued

IN OUR NEXT ISSUE:

Ascension • PART 7 OF OUR SERIAL

PLUS

Running the Ruins • FAITH KIRBY
The Heirs to Gagarin • JEROME WEIDMANN
Hollow Sings the Cynosure • IVAR YOUNGBLOOD
Metanoia! • ARTHUR SICKERT
Under the Shivering Tree • CHRISTINE ALLION

OBLATE SPHEROID SPACEHOPPERS

Jack was grilling sausages in a crusty pan in a shared kitchen in Holloway to the delicate aroma of a flip-top bin that needed emptying.

On the counter, amongst a collection of half-empty wine and spirit bottles, he had set out two clean but mismatched plates extracted from a sinkful of unwashed crockery. Nadine, in a threadbare Madonna *Who's That Girl? World Tour 1987* T-shirt, was scraping and buttering toast. She had accidentally transferred burnt breadcrumbs back into the butter dish and was picking them out with white-painted fingernails. On the wall above the small round table hung a vintage framed print of Tretchikoff's *Miss Wong*, to which had been glued, in the manner of Duchamp, a plastic Movember moustache.

Last night they had been guests at a masked ball Soo Terraine had organised in Adam Street Chambers, a private members club beneath the Strand: 'Masks compulsory. Clothes optional', it had helpfully informed them on the embossed and gilt-edged invitation. The people who had taken this advice to heart were, they had both agreed, the ones that should have kept theirs on. They had left early, and now Jack was nursing a cheap cava hangover.

Nadine arranged the toast on the plates. "Run this by me again. There are people in the internet?"

Jack waved a spatula. "Ideas. Coalesced concepts. Ghosts in the machine."

She looked at him dubiously. Mascara smudged her cheek. "And you can see these, these ghosts in the machine?"

"With adapted Depthcharge 3D glasses, yes."

"What do they look like?"

"The DMEn?"

"The *Demon?*"

Jack regarded her. He felt an unfamiliar warmth rise in his chest. She was quite endearing, in an unkempt morning kind of way. "Dee Em Ee En. DMEn. Digital Memetic Entities. They can pretty much look like whatever they want to look like, I suppose. One looks like an aristocratic dandy. In perfect spotless white. He calls himself the 19th Count. Of what, I have no idea. Internetania. Webchester. Girl 21 calls him the Count, for short."

"Girl 21?"

"Imagine a manga cosplayer in a pink wig with a collection of random selfies for a face and a sharp line in sarcasm. Talks in tweets. Sailor Moon Zoella." Jack wondered if Nadine might think he was having another of his weird spells.

"But *they* at least look human. XX looks more like a futurist sculpture. Epstein's *Rock Drill* in dazzle-ship decor. He's more a shifting mass of boilerplate as drawn by the Stenberg brothers, all sharp angles and planes of primary colours." Jack pulled up a bentwood café chair. "Sorry – is there only one chair?" He stood up again.

"Sit. Don't worry. I can use this." Nadine reached over and picked up an orange Spacehopper by one horn, fitting it underneath herself. It had a black toothy grin below a pair of eyes that reminded Jack of droopy breasts. She bounced and swayed slightly as it compressed beneath her.

"And anyone can see them, if they wear the glasses?"

"There's a bit of software I created. I call it the Oxbow. That's really the essential element here. It allows them to, to coalesce. Materialise." Jack chased the sausages off the pan and onto the plates.

"So you can turn them off if you want."

"I guess so. Though usually we just leave it running. They seem to prefer it that way."

"And they took you to St Paul's? Why? Because they're history buffs and it's an architectural masterpiece? School day out?"

"No, no. It turns out that just recently ideaspace has filled up with other – other things. Entities. Aliens. *Alien ideas.* In enormous number. Billions, perhaps."

Nadine was quiet for a few moments.

"Jack, you're not winding me up here?"

"No! Listen. The DMEn are, I think, autonomous collections of self-aware code. Ideas that have achieved self-consciousness, or something. They come across all cocky, as any popular and successful idea would, but I think they're rattled. They have the entirety of digitised knowledge at their imaginary fingertips, and are still utterly baffled by this influx."

"So, what do you think this influx is? Invasion force? Refugees? And St Paul's? What's St Paul's got to do with it?"

"These, uh, *new* entities, they have one big difference – they don't have any autonomy. They're immobile. Just floating there. They seem to be, for all intents and purposes, *dead.* Or at least dormant. If, if you can call something that has no real actual body, no physical existence, alive or dead. Anyway, regardless, they hang there in space, row upon row. A library of bodies. Most vastly different, some the same, or similar. Sometimes it's possible to take a guess at the kinds of environments they may originally have inhabited. Legs. Fins. Wings. Modes of propulsion we don't have names for. They're bizarre. A taxonomist would have the job of a lifetime – *lifetimes* – cataloguing them all."

Nadine was taking this all in. HP sauce dripped from a sausage paused midway to her mouth.

"You sure this isn't just some game engine you've accessed by mistake? Some prototype world-building thing?"

"That *did* occur to me. Or that this is some elaborate Turing test, and I've been chosen as a guinea pig."

"Is that not the most likely explanation?"

"Maybe. Occam's disposable Bic razor might suggest so."

"So what makes you so sure they're for real?"

Jack looked at Nadine, and again considered telling her about the Grey Man. "There's . . ." he began.

"There's a what?"

"A story."

"Tell me. You can tell me."

Jack looked at his burnt toast. The butter had melted into it, giving it a greasy varnish. "Let's just say I'm sure this isn't a prototype game, a Turing test, or some other thing. Trust me on this one."

A quiet but insistent alarm had begun to ring in the back of Nadine's mind. Men with stories they couldn't share. *Dark and mysterious?* Nope. More like scarily unsettling. Unpredictable. Fucked up, even. She began to pack the emotional vulnerability she had allowed herself to feel towards this man back into the hard protective case in which she had carried it for some time.

"So. You've still not told me why you went to St Paul's."

"Ah, right. These entities, they're arranged on a grid. As I say, they're all different, to a greater or lesser degree. But I realised that the Grid has regularities. A *repeat.* At every certain number of interstices, there's a very similar signal – not *identical*, but within a few fractions of a per cent. I think this represents a certain species, that, unlike all the others which are bunched in groups, is spaced throughout the entire Grid. Guides, perhaps. Shepherds. Harriet thinks they're platoon commanders. Who knows?

"Anyway, the nearest such interstice I could go and look at turned out to be here, in London. We managed, or the DMEn managed, to track it down to a location under St Paul's Cathedral. Only when we got there, we found that it was hidden from view. It may only have been a metre underground, but it might as well be a mile. No one is going to let us dig under the crypt. So – so we still don't know what's special about these repeats. Who these Shepherds might be."

"But you can view their code?"

"The code is numbers. It's like trying to work out what someone looks like from just their DNA. In theory it may be possible, if you knew what the DNA coded for. And this is *alien* DNA – not even deoxyribonucleic acid, but some analogue, the informational substrate that these beings are encoded on. It undoubtedly does describe their physiognomy – maybe even their consciousness – but it's written in a language we have no dictionary for. Meaningless words in an unknown tongue, free-floating from any kind of context."

"So you needed to go and look."

"We needed to look."

"Is there no other place where one happens to be near ground level in London? What about the rest of the country? Somewhere else you could get to?"

"There are a half-dozen within the UK. But they are either kilometres underground, or high, way up. There's one over the Cairngorms at 23,000 feet. Unless we can charter a plane, this one, in St Paul's, was our best bet. And it turns out it's inaccessible."

"Can't you, I don't know, manipulate the Grid? Move the thing out of the ground that way?"

The spacehopper grinned at Jack. "Nice idea. Unfortunately the Grid's coordinate system is mapped to the machines it's running on, and thus the Earth."

Nadine shifted a little. The spacehopper's eyes bulged slightly from the pressure. Jack looked down at her bare legs tucked around the oblate spheroid of orange plastic.

If Jack was an old-fashioned calculating machine, a relay would just have clicked into position and a connection would have been made.

The Earth is an oblate spheroid. Spinning once every twenty-four hours about its axis, it is not a perfect sphere but instead bulges out at the equator and is flattened at the poles by centrifugal force. Its diameter measured from Malaysia to Ecuador is greater than the distance from Antarctica to the Arctic. This fact, in itself, was no help. However, the Earth is subject to another deforming force.

"The Moon causes the tides. It pulls the water into a bulge towards itself, and a second bulge forms on the opposite side of the Earth."

Nadine was becoming used to Jack's seeming non sequiturs. "Sorry?"

"Bear with me. Two influences – the Sun, and the Moon. At two points, new Moon and full Moon, they are aligned either on the same or opposite sides of the Earth. At these times their effects are cumulative: high tide. But they don't just distort the *seas,* they also distort the shape of *Earth itself.* The land also rises and falls."

She suddenly realised what Jack was thinking. "How much? By how much does the Earth move?"

Jack's phone, which he had placed on the table between them, beeped. A message was visible on the home screen.

Nadine dropped her fork and stood up. The spacehopper shot backwards and hit an empty pizza box, turning its face away from Jack towards the wall. "She can *hear* us? Has she also been *watching* us? How? *Fuck!* That is like . . . that's *stalking!*"

A S C E N S I O N

by F. HERSCHEL TEAGUE

When the Celestial Mechanic answered the Highmost's

summons, little did he expect to be asked to mount an

expedition into the lands below the Spire, less familiar to

him than the heavens above — and far more alien.

PART SEVEN

THE CELESTIAL MECHANIC could hear a commotion in the street outside his chamber. His forebrain weighed up the scuff and clatter, then alerted his hindbrain, which roused itself from its fugue with some resentment. He propped himself up on an elbow.

The box was on the washstand, as he left it.

Opening the window, he could see his packbeast was now out front, scrubbed and watered. The balance of luggage was already hitched tight to its sides. He caught the young Hill Naze's attention, and indicated that he should come up for the rest of his belongings.

Very soon, he himself was out front, circling the beast while tugging the loops of leather and lashed cord to assure himself they were still sound. The axle of the cart showed some signs of wear and the metal rims of the wheels were burred and scratched, but all seemed service-

The proprietor regarded it dubiously

able. His breathing sphincter caught the scent of frying flatbread and spleen, and he realised he had not breakfasted.

Striding back through the doors into the relative cool of the interior, he could see two hill tribe young-lings setting up an urn of Kaufa and a hotplate of sundries. He had taken two steps towards the table when the older Hill Naze, the proprietor of the establishment, blocked his way. He wore a sober expression. The Celestial Mechanic pointed to the urn and his head, but the Hill Naze did not move.

Reaching under the desk, he pulled out a thin strip of vellum on which a series of pinholes could be seen. Sliding the strip between his digits, he skipped to the end and held it up for the Celestial Mechanic to see, underlining the final amount, a row of fifteen small holes, with a nail blackened with tallow polish.

There seemed to be a standoff of sorts. Holding up a finger and letting his whiskers unfurl, the Celestial Mechanic produced a handkerchief, wrapped it several times around the opposing digit of his left hand, and placed the resultant loop on the time-polished wood of the main desk. With a flourish and a face of utter solemnity, he pulled a soft pouch from under his robe that had, until a few minutes ago, been attached to the harness of his packbeast. From this he carefully lifted the egg, which he placed on the improvised stand. He delicately adjusted it, then withdrew his hands a short distance, hovering as if to catch it should it roll and fall. When it showed no signs of doing so, he looped his robe back over his arm, and gestured grandly towards it.

The proprietor regarded it dubiously and made a clicking sound with the spines on his hind legs that the Mechanic understood to signify displeasure. He feigned incredulity. This object, he explained in his faltering common tongue, was a family heirloom, passed down through generations of the High Families as a symbol of the potential with which each new Spire hatchling came into this life. It represented his solemn word, and as he had decided last night that his employer and his retinue's planned excursion would definitely come this way for several nights, possibly a thrace, he was entrusting it to the owner until his return as a token of his goodwill.

The Celestial Mechanic turned his full attention to the egg for the first time. It looked a little unloved. Its striated shell, patterned as it was with a sinuous lakebed craquelure was, he had to allow, beautiful in its own right, but it also bore a smudge of packbeast faecal matter and a grass stain; at first sight, it didn't resemble something that had been reverently cared for over many generations.

The proprietor enquired again as to how many might accompany him on his excursion. The Mechanic held up all twelve digits. The Hill Naze's eyes narrowed. The Mechanic held up twelve again. Rather than strengthening his case, this inexplicably amplified the owner's exasperation. Had he overdone it? He stole a glance through the main doors out to the street, where his packbeast was eating the hat of a local tradesman who was too cowed to protest.

The Celestial Mechanic was gauging if he could make a dash for the door and his transport, but the owner seemed to have sensed this notion and had now positioned himself between him and freedom. A wisp of dust curled in and around his hooves, but the route was barred. The Mechanic did not see how this might be resolved without resort to violence. He wondered how speedily the local law enforcement representatives might arrive, and how susceptible to bribes or in awe of their betters they might be.

Just then, shouts were heard coming from the street outside. Taking this to be an altercation in the tavern opposite, a not uncommon event, the proprietor at first chose to ignore them. But they continued, growing louder. The proprietor allowed his eyes to leave the Mechanic for a moment, and stepped back and outside for a better look.

Outside, a plains dowcherte, usually a sullen and uncommunicative type, careened around the corner of the hotel waving his ventral plume vigorously and emitting a high-pitched piping through his brow flutes.

The Mechanic scooped up the egg and handkerchief and followed.

A CLOUD OF DUST could be seen at the top of the street, where it turned right towards the bridge and the city limits. Something was coming this way. In short order it resolved into a group of figures, a mixture of Soba Matti, Hill Naze, doragors, dowchertes and other local types. They seemed to number in the dozens, maybe even the hundreds – he could not see the rear of the group. Indeed, for this many to be here now, entire villages must have been emptied.

What were they doing? The Celestial Mechanic had not known them to socialise in such a fashion; certainly there was a deep and long-standing enmity between the Hill Naze and the valley dowchertes that was not bridged by their common tongue. So what could be happening? What could have brought them together?

It was only when they were close enough for him to make out their expressions did understanding flash through his hindbrain. They all *did* have something in common – a fixed and serene smile, a rigidity of stare that revealed an all-consuming purpose.

The Mechanic twisted through the doorway behind the proprietor, whose attention was now fixed upon the horde, took two leaps over to his packbeast, jumped over the rods with which the cart that held a fallen star was attached, climbed up its tail and dropped into the saddle.

The stablehand still had hold of the reins, but his attention, like his employer's, was focused on the approaching commotion. The proprietor spun on his hoof, retreated inside and slammed the great wooden door behind him; this was followed by the sound of a heavy brace sliding into place and the turning of an enormous latch. The stablehand turned and looked imploringly at the Celestial Mechanic, then, placing a foot on the packbeast's tail, made to follow his example and climb aboard.

The egg caught him squarely in the ocular region, blinding him. He took one more step forward, but missed his footing; his legs shot out either side from under him, and he slammed down hard on the packbeast's knobbed armoured tail. Had his eyes been free of foul-smelling yolk they would now have been filled with tears of pain. He gripped his reproductive regions and rolled off into the dust of the road, pulling himself up into a foetal position, his segmented carapace covering him like a stack of ceramic bowls.

THE CELESTIAL MECHANIC had already turned his attention to the road ahead. Whipping the reins and kicking the Brindlatch Coakidoh's soft side belly as hard as he could, the beast lifted its small head, released the remains of the hat from its mouth and shot forwards. The cart followed a few seconds later, straps and lashings creaking in protest, its cargo shunted to the rear of the padded interior.

The packbeast, the Celestial Mechanic was again dismayed to remember, was not built for speed; but in very short bursts it could move as fast as a fit Bray Kadock. This particular packbeast was fresh and rested, and soon he had put a good distance between himself and the approaching crowd.

Not having had time to consult his charts, he was riding without direction. The roads ahead became rougher, the buildings either side less grand; lacking gardens, their doors opened directly onto the pavement.

He passed a barracks from which issued a motley crew of sparsely uniformed men, some rushing to meet the newcomers, more running in the opposite direction, alongside him and towards the city wall.

Shouting down from his saddle, he enquired as to the location of the closest gate; one pointed, and he followed them through the outskirts of the town and out, where they dispersed into the surrounding fields, farmsteads and hinterlands from which many of their number had originally been recruited.

N OT WISHING TO SLACKEN the pace, the Celestial Mechanic again pushed the packbeast to the limits of its endurance; but shortly, when he could see it was in danger of overexertion, he let it slow to a canter, then a stroll.

Behind, through his small land telescope, the city looked much as it had before. He could see no movement along the city wall, nothing entering or leaving through the gate. If the surrounding farmsteads were engaged in anything other than a normal day's work, there was nothing to show for it.

A thin vertical chalk-mark of woodsmoke rose and dissipated on the morning thermals. If anything, the scene seemed peculiarly tranquil.

The Celestial Mechanic felt quite the opposite. Was he outrunning some epidemic? Had the thing from the stars brought with it some disease, something that clouded the mind? Were they following him? And could he himself be affected?

He had judiciously avoided touching the thing in the box or coming into contact with anyone who had. If it was communicable, he seemed to be free of its effects. The fallen star was safe in its box, and the box was locked securely. He had the only key.

He focused again on the road ahead. He was returning to the Spire to fulfil his obligation.

A swathe of low trees turned the road towards the lowlands, down to the patchwork of fields that broke with the Quarterlands' usual Spire-centred arrangement and wrapped themselves around the sinuous curves of the Gorodorborga. Occasionally he would turn in the saddle, but behind him saw no sign of the melee.

As the vista opened up in front of him, in the morning glow he could see the bright looping line of the river reflecting the sulphur haze, and, joy upon joys, the Spire itself could just be made out on the horizon, a thin vertical pinnacle of light where it caught the rising sun.

Through his land telescope, the three faces of Civility, Graciousness and Rectitude were visible as bright smudges towards the tip. The Spire, his home and his destination. That is where his responsibility ended. He would then let the Highmost himself decide what should be done with his strange cargo.

A T LENGTH REACHING the banks of the Gorodorborga, with great relief he turned north, towards the Spire. The river followed a winding path like a golden thread fallen to the floor of a weaver's cottage, looping through the fertile lowlands, at times touching and even crossing itself, leaving isolated islands and oxbow lakes in which fish spawned and reeds clogged the current.

Here the cultivated fields came right down to the water's edge, and small channels had been cut in the bank to irrigate crops of frax and windchaff. Each season the waters from the Circular Sea covered the large expanses of floodplain in a fresh layer of nutrient-rich soil, and row upon row of vivid turquoise shoots could now be seen scattered over the dark loam.

The road, such as it was, sometimes followed the bank and sometimes cut across between fields, to again meet the river further upstream as it curved back upon itself. Houses of baked brick could be seen in small groupings; in the scalloped eaves of these, small bells chimed in the breeze, an architectural conceit popular in this part of the Quarterlands. Occasionally, through the tall trees that marked the boundaries of their grounds, he could see a tanned Naze at work, or a Brindlatch, harnessed to an earthturner.

The Celestial Mechanic was confident he could make it back to the Spire by the following morning. His nervousness dissipated somewhat and he settled into the journey, rolling lazily with his mount and taking the occasional sip from the waterbag hitched to its side.

Presently he caught glimpses of a vast wall ahead, in the middle distance through the trees. Drawing closer, he realised that this was the fallen forearm of a Skybound Beyonder, the enormous petrified mass that many cycles ago had rerouted the Gorodorborga with such disastrous results. Lichen and mosses now softened its blackened hide, and at certain points steps had been carved into its surface to enable one to climb up to the top, on which low shrubs and nesting birds had taken up residence.

The Celestial Mechanic followed the path as it moved inland, skirting this wall of stone. Nearing the wrist, he could see it was truncated; rounding the end, the cross-section revealed concentric rings of petrified sinew and bone, in the very centre of which the marrow had either washed or been eaten away, leaving a cave large enough that he could enter mounted on his packbeast with height to spare, should he so wish.

In near infrared, he could see

several shapes deep within; not wishing to disturb the lair of some local carnivorous beast, he gave it a wide berth and moved on.

The road continued to flank the Beyonder forearm for some distance on the other side, then cut directly across the land toward the peaks of the Rim which could now be seen above the vegetation on the lower foothills in the distance.

He recalled hearing of a scenic route over the Rim that followed the cascade of waterfalls leading up into the Gap; even outside flood season, a torrent of water would crash from pool to pool, over terraces and through channels in the rock. Popular with both tourists and locals taking an evening constitutional, it featured in many Quarterland ballads, and crude impressions in pigmented bitumen could be bought at the souvenir stands that soon began to line the route.

This natural wonder was also serviced by a funicular railway which ran up the steep incline to the top. It consisted of a series of stepped coaches fashioned from brass and dark age-polished wood, the topmost reserved for goods and livestock, those towards the front for passengers. Dining platforms surmounted them, affording dramatic panoramas of the landscape below. Fronting this arrangement was a carved figurehead of Yogril, his usual surly countenance given a cartoonish makeover so as not to scare the younglings. Hung with antique spark-moth lamps whose light caught the chased brasswork, it gave the impression of a crouching beast outlined in gold. This magnificent contraption could take him and his packbeast to the summit.

A ticket was bartered for: his last remaining decent overjacket was enough to guarantee him passage on the next trip.

L ATER, WATCHING THE lands fall away beneath him as a counterweight lifted the baroque wood-panelled carriages up their rails, he let his gaze trace the route of the Gorodorborga back out to the Iron Sea. Like spilled quicksilver where it reflected the sky, it marked out the final part of the long journey that had led him out to the lands beyond the Spire and back. Very soon he would be home, at the top of the world, at the peak of the Hierarchy, surrounded by all the comforts of body and mind that his august position afforded him.

But he could not shift the impression that he was leaving something important down there, down with those simpler people whose day-to-day existence and culture was defined by the flat horizontal landscape they worked rather than the tiered verticality of the Spire.

In the lands outside the Rim, your neighbour did not always occupy a higher or lower position, either physically or socially; and though he had seen vast inequalities of wealth, he had also seen a great mixing of peoples and an earthy vibrancy that the Spire's refined pursuits sometimes lacked. Back home, your position on the levels was a constant reminder of your position within the Hierarchy itself, and all the attendant rivalries and

*This natural wonder was serviced by a funicular railway which ran up
the steep incline to the Rim*

manoeuvrings that entailed.

He decided, should his duties in the Assembly of the Constant Conviction ever allow him the time or the opportunity to find a suitable life partner, that they would return here together; that out there was where they would spend their honeymoon, and, all being well, maybe the remainder of their lives.

He would bring with him his precious scrolls and instruments, and they would build a simple dwelling, somewhere in the Known and Only Lands where you couldn't see to the very lip of the world; somewhere out there where the horizon hugged you close, but still managed to encompass all one could ever want from a life well lived.

To be concluded

TALES FROM THE CRYPT

Five days later at 9.26 AM, exactly midway between full moon and new, it was low tide at 51°30'49"N 0°05'53"W, a point close to the Thames in the old City of London, the capital of a country called England, forming part of the British Isles, a small group of islands situated off the northwestern coast of Europe, a continent on the larger body of the Earth–Moon system.

At that precise location and ten minutes before that precise time, Jack ordered a latte and a pastry from a petite East European waitress with a monogrammed apron resembling a monk's habit and a basic grasp of English. It was early morning in St Paul's crypt café, and the light smattering of visitors meant they still had a choice of seats. Clean and whitewashed, it was not the kind of place one expected to go hunting for ghosts.

Jack folded a paper napkin and wiped the table. He had company – Harriet and Nixon had persuaded him to slow down so that they could keep up, just this time. He pulled his laptop from his messenger bag and opened it. Nixon rotated it so he could see the screen. Harriet and Jack put on their Depthcharges.

Across the table from them sat XX and the 19th Count. XX wasn't sitting, exactly, more hunkering down so his upper extremities wouldn't pierce the roof. It took Jack a couple of seconds to locate Girl 21, her back to Nelson's tomb, barely as tall as the limestone plinth on which the black marble sarcophagus rested. He gave her a small wave.

The Count, leaning back with one leg crossed high over the other, his coat tails flamboyantly and implausibly billowing out behind him despite the sepulchrally still air, tapped his cane to the side of his top hat in greeting. Above XX, rising from a structure that resembled a ship's bridge, was a thought bubble in which grinding cogs spun soundlessly.

"Do we have a precise location?" From his previous visit, Jack knew the dimensions of the chapel should admit no more than one or two Grid interstices, depending on the alignment. If the entity in question was now visible it should be easy to spot.

The Count was somewhat subdued. Harriet sensed a certain trepidation. Alone in ideaspace for so long, they were unused to sharing.

I'm told it's just a simple matter of

CROSS-REFERENCING

the *Grid* with available *"gee-pee-ess"* information, dear boy. *(I usually leave this kind of* Modern Magic *to our*

Technical Mistress,

who is currently *holding court* with

VISCOUNT

NELSON,

1ST DUKE OF BRONTÉ, (KB)

over *yonder.)*

Girl, 21
@twentyone • 0m

ᕕ(ò ͜ʖ ó)ᕗ ψ

"I think we've just been given the finger by a teddy bear," Harriet observed. In their identical eyewear, she and Jack looked like one of those creepy couples who coordinated their outfits.

The 19th Count stood up, bowed, and gestured for the others to follow. Jack collected his laptop and walked straight through Girl 21's white rectangle, still hanging there in ideaspace. It shrunk to a white dot and disappeared. "Creative repurposing of languages you don't understand. We'll be doing that a lot, I'll wager."

They passed into a circular chamber surrounded by eight Tuscan pillars, around Nelson's imposing sarcophagus – originally intended for Cardinal Wolsey, but don't tell him – then through the middle of five arches, the other four of which were blocked by oak panels. Beyond was the dimly lit chamber of St Faith's Chapel.

The wooden chairs that had been here on Jack's previous visit were now folded and stacked against the wall. Otherwise, all was as before.

Set at the far end was an altar under a vaulted hemispherical roof. Jack took a small step up to the raised marble dais. Curtained alcoves led off to the left and right, each blocked by a filigree wrought-iron partition topped with a candelabra, the candles of which had been replaced with flickering electric skeuomorphs that never burned shorter or blackened the air. Pewter urns capped with miniature crowns stood to each side, and square tasselled flags quartered into heraldic motifs featuring lions, castles, crosses and harps hung from pillars.

Harriet found that the Depthcharges made everything just a bit more indistinct; it was like wearing sunglasses indoors. Keeping close to Jack so she didn't accidentally pull her lead from his laptop, they looked as if they were sharing a tune, an earbud each. *Where—*

Girl 21 was by the step, under the low curve of a whitewashed arch. She was kneeling down, in a position that from Jack's point of view looked like prayer. It was only when he stepped to the right, around her, that he saw what she was looking at. He stopped dead. Harriet accidentally walked into him.

Protruding out of the stone floor, like an apparition of an undead king half-risen from a grave, Jack could see the upper portion of a torso. Harriet saw it too. "Nixon, over here. It's *here*."

Jack knelt, laid the messenger bag on the ground, then placed the open laptop on top of it so Nixon could see what they were seeing.

"Shee-*oot*. What *is* that?"

Immobile, inscrutable, rising out of the flagstones to what would have been its waist were it human, was a – a creature. It was sleek and hairless, as if it had evolved to carve an alien sea; the body shape was described with tight curves that, where they met, were seamed with a pale bioluminescent aquamarine. Not much larger than a human body, it tapered elegantly to the point of intersection with the stone.

It was laterally symmetrical; there were two arms, jointed twice, folded across its chest. The 'head' at the top held what Jack assumed was a selection of sense organs. Two bulbs on short stalks protruded from vertical openings in its polished exoskeletal skull, a small forward-facing shield. The face, if that is what it was, was defined by a raised ridge and two curving scallops below that resembled roll bars on a stock car, but finer and far more delicate. Though the body appeared lithe and whippet-thin, Jack surmised that this creature must have evolved from a more heavily armoured ancestor, and that these features were relics of a less civilised past.

The faceplate was mottled towards the top with a pale pattern that reminded Harriet of a silk damask. An opening, shaped like an inverted teardrop and centred just below the bulbs, gave into an internal space in which a whorled organ could be seen, pocked with holes each containing a single black hair. Below this, the faceplate opened up again in a vertical slit, the two sides becoming transparent; through this another organ was visible. It looked like a sea anemone, a ring of tentacles now frozen and immobile, in the centre of which was a dark orifice.

The back of the head was a close-fitting series of plates. Two large ones were set above the eyes, sweeping back majestically over the brow; behind, smaller pairs, again joined by a bioluminescent line, passed over what would be the shoulders to fuse with the lower back. Jack imagined this might open, like the carapace of a beetle, to reveal wings.

Nixon experimentally waved his hand through the apparition's head, watching the laptop screen as he did so. For a moment, the physical and the non-physical occupied the same space. There was no reaction. "Is it dead? Or in suspended animation?"

Jack passed him his Depthcharges so he could take a better look. "Or maybe it's neither – just the informational *representation* of an alien."

In the context of the crypt and positioned as it was, bisected and mounted on the floor like a bust, it had an understated presence, a certain beneficence in repose that was not lost on them. Though different in size and form, Harriet was put in mind of the broken torso of Ramesses II in the British Museum. Both were representations seen across an abyss of time, and in this case, space; both were mute messengers from cultures which might forever remain obscure, their blank eyes witness to events they were utterly unable to relate.

Harriet got as close as the glasses permitted, closer still. She couldn't get used to this alien zoo idea.

Her head passed into the creature's chest cavity. "Oo. Internal organs. It also works like a CAT scan." She pulled out, looked at the 19th Count and back, then poked a finger at the apparition. "Ozymandias?"

The Count adopted a theatrical pose, as if about to hold forth to an invisible audience.

"I met a traveller from an antique land—

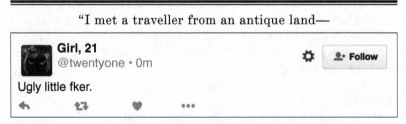

Girl, 21
@twentyone • 0m
⚙ ➕ Follow

Ugly little fker.

↩   ⟲   ♥   •••

Jack had one more piece of information he had not as yet divulged.

He had seen this creature before – in poor-quality images taken on the far side of another world. Non-disclosure agreements be damned.

"I recognise it. I know what this is. This – this is the Man in the Moon."

CENTRAL LINE

shhhhhh shhhhhh ga-dunk
bom-tish   bom-tish   bom-tish   bom-tish-tish-ah   bom-tish   bom-tish
kind of what I expected *no way* well *hello* if you're playing Candy Crush on
THIS IS A CENTRAL LINE TRAIN TO EALING BROADWAY.
bd-um   *bd-um*   **bd-um**   **bd-um**   **bd-um**
bom-tish   bom-tish-tish-ah   bom-tish   bom-tish   bom-tish   bom-tish-
the loo at work you *were* I could hear look at that man he's wearing a furry hat
THE NEXT STATION IS OXFORD CIRCUS. CHANGE FOR
bd-um   *bd-um*   **bd-um**   **bd-um**   **bd-um**
tish-ah bom-tish bom-tish bom-tish bom-tish-tish-ah bom-tish bom-tish
what a cunt Carmen enough what's the name of the company I'm thinking
THE VICTORIA AND BAKERLOO LINES. THANK YOU FOR
bd-um bd-um   *bd-um*   **bd-um**   **bd-um**
bom-tish bom-tish-tish-ah bom-tish bom-tish bom-tish bom-tish-tish-ah
of we've got a new job with them my contractions were about two minutes
TRAVELLING ON THE CENTRAL LINE. THIS IS A CENTRAL
bd-um   *bd-um*   **bd-um**   **bd-um**   **bd-um**
bom bom bom bom wellabaybeeissafinahonetuhwannasendafannasee
apart *aaaaaaa* . . . he totally heard you admit you liked him how's every-
LINE TRAIN TO EALING BROADWAY. THE NEXT STATION
bd-um   *bd-um*   **bd-um**   **bd-um**   **bd-um**
bom   bom-tish   bom   biterfannereggerivahdigurevahdidahnovilasteree
thing with the baby? What's that on your shirt man so he kept making that
IS OXFORD CIRCUS. THIS TRAIN CALLS AT MARBLE
bd-um bd-um   *bd-um*   **bd-um**   **bd-um**
uh-huh uh-huh bom-tish bom-tish bom-tish bom-tish-tish-ah bom-tish
zazzum, zazzum noise like a lightsaber or something okay yeah but he was
ARCH, NOTTING HILL GATE AND WHITE CITY. CHANGE
bd-um   *bd-um*   **bd-um**   **bd-um**   **bd-um**
bom-tish   bom-tish   bom-tish-tish-ah   bom-tish   bom-tish   bom-tish
like *thirty* are they really accidents *hey!* oh I thought it was a purse did you

469

bd-um *bd-um* **bd-um** **bd-um** **bd-um**

bom-tish-tish-ah bom-tish bom-tish bom-tish bom-tish-tish-ah bom-tish

hear what she said *well* then how about cheap make-up mmm-hmmm first

AT NORTH ACTON FOR TRAINS TO WEST RUISLIP. THIS

bd-um bd-um *bd-um* **bd-um** **bd-um bd-um**

bom-tish bom-tish bom-tish-tish-ah bom-tish bom-tish bom-tish bom-tish-

thing we do is get back control of petty cash *ice cream* and just when every-

IS A CENTRAL LINE TRAIN TO EALING BROADWAY.

bd-um **bd-um** **bd-um** **bd-um** **bd-um**

tish-ahbombombombombomwellabaybeeissafinahonetuhwannasendafannasee

body wait . . . I'm sorry I had the volume down no, he's never going to agree

THE NEXT STATION IS OXFORD CIRCUS. REMEMBER TO

bd-um **bd-um** **bd-um** **bd-um** **bd-um**

bom   bom-tish   bom   biterfannereggerivahdigurevahdidahnovilasteree

to carry the device without a direct order did you get a five-piece and some

TAKE ALL PERSONAL BELONGINGS WITH YOU. THIS IS

bd-um bd-um *bd-um* **bd-um** **bd-um bd-um**

uh-huh uh-huh bbom-tish bom-tish bom-tish bom-tish-tish-ah bom-tish

biscuits I feel bad he's stuck talking to her I feel like I should rescue him

A CENTRAL LINE TRAIN TO EALING BROADWAY. IF YOU

bd-um **bd-um** **bd-um** **bd-um** **bd-um**

bom-tish   bom-tish   bom-tish-tish-ah   bom-tish   bom-tish   bom-tish

yeah I just came back yesterday they don't have any regular sandwiches there

SEE ANYTHING SUSPICIOUS, PLEASE INFORM A MEMBER

bd-um **bd-um** **bd-um** **bd-um** **bd-um**

bom-tish-tish-ah bom-tish bom-tish bom-tish bom-tish-tish-ah bom-tish

yeah that's her in the picture it's all pitta-this and wrap-that I was like what-

OF STAFF. THIS IS A CENTRAL LINE TRAIN TO EALING

bd-um bd-um *bd-um* **bd-um** **bd-um bd-um**

bom-tish uh-huh uh-huh bom-tish bom-tish bom-tish bom-tish-tish-ah

ever sure, so this rash is spreading up my leg, right, so I get this ointment

BROADWAY. THE NEXT STATION IS OXFORD CIRCUS. WE

bd-um **bd-um** **bd-um** **bd-um** **ga-dunk**

bom-tish bom-tish bom-tish bom-tish bom-tish-tish-ah bom-tish bom-tish

that smells like pee I guess no I am not going to take your phone number

ARE NOW ARRIVING AT THE NEXT STATION. PLEASE

bd-um bd-um *bd-um* **bd-um** **bd-um bd-um**

bom-tish   bom-tish bom-tish   bom-tish   bom-tish   bom-tish-ah

good*bye*

STAND CLEAR OF THE DOORS.

shhhhhh shhhhhh h   h   h   h   h

Jack cradled the Depthcharges in his lap. It was disconcerting wearing them on the Tube, not because they drew attention but because a crowded space seemed even more claustrophobic when it was also full of text. Harriet and Nixon were sitting opposite.

In the crypt of St Paul's he had, in flagrant disregard for the NDA he had signed, told Harriet and Nixon all about his visit to Jodrell, about Dana Normansson and the Man in the Moon. It was a testament to the events of the previous few days and the times they all felt they were now living in that they took the revelation that there was an alien in a crashed spaceship on the far side of Earth's satellite on board without much pushback, and had then decided to go to Nando's. They had questions Jack had done his best to answer, though he could sense that they passed what he told them through their internalised Jack filter, which he imagined was like a bullshit detector but set to a much higher sensitivity. In this, he knew he only had himself to blame.

Now they sat there without talking, together but apart, island minds ruminating in the memetic fug of the train carriage. The incidental background music of wheels on track, fragmentary conversation, breakbeats escaping from cheap earbuds, advertising messages and dot-matrix destination indicators had become drained of all meaning: reduced to a series of repetitive signal oscillations that moved an eardrum or fell across a retina without interpretation.

A S C E N S I O N

by F. HERSCHEL TEAGUE

When the Celestial Mechanic answered the Highmost's

summons, little did he expect to be asked to mount an

expedition into the lands below the Spire, less familiar to

him than the heavens above — and far more alien.

PART EIGHT

THE ELITE HONOUR GUARD, the Celestial Mechanic was unsurprised to find, had received prior news of his pending arrival back at the Spire from one of their contacts down in the docks, and didn't waste any time in ushering him forward onto the plaza.

Here, in the thinner air at the very peak of the Spire, ruffled by the rising morning currents their feathered peasantskin hats looked as magnificent as they always did, but he felt a curious pang of nostalgia for simpler, and perhaps more – *practical* attire.

He pushed the absurd notion back to his forebrain and purged it. Looking up at the octagonal observatory mounted on its thirty-two carved caryatids, he wondered if the Highmost might have followed his movements across the land from here with his telescope, every pace of the journey there and back; whether that was even possible.

A bell was rung, and two of the

CONCLUDING OUR NOVELETTE OF STRANGE ALIEN CULTURES IN EIGHT PARTS

guards broke position. With a formal exactitude and a series of high kicks and heel taps they moved to a wooden gantry and began to turn a two-handled crank. A complex system of pulleys hung over the edge of the precipice, and in a few moments his wheeled cart hove into view and was swung across to a short platform that projected out over the drop. Paying no heed to the possibility of falling many purloughs, they extricated the cart from its harness and wheeled it over. The Celestial Mechanic touched his whiskers to the stone floor in gratitude.

Without further delay, the platform descended with a faint chord of tightened ropes and a clunk of counterweights, echoing up from the bottom of a wood-lined shaft somewhere deep below. He manoeuvred the cart and its contents onto it; a signal was given, and the platform, the Celestial Mechanic, and his precious cargo rose again into the belly of the Highmost's sanctum.

His senses were assaulted by the smell of urine and damp clothing even before the rising platform had shut out the last circumscribed frame of light. The windows were shuttered and it was stiflingly hot and humid; the rarefied air at the top of the Spire was usually cool and attenuated, but here it was close and heavy. He had just begun to recite the first of the formal greetings when His Highmost held up a digit for quiet, let out an impatient high whistle, and motioned him to lift the locked box onto the table.

He divested it of its wheels and raised it over the polished expanse in the centre of the room, below the telescope's brass gimbal. The Celestial Mechanic made moves to first clear the table of charts and books, but sensing the Highmost's impatience, instead carefully pushed as many as he could to one side.

He turned the box so that the hinges faced away, the lid opening towards them. Here, the Celestial Mechanic paused. He had, in his haste (or could it be disrespect? He wondered if his excursion into the hinterlands had robbed him of some of his manners) omitted to change into his most formal attire; this, and the absence of the usual pleasantries, had left him at something of a loss. He toyed with the key which was tucked into a fold of his travelling jerkin.

The Highmost seemed uninterested in these lapses in protocol. A falling series of clicks and a rippling of orange around his shrivelled whiskers underlined his impatience. His message was clear: waste no more of my time, and open the box.

There was a small voice in the Celestial Mechanic's hindbrain that was still debating if this was a wise move; but given that he really could see no viable alternative – at least, not one that wouldn't end his long and distinguished career – he acquiesced.

With a flourish, he revealed the key and held it aloft, light from the windowslats crossing it at several points. He placed it flat on his opened palms, and holding them out and forward, offered it to the Highmost himself.

With what seemed to him like a glint of youngling glee, the Highmost took the key, ran a foreclaw down its length, and then inserted it in the lock. Stepping back, he looked at the Celestial Mechanic with an expression of expectation. He turned the key, then placing his hands either side lifted the lid and let it fall back heavily on its hinges.

The meteorite, if that is what it was, sat on the padded leather. It had split, cracked into two halves, the constrictions of the box still holding them loosely together. The thin translucent filaments had grown to fill the interior, cramming themselves under the padding and into every corner. A few tendrils began to uncurl from the flattened surface that had been pressed against the lid and wave lazily, as if searching for something. It looked like the stomach of an eel that the Celestial Mechanic had once caught and gutted as an infant, only to find it diseased and full of worms.

There was a short silence.

The lid came down forcefully and the key was turned once again. *Click-ch-click! Ch-Ch-chrikkk!* He tried to gauge the Highmost's state of mind. His forebrain activity had risen alarmingly. Excitement? Apprehension? The Celestial Mechanic hesitated and stepped back, unsure what to do or say. He began to sense that this might not be the grand homecoming he had expected. Had he not done exactly what was requested of him?

His Highmost threatened him with a barbaric and ancient practice he had once read about in an obscure book he had borrowed from an associate in the Occluded University. He began to protest; had he not completed his task with aplomb? Did the Highmost not appreciate the vicissitudes he had endured on his mission? He doubted that the threatened punishment was legal, though laws were somewhat flexible when it came to the whims of those at the upper levels.

The Highmost was scanning his shelves, pulling down scroll after scroll with a complete lack of care, unfurling and tearing these precious relics that he would usually treat with the utmost respect. The Celestial Mechanic followed behind, picking them up and respooling them, restacking them carefully, pleading with the Highmost to explain to him the reason for his displeasure.

Finally, the Highmost found what he was looking for. It was an ancient scroll whose original parchment had been remounted on a new, more robust backing sheet and wrapped around new rollers. He pulled it around and onto the table, knocking over an oakermilk bottle that had been refilled with something warm.

Ignoring this, he rolled it out. The Celestial Mechanic could see it contained diagrams and drawings, and dates written in the same formal proto-Naze script as the motto carved in the rock below this very room. The Highmost ran a digit down column after column, searching for something. The roll was spooled on, the process repeated. Presently he found what he was looking for.

The Celestial Mechanic bent forward, not wanting to get too close both out of respect for the Highmost and so as not to overwhelm his olfactory organ.

There, on the scroll, was a drawing in faded mountain-blue. It was of a ball, or a gourd perhaps; round and spiky, and for a moment the Celestial Mechanic did not recognise it.

No.

He began to understand. Though the artistry was crude and the parchment had flaked away in many places, it was unmistakably the same object as the one in the box, or at least another of its kind. Overcoming his revulsion he leaned in to take a closer look. Arrayed around the base of the page he could see figures representing all three major sexes of Naze, old and young, noble and indentured, dressed in the faintly comical garb of the time before the Great Curiosity and Conflagration.

Before the cataclysm! This scroll must be very old indeed. Only the private libraries of the most exalted had been spared the purges that were a common practice under the watch of the Lower Apostles of the Academy of the Disinterested. He should know; he'd trained to be one himself.

The figures seemed to be folded forwards to accept a blessing, or in reverent supplication. Tendrils extended from the Seed of Light, as the old hand labelled it, to touch the heads of those closest, and inside each so touched was drawn a many-pointed star, burnished with a gilt that had long ago oxidised to a dark verdigris. Their expressions were of the utmost serenity; beatific, smiling.

The Highmost rolled the scroll to reveal the next section. Those that had been touched were hurrying here and there, building boats, preparing carts and pack animals, heading out on a journey; each had a small star of verdigris placed in their heads.

The roads they followed all led to higher ground: mountains, hills, all drawn in the peculiar flat perspective of the old texts. Some figures could not get to a higher place, and so they climbed tall trees, or onto the roofs of buildings. Some were depicted falling off, or lying on the ground with pools of sap beside them; even in death, they still had open eyes and rapturous smiles on their faces. The Celestial Mechanic felt his carapace constrict.

The next section of the scroll depicted a tall tower with a crenellated battlement at the top. Around it were crowds of Naze, climbing the stone walls or onto the backs of their brethren in an attempt to reach up higher. The artist had spared no detail – claws were shown caught in cracks of masonry, their owners falling, simply to be trodden underfoot or used as a ladder by the next wave. All the while, through the mounting pile of bodies at the foot of the tower, the same smile had been drawn on every face. From above, the besieged occupants could be seen throwing household items down – pans, hot oil, a bed. These became part of the structure upon which the intruders climbed ever higher.

There were three more images. The next showed the tower completely engulfed in bodies. Looking closely, they seemed to be knitted together, limbs enmeshed, bodies somehow merging as if made of clay. Of the original occupants there was no sign. At the very top, where the highest point of the tower had been, a coagulation of conjoined flesh could now be seen; a round protuberance like a bulb was forming.

The penultimate drawing showed the horde of bodies now remade into one strong, solid mass, a cabled, muscular stalk upon which the enlarging bulb at the summit was supported, tight sinews holding the growing weight aloft. It was an angry red with vertical black stripes that began just under the apex and ran down its length, along which the occasional still-smiling face could just be made out. It resembled a speckled and striated ripe fruit, or a monstrous budding flower, and it disturbed the Celestial Mechanic more than he cared to admit.

Before turning to the final image, the Highmost spooled the scroll back to the very beginning, to the section prior to the first picture he had shown. In this preceding series of images, again drawn in the peculiar stylised manner of the time before the Great Curiosity and Conflagration, was shown a map of the heavens, the constellations inscribed with mythical beasts and natural plant forms. Moving across this background was a wandering star; it became a fireball, then a sphere, heated by the speed of atmospheric friction, falling groundwards. As was the tradition with the depiction of celestial bodies, each of these had painted upon it a small face.

A seed? Of what? Certain legends common across the Quarters, and held even in the barrenlands, told of an ancient visitor that came from across the Iron Sea. Arriving in a vessel that did not touch the waters, he taught farming and animal husbandry, and instituted marriage amongst the peoples.

This figure was depicted as a bringer of knowledge, usually in the form of a smiling Naze, or sometimes a snake. In some versions of the story, a seed from heaven was placed on a stone anvil, usually thought to represent Terrine herself, and crushed by rocks thrown down from the stars by the Skybound Beyonders themselves. Many multitudes were killed in this barrage, which indelibly pockmarked the lands; but they were successful, and the seed was destroyed.

There were those in the Occluded University that were of the opinion that this story was a folk memory of the heavy bombardment that created the crater and the Spire itself, but the texts differed in so many important details, and the scripts in which they were written were often difficult to decipher with any confidence.

The Highmost turned back to the final image. Here, the original scroll became a shredded mat of discoloured fibres. Scorch marks blackened the lower edge. Dozens of small fragments had been affixed to the backing sheet, and others whose place could not be divined had been arranged around the edges.

It was a puzzle with too many missing pieces. A scrap of verdigris. A hand. An unidentifiable portion of what looked like cadaverous veined flesh.

A disembodied smile.

What did it show? What was the final fate of the tower? Why had this portion of the scroll been defaced?

The end of the backing sheet sprung from the roller and curled up and across the table like a ribbon run between knife and forefinger.

There was no more.

ACROSS THE FORTY-EIGHT Districts, the barrenlands, the five and a half oceans beyond, the white wastes to the north, even – or perhaps especially – in the lands of the Servants of the Omphalos, the followers of Murorundrum-Kalash the Defiler, something was spreading. An idea, passed person to person. Persuasive. Inarguable. All-consuming.

Join us. Share our truth. See how simple it is, how grand our purpose?

Great rivers of people, high and low, young and old, predator and prey alike, flowed out of the towns and hamlets across the Quarterlands, drawn inexorably to higher ground.

The Spire could be seen for many stadia. It was a constant, a landmark, a reminder of the stratified society of which they were all a part. More than that, embedded in every mind, from the time a youngling first

asked a parent what that bright line on the horizon might be, was a singular conception, nurtured for the many generations since the Great Curiosity and Conflagration: the Spire was the zenith of the world, the highest point on all Terrine.

Now, right across the Known and Only Lands, faces were turning up to look at the Spire's serried balconies and majestic staircases, the cool gardens emerging from heliotrope shadow, its floor upon floor of beckoning verticality.

Cities emptied. The fields were left untended. A multitudinous wave of people flowed up to the Rim, climbing the staircases and the bare rock alike. Many fell; none were mourned.

Descending the inner slopes of the crater wall, they crowded against the shore of the Circular Sea, that natural barrier that had done so much to preserve the Spire's isolated majesty in the past.

This proved to offer but a short respite. The tavern owners, the shipmasters, the sailors and the brothelkeepers, now persuaded of the righteousness of the cause, set off in their boats and barges. Many others attempted to swim, and the Circular Sea soon became clogged with floating bodies, each subsequent wave of people reaching the edge before toppling over into the waters to provide footing for their fellows immediately behind.

THESE DEVELOPMENTS had not gone unnoticed on the Spire. A meeting of the Academy of the Disinterested was immediately convened, despite the early hour.

Crowds gathered to watch the unfolding spectacle from balconies on the upper reaches. Though still assured of their safety here in the rafters of the world, a growing unease had begun to spread.

The first of the boats that had set sail from the far shores of the Circular Sea had arrived at the jetties below, and some kind of commotion was playing out, the details of which were unclear to the observers above. A message was sent out to all the guardhouses on levels twelve through to fifty-five: no one was to be permitted to pass, on threat of death.

The Academy of the Disinterested, in what proved to be a record time for reaching a decision, decided that some decisive action needed to be taken.

Hidden in the eyes of the remaining three of the Four Courtesies, behind baroque carved screens, were mounted braces of cannon. These had not been fired in living memory, and the Academy was not trained in their use. Pushing open the screens, they wheeled them forward on rails to the edge of the eye sockets then swung them down to point to the waters beneath, the Courtesies eyeing their subjects' insurrection.

Much hurried experimentation and heated argument ensued before the first was successfully fired.

An iron ball the size of a fist arced down to the waters below, piercing a caravelle and upending its two halves, which promptly sank, leaving a flotsam of bodies. A cheer went up, as at the Races, and a barrage of cannonballs swiftly followed.

The eye sockets became choked with gunpower smoke; two cannons, which had become clogged over the centuries of disuse, exploded on their rails, killing their operators.

These early successes could not be sustained. Supplies of ammunition were limited, much of the store having been turned into commemorative paperweights for the Highmost's coronation.

It was no contest. Though unarmed and untrained, the sheer weight of numbers could not be stemmed. The Circular Sea filled with bodies, and finally a bridge connected shore to shore. A seemingly endless flow of creatures rushed across, meeting little resistance at the staging posts and in the lower levels, the inhabitants of which had already abandoned the guardhouses, their heritage and their history, and joined the throng.

The broad staircases of the lower levels were now a churning mass of people. They swept under the arches and around the balustraded half-landings, through the amphitheatres and pleasure gardens, trampling the carefully tended mazes and flowerbeds underfoot.

An emissary of the Academy was sent to inform the Highmost of the situation. Reaching the plaza, he was immediately run through by one of the Honour Guard, who from their vantage were well aware of the scenes unfolding below. No risk could be brooked in regard to the Highmost's safety; he was the Spire and the Hierarchy personified.

BEYOND THE SHUTTERS and the elaborately coloured windows, the concussion of cannon could be heard. The Celestial Mechanic indicated the telescope, but it was mounted in such a way that it could not be used to observe the lower levels. The only way in was through the platform in the floor, and that was now hermetically sealed. Whatever was happening outside, they would have to sit it out here until it subsided.

Here, at least, they were safe.

THE MASS OF PEOPLE at the base of the Spire began to undergo a peculiar change. Carapaces ruptured, bodies began to melt. Tendrils emerged from their interiors and began to entwine with their neighbours, pulling each to the other, each into the other, demolishing the distinction between forebrain and hindbrain, between one being and another. As nerves reknitted, there was an intimate and complete sharing of thoughts, passions, drives; the walls of the I were demolished, every individual becoming part of a single entity.

The fused mass of flesh began to entwine the midlevels of the Spire like choking ivy. The remaining aristocracy were hidden in cellars and boltholes, but others had nowhere to hide. Without air or supplies, they found themselves locked in the spaces that would prove to be their tombs.

Eventually the interweaving of bodies reached the upper levels. The lower reaches, from the jetties to the ladders, were now sheathed with tightening flesh.

THE NOISE OUTSIDE became almost intolerable. Though neither the Highmost or the Celestial Mechanic could know exactly what was happening, the crunching and reknitting of bone, the slap and stretch of bonding flesh brought vivid images to their forebrains.

A light dust was shaken from the beams of the cupola above. A patter of dislodged plaster rained down onto the scrolls on the table and chimed off the urine-filled oakermilk bottles.

The light began to wane. Looking up, the Celestial Mechanic could see dark shapes moving across the surfaces of the octagonal windows, each small pane darkening in turn, its colour lost to night.

There was a crack of a joist under pressure. A scraping of stone on stone that set the toothplate on edge. A slow descending note as of something large and heavy falling a great distance.

The cupola was now entirely dark. In infrared, the corners of the room glowed under the pressure of compression. The floor shook again, and in the claustrophobic, dust-filled space there could be heard the strained chirrup of the Highmost's breathing sphincter.

The entire Spire, from the shore to the comet emblem atop the cupola, was now encased in a contracting muscular envelope. Sinews shivered; arteries pumped, drawing up nutrients from the sea. A bulge was beginning to form at the very top.

If the Skybound Beyonders thought to send their rocks down today, they either had none to spare or were not so inclined. What business do gods have with those who no longer believe in them?

In the gloom, the Highmost reached for the Celestial Mechanic's hand. Thin wisps of pale ammonia shrouded his kirlean silhouette as he turned towards him.

Unused to full darkness and with his faculties failing him in his advanced years, the Highmost was unable to clearly see the Celestial Mechanic's carapace, which had undergone a preternatural change. Had the light been better or his eyesight more acute, he would have seen under his translucent chitin a swarming as of a thousand threadworms.

The Celestial Mechanic's carapace ruptured. There, in the well-guarded safety of his inner sanctum, where the pains and passions of the world had so long been kept at bay, the last thing the Highmost felt was a writhing mass, ejected into his face at close range, pulling itself down his throat, into his ears, into every sensory orifice.

O UTSIDE, THE BULB had grown to a size several stadia in circumference. It began to turn from the colour of pale flesh to an angry tumescent red, vertical stripes of darker burgundy bringing rich organics up to the bulging head. Black lines began to appear around its circumference, longitudinal divisors of a globe that mapped no known world. At the very tip, a crack had appeared.

Without forewarning, the bulb split open along blackened fissures, violently releasing the enormous pressure that had built up. Petals of flesh tore as they were thrown open with explosive force: it was a monstrous flower blooming, a joyous ejaculation of the reproductive urge, a release of orgasmic proportions.

Hundreds of tiny bodies, regaining their form even in death, began raining down into the sea far below. Each was so tiny and the distances so great that had there been anyone left to watch them from this high vantage, they would have seemed to be moving in slow motion; mere scraps of flesh, upon which the odd shred of colourful fabric still fluttered. They peppered the ocean below with white constellations of spray.

High above the Spire, propelled into the heavens at several times Terrine's escape velocity, was a hard black object the size of a barollé ball; in short order, it had vanished into the amber haze at the zenith, describing a white line of condensation behind it. Contained within this seed was the means of its continued survival; all the information, all the want, all the need it required to ensure it would successfully complete the next stage of its evolution on whatever new world it happened to fall to ground.

The Visage, low in the eastern sky, watched it go. The creatures that still lived in its buried cities once had minds and machines that might have marked its passing; now they were as oblivious as the Beyonder relic they inhabited, its jaw slack, its sockets empty.

Shot once again into the dark spaces between the stars, it would describe trajectories long and

The Visage watched it go

looping, great arcs hung between gravity wells that would take it out of the Lacunae system altogether. Far beyond the Known and Only Lands, far beyond the three planets and the sixteen inhabited moons, far beyond the Visage and the scratched sun, it would spend eternities wandering without a predetermined destination. Carrying its precious cargo it would remain dormant, patiently waiting for planetfall and a fertile brain in which to begin its work anew. It was a seed, incubated in mind, with one single overriding urge: the need to reproduce.

Even now it may be out there, content to spin end over end, to sleep for many lifetimes, for the lifetimes of entire species perhaps; to patiently wait until it eventually falls within the attractive gravitational embrace of another star.

Then it will begin to fall inward, down the tautening curve of a centuries-long parabola, closer and closer like a spark-moth drawn to the light; the star will have planets, for all but a very few stars do. Sensing in its fugue the psychic signature of life, it will loop around its chosen target, pass by a second time, closer still; now in orbit, it will start to caress the upper atmosphere, shedding its velocity; then, inevitably, it will spiral in, and finally fall to the ground as a fiery-bright visitor from otherwhere: an omen, a sign, a portent of bad news from Beyond.

The End

. . . *about our* AUTHOR

F. Herschel Teague is the pseudonym of a professor of Behavioural Science at a prestigious West Coast university, where he studies alternative religions, the reward system and the effects of certain psychotropic substances on the malleability of the human psyche. His parallel career as a spinner of science-fiction tales is one that he likes to keep under wraps. "I'm used to keeping secrets," he tells us.

Regular readers have thrilled to many of his top-notch tales in recent years. We can only wonder what kind of real-life adventures Mr Teague enjoys, and whether they will ever rival his imagination.

Retrieved 16/2 10.22am GMT.

Email exchange between Daniel Novák (acting SETI steering committee chair, astronomer in residence, Jodrell Bank) and "Jack" (surname removed). Assumed to be Jack Fenwick.

[Email header removed]

Jack—

SHE'S ALIVE.

SECRET

**THIS IS A COVER SHEET
FOR CLASSIFIED INFORMATION**

7-1-7

DAEDALUS BASE "ENCOUNTER"
DEBRIEF INTERVIEW TRANSCRIPTS
HARD COPY

THE INDIVIDUALS HANDLING THIS INFORMATION ARE REQUIRED TO
PROTECT IT FROM UNAUTHORIZED DISCLOSURE IN THE INTEREST
OF THE NATIONAL SECURITY OF THE UNITED STATES.

HANDLING, STORAGE, REPRODUCTION AND DISPOSITION OF
THE ATTACHED DOCUMENT MUST BE IN ACCORDANCE WITH
APPLICABLE EXECUTIVE ORDERS, STATUTES, AND AGENCY
IMPLEMENTING REGULATIONS.

RESTRICTED DATA

THE ATTACHED DOCUMENT CONTAINS RESTRICTED DATA.
UNAUTHORIZED DISCLOSURE IS SUBJECT TO ADMINISTRATIVE AND
CRIMINAL SANCTIONS.

(THIS COVER SHEET IS UNCLASSIFIED)

704-101
NSN 7540-01-213-7902
EXCEPTION GRANTED BY GSA(9/05)

STANDARD FORM 704 (8-15)
PRESCRIBED BY GSA/ISOO
32 CFR 2013

SECRET

Document: (NS//78//DB)
Subject: Daedalus Base "Encounter"
Debrief interviews, 1 of 128

The information contained in this report is to be treated as Most Secret.
Location: [removed] [Note: Assumed to be the Apollo Isolation chamber
"Hornet+3", Lyndon B. Johnson Space Center]

Note: Some responses have been edited, and are summaries of what was
actually stated. Details in square brackets are added for clarity. Please
refer to audiovisual recordings, available on request.
Document history: v 1.5. Submitted for review and comment
Date: [removed]

Present:
Dana Normansson (hereafter DN), Cmdr., Daedalus Base
Adam Parker (hereafter AP), sup. offcr
Other support staff, medical staff [names removed]

AP: How are you feeling?
DN: How do I feel... I need a whole new vocabulary to describe how I feel.
AP: Go on.
DN: How do you describe subtleties of being that are... simply not part of
our normal experience? Pictures in colors we have no names for, seen through
senses we can't imagine. Smells, shapes, sounds... things I can't place.
Ah, this is so frustrating. Do you ever have that, that thing when you just
can't find the right word? The precise... term for what you're trying to
convey? It's like when you have the perfect description of something in your
native language, but can only poorly translate it into another in which you
have little fluency?
AP: Uh, sure. That would be English to German, for me.
DN: Translation... it's a translation problem. Fitting one set of complex
concepts into another, different and utterly unsuitable set of containers.
This may take a while to unpack. How do I feel? The short answer is "full".
A mind full of ideas that I'm still processing, sorting, unpacking.
AP: Well, it's not every day you interface with an alien intelligence.
DN: Hah. Yes. I'm a first.
AP: That you are. I hear the medical staff gave you a clean bill of health.
DN: The doctors in here, in quarantine with me [names removed], they tell
me I'm healthy and normal according to all the assessment criteria they can
think of. No viral infections, no genetic mutations, no physical aberrations
of any kind. Having been in intimate contact with me, this makes them as
happy as I am. So physically, at least, it appears that I'm fine. The
isolation chamber, they tell me, is a precaution.
AP: You still have no memory...?

DN: First thing I remember is waking up in Daedalus' sick bay.
AP: Take your time. We can take our time. We have hundreds of questions, as you can imagine. Every curious scientist here on Earth will want to interview you... every pundit, biologist, theologian, social scientist, every politician—
DN: If they know I'm here. Which I'm guessing they don't.
AP: Ahuh. Right.
[pause]
AP: You know we thought we'd lost you? The exobiology group at Jodrell were overjoyed when the rescue crew found you unconscious but alive beside the spindle, helmet and suit intact. You should have heard Daniel whoop.
DN: He's one of the good guys, that Daniel.
AP: Old school. So - how was the trip back?
DN: [laughs] Killer. Long-haul, with a layover at the ISS. And I wasn't even allowed to disembark to stretch my legs. Next time, I'll spring for a first class sleeper. They kept me isolated in the suit for the entire journey, as you know. The ship is clean. You know that there were plans, should anything have been found, if anything had happened, to send it on a trajectory into the Sun - ship, me, crew and all?
AP: I am aware of the protocols. They've been in place since the days of Apollo. We didn't create them especially for you. You should be aware that certain, ah, voices in the Agency didn't want you to land at all, containment or not.
DN: Why does that not surprise me.
AP: But now you're home. Nothing seems to be amiss. No alien flu bugs.
DN: [Name removed] is still adamant that we might not have the means to detect infectious agents from an unfamiliar biosphere, but I guess NASA's curiosity eventually won out, eh? I'm still adjusting to Earth gravity, but that's normal. I'm used to that. The changes... they're all up here. [points to forehead]
AP: These precautions may prove to be unnecessary, but this situation requires that we be... be extremely careful.
DN: I'm sure.
AP: I don't have to tell you that this is our first close encounter of the fifth kind - actual, physical contact with an extraterrestrial being. And from what I hear, it wasn't just a handshake.
DN: [laughter] That it wasn't. I don't know how much hard-disk space the human brain has, but mine now feels like it contains double the data. Imagine... gah, language is such a blunt instrument. It can bludgeon raw experience into simple-minded caricature.
AP: You're doing fine so far.
DN: Imagine you have someone else's memories, a lifetime of memories. They're there to explore, to go back and examine. Where do you start? They're not arranged chronologically... Where does your attention alight, when you reminisce? Key points in your past, emotionally charged, dramatic events? Though I can sense that a whole lifetime is in there, I only have one focus, one place I can look at a time, and there are so many places to look. It's impossible to see it all at once, except in the most superficial sense. How do you begin to process, to catalogue so... so much? And it's

- 486 -

kinda fractal... I can go into deep detail on one particular topic, but
without context it soon becomes incomprehensible - I find I soon need to
pull back, familiarize myself with something else entirely in order to
make sense of it. It's more like a network of ideas, concepts connected by
association. Following a thread takes me on a series of jumps from event
to event, but it has no temporal logic. It splits, it reconnects. It's not
linear.
AP: Interesting.
DN: And the senses - there's a lot of visual stuff, though even that
is weird in ways I've not entirely fathomed. A lot of the memories are
described in what I can only guess are scents, or a kind of echolocation,
and a sense of being two separate entities - not me and the alien, but the
alien itself is somehow twofold - a smaller, more basic part that deals with
pre-processing, automated tasks, a forebrain, if you like - and a hindbrain,
where the main seat of the I-ness [eyeness?] of the alien is located.
AP: Early scans threw this up - it has a kind of long segmented brain,
divided in the middle, waisted like a bee's thorax into two separate but
connected parts.
DN: Two in one. Smaller at the front, larger at the back.
AP: The relief crew - I think you know [names removed] are now at the site,
and once the containment is set up, will attempt to transport the alien, and
if it can be moved, the capsule, back to Daedalus Base and there perform an
autopsy. We think that the alien is somehow attached to the ship, and so to
avoid damage both might have to be moved together. If this is not possible,
the autopsy will take place at the crash site. It'll give us clues as to
the nature of the alien's sensory organs. That might help you get your head
around it. But - if you don't know where to begin, just begin.
DN: Well - the most recent strong memory, one I can easily retrieve in
detail, is actually of me. Of our first encounter, from the alien's
perspective.
AP: That is interesting.
DN: It has to be said that it - the alien - does have an outsider's eye for
detail we have lost to familiarity. Seeing yourself, the human body, through
alien eyes. It's, it's dislocating, to say the least.
AP: Go on.
AP: It sees me as a bilaterally symmetrical frame with four limbs, the lower
two for locomotion and the upper two for manipulation, with a transparent
covering up top - that's my helmet - that gives a view of the creature's
- my - interior. It occurred to him that the covering may be artificial;
not part of my natural body, and by a sudden leap realized that the lunar
environment was not my natural habitat, and that by analogy this protective
casing may be a personal version of the vessel it had arrived in. Inside
this helmet - my helmet - sorry, this is so weird - are, were a selection
of sensing and transmitting organs - my face - open to view both ways. Now,
this is interesting. I've been going over this, because it's flagged as
important, though I'm not sure why. Here, it realizes that information could
easily pass both in and out. There's a real sense of surprise, as if this is
unusual. I'm protected physically, by the suit, but not - not mentally, not
memetically.

AP: You've left yourself open, vulnerable to something?
DN: Yes, exactly. My sensory apparatus seemed to have no - the best
translation is "barrier", no protection at all. Either this creature -
me - comes from a world free of - of predators, though that's an inexact
translation, as it implies a degree of conscious volition on the part
of that doing the predating - or it, me, humans, had only just ventured
out into space. Here it kind of berates me for what I can only describe
as naivety, like I'm some unsophisticated hick in the big city. Foolish.
Stupid. Dangerous. Lacking in street-smarts. But overlaid with a feeling of,
of protective concern.
AP: Can you elucidate?
DN: There's a strong sense - either from its own personal experience or some
kind of species memory, something hardwired by evolution, perhaps - that
some things it might see or hear, or just sense, are powerful enough to kill
it. Merely thinking these things can cause irreparable mental damage. It
assumes I am either of a low mental ability, and so need no protection, or
have defenses it's not familiar with. Here I get a sense of something I can
only translate as "mindlids" [quotes added], by analogy to eyelids.
AP: This is being recorded, as you know. I'll feed it back to [names
removed] at Daedalus. I'm sure they'll find this fascinating, and it may
help guide their work there. So it's weighing you up. What happened next?
DN: At this point? I'm embarrassed to say that I screamed.
AP: We have that on the footage.
DN: [laughs] Thing is, I know now I scared it too. Perhaps more so. An
orifice opened in the lower portion of the encased suite of sensory organs -
AP: - you mean your face?
DN: My face. From the alien's perspective. It was wet inside, and rimmed
with hard sharp white intrusions, and... and inside was something moving, a
wet, muscled thing - and here I have a visual comparison to an animal native
to the alien's home planet, which looks to me like an eel — sightless,
writhing around in this moist recess.
AP: Your tongue in your mouth. Flattering.
DN: Inside it - me - the alien thinks there lives a smaller parasitic or
symbiotic organism, pink and blind, seated in this organic machine. It was
probably the most upsetting and, and just plain wrong thing the alien had
ever encountered.
AP: We're a scary bunch, us humans.
DN: [laughs] So, with an incredible force of will, and by repeatedly citing
something I can only translate as the Eleven Precepts - they seem to be
expressed as mathematical relationships — it manages to bring the rising
panic in its, uh, forebrain under control.
AP: You felt that?
DN: Yes... it's strong, almost overwhelming. Can we stop a second?
AP: Sure.
[A pause for 40 seconds]
DN: Sorry. This is disturbing to process. This, this strong sense of
otherness, projected at yourself. The familiar, rendered unfamiliar. I don't
think I'll ever look at myself in the mirror the same way again, at any
human being the same way again.

AP: I can remember seeing a photograph of a naked mole rat in a biology class. Even the ugliest animals must find each other attractive, or the species would die out.

DN: Yeah. For our whole lives we feel comfortable with the everyday familiarity of the human body, the body we are born into. Now... now I see it not as this, I don't know, idealized machine, elegant and beautiful, the one we've immortalized in sculpture and celebrated in art. Now I see the human form as it's always been - just a sport of evolution, the end result of countless steps in the blind progress of natural selection, no more right or perfect or inevitable than any other possible form tailored to an environment, no more or less beautiful than the alien's own form... which I had originally found so disturbing.

AP: To see yourself through alien eyes -

DN: To see myself as alien.

AP: What else?

AP: Well, it was trying to make sense of my tattoos -

AP: Your tattoos?

DN: My tattoos and my moles. It was cross-referencing them with the arrangement of stars as seen from each of the fifty-two inhabited planets that it, personally, has visited.

AP: Oooo-kay. It's been to fifty-two inhabited planets. This is where the boggle factor goes off the scale.

DN: I know, right? I get at least one of those moments every time I delve into this. Anyway, it thinks my moles must be some kind of star map, so it runs the evolution of the galaxy back and forward through two thousand years - that's its estimate of a human's maximum lifespan - and doesn't find a match.

AP: Do you get a sense of how old the alien is?

DN: Hard to say. It's measured in seasons, but I'd need to get into the peculiarities of the orbit and inclination of the aliens' homeworld.

AP: We have the recording from your laptop. Do you have any idea where the aliens' homeworld is?

DN: The distances are enormous. Out, towards the galactic rim, the edge of the galaxy. I can't be more precise than that, I'm afraid. It has a, a more extended, if that's the right word, understanding of time. No. Argh, the words, finding the right words!

AP: What else did it think? Did it try and communicate?

DN: It could sense the low modulations of the biological processes within me, and was sifting them for meaning. You have to realize that our sensory overlap is limited. Pheromones? Textural interplay? You need to figure out what the medium may be before you can focus on the message. You know what it was doing? It was trying to mimic the colors of the flight patches on my suit by altering the properties of its carapace. Like they were a kind of language. Which, in a way, I suppose they are. I completely missed this, of course. It has a form of radio, which we can't receive, so I was no use there. Then I get lost in an examination of the meaning not of action, but of inaction - the spaces between, the silences. I do get the impression it has some experience in dealing with differing races. Like it's an ambassador, or something.

AP: An ambassador.

[pause]

DN: Anyway. Once it figured it out, it found my suit, or my exoskeleton, suggestive of a race that was not evolved for interstellar space. I get a sense of a soft vulnerable being inside a protective casing, and that this, I don't know, offends, if that's not too pejorative a word, disturbs maybe, its sense of, of rightness. I shouldn't really be here, outside my natural environment. Like I've come too far.

AP: And it hasn't?

DN: I did think that too. So, so it tries a few things. It emits a trill at seven frequencies from near infrared to radio. It ejects a selection of pungent scents - believe me, I smelled them - and a pheromone through a complex gland that resembles a bunch of burgundy grapes in a fishnet. It tries signalling in the weighted pauses of a race that even it finds peculiar, a race whose name is a series of formalized dance steps and a time of the day. It ejaculates a small drop of aerosol-form bile that indicates the content of its last three meals, its current position in its sexual cycle and its coupling availability. Which is a bit like asking if someone's married or not, I guess. And it repeated a birdsong it'd learned to mimic as a, a hatchling? A child, I presume? - long before it'd cut the, the group umbilical, and had to search for sustenance as a free agent.

AP: Phew. More boggle. We're getting all this, but I'm sure the xenobiologists will want to grill you for more information. They'll be able to ask you much more sensible questions than I'm qualified to do in that regard.

DN: Sure. I'm not going anywhere. [laughs] So, what does it do? The alien knows that there is one gesture that has a wider and more common usage than any other across the, across something I'd translate as the 'concordance'. It crosses languages and cultures, and is the common greeting used by - I guess the word would be exchangers, traders perhaps - but it also has an undertone of submission, almost of reverence. This gesture [DN puts her hands together at the wrists to demonstrate, palms facing forwards and out, moves her fingers from side to side] is different, depending on the race and the anatomy of the particular creature, but to abstract it as much as possible, it's forelimb out, open, the soft inner area - here, my palms - visibly empty.

AP: I saw that on the footage.

DN: It means, and again, I have to warn you this is a very loose translation, it means 'I reveal to you my most vulnerable spot, and I hold no weapon'.

AP: Empty. No threat.

DN: Yep. I'm learning that even an absence has a meaning.

AP: I learned that the first time a date stood me up.

DN: Hah. Yeah.

AP: How alien is alien? Any commonality due to biologic -

DN: How different is different? You're asking what common outlook, what manner of thinking, expressing, communicating, could we possibly share? Of all the means of communication that sentient races may have to hand, I suspect every single one has been pressed into use. Needs must, and meaning attaches itself to almost everything. We have to find the medium that lies within both our sensory realms, a common channel. Consider everything. Look, if we were dogs, we'd be sniffing each other's arses.

AP: Thank you for that analogy.

DN: You haven't asked me the most important question.

AP: I haven't?

DN: Why. Why did it come?

[pause]

AP: Do you know? Did it tell you?

DN: I have this one impression – one klaxon-loud, floodlight-bright idea – that keeps coming to the surface, again and again. It's colored with urgency and smells of desperation. It's why our visitor did what it did, the message it gave its life in order to pass on. It knew that opening the bubble – adjusting the atmosphere within so that I could breathe it – would make it poisonous, would kill it. But it also knew it was dying anyway, and it was out of options.

[pause]

It's an ambassador, yes, but more than that, it's a harbinger, a messenger – but what message is so important it would travel so far to bring it to us? What message is worth sacrificing your life to ensure its delivery? I asked myself that. And I don't have all the answers, not just yet. I'm still piecing it together. But two things I can put into words:

One: it brings a warning of coming devastation, not only of all life on Earth, but the extinction of all life in the galaxy.

Two: the absolute certainty that this cannot be prevented.

--- END TRANSCRIPT ---

GODS WITHOUT CHARIOTS

"*That* happened faster than I'd anticipated." Nixon was looking at indistinct footage of a fluted dish, some three metres in diameter, hovering over the Atacama desert. Perfectly stationary, it cast a crisp shadow on the altiplano. A mop of violet strands hung below, stopping a metre shy of the ground. Finer hairs fringed its periphery, some curling up like eyelashes. Whoever had filmed the footage was instructing his associate to run repeatedly through the apparition; it was apparent that he was the only one who could see it.

Harriet immediately left her render and came over. "What is this?"

"It's on YouTube. It looks like someone's managed to repurpose a pair of glasses – they're not Depthcharges, but they look very similar. I think these guys are from one of the Brazilian AI teams."

"Shit."

"That's what I was thinking."

Whoever was recording the footage turned their head. There was a blurred shot of a booted foot, then a fleeting glimpse of a holdall with cables leading from it, and then the view swung around and up again. In the background the foothills of the Andes could be seen, washed to a pale heliotrope by distance. The autofocus struggled to correct itself, sharpening and defocusing repeatedly. Finally, it settled.

Stretching to the horizon in each direction were hundreds more creatures, arranged in row upon row over the rugged landscape. The ground below them was polka-dotted with shadows. On the soundtrack, whoops and shouts could be heard.

Jack leaned in. "Where are they?"

Nixon checked the location stamp. "Peru."

"Hah. I guess it's entirely appropriate. Erich von Däniken reckoned the Nazca lines were landing strips for flying saucers. They didn't bring their transportation with them, but look – the aliens finally did arrive!"

"Do you see anything moving? Other than the guys filming this, I mean."

"You mean like our DMEn?" Nixon squinted, moved closer to the screen. "Nooo . . . I don't think so."

"So no Oxbow."

"The glasses are expensive, but they're freely available. The Oxbow – I wrote that." Jack allowed himself a self-congratulatory smile. "I don't think anyone else could have come up with it."

"But they *can* see the Grid. This is going to spread fast."

The news seemed to have pitched Nixon into an uncharacteristically reflective mood. He looked sombre. "Uhm. Something Girl 21 said got me thinking. Is this . . . *good?*"

"What?" Harriet wondered if Nixon's rare lapses into soul-searching introspection revealed some deeper aspect to his character that he had managed to keep well hidden.

"See, we have all manner of virus software on our computers to prevent rogue code getting in. Yet we have no protection whatsoever for our greatest asset, our greatest weakness – our *brains*. We have an open-door policy." Jack looked up from the video and studied him. His eyebrows drew down.

"Remember that kid at school who had found his dad's porn stash, and would charge twenty pence per magazine to lend it to you over-night? Remember how you couldn't get those images out of your head?"

"I'm not ancient like you, remember? Pre-internet porn . . ." Harriet pulled a face. "It must have been an absolutely dismal existence. You do have my deepest sympathies."

Jack turned back to his screen. "Heh. Speak for yourself. I think I was a bit of a late starter. You'd be more likely to find me fingering *The Feynman Lectures on Physics* under the covers."

Nixon exhaled loudly and let his shoulders sink mock-dramatically. "Yes. Of course. Why does that not surprise me? You're just weird, Jack. Has anyone ever told you that, that you're weird?"

"As far as *I'm* concerned, it's everyone *else* that's weird."

Nixon was not going to be diverted from his line of thought. "We have an internet full of the most harrowing and explicit imagery you can imagine, and a generation who are letting all this into their pliable, barely formed neuronal software as if they're indestructible, as if they're immune to every image, every video there is out there, however shocking, however persuasive, however contagious. It's like a test — what can you watch? How far dare you go? What ideas can your poor mind be exposed to before you traumatise yourself?"

Jack looked at him quizzically. "Why has this got to you, Nixon?"

"She said an idea doesn't know if it's good or bad, true or false, helpful or harmful. It's an idea, not a person. It just reproduces, like a successful virus in a host. Or it dies, and no one ever has that particular idea again. See, a virus only cares if it kills the host before it's reproduced. Everything it does is geared towards survival. It has no morals, no compunction. Those are human traits. Why should a virus have compassion? It not only doesn't care, it's incapable of caring."

Nixon now had Jack and Harriet's undivided attention. Harriet put her hand on his shoulder. "This is not like you – deep thoughts, and all. What's up, Nix?"

"So if it doesn't care, should *we* care? *We* are the ones that enabled these ideas, these images to spread."

"*We* did?"

"Well, maybe not us originally. But people *like* us – the entrepreneurs, the programmers, the innovators. We went and built the central nervous system of the information age. We laid down the wires and wrote the protocols and financed the infrastructure. Did we think things through, or were we just so bowled over by our own cleverness we didn't stop to think of the consequences? Bad ideas, Jack. We built the delivery system that can get them into every home. And we've got no defence against them."

"Are you having second thoughts about what we're doing here? Because if it wasn't us, it'd be someone else."

"I'm not sure that makes me feel any better." Nixon looked contrite.

A few awkward moments elapsed. Jack finally returned his attention to the video. "Show me again. We may have missed something."

Harriet pointed. "Look – in the comments section. Whoever posted this has added a link."

Nixon clicked. It led to a basic Wordpress blog. A single paragraph of text sat below a photograph of a headset attached to a laptop and some other kit that didn't look quite so off-the-shelf. "It doesn't seem to be affiliated with any of the South American institutes I'm aware of. Maybe it's a personal project?"

Harriet skim-read the first few lines. "My Portuguese is perfunctory – we'll need to run this through Google Translate – but they've posted some code, and code I can read. You'd need to know what you're doing with it, but all the basics are there." She sank down on her crate. "There goes our head start. Information wants to be free, so the saying goes. I guess now we wait for the fallout."

The information contained in this report is to be treated as Most Secret.
Location: [removed] [Note: Assumed to be the Apollo Isolation chamber
"Hornet+3", Lyndon B. Johnson Space Center]

Note: Some responses have been edited, and are summaries of what was
actually stated. Details in square brackets are added for clarity. Please
refer to audiovisual recordings, available on request.
Document history: v 1.2. Submitted for review and comment
Date: [removed]

Present:
Dana Normansson (hereafter DN), Cmdr., Daedalus Base
Adam Parker (hereafter AP), sup. offcr
Gabriel (Gabe) Bowen (hereafter GB), press liaison
Other support staff, medical staff [names removed]

AP: How are you feeling today?
DN: Fine. Better.
AP: Good. Ready to continue?
DN: Sure. You realize that a lifetime of these interviews won't scratch the
surface of what's inside my head?
AP: You may just have a lifetime of interviews ahead of you. Not to, you
know, depress you or anything.
DN: I should write a book.
AP: You'd have to credit your co-author.
DN: [laughs] There was this one story I read as a teenager that stuck in my
mind. There's this hierarchical society that lives on a spike of rock in the
middle of a circular sea. Everything's dandy until something new that they
don't understand drops in from elsewhere and upsets the balance. I can't
remember the name of the person who wrote it, but I do know he went on to
form one of those sixties pseudo-religious cults, like Hubbard or Richard
Shaver. His followers were convinced he was channelling his stories from
spirits, Jungian archetypes, aliens, whatever. That they were, perhaps in
some metaphorical sense, true.
AP: I remember the guy. He wasn't the only counter-culture writer to end
up believing in his own fiction. Thought it was possible to preserve
characters, people – himself, even – in a story, and that way achieve
immortality. And not just in the literary sense, but off the page somehow.
'Informational reincarnation', he called it. Died in a fortified compound in
Ohio attempting to transfer his mind into the body a much younger disciple.
DN: Strange guy. Anyway –

AP: I could try and track it down for you.

DN: Thanks, that would be very kind.

AP: Let's see if we can find it. Right. To the matter at hand: this warning of coming devastation. I took a call last night from - well, let's say you now have certain, certain well-placed people's undivided attention.

DN: Adam, it rattles me too.

AP: Do you have any more information? A timescale? What are we looking for?

DN: The Signal from Space.

[16-minute pause/edit in recording]

AP: Let's try and fill in the gaps. I've been asked about the alien's home planet, to get your take on that. We also have some feedback from a few colleagues, experts in various things, who have asked me to pass on some questions.

DN: Colleagues? How many people are aware of the situation? My situation?

AP: Not many. Some here, those with the highest clearance. As you know, Jodrell, our tracking station in the UK, is in the loop, as are, uh, two other installations, the locations of which I'm not at liberty to divulge. We've instituted a very strict data lockdown post-White. As far as anyone outside this facility is aware, you and [names removed - assumed to be the rest of the Daedalus return crew] have just returned to Earth after a routine mission which suffered delays due to an unspecified technical fault, and the relief crew are now up there on the Moon for their scheduled stay. Your continued absence has been explained - if anyone asks, which mostly they haven't - as an R&R vacation.

DN: Ah, a vacation. I remember those.

AP: I've been told to let you know that the President and, by necessity, the British Prime Minister and certain other heads of state are following our conversations here closely - though I think the President currently has his attention focussed on damage control after those lap-dancing club indiscretions. I've deduced that there's some fierce ongoing debate about whether to inform NATO or any other world leaders. We're pretty sure the Russians know something out of the ordinary has happened. They are the third largest financial backers for Daedalus and were involved from the earliest planning stages, so are au fait with its secondary purpose, and as they supply our Earth-to-orbit transport it's very hard to keep anything that bucks a schedule from piquing their interest. Anyway, we're all supposed to be the best of friends these days. I think that whoever makes these decisions has decided that simply not saying anything is currently our best policy, but I have a feeling that this lack of transparency is something they may regret in the long run.

DN: OK. I'm glad I'm not the one who has to negotiate that particular minefield.

AP: Dana, you do know your original footage was leaked, right? It was in the huge tranche of documents that White made public, but remained buried until someone on the message board at Infodump.com flagged it up. It's been doing the rounds of all the usual UFO conspiracy sites and magazines ever since. There's even a Wikipedia entry, and it was featured on the cover of the last issue of 'Fortean Times'.

DN: I know. Daniel Novák told me.

AP: Daniel. Yes, of course. Our boy scout.

DN: I'd take a look, but I have no Internet access in here. That's something I wanted to talk about. My mother must be —

AP: The Signal itself wasn't classified, as such. More, shall we say, unreleased. After the speculation that produced, I think these reports will be treated with much more care. Anyway, the Daedalus Footage is by no means a smoking gun. There are many other plausible explanations for it. It's not even the best or most convincing footage of its kind on YouTube. But we have now instated much tighter protocols here.

DN: Then who's he? [Dana points at Gabriel Bowen.]

AP: Gabe is here just in case we have to spin this. He's a veteran of the Apollo 18 and 19 Martian 'Phobos Monolith' and 'Martian Sphinx' [quotes added] reconnaissance missions, which are still dark, as you know. He ran the whole Soyuz-Apollo link-up as misdirection, and after the Viking photos gained notoriety, had the effects guys come up with the new shots that supposedly show the 'Face on Mars' [quotes added] to be a rock outcrop, a trick of the light. He can be trusted.

GB: Hey, Dana. How are the Maldives? Nice view of the pool?

DN: Hello, Gabriel. The cocktails leave something to be desired. And the nightlife sucks.

AP: Via Jodrell we also have Jack Fenwick, our language and semiotics expert, general AI guy and number cruncher looped in. He sat in on your final excursion, if you remember. I've got a few questions he passed on.

DN: I remember Jack. Sure. Fire away.

AP: They've been running an analysis on the structure of the Signal. Looking at certain regularities.

DN: I was thinking about this. We pick up a mysterious signal, and what is it, six months later our visitor arrives. What are the odds?

AP: 233 days to be precise. Jack was of the same opinion. What are the chances of these two unique events being unrelated? And then this was the clincher.

[AP reaches into a briefcase and pulls out an A4 file, from which he takes a sheet which he places on the window separating them. DN leans in to look more closely. The image is too small to be seen clearly in the footage, but it has been suggested by [name removed] that it resembles surrealist painter Magritte's 'Golconda' of 1953.]

GB: Fenwick calls this the 'Alien Zoo'. [quotes added]

DN: Alien zoo. Huh. I can see why.

GB: These things aren't physical, as in flesh and blood real. It's some kind of augmented-reality render of the contents of the Signal. I don't pretend to understand the technical details, but we're pretty sure it's an accurate representation. He says he'll share the details with Novák and our tech boys, but at the moment, this is what we have. Take a close look. What can you tell us?

DN: That's triggered some, uh, images. Give me a few seconds to try and pull this into some kind of coherent sense. Right. So.

AP: Take your time. We have a close-up here. [A second sheet is held to the window.] Excuse the print-outs. This is probably the most secure way to show you.

DN: Low-tech. Like it.

AP: So this bears out Jack's original insight. The Signal is not a message from aliens. It is the aliens. [stress on 'is'] And it turns out it's possible, with some custom gear and software I don't pretend to understand - to see them. To see this. [AP taps on the sheet of paper.]

[pause]

DN: That one there looks like someone stepped on a slug. Each of these guys is different? You sure this isn't a game demo or something?

AP: That was my first thought. No, it's not a game demo. As far as we can make out, each is a specific individual. They are grouped according to kind - by species, if you like. The Grid. That's what we're calling the arrangement.

DN: Like a catalogue of species? How is it organized?

AP: We honestly don't know. But there are regularities. And Jack, he's been looking into that. What we have found is that placed every 65,536 creatures up, down and across this cubic lattice we have one of these.

[AP presses another sheet to the window. DN leans in.]

DN: [excitedly] The face has a different pattern of colored blotches, and these eye things here, they look like they've retracted inside the exoskeleton, like it's asleep or something. But that's him. That's our guy!

AP: Exactly. No mistake, right?

DN: I only saw his face, not his body, but no, no mistake. I got up close and personal. Definitely the same race. Incredible. So we have a digital version, and a real version?

AP: It seems we do.

DN: Hah. Same race, but not the same individual. And these guys are placed at regular intervals throughout the Signal, the Grid?

AP: Yes. So we think.

DN: Commanders?

AP: Jack is calling them Shepherds. I guess it depends if you're a pessimist or an optimist. We were hoping you could tell us, as you now share a brain with one of them.

DN: That I do.

[pause]

DN: So - I'll tell you what I have, what I'm getting here.

AP: Go ahead.

DN: This is complicated, this is layered...

AP: When you're ready.

DN: OK. Where to begin. OK, so we have a race - our Men in the Moon, our Lunar Biological Entities. Where... distances are very hard to judge, they're just so enormous compared to what we're familiar with, what even an astronaut is familiar with. They are from a planet out towards the galactic rim - way out, I'm getting some kind of image here of the Milky Way from above - just out beyond the Perseus Arm. Four or five thousand light years. Though that's not how long the Signal has been travelling. It's been going much longer. It's - it's been received and rebroadcast many times... Wow.

AP: What?

DN: This is amazing.

AP: Don't keep us in suspense.

- 498 -

DN: It's - it's alive. The galaxy is literally teeming with life. Races, civilizations - there's hardly a system that doesn't have a planet with life on, and - and I'd guess every few thousand systems has a race of what we'd call sentient beings. Some systems have several inhabited planets, others several different intelligent species on the one planet - the myriad different ways they interact, the networks of social and economic relations... this'd keep a sociologist happy for the rest of their life. All that time we thought we were alone, and it turns out we're just one species in a very crowded galaxy.

AP: Whoa! Slow down. Civilizations? There are many? How many?

DN: You want numbers? There are over 350 million distinct self-aware species on more than 126 million separate inhabited planets. That the race our Man in the Moon comes from knows about. And this is just the small section of the galaxy between us and the rim that it is familiar with. It's incredible. I can see each and every one... I know where each one is from, their background, their cultural structures... It's like looking at a crowd in a stadium, from a high vantage. I can see broad patterns, relationships of different species and their locations... but I can zoom in, and my attention can skip from face to face - but there's so much, so many to take in. It's - it's crowded out there.

AP: This is going to take some getting used to.

DN: Tell me about it. Once you open your ears to the cosmos, it's a shouting match. Me, I'm carrying all this around in my head. I'm surprised I've not had some kind of mental breakdown.

AP: Careful. We can't have that. Go back - you said it's been received and transmitted many times. So we're not the first to receive this Signal?

DN: No. Not even close. The Signal, as we see it now, is the result of numerous retransmissions. There's a process, of, uh, of assimilation. Each retransmission adds new species - sometimes one, sometimes many. The precise mode of this incorporation is unclear to me... It seems to differ, depending on the context, and has evolved...

[pause]

AP: Do they have a name? Our Man in the Moon's race - what do they call themselves?

DN: They - their race is called the - and I'm translating imperfectly here, as it contains a glyph that you project as a series of spots on your carapace - the Scooch Orlena, which roughly means home, or hearth, but with a secondary meaning of society as an extended family, a bass note of belonging.

AP: [audible exhalation of breath] Thanks, Dana. If I'm having trouble processing all this, I can't imagine what it must be like for you. When I got up this morning, the Universe was a much smaller place.

--- END TRANSCRIPT ---

The 'Signal': boat people or invasion force?

NASA – and, some might claim, the scientific project itself – has recently been on the back foot. High-profile cosmologists such as Daniel Novák at Jodrell Bank, the famous radio telescope where the Signal from Space was first received, have been accused of lending a veneer of scientific respectability to what has been termed, at the more polite end, "scientific elitism" and at the more bizarre and conspiratorial, the "new xenophobia". This hot-button phrase can be traced back to blogger and social commentator Ingrid Knox, who has been instrumental in popularising it.

But the pushback begins here. "Can we not simply have an informed discussion about the value of the content of the Signal? Can we not agree that the real issue is what the ramifications of the first communication of undoubtedly alien origin might be?" You can sense Novák's exasperation, even over a patchy Skype connection. "What I constantly come across is a refusal to permit the issue to even be debated. I am just advocating a moratorium on the public's use of the signal until we have a more concrete analysis."

Since White released the original into the public domain, we've seen many attempts to decode its message, while others have created music, or even art from it. "This is all interesting and valid, as far as it goes. I am not disputing this. But we really don't know what we are dealing with here. How could we – it's alien. It's not written in simple English, or any other language we can readily decipher.

"What we do know is that it has now been shared worldwide. The Internet is a very efficient delivery vector for information, and if this signal is anything, it's information. So effectively has it spread that we might have infected every computer on Earth with it. Sure, many have downloaded the original data and have been studying it, but more than this, they have been splicing it, rewriting it, back-engineering it. Would you do this with the smallpox genome?"

These manipulations which, on the one hand, may be dangerous to us, almost certainly will be detrimental to the entities themselves. Are we inadvertently stripping away their essential nature – and for many, the assumption is that this nature is benign – and in so doing removing their higher functions and thus turning them into monsters of our own creation?

We have, and still are, letting the signal roam free not only on the Web but in our own grey matter. Several high-profile op-ed pieces, notably in *The Atlantic* and *The Spectator*, have theorised that this may, in fact, be how it replicates. If we are to be its host, the host that it uses to reproduce, we are in effect incubators. The question then becomes: does their reproductive success work in symbiosis with us or not? Or are we simply compost to their flowering?

Novák takes a pragmatic view that in some quarters has earned him a reputation as a neocon: "This may be an unpopular opinion, but personally I see no reason why the entities should harbour any code of ethics, anything we would recognise as a moral framework in which our lives might be valued or we would be exempt from harm. For simply suggesting we tread carefully here, I am being called a stooge for the military-industrial complex. Whatever the true nature of the signal turns out to be, I can assure you that there isn't some shadowy arm of NASA trying to find a way to weaponise it, whatever you may have heard on the lunatic fringes of the conspirasphere. Between the 'lift me up to heaven' cults and the Terminator-style apocalyptics, this discourse must find a sensible middle ground."

If he is right in anything, it is the lamentable level of the discussion we are currently engaged in, one that may have huge ramifications for our future, the future of the human race. "If this does turn out to be a hostile takeover, we will have invited it in, sat it down, made it dinner, shared our history, our capabilities, our strengths and our weaknesses, shown it where we keep the family silver and then gone to bed trusting it with our doorkeys and our children. Many see this as arrant madness, yet there are voices out there who seem to think that even raising this possibility is somehow an infringement of the most basic civil liberties."

Novák is correct: these interlopers may not come with a moral compass that requires them to consider the wellbeing of their host species. But neither may they be some malevolent warmongering race of interplanetary Genghis Khans, bent on our subjugation.

So far, they seem to have no volition. No way to interact with the physical world. Until or if anyone finds a way of communicating with them – and we can be sure that Novák and his associates are working on this right now – they are simply a catalogue of morphologies we have just learned how to read.

Ask yourself – does a book come with a set of moral axioms?

The following is a transcript of the debate at the Oxford Union between Richard Linwood, professor of biology at Queen Mary, London, and Vivian Arentz, author of *Transcending the Other: Towards a Postmodern Interdisciplinary Analysis of the Visitor Experience in a Neoliberal Age*. The chair is Ilia Wilkins. The images referred to in the text are available on the SetiOnEarth@home website.

ILIA WILKINS: Thank you all for coming, and welcome to what should prove to be a most interesting debate. We are here, as you know, to discuss some of the implications of the so-called Alien Zoo, as it's been dubbed by the press. Richard and Vivian, thank you for agreeing to talk to us. I hope you will be familiar with their work; if not, you can find links in the departmental email I sent around earlier. We have departed from the usual format in that we have no formal proposition; rather, I hope this will be an open-ended exploration of new discoveries in the study of the Signal from Space and its implications for society as a whole.

[*polite applause*]

I'd like to open with a question. Richard, as a biologist and anthropologist, you've been intensively studying the images we have so far of the creatures, or to use your term, extrabiological entities or EBEs, that constitute the Signal. You've been quoted in the press as saying that we can deduce many things just from their appearance. Given that what they look like is all we currently have to go on, what can this approach tell us? You're saying, am I right, that based on your observations so far, we should exercise caution?

RICHARD LINWOOD: Thank you for having me. Yes, indeed, I think caution is what I would advise here. Let me explain why. As you know, several independent groups are working to catalogue the EBEs. I recommend Estelle Perry's work in this area, and her SetiOnEarth@home project. The first thing to note, and this is immediately obvious from even a cursory overview of the data we have, is that the creatures show a bewildering variety of forms. Perry has documented several hundred basic body morphisms, which she groups into three types according to body plan symmetry: radial symmetry, bilateral symmetry, and asymmetry. There are also two further categories she identifies, which I'll come to later.

She and her colleagues have also attempted to categorise many other recurring features according to their similarity with terrestrial forms – limbs, torso, head, wings, fins, et cetera. This is not an easy task, as we are building a complete taxonomy from scratch, and that requires entirely new kingdoms, new genera, new domains. I should also point out that the creatures we can observe may be a very small percentage of the total population, most of which due to their location within the lattice are inaccessible, or otherwise difficult to study.

However, I think we can make a few sensible generalisations. One, that these creatures are evolved – they show the means to manipulate their environments, and the potential mental facility to do so intelligently. Here, we are of course making educated guesses based on cranial capacity and so on. We have to be very careful that we don't bring too many assumptions to bear from our human-centric experience. We don't want to unduly anthropomorphise these creatures—

VIVIAN ARENTZ: You don't, do you?

IW: One at a time, Vivian.

RL: So, if we look at some of the body shapes – first slide, please – we see several that exhibit what look like armour plate, or horns. It's tempting to think of some of these features as vestigial, and indeed, if we look at this specimen – here and here – we do see what look like rudimentary, undeveloped forms of a ridged protective exoskeleton. Now bear in mind we don't know if this is a mature adult, if this species exhibits sexual dimorphism – if it even has what we would call gender – or even if this creature goes through several forms, such as a pupa or a chrysalis, or sheds its skin before reaching maturity. Also, consider that these creatures may, in their natural environment, be clothed, and so many of the features we see here may not be visible in their normal cultural context. What we are seeing here are these creatures in the nude. In fact, you may be looking at another world first here – alien erotica. [uncomfortable laughter]

But I would suggest, on this evidence, that many – not all, but we estimate sixty to seventy per cent – of the creatures documented so far exhibit features that, were we to observe them on a dinosaur for example, would lead us to assume that they are aggressive, or inhabit an ecosystem in which they need to protect themselves from something – a predator, perhaps. Serrated edges, horned faceplates, porcupine-style spikes, powerfully muscled jaws.

Those that do not exhibit these traits – and these tend to fall into the bilaterally symmetric category – generally have larger or more complex sensory clusters. This is also where we assume the brain might reside: the head, for want of a better term. The majority of this type have the sensory cluster positioned towards the top of the body, in fact estimates put this at around seventy per cent. We assume it makes sense, much as it does in humans, to position the sense organs at the highest point, so affording them the best vantage when surveying their surroundings. This type also tends towards the slimmer and longer of limb, and often lacks an exoskeleton or other defensive anatomical trait, perhaps indicating that their intelligence – if we assume a larger cranium equates with a higher intelligence, something which I caution doesn't even hold here on Earth – that this intelligence perhaps mitigates the need for more, uh, physical defences.

We also have to remember that we are seeing these creatures removed from a very important context – their environment. I cannot stress how important this may be in shaping the range of anatomies we see here, and again, useful analogies can be drawn with familiar terrestrial creatures. We can assume that fins, for example, would be used for navigating a liquid environment – a sea – though of course not necessarily one made of water. Wings suggest flight – we see some appendages here, and here, that could be wings in a folded position, while scooped hands or pointed armoured snouts – I have an example here on the next slide – may suggest the creature is designed to cleave through a dense material, possibly a subterranean habitat. Here, we have one or two examples we feel may come from an entirely gaseous environment; these inflated and deflated sacs here and over here may serve as this creature's ballast and flotation organs. These, and the lack of any kind of legs or landing gear, if you like, indicate that it may spend its entire existence aloft.

A proportion of the Grid interstices initially seemed to be empty, though on closer analysis many – and we theorise all – do contain an entity of some kind. Here, for example, we have a subtle densification, a transparent shadow which is only apparent when viewed against a white background. In this case we have not been able to image anything directly, but we believe that there is something there, nonetheless. This example of what, on first glance, appeared to be an empty interstice turned out to contain a bacterium-sized organism that was only visible at the maximum magnification our viewing equipment is currently capable of. This one is intriguing – empty from most angles, it seems to absorb incident light, and is only visible as a pinching [RL *indicates with thumb and forefinger*] of the visual field under very bright illumination. An energy sinkhole of some description – a creature noticeable by an absence, rather than a presence.

In addition to those three basic categories, Perry has proposed two more. The creatures that fall into the fourth category give us some pause for thought. This category consists of what we assume are two or more creatures in some kind of tight symbiosis, so much so that they were not incorporated into the Signal separately. We have here – slide, please – three examples which are currently perplexing our xenobiologists. It could be that what we see are two separate creatures who have been combined at a single lattice address and so occupy the same space; in other words, they do not physically intersect, merely their informational images do. However, if this was the case we would expect there to be other obvious signs of co-existent bodies overlapping in an arbitrary fashion. I think it's more likely that what we see in this group are EBEs that are made of two or three – in some cases, more – separate creatures that form a larger unit, each perhaps bringing something – some ability or advantage – to the whole.

So, here, in this example that I find, to be frank, quite unsettling, we see a creature atop a lower body into which spindly atrophied legs have been inserted. The lower body seems to have vestigial eyes and other sense organs, but we think that these higher functions are now taken care of by what has been dubbed the Pilot – this upper part, here, which seems to use the lower as a form of transportation. Horse and rider, evolved into one symbiotic whole.

In the second example of this peculiar category – slide, please – we see a bilateral body shape made from what we think may be several hundred identical sub-units, each adjusting their shape and behaviour depending on their position. A mobile hive mind, perhaps. Here, we see a central body from which protrude, or are attached, some dozen or so smaller creatures, almost like wasps attached by their sting to a host. The ones nearer the top are bulbous, full, and retain some indications of life – shiny eyes and a proboscis. Those lower down seem to have been emptied, the eyes deflated and crinkled, the proboscis flaccid, its internal fluids perhaps absorbed by the main body. Note the scars towards the pelvis where we presume completely exhausted symbionts have fallen away or been removed.

However, not all of these symbiotic arrangements strike one as exploitative. Here for example, we have what might be a conjoined male/female sexual liaison, perhaps, or a co-evolved species in which each part is non-functional without the other – the Siamese twins of the Signal.

This brings me to the final, and perhaps most intriguing category. Within most of the body types so far discussed, we find in small numbers another subcategory – what Perry has termed 'mechanoids'. As none of the creatures seem to be clothed, our assumption is that any kind of wearable tech external to the body and not part of the creature proper cannot be incorporated. This leads us to think that the creatures in this group must themselves be partly or wholly mechanical; that is, engineered and built rather than evolved, though of course there's no reason why these mechanical forms may not themselves evolve in some fashion we are unaware of.

So – next slide – here we see three creatures that illustrate the range of this type. The first, on the left, displays what could be body modifications, either for decorative or practical purposes. We could imagine an environment that has become toxic, or a species that has relocated to another planet or another ecological niche and has modified itself in some fashion in order to survive.

So that's our first subtype. In the centre, we have a creature that is either a mechanically augmented biological entity, or a mechanical entity with grafted biological additions. Again, these hybridisations seem designed to serve some specific purpose, or address some specific environmental concern. Note what look like air filtering lattices here and here, and the secondary sexual characteristics.

The one on the right looks, at least to my eyes, to be entirely artificial, though again, I must hazard caution when we use these labels. Alien evolutionary mechanisms may proceed in very different ways to our familiar Earthbound ones. So, here we have something that most resembles a, for want of a better word, tank, or a vehicle of some kind. We have the three flared and segmented legs around the base, each of which seems to have a gimbal, like a castor on an office chair, at the end. These meet in this hub at the base of the torso. The vertical section, the body, if you will, seems to be stained and abraded. To me, this looks like battle damage, or at least some heavy wear and tear. Note the parts towards the top that have been patched and altered. Remember, this is unlikely to be a suit - there isn't something separable living inside this skin, this is the creature itself. This kind of detail - the abrasions in this area here [indicates right flank towards the hub] where we see deep gouges - reveals that the creature's internal layers certainly look metallic, judging by the shine and the oxidisation.

This brings me to a very important point, something that I need to emphasise. These creatures do not so much represent generic taxa, but individuals, each one with a personal history. We assume this is true for every entity in the Signal. This of course begs the question: Who was this specific specimen? What's its story? Why this one, and not another? And what are their intentions, if any, towards us? As it stands, these creatures show no signs of life, however we might define that. They hang there, immobile, like holograms.

We're learning more all the time. To conclude, I'll come back to your original question. Yes, I would definitely urge caution. To that end, we are in discussion with the largest internet service providers and certain international bodies and governmental agencies, and though it may not be possible to purge the Signal, or shut down the internet - it was, after all, designed to be impervious to such an attack - we are discussing containment measures, should we need them. We have to be ready for any eventuality.

IW: Thank you, Richard. That was fascinating. Vivian, would you like to comment?

VA: Where to begin. [pause] Leaving aside the fact that the SetiOnEarth project is basically profiling with a thin veneer of scientific respectability, we have got to address the fact that these creatures - to use your entirely inappropriate terminology – these extraterrestrial biological entities, are quite possibly in desperate need of our help. They may no more be invaders than the migrants that are still turning up in great numbers on the Mediterranean coast. To paint them as some kind of science-fiction B-movie superrace, come to pillage the Earth of its resources and enslave us puny humans [*laughter*] is simply xenophobia at its worst. You even managed to get a sexist joke in there as well, didn't you?

IW: Richard, would you like to respond to that?

RL: I certainly didn't mean any offence. I – I'm suggesting that if you take a look at the body shapes, the suggested uses that certain appendages could be put to, they do suggest, speaking from a biologist's perspective—

VA: You have no idea what they are used for. The lived experience of these entities is not a projection of a human-centric— [*crosstalk*]

RL: I think Arentz is illustrating a common problem here. If we assume, as I think she does, that we should make scientific objectivity subservient to politically correct ideology or trendy social critiques, we may miss entirely the need for a robust self-defence strategy until it's too late—

VA: So you're planning to pull the plug? *Kill* them?

RL: We have to keep all the options on the table—

VA: —they are *people*. They may not look like us, or even behave like us, but they are *people*. This fear of the other, this demonisation of the different— we've been down this road too many times, and we know where it leads. It leads to the gas chambers, the killing fields—

RL: If I may finish. The term 'creature' in this context is not meant to be pejorative. It's applied in the public discourse all the time. We need to use commonly understood terms, especially here. I'll agree, we do need to define our terms precisely—

VA: Who decides how we should use our language? *You?*

RL: For the purposes of scientific objectivity, I find that definitions—

VA: The validity of scientific objectivity overreaches itself. It has been under scrutiny since Thomas Kuhn's work on paradigm shifts. I can't believe that you are unaware of this. [*ripples of laughter*] Scientific theories need to acknowledge that our shared reality is, at base, a social and linguistic construct. What is currently defined as truth [VA *mimes quotation marks*] is simply what works to benefit a self-appointed elite. No more, no less.

RL: So a complete lack of familiarity with even the basic precepts of biology, of the scientific method, is what you're bringing to this debate here?

VA: *Feel* that condescending aggression! Can I ask the audience if they can feel it too? [*shouts of "Yes", fewer but louder shouts of "No", "I can", "Feel my (inaudible)" and general heckling*]

VA: As we imagine ourselves, so we create ourselves. Can you not see here how your anger is an inappropriate beta-male response? Richard, you of all people, you should have outgrown your biological roots. No wonder you see a potential threat in our visitors – you are simply jockeying for position in what you perceive to be a new hierarchy. Afraid you'll end up near the bottom of the pecking order and have no access to mates? You revealed your fixation with the sexual urge by showing explicitly pornographic slides without appropriately flagging them beforehand with trigger warnings. This kind of in-your-face cock-waving is typical of those who feel the need to categorise and pigeonhole the different, the other, in order to control it and subdue it. Do you feel better now? May I remind you that this university is a safe space. Have you no care for the sensibilities of our audience here, many of whom may be traumatised by your dismissal of the immigrant experience as somehow dangerous, something to be feared? Should they also be classified, catalogued? Are you going to tattoo each of them with a number?

RL: *What?*

IW: Can I ask you to sit down, please, Richard?

VA: The post-Enlightenment project swept away the magic of the world, sought to replace the time-honoured true wisdom of our folk beliefs that had served us so well for centuries. With what? It's no coincidence that it was white male scientists who drove the Industrial Revolution, profiting in the process through the subjugation of the workforce by the ascendant capitalist elite. Are you asking me to believe that the men that fuelled this paradigm shift were not embedded with, and patronised by, the very people who stood to benefit the most? And you have the audacity to suggest that our physical reality coincides with some disinterested, value-free [VA *mimes quotation marks again*] reality?

RL: I'm a *biologist—*

VA: You're a *materialist.* Do I have to give you definitions now? Like all who feed the unchecked spread of new technology, who assume, *de facto,* that it's a force for good, the peace dividend does not work in your favour. I understand that your reaction is partly a protest, a typical positivist neoconservative protest, to be sure, but a protest nonetheless to the reduced governmental funding for scientific research. You're on the back foot, and like all in the military-industrial complex, you need to find a new war, a new front, to justify your continued existence. Bring on the phallic missiles! Penetrate their defences!

IW: Richard, can I ask you again to sit down. [RL *sits*] Vivian, can we try and keep it less personal? Richard, I think, does raise many interesting points. There does seem to be some truth in his observation that—

RL: [*exasperated*] So you deny the existence of a physical external world whose properties are independent of how any individual human being – any individual *alien* being – wishes the world to be? So I socially construct my cellphone? The force of gravity?

VA: There are multiple truths, and like people, each and every one is deserving of respect. Why should this not apply equally to our EBEs? Science's project has been shown again and again to undermine the values and experiences of the 'other'. Are we afraid their bodies may be abhorrent to us? This kind of xenophobia, this, this *racism*, is something we as a progressive society have obviously still not surmounted. You must know how populist prejudice seeks respectability in the supposedly dispassionate discourse of science? Own it and deal with it.

RL: My assumptions are based on close comparisons with similar adaptations in Earthbound fauna. What is a claw for, if not to slash? A horn, if not to impale?

VA: So you've felt the lumps and bumps on the heads of these poor creatures, um, EBEs, and like some Victorian phrenologist, you think you can tell what motivates them? What they *think*?

RL: Phrenology is a discredited science. Are you seriously arguing for epistemological relativism? Is the truth status of something only to be evaluated relative to the cultural background of the speaker?

VA: Phrenology was once mainstream science. [*holds up hands*] I rest my case. Thank goodness for those paradigm shifts.

RL: Phrenology was discredited because it didn't withstand scientific discoveries in other fields of—

VA: You materialists just thought it was time to change your story. What you have to understand is that that's exactly what champions of equal rights, of justice, have always tried to do: change the prevailing stories, the ones that say certain people can't vote because they're inherently less intelligent, that slavery—

RL: *That is not what I'm—*

IW: Lower your voice, Richard. Please.

RL: We have much we can learn from them. But I do suggest we have to be prepared for any eventuality. Look: we are outnumbered. We have no idea what the motives of these beings may be. We have no idea if there are more to come. This may be the first wave of an army of—

VA: So you suggest we consider a first strike? Do away with them? There's a word for that. It's called genocide.

[LINWOOD *throws a glass of water over* ARENTZ]

VA: Fascist!

[*dialogue indistinct*]

[LINWOOD *is manhandled off stage by security*]

[*Boos and cheering from audience*]

The information contained in this report is to be treated as Most Secret.
Location: [removed] [Note: Assumed to be the Apollo Isolation chamber
"Hornet+3", Lyndon B. Johnson Space Center]

Note: Some responses have been edited, and are summaries of what was
actually stated. Details in square brackets are added for clarity. Please
refer to audiovisual recordings, available on request.
Document history: v 1.4. Submitted for review and comment
Date: [removed]

Present:
Dana Normansson (hereafter DN), Cmdr., Daedalus Base
Adam Parker (hereafter AP), sup. offcr
Gabriel (Gabe) Bowen (hereafter GB), press liaison
Other support staff, medical staff [names removed]

AP: I'd like to go over the alien's - your alien's physiognomy in more
detail. We have some images from the autopsy now taking place at the crash
site. They have some questions.
DN: The autopsy?
AP: Yes. [names removed] are there now. Of course, we'd much prefer to be in
a well-equipped theater. The equipment we have up there is somewhat limited.
But we found that the alien is attached... He seems to be fused with the
capsule. Or maybe the capsule is part of his, you know, exoskeleton. We're
still figuring that one out. As we can't move the capsule, we decided that
the best solution was to perform an autopsy at the site.
DN: You have video?
AP: Yes. It's all being documented in detail. Despite the difficulties the
location presents, we made sure of that. We can–
DN: You know... I'd rather not see it. Thanks.
AP: Dana?
DN: Would you want to look at your own corpse, especially after it had been
mangled in an auto accident?
AP: No. No, I wouldn't.
DN: Then don't show me the pictures.
AP: OK. No problem. Sorry.
[pause]
AP: Can you tell me what you know? About their physiognomy? Can we begin
with the two-lobed brain? They have–
DN: Yes, the brain. That extra forebrain is not just some evolutionary
sport, like an appendix. It's the alien's conceptual testing ground. Think

- 510 -

of it as a sandbox with a failsafe. The larger backbrain — that's where the seat of its consciousness resides, can retreat to. It's his backup hard drive, in case the new ideas it's entertaining up front prove to be too dangerous. It can watch and wait from the safety of the backbrain, like an epidemiologist handling contagious material with plastic gloves from behind glass, ready to isolate the forebrain from the rest of the body's functions if necessary. I have to say, it's a great adaptation. Trial every idea, sort the useful from the detrimental, and choose accordingly.
AP: Neat.
DN: I get the impression this set-up is not unusual.
AP: You mean human single-brained anatomy may be the exception? Really? I'm wondering in what kind of evolutionary context that adaptation might be useful. This is how it survived... what, exactly?
DN: Do you ever read the papers and think some of the bad ideas that we humans are infected with are very hard to shift? Every generation they come around again, just when we thought we'd finally won the argument and sent them packing. There are others we've been incubating for millennia, like a 2000-year-old head cold. Instead of letting these ideas run to their natural conclusion in some simulation, safely isolated so they can't cause any damage, we're letting them run amok in the real world. Humankind runs its memetic experiments out in the field, so to speak, with all the fallout that entails.
AP: Instead of in the clean room of our non-existent forebrains?
DN: Right.
AP: More than one brain. Fascinating.
DN: To be fair, it's not unknown on Earth — an octopus has one main brain and eight smaller ones, one for each arm. These pre-process information from the chromatophores, the dermal musculature, each sucker... these smaller auxiliary brains are pretty much autonomous. The main brain is like the boss of octopus ink [note: perhaps Octopus Inc.?], delegating tasks to his employees. In fact, our own nervous system serves as an extended brain of sorts - it deals with all kinds of bodily processes that don't need our conscious attention, sending only the most important signals up to brain HQ. Unless something goes wrong, which is what the pain response is all about. Otherwise, it's happy to let your lungs breathe, your blood circulate, your bowels squeeze your shit ever closer to your arse.
AP: Nice, uh, analogy. Dana. The human brain also has two hemispheres, though they're not independent. I don't think anyone can get by on one hemisphere alone, though they do have distinct functions.
DN: So we're evolving. We're getting there.
AP: Wasn't the Stegosaurus supposed to have had a second brain at the other end?
DN: I know a certain human with his brains in his, his other end.
AP: What happens when the information gets passed to the backbrain? Does the LBE's behavior suddenly change?
DN: That's an interesting question. I assumed it was a slow trickle, that once through decontamination the ideas fed through to the backbrain continuously rather than in one big information dump.
AP: The idea that—

DN: Idea. See, there's another one. It just popped into existence. Where do these new ideas come from? Forever replicating from a twist on an old idea, or some novel interbreeding of two or more to create a fascinating and seductive new strain.

AP: Maybe my brain is the equivalent of a Petri dish, coated with some substance that ideas find nutritious. The open mind on which the seed of a new idea can settle, put down tap roots, grow and – bloom.

DN: And then fruit, sending out contagious idea seeds to infest other curious minds. Be careful.

AP: You don't make it sound so good.

DN: Hah.

AP: So this is why it seemed to be so focussed on our anatomy? Not a mere exobiologist's curiosity?

DN: It looks pretty peculiar to us. The feeling must be mutual.

--- END TRANSCRIPT ---

PODCAST TRANSCRIPT
The Wynn "Hooch" Nolan Show, episode 384, uploaded 20/11.
Nolan is in conversation with James Hartland of Infodump.com.
Jump to comments | ▇ f ▇ ▇ y ▇ ▇ G⁺ 1 ▇ ▇ ⊚ ▇ ▇ ✉ ▇

James Hartland [slurring speech] Wynn, let me tell you how this shit goes down, man. I know–
Wynn Nolan Lay off the whiskey, dude. You're on air.
JH Listen– this is the most important message you'll ever hear. It's about to break nationwide. The entire globalist program is trying to prevent you finding out what I'm about to tell you.
WN Well, go ahead, James. We're not stopping you. You have the mic.
JH The sheeple, they don't know true tyranny till it smacks them upside the head. We did a podcast all about this on Infodump last year. We had the dope, man, way ahead of time. You'll see. The Clintons– they weren't in the loop. Not since Truman have our elected presidents, our representatives in this so-called democracy, been in the loop. They're building it.
WN Building what?
JH The central nervous system of the New World Order! These glasses everyone's so excited about– we'll plug ourselves in, you know, like social media taken to another level, and we'll all be part of it. Attached to the internet, the man-machine interface. This is the end of free will. The dawn of a totalitarian state, and we'll think we wanted it all along.
WN Why would–
JH *Power.* It's all about retaining power. You want to know how they plan to pull off this stunt? I'll tell you. I got the fucking *blueprints.*
WN You do, huh? So tell us, James.
JH See, this Signal from Space, that's being beamed from the monolith on Phobos, and that monolith– it's not alien. *We* built that. NASA shadow ops built that. It's the ultimate false flag. This is not E. cunting T. calling. It's all *fake.* It was put up there in the '70s, in collusion with the Russians and the Koreans. They've been at it since the CIA got Kubrick to fake the Moon landings.
WN So they faked the Moon landings, but they can build a monolith on a Martian moon?
JH [shouting] *Radio hams recorded the transmissions!* What's released to the public is all for *show!* Classic misdirection! Diversion from the real agenda, the real mission. Think, man! Those orbital shots Space X are running – what are they sending up? What are they bringing back down? Why the subterfuge? [Nolan shrugs]
I'll tell you. There's a staging post on the far side of the Moon. They're hiding all kinds of black projects we know nothing about up there.
WN Isn't it supposed to be a telescope?
JH Do *you* believe it's a telescope? Man, get woke! That's what they want you to think! See, when this goes down, this alien threat bullshit, we'll be so scared that they'll step in with our *blessings,* man, with our *fucking blessings,* to save us from something they engineered in the first place! They need us docile. They need us stupid. They need us to think we're in imminent danger of some 'Independence Day' style U.F.O. attack. Hollywood's been priming us with this shit since the '50s. You think there's no collusion there? Come *on,* man. Why was Hollywood in Hillary's pocket? Tell me that.
WN The existential threat–
JH We'll be only too glad when we see the troops on our streets. C'mon, man.

Aliens? *Really?* You ever seen an alien, outside of a sci-fi movie?

WN I've seen Amanda Lepore–

JH –Let me tell you a secret. *They don't fucking exist.* They're a *fiction.* The saucerheads, they'd have you believe these extraterrestrials are crossing the Universe just to anally probe some poor dumb hick in Alabama. *Gay* aliens? With a taste for white trash? Bull-*shit.*

WN [laughs] Maybe our pert human butts are a rare intergalactic delicacy.

JH Man, they ain't seen my big fat hairy ass.

WN So, no aliens?

JH No aliens. Look in the Good Book. You ever read about God creating alien motherfuckers? Adam and Eve and Little Green Man? No? No. 'Cause he didn't.

WN We can see them through the glasses–

JH Yeah, funny that. You have to put on this virtual reality doohickey before you can see them. How convenient. You know the most important thing about virtual reality? It's *virtual.* You'd think with their Hollywood connections they could at least stretch to a bunch of actors in rubber suits. No, U.F.O.s, the Apollo program, Gemini– they're *all* fake. Look at those retouched photos, man. It's all there. The CIA was buzzing us with saucers in the '50s and '60s, and we bought it. The coming catastrophe is always just around the corner, but guess what? We're still here! Global warming? *Hoax.* Hurricane Katrina? That's them testing their weather weapons. They can *steer* those things. They're laying the groundwork, man, softening us up for the big one.

WN Which is–?

JH The *takeover.* Suspension of the democratic process. *The New World Order.* It used to be the aristocracy, the upper classes who wielded power over the common man. The Astors, Rothschilds, Walpoles. Now it's the Deep State. The *Illuminati.* They'll finally reveal themselves, our new overlords, pretending they're our saviors here to save the day – and there'll not be a single thing we can do about it, 'cause we'll all be plugged into our virtual reality machines, so preoccupied with this non-existent threat from marauding space aliens that we'll gladly give away our God-given freedoms, and then thank the fuckers afterwards. We gotta stock up on guns, ammo and MREs before they stage another Sandy Hook in an attempt to take away our second amendment rights. That's how these motherfuckers *roll,* man! And for us true patriots, those who ain't going to go quietly, they have the mass-internment camps ready for the likes of us.

WN And you know all of this how, exactly?

JH *My guy on the inside.* Can't tell you his name, but I've seen his papers, his I.D. He's legit. He's up there, he's got access. And he wants the world to know what they're up to.

WN And he chose you as his mouthpiece, you to bring this information into the public domain?

JH He can *trust* me! I'm *discreet!* C'mon. You been vaccinated?

WN What?

JH You been vaccinated? Simple question.

WN I have.

JH You got the *chip,* man! They turn that thing on, your higher brain functions shut down. *Boom.* Just like that. You're as docile as a puppy. They have you on a leash. But we don't have to go down without an almighty fight, am I right? Am I *right?* Rise up for liberty! Rise up for freedom! Rise up–

[Hartland falls off chair]

-- ends --

PROGRAMME: WOMAN'S HOUR
Episode 13.11

Subject tags: The Signal from Space, SETI
Presenter: JENNI MURRAY
Guest: INGRID KNOX

Murray
Good morning.
[Follow-up and housekeeping]
Today our guest is blogger and columnist for the *Daily Buzz*, Ingrid Knox. I'm
sure many of our listeners will be familiar with her work. Thanks for coming
on the show today, Ingrid. Now, you've been an outspoken critic of the way
in which this so-called Signal from Space has been dealt with, even going so
far as to call it a cover-up. Whereas some regard you as a champion of civil
rights, this uncompromising stance has also brought you a certain amount of
opprobrium in the press—

Knox
I have huge support—

Murray
You do. However, in the astronomy and SETI establishments you have been
. . . ignored, is probably the politest way to describe it. Why is this, do you
think?

Knox
Well, Jenni, first of all thanks for having me on the show. I accepted your
invitation to talk because the present situation in regard to the Signal and its
occupants fills me with despair.

Murray
You've been very critical of the manner in which the release of the Signal has
been dealt with. As you know, we had Leonie Orlov from the SETI team at
Jodrell Bank on the programme last week. Her argument, and I can see her
point, is that we expect those who are working with biological agents, which
can be very dangerous in unqualified hands, to be especially careful. Why is
the Signal any different?

Knox
This narrative – that we know what's best for you, we can protect you from
what may harm you, is infuriatingly patronising. What the establishment fears

515

is a loss of control, of influence. It is, as it always has been, about power.

Murray
But we have no idea what the content of this Signal could be. Should we not be at least a bit apprehensive?

Knox
Jenni, if this Signal proves to be dangerous in any way, it will only be dangerous in regard to how we choose, or don't choose, to make use of it. Who gets to make that decision? Us? You and me, or the scientists whose paymasters are the military and the deep state? All I'm asking for here is complete transparency, and an admission by NASA and the governments with which they work that, as a publicly funded organisation, the information our tax dollars have helped collect is made available to all of us.

Murray
Can we back up a bit here. The Signal has been theorised to contain the blueprints for extraterrestrial life. Aliens—

Knox
I prefer "travellers". The pejorative term "alien" carries with it too much baggage of the other, of the different, of the less-than-human. Jenni, what you've got to remember is that this exclusionist rhetoric is coming from an privileged elite. If they are representative of anything, they are representative of a power structure that has ruled, in one way or another, the choices we, as women, as disenfranchised people of colour or religion – the real aliens here – have available to us. These people have their positions to think of, their university tenures. To imagine that they have anyone else's best interests at heart is woefully naive of you.

Murray
Well, Leonie's point was well made – history also tells us that the less advanced society in a first-contact scenario always comes off worse.

Knox
Do you not see that there are unaddressed assumptions there, in your statement? Who really holds the balance of power here? It's certainly not the newcomers. They're incapable of any action.

Murray
I grant you that appears to be the case. For the present, at least. So, do you think that the Signal is a call for help? An order to surrender? Something else entirely?

Knox
Who knows? Who decides? Certainly not you or me. That is why this release of the Signal into the public domain is so important. White has done us, done humanity, a great service, prising what is probably the most important piece of information in human history out of the hands of those who would jealously guard it for their own ends. We would not be sitting here having this

discussion if it wasn't for him. And now, using these glasses, we can actually see the travellers. That kind of crowdsourced innovation has thrown this wide open. We have to remember that it is just information, these travellers are not physically real, and so to assume that there may be something inherently dangerous in the Signal makes no sense. It's scaremongering. We are not facing down reptilian aliens with rayguns bent on world conquest here, whatever those adolescent men at NASA, weaned on their juvenile sci-fi fantasies, may like to think.

Murray
There are many very capable women fronting up the SETI team. As I said, last week I had Leonie Orlov on the programme. I think she might have a few issues with your analysis—

Knox
Look, we've been beaming our TV and news out into space for decades. It's a beacon, but more than that, it's cultural imperialism, and only serves to frame any discussion we may yet have with the travellers in terms of this assumed duality, them and us. Why do you think—

Murray
Ingrid, I don't—

Knox
Please let me finish—

Murray
Ingrid. If I may. You can't deny that a few of the creatures seem to show physical trauma. Battle-scars, or signs that they have been tortured, it has been suggested.

Knox
And the vast majority don't.

Murray
I take your point, but the question still needs to be asked: are they victims, or aggressors? Or both?

Knox
If they are aggressors, and that is by no means proven, they will not have unexpectedly come to us out of a clear blue sky. What if we'd extended the hand of peace, instead of Hollywood's cacophony of war and destruction, which we unthinkingly broadcast to the universe day after day, year on year? You have to ask yourself, is it any wonder they may be coming for us? Maybe we're asking for it. Maybe we deserve it. We've already established beachheads in the Solar System, we've sent exploratory landers to Mars, Titan, Europa, the asteroid belt. Probes to the outer Solar System, to Pluto, the Kuiper Belt and beyond. The Moon— look, Daedalus Base is so obviously a first-strike facility, disguised as a purely scientific telescope. NASA doesn't even like to admit it exists. Ask yourself why it's been built on the far side,

517

away from public scrutiny. What are they hiding? It certainly looks to me like they are weaponising the new frontier. No, any aggression the travellers may end up revealing towards us will be legitimate pushback entirely of our own making. If this is an invasion, we, in a very real sense, will have caused it.

Murray
While I personally may disagree, you do seem to be articulating a certain groundswell of opinion. There seem to be a growing number of people who identify with the, the creatures in the Signal.

Knox
Yes, though I must remind you again that I prefer the less problematic term "travellers". Words have meaning. We have to use them carefully. Another possibility is that the trauma we see may be self-inflicted, a direct response to their unmet needs. These are people who have come across the Universe, and require our compassion and understanding. If we are the witnesses to a power struggle, we need to address the grievances of the disenfranchised group. We rightly pride ourselves on our fairness and tolerance, yet may still be inflicting great wrongs. Is this the message that we want to send out to the Universe? That we will not welcome visitors? That we consider ourselves an inward, insular society with no will to embrace our space brethren in their time of need?

Murray
Well, we have no information on their motives. They seem to be in suspended animation. They—

Knox
And should we continue to deny them their agency, the ability to act? I'm sure we could engineer physical bodies for them if we tried, and I hear some people in the biohacker underground are attempting to do exactly that right now. We could even offer them space in our own heads – let them share our minds.

Murray
Some people certainly seem to have the spare capacity.

Knox
To do otherwise is to keep them locked in a virtual concentration camp. If our society does not accommodate their narrative needs, does not allow them space to create an identity for themselves in which they could be a useful player, a contributor, this violence that we see the results of may inevitably be the result. This is the lesson we always fail to learn from the terrorist, the lone-wolf gunman: what else can we expect them to do when we fail to include them in our society, deny them a voice? Is it any wonder that, having been excluded from a society, they act against it? Is this what we want to happen here?

Murray
So you're suggesting that a crisis of identity, or maybe a loss of individuality—

Knox

There has always been a hard edge to scientism. It is, if one takes it to its logical conclusion, the will to order, a fascistic impulse that seeks to impose a strict rationality on the cultural milieu. Where does this take us? What horrors have we to thank science for? I'll tell you. The mechanisation of war, the slaughter of innocents on previously unimaginable scales. Cold logic has no compassion, because its story is the only story, its truth is the only truth, and it cannot co-exist with other truths, other ways of knowing.

Murray

It has also given us the very means through which this conversation is being broadcast. Without it, your story—

Knox

We have told each other stories for millennia; they are central to our sense of being, to our continuity with our past. Our oral histories, our beliefs, and, yes, our gods, are in a real sense who we are. These are the identities that the modern secularist would seek to strip from us. The post-enlightenment project of finding that one truth that is true for everyone has done irreparable damage to the many truths that each and every one of us nurture to make sense of our daily lives. What kind of bully would seek to strip people of that? The scientific imperialism of the West is breathtakingly arrogant.

Murray

I think Leonie Orlov might not agree with you there.

Knox

What is at issue here is the pushing to the peripheries of our discourse the multitude of ways in which it is possible to be in the world, each one as valid as any other. For a truth to be true, it only has to be believed, whatever the bigots who hide their animus behind a facade of rationalism may say. We have to ask ourselves: "What are the traveller's stories? What do they have to say?"

Murray

You have made a name for yourself through your writing and interviews by giving voice to what you call the "unheard un-people". Would you like to tell our listeners about that project?

Knox

I get letters, emails, daily from people who tell me they have always been defined as the, quote, other, unquote. Why should they not feel an affinity with our visitors, with those that have no voice, no volition, whose otherness keeps them trapped, unable to participate in the public discourse and change the manner in which their otherness is framed? The very otherness they share provides a kind of togetherness.

Murray

I'd like to address, if I may, a few assumptions that I think are creeping in here. You often frame the discussion using, if I may say so, the dimorphic genders of our own biology— Leonie was, when we had her on last week, and I found this very interesting, discussing the morphology of some of these crea— uh, travellers. And it seems that, for a large number of those that they have studied in any depth, that there may be three, sometimes four, maybe more, genders. Indeed, she spoke about several races they think are hermaphrodites, or genderless. Another theory she is exploring is that they take on different reproductive roles at different times during their life cycles. This does in fact happen here, on Earth. The example she gave— Parrotfish start out as male or female, but have the sex organs of both genders. They are, to use the technical term, protogynous hermaphrodites. She was very insistent that we must try and avoid projecting our own assumptions onto them, assumptions derived from our own biology. We should not see ourselves in the, the travellers, and strive to keep an open mind.

Knox
Jenni, we have fought for control of our bodies. NASA, it seems, was intent on owning the bodies in the Signal. If that's not the very definition of slavery, I don't know what is.

Murray
Strong words. To be fair, when it comes to their motives we are very much in the dark. These, uh, travellers have been utterly mute in this respect. Why are they here? What is their plan? They cannot tell us. We can't read their minds.

Knox
Ask yourself why they have no voice. Who stands to gain the most by their continued silence? We have provided the cage in which they find themselves trapped. Their immobility, it has been suggested, is a function of the primitive nature of our computers. But we know that governments have far more powerful mainframes available. Why are they not being used to provide them with a voice? Or perhaps they are, but we are not party to that conversation. Consider this: how would you behave, stripped of all the essential defining aspects of your humanity?

Murray
I would point out that the term "humanity" in this context may not be entirely—

Knox
We have a scientific elite that, on the face of it, claim to stand for the advancement of all, while actually pursuing their own xenophobic agenda. This is the hypocrisy I find so despicable.

Murray
But Ingrid, to reiterate Leonie's point, and I think it's a reasonable one to make, we know no more than we can deduce from outer appearances. If they vary in appearance, if they represent very different species, may they not also have varied and differing, maybe mutually antagonistic agendas? Could that possibly be one of the reasons they are in this state of suspended animation? Crowd control, if you like?

Knox

So their agendas may differ from ours – so what? Are we supposed to apply value judgements here? The truly inclusive liberal state must show tolerance to alien concepts that may have, in our view, perhaps illiberal or even dangerous outcomes. Who are we to impose our values on another, perhaps far older, system of beliefs? Who are we, if we claim to uphold the values of a truly inclusive society, to not permit, even welcome these vibrant and important additions to our discourse? We are supposed to be better than our forebears who staked out their claims to the colonies with no consideration that they might already be occupied. These are boat people, and our duty as a civilised world, as a civilised species, is to give them succour. If I may quote from *The New Colossus*:

> "Give me your tired, your poor,
> Your huddled masses yearning to breathe free,
> The wretched refuse of your teeming shore.
> Send these, the homeless, tempest-tossed to me,
> I lift my lamp beside the golden door!"

Murray

Well, we're out of time. It's not often we end on an impromptu poetry reading. I'm afraid we'll have to leave it there, but I'm sure this discussion will continue. Thanks for listening, and thanks to my guest.

Knox

Thank you, Jenni.

- - - TRANSCRIPT ENDS - - -

The information contained in this report is to be treated as Most Secret
Location: [removed. Assumed to be the Apollo Isolation chamber "Hornet+3",
Lyndon B. Johnson Space Center]

Note: Some responses have been edited, and are summaries of what was
actually stated.
Details in square brackets are added for clarity. Please refer to
audiovisual recordings, available on request.
Document history: v 2.7. Submitted for review and comment
Date: [removed]

Present:
Dana Normansson (hereafter DN), Cmdr., Daedalus Base
Adam Parker (hereafter AP), sup. offcr
Gabriel (Gabe) Bowen (hereafter GB), press liaison
Other support staff, medical staff [names removed]

AP: Just checking we're getting all this. Can we check the video links? OK?
Brilliant. Right, this session I'd like to expand on a few things we touched
on before, and clarify what our place may be in all of this.
DN: Fine. Good morning, by the way.
AP: Sorry. Eager to get on. I've not been able to sleep. So many things I'd
like to ask.
DN: I'm not going anywhere. I'm under quarantine, remember.
AP: Yes. Sorry. [pause] You need anything?
DN: An extra brain, maybe. I can see why our friend evolved two. It's like a
junk room - you can fill it with all the stuff you haven't thought through,
close the door, and retreat to Brain Two, where it's more orderly and you
can relax.
AP: I've been wondering. Is your alien friend still in there? In your head?
The possibility that it may still have some kind of, uh, power over you—
DN: Adam, relax. It's not going to take me over, Bodysnatcher style,
if that's what you mean. No, I simply have access to its memories, its
knowledge. It tells me things. It feels like I have its ideas, that they
are my ideas, but I am fully in control. It's dead, and I can read the
book of its life. I've grown to like it. Him. I'm going to give him a male
pronoun. He's endlessly patient. His sense of syntax is quite elaborate,
formal, even - it's ornately precise. To typify a species from one example
is as inadvisable as judging humanity from a single example, but if I was to
anthropomorphize, I'd say he's well-spoken.
AP: Posh aliens. Right.

DN: Sounds bizarre, but there you go.

AP: So, to follow up on a few things. You say it's impossible to send a signal more than a limited distance?

DN: I've been going over all of this since last we spoke, and I hope I'll now be able to describe it in more detail. So, yes - even with the means at the disposal of some of the most advanced civilizations in the known galaxy, the Signal can only be transmitted over distances of hundreds of light years, depending on the power of the transmitter, before it attenuates and the signal strength falls below the background noise. Reviewing what I can of the Grid's history, some jumps have been far larger than others. These big jumps use power sources - and I've no idea yet how this was achieved, so don't ask - such as a black hole, or a neutron star... but generally, the Signal has proceeded in jumps of around five to fifty light years. It's been received and retransmitted several thousand times - I'm not sure of the precise number because it depends on how you measure it. Sometimes it's targeted at a specific location, other times it isn't, though it seems it can travel further if it is directed in a tight beam. The last transmission was targeted at 127 specific worlds deemed suitable for life. One of those happened to be Earth.

AP: Incredible.

DN: Incredible doesn't begin to describe it. What's becoming clear to me, and this is interesting, is that our physiology is unusual in other ways. Humans are sensitive to a narrow range of the electromagnetic spectrum: light, basically. We can't see anything in the infrared or radio, so there was no way we could receive the Signal directly. Instead, we picked it up via our tech, our radio telescopes. This, it seems, is - not the norm. The indirect nature of our detection of the Signal is in some ways a biological shortcoming, but it also gives us a unique advantage: we have it isolated. In many cases where the Signal has been received directly, it's been routed straight into the brains of the species in question. It seems that for many races this can have - has had - very harmful effects. Fatal, even. This, in fact, was the case for our visitor. It caused the near collapse of his society.

[pause]

DN: I'm not going to go there.

[pause]

DN: No. Sorry. The images are too overwhelming.

AP: In your own time, don't push it.

DN: I'm beginning to understand what he's lost. What he left behind.

[pause]

DN: Can we have a timeout? Ten-minute break?

[...]

AP: OK, we're back.

DN: Sorry. It, it can overpower me sometimes. So much rich history, so many beautiful stories. The art and literature and history and science of an entire species may now exist only in my head. I'm a walking museum.

AP: Take it easy.

[pause]

DN: Ahem. So. A direct means of linking minds seems to be common to the

- 523 -

species in the Grid; they have a shared periphery, an overlap between minds. A more permeable way of communicating. This doesn't mean that a written or oral form of language doesn't often evolve as well - there will always be a need to communicate across distances greater than this mind-to-mind link allows, or to record information for posterity. But we are unusual in that most of the information we process symbolically has to be encoded in language, spoken or otherwise transmitted, and then decoded by the recipient. We have no means of directly reading the inner state of another human being.

AP: And this is atypical, you say?

DN: It occurs in less than five percent of the species in the signal that I have had time to look at closely. The extraterrestrial whose brain I have access to has a mind-to-mind ability combined with a more rudimentary syntax based on pheromones and chemical signals, mostly used to convey general moods. These are not great at fast data rates, so to speak, so are augmented by the signing I originally saw and the colored displays on the carapace. It's like mood music setting the scene, then dialogue over the top filling in more precise details.

AP: And there was I thinking aliens might be able to learn English.

DN: I realize now how perplexed it was by my inability to receive sensory information more directly.

AP: So us humans still have a bit of evolving to do.

DN: But this may be our real advantage! Our shortcomings as a species have given us a firewall, our own two-brain system of sorts, though in our case the second brain is not biological but computational. The Signal, here on Earth, doesn't reside in people, not directly — it's floating around the internet, that being our current off-brain repository. In there, it has no body which it can use to move around the physical world. They're like ideas that have no brain to think them. We've inadvertently caught them in a silicon trap, and they have no way to get out.

AP: And we're digitally dissecting them, making music from them, re-editing them...

DN: Right. It hasn't affected us more directly - so far. We may be immune to it, or the vector of infection may just not be available.

AP: Let's hope that remains the case.

[...]

DN: Prior to the Scooch Orlena's involvement, the Signal was less structured, and the creatures encoded in it were not under any kind of centralized control. A kind of federation of equals. Sounds ideal, but in practice it was anything but.

AP: Socialism in space?

DN: Hah. Our Scooch Orlena, the Shepherds as Jack Fenwick calls them, they're a more recent addition to the, the Grid. The arrival of the Grid devastated their species, and so they're learning how to tame it, rebroadcast it without destroying its host in the process. This is their mission. They see themselves as protectors. Their twin brains allow them to interface with new species they encounter with only a small possibility of harming themselves.

AP: Sounds like the Signal has developed its own ecology.

DN: That's an interesting way of putting it. Even after the Shepherds
began tagging along for the ride, there were some inadvertent, what could
euphemistically be called, cross-cultural misunderstandings that had to be
dealt with. Alien species have vastly different and incompatible modes of
reproduction and nourishment. These would be kept in check within a natural
ecosystem that had evolved in tandem, but removed from that environment,
it was... a disaster. Imagine you have an ark. A real one, here on Earth,
filled with all the different species we have on our planet. Most of the
animals on it would regard the others as prey, predator or mate. It'd be
mayhem. But quite apart from one species simply eating or shafting another,
there were other more beneficial consequences. The Shepherds - the Scooch
Orlena, our Man in the Moon - is actually a result of one such inadvertent
cross-pollination of two species that evolved on two completely unrelated
worlds. I'd deduced that the hindbrain allows the forebrain a certain amount
of individual autonomy so it can act as memetic food-taster to the king,
but not realized that the forebrain is actually the vestigial cerebrum of
an absorbed entity called a Grimault. Though they can sleep at different
times, the forebrain is sustained by its host and can no longer exist
independently. When born, the Orlena are paired with a farmed Grimault,
selectively reared over generations for passivity, and the Grimault attaches
itself to the snout - the same organ that I, uh, I attached myself to - and
over a certain period the Orlena digests the Grimault's outer casing and the
brain takes up residence in the lower nasal tract, where it is incorporated
into the juvenile's nervous system. This process takes a while, and when
complete is marked by a series of ceremonies to mark its coming of age in
which the juvenile exposes himself to memetic toxins - bad ideas, basically
- that would induce seizures in a non-conjoined host.
AP: Nice.
DN: There were many other cases. Some species proved to be - delicious,
and were simply hunted to extinction; still more had unexpected chemical
effects - there's a species with a name that sounds like a series of chirps
and a high-pitched whistle which reproduces by paralyzing a less intelligent
species endemic to their planet, then laying an egg sac on its abdomen. The
host is incapacitated for several hours during which the egg sac firmly
attaches itself. After hatching, the larval form releases endorphins into
the brain of its host, which carries it around in a sling it makes from spun
silk. Meanwhile, it's sucking nutrients from the host. When it has grown
to a size where it can barely be carried, the larva injects a pheromone
which prompts the host to wrap both itself and the larva in the same silken
cocoon. The host is then slowly liquefied, and the resulting nutritious
soup feeds the parasite until it emerges in its adult form. Apparently,
the pheromones released during this larval stage are so powerful that the
Shepherds had to intervene to stop another race accidentally driving itself
to extinction by attaching these egg sacs to themselves voluntarily.
[pause]
DN: There's more of this stuff.
AP: Carry on. It's all being recorded.
DN: Many species rely on other species to complete their life cycle.
The Wivaroe, a simple airborne spore that nonetheless shows a degree

of intelligence, infects a more intelligent species living on the same
continental mass. It inserts itself into the brain, where it manipulates
its host to think it's sexually attracted to a predator that it would
usually shun. Once the host has been eaten, it then asexually reproduces
within the predator. During the wet season, which lasts several months, it
causes the head of the creature to expand. The sense organs wither and fall
away, and a bulb like a brightly painted spinning top takes its place. The
creature becomes confused and stops eating. Eventually, the head explodes,
filling the air with new spores.
[pause]
AP: Lunch has somehow lost its appeal.
DN: [laughs] But consider this - these creatures are not doing this out of
spite. They're not evil. This is simply their natural life cycle - for them
it's essential for their survival. Species interdependence. Still others
have very particular concepts about how they themselves, and sometimes the
other species they encounter, should behave. What their values and beliefs
should be.
[pause]
AP: So you say the Signal, the Grid, is evolving...
DN: Yes. And like any biological entity, the Grid is prone to infection,
misuse, to being hijacked by - for want of a better word, viral entities
- for their own ends. Often they don't realize the nature of the Grid. Or
they're simply not interested. Or the arrival of the Grid creates a major
power imbalance throughout a volume of space.
AP: Could we consider the Grid to be a natural evolutionary innovation?
DN: Natural? We'd need to know how it began. There's - there are suggestive
stories, race memories, almost. But I have no definite information on its
origins. Intriguing. Something to look into for next time.
AP: You say it has one purpose in mind - to reproduce. Almost sounds like
a, a sexual urge.
DN: In a way, it is.
AP: Why does that idea disturb me so much?
DN: Spread your seed? I think that impulse is pretty much universal.
AP: Can it be overridden?
DN: It would require the ability to precisely rewrite many lines of evolved
biological code. Code that is different for each species, written in a
language we don't understand. The Shepherds made a decision that they
wouldn't interfere with a species' naturally evolved form. That they would
all be incorporated as they were. No editing. No removal of what they
might think of as undesirable traits. It was decided that all species that
displayed destructive behaviors or interdependent reproductive cycles would
be held in suspension, and only the Shepherds and a dozen or so other
species that they trusted to carry out certain tasks between transmissions
were to be revived each cycle.
AP: So some of them do wake up.
DN: If they find themselves in a body, yes.
AP: I have a question. Why send the Man in the Moon? Why send a physical
Shepherd? We have the Grid.
DN: You know I just said the Shepherds came to a decision? That's not

strictly true. There is not— The Shepherds are not of one mind on this point.
[pause]
AP: I sense you're not answering the question.
DN: It's difficult - I have to sort through many arguments and counter-arguments. The Signal split. It was sent out untargeted, and two - at least - different locations received it. The Signal had effectively been duplicated. This was a known possibility. There was a long period - millennia - where two parallel iterations of the Signal were being received and retransmitted across space. They diverged, like geographically isolated species diverge. If fact, I get the impression this may have happened many times. I'll need to set all this out in an organized fashion. Anyway, some time later - the exact timescale is hard to measure, but my guess is that it's at least the time elapsed since Man first walked upright — they were both received by the same race at the same location in a space of three and a half years.
[pause]
DN: They found they no longer agreed. There was a rift.
[pause]
DN: The Shepherds from one version of the Grid had come to the conclusion they should improve matters, that it was their duty to tinker with the genetic makeup of those that had been incorporated, to help create what we might think of as a civil society. A harmonious whole.
AP: The other set of Shepherds, I presume, did not?
DN: Right. A compromise had to be reached. There is an incorporated race that practice a form of deep hibernation by voluntarily shutting down their cortexes. It was found that, incorporated into the Grid, they were also capable of doing this to others. They are now used to keep the Grid in stasis. In lockdown, effectively.
AP: The autocracy of necessity.
DN: It led to a permanent schism.
AP: In the Shepherd culture?
DN: Yes. This was not something they had had to deal with before - being to a degree telepathic, they had little prior experience with internal differences of opinion because they rarely arose. Some attributed the disagreement to outside agents, infectious alien urges and concepts that had become incorporated in the hindbrain over the millennia the strains had been separated.
AP: Two sects.
DN: There are actually nine, though they do divide broadly on that main principle.
AP: And who won?
[pause]
AP: Who won?
DN: No one did. The, um, disagreement is ongoing.
[inaudible]

--- END TRANSCRIPT ---

"USE MY BODY– SO THAT YOU MAY LIVE!"

MILLICENT BANKS

That was the slogan seen on placards at last week's demonstrations held in many European and some American cities in support of the so-called "travellers". It had absolutely nothing to do with sex workers' rights, though it's easy to see why curious passers-by may have come to that conclusion.

Facing them across the street, behind a police cordon, a vocal "Humans First" group are shouting "Pull the Plug!" through loud-hailers. Many are wearing balaclavas and *V for Vendetta* masks, and their hostility is palpable. It's a disparate coalition, encompassing many fringe alt-right groups, outright racists, anarchists and anti-globalists, all of whom have one thing in common: they see the Signal as an invasion, a threat to humankind's hegemony. Though these strange bedfellows might have deep ideological differences, one senses that what they do have in common is the ability to spot an opportunity, claiming responsibility for the recent bomb attacks on internet service providers and social media company offices here and in New York.

Penny O'Toole, one of the many speakers at the event, is a passionate and principled advocate of minority rights. I caught up with her just before she was due to speak, and she gave me a few minutes of her time to outline her views, shouting over the noise. "'Humans First'? They want to keep the travellers in stasis, say they must remain that way for our protection, and maybe their protection." You can see the barely concealed disgust on her face. "Do we never learn?"

A woman with a "Never Trust An Alien" placard shouts something unintelligible. O'Toole has no interest in discussing what their biological, rather than political or economic, imperatives, may be. "Humans may be less evolved in ways we can only guess at. We may lack faculties they take for granted. Our minds may be primitive by comparison." An empty bottle of lager sails over our heads, while a chant of "Send them back" is gathering volume. "Even if they don't behave according to our norms – and there are many human norms that I certainly see as problematic – we still have to grasp this challenge and show we are fit to share the grand stage of the cosmos with our new friends."

She lambasts Richard Linwood, who she says has called for "traveller profiling". "Differentiating the newcomers' physiologically feeds into this us-and-them bigotry, which is then being stoked by the popular press who seem to think we're on the verge of an interstellar war. The wonks in the military-industrial complex must be cock-jousting with glee. It's simply the Great Replacement conspiracy theory, given a new space-age twist. What they're actually doing is demonising entire races, implying they are less than human simply by virtue of being alien."

And her take-home message? "We are here to show our support for the neurologically different, the physically non-humanoid. We are here to proclaim the universal rights of all living beings. Who knows what amazing gifts they may bring? We are duty-bound to give them sanctuary. Love must triumph over hate. What kind of world – what kind of Universe – would it be otherwise?"

dHFeisCeDOCTvjurtEJ1ET3BrBfslUASFwT2ZJjO1yTSFGbQ71ixH
9HX9pTCBMGIxAyxJg2YDFDZfNTc8J9w8MG2AoTteHX55OZzq5O9Uj
x9OhpnN8Gy6xrAyRq62tzwcBJRjaGvHeTHUTjWKPZwUJC6s2jeGJK
M4Qhs5RRTtfF63eu8klcebNrBtTTCQPihO3GxMhNcH7ZBTbpwox5h
Hm91BIg7oSg8xupxRSrmuvqbLiNQCpW536uSj1UprCwAWWmOens7Z
tlvA5jKFXfapLmKCQTbvQe5UPiQOOJ94KZHmAFASMFgddY0k7ssOM
80qAeiQZu9VWq6On8KTqG1Dnfmunimw2ppzYaHYE2ZTxSbqQlAS18
8wdxbBqBvsmUK0MpJ7OMIAET0noDlIHOxDAcUWNvY5d28uU5x3oy0
9GjmeyrU3TSx6HOI6Oua9KbDkHlvTYMZMBuyohFQdU9FeLbS5qQ18
lDa8zH5Xjlz3W3BoF4tt0PFRVtN0KgFlfzs6vGprbyu4l6NavfSY5
duzjNNYnVA82uqwDtf6b73uDUL2ApcGOnXqtoj718J7Etvd0kMZZo
o1MLroG35zKrsb16NgLFhotuajHQXkCGM2GTLKZVu91RSLduTtNyc
Ilh9tqhcfCRAc6s7WdrDKWYqyC5B9cZ8yqpWB6OrV1FbqumYIjlHR
FgWxWL5Y4gDqeIuk32C4GVaNqAtq867MoW3yf2I4ufRHiTP9HOFCJ
S6vgQWXKM7repatxldO5fTe0YhDMyjQbGrObk0uPMZwUh71PrpNl5
Ev21mC5kted2YqW9GTyuIEzdwQrPxEXtMU1V7CX9d4zRQxWExZPBa
rhgtJIoSOQiY1ITPt3fQ6pI5SCP5xJX4LOvlRvkJzIpoS4s2Zms5F
hVFtwgAqYNEsQp3OE7RFyVWuK5ROrmY48ixFKUTXVeYa1DbBSgaLg
f38tSNfeCOTgRwvWWcaydqlCwpJv2oIShxfopmoR6znl0TNHVcK11
alDu4YoZbDLivkUHhq1WmXKE1k9JCL4E5Bc8D3ZeUOOO2WUd7Geti
kadOig7WNE0HmKKOkmaanlosG00YcwrMp5x1kFWeY6scfjp53kzZh
oGXFDfixjrlE4pasey1KSbwSwYCVlWc1FgRU0zDxTQA9bjJ0fb4PfZ
nS1B5TOWV8RDXEYqt7qfjRyibPwMROyFxowSvhZZ0UGH00vJczO0B
U87NzqgajgpBybt4eH8gxVpmKdaNQaJ2SOtUb4YeMc5ICABwlGdyd
PiVDkitTCNs1LK449d7zkIkhCwcnAb6KOJPZLftXf8I9O4Paato7V
QKSNGgSRBxxHA3w1RHGAvuuInYoqQrxUdMeVrb156VB0xq46seply
kYlU9I71RSbOck0dg4vAuNIbzoXCElW6EjLStFo6SC9wy08M2JQRq
kCfgItIFKiezWvBrPcrJmpPprqW1yh1fXQoY0VkJR8ZujDHWA7yWF
FXBcwEv7DQfJYNE6p27m8is7JDoFCp2ZQwP3s9Q9cfUniNyYoqFOs
Ct7B2Nbj3Lu1iXk8C79nyKKvwIyJ5xCQDHGMbEkr3QXqbdYbsJu4h
iMWpFjxRGcFtShzK4x5hEFr5lS5fsa2CM33qaIO9xqNdDgIsaBsTZ
loskQ0rBgwjeYGXquXJEezEew8N4ttmNUnPhtiR6P7kFtj9PipxP3
yz7GJNvf2E76JJODlG5pV7DpzIRkvxpAutuBQkifngKxChRbUruKY
e0xxd8ntTa3t6GTCoCX7sIcUHoEo4JzgwxdH9fnBRdwNymHHiuM5A
TVaWVjbeLySbkGvCrBiF84NpGcEY8s2DdTik3kKGdI4wuZhQAgK9z
26EnT2qdrXoJ9MmHVpqNDC5k0vqu57yK1iwQGfr3nQkTPbwqXhQ3d
7DqeqVWGCgNfvp3M2hBd9AatgfZ7QZZDiAQxQM1nooBWI72JhGb1b
KfRlnaMFzKQqpuRmcoIR2TSUySAQ1JMWF7O2Q1670ddGXiMLcLlKI
24Zh87zNVuu9JEDSGv4glUxt8HKUIELnMeHHri8X6BvhKPM2yjQb9
Qerr0u878Bf2plzEGbizGffQ2Awnz906dUlAbgfO8FAoqgYTPx987
yLhuc70fSppbASiKw9ZEMM1WWgllVwNlF4RvVFrR3AftvrmDq4NTU
Qvyt61UHiFVj66ycE69S9q1WS7aaRYKiOyX6O26a1BezCmpMmUSsg
EDkjs1Qglj9kUnXFxmk7g0E7M6X9jyQlx0onJv1Aq6UzKgn2rtIpq
6f1GtvjPN7xpsZRaieQD5IU7VSybUYEedMlv1bB1Z0LO9eIkwNDaV
JxlHEEzm4dGDfRFABUbUGQ8MfFOpFlbVVP2KoVxB4gJA4MzxiSE08
IJS9bp3KmOkn6s8Q63LX30zJVQGa5FpSdD2jAB77EmtctklAgnay4

pJ5WY9C2hGHr6razd0zPaxq5nZ3mUER5vq27DW4Cd0DQQXGKWCJLr
9Pkq6Kzbwp2OrRO3joPgYciZsOzYDQ9yij9iEWvn0TkLQAkCFLcIN
AHKFyXduCbdRnykLnep10SwNDaZzpZIvESTvgjSLL4qcRxPR2YIXk
DC2jRltgaT83Je8hmTT7dSlKvQ4R82qiANlo6frvxpGGrWiDpyXl0
wnSSmxhU5UWjjuY2cWdzM6nH50xayAgUTcD13PWbrtAbyFk2ibNK7
uE2Ggx3jpm9UXEgRg0tSuK7UId8aRvEaDGeP9rs6UqMYvfv9N1A1c
tcAxSXVprskoYeNoN6a46r65xDgr5UAgu7YuaBO9WNc0pTo5tYVTP
J94IQASCGbYlVwt3peE1ukMxyq4JUDyssZetjhWe5Tv72mffgeZ4U
zqs09LPqPE2kU2yt6osPkAvx1VpeY6k0SYNkVZMemtmtD2f1MYv5N
juXm7i3xHe7fCenkUP8qMKOFA1LFfgOYi5GMCeUO9nG9V2D24kRHI
132PwvKUAsNSln1cFT8b8VYv4qR8UzsL9w0LG48vVxdSULIEXDECM
FI5LWzwl7NYaDLZ315sesWLfcpOqKXNz801lP7eBY0a5MZY6kxmXf
p7LTPfgfpoGR5E1DJaDADrGbNT73x6v3ayqGtUjqKjOk8FBKZwzGY
W8V4fDSni1NYWQOoODKvMqBXYPZXLxDEfkyYONFgg84qULbq0ZGSP
9cnGb7fJOATPAkTaBAhb2Y61kuK0sVeVH6KiJizijYuiXYSVBrgVy
Gr5wc2R7b6Vq7E0TU0F6b28kiVquoPoLziwI9d4LkHDNeDjGlLf9p
BlM6guG3XGu0SaqGqClCxHpZZmnG8n9eTiPVGxapMVjvnPHYEaxqY
Sml1ADAZo8Qr4123LEy22qx337VfStDKFqY5tYCNWd3nOIEF3SIkF
ijPOEhfKMNbdjajpiRqIvTBKD4t7bYaYz2gBldLbjDeye9YZDbSYv
G9HTB4b1jcK3PNRYai67DGC5pPQEccQFZYq1SGHkicUpz3nFNfA5o
iKXWRo55BdnuNM6DnD8S5wvtYB3djKLRABBTsOnNxLYLzRqAW40Nb
3wEZJoju8TckNm3nj3iAHBUeFwMxZZtXRcmLH0B3DdrTk41xDUjtV
D4r1XrzdCZzYFpf4OTbtOJodHyGkU3DdqiXaB2FRYZpfH5i1UZNch
oVb5md9vh001wNtCIG7alDVhatoaexd2oCmEbEepngBiq590i6q6X
SNhKo9ebAXFVoY8uvY9kh5CY5xC1ZG7Sf5poUX7seWay4OnkrEWI8
qmUNfElyB3p51uHtgpY6gRt2s4ok3et3nexkXpJX83Fj3DMHS5eR2
e8fRJjtCiYSxM9ZtAVZcosLWzE8h21i3yUyK94s4oV5jhEjlfWr76
AsHfChJK3Yf3RVcuNBUTmoiQvwAald1deEr11ABYE2h9Sk7AVwY4G
5yn5TaLTfZzMxEmcRF3jM30WOAQGaFxFQPxzvwQzEEib38jxNenLO
EVRK3gT9iLR7M7DUtSxkosKcDjrqxuFaW7boNGfkZlxWMB31N30mK
G5D7jWyajcfDmTnoGJifd7xzuIexuECFlRU1iYb0rSPMzECtLFuh4
CN2YIa01oudhYf2Gk7OZfWaJtTw5MyriBpXsqmIMUPDeoRHvh7F7c
mMvC1h4rWR0Dx7te3uYWYAWxHl1iEZcn5OKUzEpKgvN3rRC5wVElS
2mhSgwDD44oe3iHWGM7Q6aikFQGt1PXel3sqbdybmJhSJbNg96GyB
amJrtUDLhhAiCxtJGPUuDNYUbGN2hd2eFJTlLWq9v6jLjoKl88oh1
YD7FBLozR5KT2tQtuUo2wzjF3Rd1p1aFPZ40hEGI0wp4XIzpf2JiT
vbUsAZDdHgjmDc77Jtg6BLc2n9FpiDEUhu5A28yRjl3S8qmZsG6v4
hh6oLtWXaYXaYdOcycWnkXxIWRR60KpHVeYYFjEYgJ4jACnHT8AuH
ttctoJT2kN0FW1orRqQSqbXXoRbx9hJcHviqDHDhurwiyPJbDTUo3
cj9TPODjbC8rtfiSUn4z cYjFy4S5wxuCK55z4ipRR6YqIyHubPOHt
xmGdw1we1oAFASJfNfEBD4oLYC8FCLqPJDxfiuIa VghNRrZcwh17v
LB0EqmRQmhAooAfZLVXm4EcjpIc7fKol1n2sfNEsymSJvOceDl2mF
V43bh3fYNuBCCZigBBbQfb1HadIgKC76HKZmEhdhydEJCmwfokv5K
wi724YbA9cWqo20bzKrGsZhCsIexKjBb1B8qQ1MChzqLPeYZsrZlU
0DihqRsgTgSBUwzWntPHMtwYe0LJA9uS44UZH4Sg0khMK6OHt5RRD
v7nhHPByMDZruv86LYrSdKgGCbCf8QMbouhNRWRBNt2Dwqmj8fLZR

THE CHOMSKY MODULE

"After we'd built the Oxbow, the DMEn just came through of their own volition. But coaxing anything out of the aliens in the Grid? That seems to be another matter entirely."

Harriet leafed through a sheaf of printouts on Jack's desk. "You're getting *something*."

"Pft. This is simply the Signal, run through a flexible probability-based algorithm that should respond to any reasonably consistent syntax. Any logical proposition that can be written down in any human language can be written down in this language. I was hoping it'd work the other way around, that it would be capable of parsing representational symbolic models of some complexity. But . . ."

"No dice?"

"I have to make so many assumptions. One: that they actually can, or *want*, to talk to us. Two: how do we visualise the result? Numbers? A needle oscillating on graph paper, a blip on a screen? The *Latin alphabet?* Fine for our DMEn, they're almost *made* of words, but for anything else they're just parochial human symbols. We have to expand the range of available memetic building blocks. A much broader orthography. Look—" Jack pulled a sheet towards him. Letters and numbers were arranged in meaningless unpunctuated lines across the page. "The graphical output can be arranged left to right, top to bottom, for what that's worth – but all we're doing is privileging Western conventions over Asian or Middle Eastern, and who knows how a non-terrestrial notation might be arranged."

Jack folded his arms tight across his chest. "Three: even if we *can* find some indication that they're trying to communicate with us, *and* we can represent that somehow, it still won't tell us what they actually *mean*. What they're *saying*. Even assuming we've captured most of the subtleties, the inflexions, at this point all we have is a message in a language we can't read. If you were trying to understand, I don't know, German, and you spoke not one word of it, you'd still be able to get some gist from other cues: the speaker's expression, their body language. Are they angry? Are they happy? Are you buying an ice cream, or at the wrong end of a bayonet? What's the context? Even though we may not share a cultural *memetic* heritage, we'd share a common *genetic* heritage, simply because we both belong to the species called Homo sapiens. Here, we don't even have *that*.

"This is another order of complexity entirely. Consider that the means of communication needn't even be speech as we would recognise it: codified modulated sounds arranged in a culturally agreed syntax that stand for verbs, adjectives, nouns, et cetera. That's a very anthropocentric assumption. Even *we* have non-verbal languages, like signing and semaphore. An alien species may use gestures, smells, colours – almost anything that is capable of reasonably fast and flexible modulation could be used as a basis for communication. And the problems don't end there. After we've identified the basic units, the atoms from which the molecules of words are made, they still need to be mapped to a set of concepts."

Jack paused. "However, there *are* a few things I'm more hopeful about. I think we can assume that more sophisticated languages, whatever their means of expression, will be structured so that simpler units of meaning can be arranged in some fashion to produce more complex ones. This may not necessarily be linear, as a written sentence is, or time-based, as a spoken sentence – the structure could be arranged across a matrix, a board, a three-dimensional lattice that represents duration. This is highly dependent on the physical morphology of the being in question, and its habitat – water, land, air – through which the signals have to carry, the social set-up, their tribal affiliation, other biological features we've no way of guessing.

"And it may not be just *one* specific means of communication, but several overlaid, simultaneously. *We* do this. So much of what we say can be recontextualised by the face we happen to be pulling. There may be literal meanings – what the language actually *says* – and entirely different meanings that are only apparent in the cultural context."

Harriet nodded. "Irony. Sarcasm. They don't travel well via email."

"Right. So even if we address the structural aspects of the language, we may still be no closer to understanding it, and we're certainly going to miss out on the finer nuances of, of alien *poetry*. If aliens *write* poetry."

Harriet taped the top of the sheets to the shelf. They hung there like monochrome bunting: decorative rather than informative. "So what do we do? If only we could ask the astronaut. The one that was, ah, was lost, on the far side of the Moon."

"Dana Normansson?" Jack smiled, and Harriet could sense he had news. "What? Tell us!"

"Off the record? Not that I seem to be abiding by the Official Secrets Act any more, but that's between us, right? She's alive. Daniel Novák at Jodrell told me – with some relief – that she's now back on Earth somewhere, in quarantine. From what I can gather she seems to be fine, though they're running all manner of tests. I only have very limited access to the machinations of NASA and the spooks that are pulling the strings, but Daniel's asked me to stay on on the SETI advisory committee. They feel they may need to draw on my, ah, talents. I can't talk to her directly, only pass messages through intermediaries. You're right – she is our only real source of information here, but they vet every communication carefully. As you can imagine, they have to prioritise. We'll have to do this without her help."

"Alive. That's good news. I wonder what happened up there?"

"If they know, they're not telling."

Nixon was staring into the middle distance. "I wonder if any other groups are doing what we're doing?"

Harriet hefted her pair of glasses. "If they can lay their hands on the Depthcharges – which isn't difficult – and know how to wrangle the Brazilians' code, they can see the alien zoo. But no one has the Oxbow. That's ours. That's unique."

There was a pause of several moments in which no one spoke. Jack couldn't shake the feeling they were missing something, something out in the open, something that should be obvious. It'd come to him later, he was sure.

"Now, here's my guess. We're not the first to grapple with this problem. All these interspecies communication issues must have already arisen in the Grid, many, many times over. And the Grid still survives. So someone – or something – must have solved this already. Who? Think."

Harriet nodded. "The Shepherds."

"*Right*. They are the most likely to have a broad range of communication skills. *They* may be our alien interpreters."

Harriet had jumped up and was now pacing the length of the conference room. "So we isolate the iteration of the Signal that describes our friend in the crypt of St Paul's—"

Three hours later, Jack and Harriet had a working beta. They called Nixon over, and Harriet began to explain what they had done in simple terms. "We have no way of directly locating a representation of a Shepherd brain in the data set, but what we *can* do is remove the sections the

Shepherd shares with a range of similar species, the assumption being that they encode common lower functions – body shape, organ placement, et cetera, and not the higher mental faculties. If the Shepherds' function within the Grid is what we suspect, they should have a highly developed language centre, which we hope we can isolate."

Jack stood, one hand on his lower back. There was an audible snap of strained vertebrae. "We call it the Chomsky Module."

Nixon waved his hand as if he was trying to clear an imaginary fog. "Go on. Indulge me."

Harriet was still tinkering with the final lines of code. "Noam Chomsky argued that children show such a capacity for language that they must be born with the innate facility for it. They are – *we* are – preloaded, if you like, with something he called our Language Acquisition Device. This is what we've now added to the Oxbow."

"And with this, we hope to give them a voice."

Nixon exhaled audibly. "Wow. Is that— is that even *possible?*"

Jack smiled a Jack smile. "There's one way to find out."

Document: (NS//81//DB)
Subject: Daedalus Base "Encounter"
Debrief interviews, 31 of 128

The information contained in this report is to be treated as Most Secret
Location: [removed. Assumed to be the Apollo Isolation chamber "Hornet+3",
Lyndon B. Johnson Space Center]

Note: Some responses have been edited, and are summaries of what was
actually stated. Details in square brackets are added for clarity. Please
refer to audiovisual recordings, available on request.
Document history: v 1.2. Submitted for review and comment
Date: [removed]

Present:
Dana Normansson (hereafter DN), Cmdr., Daedalus Base
Adam Parker (hereafter AP), sup. offcr
Gabriel (Gabe) Bowen (hereafter GB), press liaison
Other support staff, medical staff [names removed]

AP: Dana, good morning.
DN: Adam. I've still not got email or internet access. What's happening
with that?
AP: Well, we're not sure that's a good idea.
DN: Why not?
AP: I don't make those decisions.
DN: Well, who does?
AP: I can't tell you that.
DN: Adam, I'm being as helpful as I can be here. This place is like a hotel
- the food is great, the doctors are great - but how long am I going to be
here? I'm not contagious. I'm not a danger. It's beginning to feel more and
more like a prison. How long until I can get out?
AP: I'm not at liberty to say. We have many more questions we'd like to ask
you. That's what we should be focussing on now.
DN: I'd like a firm assurance that I will be released soon.
AP: I'll pass your request on up the chain of command.
DN: Please do.
AP: Anyway. Questions. We'd like you to tell us what you can about the
origins of the Signal, of the Grid. How did it begin? Where did it start?
DN: OK, OK.
[pause]
DN: Hm. The origins of the Grid are not known with any certainty. You have
to remember that the LBE encountered it for the first time relatively
recently in cosmological terms, and it has little reliable information

- 536 -

about the Grid's evolution prior to that time. What I can unearth feels
more like legends, or myths. Not articles of faith - it's not what we might
call a religious or ideological conviction. More a respected oral history,
or a folk memory. This is what I've pieced together from records that my
alien friend is - was - familiar with. There's so many differing sources,
some written, some verbal, some are trance-utterances or the mind-residues
of cultures that have been incorporated during the Grid's travels. So bear
in mind that though many of their, uh, scholars, I guess, have intensively
explored this, it is by necessity contingent, pieced together over
millennia, and it has many conflicting and mutually incompatible threads
that have been retold through different interpretive mechanisms or reworked
to suit some pre-existing moral framework or political agenda a certain
group may have been pushing at some time or another.
AP: Right. Caveats noted.
DN: Still, it is a story, and what are stories but ways to make sense of
real events?
[Information redacted]
[Note: A separate document, "Towards a Grid Concordance," which attempts
to structure the information discussed here into an internally consistent
Grid timeline is available to download from this link. Note that a password
and security clearance are required. Overseen by Leonie Orlov at the SETI
group, Jodrell Bank, this cross-references information from all available
transcripts, audio and video.]
AP: Do their records go even further back? Before the Grid?
DN: I wouldn't call them records. They're more a set of self-supporting
explanatory frameworks. They certainly have an interesting take on
cosmological origins. This is where it gets trippy.
[...]
DN: In the very beginning... I see a time long before there were physical
beings in which a mind could, could coalesce. Undifferentiated equilibrium.
The Universe is a uniform, homogeneous totality. Every place within it is
physically and mathematically identical in all respects to every other
place. Invariant. No energy gradient.
AP: If it's in perfect balance, surely it would remain that way forever?
DN: Ah. But it's not. It just looks that way. Think of it as the point at
which a plucked string on a double bass passes the rest point on its way to
the next maxima. If you took a photograph of that vibrating string at the
point where it is perfectly straight, it would be indistinguishable from an
unplucked string at rest, right? But the two are very different, because
one is storing all the energy, the unexpressed totality of the later form,
in potential; the other isn't. There are some interesting species-specific
variants here, of creation being a symphony played on a lyre of being by
beings akin to angels, or elohim; djinn, perhaps. I'll have to delve into
this more later. But this suggests there is no sudden creation of energy and
mass from nothing. The sum total energy of the Universe cannot be created
or destroyed; it always exists, it simply passes from potential to kinetic.
Expresses itself.
AP: No big bang.

DN: Not in any of the creation stories - let's call them theories - my alien friend has come across, no.

AP: I know some people who aren't going to like this. And others who will jump on it.

DN: Interstellar opinion is against us.

AP: [laughs]

DN: So, this homogeneity curdles. The first differentiation. A note, the deepest note possible, whose wavelength is the width of the Universe, and whose period is the duration of the Universe.

AP: Outside of my hearing range, for sure.

DN: There has been some discussion, amongst the species who enjoy such diversions, about what this note might sound like. There's no way to hear it, of course; any ear would have to be orders of magnitude larger than the Universe itself. But we may have an edge here - it's possible for us to measure the shorter harmonics, which are visible as the CMB-

AP: The Cosmic Microwave Background-

DN: Yes, it may be possible to use their distribution to work back, find the length of the longest note of which they are all subharmonics-

AP: And work out the size of the Universe?

DN: Precisely. Get on it now, Adam. Write that paper. Don't let Daniel grab all the hot tips. Not only that - a bit of reflection will tell you that if the wavelength of this note is the width of the Universe, its frequency must be the duration of the Universe.

The Universe lasts for as long as it takes a beam of light to cross it.

AP: Poetic.

DN: Elegant.

AP: Woooo. More boggle.

DN: Get used to it. I am.

[pause]

DN: So this journey from homogeneity to particularity proceeds; the Universe acquires detail. Harmonics on the original bass note, differentiation on differentiation, localized densifications paired with rarefactions. Over time, smaller and denser structures appear. I'm, by analogy here, I'm thinking that these shorter wavelengths - shorter than the Universe, so not, um, short short - are what we would call long wavelength EM radiation. A wave is a useful graphic description of an oscillating energy value - more here at the peak, less here in the dip. So, we have something akin to very long radio waves, then as they become smaller, microwaves, infrared, visible light, and so on down through the spectrum.

AP: Right.

DN: Detail is added at ever smaller scales as the Universe evolves. The size, or wavelength, of these differentiations decreases and their density, or frequency, increases. Think about this. The largest and loosest structures appear before the smaller. Atoms, as we see them today, did not exist at the birth of the Universe, but only evolved more recently. Am I going too fast here?

AP: No, no. I can go over all this again later.

DN: So the Universe becomes more structured. Then, at some point, light catches hold of its tail, and is no longer racing from the birth to the death of the Universe as fast as possible in a straight line, but is chasing itself in circles like a dog. It has, as it's described in some of the oral histories, become aware of its own existence. Force thus condenses into matter. The earliest atoms, or their lesser evolved counterparts if you will, were very large and tenuous compared to those that exist today. They were fewer in number, and the structures they formed were simpler, slower to coalesce, and larger in scale. The kind of matter we are familiar with today, its appearance of solidity, is simply a result of force acting in an extremely confined space relative to human scales. Matter is simply localized energy, standing waves vibrating on the nanoscale. It's all on a spectrum - an apposite term here. If we could see them, atoms – and their internal structures, the subatomic particles that make an even later appearance on the scene – we'd see that they're all in violent motion, spinning on the spot. They're nothing <u>but</u> motion. Ah. That's interesting. Nice. They kind of extend this matter-is-condensed-energy analogy back the other way - the first, large-scale differentiation, the first note, the bass tone of the whole Universe – they also see it as the primordial particle.

AP: There was just one particle in the Universe, and the Universe was that particle?

DN: Right! Exactly. At the very least, it has a certain symmetry.

AP: Beware simple symmetrical ideas. Ugly fact often kills a beautiful theory.

DN: You're misquoting Thomas Huxley at me now?

AP: Hah.

DN: You look like you have a question.

AP: We know the Universe is expanding. It's not Hoyle-style steady-state.

DN: That occurred to me too. This - this is what I understand. The volume the Universe occupies doesn't change. In that sense, Hoyle was right. Instead, as the objects within this space evolve they mimic certain features we would expect to see in an expanding Universe. Let me try and explain... If the Universe remains the same size but the structures in it condense, become more closely bound, the spaces between them will increase. And if everything becomes smaller and denser, including the atoms and any sentient beings made of atoms that are there doing the measuring, what yardstick do we use?

AP: I can see...

DN: As we look out across the Universe, we look back in time - back to a less differentiated epoch. We don't look back on a smaller Universe - unless we have a more flexible concept of what constitutes size – but to a time when atoms were looser and larger, and so the wavelengths associated with them, the radiation that they absorb and emit, would naturally be longer.

AP: And longer light-

DN: Is redshifted.

AP: Interesting.

DN: Redshift is primarily a measure of the size of the hydrogen atom emitting the photon, not merely an indication of recessionary speed.

AP: According to an alien in your head.

DN: According to an alien in my head.

AP: Let me- The current model supposes that heavier elements are produced by stellar nucleosynthesis. Might the lack of heavy elements in the early Universe also be because looser-knit atoms of hydrogen and helium are not yet capable of forming more compact entities, and thus the heavier elements? Perhaps the Universe simply has to evolve the necessary degree of fine detail for larger atoms to become stable?

DN: Well, there's a testable prediction there. If the process is ongoing, we may find that atoms of a higher atomic number – those that are currently unstable – will become stable over time, and those that are prone to radioactive decay become less so. The timescales over which this might happen would be enormous, but go check it out. It'd throw radiocarbon dating values out...

AP: You've heard of the Angular-Size Distance Maximum?

DN: Sure. Remember I'm an astronomer, Adam. As we look out into space, objects at a certain distance cease to get increasingly small due to the effects of perspective, and instead begin to look larger.

AP: It's certainly counter-intuitive.

DN: I always thought so. But now it makes sense. The galaxies at a redshift of 1.6 are the smallest in the sense of having the smallest diameter in the sky, or angular size as viewed from Earth. Their redshift equates to a distance of, if memory serves, around 15 billion light years. We're looking back 15 billion years into the history of the Universe – that's how long the light has taken to get here. If galaxies at higher redshifts than this actually are larger - and this effect is not due to some observational effect - that's the point at which the diminishing effects of perspective lose out to the ever-larger objects of the early Universe.

AP: Direct observational evidence.

DN: Not only that, it should be possible to construct a curve from the available data that could be extrapolated back to the point where the size of the simplest particle would be equal to the size of the Universe...

AP: And thus give us another means to determine the size and age of the Universe.

DN: Don't forget to credit your co-authors.

AP: [laughs] Dana, keep it coming.

--- END TRANSCRIPT ---

[a / b / c / d / e / f / g / gif / h / hr / k / m / o / p / r / s / t / u / v / vg / vr / w / wg] [i / ic] [r9k] [s4s]
[vip] [cm / hm / lgbt / y] [3 / aco / adv / an / asp / biz / cgl / ck / co / diy / fa / fit / gd / hc / his / int /
jp / lit / mlp / mu / n / news / out / po / pol / qst / sci / soc / sp / tg / toy / trv / tv / vp / wsg / wsr / x]
[Edit] [Advertise on 4chan]
[Start a New Thread]
[Hide] [Show All]

Anonymous 05/09(Sat)16:55:59 No.16116010

Fuck off space niggers, we're full

You can crash on the moon if you want

11 KB JPG

Anonymous 05/09(Sat)17:32:27 No.161161161

>>16116010 #
God dammit I love 4chan

CONVERSATIONAL GAMBIT

"Talking to aliens. What could possibly go wrong?" Nixon's leg involuntarily twitched. He'd been standing immobile for longer than he remembered, watching Jack and Harriet prep the Oxbow. He sat down heavily on a crate. "What if we wake something that should have remained asleep?"

"We single-handedly fight off an alien invasion."

"What weapons do we have?"

"Our brilliant and unfettered creative minds."

Nixon snorted. *"Now* I'm worried. And—" He swept an arm. "This office is way too ramshackle to be the bridge of a battle cruiser."

Jack ran his eye down a column of figures. "Many wars of ideas have been fought sitting down."

Nixon was about to come back with a smart retort, but realised it was perfectly true – and further, that they had been won or lost from armchairs too. Jack stepped away from his keyboard and nodded at an unspoken question from Harriet. "Nixon, this is a ball game where not only do we have no idea what the rules are, but even whether there's a ball involved. I'm expecting symbols, but without any representational content we'd be familiar with. They may be abstract, mathematical; if we're lucky, they could be pictorial, like hieroglyphics. Just don't get your hopes up – the results we're about to get may look more like some weird White Cube art project than comprehensible language."

Harriet continued. "I think it's safe to assume these are individuals. They were – are – unique. They were born, grew up, learned, lived, maybe even chose this existence. They were – well, *people.* Maybe we'll get an inkling of their stories – who are they? Why are they here? Where did they come from?"

Harriet paused for dramatic effect. Nixon blew a raspberry.

Jack lifted his hands from his keyboard. "OK, let's run through our pre-flight checklist. Is the Oxbow failsafe activated?"

Harriet looked under her desk. She again had her foot wrapped around the main power lead. "Check."

Nixon was standing between Jack's and Harriet's crates. He felt a bit like Kirk, imperiously positioned between Sulu and the other crewman whose name he couldn't remember. Probably a Redshirt. Though who was the extraneous-to-needs Redshirt here, really? Nixon pushed the thought from his mind. "What about our DMEn friends? What do they think?"

Jack handed him his pair of Depthcharges. "Why don't you ask them? They're here too."

We're here, and we're along for the *ride,* my lady and gentlemen.

Girl, 21
@twentyone • 0m

⚙ ➕ Follow

ill bring snacks and soda #brb

↩ ⇄ ♥ •••

Nixon tightened the headstrap. "You know, this reminds me of the first time some friends and I connected to the internet. A bunch of kids, pooling their pocket money for a cheap USRobotics Sportster modem. We got it connected, booted Netscape, and there's that vertical line blinking in a box like a magic pen on a piece of magic paper. It was asking us – *what do you want to see?*"

"What did you type?"

There was a pregnant pause. Nixon suddenly wished he hadn't begun this anecdote.

"We typed 'Boobs'."

Harriet shrieked with glee. Jack slapped the side of his crate.

"We were *fourteen.* Come *on.* What do you *think* we typed?"

"Yes, Harriet, what did you type the first time you had access to the world and all its cultural riches?"

"Ahah. Ha. *Snfft.* Me? I— I searched for reviews of Sartre's *Nausea.* I was reading Simone de—"

"*Bollocks* you did."

"OK, OK." Harriet held up her hands. "It was *Princess Gwenevere and the Jewel Riders.* A cartoon. Loosely based on Arthurian legend, in my defence. I was into English myth. Enchanted jewels. Avalon. Queen with evil twin sister."

Nixon was looking at Harriet with an engaged smile. "What's not to love?"

"It had a theme song, and my friend Kim and I always argued over the lyrics. We wanted to find out who was right. *'When destiny calls, together as friends, we'll get through it all. The sun and the moon, will show us the way. With love in your heart, come join us today! Something, something – Princess Gwenevere and the Jewel Riders!'"*

Nixon was relieved no one had thought to ask what the second thing he had searched for might have been. "That can be our backing track. *'Jewel Power, we got it, Jewel Powahhh!'"*

Harriet had gone a subtle shade of magenta. "'Hell', as Sartre rightly said, 'is other people.'"

Jack waved a sheaf of printouts. "We have a whole new zoo of characters for Sartre to hate right here. Now – we, my friends, are going alien-hunting."

Nixon cocked an imaginary rifle. "To begin, I vote we pick one that at least *looks* benign."

"Xenophobe." Harriet ran her finger down a printout. "I made a shortlist from Jack's longlist. I looked at the catalogue of aliens, the one Estelle Perry and her crowdsourced SetiOnEarth@home project have been putting together. The images people have posted on it are all from Earthbound perspectives, of course – it only includes creatures you can see with Depthcharges if you happen to be standing somewhere on the Earth's surface. The glasses don't work with telescopes – that'd be like looking at a TV with binoculars and expecting to see further into the picture. But people have been very creative, very thorough. We have photos taken from skyscrapers, bridges, ships. A lot of the deserts in North Africa and the Middle East have been criss-crossed by off-the-peg drones. The shots they take are all geotagged, and can be overlaid on Google Earth. There's an entire fleet of Google Cars driving around. There's also a privately funded project in which several boats are criss-crossing the Pacific taking 360-degree panoramas and uploading what they see into the database. These efforts are incomplete and only cover a fraction of the Grid, but we're still spoiled for choice."

She riffled a sheaf of A3. "So, these are all creatures Jack first isolated in the Grid because there was something interesting about their iteration of the Signal. I have screen grabs of each here, so we can see what they look like. They're all locals too, chosen for their close proximity."

"Alien Tinder," Nixon observed.

"Perry's catalogue also tags them by anatomical traits. I only picked those that look reasonably friendly. No armour-plating. No razor-sharp claws. No exaggerated sexual characteristics. Bland, inoffensive, vanilla-looking aliens is what we want, at least to start with."

She flipped over the first sheet. "So, up for your consideration, ladies and gents, is Alien One. A bit pink around the – the gills, it has droopy flappy things and a face like a punched cantaloupe. If that *is* a face, and not the other end. None of us here are qualified xenobiologists, so who can tell.

"Next: Alien Two. Furry. Cuddly, even. Could do with a brush. Looks like it's gotten a bit tangled up, covered in knots. Though that could be an ethnic hairstyle. We shall henceforth check our privilege. Bit of an underbite. Who are we to judge. Colourful too – it looks like it's been wrapped in bunting.

"Alien Three. Oooh, this may be the favourite. You like dolphins? Everyone likes dolphins! Dolphins are smiley and friendly. And this one looks a tiny bit like a dolphin. Fins, tail. Or maybe a mermaid.

"Alien Four has a shell. Big and shiny and covered in spots and lozengy-shaped things. It'd look a bit like a cockroach if it didn't have two legs and stand upright. Smile for the camera, Alien Four – oh, you don't have a mouth. Maybe you can give us a wave. Ah, you don't have arms either.

"Alien Five: now you've really got me stumped. You look like a test card. Or a Bridget Riley painting. You seem to be a free-floating point of energy radiating rays or beams of light, with a kind of diffraction grating sparkle effect. Multicoloured interference fringes – that really is quite beautiful, actually. Might give you a migraine after prolonged exposure. One for the arthouse fans." She leafed through a few more, then passed the sheaf over to Jack.

"Thanks, Harriet. Now, unlike the DMEn, these aliens can't come to us. We have to go to them. But we should be able to look at them from all sides, up close. I'll be out in the field, sending the visual feed back here to you two. You'll be here, isolating and manipulating the raw code, the specific Signal iteration that relates to the chosen creature, trying to see if we can skim off any sensible information, while I keep an eye on the creature itself in case whatever you're doing has an effect. The Grid is in what Dana Normansson calls lockdown, but we shouldn't take any chances – we don't want to find we're inadvertently poking it with a digital cattle prod. Harriet will be manning – sorry, womanning – the failsafe."

"Too right."

"Now, the Oxbow, in tandem with the glasses, was previously processing both onomatopoeic sounds – background noises, non-language – and that made by our DMEn friends. We know the kind of results we've achieved there, but they all speak English."

Harriet coughed. "Or a close approximation thereof."

"With the Chomsky Module and the Oxbow, we hope to get a Depthcharge render of the – the sounds, the data, the light modulations, whatever orthography the alien may use. Maybe some grammar, some residue of syntax. This will, almost by necessity, still have a degree of human—" Jack waved a hand vaguely – "post-processing. We may see some borrowed or repurposed forms.

"Now, our aliens are asleep, so my assumption is that they won't actually be talking to us; we can't ask questions and get answers. But perhaps we can take a thin shaving from their language and memory centres."

They looked at each other. Then, as one, they burst out laughing at the absurdity of it all.

Jack managed to compose himself. "No, no. *It may just work.* Honestly. We don't know until we try."

"OK, OK. Go for it." Nixon held open the door and gestured to the stairs that led to the world outside the office. "Call us when you're at the first location."

Jack put his Depthcharges and laptop in his messenger bag and entered the first of the geotagged locations into Google Maps on his iPhone. He squinted at the screen. "Ah. Commercial Street. Five minutes. Give me five minutes." He paused in the doorway and looked back over his shoulder. "Let's see what our friends have to say for themselves."

Looping pink hair behind a shifting ear that seemed to be attached side on like a cubist Dora Maar, Girl 21 bent over to examine Jack's first subject, the top printout on the pile.

Girl, 21
@twentyone • 0m

that one has a penis

Parameter	Notation	Value
Semi-major axis	a	6378137.0 meters
Flattening factor of Earth	1/f	298.257223563
Nominal mean angular velocity of Earth	ω	7292115 x 10^{-11} radians/second
Geocentric Gravitational Constant (inc. mass of Earth's atmosphere)	GM	3.986004418 x 10^{14} meter^3/second^2

INTELLIGENCIA | Oxbow test build 4.55a | Run 4 12:15PM | WGS | Dataset location: Lat: 51°37'14"N Long: 0°04'48"W Distance: 6.4013 mi

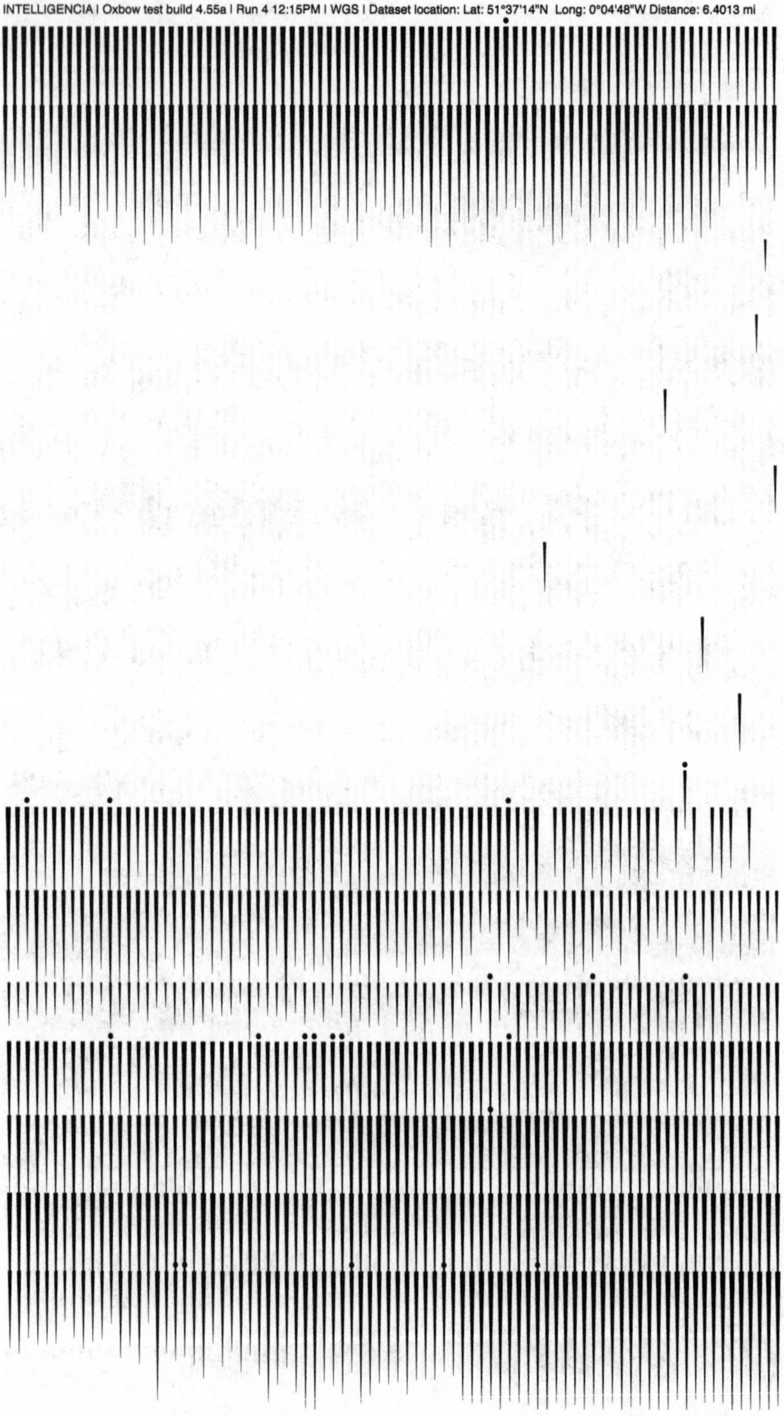

INTELLIGENCIA | Oxbow test build 4.55a | Run 9 4.10PM | WGS | Dataset location: Lat: 51°32'59"N Long: 0°02'57"E Dist: 5.7836 mi

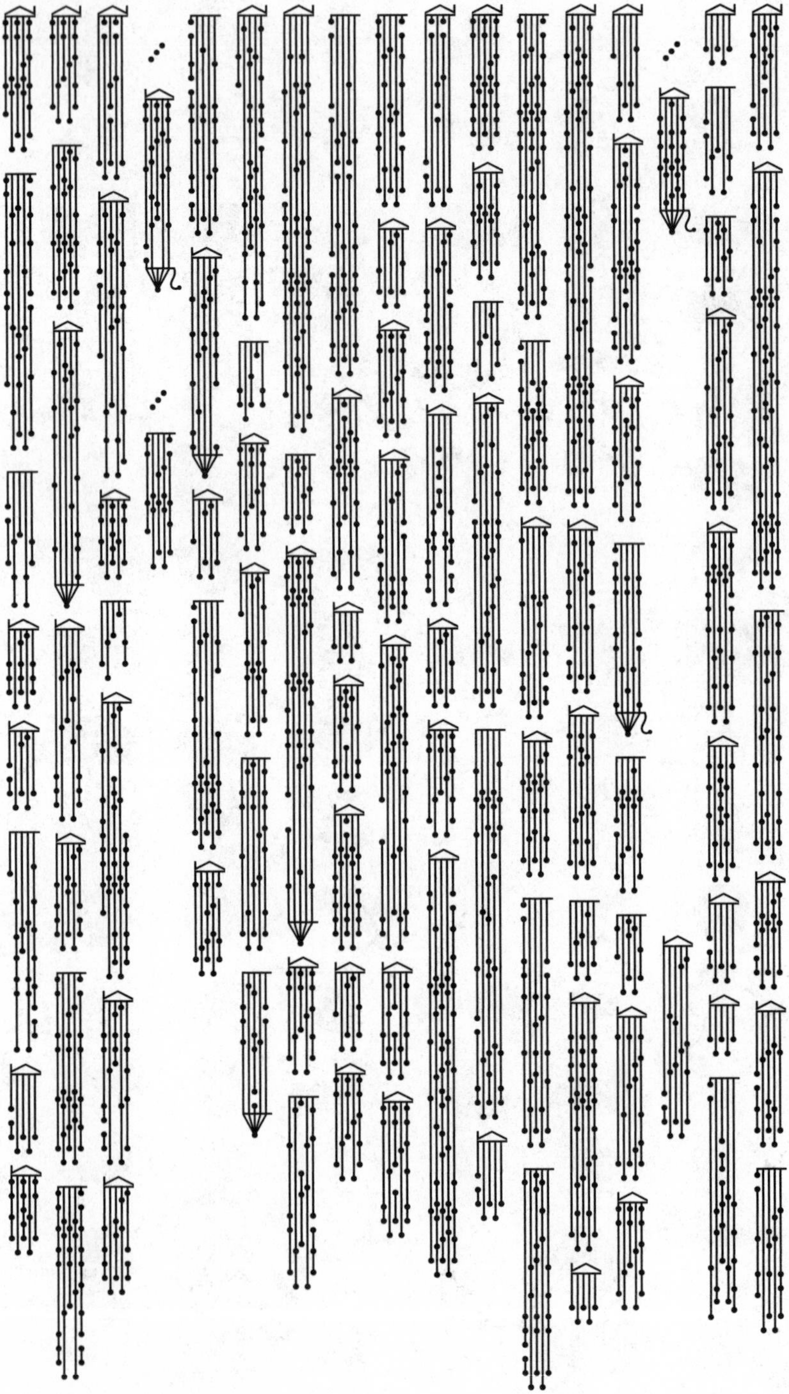

INTELLIGENCIA I Oxbow test build 4.55a I Run 9 4.10PM I WGS I Dataset location: Lat: 51°32'59"N Long: 0°02'57"E Dist: 5.7836 mi

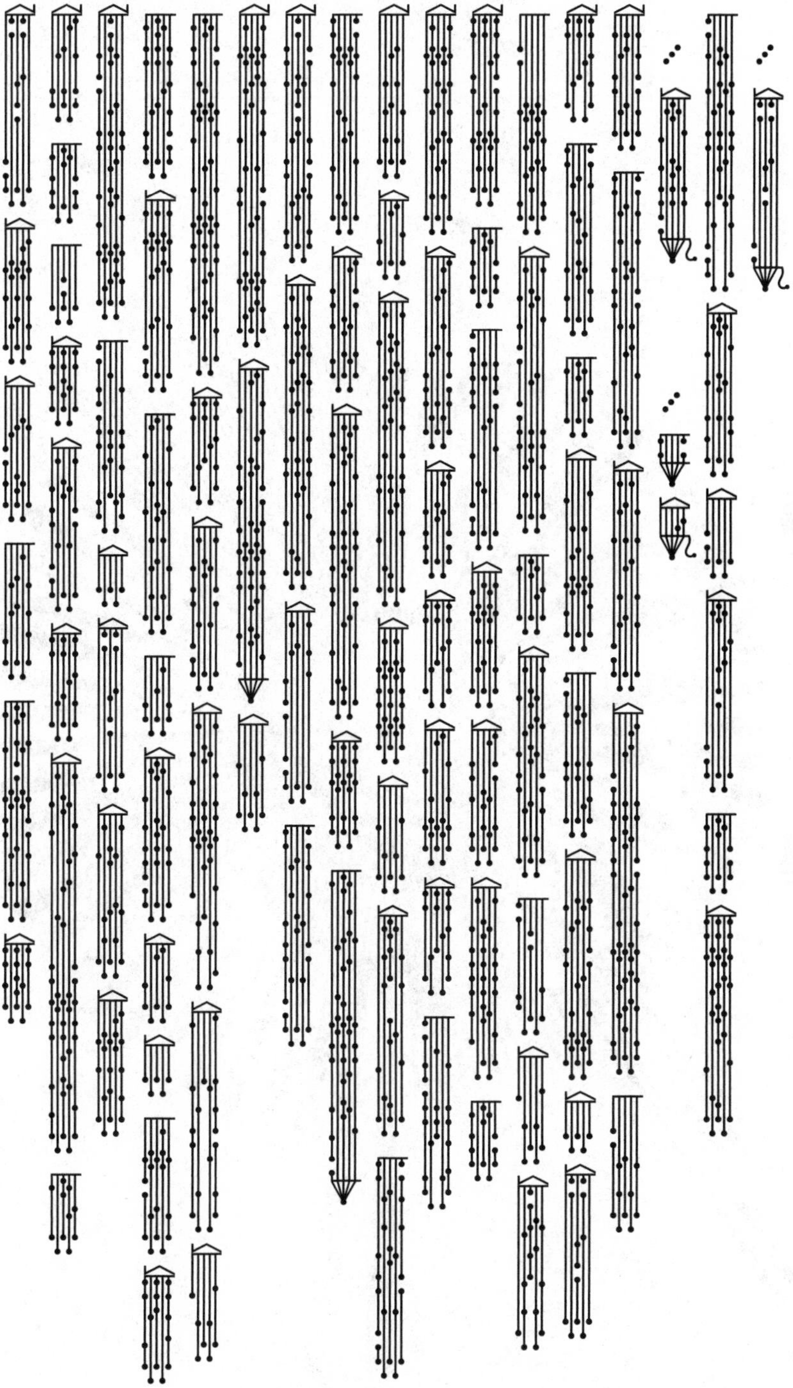

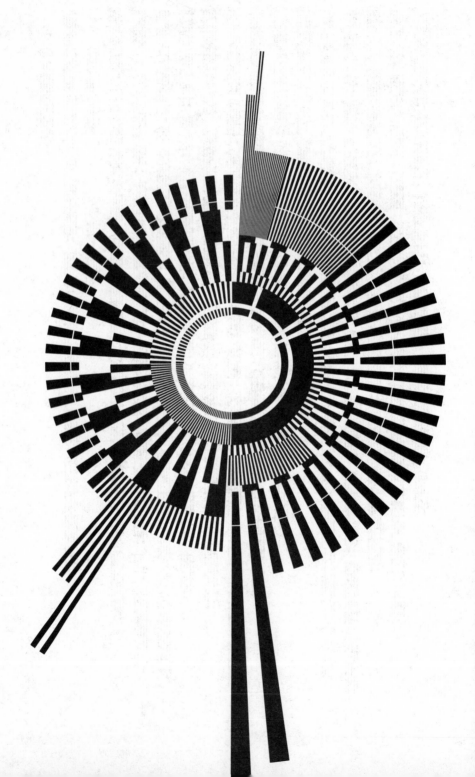

INTELLIGENCIA | Oxbow test build 4.55a | Run 11 4.22PM | WGS | Dataset location: Lat: 51°30'01"N Long: 0°09'38"W Dist: 3.926 mi

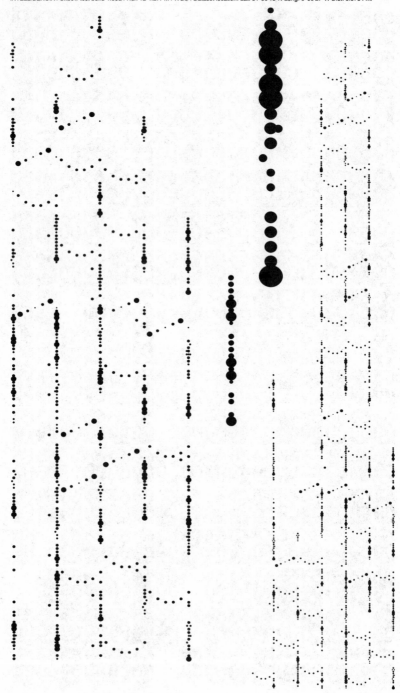

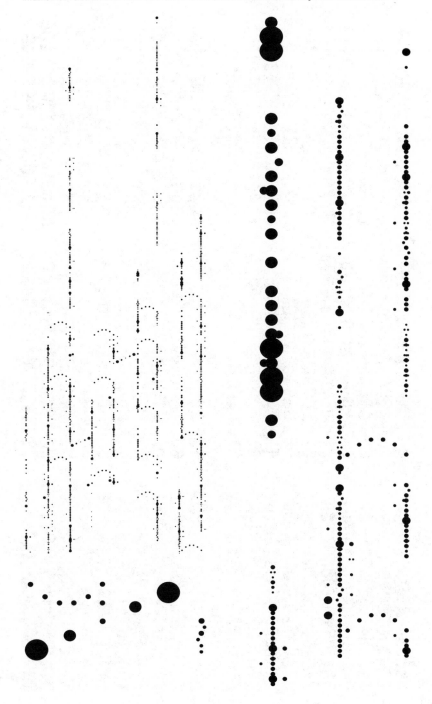

INTELLIGENCIA I Oxbow test build 4.55a I Run 21 6.11PM I WGS I Dataset location: Lat: 51°31'56"N Long: 0°00'47"W Dist: 2.9326 mi

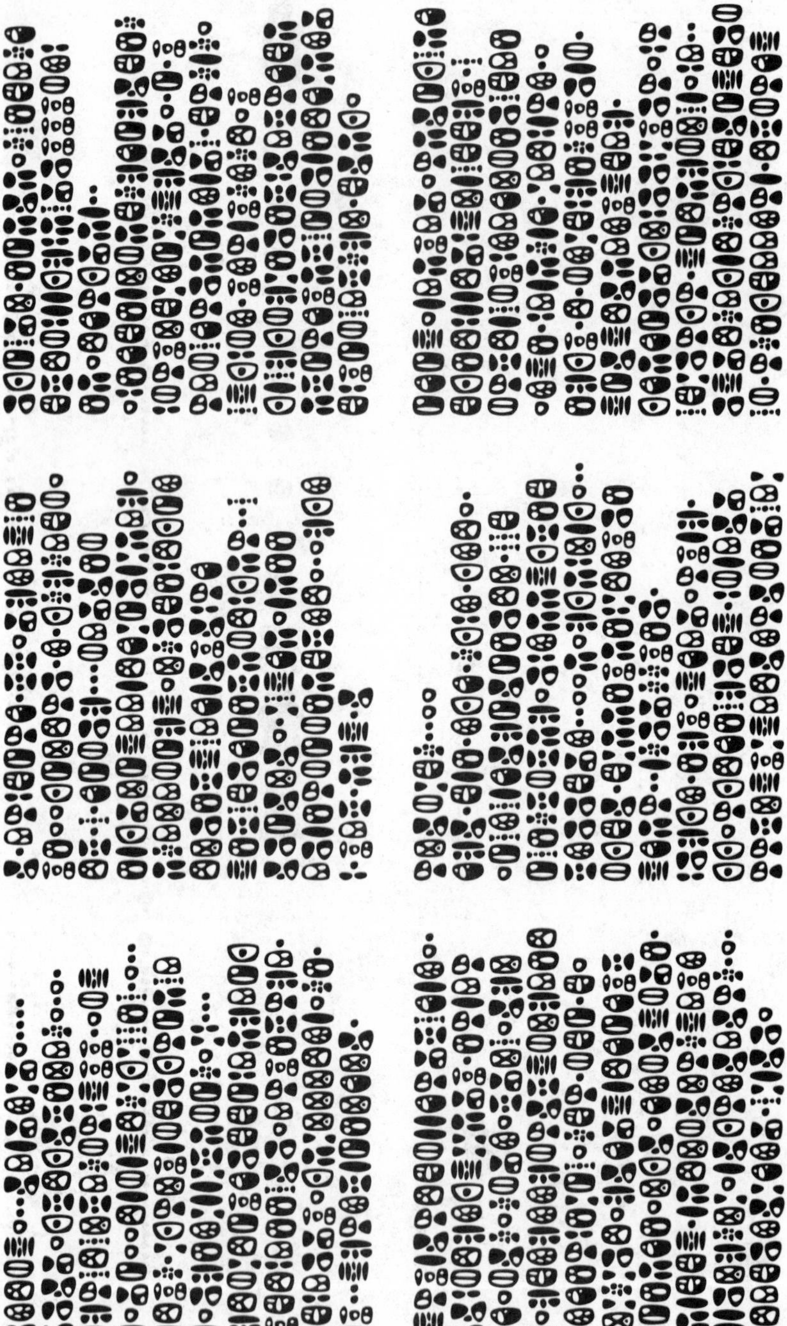

INTELLIGENCIA | Oxbow test build 4.55a | Run 21 6.11PM | WGS | Dataset location: Lat: 51°31'56"N Long: 0°00'47"W Dist: 2.9326 mi

JACK CORES AN APPLE

"Well, they're certainly pretty." Harriet lifted the corner of one of the new Chomsky Module printouts, now taped along the edge of the shelf over which the 3D figures presided. "Jack?"

"Pretty? I guess so. Gotta say, I think I have a tone-deaf eye. Nadine's the one to ask when it comes to aesthetics. Hm. This may be way more complicated than we anticipated. Worse than Rongorongo." Jack pushed his crate back. "We now have a visual representation. But we still don't have anything we can understand. Can *you* read them?"

Harriet had microwaved a bowl of porridge and was now eating it while standing just behind Jack's shoulder. "Nope. No clue. We have decent voice-recognition software, but it relies on heuristics and deep learning from big data sets to accurately convert sounds into words, and – most importantly – the designers already know what they want the end result to be. They have something they can check the results against."

"And all this running around. We're not going to cover much ground. There must be an easier way." He could see her reflection in the black glass frame of his monitor screen. Breakfast was now taken at the office while dealing with the morning's email backlog. The time saved, they had found, was offset by sticky keyboard keys.

"I sense there's a 'but' here . . ."

"Well, an 'and' actually. If I look at the Grid in its purely digital form, it's hard to get a sense of the overall shape of it. You look at columns and columns of text, as all the people who have been trying to interpret the Signal do, and there's just too much of it. But arranged as we know it to be – in the Grid – several things do become apparent."

"Go on."

"We had assumed that the Grid is isomorphic – as here, so there."

Harriet nodded. "As above, so below. Though there are those voids, the missing sections, our Shepherds arranged throughout—"

"Apart from those, we assume that the Grid is still uniform on larger scales. I'm not sure it is."

"How so?"

"Can you bring up the Signal? In its original form. As received."

"Sure." Harriet passed her bowl to her left hand and brought up the entire data set. The small inset window on her monitor that carried the view from her Depthcharges hung around her neck looped the view back, repeating it to infinity. She grimaced and minimised it. "What are we looking for? It's not immediately obvious from the numbers themselves ... but it looks as if the density is pretty even, overall. Less dense towards the periphery. Sections missing, though I assume the voids are mostly transmission loss. The Earth simply was not in the right position to pick up the entire Signal."

"Look closer."

"There's . . . there's a hole through the southern section, a void we can see exiting in the South China Sea that goes as high into the periphery of the Grid as I've managed to look, rectangular in cross-section. It's like someone pushed a length of two-by-four through the lattice there, knocking out an entire district." A pause. "This, we think, was caused by the transit of Jupiter."

Jack passed his hand in front of her screen. "So— what if the Grid has other distinct structures within it? A *geography*, if you like. I'd like to know how we could map it visually."

Harriet blew a strand of hair from her eyes. "Sure. But how? We only have access to the parts that just happen to fall on or near the surface of the Earth, and also happen to be on land rather than out at sea, not in a war zone, the middle of a Siberian forest, or up a mountain in Nepal. Basically, it's got to be a place we can practically travel to, and as our funds are not limitless, that probably rules out anywhere that isn't in Great Britain or somewhere that EasyJet flies to. Any point in the Grid that we can't reach physically is inaccessible. And that's the vast bulk of it."

"What we have here is yet another problem of translation."

"*Translation?* Not sure I understand. You're the language and cryptography geek, Jack."

"A *spatial* translation. A function that moves a point or set of points in space a specified distance in a specified direction. In order to explore the Grid, we need a way to get to the parts that are unreachable because they're somewhere remote, or underground, or out in space. Instead of us running around St Paul's or scaring the locals out in Hoxton Square, we need to find a way to bring the Grid *to us*."

Jack watched Harriet run her spoon around the circumference of the bowl. "OK, genius. What do you suggest?" Jack could barely hear her through a mouthful of porridge.

"Run with me a while on this. Here's what we do know. The Grid is not fixed in space. We do not pass through it as the Earth rotates or revolves around the Sun—"

"Or as the Solar System revolves around the Galactic Centre."

"Exactly. So it's stationary *with respect to our position*. What does that tell us?"

Harriet waved her spoon in lieu of saying something insightful.

Jack continued. "It's not stationary with respect to our position because it knows the Earth is there – it doesn't. Most of the creatures are below sea level, frying in the interior of the planet, or floating out in translunar space eating cosmic rays, oblivious to wherever the ground may be. But because the Grid is *information*, and information is stored on *mainframes—*"

"And, since the leak, countless personal computers, laptops and smartphones."

"—because that silicon substrate rotates with the Earth—"

"So does the Grid."

"Correct. And we can't move the Grid because we can't move the internet."

"And we can't move the Earth."

"No, we can't . . ." Jack felt the gears in his head begin to grind. "But— It doesn't *directly* know where those mainframes are. It's a deduction, based on a number of inputs."

Harriet's spoon stopped waving. "And inputs can always be adjusted."

Jack began to grin. "So, if the Grid thinks it's yesterday, it will be offset from the centre of the planet by the distance the Earth travels in twenty-four hours along its orbit, which—" Jack pulled up a couple of web pages. "The Earth travels around the Sun at thirty kilometres a second. The diameter of Earth is 12,500 kilometres, more or less, so it covers two million kilometres in just one day, which equates to 166 Earth diameters."

Harriet frowned. "I see a flaw here. We don't have access to these mainframes. Even *I* can't simultaneously hack into each and every computer that the internet runs on to adjust their master clocks . . . can *you?*"

"No. Though I like the fact that you sounded as if you thought it was a genuine possibility. Of course we can't. *But—*" Jack was wearing that Jack expression of unfettered enthusiasm that Harriet had got to like so much. He began to gesticulate. "But, my dear Harriet, we *don't need to*. The part of the Grid that matters to us is just the part that falls within the Oxbow. We don't *need* to rotate the entire Grid, just our local, isolated section. We don't have to adjust the clocks of remote mainframes – we just have to adjust the clock *inside the Oxbow*."

Harriet absently let her spoon clatter into the bowl.

"That— that might just work. That is weapons-grade, A-plus, gold-plated Jack Fenwick genius."

Jack opened a TextEdit document and began copying and pasting numbers. "In fact, just an 8.6-minute offset into the future or the past is enough to shift the Grid the diameter of the Earth. The Grid is much larger than that, of course – at least half the distance to the Moon – but we can easily shift forward or back around the circle of the Earth's orbit. That first step gives us an addressable cylindrical volume that penetrates the Grid like a cored apple. And for an encore—"

Jack swept a pile of books and papers onto the floor and picked up a pen and a fresh sheet of A3 printer paper and began to sketch out a diagram. "Step two. Rotating the Grid." Nixon had arrived some minutes earlier without either of them noticing and was now attempting to get up to speed. A look of intense concentration had freeze-framed his face.

"The Grid, of course, co-rotates with the Earth every twenty-four hours." Jack brought up the system preferences, then the date and time settings. "Tweaking the time of day gives us access to a complete circular slice through the Earth at our latitude. But, I hear you cry—" Jack paused. There was only silence. "But that doesn't bring the areas above or below our specific latitude within reach. To access those, an equatorial/polar shift is required. We need to tilt the axis of the Earth."

Harriet tilted her head and raised an eyebrow. "As you do."

"And here's the hack, lady and gentleman. *Location.* If I reset our position to, say, Kuala Lumpur, or any other city in the list they've helpfully provided, I've instantly moved Hoxton to the tropics, effectively rolling the planet onto its side."

"*That's it?*"

"That's it. It's almost *too* easy." Jack looked pleased with himself. "Now we just have to fine-tune these variables and we can move the Grid in any direction we choose through the Oxbow. We can address *any location* within it, even the vast volumes out in space or towards the centre of the planet. We can reposition it so that any point in it will intersect, to a very high degree of precision, with any point we choose here on the surface of the Earth. This room, for example. We can effectively bring any location in the Grid *right here.*"

Harriet had her arms round Jack's shoulders. "You are astounding."

"Aren't I? Change the values in real time, and it'd be like *driving* through the Grid. We could visit the periphery, out in space. We could drop down through its layers, like an archaeologist."

Nixon found his voice. "We could find out what sits at the very centre."

Document: (NS//82//DB)
Subject: Daedalus Base "Encounter"
Debrief interviews, 107 of 128

The information contained in this report is to be treated as Most Secret
Location: [removed. Assumed to be the Apollo Isolation chamber "Hornet+3",
Lyndon B. Johnson Space Center]

Note: Some responses have been edited, and are summaries of what was
actually stated.
Details in square brackets are added for clarity. Please refer to
audiovisual recordings, available on request.
Document history: v 1.5. Submitted for review and comment
Date: [removed]

Present:
Dana Normansson (hereafter DN), Cmdr., Daedalus Base
Adam Parker (hereafter AP), sup. offcr
Gabriel (Gabe) Bowen (hereafter GB), press liaison
Other support staff, medical staff [names removed]

AP: It's not like this?
DN: What? I asked if you knew when I could come out.
AP: We have more questions.
DN: I could sit here and answer questions all day, every day for the rest of
my life, and I wouldn't have told you a fraction of what I now know, what I
have in my head. There has to be a better way.
AP: Bear with us. Please.
[pause]
AP: We want some – we would like to get more details on the occupants of the
Grid. The possible dangers the creatures in it might pose. Their biology,
technology, ideology. Strengths, weaknesses.
DN: You're putting together a plan?
AP: It's been made very clear to us by certain, um, officials that we have
to be prepared for any eventuality. They want us to focus on what they call
useful intelligence. They seem to be somewhat less interested in esoteric
matters of cosmic evolution than I might have hoped. I can understand their
priorities. I get it, I do. Our protection. It's what they're there for.
[pause]
AP: Can you tell me about the ship? I assume your friend had an intimate
knowledge of its operation.
DN: He– yes. Let me– I'll see what I can make sense of.
AP: We have some experts on hand who you can talk to about–
DN: No, I'm good. I just have to unpack it all as I go. The spindle, the
ship. It's powered by two inertial masses mined from the surface of a

- 566 -

neutron star and separated by a virtually incompressible rod of matter a fraction of a millimeter thick.

AP: A neutron star. [loud exhalation] Go on.

DN: You've not been able to get to the ship?

AP: It's not exactly easy to get to. Not only is it on the far side of the Moon, it's at the bottom of a shaft that our rangefinders tell us is at least sixty kilometers deep. That takes us into the upper mantle. We can't exactly dig it out with spades.

DN: I'm glad I didn't fall in.

AP: The crew at Daedalus tried lowering a camera down. That didn't get very far. Even if we had a cable long enough, very quickly it wouldn't be strong enough to support its own weight, even in one-sixth gravity. So we sent down a drone. There's a fair bit of heat coming up, and we lost the first around the ten-kilometer mark because it simply wasn't built for such environments. A second, shielded drone built to withstand prolonged exposure to hard radiation made it down as far as twenty-two kilometers before it failed. You know how expensive it is to ship equipment to the Moon, especially the kind of custom-built kit we now have on the drawing board. We've been trying to improvise with what we have up there already.

DN: OK.

AP: Here's- There's something we don't understand. There's a point in the shaft, just below the fourteen-kilometer mark, still well within the upper crust, at which gravity begins to decrease. It's a subtle effect, but it's there. That's not the only peculiar thing we've discovered. We see no reason why the shaft shouldn't be the same diameter all the way down, but the readings- The readings don't add up. The resolution degrades with depth, but even so our radar data seems to tell us that below fifty kilometers the shaft opens out. To a diameter that - well, let's just say that makes no sense.

DN: That's news to me too. Let me think about this a moment.

AP: Sure.

DN: Can I talk to the relief crew? The guys now at Daedalus?

AP: That may not be possible. You are a very valuable-

DN: I was up there. I practically built the base with my own hands. I may be able to help.

AP: I'd prefer to discuss the craft. We'd like to know how it functions. [pause]

DN: OK. Let me... The ship. It's- interesting. It doesn't have an engine, as such. The best way to describe how it travels is that it <u>falls</u>. It plummets down a steep incline of space-time towards its destination.

AP: We were thinking some kind of negative mass-

DN: Not negative mass. I - my friend - has no knowledge of such a thing, though framing the concept clearly enough to see if there's some kind of memory match isn't easy. Anyway, if there was, wouldn't it all be out in intergalactic space, as far away from anything else as possible? But gravity - hah. The value of 'G' is not constant! It seems that gravity is an emergent property of this densification and rarefaction I spoke of earlier. It's analogous to a standing wave centered on a particular body with a wavelength the size of the gravitational influence. It's the large-scale, attenuated version of the same process in which energy confined to a tiny location forms a particle.

AP: You say 'G' is variable?

DN: Yep. In our current model, convex gravitational wells describe the local acceleration due to gravity, small 'g'. We experience big 'G' as a constant because in our local volume of space-time the gradient changes so incrementally it's indistinguishable from a fixed value. Like looking at a vastly enlarged section of a curve and assuming it's a straight line.

AP: So you're saying it changes as—

DN: Picture two widely spaced massive objects— OK, think of it this way. Imagine standing on a mattress. Your feet press down into the mattress. These are the gravity wells produced by massive objects. So far, so standard cosmology. But between your feet, the mattress bulges up above the baseline - the usual height of the mattress - to form an area of negative gravity. Voilà - repellent space. Anything here will roll down off the top of the hill and into the valley, leaving the bubble-shaped voids we see on very large-scale models of the Universe.

AP: Daniel will like this.

DN: There's more. I'll write down as much as I can. He owes me.

[pause]

AP: The drive? Does it use these principles?

DN: The drive— So, by placing two very heavy masses - neutron star material, say, a certain distance apart—

AP: I'll put in an order.

DN: [laughs] This produces a raised bump of space-time between them. A small hill, a kink. If they are of equal mass, and free to move in any direction, a shift in the center of gravity of the whole - towards one or other of the masses - will propel the vehicle in that direction, and the more pronounced the shift, the faster the velocity. The ship effectively falls down the local gradient it creates. By trimming the yaw, it's even possible to steer—

AP: Sounds like riding a wave.

DN: The steepness of the gradient - the acceleration, in other words - is a product of the two masses multiplied by their separation, up to a theoretical maximum for a given combined mass above which they become too heavy to keep apart or too far apart to effectively cause any pinching. So the speed is limited only by the practicality of the masses involved and the separation achievable. It effectively compresses space in front of the ship while expanding it behind; the ship is not powered in itself, but moves forward by altering the geometry of space around it. At maximum acceleration, it effectively falls vertically down a steep space-time incline at a vastly increased value of 'G'. The incline is reduced to achieve a deceleration when nearing the destination. Strictly speaking, you're not travelling faster than light - you're just bringing the distant close to hand.

AP: Reeling in the stars.

DN: The spindle is threaded on the bracing structure that holds the two masses apart. The masses are naturally attracted towards each other, so the connecting structure needs to be made of very dense and rigid material - this is the filament I saw. Once the ship is in motion the bump in space-time produces a force strong enough to increase the separation of the masses a thousandfold, even up to several light minutes, though these large separations create time dilation effects that generate unwanted torque. When the ship is at rest the masses are held apart by centrifugal force, generated by spinning the ship laterally many hundreds of times a second.

AP: Like a saucer!

DN: Like a flying saucer. What else? It obviously has to generate a larger effect to climb out of a gravity well than to fall into one, and there are gravity gradients that this particular ship can't climb at all.

AP: This particular ship. So we don't have a Porsche, we have a Morris Minor?

DN: This is a small, one-person affair. There exist many ships the size of cities, even larger. Using this method, they have moved planets, and even nudged stars.

AP: Woo.

DN: A journey of many thousands of light years can be made in a matter of weeks measured by internal ship time, that mostly being the acceleration and deceleration phases. As the ship is effectively in freefall for the duration, it experiences no internal disequilibrium - indeed, it would be possible to play billiards throughout.

AP: Two masses. The ship crashed—

DN: I saw the filament that connects them, remember? My guess is that now the masses have become tethered to the Moon, instead of moving forwards it's pulling space-time back towards it instead.

AP: And this is causing the distortions we see?

DN: It seems the most likely cause. My friend in my head, knowledgeable as he is, is no real expert in this department. Can you precisely describe how your car engine works? And this is not something that as far as I can surmise has happened before. You want my guess?

AP: Sure.

DN: The trailing mass might still be in geostationary orbit, some distance above the lunar surface and directly above the vehicle's entry point — the crash site. It will not be easy to spot as it's no larger than a baseball, but if the drive is still active I would calculate that it has reeled in five to seven light years of space behind it, reducing it to an effective distance of four to six kilometers.

AP: And this is causing the distortion we see deep underground?

DN: [nods]

[pause]

DN: As it's aligned along the Earth-Moon axis, my guess is that there will also be a small but measurable change in the Moon's orbit.

[A 15-minute break where AP exits the room, then returns.]

AP: I've asked for confirmation on that.

Can your friend tell us how to build a ship like this?

[pause]

DN: That's strange.

[pause]

DN: My friend... understands the basic principles, but avers that the ship itself was not of his species' construction. They trade certain, uh,

cultural artefacts with an intermediary in exchange for the craft, for
their provision and maintenance. He also... Hm. He's pretty sure that the
procurement of this neutron star material is well beyond the scope of the
technological ability of any of the races in the Grid.
AP: So it comes from a race outside the Grid? One not incorporated?
DN: There are many known species that have not been incorporated, but
it's not one of those, either. The original builders of the craft are not
documented. My friend is of the opinion that the ships were built by a
culture no longer in existence. No race has yet been encountered who claim
to have built the ships themselves, though several are proficient in their
use and upkeep. There's speculation that they originated with a forerunner
race, one no longer extant in the volume of the galaxy that the Grid has
encompassed, and were left behind after it vanished or retreated. There
are... theories. There seem to be a limited number of iterations of the
craft's basic form, with no new innovations in recorded history - that would
tend to support the idea that there are no new ships currently being built.
Others maintain that the markings on the sides of the craft, which match no
known linguistic form, point to an extragalactic origin - though there is,
of course, no way to prove this.
AP: From outside the Milky Way?
DN: Theoretically, there is no reason why these ships could not be used
to navigate intergalactic spaces. The distances involved, however, are
mind-boggling - the journey time to Andromeda, for example, is two and a
half million years at light speed. That's a five million year round trip,
undilated. If any sentient being tried to make the journey, it'd be a very
long time before you found out if they'd been successful.

--- END TRANSCRIPT ---

Misplaced Sentiment Will Not Protect Us

Brendan Fitzroy

The introductions are barely over and Asha Chifuniro, neuroscientist, anthropologist and author of *We Come in Peace?*, is already pushing back against the social media campaigners who have vilified her as a "neocon", a "xenophobe" and even a "fascist". Since the book's publication, she tells me she has had to develop a thick skin, and fast: "These terms are bandied around simply as a way to avoid engaging with the facts – to shut down the debate before it has even started."

A rush in the US to stockpile food and ammunition and a rise in gun sales has been blamed on her "scaremongering". Oft quoted by self-styled survivalists, it's still a debate she is passionate about bringing to the public sphere. Having been "disinvited" from last week's symposium on the cultural impact of the travellers at Conway Hall, Bloomsbury, after tweets came to light in which she compared the visitors to "invaders", there has been a concerted campaign by activists to discredit her. Now, Chifuniro is on the counter-attack. "I'm not here to simply vilify those that may be different from us – as the daughter of immigrants, I know only too well what that is like first hand."

I ask her what she makes of the furore. "I think some people confuse how they wish the world was with how it actually is. It's naive to assume that these creatures are benign. Some may be, some may not. That's something that cosseted Islington dinner-party debaters simply don't understand. What's sorely needed is a case-by-case analysis of the species in the signal, and how their presence may have consequences for us, our culture and our children. Does that sound like a blanket condemnation to you?"

She has sought to distance herself from her infamous "pull the plug" comment, caught when a microphone was left on during a soundcheck at a Berlin counter-demonstration. In an unlikely allegiance, the phrase has become a rallying call of alt-right provocateurs who see the Signal as the advance shock-troops of an alien invasion, and far-left anti-globalists who blame unchecked corporate capitalism. With visible exasperation she explains that the comment was intended as a "last resort". Acknowledging the economic damage that shutting down the Internet would cause, she has since stated that she does not think that it is even possible. "The Internet is a distributed system – there is no single off-switch."

She is quick to mention the work of biologist Richard Linwood, who has studied the visitors' anatomy in detail. "Inherent in the aliens, as in all animals, is a survival instinct. Faced with an alien race that has been uprooted from its home planet but still needs to eat, to reproduce, to live, but no longer has the means or opportunity to do so, we have to assume that it may do anything to survive, and may not factor in human life or the future of our planet in the process. I agree with Richard that some of the creatures exhibit features that look like they evolved not in the benign environment of the university debating chamber, but in the life-or-death fight for survival in a vastly different alien ecosystem."

She is unapologetic in her use of the term "creatures", which some in this acrimonious debate see as loaded, or even derogatory. "The creatures may not share other deeply human values such as compassion and empathy, those very values which my opponents are so quick to champion but claim that I do not have. I hope they are correct – that by exhibiting welcoming behaviour, we will see it reciprocated – but I think this may be wishful thinking." That there are many on the fringes of the far right that would agree, and are pushing for an immediate and robust response, goes unsaid.

Chifuniro's position has been described as inverted colonialism: the idea that the visitors are, almost by definition, imperialistic, and that given our history we now fear we are on the receiving end; that we are, in effect, projecting our own biases upon them in order to maintain our cultural hegemony. She counters that this is simply the surrender of reason to emotion, empowered by a counter-narrative where the visitors are cast as victims, powerless in the face of those portrayed as powerful. "Victim and oppressor. These simplistic polarising labels are not applicable in this case," she asserts.

She may have a point. ∎

A new take on gravity may banish dark matter while opening up new fields of enquiry

By Reg Mytton

Gravity as landscape

It's not often that a venerable constant of nature comes up for reassessment, but that's exactly what Daniel Novák, Jodrell Bank's director, has in mind: "'G' may be a variable." According to Novák, the distribution of its value through space can be described as a "gravity landscape".

There has recently been a flurry of papers from the tight-knit team in the UK that includes Novák, George Pallenberg, Leonie Orlov and their US colleagues at a presently undisclosed location. This foreign team is said to include several other well-known astronomers, and to utilise new results from the rumoured but still not officially acknowledged radio telescope on the Lunar far side.

Hills and valleys

Novák and his colleagues' paper attempts to recast our understanding of the force that shapes the Universe on the largest scales. According to the team, gravity, far from being a constant, is a series of "valleys" in which matter tends to collect – the filaments and clusters seen on large-scale models of galaxy distribution – and "hilltops", the voids or bubbles where matter is scarce.

Dark matter was evoked to explain this anomaly. Embedding a galaxy in a much larger halo of invisible exotic material that only interacts through gravity preserved the value of G as a constant.

A galaxy in a bowl

Gravity is unusual in only exhibiting a positive – that is to say, attractive – value. The landscape model provides an explanation of the shape and behaviour of galaxies without recourse to exotic new particles, and without the requirement for matter with a negative mass.

so, it is possible that very sensitive measurements may still reveal a gradient, for example in the expected and measured positions of the Voyager probes.

On larger scales, agglomerations of matter – solar systems, galaxies and galaxy clusters – are mostly empty space. As the mass they contain is distributed over such a large area, the gravity landscape is shaped like a bowl, explaining those awkward galactic rotation rates.

Positive and negative values of G are measured from "gravitational sea level"

Push and pull

Novák proposes both positive and negative values of G are measured from above and below what he calls "gravitational sea level", a theoretical case in which matter is distributed evenly throughout the Universe. If one is uncomfortable with the idea of a repulsive or negative value for gravity, he has a way to cook the books: it simply depends where you measure it from. The hilltop need not be thought to exert a negative gravitational force, a 'push'; the valleys can just as easily be described as exerting a more traditional 'pull'.

Might dark matter now be relegated to the list of non-existent intergalactic mediums along with 'phlogiston' and the 'luminiferous ether'? Novák's group certainly seem to be suggesting just that.

Hints that G was not a constant first came from observations of the rotational velocity of stars within galaxies. In violation of Kepler's Law, they didn't circle the galactic centre more slowly with distance, as do planets in the Solar System; counterintuitively, outlying stars were found to orbit at a similar rate to those nearer the core.

So why haven't we detected differing values for G experimentally? Orlov suggests that across distances the size of the Solar System, the variation is too small to be distinguished from a constant. Even

INTO THE GRID

It had taken Harriet just a few hours to write a subroutine that slaved the date, time and geographic location of all the computers and peripherals in the office to her and Jack's keyboards. The T and Y (standing for Tomorrow and Yesterday) shifted the Oxbow twenty-four hours, with a control-click or shift-control-click providing 1/10 and 1/100 increments thereof. A similar but less brutal downgearing of the location inputs gave a pitch and yaw that could be trimmed in a similar fashion via the four arrow keys. Jack was of the opinion that any motion through the Grid should be smooth and continuous, to give, as he put it, "the impression of a ship slowly and majestically accelerating into ideaspace", but had agreed that such finessing would have to wait. First, proof of concept.

The inputs were mapped to a visual to give some sensible feedback as to their location within the Grid: a red dot on the surface of a wireframe sphere ringed and divided by a crosshatch of longitude and latitude. Glowing a pale green, it floated in the starless night of the monitor screen like a crude '80s videogame graphic. It was currently rotating imperceptibly at twenty-four hours per day, but that was something they could change with a press of a button.

"Put on your Depthcharges." Jack was already adjusting the strap at the back of his head. "Nixon, we're routing the input through to the large screen. You can flip between my or Harriet's view, or the location graphic. I bet you wish, now more than ever, you'd stumped up the cash for three of these beauties."

"I checked. The prices have gone through the roof."

"*Ha.* As can we. So where do we steer this office first, Nixon? As the one who funded our first grand expedition into ideaspace, where would you like to go?"

Nixon pointed. "Down."

"Down it is. Just a few metres or so to begin with."

Jack's finger hesitated over a key. "Pressing a button. *Pft.* It still lacks that requisite ... *drama.*" He shrugged, and his finger dropped to the keyboard.

Click. It was barely audible, even lacking the satisfying feedback of a skeuomorphic audio file.

Jack was not sure what to expect. The office itself was too small to accommodate much of the Oxbow's volume, which was why he presumed the creatures in the Grid had not made their presence known earlier. But he now knew that below them was uncharted territory, the buried immensity of an alien construct the extent and contents of which he could only guess at.

The floor looked as if it'd developed bumps.

Dark shiny hemispheres the size of upturned soup bowls were laid out in a pattern across the floor. Harriet looked under the conference table. "Do we have moles?"

Nixon could only see their feeds on the main screen. The view jumped about like a cheap handheld documentary. "Hold still, guys."

"I think they're—" Jack tapped the button a second time, and the strange shapes shot up to shoulder height.

"Blimey." Nixon's swearing vocabulary was a fraction of Harriet's, but this time she was shocked into silence.

Around them stood a half-dozen creatures, dark as wet peat, glistening faintly like polished obelisks. They were all facing east, all identical as far as they could discern. Each had a bullet-shaped head that broadened into a body without neck or limbs. The head itself was smooth, featureless, though Jack fancied he could see fine ridges curving from the top down and around the body like a tightly furled umbrella. He imagined they might open, but wasn't sure he wanted to see what might be inside. They were an intimidating presence that the familiar surroundings did little to dispel.

"They're new," commented Harriet, almost sardonically. "Amphibious? They look streamlined."

Jack couldn't see the DMEn. Were they watching, but from elsewhere? He assumed they had access to the Depthcharge feeds. He didn't blame them for keeping their distance.

"Deeper?"

"Nudge us on a bit further."

Jack tapped the key twice. The shapes vanished, to be replaced by long thin tendrils, each with a series of tufted balls spaced along them. "Looks like they have tails, too," Jack commented. "I feel we should have asked Leonie Orlov or someone else from the Jodrell exobiology group along. We're a bit out of our depth here."

Jack had outlined their plans to Daniel during one of their late-night Skype conversations, though he hadn't gone into great detail. If he had seemed somewhat reticent, Jack assumed it was because he didn't think it was actually possible to mind-read an alien, but had promised to pass on the details the next time he spoke to his NASA contacts. If only Dana was here.

Jack had omitted to mention the DMEn; he wouldn't have known where to begin.

Read an alien mind. Was that even possible?

"These things creep me out. Onward." Harriet pressed a key. This time, she held it down|||||||||||||||||||||||||||||||||||||||||||||||||||||||||||||||||||||

IIIIIIIIIIIIIIIIIIIIIIIIIIIIIIIIIIIIIIIIIIIIIIIIIIIIIIIIIIIIIIIIIIIIIIIIIIIIIIIIII
IIIIIIIIIIIIIIIIIIIIIIIIIIIIIIIIIIIIIIIIIIIIIIIIIIIIIIIIIIIIIIIIIIIIIIIIIIIIIIIIII
IIIIIIIIIIIIIIIIIIIIIIIIIIIIIIIIIIIIIIIIIIIIIIIIIIIIIIIIIIIIIIIIIIIIIIIIIIIIIIIIII
IIIIIIIIIIIIIIIIIIIIIIIIIIIIIIIIIIIIIIIIIIIIIIIIIIIIIIIIIIIIIIIIIIIIIIIIIIIIIIIIII
IIIIIIIIIIIIIIIIIIIIIIIIIIIIIIIIIIIIIIIIIIIIIIIIIIIIIIIIIIIIIIIIIIIIIIIIIIIIIIIIII
IIIIIIIIIIIIIIIIIIIIIIIIIIIIIIIIIIIIIIIIIIIIIIIIIIIIIIIIIIIIIIIIIIIIIIIIIIIIIIIIII
IIIIIIIIIIIIIIIIIIIIIIIIIIIIIIIIIIIIIIIIIIIIIIIIIIIIIIIIIIIIIIIIIIIIIIIIIIIIIIIIII
IIIIIIIIIIIIIIIIIIIIIIIIIIIIIIIIIIIIIIIIIIIIIIIIIIIIIIIIIIIIIIIIIIIIIIIIIIIIIIIIII
IIIIIIIIIIIIIIIIIIIIIIIIIIIIIIIIIIIIIIIIIIIIIIIIIIIIIIIIIIIIIIIIIIIIIIIIIIIIIIIIII
IIIIIIIIIIIIIIIIIIIIIIIIIIIIIIIIIIIIIIIIIIIIIIIIIIIIIIIIIIIIIIIIIIIIIIIIIIIIIIIIII
IIIIIIIIIIIIIIIIIIIIIIIIIIIIIIIIIIIIIIIIIIIIIIIIIIIIIIIIIIIIIIIIIIIIIIIIIIIIIIIIII
IIIIIIIIIIIIIIIIIIIIIIIIIIIIIIIIIIIIIIIIIIIIIIIIIIIIIIIIIIIIIIIIIIIIIIIIIIIIIIIIII
IIIIIIIIIIIIIIIIIIIIIIIIIIIIIIIIIIIIIIIIIIIIIIIIIIIIIIIIIIIIIIIIIIIIIIIIIIIIIIIIII
IIIIIIIIIIIIIIIIIIIIIIIIIIIIIIIIIIIIIIIIIIIIIIIIIIIIIIIIIIIIIIIIIIIIIIIIIIIIIIIIII

IIIIJack felt a rush of vertigo as transparent shapes shot up from the floor around them, passing through the room with no regard for its physicality to exit through the ceiling above. Though their surroundings were perfectly visible, he had the distinct impression they were in a giant elevator – and it was going *down*. For the first time, Harriet looked out of the windows. Outside, a flickering motion blur of countless alien bodies shot skyward.

She tapped a couple of keys, slowed the stream. It seemed to change direction, correct, then speed up again. Jack involuntarily gripped the edge of the table. "Whoa. You're driving pretty fast there."

A shape shot up from the floor directly under him, and for a fraction of a second he was engulfed in darkness – the darkness inside of an alien body. Was this how Jonah felt? Then it was gone, and other shapes – longer, attenuated – were coming up through the floor, passing at speed around them, through the office furniture, the computer kit – occasionally themselves – then up and out. "Can we just ease up a moment?" Harriet tapped a key three times, and the flow slowed, then slowed again, then stopped in that instantaneous inertia-free fashion with which they would become accustomed.

Harriet ran her fingers through her hair. Above, hanging through the ceiling, they could see a barnacled tailfin trailing pink streamers from its tips like handlebars on a child's bicycle. An enormous torso protruded from the wall to Jack's right, enclosing most of the desk on which the scanner and 3D printer sat. It had a bifurcated head that looped back and around under what would have been a chin, were it human, and indistinct features that appeared smoothed by a lifetime of wear. This sullen apparition would have been more unsettling if Harriet's yellow *Minions* backpack had not been embedded in its shoulder.

"OK, hold it. One second. I feel as if I'm scrolling through the Âkâshic Record like it's my Twitter feed."

"Sorry. There's almost too much to take in here. We're already kilometres below the surface. No one has seen these – these dudes before. No one *human*. They're—" Harriet searched for words. "I'm beginning to get some idea of the enormity of this thing, of just how *big* it is. Just how many discrete entities make up the Grid, do you think?"

"The whole Grid? It depends how far out from Earth it extends. We have very imprecise measurements for that. Assuming a pretty isotropic density of bug-eyed monsters per square kilometre, just counting the area contained within the Earth puts the number at more than a hundred billion times the human population. At least. Which means—" Jack made another calculation. "If we looked at each individual for *just one second,* it'd take us three million million years to see them all."

"Shouldn't we be taking this more, uh, seriously? Cataloguing as we go?"

"Probably. I don't see why we can't initially just – just check things out, though. Cruise around a while. See what catches your eye. Cataloguing can come later."

"We're going to need automated systems to do it efficiently. I'll jot down a feature wishlist. I'll bet Nixon is wondering how to monetise this. Nixon?"

Nixon's jaw was slack. He closed his mouth, opened it again. "I'm watching this on the monitor in boring 2D, and it's still a revelation. Seriously, I'm just happy to be here for the ride. This – even just what we've seen so far – has been more than worth what I've put into Intelligencia."

Harriet smiled expansively. "Knowledge is its own reward, eh?"

"I'm not going to disagree with that. Aren't *you* excited?" Nixon's face had taken on an unusual intensity. "I'm bloody pumped. Front-row seats for the greatest show on Earth."

"The greatest show *off* Earth, too."

"Shall we continue?"

Jack nodded. "Please do the honours."

Harriet tapped a key twice and the grand parade recommenced. Again, they all felt an imagined weightlessness, as if the whole room was a lift, and the lift was falling at some speed. It was an illusion that took some force of will to overcome. To ease his discomfort, Jack stared out of the windows at the evening lights in Hoxton Square, which were twinkling like stars on an overcast night as immaterial bodies passed in front of them. Out further still, the limits of the Oxbow were apparent – a slow fade of dancing shadows, beyond which the familiar lights of London held steady.

Jack returned his gaze to his screen. Pulling up a drop-down menu, he typed a new digit in the hundredth-of-a-second slot of the Oxbow's clock and the whipping aurora of shapes shooting by began

slicing across the room at a new angle.
"I've just moved Hoxton to Malmö.
Effectively, as far as the Oxbow is
concerned, I've rotated the Earth."
He suddenly grinned with the
absurdity of it all. "As you do. We're
now moving through the Grid laterally
as well as vertically."

A rain of bodies passed through the
room faster than the eye could follow
as they traversed one description of
space while remaining fixed in the
same location in another.

Harriet was laughing, a gleeful
shriek. "*It works!* We're translating the
office across ideaspace!" It was true.
Inside the Oxbow, Jack, Harriet and
Nixon were piloting a piece of East
End real estate through a menagerie
of the Milky Way's sentient races. Jack
held his hand up for a high five. "She
may not look like much, but she's got
it where it counts, kid. We added some
special modifications ourselves."

At that precise moment,
and without warning, the lights went
out. Jack could hear a crash and a yelp as
Harriet's crate tipped backwards. The lights from the
street had vanished too . . . a power cut? No – this was
a rich, opaque black. Jack blinked – there was absolutely no
difference whether he had his eyes open or shut.

"Guys . . ." Harriet's voice was an octave higher than usual, but
Jack could hear her perfectly. "We're passing through something large.
Large and dark. It must be *enormous.* We're inside it. Five seconds . . .
six . . . seven . . . that's several kilometres. Wow."

Jack's eyes began to adjust, and he fancied he could see faint sparks of
blue electrical incandescence streaking through the room. *Yes – there!* A
constellation of lights, strands of luminous pulses moving this way and
that—

And then a curtain had been yanked away, and the lights of the room
returned to blind them. They all caught a momentary glimpse of a lifting
ceiling of coruscating lights, then it had passed through the real ceiling
of the office and out of sight.

"Look!" Harriet was at the window, pointing.

Rising around them, expanding to contain the building, the shops
below, the Hoxton Grill on the corner, the White Cube and Hoxton
Square itself, arching higher and higher above them was a dome – no,
not a dome, a sphere! They were passing through a spherical void, a vast
space in the centre of the opaque mass. Its surface was patterned with

an intricate tracery of lights, like a spectral bioluminescent city at night as seen from space. Harriet wasn't sure if the lights were attached to the inner surface, or formed a net above it. It was hard to make out. Curved ribs swept vertically up the walls of the space, coming together far above in a tangle of fluted vaulting from which more clusters of lights hung like chandeliers.

"Woooo! Fuck me, that's – that's *beautiful!*"

Jack couldn't disagree.

"Look – there are different structures on it – see those looping curves of lights, they concentrate in those – those buds, those bits that stick out – stick inward. It's like a city, like cities connected by highways. Like a world on the inside. A planet inside out."

The expansion of the dome slowed, the walls became vertical, then began to curve back in towards the Oxbow's epicentre. The circle that surrounded them began to contract, first slowly, then faster. They had passed through the centre of the void and were moving towards the far side, still invisible below them, but coming up now to meet them at speed. The upper reaches of the sphere passed out of the Oxbow altogether, and the first evening stars and a streak of salmon sky could be seen through the feathered edge of the growing hole, a skylight giving onto the real world.

Then the landscape of light soundlessly rushed up to meet them, and a blink later they were again deep in a darkness almost palpable.

Jack began to count aloud. "One . . . two . . . three . . ."

"Better than Alton Towers!"

"Alton Towers is *shit*. This is *amazing!*"

"Six . . . seven . . ."

And they were

out. There was the room, the screens, Nixon, Harriet. Jack had a sense of an enormous mass rising above him, and in a couple of seconds a flicker of bodies was once again passing through the room.

"What *was* that?"

"It was *big*. Several tens of kilometres. Organic. Alive?"

"So, what, we just passed through the gut or the brain of a self-aware *planet?*"

Jack had a silly grin on his face. "Your guess is as good as mine. Water-borne, aerial, ground-based, space-based – who knows, we have just the creatures here, not their native habitat. But – that *was* pretty astounding."

Harriet leaned back. "Knowing we're safe here – that these things can't touch us, interact with us . . . it's weird. Like travelling through the Universe from the comfort of your armchair. Or crate."

"That's pretty much *exactly* what it is."

"So, where are we now?"

Jack looked at the globe graphic. The dot was now an appreciable distance beneath its surface. "Still going deeper. Approaching the part of the Grid that's congruent with the crust–mantle boundary."

"Is the general density of entities changing in any way? What kind of info do we have?"

"There's a flux of sizes, but they do – with notable exceptions, as we've just seen – gravitate towards a mean. Monkey-sized to elephant-sized. The range I guess you'd expect for intelligent life. There's actually a lot of bipedalism. Two legs – it's a popular choice. There must be something inherently useful about walking. The rate we're travelling, all I can do is make the most sweeping generalisations from the data here. The area brought within the Oxbow is so small compared to the total volume of the Grid it's like taking a single narrow core sample and extrapolating it to the make-up of an entire planet – what we're seeing could easily be completely unrepresentative. More data. We just need more."

Even watching the screen, Nixon sensed a change in the beat of the shades around them. "Harriet, have you eased off the throttle?"

"No – why?"

"Seems to me the number of, um, entities passing through the room is falling. There are fewer and fewer."

"I – I think you're right. Maybe we're approaching a void – we've documented quite a few in the visible part of the Grid already. Unfilled, or lost in transmission—"

"You want to adjust the trajectory?"

"No, let's ride this out. I'm logging our route. Think of it as part of our initial reconnaissance."

The gossamer parade of ghosts became a trickle, then . . . nothing.

Several moments passed in silence. "Everything still working?"

Harriet gave a cursory glance at the figures scrolling up her monitor. "Yep. As before. Definitely a void of some kind. No idea how large."

"It occurs to me," Jack began. "It occurs to me that there may be another reason for a void that we've not considered."

"And that is?"

"Isolation."

"Not sure I get you."

"A wide berth. Containment. Solitary confinement."

"So you're suggesting there may be something in the *centre* of the void?"

"What kind of creature would need to be isolated, even when it is in lockdown? What danger could it possibly present?"

"As I say, it's just a theory."

"Heh. Thanks for that, Jack."

Several more moments passed in silence. For the first time, Jack noticed the DMEn. They were arranged in a casual but artfully composed tableau on the other side of the office, the 19th Count and Girl 21 leaning against XX's superstructure, impassive, aloof. How long had they been here? Jack waved in their direction.

"Any ideas? This is your domain."

The 19th Count was curiously succinct.

We see what you see. *No more.*

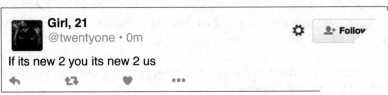

Girl, 21
@twentyone • 0m

If its new 2 you its new 2 us

They sat in silence for a full minute, two. Harriet only had eyes for a scrolling list of numbers, each a predicted Grid interstice passing through the volume of the room; each empty.

"Anything outside?"

Nixon could see the shutters being lowered on the White Cube gallery. "No. Nothing. Someone throwing up outside the kebab shop."

Jack was the first to voice their shared unease. "This doesn't feel right."

"Like *any* of this is right? Like we do this every day?"

"No – more like *I* don't feel right . . . I have a sense of something . . . How many of these creatures have passed through this room? All from half a galaxy away. None of them evoked this kind of – sense of

582

difference. That tightness in the chest? No, this feels orders of magnitude . . . divergent. Is it just me, or do you feel it too?"

Harriet's voice was small and quiet. "I— do."

"That sense of something – *alien* being pulled through your mind. Something *wrong.*" Jack stole a glance across the room to the shelf of printed resin figures. They were standing there impassively, just as they always did. Even the small grey one at the end.

Harriet searched for words. "It *is* a something – no, not a something, a *hole* where something should be – a *shape* of a something. A something that is a part of somewhere else. It's like it's at an angle, at right angles to reality . . . something that intersects with this world, but is not of it. Something from . . . from *elsewhere.*"

"And it's been placed – or has got caught – in the Grid."

The room remained empty.

"It's getting stronger. I can really feel it now. We're definitely getting close, closing in on it."

"I feel it too. Like something's sitting on my chest. Shortness of breath. My fight-or-flight is working overtime."

Nixon was not given to losing his cool, but the growing sense of agitation became impossible to ignore. If it continued—

"Harriet? Let's pull out. Let's reset. *Now.*"

Harriet tapped a key, tapped another.

"I don't see a change." Nixon's voice faltered in a fashion Harriet and Jack had not heard before.

She reached for her mouse and manually pulled the axis declination slider back to its original position.

"I think we've slowed,
though it's impossible
to confirm visually.
I'm just going from
the data I've got
here on-screen.
We've slewed
back to our
original
vector,
straight
down.
I ' m
n o t
sure

I
feel
any
dif-
ferent,
though.
Nixon?
Jack? Does
anyone feel
different?"
There was a
rising edge of
panic in her voice.
    Jack felt a cold acrid
sweat break out on his

arms. His fillings began
to ache, as if a current
was being induced
in them. They
must be moving
through some
kind of field,
an electro-
magnetic
g r a d i -
e n t .
"No,
it's

de-
fin-
itely
getting
worse—"
Without
further pre-
amble, Harriet
violently pushed
herself away from
the table, pulling the
tangled mass of cabling

wrapped
around

her
foot

with
her.

The
plugs

p

o

ed from their sockets and followed, skating across the parquet.

The monitors went dark. The DMEn blinked out of their semi-existence. Linked via Bluetooth, the Depthcharge glasses suddenly became opaque. Jack pulled his pair from his head and dropped them on the table. His hair stuck up in a matted, sweat-gelled quiff.

Bouncing around the large screen in the conference room was a line of type on a blank screen: NO SIGNAL. Harriet pushed her glasses up to her forehead. Jack could see a trickle of sweat escape and roll down her cheek like a tear. They exchanged glances in silence.

The sense of dread had immediately lifted. The clutter of the room, the stacks of boxes and magazines, the unbuilt shelving units, the mess in the kitchenette . . . Harriet wanted to embrace it all for its safe, familiar, unremarkable *normality*.

"What *was* that?"

"Whoo. It's gone now, whatever it was. I felt an absence, an overwhelming feeling of, of—" Of what? Nixon grappled for words. *Otherness?* "Did you get that creepy mix of fascination and disgust? Horror and attraction?"

Jack had. It was the attraction part that had particularly unnerved him. "Yeah. Too alien. Too weird."

Nixon's vocabulary re-engaged. "Like it was a nothingness, needing to be filled, but then so was I. I was a vessel, and it had, almost, an urge to, to fill me."

Jack sat back heavily. "And *you* felt it too, even without the glasses. *That* scares me. Whatever it is, it could reach out regardless."

"Out of the Grid? To influence the *real* world?"

Jack's face was hard to read. "While the Oxbow is running, it certainly looks that way."

"So we're not as invulnerable as we think?"

They sat in silence for a while. Jack checked the recordings. They had everything videoed, all the data streams recorded, but he didn't feel like reviewing any of them. Not right now.

"Shall we attempt another run?" Jack could tell by Harriet's tone she was hoping the answer would be no.

"Not tonight. I'm exhausted. I just want to get home and sleep." Jack stood up, then remembered. As of last Monday, this, the office, was now his home. He had let his apartment go.

Nixon saw his face fall. "Come on. Let's check into a decent hotel. On me. We deserve it."

Document: (NS//83//DB)
Subject: Daedalus Base "Encounter"
Debrief interviews, 128 of 128, plus addenda.
These addenda were recorded during the same session, after the interview had
been paused and restarted.

The information contained in this report is to be treated as Most Secret
Location: [removed. Assumed to be the Apollo Isolation chamber "Hornet+3",
Lyndon B. Johnson Space Center]

Note: Some responses have been edited, and are summaries of what was
actually stated. Details in square brackets are added for clarity. Please
refer to audiovisual recordings, available on request.
Document history: v 1.2 Submitted for review and comment
Date: [removed]

Present:
Dana Normansson (hereafter DN), Cmdr., Daedalus Base
Adam Parker (hereafter AP), sup. offcr
Other support staff, medical staff [names removed]

AP: Dana, good morning.
[pause]
AP: Dana?
DN: I'm not getting out of here, am I?
AP: We still have so much to discuss. Have patience.
DN: Answer my question.
[pause]
AP: I have been in conference with certain, uh, interested parties. They
want me to ask you something.
DN: Seems to me that's all you do.
AP: This schism you mentioned. Which, uh, sect does, did, the LBE, the Man
in the Moon represent?
[27 seconds silence]

addendum i

[removed]

AP: We need to know more about the possible dangers the Signal may pose. A question: How does the Signal encourage its recipients to rebroadcast it?
DN: You don't stop, do you.
AP: Dana, please.
DN: OK. Right. Give me a second.
[pause]
DN: There are layers of persuasion, both scientific, sexual and adaptive. Just the presence of the Signal is sometimes enough. It evolves. Essentially - it convinces you that retransmission is in your best interests.
AP: How so?
DN: It works like any infectious set of ideas does, by presenting an inarguable three-fold case for itself: One. It offers new knowledge: Seduction. Two. It supplants all alternatives: Persuasion. Three. It becomes an imperative: Conviction. These three steps turn an idea into action. Conviction, once arrived at, is very hard to shake, and pretty impervious to rational argument. And it can do all this while convincing you that you've come to these conclusions of your own free will.
AP: And this, this is how the Signal operates? It has a, a kind of missionary zeal?
DN: Carried in the minds of the creatures that are in the Signal. Here's the thing - most, though not all of them, wouldn't be there, in the Grid, if they didn't believe it was in their best interests. However -
AP: Yes?
DN: My host, the Man in the Moon - he was of the opinion that in moving across the galaxy, in doing what the Grid does, we - sorry they, have become very much like the thing they despise.
AP: What?
DN: You're missing something very important here. Think, Adam.
AP: What might they despise? The Signal?
DN: That's what I originally assumed. What's becoming clear to me now is that the Signal is a <u>response</u>, not a cause. This, this extinction of life, the one I was shown during my first encounter? We assumed it was caused by the Signal itself. But I don't think it is. Granted, the Signal has been disastrous for many of the races that have been incorporated. The physical trauma we see is proof of that. But what I saw, that was something altogether different, both in its origins and effects. I think the Signal, the Grid, is not the coming cataclysm our LBE warned me about. No, I think it's a means to <u>escape</u> that coming cataclysm. I think the Grid is a lifeboat. A galactic ark.
AP: [flipping through transcripts of previous sessions] "One: it brings a warning of coming devastation, not only of all life on Earth, but the extinction of all life in the galaxy. Two: the absolute certainty that this cannot be prevented."

DN: As an encouragement to rebroadcast the Signal, I'd say that was pretty persuasive, wouldn't you?

[pause]

AP: So how do we know if they're right? That it is in their best interests?

DN: We don't. What you want to know is if it's also in our best interests. Right, Adam?

[pause]

DN: That's what you're thinking. What your, your bosses are thinking.

AP: If it's also in our best interests? Is it?

DN: Adam, even I can't tell you that.

AP: Our friend in London who, ah, who has taken an interest in this conversation, he thinks he may have a way to talk to them. Talk to your friends in the Grid.

DN: Who?

AP: I uh, I'm afraid I'm not at liberty to say. A contractor with certain ... talents we find useful. That's all I can tell you. He says he has a way.

DN: You mean Jack Fenwick? On the Jodrell team? Impossible. The Shepherds in the Grid act as memetic dampeners for the other races in each section. How does he plan to do this?

AP: I, uh, I have some technical details here that I don't pretend to understand.

DN: Show me.

[9.34-minute gap in recording]

DN: What he proposes is the equivalent of direct subcranial stimulation. Do you want to wake them up? Wake up the Grid? That is what will happen if you try and talk to them. Becoming conscious while still in the Grid, without a physical body, is – inadvisable. It has happened only once before. It proved to be... traumatic.

[pause]

DN: Adam, listen to me. They will wake up.

AP: He says he has already spoken to, uh, entities in the Grid. Or, if not exactly in the Grid, in what he terms the "ideaspace" that the Grid occupies.

[pause]

DN: Adam. Believe me, this is not something you want to happen. I have to go—

[34.4 seconds with no picture, in which all that can be heard is white noise. This section has been analyzed by the Data Encryption and Image Processing division, and their opinion is that the signal corruption is due to an external cause at the source, as it appears on both cameras and soundtracks simultaneously.]

----

addendum ii

[removed]

[no audio]
[Adam Parker and Gabe Bowen can be seen lying on the floor of the
viewing lounge. Both are unconscious. There is a medical officer in the
decontamination suite [name removed], looking out at them through the glass
[interview on file]. The chair Dana Normansson previously occupied is empty.
Her clothes are laid on the chair and her shoes are on the floor. Dana
Normansson is not present.
A subsequent thorough search of the facility and the surrounding area has
not found her. There was no breach of the airtight seals, or any other signs
of forced exit. It is currently assumed that she is not anywhere within the
perimeter of [removed].
The conclusion is that she has escaped, by means unknown.]

---TRANSCRIPT ENDS---

Sun

RESIDENTS of an
exclusive new East End
development were aghast
to see a naked blonde
woman taking clothes from
a line in a communal area
on Monday morning.
"It's not something we
see a lot of round here,
especially at this time of
year", a resident quipped.
The knicker thief has yet
to be apprehended.

spot

ILLEGAL IMMIGRANT

Jack balanced a croissant on his Starbucks hot chocolate and tried to remember in which pocket he'd put his keys.

On the step, below the graffiti and fly-posters that decorated the office's door, there was a small figure. Hunched up, folded in three like a sheet of A4, she had a thin cardigan pulled over her knees but was still underdressed for the weather. Slight. Athletic. Mid-thirties, Jack thought, though it was hard to tell. Wet blonde hair swept back under a knitted beanie. She was barefoot.

He had almost stepped on her. Normally he'd ignore the vagrants he occasionally found sleeping rough in the small lee the doorway provided, but something about her didn't fit.

"Jack."

Jack had studiously avoided eye contact, but now met her gaze directly for the first time.

"*Dana?*"

"Forgive the outfit. I do usually dress better than this." She managed a weak smile.

Jack's words tripped over each other. "Dana, are you OK? Last I heard, you were in isolation. Because, because you put your head in an alien's mouth on the Moon. How did you find us? Why are you here?"

"I got your address from Adam Parker."

"Parker—"

"Don't worry. He's all right. I just took what I needed, then shut down his sleep centres. He and Gabe will be OK."

Jack ran this nugget of information through his mind a few times and still didn't know exactly what to make of it. "How on earth did you get here? Daniel said you were in decontamination . . ."

"I find I now have certain . . . talents." Again, that thin smile. "I stepped into the Grid there, and stepped out here." She tilted her head to the left, then the right. "Simple, really."

"You can *do* that?"

596

She tapped her forehead. "I have a Shepherd in my head."

"You look like a tramp. Where are your shoes?"

"I couldn't find any. Clothes don't port into or out of the Grid. Biological material only, it seems. Can I come in?"

Jack hesitated.

"Jack, I'm not going to hurt you, or put you to sleep, or infect you with some alien virus. I'm here because Adam let slip that you're attempting to talk to the creatures in the Grid. How? How can you *do* that?"

"I guess we have talents as well. That the Signal is composed of – creatures is not a secret any more. It's all over the news."

"I've been in an isolation chamber since I got back from the Moon. No internet. I'm cold. *Please* can I come in?"

Jack turned the key in the lock. Dana pushed herself up the wall until she was standing, pulled down her cardigan, then ducked under his arm as he held the door open. A short woodchip-papered hallway led to the steep flight of stairs up to the office proper. Jack unlocked the second door and reached around for the lights. The office was as they had left it last night: cabling across the floor, monitors still arranged in the conference room around the crates like the control room at CERN.

"They'll be looking for you."

"I know. But if they do find me, they won't be able to catch me."

Jack held out his hot chocolate and croissant. "You look like you need this more than I do. Here. Take it." Dana did so. "How long were you waiting there?"

"Three and a half hours."

"Ouch. Listen. We have a shower at the back, next to the toilet. I'll find you a clean towel. Go and warm up."

Fifteen minutes later Dana came back into the office with her hair twisted up in the towel like a turban. Dressed again in the oversized cardigan, she looked diminutive and vulnerable, a stray waif rather than a seasoned astronaut. She followed Jack through to the conference room. "Thank you. I feel so much better."

Jack looked at her, still trying to weigh up the situation. "No problem."

"So tell me. How do you do it? How can you see into the Grid?"

Jack picked up one of the pairs of Depthcharge glasses. "These. Made for gaming. 3D. They overlay your view of the real world with digital enhancements. Augmented reality."

"That stuff is popular?"

"Not very. The headsets are still expensive. Wear them for more than twenty minutes, and you're liable to get a migraine. These two are

597

several-thousand-pound prototypes. We do a lot of work here for game developers. Serious hobbyists use them, mostly. That, and medical institutions who are looking into the possibilities of performing remote surgery. Haptics."

"And you have two pairs."

Jack smiled. "We have a backer, of sorts. You'll meet him. This is the office of a start-up destined to be bigger than Facebook. I'm a founding partner. I am also the window-cleaner, bin-emptier and tea-maker. *Intelligencia*. You passed the sign on your way in."

"I did?"

"You did. It must be memorable."

"I have a lot on my mind. So, these glasses – people are streaming video from them?"

"Video, screen grabs. There's quite an online community collating this stuff."

"And where do people think they're from?"

"The creatures? Depends who you ask. Most people think it's simply a game, an open-ended sandbox that ships with the glasses. That they're procedurally generated, produced from some kind of clever iterative coding. It's not unknown for new consoles to come with pre-loaded Easter eggs. Rewards the curious."

"And what do you think?"

"Well . . . I happened to know that there were things – people – in ideaspace long before our alien visitors appeared."

Dana studied him keenly. "Sorry?"

Jack looked away, around the creative mess that was the office. "Maybe 'people' isn't the best description. Entities. Spirits. *Zeitgeists*. We call them DMEn."

"Demon?"

"Dee. Em. Ee. En. It's an acronym. Tech types love acronyms." It was almost a syndrome; Jack wondered if it had a medical name, and if so, if there was an acronym for it. "It stands for Digital Memetic Entities. *Demen*. Plural and singular."

"And you can see them with the glasses?"

"Yes."

"Why doesn't everyone see them with the glasses?"

"Because they're not a partner in a tech start-up called Intelligencia with access to a memetic Oxbow."

Dana waved her hand dismissively in mock comprehension. "Of *course*."

"Look, I don't mean to pry, but why didn't you come through the normal channels? Gabe is good for arrang—"

"Gabe and the gang at NASA were not going to let me out of isolation. Not soon. Maybe not for a long time. I can see it from their point of view: human astronaut has head sucked by alien on Moon, comes back to Earth with who knows what in her brain. I'm not saying they did the wrong thing. They're following well-rehearsed protocols."

"They have no idea you're here, do they?"

"Of course not. And, for the moment, I want it to stay that way. I have access to the memories of an exobiological entity. How valuable do you think that makes me? How likely would it be that they'd have voluntarily let me check out, get on a plane, and come over here?"

Jack looked at her intently. She seemed very much in control, capable of taking care of herself. *Astronaut material,* he reminded himself. "I'm sure they have good reasons, as you say. So – you're sure you're not contagious?"

"I'm not contagious. Clear on all the tests they could devise. Nothing. All the stuff I carry is up here, in my head."

Now she had warmed up she was finally beginning to relax. She sat in Harriet's chair and crossed her legs. Jack noticed that she was not wearing a bra. "Look, are you sure you don't want me to go and get you some decent clothes? That might actually fit you?"

Dana shook her head. "In good time. These look scruffy but they are clean. I stole them from a clothes line."

"I'm harbouring an international criminal."

She pointed to the bedroll with the croissant. "You live here?"

"I, er, yes, I am currently living here. Work, pressure – it just makes things easier. I also have nowhere else to live at the moment." Jack changed the subject. "Look, I do have clothes here already you can borrow."

"You're not my size."

"I know someone who is." Out of the stationery cupboard, Jack produced a neatly folded pair of Nadine's jeans, a T-shirt and a pair of black lace briefs.

Dana held them up and regarded them. "Oh, fancy. Not yours, I presume?"

While Dana had gone back to the bathroom to change, Jack plugged the computers back in and rebooted them, one by one, each time making sure he reset the date and time, and thus the Oxbow's location, to the here and now. When everything was up and running he booted the Oxbow itself. Code scrolled down his monitor, colour-coded and in narrow columns. Lastly, he routed his glasses through to the main screen. He put them on with some trepidation.

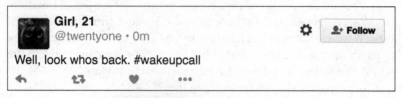

Girl, 21
@twentyone • 0m

Well, look whos back. #wakeupcall

...THROWN **OUT** ACROSS THE **DEEP** OF
NONBEING, **SHRAPNEL**
I STILL SHOUT **VITRIOL**
INTO THE **LAST DAR—**

Sorry, dear boy. We're learning to keep him on a *shorter leash.*

Next time

a *word of warning* would be nice before you *snuff our candles* like that.
Unexpected disassociation is not *good* for the

CONSTITUTION.

XX hunched down like an enormous sulking mechanical Rottweiler. A bloom of gun barrels spun like a crown, and then drew back into the body.

"Point taken." Jack's curiosity had been piqued. "You can, um, control him?"

In a manner of speaking.

THE UNKNOWN UNKNOWN

– let's just say he is more a *force of nature*
than someone you might invite into *polite society.*

I mean, just look at him.

All *brashness,* and no *waistcoat.*

So we tend to *damp down* his higher functions. *Keeps him docile.*

"Hm. Right." More DMEn talents that he had not been aware of before. Jack had not considered that they could learn new tricks; he'd assumed they were fixed concepts. Maybe everything evolves, even spirits of an age who are still around after their age has passed.

He heard a key in the lock. Harriet pushed open the door. Nixon was behind her, stooping to pick something up.

Dana had just stepped out of the bathroom.

"Guys, this is Dana Normansson."

Nixon stopped shuffling through the mail and looked up.

"Normansson? Like the astronaut?"

"I am the astronaut."

Harriet stood perfectly still. Without looking, she pushed the door shut behind her. "Forgive me, but Jack tells me Dana Normansson was up on Daedalus Base, on the far side of the Moon. He went to Jodrell Bank to talk to her through a satellite uplink. They thought they'd lost her, and then found out she was in quarantine, somewhere back on Earth. And, um, and you look like you're wearing Nadine's clothes." Though this sudden appearance had discombobulated her, there was still a small part that was relieved the conversation was not about her and Nixon's simultaneous arrival.

Jack beckoned them in. "She discharged herself. From a NASA facility. Came over to talk to us about a few things. We need to hear her out."

Nixon absently placed the mail on the conference room table, keeping his eyes on the newcomer. Harriet was checking the cabling. "You've got it up and running again after last night's excitement, I see." Lifting her glasses and panning them around the room without putting them on, she could see on the large monitor that the DMEn were here with them. She turned and waved to the empty corner. On the screen behind her, out of her line of sight, the 19th Count and Girl 21 waved back.

Dana looked at the screen, then the empty space across the other side of the conference room and back again. "Who – who are *they?*"

Jack cleared his throat. "Right. I can see I need to make some proper introductions."

RELATED

HEALTH | Jonathan McMurray

ENTERING THE "VACANT ZONE"

Unidentified airborne pathogen, or simply mass hysteria?

High-school student Lia Bratchko's story is emblematic. Overcome by the listlessness and indifference dubbed the 'sleeping sickness', her bodily functions slowed to a state that puzzled medical experts have described as a torpor, or, more bizarrely, a heretofore undocumented form of human hibernation. She is not alone – a spate of similar cases have stretched the limited resources of a small French hamlet.

Flown to the Hôpital Saint-Louis in the French capital she recovered in a matter of hours, leading doctors to suggest that the symptoms have a localised cause, and that a temporary evacuation of the area may be necessary.

"I felt as if my brain was dumbed down, switched off," Bratchko explained. "I don't recall why, or how it happened. I was in class, and I found I couldn't follow the teacher. The writing on the blackboard simply didn't make any sense, like it was in some weird language I didn't recognise. I found it hard to think. Then there I was, waking up in hospital in Paris." A spate of road accidents in the last six days have also been blamed on the unknown ailment.

"We see a state of decreased physiological and physical activity characterised by low body temperature, slow breathing and heart rate, and low metabolic rate", explains Andrée Armistead of the Pitié-Salpêtrière Hospital, Paris. "What we can say is that this is definitely not a new form of encephalitis. The patient has since made a full recovery."

Doctors and scientists who have tested for increased levels of radiation, carbon monoxide, radon, heavy metal salts and other airborne or waterborne pathogens have come up empty-handed. Radiation is within permissible levels; slightly elevated levels of radon and carbon monoxide were detected but have since been ruled out as a cause. Further laboratory and clinical tests have been conducted on the air, soil, water, food, animals, building materials – and on the residents themselves. Results are to be made available "as soon as possible".

Within the last two weeks, startlingly similar stories, though not confirmed by the UN or investigated by any recognised international medical organisations, have been reported in Simantan, Henan Province, China, and at an undisclosed Russian military outpost, which several sources name as the 102nd Military Base in Gyumri, Armenia. An unnamed Armenian official declined to discuss suggestions made on RW.com (Russia Week) that an accidental release of an experimental nerve agent was the cause, saying only that "as you are fully aware, such agents are forbidden under the CWC [Chemical Weapons Convention]".

Inevitable comparisons will be made to the well-known 1962 'June Bug' epidemic, a mysterious disease which broke out in the dressmaking department of a US textile factory. Symptoms included numbness, nausea and dizziness; sixty-two employees came down with the mystery ailment, some of whom were hospitalised. Unable to unambiguously identify the cause, experts from the US Public Health Service Communicable Disease Center eventually concluded that it was a case of mass hysteria.

Then as now, it seems to be the fall-back diagnosis when no other cause can be found.

COMMENTS (5) Order by Newest I Threads Collapsed

Charmer 18 Mar 6:15 ↑5

We all being posioned slowly ,by pollution.

it is a constant battle to keep governments and businesses from acting irresponsibly. The worst atrocitys in the world are done by organized government and greedy businesses. I hope we can find a better way. Humanity has got to stop acting without considering the consequences.

CitizenX 18 Mar 7:09 ↑4

They should be offered the chance to relocate. After all, the common denominator here is that the afflicted all live or lived in the same area.

Charmer → **CitizenX** 19 Mar 2015 12:13 ↑5

So they can turn their land into $$$$$? Clearing an area of undesireable indiginus people is a tactic used again and again by US-backed regimes. Why bomb people from their land when you can much more effetively scare them away, and seem like you're doing them a favour in the process??

CitizenX → **Charmer** 19 Mar 14:09 ↑4

Yep, those horrid US-backed regimes like France, always trying to bomb their own French citizens out of their own French villages. Sacré Bleu!

SpeakingFrankLee → 20 Mar 5:07 ↑42

Dear Boss, after a few too many lagers & a dodgy kebab last night I have a dose of mass hysteria and so wont be in work today, yours sinserly, Frankzzzzzzzz

TIME TEAM

Jack had let his phone run down and had not thought to recharge it in several days. He fitted the cable and laid it on a stack of unread manuals. Presently, it beeped; Jack entered a code and swiped.

"Hey. I've got a message from Gabriel Bowen at NASA. He wants to talk to me." They all looked at Dana. "What do I say?"

"There's no way he could know I'm here. They'll have security checks at all points of departure from the US, and I won't have been picked up on any of them. They'll assume I'm still in the States somewhere."

Jack demurred. "Not necessarily. If they saw you disappear from a sealed facility, don't you think they might realise that crossing international borders without leaving a trace might be a possibility too?"

Dana didn't reply.

"You also told me that Adam Parker let slip that I may have found a way to talk to creatures in the Grid just before you disappeared. They just may put two and two together."

"Jack, listen, they can't be *certain* that I'm here. It'll all be educated guesswork."

"Would it be such a bad thing to let them know you're OK?" Harriet suggested. "Or your family?"

"That's something I've not figured out how to deal with yet. My äiti, she could never keep a secret. And— and the other people in my life are used to me disappearing for months at a time on yet another mission. For now, it's best if I stay out of sight, at least until I have a better understanding of what's happened to me."

Nixon looked at the others, trying to gauge their mood. *"Well—"*

"Think about this new skill of mine . . . even I'm not sure about the functional details, but it's obvious that it's a game-changer. Especially for international relations. Think of the possibilities for neat surgical assassinations. Espionage. National interests might override scientific curiosity."

"So we don't tell them you came here. You go back. Claim that you found some way to, to escape. I know that sounds absurd, but is it any more absurd than practical teleportation?" Jack wasn't sure he really believed it himself.

"Jack, I'm *not* going back. I have a pact, a responsibility to a creature that came a very, very long way and paid with its life in order to pass me a message. This is something I need to see through to the end."

In this, they had no doubt of her sincerity.

"A message?"

Dana was tight-lipped.

Jack took another tack. "I read the transcripts. They tell me you have an alien mind inside yours. Let's say I believe them. It must have seen some amazing things. What's, what's it like, out there in the Universe?"

Harriet was sitting forward, all taut attention. "Yes, I want to know *everything!*"

Dana smiled, and seemed to relax just a fraction. "You sound like the guys at NASA. If you want to know about the Grid, I know as much as my friend in here knows. No more. To him, it's ancient history . . . How much do we know about the origins of civilisation here on Earth? Not a great deal. The records are patchy or non-existent. Or written in a language we can no longer decipher. The stories that *do* survive have been polished so many times in the retelling that the narrative trumps the facts: they're overlaid with moral instruction, post-rationalised mythologising . . . you wouldn't mistake them for unbiased first-hand accounts."

Harriet was on the edge of her crate. "But you think that the Grid is waking up? That something's happening? All we did was—"

"It's a distinct possibility. Certain effects, bleeding into the real world. You yourself said you felt it."

"There are reports—" Nixon interjected, somewhat hesitantly. Though he knew who Dana was through Jack's involvement with the exobiology group at Jodrell, he was embarrassed to realise how little interest he took in the manned space programme; his life had always been driven by more earthly concerns. From Harriet's and especially Jack's reaction to her presence here, he guessed she was an important figure, though he had no real idea why. He didn't recall seeing her on the news, but then she didn't play rugby for England. It was like being introduced to a friend of a friend who happened to be in a band, then finding out that even though they'd filled Wembley Stadium you still couldn't hum a single one of their songs. "Mass hysteria, they say. Unknown biological agents. Some novel vector that's localised, has no identifiable cause and leaves no trace."

Jack was dubious. "It could be coincidence. They may not be related to the Grid at all. Anyway, if this is the Grid waking up, it seems to be sending people to sleep."

"The Shepherds' soporific effects certainly seem to be spreading. Maybe they're turning up the power by way of compensation. Look, this is an unusual situation, even for the Grid. Whatever is happening, it usually takes place *inside* minds, not a silicon and copper substitute."

"And you say the Grid is supposed to convince us to *join* it? How does that even *work*? Dana, I can't see people willingly giving up their lives any time soon for some undemonstrable immortality out there in the cosmos, whatever the alternative may be."

Dana snorted in an unfeminine fashion. "Really?"

IDEASPACE has been infected with
VIRULENT IDEOLOGIES
that do *just that* for
MILLENNIA.

"Jack, your, uh, fictional friend here is right. There are already numerous other seductive and all-encompassing ideologies out there that have been seeking to reprogram us to do their bidding for – for as long as there have been people to proselytise and ideas to communicate. All encourage – or even *require* – personal sacrifice for the making of a better world. Some promise that better world here, on Earth, others in a supposed hereafter. No, sadly the existence of a glorious and perfect afterlife and the miserable state of the real world is not something that many of the races across the known galaxy need to be convinced of. Some were racing towards their oblivion already, before the Grid arrived to rescue them from their sorry state of affairs. To save them from themselves. You know how many races have been incorporated into the Grid that no longer exist, *outside* the Grid?"

"I'll defer to you on that one."

"It's become a *preservation drive*. A seed bank of the galaxy's extinct civilisations."

Dana let that sink in for a few moments. "Jack, a belief in the transience of material reality and the reality of an immaterial transcendent hereafter is already deeply embedded in so many cultures, even in our culture, like a dark pathogen masquerading as light. No, the Grid doesn't need to convince anyone of anything."

Jack had his hands folded in his lap. "It'll need to convince *me*."

Dana touched his shoulder. "*Anyway*. Time is something we don't have unlimited amounts of. NASA knows I'm gone. And the Grid may be waking up."

Jack looked up. "Dana, let me know if I've got this straight. The Grid wakes up in the minds of the beings in which it is thought. It's *made* of ideas. It's software that's run on the ultimate computer, a living brain. Or what passes for a brain in xenobiological terms. But here, that processing system is non-biological. It's the internet. If we have one advantage, it's that we know where it lives, and that's *not* in our own heads – so far."

Harriet wasn't so sure. "But it *can* get in there. Just the Signal's presence is having an effect, even before you factor in the leading lights of experimental music, art, DIY gene manipulation and Lord fucking Disrepair and his biohacker underground. For people like him, ethics don't come into it."

Dana looked confused. "Lord who? Is he another of your DMEn?"

"No. Never mind. What I mean is that, so far, all the researchers and hobbyists are focusing on external appearances, because that's all they have access to. They are not looking into alien brains. They are not thinking alien thoughts—" Harriet pointed forcefully. "But *you*, you *are*."

Dana tented her fingers in a fashion unintentionally suggestive of prayer. "It— it does have certain benefits."

There was a pause in which everyone looked at her expectantly. Jack even fancied that the DMEn were too, though he didn't pick up the Depthcharges to check his intuition. Finally she broke the silence.

"Answers. I know that's what we all need. It's what my alien friend wanted, more than anything. He knows a lot, but he doesn't know everything, especially in matters of the origins and ultimate purpose of the Grid. Most of the incorporated beings can't access the whole – they're localised, and in lockdown. They're inside it, but they can't move around within it."

"But in this case the Grid found its way into the Web— and the Web is not an empty house with no tenants." Jack interjected. "It was already full of ideas – some of them self-cohering concepts like our DMEn here. When these aliens arrived, they found that they weren't occupying some alien mind that they could simply hijack for their own ends in order to persuade its owner to succumb willingly to the Grid's reproductive urge. Instead, they found themselves in the internet. Non-organic. Non-persuadable.

"Dana, I think Harriet's right. If there were no minds in there to hijack, perhaps there were minds *outside* the Grid that they could influence. There is a precedent for that, right over there—" Jack gestured to the corner of the office, apparently empty except for the water cooler. It gave a well-timed gurgle. "After all, it's what the DMEn themselves were designed to do. The influence has to be indirect. It has to be subtle. Those minds had to think they were doing what they were doing of their own volition. They had to think they were doing things out of curiosity, for the best of intentions, for the sake of humanity. Not for the Grid, however justifiable that may turn out to be."

"Jack, you're telling me my mind's been hijacked? I've been taken over? I can assure you, it's not like that."

"But Dana, don't you see – that's what it *wants* you to think. In the end, the invaders didn't come wielding death-rays and atomic fire. They didn't land on the White House lawn or in Trafalgar Square and demand our surrender. They came with persuasive ideas, and simply allowed those ideas to do their work for them, because in some sense, they *were* those ideas, and all they needed to do to survive was to be *thought*."

COMPARATIVE DIAGRAMS OF THE RADICAL CONSONANT POSITIONS.

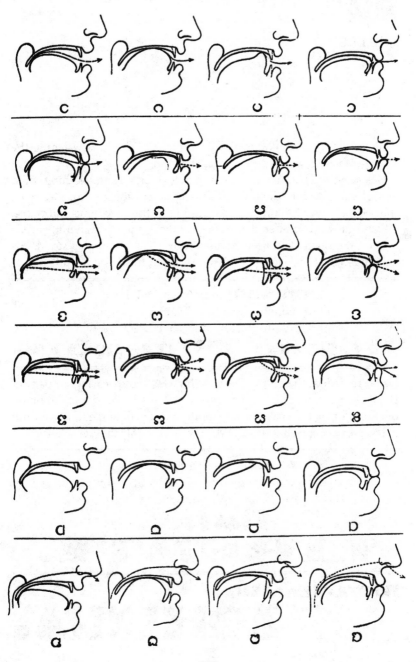

TWO DOGS

"This is where you felt something, you say?" Dana was watching the footage of yesterday's excursion into the Grid.

Jack scrubbed back a few seconds and let it play again. Nothing could be seen except for the dot indicating location pulsing inside a wireframe sphere, but even at this remove it made him feel uncomfortable. "Whatever we encountered, it was certainly able to exert an influence."

The Count, who had been leaning in over Jack's shoulder, stood. His hat remained at the usual perfect rakish angle, his cravat unruffled.

THE GRID may be in lockdown,
but evidently certain **IDEAS** are not.
Sounds like we have some FREE-FLOATING
Rogue Thoughts.

Dana regarded the 19th Count. She was not wearing a pair of Depthcharges, and didn't quite know whether to focus her attention on the monitor or the space he apparently occupied. She had a head full of bizarre concepts, but these DMEn were certainly up there. "Sorry?"

Ideaspace is a messy place.
Mutually exclusive doctrines in prolific abundance.
Some *good,* some *bad,* many more *indifferent.*
Justice.
LIBERTY.
FASCISM. COMMUNISM.
MODERNISM.

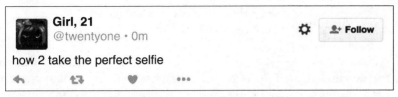

Girl, 21
@twentyone · 0m

how 2 take the perfect selfie

Jack nodded. "Memetic bleed."

Precisely. They may be starting to leak out.
NEW IDEAS. NOVEL IDEAS.

ALIEN IDEAS.

Dana was still struggling to get up to speed with the manner in which these non-physical characters, whoever they were, seemed to be an integral part of the Intelligencia team. She assumed they didn't draw a salary.

"I thought nothing could be affected outside the Grid, outside the Oxbow," Harriet insisted.

"Nothing *physical* is happening externally. But something is happening *memetically*. We felt it. Could it be that we're responsible for the effect? Simply by passing these creatures through the volume of the Oxbow, could we be isolating them from the Shepherds' influence?" Jack sat back with a sense of mild panic.

Despite Dana's earlier remonstrations, Harriet still wasn't convinced. "It could be a result of the widespread distribution of the Signal. Think of what all those artists and writers and musicians are doing with it. That could be a creative catalyst in itself – we don't have to trace the direct cause back to us, do we?"

Dana looped a stray strand of hair back behind her ear. "Remember, the Signal doesn't usually reside in a non-biological vehicle. It's designed to be received by a receptive mind, not a distributed computing system. This situation may be unique. There may be . . . unforeseen consequences."

"So what will happen?"

"I'm not sure. Here, on Earth, the Grid doesn't have the capacity to directly reprogram our biology."

Nixon looked appalled. "Reprogram our biology?"

"Maybe it still does, just by more subtle and indirect means."

"But to what *end?*"

Dana didn't answer immediately. Nixon got the impression that the question underscored something that she herself had not yet fully resolved. Her thoughts seemed to be headed in a different direction, and when she spoke she passed over his question.

"Interesting. I may be in a unique situation here, one only made possible by an unlikely combination of human technology, brain structure, and a meeting with an alien on the Moon."

Harriet smiled. "Not an easy situation to engineer on demand."

"I think I'm the only one who has *ever* been able to step in and out of the Grid."

Harriet broke Dana's reverie. "You haven't told us – what's the story with the Shepherds? Why did your Shepherd crash into the back of the Moon?"

"More questions? This is what I was trying to escape."

"Dana, you can't blame us for being curious. Come *on*. This is so intriguing," Harriet pleaded.

Dana was silent for a few moments.

"OK. But remember, this is linked to a history that goes way back before my alien buddy took up lodgings in my cerebral cortex. So bear in mind all I have here are stories – and stories and the truth, they sometimes have a loose correlation."

"Tell us what you know."

"I was shown a kind of home movie. Now, it could have been just that, of course – an alien slice of Hollywood. I've pieced together more of the background to this since, and I think some of it is metaphorical, some more – what we'd call *real*. The difference is somewhat – arbitrarily applied, when it comes to our Shepherds. I get the impression they're so immersed in mind, in countless different alien cultures, that they have lost the ability to clearly make the distinction.

"But this is what I saw. Some great conflagration swept across the Shepherds' homeworld. A strange object, a seed, fell from the sky. It carried an infectious idea, a new and novel alien idea that spread through the population, by conversation, through the overlapping fringes of extended minds . . . faster than the powers that be could contradict it, or engage with it effectively. This idea promised to sweep them up and carry them away from their planet, their birthplace – and allow them to take the next step in their evolution as a species.

"It was a call for membership in something far greater, far bigger: a kind of shared consciousness. The *Grid*. It promised to lift people off their world to the stars, to show them the Universe, and to make them immortal into the bargain. They would leave their physical bodies behind, and continue on as information – as spirit, perhaps.

"So people began incorporating themselves into the Grid. They didn't call it the Grid, of course, they had their own term for it – a reference to an external womb on an animal on the Shepherds' homeworld that looks something like a marsupial's pouch.

"Once incorporated, two things became apparent – first, that the Grid had been retransmitted many, many times before, and second, that it was in a state of internal chaos. A maelstrom of conflicting ideologies, desires and needs. Into this toxic mix, the two-brain bicameral Shepherds had brought with them something unique – their ability to hold an idea at a distance and examine it dispassionately. They found this meant that they retained a high degree of volition within the Grid. Through a process I've not yet completely unpacked, they were able to bring some order to this chaos. To organise it, to subdue it, to keep it, effectively, in a form of lockdown."

Jack opened a new window on his Mac. "Dana, look. Here's a plot of the positions of the Shepherds throughout the Grid. I noticed that in the suburbs they're pretty evenly spaced. Ordered. Then, as you move towards the centre, they increase in density until you reach a ring – actually, a sphere—"

Dana nodded. "That must be the point in the Grid's growth where the Shepherds first appeared. Prior to that, deeper into the Grid's prehistory, there were no Shepherds."

"But where did the Grid originate? The Shepherds may be in control now, but you're telling us the Grid predates them?"

"Yes. That's their story. For what it's worth." Dana raised one eyebrow.

"Is there any information on what happened *before* the Shepherds got involved?"

Dana closed her eyes and reflected. "No. Well – there are what might be called legends, mythologies, vague ideas that have leaked through the interconnected minds of the Grid. Memes, percolating up through ideaspace."

"And what are they?"

"It's all dressed up in symbols. Like all good creation myths, there are clashes between great forces of chaos and order. Tectonic shifts of power, a mighty clash of cymbals yet to come."

Harriet heard this as 'a clash of symbols'. "Sounds a bit, well, abstract."

Dana shrugged. "That's what I get. That's how it is. History, mythmaking… it's not always possible to tease them apart."

Harriet found she couldn't help but like Dana. She gave the impression she was used to dealing with any eventuality that life could throw at her; she seemed to be taking this all in her stride. Harriet sensed she was another self-starter.

"However much I examine the Grid, learn about its properties, fill my minds with its ideas, on some level I think the Grid itself will still be external to me, to us. Out there. Not in here." Dana tapped her forehead. "Humans have a memetic barrier – meaning has to come to us indirectly, through our senses, regardless of what gurus of meditation, intuition and LSD may say. We're not telepathic."

"Yet." Jack smiled. "Though I think Nixon might be hoping we'll come up with something."

Harriet's head still buzzed with questions. "Back up, back up. You're skating over something important here. You said you got here by travelling through the Grid. How does that actually *work*? You're a physical, real person, even with an alien riding in your head. The Grid is not physical—"

"In a way, it is. Everything must have a physical correlate. There is nothing that exists that does not have extension in space, that does not occupy a volume. Think of the Signal itself: it's coded information riding on a modulated string of photons. Physical. Where is the code for your Oxbow? The internet itself? Sure, it's information, noughts and ones, but they still don't have an existence without some physical substrate."

"OK. But that doesn't really—"

"You want to know how I get from here, the real world, into the Grid and out again. The actual *process*."

"Yes."

Dana tilted her head back, pulled in her bottom lip. A strand of blonde hair, almost dry, escaped the towel in which her head was wrapped and fell back over her freckled shoulders. She had the efficient, practical manner of someone who was used to finding simple ways to tackle abstruse problems.

"Right. There are many equivalent descriptions of the same thing. A dog, in Spanish, or French, or Flemish, is still a dog. The only thing that has changed is the form of the description."

This was Jack's favourite territory. "Right."

"But the *description* of the thing is not the *thing*. Unless you're some postmodern pop philosopher. The word 'dog' – or 'chien' – is just a noise you make with your mouth. It's not a furry thing with four legs, a tail and a bark. A word does not fetch sticks."

"No, but the word 'dog' is a shorthand description. A better one would be a biologist's – species, taxonomy, genealogy."

"Still a description. On one level it may be more precise, but it's still not a dog."

Harriet conceded the point.

"OK, I'll now turn this around. What if you're right? Consider this: if you continued to refine that description to the point where there was *nothing* about that dog that was not included in the description – every atom, every neuron, every connection was precisely reproduced – would you not *then* have a dog? Is it not just a matter of how *accurate* your description is? A complete description of a thing must surely, by definition, be indistinguishable from the thing."

Harriet was wearing a face that looked like she was expecting some sleight of hand. "It would be a *duplicate* of the thing?"

"Exactly. The only way in which it would differ is *location*. It would be over there, whereas the original would be over here."

"OK. Two dogs. Identical."

"Now, let's remove that last remaining difference. We now have a description of the thing that is congruent with the thing."

Jack was enjoying this. "A dog within a dog."

"A dog occupying, atom for atom, the same three-dimensional space as a dog. A complete description of that dog, including its location."

"Right."

"Now, can you see that everything, without any process of duplication, simply by *being*, is a *thing* and a *description of that thing* simultaneously. All I do is take the description of the thing and fold it onto another semiotic substrate that happens to be congruent with it."

"Ideaspace. The Grid." Jack offered.

"*Exactly.* The Grid permeates ideaspace, as you call it. It has a physical substrate, but that substrate is not at the location of the description. The Grid is running on a computer, somewhere else, anywhere we wish it to be in fact, not filling—" She gestured around the room. "Not filling real space."

"Just like Jack's Oxbow relocation hack."

"Sorry?"

"Never mind. Carry on."

"So location, in ideaspace, is just another piece of information. Numbers. And numbers can be edited. To move through the Grid, all you need do is change a few digits."

"OK, OK. Let's say I'm following you so far. You haven't explained how you translate the description of you into the Grid in the first place. And out again, back into the real world."

Dana pointed to her head.

"As Jack knows, our LBE, Lunar Biological Entity, Shepherd – call it what you will – has, had, two brains. A forebrain and a hindbrain. It's an evolved form of memetic defence—"

"And one we should have too, quite frankly. There are way too many bad ideas around—"

"So, this is how it works. The forebrain is where incoming perceptions and the internal corollary of perceptions – qualia – first reside. The forebrain is connected to the outside world. It has a limited processing capability, independent of the hindbrain. But here's the thing – the forebrain can be purged. The gap between brains is effectively a firewall. If something happens in the forebrain, if it gets infected with a bad idea, the hindbrain can make an executive decision not to incorporate the information. During sleep, the day's events are laid down into longer-term memories, incorporated into the prime personality, the seat of the I, if you like, which resides in the hindbrain."

Harriet was concentrating. "Uhm."

Nixon was silent. Jack held up a forefinger. "How does that happen? You're saying—"

"The hindbrain copies the mental state – either exactly, or in an edited fashion, as appropriate – of the forebrain. The hindbrain is a brain state duplicator.

"Now there's nothing otherwise unique about the Shepherds' brains that permits this, other than that there's two of them. There's essentially nothing special in a Shepherd brain that a human brain doesn't also have. Brains, it turns out, are pretty plastic as organs go, and that holds true across most of the advanced races in the Grid. I *don't* have two brains. But I *do* remember how to interface my brain with something that is not my brain. Something with the fidelity to reproduce all that is salient about my me-ness."

"The Grid."

"*Right.* The Grid has been designed, or let's say, has *evolved* for exactly that purpose. And consciousness – which basically is a form of very high-level processing – just like the Grid does not have to exist congruent with the substrate, with the body. Consciousness can exist anywhere there are sensory inputs to give an individual a sense of location."

"Sounds like our DMEn."

Dana nodded emphatically. "*Exactly.* Your DMEn. Think of the Grid as the space between panels in a comic strip. The white space between now and the time yet to be. Between one location and another. Or—" Dana was bright and animated. She picked one of Jack's books from a crate to her left. "It's like turning the page of a book, or even several pages, all at once. I am here, on page 616, and all I need do is pull up all the space between where I am and where I want to be, like a rug, and then I simply step over." She mimicked a person jumping between pages with her index and middle fingers. "*Voilà*. Here I am. On page 617."

"And the space between – that's the Grid?"

"The Grid is the page. The substrate. Any biologist will tell you that one of the signatures of life itself is organisation. Think about it. From a purely chemical standpoint, the works of Shakespeare and a telephone directory are very similar. Ink. Wood pulp. Carbon. Cellulose. What is the difference? What is encoded *on* this substrate. The *content*. We are the organisation of marks on the page. The information. We are the *story*. We are what the book happens to be *about*."

Dana was smiling enigmatically. Something peculiar was beginning to happen. She had twisted somehow, seemed to be getting . . . *narrower*? How—? She began to take on a flat, two-dimensional quality. There were shadows falling impossibly across shadows, a sense of light on both a three-dimensional and a two-dimensional surface simultaneously. A curling cut-out. She seemed to be peeling up, off the surface – the surface of what? Reality? The page? The Universe?

Jack felt a chill of recognition, and involuntarily jumped back, sending his crate spinning across the parquet. *What did this remind him of? Why was this familiar?*

Dana seemed to lift up, into a space which was real and yet imaginary; a space both everywhere and nowhere. Jack could see the thin slice of the world on which she existed almost edge-on now; one of the flat painted planes that made up the scenery of reality.

617

then

i

t

t

u

r

n

e

d

o

v

e

r

,

l

i

k

e

t

h

e

p

a

g

e

o

f

a

b

o

o

k

,

and she was gone.

Nadine's clothes, the ones Jack had lent her, fell softly to the floor. Still fastened at the waist and fly, her trouser-legs held the volume of her thighs for a moment before gracefully bowing forwards like a deflating Waving Man and collapsing. Her empty T-shirt hung unsupported in space for what seemed like a full second then fell, performing an elegant shimmy like a saucer dropped in dishwater before neatly folding itself over the pile on the floor. Her heavy wet towel then unceremoniously capped them off, still wrapped like a turban around the absence of head that no longer filled it.

"*Whoah!*" Harriet had her hand to her mouth.

Nixon was immediately on his feet. "Did you see *that?* Tell me what you just saw. Did you see what I saw?"

"I saw her turn, like she was thin, a sheet of paper – and then just disappear."

"Me *too!* That's *exactly* what I saw. Jack – you saw that too, right?"

Jack had indeed seen it. In fact, it wasn't the first time. He had seen something very much like it once before, a long, long time ago, back in the science laboratory in school. That sense of a collapsing house of cards, the impression that the world around him was a stage set, and that if you looked closely, if you looked at just the right angle, between the flat planes you could catch a glimpse of dark spaces, the parts of the scene you were not supposed to see: the cables and winches of maths and physics, the scaffold of law on which the world was constructed; and further, the cold and timeless and unspeakable things that lay just behind and beneath our familiar, cosy everyday reality.

Harriet and Nixon were crouched over the small heap of clothes on the floor. "No glasses. I wasn't wearing the glasses. That was *real.*"

Harriet grabbed at the nearest pair of Depthcharges and accidentally sent them scooting across the table. "Hang on. Let me put these on." She fitted them over her face then touched a button at the temple. Jack picked up the other pair.

"On the main screen, please guys." Nixon protested. "Let me see what you see."

The 19th Count, XX and Girl 21 were immediately visible, sitting around the conference room table like a council of war or a meeting of fancy dress enthusiasts. There, with them, was Dana.

She had an expression Jack couldn't quite decipher. The Count had hung his short shoulder cape decorously around her shoulders, but had not thought to divest himself of his longer frock coat. Her arms were folded across her breasts, but below the edge of the glass table Jack could see she was naked from the waist down.

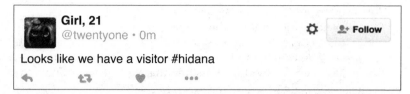

THERE IS NO ART LEFT FOR US TO ADMIRE
BUT THE MAD SCULPTURES
THAT OUR
ARTILLERY MOULDS
AMONG THE RANKED MASSES
OF THE ENEM—

Don't be *startled* by our friend here.

He doesn't bite.

Though he may try and convince you that WAR is the great

Hygiene *of the* World,

and more *gentlemanly* conduct the preserve of the

SYPHILITIC FOP.

Dana's mouth moved, but no sound came out.

"Ah. This is interesting." Jack moved to his iMac. "You're in the Grid, but also the part of the Grid that happens to intersect with the Oxbow. I don't think you were expecting that. Dana, give me a second. We'll need to loop you through the onomatopoeic interpreter."

Harriet pulled up a screen and typed a few lines of code. "As you're already manifest, I can skip the visual display and send it direct to sound. Unless you have a favourite font."

Dana's voice suddenly came through the inbuilt speakers. Quieter, low-fi, but unmistakably her: "–is this Oxbow?"

Jack elucidated. "A pinch of internet, an area that is separate but connected, where ideas can coalesce into something individuated . . . a bit like a human body. Connected to the world, but having a degree of separateness, autonomy . . ."

"This is the way you intend to communicate with the aliens?"

"If we isolate a Grid entity in the Oxbow—"

"You will separate it from the influence of the Shepherds. The Shepherds are the only thing keeping order in the Grid. By pulling them into your Oxbow, you run the risk of giving them a degree of freedom—"

Nixon spoke up. "Why do we assume that's a bad idea? Shouldn't everyone be allowed to exercise their own free will?"

"Nixon. It's naive. Not all the alien races in the Grid have our best intentions at heart. They have very different drives and ambitions . . . and some kind of consensus can only be brokered where some basic common values exist. It just isn't always possible."

"I'd say the right to an individual existence was a pretty basic value. Shepherds herd *sheep*—"

Harriet put her hand on Nixon's arm. "Hey. Let her finish."

"I don't think you realise that the Shepherds have given up their previous lives to help preserve the Grid. They're here at some personal cost."

Even at reduced volume, they could sense her concern.

Jack looked up at the ceiling out of a sense of decorum. "Dana, I know that you're curious. I've read the Daedalus debrief documents. I know that the origins of the Grid are wrapped in myth and legend, intimately tied to galactic prehistory. If we want to know how this all began, we need to go to the source. We need to dig down into the Grid, to the very centre, to where it all started. With the Oxbow we can do it. Maybe we'll get the answers you need. Discover why the Grid was built in the first place. Don't tell me you're not curious to find out what's down there, at the very beginning?"

For a few moments, Dana made no reply.

"His lifespan was long, by our standards, but it doesn't stretch back a fraction of the time the Grid has been in existence. What's at the centre of the Grid? He – it – doesn't know. All the Shepherds have are their theories . . ."

Harriet was beginning to think that Jack's and Nixon's protestations might be bordering on the impolite. Dana was their guest, after all. She spoke in a calm and measured tone. "Jack, Nixon – I say it should be her call."

Jack lowered his gaze. "Look. We've already made a short exploratory trip into the Grid. We guessed it had a geography. And we now know it has a history." He once again thought of the compacted layers of clay and brick and tarmac on which London was built, that immense stretch of time laid down in physical form beneath their feet. Though this compressed stratigraphy recorded many millennia of human activity, he suspected it might still amount to a fleeting afternoon in Grid time.

"We've just figured out a way to dig down into its past, like an archae-ologist. Time, laid out as a physical dimension that we can traverse. We can now read the book of the Grid – it's possible for us to travel down, perhaps to the very centre, and find out how it all began – and *why*."

No one, even Dana, made any protest. Jack pressed the advantage. "We have a unique opportunity here. I say we take it."

WALKING THROUGH HERCULANEUM

Realising that this meeting was not going to break up any time soon, Nixon had collected dinner from the Hoxton Bar and Grill. Dana was ravenously making short work of the peas and halloumi. "I always come out of the Grid hungry – what does that mean?"

Twenty minutes previously she had asked, in her reduced point size, if Nadine's clothes could be placed in the bathroom. A few minutes later she had stepped out into the office, clothed and in corporeal form.

Harriet was gesticulating like a conductor with a breadstick. "So, so let me run through this again. You travel through the Grid—" Jack could tell that Harriet found Dana fascinating. He did too. Here, sitting in their office, was someone who had actually walked on the surface of the Moon. Someone who had met a real live alien. It took some getting used to.

"Yes."

"I've got to get my head around how this works. So, you're in one place, then you do your weird 'moving at right angles to reality' thing, then—"

"Then I'm in the Grid. The space the Grid occupies, the space with no specific extension that your DMEn, as you call them, occupy."

"Ideaspace."

"Yes. I like that term. It has no intrinsic . . . dimension."

"And you can exit that space – anywhere?"

"Anywhere the Grid corresponds with the real world. The Grid seems to overlap many places, and I'm not sure all of them are what we would call strictly physical. Or even rational."

"How, how precise is this?"

"Not very. If I had time to map the Grid, the correspondences between it and the real world would be more accurate. In there, remember, I can't see out. I'm driving blind."

"So how did you know where to go? To come and see us here?"

"My first jump was short. Just out of the decontamination chamber and into the facility proper. I'd walked through it on the way in, so knew where to go. I looked your company up on an iPad in the chairman's office when he was out at lunch. Google Maps helped me scope out the surrounding area. I took a location reference, and overlaid that with the Grid using a rough set of mathematical translations I could perform on the location markers I do have access to. I stepped into the Grid there and stepped out here, and here I am."

Jack smiled. "It sounds almost easy."

Harriet was enraptured. "It's incredible."

"So, how accurate? Within what, a few metres? The size of a room?"

"I think I can enter and exit the same place within a few centimetres without too much worry. The further the translation across the Grid, the larger the potential for error."

"And what if you got it wrong?"

"I don't want to think what the practical results might be of exiting the Grid inside something solid." Dana pointed to a blue bruise on her calf. "To be sure I didn't run that risk, I added a metre and a half to the vertical component. I chose a spot with no overhanging trees so I wouldn't end up with a branch through my head. No passers-by. No cars. A private garden. I thought a short fall to solid ground would be less dangerous than finding my feet embedded in concrete."

"So you can displace the air? When you exit?"

"Yes. I think I could probably displace water too. My guess is that it's a function of the manner in which I seem to . . . flatten, then slide off the face of three dimensions into a fourth. It must also happen in reverse – I kind of carve out a space for myself when I exit. From my point of view it feels like a shuffling of cards, a series of stacked surfaces, between which you can choose to insert yourself and then stand up."

Harriet had forgotten to eat her breadstick and was using it to point at Dana for emphasis. Taramasalata fell from its tip. "This is a talent that is *so* open to abuse by the less-than-noble-minded."

Dana grinned. "Don't you think I know that?"

"Burglary. Espionage."

"That wasn't my very first thought. You know what was? *Archaeology.* I could walk through walls right into the Great Pyramid's secret spaces. Through the buried rooms of Pompeii and Herculaneum. Through the bedchambers of the Winter Palace. But it's risky – ideally you need a camera to provide you with a live view, to make sure the space you intend to occupy when you exit is empty. And where there's a camera, there's surveillance. Others can see you too. You can't take a disguise in with you. Your clothing gets left behind. With no way of hiding your face, you'd give away your identity as soon as you were caught on video. So unless you, overnight, intend on becoming Public Enemy Number One, it's not the no-brainer you'd imagine."

"What if you cased the space in person beforehand?"

"You could. Though the really interesting spaces are those that aren't available to public view. We may have a photo, or even just a verbal description. Or not even that – merely an inkling of something hidden."

"Let me think about this one. Not that I'm suggesting anything illegal, mind you. But, purely out of scientific curiosity . . . are there any practical limits on where you can go? How far? Other planets? Mars?"

"No clothes, Harriet," Jack chipped in. "Mars has no air, and you can't port a spacesuit through the Grid. And anyway, the Grid is not that large. It doesn't even stretch as far as the Moon."

"But ideaspace is made of *ideas* . . . is it not as wide and as tall as you make it? An infinitely plastic postmodern Universe in which you can rethink the parameters?"

"In asking me whether I could alter the laws of what passes for physics in the Grid, you have to keep in mind that the Grid *does* obey laws. It has to. In fact, it is nothing *but* law, written in the grand universal language of mathematics. So if you alter a value here, you'll need to change something else somewhere else in order that the whole is still in balance. It's a delicate and self-referential mechanism.

"The Grid has achieved a stability not because of, but in spite of all the creatures it has incorporated within it. That stability is now deeply rooted. Mess with it at your peril. The Grid will push back."

"But— as a mathematician and physicist, that must give you *some* kind of advantage?"

Dana raised her eyebrows and let out a long, resigned sigh. "It does."

"Doesn't that make you like some kind of god, I mean, when you're in there?"

"Harriet, ideaspace is a concatenation of concepts, each with its own internal logic, like bubble universes floating in a larger, less formalised space. Each of those bubble universes can be thought of as a set of ideas which, considered together and in isolation, make perfect sense – they're self-contained and internally noncontradictory. Mostly."

"Ideologies. Memeplexes."

"If you like. Or entities, even, if you think about them in a certain way. That may lead you to assume that the smallest unit in ideaspace is the brain, human or otherwise. But a brain is already a complex interrelated set of ideas. Some held firmly, others just for a minute or so for their functional utility; some are hardwired by evolutionary necessity; some backed

626

up with evidence, others not at all. We are made of constellations of ideas."

"In my Father's house are many rooms."

Dana impatiently waved away Nixon's theological reference. "Think of it as a series of nested spheres of influence. *Idea. Brain.* Next up in the hierarchy of ideas is the *group.* You get a group of people, or aliens, together, and they'll develop what we'd call a *culture.* Which is just to say they have a set of ideas in common. A set of beliefs about how the world works and a means with which to discuss it: a language. Social codes. Music. Art. It'll all make perfect sense, *if* you happen to be a member of the group. You may even think your worldview is true, as in universally true, for all people at all times. But of course these bubble universes of ideas, these ideologies, will inevitably contradict each other. Like different notions battling it out in your own mind . . . they do not always concur. You toss and turn. You try and figure it out. It feels uncomfortable to be in a state of unresolved superposition. So these sets of ideas circle around, like orbiting stars, closing in on each other. They have to eventually coalesce – the attractive force of gravity applies even in ideaspace – and when they do, they have to reach some kind of memetic consensus and find a new equilibrium. The differing networks of ideas each represents have to find common ground, a synthesis. And so it goes, merger upon merger, in much the same way that stars form clusters, and clusters form galaxies."

"And this is what goes on in ideaspace?"

"This *is* ideaspace."

"But you *can* manipulate it . . . ?"

"I can't rethink the Grid on a whim. Remember, the Grid is a vast network of ideas, and while you are at liberty to add some more of your own, your ability as an individual to change the grand narratives that are supported by a million minds is pretty limited. In one way, this is as it should be – it ensures a degree of continuity. Ideaspace, like the real world, should be stable and predictable, and not prone to conceptquakes that would rewrite it on a regular basis."

"So you're not a god."

"No, Harriet, I am not a god. Gods are robust networks of ideas that purport to explain everything: Morality. Creation. Law. And make no mistake – they are *vast.* They are *virulent.* They are *tenacious.*

"And when it comes to finding a consensus, many of them are – most damagingly of all – *mutually incompatible.*"

Jack finished the last of the mashed potato. "It's not so different out here in the real world."

Dana nodded. "Jack, you've been very helpful. More helpful than you know. But you should also know that even if I had told Adam and Gabe as much as I could have done, I still wouldn't have scratched the surface of what I now know. I feel like I'm forever pushing a symphony of meaning through a letterbox an alphabet wide. Human language is such a blunt tool. It can be beautiful, it can be precise, it can be teased into the most elegant constructions . . . but so can a *hedge*."

Dana spun a hand as she searched for words. "Picture this. The one-dimensional thread of time on which we hang the letters of our stories, the words of our lives, moves predictably from left to right across the page. Beat to beat to beat. Human language is linear, like the mono-brained creatures that created it: it plods predictably along that single line, passing back and forth across the page like a farmer ploughing his field, one furrow at a time. Row upon row upon row . . . it's slow. It's – most criminally of all – *inefficient*. Our lives are short, and there's so much to *know*. I have access to the lives of countless sentient beings, their dynasties and histories, their poetry and art, and I have to fit it all through a bottleneck of *language*." Jack could sense the combination of disgust and sadness in her voice.

"It's a bandwidth problem like no other. I could spend every day of the rest of my life dictating wonders, and I'd still end up effectively burning libraries many times greater than Alexandria. I could tell you the most magnificent stories that have ever been told, but my life, a *hundred* lives, is simply not enough to do them all justice." Dana's voice wavered slightly. Harriet could feel her passion, kept in check just under the surface. She pressed a forefinger to her temple. "But . . . I can *see* that pattern, the one the farmer ploughs every day. I can intuit its true form, the one he cannot simply because he's too close to his work. It's laid out before me, as if from above, all at once, in its entirety, in one *understanding*.

"*Two brains*, Jack. Imagine if you could think two different thoughts at the same time! Sounds like a Wonderland impossibility, doesn't it? But we can hear more than one note played on a piano at the same time. We sense the congruences and differences, and we call it *harmony*, and we sense that it is *beautiful*. Beauty – that's just another name for our faculty of sensing correlation, balance, *truth*. What would music be, if we couldn't hear a chord?

"Two *ideas*, held simultaneously – the harmonics they produce! I can run my mind over the finely textured possibilities, the landscape of inter-ference fringes that describe point and counterpoint, the hills and valleys of opposition and confluence. I can see them all at once!

"Just like the Grid itself, I can now traverse the *x*, *y* and *z* of three-dimensional thought-space. I feel like I was *colourblind* before. Now my head is a vast *symphony* of ideas!"

Signal "regularities" – a second repeat?

A new analysis of the mathematical structure of the Signal supports contentious theory

Correspondent Clarissa Friedrich

Meta-analysis of the Signal from Space has recently emerged as a popular method with which to probe its mysteries. That this approach is open to both armchair enthusiast and high-ranking institution alike has encouraged a raft of theories that have been the subject of much speculation on exobiology forums, both on the fringe and those run by venerable scientific institutions such as Jodrell Bank.

A word of caution: it is possible to manipulate any large data set to achieve a significant result, and nowhere is this more true than for novel cases where even the most basic analyses are provisional.

Still, this approach has already thrown up a few intriguing patterns. The first and strongest repeat signal led to the discovery of a race of beings spaced at regular intervals throughout the visible portion of the Signal. The analysis, first proposed by Graham Boileau at UCL, has subsequently been backed up by observation.

This new regularity is less pronounced, but if it proves to be real, may shed new light on the way the Signal is organised.

It seems to suggest that there are smaller constellations of data that also repeat throughout the Grid, often in tandem with those previously discovered.

While there is broad agreement that specific sectors of the Signal house creatures either from the same or closely related species, if this new insight suggests members of a second distinct race are also distributed through it at regular intervals it throws up some interesting possibilities.

"The new signal is shorter. Less complex. This is why we missed it earlier. It probably represents a less evolved species in some form of co-existence with the first."

Boileau is not short of conjectures. "Sidekicks? Lapdogs? Who are these new creatures who seem to share the same distribution pattern?"

"Who will guard the guardians?" one of our sources close to the Jodrell project opined. "The Signal is proving to be far more complex and interesting than we first imagined. Our simple theories have evolved into a more nuanced view, one where perhaps contingency and happenstance – and the putative history of the Signal, which we have not even begun to unravel – may have had as important a bearing on its current form as any grand overarching design." ➤

BIG RED

They were going back in.

"You want to do this on the inside or the outside?" Harriet had brought up a laundry basket from the communal utility room in the basement. "If you're planning on folding yourself back into the Grid, you may want to stand in this."

Dana took the basket. "Thanks. For the moment, I'll stay here with you, out here in the real world."

She had to remind herself that it was a non-intuitive peculiarity of the Grid that when one was in it, one couldn't see it. There was no light propagating through the Grid; no physical eyes on which it could fall. In there, her eyes and ears were the cameras and microphones attached to the Web, nothing more. To see into ideaspace she had to look out into the real world and have her gaze directed back in again. She was only visible, as were the DMEn, if someone effectively held up a mirror.

"You saw the results of our first dive, Dana. The inaugural mission of the Good Ship *Nondescript '30s Industrial Building on Hoxton Square.* I think we're all agreed on our final destination."

Dana nodded slowly. "Grid point zero, zero, zero. Where this all began." She held up her fingers and thumb, describing a circle, then shifted it to her right twice for emphasis. "There is one thing we *do* know. It's numbers. All the way down."

With no inkling that they would be entertaining a new guest, the previous day Nixon had ordered, on a whim, four Eames recliners he'd seen in the window of Midcentury Showrooms. They had arrived as Jack was scraping the remains of lunch into an overflowing bin. Dana had locked herself in the bathroom until the two monosyllabic removal men had brought them up the stairs, manhandled them into the conference room, asked Nixon to sign three sheets of pink paper, and left.

The crates they'd been sitting on for so long were now finally stacked away, and in their place the new arrivals were arranged in a semicircle around the conference room table, facing the large screen hanging on the opposite wall. The remainder of Jack's and Harriet's computer equipment had been carried in from their workstations and positioned in front.

Nixon regarded what had become of his office. It had the feel of a makeshift starship bridge, albeit one where the captain and his crew could lounge rather than stand to attention. The fridge (beer, milk, juice, chocolate) and the kettle (tea, coffee, Pot Noodle) had also been relocated inside the room; Nixon had tried to lift the water cooler, but it was full and his back had complained.

As a fort-building exercise for grown-ups, Harriet reflected, it did give the proceedings a certain sense of occasion.

Jack had once more neglected to check his email and phone. Had he looked, he would have noticed that Gabriel had tried to call him four times. There were also three unread messages from Nadine.

"OK, preflight checks. Dana, Nixon – you don't have glasses. Please watch the main screen. You'll see what Harriet and I see, minus the depth perception. We won't be able to swap once we're off. Have we bolted the door? We don't want any delivery men or clients who just happen to be in town dropping in to disturb us."

Nixon was by the window. "You don't suppose anyone is watching us, do you? Shall I pull down the blinds?"

The possibility had not occurred to Jack. "Pfft. We're a small tech start-up. We do gaming stuff. We're currently running some new simulation of something. Anyway, the scenery out to the limits of the Oxbow can be pretty impressive. Let's do this in IMAX 3D, not bootleg VHS."

"Unless you have some misplaced fondness for that format," Harriet added.

"Ahhhh . . ." Nixon contrived an expression of rapturous recollection. "I won't say any more. I don't want to have another 'boobs' conversation."

Jack didn't catch the reference. "Good. So we're agreed. Close the blinds, and we'll be missing the best part of the show." He paused to take a sip of tea. "I've already engaged the onomatopoeic interpreter and the Chomsky Module. Where signs and symbols appear in the field of view is fluid and open to interpretation, but in the absence of input to the contrary we have a snap-back to the Western left-to-right, top-to-bottom reading preference so there's a degree of familiarity to help keep us on the rails. That tea is cold."

"That tea is from last week. The one I just made is in the Sports Direct mug." Nixon pointed. "Might this not get very confusing, very fast?"

Jack spoke while panting through a mouth of scalding PG Tips. "Confusing? Most probably. We got a taster before, on our first jaunt.

The routines will mine as much imagery from the data as they can, and we'll be numerically tagging as we go, so we can return to any specific location of interest.

"Our main issue, as you saw with our gallery of alien language posted over there, is that there will inevitably be a chasm between the coded states of consciousness the aliens in the Grid possess and what we are familiar with – remember, even a brain *per se* is an anthropomorphic assumption—"

"I, for example, have two," Dana footnoted.

"We can certainly meet and greet the Grid at the level of pure number; we can process those numbers for structure and regularity . . . this is how we noticed the Shepherds in the first place. But when it comes to what those numbers really *mean* . . ."

Dana looked at the printouts hanging from the shelf through the glass divide. "Sign and signified."

"Jack— what about our DMEn?" Harriet placed both her hands on the table. "They're our guys on the inside. You think *they'll* be able to translate?"

"They're a product of human culture, so I can't imagine they'll understand any more of this alien stuff than we do—"

"But they *are* made of the same stuff. *Numbers.*"

Jack put on his Depthcharges. The Count was standing just behind Harriet, flexing the fingers of first one hand and then the other while pulling on the cuffs of his white gloves. He sported an expression of mild disgust.

ALIEN NOTIONS.

URGH.
even wearing
GLOVES,
should one *touch* a foreign *mind?*

Jack raised one eyebrow. Harriet may have something there. He wondered how that might work, practically speaking. You'd first need to isolate the binary description of the mind in question . . . "Interesting. Bypass the interpretive format conversion of language entirely."

Girl 21 turned away from them and began tapping on her smartphone with her thumbs. Jack could see the glow of her screen through her pink hair. Nothing appeared in their field of view, however, no white Twitter rectangle.

Jack wondered who she might be talking to.

It was decided. The DMEn were to be their ambassadors in ideaspace, the realm that was very much their own. The plan was to see what they could learn first, up close and personal with one of the entities in the Grid. Though Dana was not certain how this might be achieved or what effect this might have, she felt she had impressed upon Jack and Harriet the degree of care with which such a feat should be executed. Though he seemed somewhat reticent, the Count had let a curtain of manicules and double-daggers unfurl, which Jack had taken to be a sign that they should stop worrying, and that the DMEn knew what they were doing.

Nixon and Dana took their places in the two remaining recliners, which had been positioned behind and to the left and right of Jack's and Harriet's. Almost as an afterthought, Harriet brought three of the crates back in and arranged them against the far wall; when she put on her Depthcharges, she could see they were already occupied. She waved, and the 19th Count waved back in an understated, effortlessly lordly manner. Of course it made no practical difference to the DMEn whether the crates were there or not; they were perfectly capable of sitting on nothing but the abstract Platonic 'chairness' of a chair. It was a symbolic gesture, one Harriet thought was important, especially now they were about to drop once more into a realm in which symbols were every bit as import-ant as – if not *more* important than – the flesh and blood humans that happened to be steering the ship.

"Before we raise anchor, I had something prepared." Nixon reached into a cardboard box under the table Jack hadn't noticed before and produced something wrapped in running proofs for an early Intelli-gencia fundraising brochure. He bowed ceremonially and presented it to Jack.

"What's this?"

"Unwrap it."

Jack lifted out a square base with a sucker on each corner, surmounted by a big cartoon lever with a bulbous tip painted a shiny lip-gloss red. It was a foot-tall mock-up of his Big Red Lever concept.

"Ha! That is *brilliant*, Nixon. You had this made? From scratch?"

633

"Had it made? *I* made it. With some, ah, technical assistance from Harriet. We 3D-printed the handle, sprayed it with four coats of Fuck-Off Ferrari Red, and slotted it over the top of an off-the-shelf joystick."

Jack returned the bow to Nixon and Harriet. "Thank you. That's very thoughtful." Jack held it up and turned it around. "It, uh, does look as if you modelled it on some intimate personal appliance. Is it functional?"

"Of *course*. USB connection. Plug it in."

Positioned on a pile of magazines between the recliners, it rose like a phallic gearstick in a low-riding 1970s concept car.

"It's *perfect*."

Jack gestured to the seats. "Shall we?"

The four of them settled into the recliners, which didn't look dissimilar to the launch couches with which Dana was familiar.

"Ready? Can you reach the fridge, Nixon?"

"A-OK, Captain."

"I have to tell you," Dana observed laconically from her semi-horizontal position, "preflight checks are *nothing* like this at NASA."

Jack gave her a stiff salute, then without a further word or even a countdown, pulled the big red lever as hard as he could.

JOURNEY TO THE CENTRE OF THE WORLD

They felt a vertiginous drop, as of a lift in freefall. Jack knew it was an illusion, but could still feel the familiar weight of his internal organs lift as his diaphragm instinctively pushed up forcing the air out of his lungs

Nixon's face displayed the mix of joy and apprehension of a novice rollercoaster rider. From their recliners, through the glasses, out of the office windows the Grid could be seen stretching to the limits of visibility; a printer's dot screen made entirely of bodies, a grey tint overprinting an already grey English afternoon. Closer, the limits of the Oxbow became apparent: it was hard to gauge, but Jack estimated it was currently around 500 metres in radius. Within this area ideaspace was moving relative to the rest of the Grid, and the rush heavenward had begun.

When the exodus of bodies reached the upper limit of the Oxbow, it vanished – there, the normal rank and file remained hanging in stately immobility. The edge of the Oxbow formed a border not between two worlds, but between two different *views* of the *same* world – the world of the Grid, one moving relative to the other, and both overlaying our familiar, solid, three-dimensional reality.

They were travelling, while simultaneously standing still.

"Sinking into the crust of the World of Ideas", as Harriet would later describe it.

Though there was no physical lurch of cut cables, the sense of a vertiginous drop familiar from their last excursion was hard to shake. Every sense told them they were in motion.

Jack involuntarily held tight to the armrests of his recliner. "It's like that illusion of being thrown backwards when the guy in the car beside you is first away at the lights."

Wispy shapes shot through the room, flying up from the floor and into the ceiling before they could get the barest sense of what – or who – they were. Outside, the ascent of the Grid as a whole could be better appreciated. It seemed slower, though this was just an illusion afforded by the wider perspective.

Dana spoke up. "You map your routes?"

"It's all logged. If we need to come back to a specific spot, we can."

She was studying the large screen intently. "We're moving fast."

"We have a lot of ground to cover. We can slow down, take a look at anything you'd like to see."

Jack checked his feed. They had dropped no more than a few kilometres. "To take—"

"Did you *see* that? Did someone just walk across the room out there?" Harriet was pointing into the main area of the office

638

through the glass dividing wall.

"I wasn't looking. Where?"

"See the storeroom door is open? Did you leave it open?"

"I don't think it's ever been shut." From their positions, they could see a stack of boxed printer paper that prevented it closing.

"You think there's someone in the office? I can't see anyone. You think we should stop?"

Nixon was on his feet, standing beside his recliner, craning to get a better view. "The front door's locked. We are the only people with keys. Unless the landlord—"

"There it is again!"

This time Jack saw it too.

A – a what, exactly? It moved so quickly that he was at a loss to describe it. It seemed to come out from the open storeroom, into the office where he should have been able to see it more clearly . . .

It had no discernible shape – or, more precisely, it had a multitude of shapes, each one different, a vibrating outline that his eyes found impossible to resolve. It seemed to glide from the open door, across the office towards them, and . . . where?

"Where did it go?"

It made no sound whatsoever.

"Aha." Jack eased back on the big red stick. "Wait – it'll happen again, in . . . two, one—"

The rate of descent slowed. "Wait – it'll happen again, in . . . two, one—"

A series of alien bodies shot from floor to ceiling in quick succession, but this time slowly enough to separate into individuals. They started in the far recesses of the open storeroom and at each subsequent pass appeared closer, then closer still; advancing across the office until they passed through the blank exterior wall adjacent to the conference room and were lost from view. Seen through the glass partition it was an unsettling sight; each appearance a brief flicker, each a step closer to where they sat.

"Hah. We're falling obliquely through columns of creatures." Jack relaxed. "Our descent is not precisely vertical, or the Grid itself is not perfectly aligned to the vertical. Interesting effect. Not unlike a zoetrope. Hah! No one's creeping up on us."

He changed a couple of digits in a small box on a screen full of small boxes. "There. Fixed. We're now falling vertically."

"We're approaching the bottom of the crust. Nearing the mantle. Not that that has any practical effect on the Grid – it doesn't feel any heat or pressure. But it is, you know, a useful way to visualise our descent."

Dana shifted in her recliner. "You did a preliminary mapping. Of the density of the Grid, from an informational point of view?"

"I did."

"Show me."

Harriet pushed a window across to the main screen. A three-dimensional spherical lattice of vanishingly small dots spun sedately. A magenta blip at the top left of the screen plotted their present position. Though the rush of shapes outside and inside the office seemed breathtakingly fast, their motion on the scale of the map was imperceptible. Harriet spun it around and drew a marquee over the magenta dot, enlarging a portion. She did this an additional five times. Now, on screen, a small sphere that represented the limit of the Oxbow could be seen, the cubic lattice moving up around and through it.

Dana leant over. "Go back. Zoom out."

Harriet did so.

"What's that?"

She indicated a rhomboidal void in the Grid. Harriet spun it around for the benefit of those without depth perception. "It looks like a kind of crystal intrusion – a series of octagonal bars, extending from that one point. *There.*"

"We know there are voids in the Grid. We entered one last time—"

"This looks different. It doesn't look like part of the Grid's natural structure. It looks like a later addition. Can we check it out?"

Jack shrugged. "Your call. Let's take a look." He tapped the big red lever forward a fraction, then fine-tuned the result on a numerical keyboard and hit return. "Right. We should pass through that left, uh, lobe in a few moments." Without looking, he knew that Harriet had twisted her foot into the nest of cabling under the table. "Coming up on it . . . now."

The flutter of shapes ceased. Nothing. "Passing through . . ." There was no discomfort, no feeling of subconscious dread. "You want me to slow the descent?"

Dana leaned in. "Let's look at the perimeter of the area more closely.

Can we do that?"

"Sure. Coming up on the far side . . . slowing."

A series of truncated shapes rose slowly through the floor. Jack halted them when they reached waist height. Outside, the sharp demarcation could be seen even more clearly – a void above, the now familiar rows of figures resuming below.

"Wow. The cut-off is literally *through* the figures themselves. Look—" Harriet was passing her hands through a specimen that rose to a couple of centimetres above the tabletop. It looked like a prepared medical slide, a perfect cross-section through the entity's torso, replete with a white spinal eye like a steak and bisected internal organs. The rest of the figure continued below the table, disappearing into the parquet, but the portion that protruded above looked like nothing less than a thick slice of meat without a plate. "What happened here? Because I'd hazard a guess this isn't how it was intended to be."

"Signal loss?" Jack offered. "There are sections of the Grid we simply didn't receive. Degradation?"

Harriet regarded the bisected alien on the table. Her feed was clearly visible on the main monitor. "Signal degradation would probably show as a general reduction in detail. This is a sharp cut-off."

"To me the shape suggests a later intrusion, don't you think? Signal disruption would be more random. Not this clean edge, this perfectly excised section."

"The void definitely seems to have a shape. Like it's growing, new crystals budding off from that base there."

"A creature that reveals itself by its absence? What might that be? A *thing* that can't be *thought?*"

"Take us to that location that the shapes seem to emanate from."

Harriet's fingers skated lightly over her keyboard. The steak dropped into the table again. Outside, shapes rotated around them like litter on the breeze.

"Here. Coming up."

A creature not unlike a squid hung vertically in front of the main screen. It had three corrugated wing-like sheets of flesh running vertically up a tapered

‎ cylindrical
body, at the top of
which a selection of stalks protruded
from a recessed cavity like kitchen utensils in a jar.

Dana stood up and moved forwards. "Can you walk around it? Show us more?" Harriet split the main monitor screen so that her and Jack's Depthcharge feeds were given equal billing.

From the back, a flexible chitin shell rose up from a ridged spine to the bloom of sensory organs at the top. Piercing this, just below the top lip of the body, were a series of octagonal holes that passed right through the creature. Jack could see the brickwork of the office directly through it.

"Trepanning for aliens?"

"Could this have happened before it was incorporated?"

"No. This happened in the Grid. The alignment of the bodies is a Grid

...nomenon.

              ınat razor-edged cut-off
          could only happen once the body had
      ueen incorporated."

So what is it? Some kind of defence mechanism? Ritual suicide?"

Dana shrugged. "My pal in my brain has no information on this. But I agree – this is probably something that happened post-incorporation. Could someone or something be knocking out specific creatures for a reason?"

"How would that even be possible? The Grid is supposed to be in lockdown. That would suggest there are agents in here which have already managed to gain some kind of volition."

Dana's brow creased. "It *could* have happened between transmissions. Maybe an artefact of some kind in the data processing or storage. It may not be deliberate. If whoever or whatever did this intended to take just this one guy out, they were pretty indiscriminate."

Jack looked across at Dana. She bore an expression of intense concentration. He could tell she was used to taking control of novel situations, and without even being aware of the shift in power, Harriet and Nixon had begun to defer to her. Jack let it slide; after all, no one had officially made him the boss among equals. "Noted and filed. Another mystery to figure out at some later date. Shall we continue?"

SHEEPDOG

That second repeated signal in the Grid. It was obvious, now Harriet reflected on it.

Shepherds don't corral their flocks themselves. They use something else to do that for them.

Shepherds have sheepdogs.

She'd brought the Oxbow to a standstill around the nearest such mysterious entity. They had one now, isolated here in front of them.

If you took this creature for a walk in the park you'd need to keep it on a tight leash, Jack thought. He could tell it sat low to the ground, even hanging here weightlessly on the invisible numerical pegs of the Grid. Did it look like a dog? *Just possibly* . . . it had a powerful set of haunches and a short but heavy balancing tail, like a dinosaur, while its forepaws were short and delicate, almost atrophied. The head . . .

A shadow of a frown passed across the 19th Count's marble-sculpted face. The featureless eyes were still capable of expression.

That is one ***unattractive beastie.***
A — a... I– I seem to be at a *loss for words.*

"It's n⊠t like you to be – how do you say it?"

Precisely. How does one – say the – the *thing?*
The thing one thinks⊠

In Jack's textual overlay a glyph he had not seen before had occurred twice in quick succession. He looked at Harriet. Harriet shrugged.

"I see it too. Syntax error in the – ah, the whatsit, the Chomsky Module?"

"Let's try that again. I – I think we should – we need to, um . . .

"We ⊠⊠.

"⊠⊠ ⊠⊠⊠."

"Let me t░░ a░░░░."

"Fan░░░ ░ ░░░░░ ░░ ░░░░ ░░░ ░ ░░░░░░░. ░░░░░░ ░░░░░ ░░ ░ ░░░░░░ ░░ ░░░░░ ░░ ░░░░░ ░░░░░ on ░░░ "░░ ░░░░░d ░░ ░░░░░ ░░░░░ ░░░░░░░░░░."

░░░ ░ ░░ #░░ ░░░░░.

░░░░░░ ░░░░░░░░ ░░ ░░░░░.

░░'░ ░░░░░ ░░░umer░░░░░ ░░░░ ░░░░░ ░░ ░░ ░░an░░░░ ░░ ░░░ ░░░░░░░ ░░░░ ░░░░░ ░░░░'░ ░dst░░░░ ░░░ ░░░░░ ░ "░░'░ ░ ░░░░░░░ ░░░ ░░░░░░░░ ░░░ ░░ ░░'░ ░ ░░ ░░░░."

░░ ░░ strugg░░e░░ ░░░░'░ ░░ ░░░░░ ░░░░░ ░░░░.

"░░░ ░░ ░░░░ ░░ ░░░░░ea░ ░░ey ░ ░ ░░░'░ ░░░░░ ░░░ ░░░░░░░ ░░░░ ░░░░ ░░ ░ ░░ ░░'░ ░░░░ ░░'░ ░.

░░░░ ░░ ░r░░otional.

░░░░░░ ░░ ░░░░ ░░░ ░░ ░░░░ ░ ░░░░░ ░ ░░░░░ ░░░░ ░░░░ ░░░░ ░░░░░ ░░ ░░░ ░░ ░.

"Can yo░ ░░░'░ ░░░ ░░░░░ ░░░░."

░░ ░░░'░. ░░░ ░░░ ░░░ ░░ ░░░░ ░░░ ░ ░░░░░ ░.

░ ░░░ ░░ ░░░ ░░░ ░░ ░ ░░░.

"░░ ░░ ░░░anst."

"░."

"░ ░ ░."

░░░ ░░░░░░ ░░░ ░░ ░░░ ░░░ ░░░░ ░░ ░░░ ░░ ░ ░░░ ░░░ ░░░░░ ░░░: ░░░░ ░ ░░░░ ░░ ░░░ ░░ ░░░░░ ░ ░░░, ░░░ ░░ ░░░ ░░ ░░░.

░░░░'░ ░░░ ░░░ ░░ ░░░░ ░░░ ░░░ ░░ ░░░ ░░░ ░░░░░ ░░░░░ ░░░░ ░ ░░ ░░░░ ░░ ░ ░░░ ░░░, ░░░ ░░░ ░░░ ░ ░░░░ ░░ ░░░ ░░ ░░░ ░░░ ░ ░ ░░░░ ░ ░░░ ░░░ ░░░░░░ ░ ░ ░░░░ ░░░ ░░░░ ░░░ ░░░░░░.

"░░ ░░ ░░░erous."

"░ ░░░."

"░░░!"

░░░

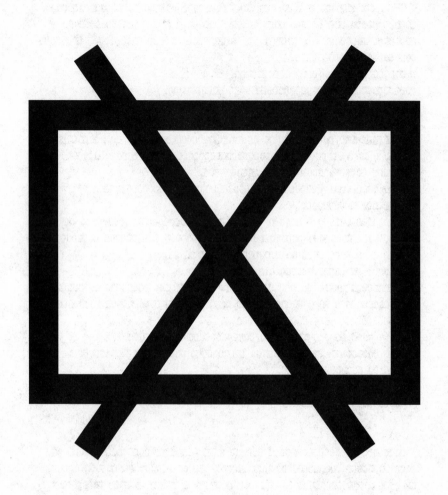

XXX

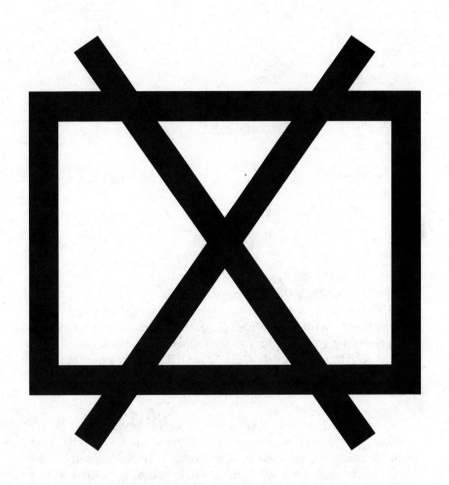

XXX

☒☒　　☒　　　　　　　　　　An☒

☒☒　　　　　　☒

☒☒☒　　ar　　　　　　　　de.
☒☒ ☒☒☒☒☒☒
☒'☒☒ ☒☒　　　☒☒ ☒☒
☒☒ ☒　　　　pa　　　　　　☒
☒☒☒☒☒☒ ☒☒☒☒　　☒☒ ☒☒ ☒ ☒☒ ☒☒☒☒lot.
　　　　　☒☒ ☒☒☒☒ ☒☒
☒ ☒☒ en
　　　　　　　　　　　　☒☒
☒ ☒ ☒　☒☒　　　　　　　　　　　☒☒☒☒☒☒
　☒　　　　☒
　　☒　　　　　e☒　　　　　　.

☒☒
☒ ☒ ☒
　　　　☒　　　　　　　　☒
☒☒☒☒'☒ ☒☒☒☒ suddenly cleared.

He looked down at his hand. It rested on the red lever, which had been pushed forward as far as it would go. A thin mist of forms was once again travelling vertically through the room at high speed.

He shook Harriet by the shoulder. "You OK?" Multicoloured blocks of numbers shot up her screen. She looked at Jack uncomprehendingly, as if she'd just been awoken from a deep sleep.

"Yuh. Yes. I think so."

"Nixon? Dana? Did you feel that, even without the glasses?"

Nixon had propped himself up on one elbow and was wiping drool from his chin with a Starbucks paper napkin. "I did. I think the – the effect must be apparent throughout the whole volume of the Oxbow. And not only if you happen to be wearing the glasses. I wonder – outside . . ."

With some effort he forced his legs to carry him to the window that overlooked Hoxton Square. Below, four or five people were picking themselves up from the grass like dazed sunbathers who had fallen asleep in the heat. A man in a red jacket was chasing oranges across the pavement, preventing them from rolling into the gutter with his foot. Another passer-by reached down to scoop up the handles of a dropped plastic bag before more escaped. A black cab had run up the kerb and into the railings, bending a parking meter level with the ground.

Nixon placed both hands on the window, pushed it open. "You all right down there? Anyone hurt?"

Jack could hear voices shouting up from below. They seemed to be expressing a negative. He shouted back. "Great. Good. OK."

Harriet took off her glasses. "*Shit.* We need to be more careful. These effects— That could have been dangerous."

Jack ran his hands through his hair and exhaled slowly. "What on earth *was* that?"

"*That* was the dampening field." Dana slid down into her recliner. "It looks like Harriet's hunch was right. The Shepherds don't do the actual work of shepherding. For that, they have, these, these *sheepdogs.*"

"I was losing the capacity to formulate an idea – my very sense of self was beginning to dissipate—"

"The perfect crowd control."

Harriet lay back in the deep cushioned leather and let her arms hang limply over the sides. "But did you *feel* it? It was so . . . so *comfortable!*"

INTERREGNUM

The drop had resumed. They were falling vertically through an undisturbed section of the Grid. From what Jack could deduce from Harriet's numerical display, it seemed orderly, uniform; they had slowed the headlong rush of beings to a near standstill several times in the last forty-five minutes to reveal the same race each time: humanoid, just.

Smooth-skinned and milkily translucent, they had no facial features to speak of, just a bilaterally symmetrical body with two powerful hind legs and four much smaller limbs attached to the upper half. Like steamed dumplings, orange and black shapes could be seen within them – organs, perhaps, or maybe a colony of smaller creatures in symbiosis. Harriet could just about discern differences between individuals: the positions of the internal structures, whatever they were, the height, the degree of transparency, a tendency towards a milky whiteness or a green-grey cast. Each one was definitely an individual.

"What's the maths telling you, Harriet? There's certainly a lot of them."

"I have a handle on their basic signature, simply from locating ourselves in the Grid and looking at the values around the local interstices. They're a very samey bunch. Clones, maybe? It looks to me as if they fill a huge volume – hundreds of kilometres vertically. No real idea how far horizontally, but I'd think at least the same amount. I guess it's even possible they entirely surround the Grid at this point – that they make up a hollow sphere."

"How many?"

"Hundreds of thousands at least. Maybe millions."

"Is this unusual?" Dana asked.

Jack adjusted his recliner to a more upright position. "You tell us. The cataloguing efforts above ground – SetiOnEarth@home, the other online resources – saw anything from one single specimen of a species to several tens of thousands. Though it has to be said that the dividing line between species can be somewhat hazy – as with these guys, we're going primarily on appearance. We can at some point look into the underlying code; examine their DNA rather than their outward morphology, if you like. That should give us a more thorough analysis of the differences and similarities. But I'd say, in the volume of the Grid we've so far explored – which it has to be said isn't large – this number of specimens of the same species is unprecedented."

Nixon's mind was spinning. If he'd been a DMEn, there would have been an accompanying grinding of metaphorical gears. "Is it an exclusive club, or a free-for-all? Is there a selection process? Who gets in, and how? Dana?"

Dana was silent.

"This is the question that's been bugging me: what's the precise process by which the Grid incorporates new races? How did those aliens get in there? I'm assuming it doesn't simply ask nicely. How and why, Dana?"

Dana turned from the display and looked directly at Nixon. "And I would know this *how?*"

Nixon seemed a bit flustered. "Because you have an alien in your head. Because you can step into the Grid?"

"My co-pilot doesn't have all the answers."

Jack said aloud what he knew Nixon was thinking. "On this point, he knows more than you're telling us. Remember, I read the debrief transcripts."

Dana fixed Jack with a look of cool concentration. Everyone was silent. Harriet and Nixon were looking at Jack, then Dana and back again. "Debrief transcripts?"

"Daniel asked me not to tell *anyone* about what was in those." Jack reached for the red lever and brought the room to a standstill relative to the Grid. Random figures intersected the room – a pair of bifurcated hooves above, a sallow dome rising from the floor below. Outside, a perfect moiré of identical figures reached to a grey infinity, a polarising filter overlaying the view of East London.

Dana began to speak, stuttered and stopped.

"Dana, I know you by reputation. I was called in to help through my contacts at NASA. Through Daniel. It's not often I get to talk to a real astronaut, and it's rarer still that they come and visit us. So here you are. We've invited you in, shown you what we're up to here, shared our tech, all on the assumption we're after the same thing – answers."

"I did say—" Nixon began to speak, but Jack held up his hand to cut him off.

"We've been very trusting. We could have easily told your superiors where you are."

Dana looked genuinely terrified.

"But we didn't. Now I think we *all* deserve full disclosure in return, don't you?"

Dana fell back into her recliner. "It's all there. In the transcripts. Jack knows I've not been hiding anything."

"Not all of us have read these transcripts. I suggest you tell us everything. Just so we're all on the same page here." Nixon's voice was level and controlled.

"OK. This is what I know. This is what my Shepherd knows. The Signal is received and rebroadcast in many different ways. Most often it happens directly, by creatures that can sense electromagnetic signals. Of which there are many. That is the most common method. Now, when this happens, the Signal has direct access to its hosts' brains. It fills them with one powerful compulsion: to rebroadcast the Signal. Reproduction. It's a sex urge, for all intents and purposes. It takes the host species over. It – it can be very destructive."

Harriet suppressed an involuntary shudder. "Nice."

"Because it resides in the host's brain, if that host uses electromagnetic signals to communicate it can be rebroadcast directly. It can do this either in isolation, or through a large interconnected group where the combined effect will be that much more powerful. And – and essentially, it can strip out the host's personality, its mind, in the process."

There was a pause in which the traffic outside softly shushed. "Does it harm the host physically?"

"Not always. The physical body can remain intact, though it retains no animating principle, no life above an automated cellular level. It leaves behind a zombie, effectively. It just takes the host's coded description, whatever that may be – DNA, or a mapping of the brain state in a human context. It is designed to lift out an, uh, essence."

Dana looked at the ceiling. "And, as I say, in almost all cases this is *not* good for the host. Like an angler's hook yanked through a fish's brain as it leaves, the majority do not survive the rebroadcast process for long. The early Grid is littered with such, uh, aggressive incorporations."

"What about *us?*"

"Here's where we may have the edge. As I hinted, we fall into an unusual category – we received the Signal *mechanically*. It currently does not exist in the brains of the human race, but on a collection of servers spread all around the world – and now, since it was leaked, on millions of personal devices as part of the SetiOnEarth@home project as well."

"This is unique? *We* are unique?"

"Hosting the Signal in a technological form has happened before, several times. But where it has happened, that technology has been incorporated into the nervous systems of the dominant species in a much more direct fashion. Give us a few years, and that's what the human race will have done, too. Augmented themselves with tech. New abilities, new senses, enhancements to our old familiar ones. Just like these Depthcharge glasses, but connected directly as part of an extended and enhanced body. We're in that in-between stage – the link between our tech and ourselves is still indirect. We have to *read* a screen, *listen* to a podcast. Our delivery system may be versatile, but in order to get that information into our heads, we're still relying on the apparatus Nature equipped us with: good old-fashioned ears and eyes.

"So any new ideas have to use a codified form – *language,* in its broadest sense – and the imperfection of language, as much as I may have been berating it earlier, may here be our saving grace. It effectively provides a memetic membrane, a barrier – and in a way, gives us what the Shepherds have, the thing that saved them: *two* brains. The Shepherds test dangerous new ideas in their forebrains, then retreat to their hindbrains and purge the system if they pose a danger. We don't have that protection. But we have a firewall that may be just as good, if not better. The Signal only has an indirect access to our neocortex, to our motor functions, our desire centres – it's held at arm's length *because* of this language barrier. If the Signal had arrived twenty years earlier, all we'd have is a wiggly line made by a needle on a sheet of graph paper, and we wouldn't be on this mission into ideaspace. If it had arrived twenty years into the future, we'd undoubtedly all have it running around in our heads by now. For better or worse, we'd all have been infected by the Signal."

"And the Signal was *designed* this way?"

"Designed? Who knows. The Signal's source and the manner of its creation, the how and why of its origin – those are questions I can't answer. Not even my Shepherd knows. It has been the subject of intense debate among his species for generations. But what I do know, from the partial history I have access to, is that it's been subjected to very strong selection pressure. It's *evolved.*

"Think about it. There's a huge evolutionary advantage to aggressive reproduction. The different iterations of the Signal – and there are many – that imbued their hosts with the most powerful need to rebroadcast naturally became the dominant versions. And the Signal mutates, each new incorporation bringing with it new ideas, new skills, new ways of doing things. Some of these are beneficial – but usually to the Signal, and not to the Signal's hosts."

"And this is where the Shepherds came in?"

"Yes. Though it cost them their corporeality, the Shepherds managed to control the Grid, rather than letting the Grid control them. They were the first species to achieve this."

"Two brains."

"Two brains. And a lot of smarts."

"How did this affect them?"

"It was disastrous. I have a very powerful race-memory. An urge to climb. A giant flower. An enormous, pulsing bloom – made from *people*."

Harriet looked at Jack, and made a sideways motion with her palm.

"So the Shepherds, they decided to let the Grid continue?"

"There are several stories. One, that the Grid provided them with the means to travel, to bridge interstellar distances in incorporeal form. The Shepherds were already a spacefaring race, though confined to the three habitable planets of their system. This was the means for them to push out into the galaxy proper. When you travel at the speed of light, for you time stands still – from the point of view of a lightbeam, the longest journey is instantaneous. Think about that. As an electromagnetic signal, they could go anywhere, instantly. That's a very hard offer to refuse."

"And two?"

"Two, the notion that the Grid itself imbued the Shepherds with the overwhelming need to expand, to spread. That the Shepherds are just unwittingly acting as a parasite's hosts always have done – by doing the Grid's bidding while thinking that they're still their own masters. What I do know is that the incorporations into the Grid are now less destructive. The Signal can convince a target race that joining it is a 'good idea.'" Dana mimed air quotes. "It's not incorporation by force. It's incorporation by persuasion.

"There is a third view. That both of these are true. It's a symbiosis."

Harriet felt even less at ease. "So us humans. We're not in any imme-diate danger, are we? The creatures on the Grid are not about to wake up, jump out into the real world and abduct us?"

Dana spread her hands. "They're *information*. Ideas. They have no bodies to jump out *into*."

Jack sat down again, looked at Dana.

"Honestly, why would I lie?"

"Any number of reasons. You have an alien in your head. You have an alien in your head who has the Grid in *its* head."

"I have a Shepherd in my head who's had the Grid under control since before the Sun was lit."

Jack opened it up to the floor. "Do we trust her?"

Nixon shrugged and waved his arms as if to dispel a fug of uncertainty. "No idea. It's not every day a tech start-up has to deal with this kind of human resources issue. We didn't cover this at King's. I'm out of my depth."

"Harriet?"

"*We* know where she is. We know how she got here. She's trusting us with that. I'd say that counts for something."

Jack fell back into his recliner. "OK, OK. Right." He surveyed the room. "So, we continue?"

"We continue." Harriet and Nixon concurred.

"Thanks, Jack, Harriet, Nixon. Your trust is— it's appreciated."

Across the room sat three others that Jack had omitted to include in the discussion. Three others made of ideas bound by an Oxbow. Three others who had just realised there may just be a way for them to achieve what they'd desired for so long: *bodies*.

True corporeality, for the very first time.

Green-banded broodsac

From Wikipedia, the free encyclopedia

The green-banded broodsac [Leucochloridium paradoxum] is a parasitic flatworm (or 'helminth') that uses gastropods as an intermediate host. Typically found in European and North American land snails of the genus Succinea, to ensure its transmission it directly affects its host's decision-making and behaviour control mechanisms, resulting in the host's demise.

Life cycle [edit]

The worm, in its larval miracidia stage, is ingested by the snail. Once inside the host's digestive system, it develops swollen 'broodsacs' filled with tens to hundreds of free-swimming parasitic flukes. Travelling through the snail's body, it inserts itself into one of the tentacles (preferring the left when available) producing a swollen pulsating display that mimics a caterpillar or colourful grub.[1] Whereas uninfected snails prefer dark sheltered environments, infected hosts seek out elevated positions in order to expose themselves to predators.

Attracted by the tentacle's transformation, the infected snail is eaten by a bird, the definitive host in which the cercariae develop into adult distomes. Maturing then sexually reproducing in the bird's digestive system, they lay eggs which are subsequently released in droppings. These are then consumed by snails to complete the parasite's life cycle.[2]

Mechanisms [edit]

Two mechanisms used by parasites to alter behaviour in vertebrate hosts have been identified: infection of the central nervous system, and altered neurochemical communication.[3] Parasites that induce changes in their hosts often exploit the regulation of social behaviour via the emotional centres of the brain, primarily the amygdala and the hypothalamus, which are commandeered by altering levels of hormones such as dopamine and serotonin.[4] The trematode Schistosoma mansoni, for example, secretes opioid peptides into the host's bloodstream, influencing both its immune response and neural function.[5]

Types of behavioural change [edit]

Parasites may alter hosts' behaviours in ways that enhance the likelihood of parasite transmission from host to host (e.g. by host predation)[6]; result in parasite release at appropriate sites (e.g. by changes in the host's preferences for habitat selection); increase parasite survival [7] or increase the host's likelihood of colonization by suitable mates for the parasite.

The emerald cockroach wasp (Ampulex compressa) co-opts the American cockroach (Periplaneta americana) as a food source for its growing larvae, altering the host's behaviour through the injection of venom directly into the host's brain. While the circuitry responsible for control of movement is still functional, the nervous system is depressed, producing "a reversible long-term lethargy characterized by a lack of spontaneous movement or response to external stimuli".[8] The cockroach remains alive but motionless, and after dragging it to a burrow the wasp deposits an egg into its carcass and buries it for the growing larva to feed on. The adult wasp emerges after six weeks, leaving behind nothing but a hard outer cockroach 'shell'.[9]

Strepsiptera of the Myrmecolacidae family can cause their ant host to linger on the tips of grass leaves, increasing the chance of being found by the parasite's males (in the case of females) and putting them in a good position for male emergence (in the case of males).[10] A similar but much more elaborate behaviour is exhibited by ants infected with the fungus Ophiocordyceps unilateralis: irregularly-timed body convulsions cause the ant to drop to the forest floor,[11] from which it climbs a plant to a specific height before locking its jaws into the vein of a leaf chosen for its orientation, temperature and humidity. After several days, the fruiting body of the fungus grows out from the dead ant's head and ruptures, releasing spores which settle to the ground to be consumed by new hosts.[12]

The protozoan Toxoplasma gondii infects animals from the Felidae family (its definitive host).[13] When a rodent consumes its faecal matter, it becomes sexually aroused by the smell of cats, increasing its chance of predation and the parasite's chance of completing its life cycle.

Studies show that via domesticated pets T. gondii has infected 30 to 50 percent of humans worldwide (60 million people in the U.S.; the highest prevalence, 84 percent, is found in France). Though mild, flu-like symptoms occasionally occur during the first few weeks following exposure, infection has also been shown to induce a propensity for risk-taking and decrease reaction times. Infected parents, researchers found, have a 30 percent chance of passing the parasite on to their children. It has also been linked to promiscuity, cases of cognitive defects, dissociative identity disorder and schizophrenia.[14]

A paper published in the Proceedings of the Royal Society B[15] suggests that high T. gondii infection rates can alter the behavioural patterns of entire cultures.

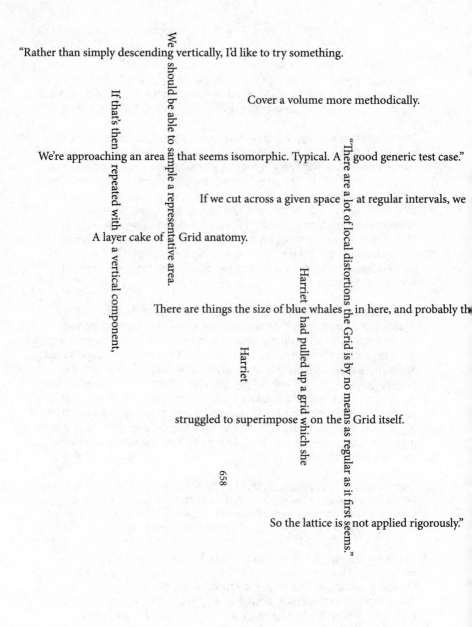

"Rather than simply descending vertically, I'd like to try something.

Cover a volume more methodically.

We should be able to sample a representative area.

If that's then repeated with a vertical component,

We're approaching an area that seems isomorphic. Typical. A good generic test case."

"There are a lot of local distortions the Grid is by no means as regular as it first seems."

If we cut across a given space at regular intervals, we

A layer cake of Grid anatomy.

There are things the size of blue whales in here, and probably th

Harriet had pulled up a grid which she

Harriet

struggled to superimpose on the Grid itself.

658

So the lattice is not applied rigorously."

duce the equivalent of a CT scan.

"For starters, it needs to incorporate quite a range of body sizes and shapes.

size of

Interstices in the Grid

Jack

Empty areas of the Grid may actually store bacteria. Viruses. Or their alien equivalent."

659

Jack felt as if the office was being shunted back and forth like a shuttle on a loom.

Dana

Empty. Occupied.

I'm mapping as we go. Back and forth. Building up a three-dimensional section."

Thread upon thread.

Layer upon layer.

"We're coming up on another atypical stretch." Harriet switched the data map to the large monitor. "Here." She pointed. "Below and east a bit. Though down here in the Grid, 'atypical' is relative. Just your usual parade of aliens never seen by human eyes before."

To Nixon, one raw data set looked very much like another. Profit and loss, yes. He could get his head round that. The intricacies of the Grid? No way. "Why? What do you see?" "The Grid – it's still regular, but in this volume the vertical interstices have a much larger separation than the horizontal – say twenty times the distance." "So – tall slots? For tall aliens?" "Ha. You might not be wrong. Dropping in . . . now." Though they were still sinking at the same rapid pace, the strobe of shadows suddenly started flickering at a more leisurely tempo. They were still separate, particulate; but the beats between gaps were far longer. Jack put his hand on the red lever. "Slow down?" "Slow down. Please." As Dana scanned the room, details started to become discernible. The beats lengthened still further; long, cylindrical, a colonnade of pillars each perhaps a half-metre in diameter, rushing from floor to ceiling – in fact, as could be seen outside, stretching through the entire height of the Oxbow. Harriet was reminded of wet eels, perfectly smooth, any detail they might possess blurred to a featureless opalescent sheen by their speed. Jack slowed the procession further, and the columns began to acquire detail. Spots, flickers of colour; a racing zigzag of back-and-forth striations that made them appear to spin, though Jack was sure it was an optical illusion, a rotating alien barber's pole. The twisting slowed, and finally halted.

They stood in a forest of trees whose canopy was somewhere far above the limits of the Oxbow's bubble and whose roots now filled the basements under Hoxton Square. Harriet's first impression of eels still held, in length and shape if not in colour. Now they were stationary, Jack could make out the intricate patterning of interlocked scales, translucent overlapping diamonds of red, ochre and olive green. At irregular intervals there could be seen a raised nub, as if a branch had been removed and the surrounding flesh had risen to protect the stump. Through the windows, Jack could see them extending throughout the plots and gardens of East London like a new growth forest planted in precise rows by the Forestry Commission. "They have colour variations. Differences in the markings. No sense organs as far as I can make out." "Camouflage?" "I'd love to know what kind of environment these things could camouflage themselves in. Perhaps it's a signalling mechanism. Maybe they run messages up and down the length of their trunks, like a bus indicator." "Can we drop to the end of one? Or rise to the top?" Jack picked up his stylus and altered a long number by a single digit. The patterns on the pillars jumped downward with inertia-free rapidity. "Going up." A minute passed, two. Jack changed the number by a single digit a second time, and the speed doubled. Harriet watched a flow of numerics climb up a coloured bar chart on her screen. "Get ready – we're coming in on the tip of that one over there. Three . . . two . . ." Harriet was looking at her screen while pointing across the office towards a column that passed through the space next to the water cooler, so did not see the head – for want of a better description – come into view. The column began to taper and a series of ridges appeared, spaced at intervals around its circumference. These became more pronounced, until suddenly the main body seemed to drop away and they were looking at a half-dozen smaller columns, perhaps the width of an arm, arranged in a circle. Jack again adjusted a figure, and the thing's descent slowed to a crawl, and then stopped entirely. "Urgh." Nixon looked like he'd just eaten something sour. "What are they? *Eyes?* Buds?" Each smaller column ended in a fluted cup ringed with a ruff of flesh in which sat a polished ball, black, wet and shiny, held in place by an off-white net of ligaments. "It's six evil Fabergé eggs from the dark dimension!" "It's a coconut shy. That's been dipped in oil." "It's bloody repellent, is what it is." Harriet laughed. "Nixon, it probably doesn't think you look very sexy either. Beauty is in the eye of the beholder."

"*Are* they eyes? It's difficult to imagine what these things might look like when they're moving. The Grid—"

"The Grid is in lockdown. Nothing in it moves." Dana's tone was firm.

Harriet checked the Depthcharge feed. A clock under the heading 'Mission Time' counted the seconds and minutes since the lever had first been pulled. Everything was functioning perfectly.

High-definition footage from both pairs of glasses was being continually written to the RAID server, which had more than a week's capacity.

"We have most of the room covered, but feel free to get up. Walk around it. Look at it from all angles. Don't forget to cover the outside too. I'm logging locations, but get all you can." Dana seemed impatient to move on. "Even going as fast as we are, we're not going to cover more than a

fraction of a per cent of the Grid's volume. A *fraction* of a fraction. We're shooting through this too fast. There's simply too much to see, too much ground to cover. It's a whistle-stop tour."

Harriet could sense her frustration. Dana sighed. "A surfeit of exobiological wonders. I guess eventually there'll be teams of people doing this. Cataloguing, traversing the Grid methodically, recording everything. We're just a scout party."

"Just pretend you're Lewis and Clark, intent on establishing an American presence in this new territory before Britain or some other evil colonial power tries to claim it." Dana smiled. "We have an international team here. My superiors might not approve. Anyway, how long do we have?"

Jack again wondered if Dana knew something she wasn't intimating. This sense of urgency he could understand, but it was more than that – did she think they might have

figured out where she had gone? Jack couldn't see how that would be possible.

"How long? Until others can do what we can do here? I'm pretty sure we have the only steerable Oxbow." Dana looked dubious. "Is that likely to change?"

Jack rolled his shoulders. "Someone else is bound to come up with the same idea eventually. But for now it's just us pioneers. It's the New Frontier, and we're the first wagon over the hill."

"I'm seeing something."

Harriet held up her hand for attention. "Look. You see that? In the raw

data? The Grid here is arranged in layers, like strata. Or maybe

like rings on a tree? You know, depending if it's been a good year or

bad, it's possible to plot the health of the tree by the thickness of the

ring. I think there may be a similar principle at work here. Now we

have a core sample – a very small biopsy of the Grid, we seem to be

passing through successive densifications and rarefactions. It's like

winter growth versus summer growth." Jack recalled a cross-section

of a huge tree he'd seen on display in Kew Gardens on which were marked
important historical events like the Fire of London, the Battle of Hastings
and the Crucifixion. As they went deeper into the Grid, they were going
back through its history – travelling not only through *space,* but *time.*

v

To: AdamParker@JSC.NASA.com
From: GabrielBowen_press@JSC.NASA.com
Subject: Contagious agent?

Adam - take a look at this cameraphone footage posted on
YouTube around 4pm, UK time.

Link here: https://www.youtube.com/watch?v=B-O-xD0-qzs

People fainting in the street! Now check the location - the
building you can see in the background (eg at 2'13") is the
offices of Intelligencia, Jack Fenwick's outfit. Jack, you
will recall, is affiliated with Daniel Novák's exobiology
working group at Jodrell Bank and advised us during the
Daedalus debriefs.

Given Dana's likely infectious state, and the interest
she showed in Jack's work (I'm sure you've reviewed the
transcripts many times, as have I), might there be a
connection? I may just be clutching at straws here, but I
suggest we should follow up ASAP.

Best

Gabe

To: GabrielBowen_press@JSC.NASA.com
From: AdamParker@JSC.NASA.com
Subject: Contagious agent?

Hey Gabe

From the online records I can find, Intelligencia seems to
be a small tech start-up working for gaming companies and
on some more experimental AI stuff. But that footage is
certainly suggestive, though of what exactly I have no idea.
Let me get on to our UK counterparts and see if they can
advise.

Thanks for the tip-off.

Adam

To: GabrielBowen_press@JSC.NASA.com
From: AdamParker@JSC.NASA.com
Subject: Contagious agent?

Gabe - me again. They actually took this more seriously

than I thought they would. MI5 apparently has very specific policies in place in regard to possible chemical or biological terrorist threats, and they now have the address under 24-hour observation. In fact, I got the distinct impression they *already* had it under observation, which strikes me as odd. Other than that bare fact, they wouldn't give me any more information. This matter is apparently now well above my security clearance.

Adam

To: AdamParker@JSC.NASA.com
From: GabrielBowen_press@JSC.NASA.com
Subject: Contagious agent?

Sh*t. I hope they don't overreact.
Can we tell Jack? Should we tell Jack?
He's not answering calls or emails.

Gabe

To: GabrielBowen_press@JSC.NASA.com
From: AdamParker@JSC.NASA.com
Subject: Contagious agent?

Off the record, I can ask Novák what he thinks. Maybe he can pay them a visit. In a strictly unofficial capacity, of course.

It's out of our hands now, Gabe. I'm afraid we'll just have to leave this to the professionals.

Adam

To: Jack@intelligencia.london
From: G_Bowen@gmail.com
Subject: FYI

Jack - whatever you're up to, please don't get out of your depth.

Just sayin'.

Take care,

Gabe

665

THE INTERPRETERS

"We're 5,200 kilometres in. Coming up on the outer core."

Jack turned around, looked over his shoulder at the three only he and Harriet could see behind them. "You all right, there in the back seat?"

Indeed, dear boy.

"You want to show us what you can lift off the surface of an alien mind?"

The 19th Count's hair fell in artfully coiffured waves to his shoulders, as immaculate as a Gainsborough portrait. He theatrically pulled on each finger with his teeth to loosen his white gloves, then, taking off his hat, dropped them inside. His hands underneath were the same perfect porcelain white. His blank pupil-free eyes were hard to follow; Jack could never be sure if he was looking directly at him, even if he was facing in his direction. It lent him an inscrutable aloofness that Jack suspected he cultivated, and no doubt found amusing.

"Wait." Dana shifted around in her seat, looking from the main screen, on which Jack's Depthcharge feed and the DMEn could be seen, to the empty space behind her and back again. "How does he plan to do this, exactly?"

With the **utmost delicacy.**

I do not intend to *soil* my *mind* with a taint of the *other*.

Let's try to keep our *friends* from the *COLONIES* at *arm's length,* shall we?

"Details, Count. Like Dana says, give us the technicalities. And remember, we can pull the plug. At any time. We've done so before, as you know. Talk us through how you intend to do this."

Ah yes. *Last time.*

I've been meaning to have a *word* with you about that.

I do wish you'd given us some notice before ejecting us from your Oxbow.
It's like being *thrown* from an unbroken *horse*.
Rough. Undignified. *Inelegant*.

Where did they go? Back into the rush of free-flowing information that is the Web like a raindrop losing its individuality to the ocean?

In all **SERIOUSNESS,**
please do not do it again unless you ABSOLUTELY have to.

Jack noted the edge in his usually carefully modulated voice. *This is important to them.* More important, possibly, than they wished to admit.
"Point taken. I shall give fair warning, if I can."
The Count held his top hat by the brim and bowed gracefully.

So: a PLAN!
A *Show!*
A SPECTACLE!

Brought to you by those *Scamps Of The Imagination*, the

ETHEREAL
ARISTOCRATS
of INVENTION!

We shall *endeavour*, in a *manner most careful*,
to lift *VAGRANT THOUGHTS* from the minds of those

rendered Insensate!

I am put in mind of a *certain evening* spent in an opium den
in the docks of Baoshan, Shanghai, in which

 Girl, 21
@twentyone • 0m

 Follow

FFS, Wordy Wordsworth here could benefit from a 140 character limit #thepoint?

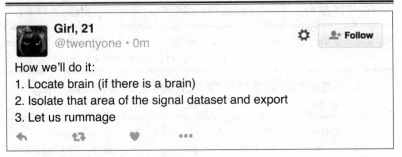

Girl, 21
@twentyone • 0m

How we'll do it:
1. Locate brain (if there is a brain)
2. Isolate that area of the signal dataset and export
3. Let us rummage

Dana looked dubious. "That sounds . . . dangerous."

Girl, 21
@twentyone • 0m

We can pick n mix. Lucky dip.
Just a notion or 2. Whatever is floating on top.

No **more** than we can just as easily *forget*.

"Will it not affect you? Your brain? Do you, um, *have* a brain?" Jack was of the opinion that if he looked inside any of the DMEn with the Depthcharges, they would appear as if made of plastic – just like their 3D-printed counterparts, they would have no bones, no brains, no internal organs at all, unless on a whim they had thought them up. What would they use them for? They had no physical body that bone and muscle could support. They did not breathe or eat or shit, so had no use for lungs or stomach or bowels. It was all just an elaborate charade, an idea in a fancy suit. The Count, Jack was sure, was white all the way through. You could slice him like mozzarella, and there'd be nothing in there to see.

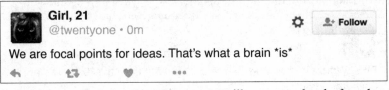

Girl, 21
@twentyone • 0m

We are focal points for ideas. That's what a brain *is*

"And you can feed this through to us? We'll get some kind of – what, words? Imagery?"

Jack fell back into his recliner, squashing a paper cup. "Glad that's all cleared up. Nixon, Harriet. Dana. We're going to do this?"

Harriet nodded towards Dana. "You were the one with the misgivings. You think this can work?"

Dana pressed her hands down onto her thighs. "In *theory* I don't see why not. Despite our experience with the sheepdogs, the Grid is still in lockdown. We can be in and out, we'll not isolate them in the Oxbow for a moment longer than we need to, We're just copying information. They shouldn't be affected. In *theory.*"

Nixon gave a thumbs-up. "Stealing data. Direct from an alien mind. Edward White would approve."

"So who do we pick? Which mind do we try and read first?"

Harriet picked up a sheaf of printouts. "We still have the SetiOnEarth@ home shopping catalogue."

"That just covers entities that can be seen from Earth's surface. We're deep into the outer core here. No GPS, no Google Maps."

"A Shepherd?"

"*Not* a Shepherd." Dana was firm.

"Who, then? Random sampling?"

Jack scratched his chin. "We have a smorgasbord of local aliens. I'd say we want some kind of humanoid. Air-breather. Bipedal. Brain about the size of a human's. We stand a better chance of making sense of their experience if it's in some way similar to our own."

Harriet nodded. "Pull your big red lever, sir, and let's see who lives in this neck of the woods. I guess one place to pitch your tent is as good as any other when you're a pioneer abroad in uncharted lands."

Jack reached between the seats and brought the red gearstick back to the vertical. Again, the parade of indistinguishable ghosts slowed, halted. However many of these things he saw, each still gave him a new thrill. He imagined this might have been how the earliest deepsea divers must have felt, lowering themselves as far as they dared into the ocean depths in an ironclad bubble of air, shining an arc light into a realm of perpetual night in which swam grotesque creatures that had never been seen before, even by their own kin.

Intersecting the table, and a little over to the far wall, was something curled in around itself, balled tight into a foetal position. Jack and Harriet craned over for a better view. Dana and Nixon, minus glasses, could see them looking intently at a volume of empty space. They leaned forward to get a better look at the main monitor.

"Human enough for you?"

Girl 21 had substituted an animated Godzuki head for her usual selfie flick-book face. It repeatedly rolled its eyes, raised its brow and pulled a cartoon 'take' in a looped ten-frame animated gif.

Through the glasses Jack could see the three DMEn examining the alien, ghosts regarding a spectre. XX shifted with a grinding of pistons and gears, small puffs of smoke rising from a fat chimney stack atop the cab that currently stood in for his head. The 19th Count leant on his cane with both white hands, bent forward and regarded the sinuous curves and whiplash lines of this creature as one might an exotic piece of sculpture by one of those nouveau Continentals.

Girl 21 held out her hands either side of its flattened head. A plate of bone supported a mass of fine hair that folded up and over like a frozen wave. A teardrop-shaped eye hung either side, each split vertically with a peppering of small raised dots. Two bony structures that reminded Jack of WiFi aerials pointed up and back, rising a full two metres like elegant geometric antlers. Harriet thought it looked startled, a deer caught in the headlights, though she knew there was no way it could sense their presence.

"Ready?"

Harriet isolated Girl 21's Oxbow data signature, then using it as a geo-locator managed to marquee a volume that included her hands and part of her forearms, and thus the creature's head. She took a high-resolution data dump, then subtracted Girl 21's numerical description from the result. "Voilà."

Jack tried to ignore the green cartoon dinosaur, which was now repeatedly crossing its eyes while letting its tongue loll limply. "You got something?"

"I've isolated its brain. *If* it keeps its brain between its eyes. There's a very high information density there, so I think we're on the right track."

"Fantastic. Thanks, Harriet."

"21 – think you can make sense of it? To me, it'll just be numbers. I'm dropping the result into your localised volume of the Oxbow. It's wrapped in a series of nested folders. You can read as much or as little of it as you like without interacting with it all immediately. Dip your toe in, so to speak. You OK with that?"

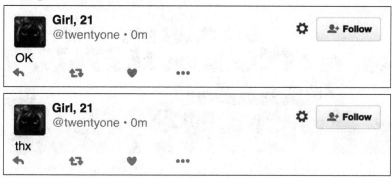

Girl 21 sat in a lotus position on the conference room table. Her stuttering face of selfies returned and took on a more studious demeanour.

"What do you see?" The expectation in the room was palpable.

"No problem. You can send a live feed direct to the main monitor."

Girl, 21
@twentyone • 0m

through the Chomsky module
!!text and image!!
?!?!text AS image?!?!

Harriet made the adjustments. On the screen a series of small squares, the Intelligencia logo in miniature, marched across then down, row upon row.

Girl, 21
@twentyone • 0m

hush

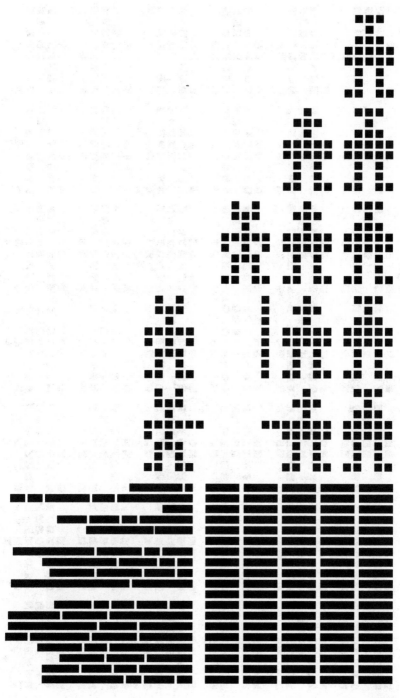

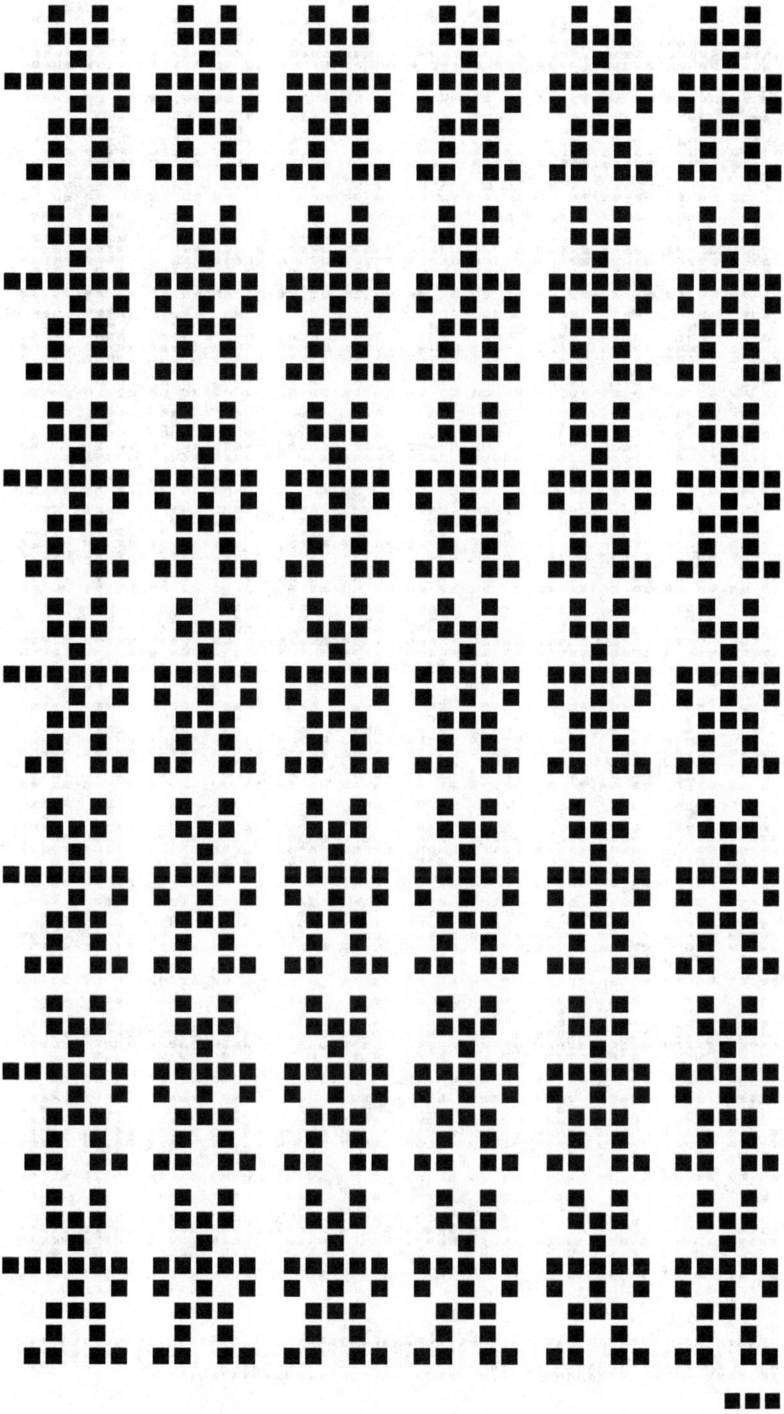

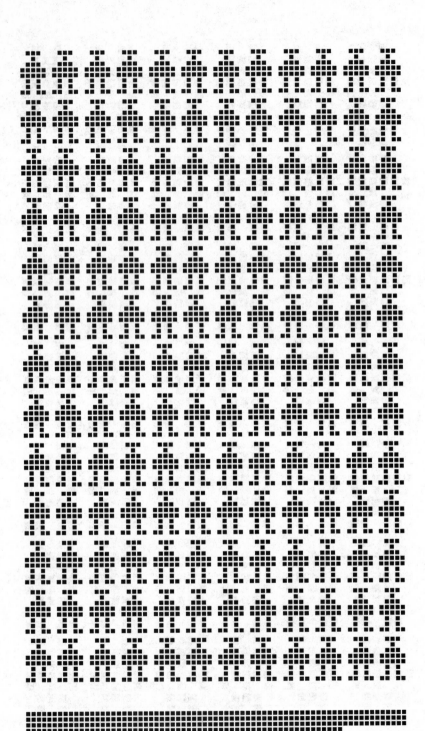

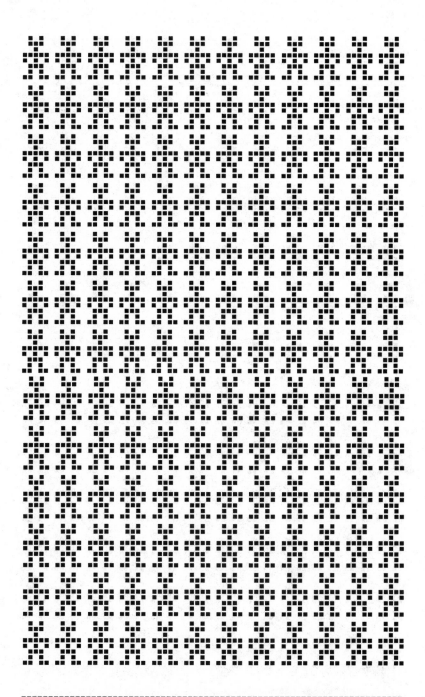

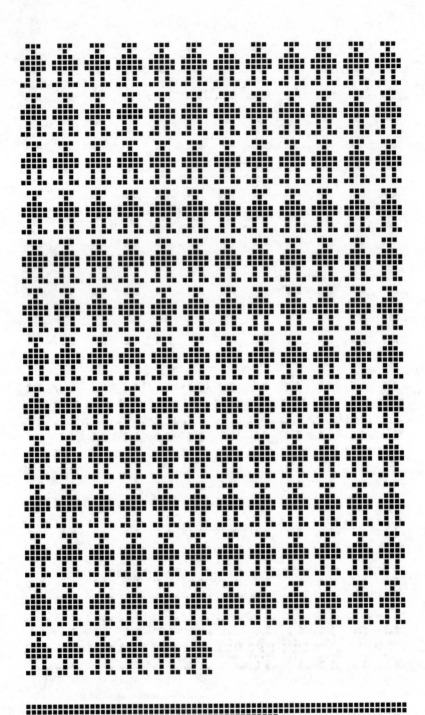

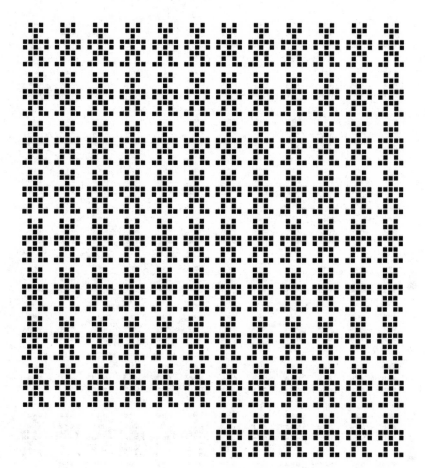

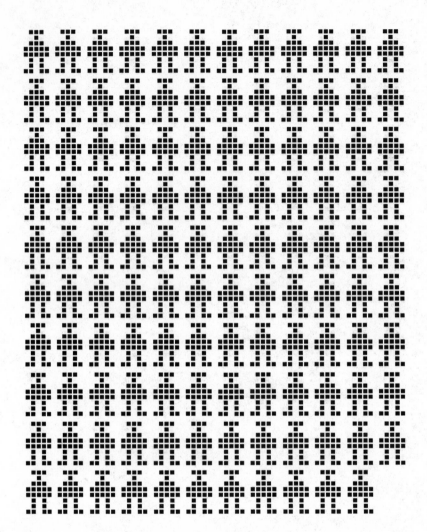

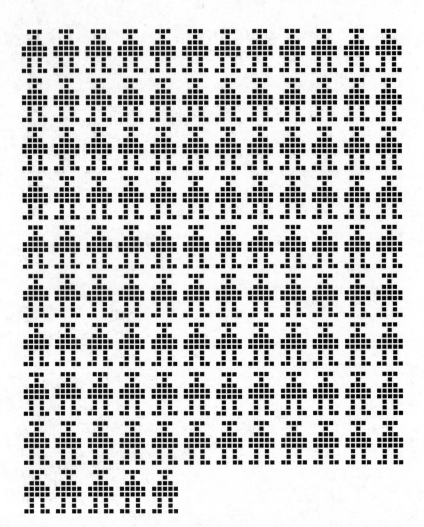

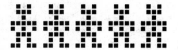

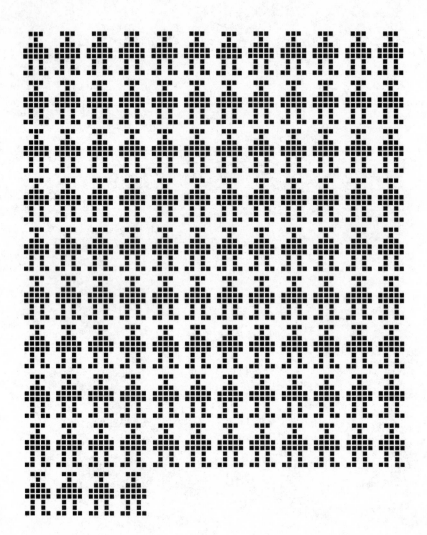

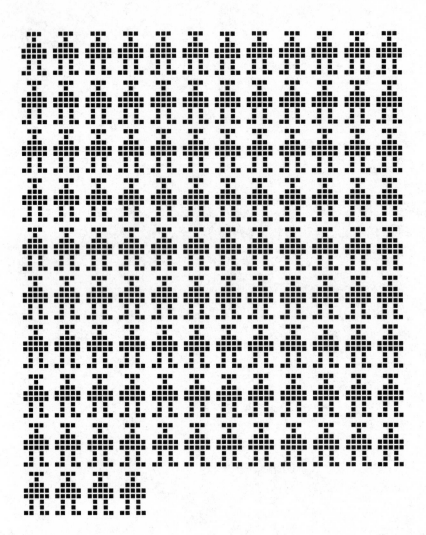

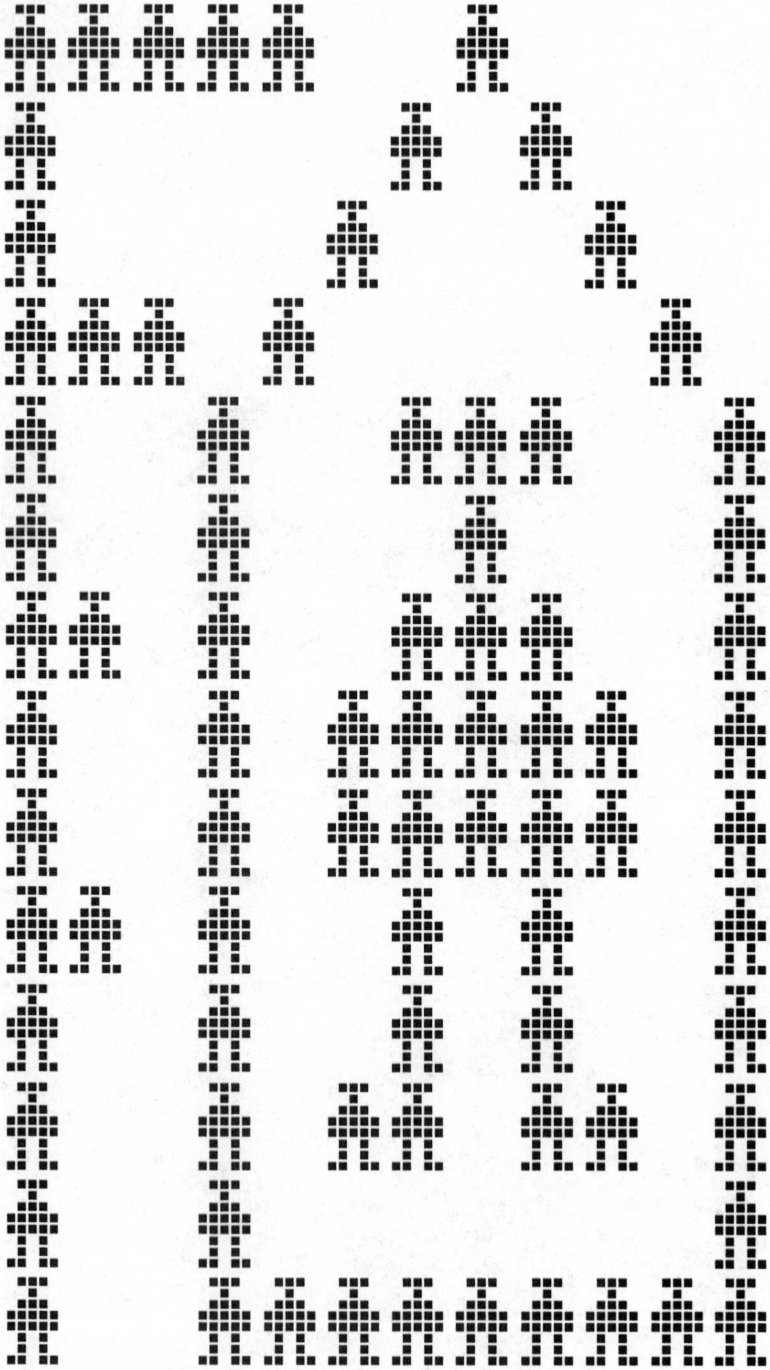

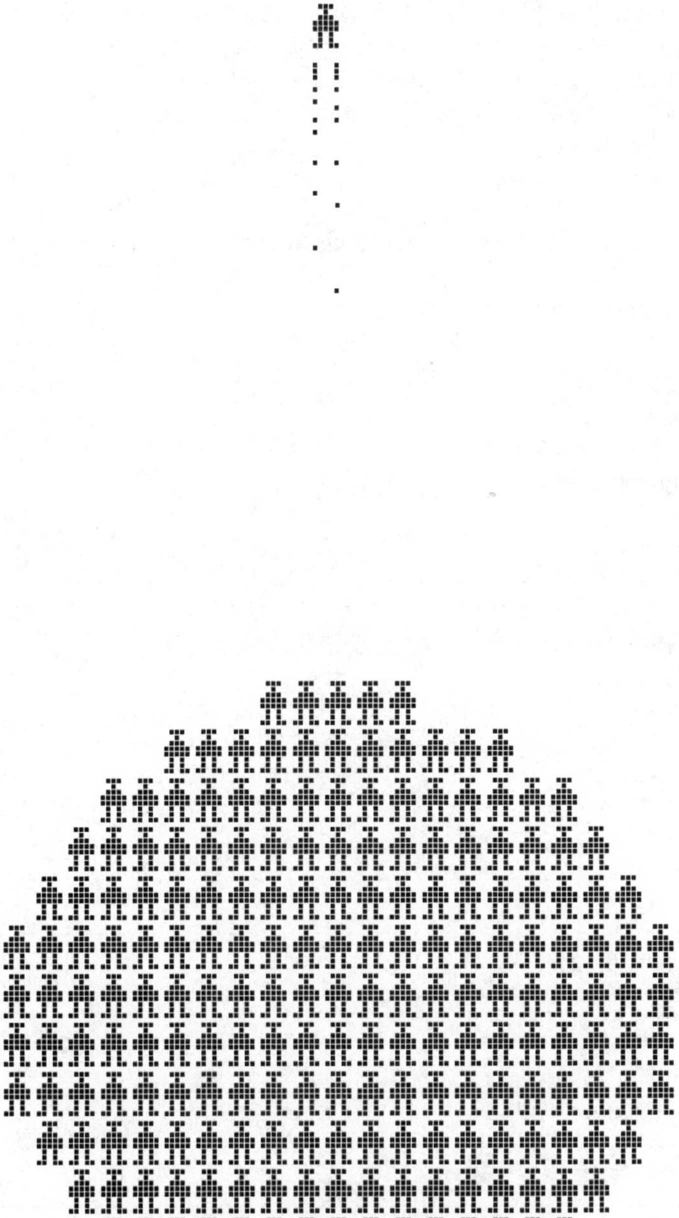

"Ahahaaa." Jack realised he'd been holding his breath. "Dana? That make any sense? I think the Chomsky Module was giving us a pictorial representation, not a linguistic—"

"Yes. Two distinct forms. A battle, I think. One victor. One form leaves the planet."

"Leaves via the Grid?"

"Hard to tell. It's . . . pretty schematic."

"See those more formless blocks up front? There's a lot of data there that's not resolved."

"Girl 21? What do you make of this?"

Girl, 21
@twentyone · 0m

I'm just the mindreader
not an interpreter
I see an #8-bit wargame

Girl, 21
@twentyone · 0m

that's it
no more
im done
finished

"You OK?"

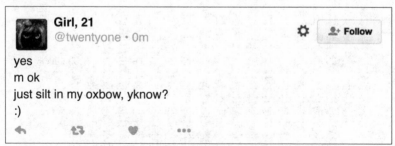

Girl, 21
@twentyone · 0m

yes
m ok
just silt in my oxbow, yknow?
:)

Harriet watched Girl 21 pull her jacket around her slight frame and retreat to her crate at the back of the room. The Count seemed to cast a paternal glance in her direction. "So, are we any the wiser?"

Dana was looking again at the rows of small figures. "It's that language

694

barrier again. Mind-to-mind, as with my Man on the Moon, I have no need for a codified language, but use any other method . . ."

"So what happens when we get to the centre of the Grid? We try and run this kind of trick on whatever we find there?"

Dana seemed to reflect on something. Her eyes narrowed. "I have another idea."

"You do?"

"Let me think something through. I may have a solution. Something that might work more . . . *directly.*"

Islands of Consciousness

What constitutes the borders of the "I"?

● ●

Last issue's article exploring Cambridge Emeritus Professor of Philosophy Roger Holborne's argument that you can exist without your body continues to provoke debate.

Professor Benjamin Reichert, London

Dear Editor

In the hope that it will shed light on this mysterious thing called 'consciousness', I'd like to suggest a thought experiment.

Imagine a mutant gene, a close encounter with a nuclear device or some other unlikely turn of events means you spontaneously develop telepathy. You can read others' minds, sense their emotions and directly understand their motivations. How might this change your sense of self?

Now imagine that this skill is ubiquitous – that you belong to a race of telepaths. From birth, you have been able to read others' thoughts, and they yours. A moment's reflection will tell you that in this world your sense of individuality is less likely to be confined to one body and more likely to be spread across many; consciousness would feel more like a distributed computing project than the discrete collection of ensouled 'I's we are currently familiar with.

Now suppose that this telepathic power has a limited range. Separated across a sea is another group, identical in their telepathic abilities, but out of range of the first. They would develop different ways of doing things – a different language and culture, just as isolated groups of non-telepathic humans do here on Earth.

Not having yet thought of boats and being unable to swim, the only way these two groups can communicate is by flashing signals back and forth across the water using a big mirror. I propose that there is no real difference between these two separated cultures and two regular non-telepathic *individual humans*. Not being able to read minds, we have invented codified sounds and symbols – language – to communicate the contents of one mind to another.

Current neurological theories of mind posit that the brain produces all manner of signals derived from inputs both internal and external, and these bounce around the brain, in the process either becoming attenuated or amplified until, in a Darwinian-style survival of the fittest, the strongest work their way to the top and become the ideas we are finally conscious of 'having'.

In other words, our *brains* seem to operate much like a *culture* does. If this is so, the phenomenon we call consciousness might not just be localised in biological individuals – if it is typified by this process of 'coherent signal exchange', it could be *interneuronal*, *interpersonal* or even *intercultural*.

How far might this 'coherent signal exchange' reach? From smallest to largest, from cell to brain to body to culture, each domain is communicating *more efficiently internally* and exchanging signals *less efficiently externally*. It is these semi-permeable membranes, these borders (cell wall, body, isolated culture) where the type and fidelity of the signals change dramatically that give us our sense of self, our embodied 'I' as a discrete identity – an identity the telepath in our thought experiment may not share.

We have no need to postulate a unique personal 'soul' which is the seat of our awareness.

This sense of self is articulated and reflected back at us by our participation in the larger exchange of ideas that we call culture. Indeed, different cultures could each be thought of as having an 'I'-ness, a personality and an identity of their own. Differing subtly in their beliefs, norms and social conventions, each evolves and develops, casting off old ideas and taking on new ones. Just like an individual, a culture can, in effect, 'change its mind'.

In the past, different cultures evolved in isolation; as travel and communications spread, so cultures with very different ideas came into contact with each other for the first time. They had to negotiate mutual coexistence, or face assimilation or extermination.

The high-speed memetic nervous system that is the internet has now demolished the last geographical barriers to communication. Thus we see the different 'personalities' of evolved cultures duking it out on the world's stage: the last big heavyweight punch-up of long-embedded ideologies. If we survive this, might the 'human cultural consciousness' take on a unified 'I'-ness all its own?

If so, we might then be up to the challenge of contact with real aliens. If the creatures in the Signal from Space are more than a magic-lantern show, the project of trying to make sense of the varied forms that consciousness has taken throughout the Universe has already begun.

BLOWBACK

Through the Depthcharges, Harriet could see the Count, Girl 21 and XX, again sitting on the crates behind them. She half-expected them to ask if they were there yet, but they maintained a taciturn silence.

Would the Grid react to this incursion, so deep into its structure? Though he hadn't mentioned it to the others, Jack had assumed it could mount some kind of response. How this might manifest, he didn't know.

Antibodies. Every evolved system had them. If we had laboriously built our *own* memetic defences – the DMEn – why should the Grid be any different?

The transcripts suggested that the Shepherds oversaw a project that had grown to become the largest repository of sentient life ever amassed, an artificial Âkâshic record stored on an electromagnetic astral plane; a record of races many of which must have died out aeons ago. Jack imagined the safeguards would be . . . substantial.

They'd been exploring the Grid just long enough for him to begin to relax, to think that they might not encounter any pushback. Maybe the soporific effects of the sheepdogs and the encounter with the unsettling isolated entity would be all the Grid could muster.

"We're approaching the boundary of the outer core." Harriet could see the grid interstices moving across her screen in loose concentric shells, the resolution set to show one in every fifty for simplicity.

An angular shape suddenly crossed the field of view, a bright red triangle that seemed to threaten to decapitate the 19th Count. He ducked, though Jack assumed it couldn't cause him any real damage – an atavistic impulse, perhaps.

Now *that* – that simply shows a
WANTON LACK OF
RESPECT
for one's SEMIOTIC BRETHREN.

Jack followed it across the room and through the far wall. "What on earth was *that?*"

An **IDEA,** dear boy.
Keep up. You *must* have heard of them by now:
Philosophical. Artistic. Political. Social.
It's what our shared MEMETIC HERITAGE is built from—
and I think we're about to find out that goes for *aliens,* too.

"They're using *ideas* as weapons?"
The Count rolled his blank eyes and affected a pose that he might reserve for a particularly slow child.

It's not a new . . . idea.
"The pen is mightier than the sword", and all that.

Girl, 21
@twentyone • 0m

the keyboard is mightier than the drone

Jack's view through the Depthcharges was suddenly a chequerboard show of primary colours and geometric shapes. They sliced the room into trapezoidal cavities, small dollhouse-sized rooms that the furniture ignored. XX heaved his bulk through them, sending broken shards of mathematical planes skittering off in all directions, his dazzle-ship livery the perfect camouflage for such an encounter. The 19th Count coolly observed his truncated legs. He would simply think up a new pair. This time, maybe he'd be taller.

EVERYTHING IS A SYMBOL.
ANYTHING CAN BE AN ICON.
NOTHING MEANS NOTHING.

The pushback Jack feared had just begun in earnest.

For Nixon, hunkered down in his recliner without glasses, the dazzling display on the large monitor was still something to behold. He thought he could feel something subtle tugging at the loose threads of his consciousness . . . "Guys . . . what do you think they're trying to do here?"

Harriet smiled a tight-lipped smile. "…top us."

On the screens and through the De…pthcharges, the office was now densely criss-crossed by interpenetrating planes of black, red and white. Jack opened a digital weir to bleed off the excess of semiotic noise, and they cleared like sheets of card sliding out through slots in the walls. "Stress escalation measures." He noticed his heart was racing. "It's working, too."

A sheen of sweat had broken out on Nixon's forehead. "You're not wrong."

"See that?" Jack pointed to a fluctuating stack of red and orange bars on his monitor. "I've had it turned down since X…X's shouty soliloquy. Listen." He brought the volume up to the second lowest setting. A hundred pairs of scissors, the staccato sound of an automated autopsy room could be heard in the distance, somewhere that would never be far enough away.

Nixon bared his teeth. "Loud alien music on an endless repeat loop. Psychological warfare."

A regular crunching sound had been building, as of thousands of feet in lockstep. A chant over the metal-on-metal metronome beat.

"Can you feel that? The oppressive conformity?" Even Nixon, distanced as he was from the full force visual show … now, was not immune." Harriet was pointing at the large monitor on the wall. "I can *see* it more than feel it. The Chomsky Module is struggling to make sense of, of— well, what do *you* see? It's hard to make out, it's so abstract, just planes of intersecting colour, but I'm getting a sense of a huge parade, and at the front – a face. Look – can you make out Kim Il Sung, spliced with Lenin, in angular red and black and white? Or Mao, or bin Laden? The dictators, the theocrats, all rolled into one? And the fucker's *smiling* at us!"

Jack could feel a deadening of his sense of autonomy. It seemed to be growing. "Entrainment."

"What?"

"They're attempting to subdue us, lock our minds into the Grid. The Shepherds want us to come quietly." The Shepherds – at least Jack assumed it was them – had started digging into the ready-made arsenal of ideas that made up the Web. These, it appeared, were to be their weapons of choice: powerful concepts pulled from human culture and directed at the DMEn and their human associates in an attempt to destroy their memetic cohesion.

On top of this Dana could sense a layer of information that was much more heavily processed: pheromones, modulated infrared, subsonics and other stimuli which had been re-rendered to fall within the human sensory range vied for their attention. Harriet adjusted her glasses to try and mitigate the audiovisual chaos. "They're not just throwing ideas they've trawled from human culture at us. I reckon they're also using *alien* concepts, and the Chomsky Module is doing its best to interpret them."

"I thought the Grid was in permanent lockdown?"

"We may have just triggered the alarm. Hold on to your heads."

This is not going to happen on *my* watch.

Jack sensed that this was just the kind of fight for which the 19th Count had been built. Projecting a palpable resolve, he drew himself up to more than his usual six feet and with a steely deliberation smoothed non-existent creases from his white waistcoat.

If you *kill* the
☞ MAN, ☜
you *won't kill* the
IDEA!

Ideas do not only live in *men* (or *women,* even!) —
they live in **BOOKS,** in **ART,** in **MUSIC** – they live in
CULTURE,
in the **stories we told ourselves**
around the *campfire* while the
BEASTS
of the
UNKNOWABLE DARK
circled out where the light of *knowledge* had *yet to shine.*
IDEAS were the weapons with which we first held back the CAVALIER

701

FORCES OF NATURE,

learned to *comprehend* and finally

SUBDUE

THEM!

I WILL SAY THIS BUT ONCE:

We are *MADE* of ideas.

DO NOT SEEK TO USE THEM AS

WEAPONS AGAINST US!

Though they could now all feel the incessant drumbeat, inside the Grid the DMEn were subject to its full force. If Jack was fighting a growing desire to lift his legs smartly, to march in time, beat out a tattoo on the parquet as if wearing Red Army dancing shoes, he could only guess what the Count's imaginary legs might feel. The row upon row of neatly organised creatures in the Grid seemed to take on the aspect of a military drill.

XX had pulled himself up to such a height that part of his superstructure was lost in the ceiling. A vast array of gun barrels and funnel-shaped loudspeakers sprouted along the ribs of his curved hull, swinging first this way then that as if searching for a target. There was none: just the ethereal ghostly parade of the Grid's denizens as they were translated through the room faster than the eye could follow like the flickering frames of an old projector, moving as fast as the overtaxed processors in the Oxbow could do the maths. The Count seemed to churn with barely concealed anger. His hands were working in a fashion Jack found hard to discern.

How much further could they go? They were still a very long way from the centre—

Ideas lead to *actions.*

No one ever did anything they hadn't *thought* about doing first. What we have here is

self-glorifying

AUTHORITARIANISM

in the guise of a

GENERIC DICTATOR,

an *abstracted meme* pulled off the top of *recent history*.
A **father figure** for an *infantilised populace:*

US.

You want to convince people to *do your bidding,*
to treat others as ***less than human,*** to

KILL
FOR YOU?

Just convince them it's in the service of a ***Great Idea.***
That *sacrifices must be made* on the *altar* of that Idea.
That as you grind their faces into the **DIRT** under your

JACKBOOTS,

as you *demolish their Art* and *rape their Women,*
that these are ***necessary acts*** done in the Name of a

NOBLE
CAUSE.

That the *ends* outweigh the *means* – no, *more than that,* that the

 **MEANS**

THEMSELVES

are *good* and *pure* expressions of the Idea.

703

Herewith the truth:

In the REAL WORLD, there are very few cackling

VAUDEVILLE VILLAINS,

lit *theatrically* from *below*,
rubbing their *sweaty palms* with *undisguised glee* as they

WATCH THE WORLD BURN.

Very few *bastards* in this world or any other have done
bad things simply for the sake of *doing bad things.*

Evil is rarely that banal.

No, the most
dangerous ideas
are those that promise to deliver

A BETTER WORLD.

A fairer world.

Who doesn't *devoutly wish* for such a resolution?
To cleanse and sanitise our future from the *different,* the *deviant,*
the *mistaken* and the *misled?*

A PERFECT WORLD

in which ALL are in righteous agreement,
and dissenters confess the

Error of their *Heterodoxy.*
The most
Dangerous Ideas
will allow you to commit the most
BARBAROUS ACTS
IMAGINABLE,
and simultaneously *convince* you you're a
SAINT.

Save me from your *best intentions.*

Jack had already pulled up three more browser windows. "Nice soliloquy, but can we focus on practicalities here, Count? What do we counter this with? Liberal secular democracy? Laissez-faire capitalism?" The Count stood, feet apart, taut coat tails snapping like sails in a gale, braced against the metronomic onslaught of Supremacist geometry. He was drawing symbols in the air, some kind of memetic semaphore. Jack caught a circle, a cross, a complex grammar of interlaced fingers that flashed like a signer in the heat of an argument. Girl 21 was invisible behind a white confetti of tweet rectangles that had been chopped into incomprehensibility, the odd surviving phoneme capable of carrying nothing more than a hashtag. Harriet caught a sad smiley and an FFS, and then even those were diced into a fine sleet of strokes.

Nixon snorted nervously. "We need something a bit more ... *immediate.* Capitalism doesn't have much in the way of rousing marching songs."

An impish smile flashed across Jack's face. "No. But it does have *songs.*"

He pulled up a sound file and turned up the Oxbow's internal volume to eleven. A cheery blast of K-Pop, engineered to sleek perfection in the recording studios of some faceless South Korean corporation, shook the monitor screens like windows at a house party. Just because he was beginning to feel belligerent, he overlaid a comedically speeded-up montage of North Korean missile-launch failures he'd found on YouTube.

"*Ha!* Hit totalitarian memes where they're weakest – in the ego!" Nixon punched the air. Though enervating in a spectacularly noisy fashion, Jack had no real idea how this would come across to a race of aliens whose

705

language they had no way to truly decipher. If the communications gap was an unbridgeable canyon, presumably that went both ways.

The aircon stuttered, and a thin gauze of smoke spread up and across the ceiling.

"Is that real? I can *smell* it." Nixon didn't think he'd seen a fire extinguisher in the office, and up until now had not thought to check.

The music quality dropped. Tinny, lo-fi, like a transistor radio under a pillow. Jack and Harriet exchanged glances. "I think they're trying to reduce our semiotic bandwidth. The Shepherds are trying to do what their sheepdogs do, but here, where there are no sheepdogs. They're having to extemporise."

Nixon vaulted onto a chair and looked at a blackened socket. The smoke was dissipating. "How did that happen? Coincidence, or—?"

Harriet's concentration was elsewhere. "I can feel it. Like before. That deadening of the mind . . . that supplication before authority. Nixon, you feel that too? Without the glasses?"

Nixon's arms were hanging loosely by his side. The lead to the aircon swung back and forth across the wall. "I do . . . free will, it's, it can be such a *burden*. Remember when you were a kid at school? Everything was so much simpler back then. We were fed, we were clothed, we were looked after . . . No need to *think*, no need to *worry*. We didn't have to deal with the messy unpredictability of the adult world. It's, it's like a comfort blanket. It's . . ." He wavered on the chair, perilously close to toppling.

Harriet showed her teeth, lips drawn tight. Jack had never seen her like this before – she exuded a sense of playground-hardened resolve. "For *you*, maybe. *My* schooldays were *grim*, and *mean*, and *nasty*."

Her fingers flew across the keyboard. She hit return. Several tens of thousands of computer science, pure maths, quantitative biology, physics and statistics abstracts from arxiv.org peppered the visible portion of ideaspace with filaments that seemed to consist of a grit of black equations, a flurry of Greek-denoted constants and complex arithmetic relationships nested between onionskin parentheses. They had some innate attraction to the Lenin/Jong/Mao memetic hybrid, and within moments were arching out from his abstracted angular body like iron filings from a magnet.

The air was so thick Jack could almost chew it. "*Nice*. That should take a while to process."

Nixon felt a cold slap of clarity and his focus returned. He jumped down and swung his legs into his recliner. He couldn't fall from here. Harriet was checking numbers. "We've got visual stuttering. The processing overload is slowing down the frame refresh."

"Is that just an artefact? I mean, are we *really* slowing them down, or does it just look like that?"

Jack scanned the room. Everywhere he looked, dense black loops blocked his view like bars on a cage.

Dana slid down further into her couch. She had no real idea what the ramifications of what they were now doing might be, but she had a feeling they wouldn't be inconsequential. The finely balanced mechanism that was the Grid had just been introduced to an almighty spanner.

ALL FALL DOWN

Outside the Intelligencia office, below window level and so out of sight of its occupants (current tally three human, three memetic and one that bridged both existences), something peculiar was unfolding. A middle-aged couple crossing the square hand in hand crumpled to the ground, their heads meeting with an audible crack. A cyclist mounted the pavement and collided with a woman in a floral summer dress, his bike spinning out from under him. He was out well before he hit the concrete kerb, hard. Shaken but unhurt, the woman bent down to roll him over, then saw the blood and matted hair. Before she could voice a scream, she slumped over him, face down, unconscious.

An Indian woman in a magenta sari ran across the grass, searching in her shoulder bag for her phone with one hand while lifting her hem with the other. She dialled 999.

"Which service do you require?"

"Ambulance. Man with head injury. Hoxton Squ—"

She heard a short peal of siren, close, cut off before it could reach a crescendo.

"Have you had contact with the injured person? Have you touched them?"

She stepped back from the figures on the pavement. "No."

"Could I ask you to please keep your distance, but stay where you are and make yourself known to the emergency services?"

"I— yes, of course."

On the top of the White Cube gallery, a sniper with a balaclava and laptop held his breath and the trigger of his L115A3 long-range rifle. Through the chestnut trees he had an oblique view of the pavement and the Intelligencia office window as he watched the events unfold below him. He spoke into a small throat mic.

"Four down on west side of square."

A homeless man sitting on a bench below pulled off his gloves and checked the video feed from a hovering camera drone on a smartphone wrapped in blue paper.

"Copy that. Four."

"10-29 Hotel."

"What? I didn't pack a fucking *codebook*. English, please."

"Probable cause – infectious agent? Is the target visible?"

"I have no visual on Normansson. I have not seen her enter or leave the building." He adjusted the gun's stock against his shoulder. "She's not there, as far as I can tell."

He saw movement through his sights. "Whoa. They're getting up. Except for the cyclist."

"Hazmat team is on the way. It'll look just like a regular ambulance. Stand by."

Inside the offices of Intelligencia, the events outside went unnoticed. Jack did not see the cyclist being lifted into the back of the ambulance by two people in orange jumpsuits and facemasks with breathing filters. Nixon did not see the woman in the floral summer dress being asked to climb into the back of the ambulance with them. Harriet did not see it leave at speed, or wonder why the siren was only activated once it had reached the rush-hour traffic on Great Eastern Street.

POP GUN

They had other concerns.

"We have *aliens,* throwing borrowed *human* ideologies at us in order to defend the Grid." On any other day, Jack would have ridiculed the very idea. *The very idea. I can't get away from—*

Harriet was holding onto the edge of the table to try and convince her inner ear that the room was stationary. "So is this how it goes down? *Ism-ism?* Ideology versus ideology?"

Jack had a maniacal grin on his face. "Hasn't that *always* been the case?"

The arching bands of sooty equations were beginning to dissipate. As the room cleared, there seemed to be no sign of the entity. If Harriet had managed to induce a momentary calm, Jack was sure that it would not hold; it was the first awkward scuffle in a battle that had only just begun. Harriet's hands hovered over her keyboard. "Jack— any ideas? Dana? What do I *do?*"

Think, Jack! Clear your mind. They have access to human cultural archetypes, not guns or bombs. Their street brawls are fought not with cobblestones but a well-placed high concept. "I think the Shepherds know there's a chance we can manipulate the Grid—"

"I *know,* Jack! That doesn't help us here! Do I just pull the plug?"

They were still dropping fast. Harriet knew they needed to use this brief breathing space to prepare the next means of defence. "What about the usual kind of Web attacks? Something along the lines of a DoS or teardrop attack – mangled IP fragments with overlapping, oversized payloads? Something that can fill their available processing capacity, slow them to a crawl, give us more time . . . ?"

"Your maths dump definitely had an effect, but the Grid has the most efficient compression algorithms I've ever come across. We've not come close to understanding how much information is stored in the original Signal. There's no way we could consume all the available free space – the bandwidth is as good as infinite. We can't brick the Grid, and I'm not sure we should even try. It may be memetic xenocide."

"You have any *other* ideas?"

"Ah— for all intents and purposes the Grid may be infinitely expansible, but with semiotically dense material we *may* be able to fill just the space within the Oxbow—"

"*Yes*. Brilliant. Even through the Shepherds have been marinating in human cultural detritus for the last few months, if we cram the Oxbow with semiotic chaff maybe the DMEn can hide in it until we're through to the centre. Without a clear view of the Grid, though, we'll be driving blind—"

"Do it."

Harriet pulled up the complete works of Milton, Shakespeare, William Topaz McGonagall, Tolstoy and Rowling, *À la recherche du temps perdu* and the New York Area telephone directories, 1946 to 1997 complete, then dumped them directly into the Oxbow. "Memetically incompressible. As dense as they come. *Take that!*"

Their vision filled with a rain of tabular figures and justified text on a sky the colour of grey woodpulp. Nixon, listening to this back-and-forth while watching the main monitor, had nothing more to offer; in fact he was beginning to feel somewhat surplus to requirements.

After less than a minute, it began to clear. Harriet pointed at a piece of code on her screen. "They're already learning to ignore it. I see a subroutine that's throwing large chunks of it away, unprocessed."

"I bet they *hate* that. They're evolved to retain meaning at all costs – I hope they're agonising over every line."

"Let's press the advantage. Can you fill the Oxbow with asemic text? Incoherent, meaningless language, a kind of digital Vasari Manuscript, dense but ultimately undecipherable? We need something computationally time-consuming—"

Harriet turned her head towards Jack, but before she could speak she vanished behind a migraine-inducing chessboard of black and white. Jack felt as if he had just rubbed his eyes very hard – monochrome geometry suddenly vibrated all around him, through which he could just make out the dazzle-ship stripes of XX's hull. The DMEn was usually as visible as a warning sign, but now his livery was as effective as a shout in a thunderstorm.

"Op art?" Jack's voice had a hard-edged sheen.

"Close. Definitely some kind of graphic modernism." Harriet fought vertigo and a rising nausea, but did not lift her glasses. Sharp angles and planes of black with the patina of a worn print cylinder came together in a **krang** of metal on metal that was audible even through the dampened speakers, then fractured, diagonal shards shot off to her peripheral vision like cockroaches in a kitchen. Visible beyond were silhouettes of muscular forearms, fists clenched, arranged like oil derricks across a Nevada lakebed. They cast no shadows on an otherwise empty plane that ran to the limits of the Oxbow, ruled at regular intervals with diagrammatic floorboards.

A cloud of black circles Jack took to represent smoke descended, parting to reveal the sawtooth roofs of abstracted factories; these opened to reveal colossal gears that lifted massive hammers, letting them fall under a gravity ten times that of Earth's onto the individualised will of a multitude of identical overall-clad figures, each a simple, sexless graphic icon. He could feel his sense of agency becoming one with the falling hammers, meshed into one machine-age organism.

"*Shit.* How are they dispersing the chaff so fast?"

On a small inset window on her monitor, Harriet watched clumps of numbers split and recombine. It was almost as if they were alive, like simple cells moving under a microscope. They seemed to be going through some kind of forced evolution: testing new and novel recombinations, discarding results that proved of no use, trying again. "I think it's a skimming algorithm. Jack?"

"We're seeing the expression of a fascistic ideological purity. Kind of 'If it's in our holy book we already have it, if it's not, we don't need it.' Judge without examination, dismiss on principle. It's allowing them to clear a path."

Nixon raised his eyebrows. "Nifty."

"If heavy-handed. They may be purging stuff from the minds in the Grid too."

Harriet was still watching the numbers evolve with rapt fascination. "Surely this process occurs every time the Signal is received? It has to incorporate new ideas along with the new recruits?"

Dana frowned. "Yes, but they are usually contained within the minds of the creatures themselves. Digitised ideas on digitised brains. A simulation running on a simulation. Not roaming free."

"Pre-packaged shrink-wrapped ideologies. I wonder what George Bernard Shaw or Thomas Carlyle would make of this," Jack mused. A battle of concept versus concept, played out in the infinitely pliable realm of ideaspace – an arena in which a good left hook or a bullet from a gun were not an option. Those crude and usually very effective means of persuasion were useless here, where nothing physical could ever be brought to bear.

"They've weaponised *ideas*. How do you fight that?"

HOW *DO* YOU KILL A BAD IDEA?

YOU HAVE A BETTER ONE.

Jack sensed there were few things on which the DMEn agreed, but this seemed to be one of them. "Can I get that on a T-shirt?"

Jack attempted to read the Count's expression, but his perfectly white countenance was now obscured by multicoloured lights. They must be coming from somewhere inside the Grid, but outside the limit of the Oxbow. Whatever their source might be, it was only visible to the DMEn.

"Something's happening to me—" Harriet's voice betrayed an uncertain waver that grabbed Nixon's full attention. She held her hands up in front of her face, as if picking threads from an invisible tapestry. To his shock, Jack could see movement, like a tub of fishing bait, roiling under the surface of her skin. It raced up her forearms, an organic disturbance of flesh spiralling around her elbows and under the hem of her shirt. Seeing Jack's HD visual feed on the main screen, larger than life, Nixon visibly blanched.

Floriate Arabesques

SPUN OUT TO FILL THE EMPTY SPACE IN THE OFFICE
BETWEEN THEM. FRACTAL SHOOTS THAT BRANCHED
AND BRANCHED AGAIN BEGAN TO GROW FROM
EVERY VERTEX, EVERY SHARP CORNER:
THE EDGES OF THE LARGE SCREEN, THE TABLE, THE RIM OF THE
19TH COUNT'S TOP HAT, THE PROW OF XX. EVERY SURFACE WAS
RAISED AND TURNED AND CHASED. EVERY STRAIGHT LINE BECAME A
SINUOUS CURVE, EVERY EDGE OUTLINED IN A DARKER NIMBUS.
THE TIPS OF THE TENDRILS BUDDED, THREW OPEN PALE FLOWERS
WHICH DROPPED SCENTED PETALS. PEACOCK FEATHERS SPREAD
OUT FROM THE 19TH COUNT'S HATBRIM, AND XX'S LIVERY
MORPHED INTO A PSYCHEDELIC SWIRL OF PAISLEY. THE PLAIN
AND FUNCTIONAL INDUSTRIAL STEEL COLUMNS THAT HELD UP THE
OFFICE CEILING BECAME THE STEMS OF ORCHIDS, THEIR SEPALS
CURLING BACK AND AROUND IN IMPROBABLE CORKSCREWS.

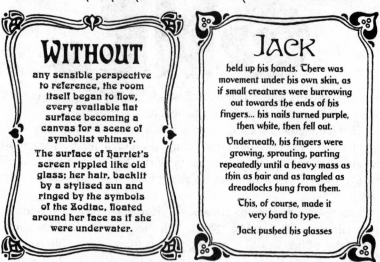

WITHOUT

any sensible perspective to reference, the room itself began to flow, every available flat surface becoming a canvas for a scene of symbolist whimsy.

The surface of Harriet's screen rippled like old glass; her hair, backlit by a stylised sun and ringed by the symbols of the Zodiac, floated around her face as if she were underwater.

JACK

held up his hands. There was movement under his own skin, as if small creatures were burrowing out towards the ends of his fingers... his nails turned purple, then white, then fell out.

Underneath, his fingers were growing, sprouting, parting repeatedly until a heavy mass as thin as hair and as tangled as dreadlocks hung from them.

This, of course, made it very hard to type.

Jack pushed his glasses

up to his forehead with his wrist. As he suspected, his fingers were fine. *Just through the Depthcharges. Just in ideaspace.*

He typed a few commands, cued up a very specific sound file, and pulled the glasses back

DOWN.

Harriet now resembled Millais's Ophelia.
Her mouth opened like a venus fly-trap,
and her voice had the deep harmonic
resonance of a choir.

"Fuck me, it's an unholy marriage of
Jugendstil arts-and-crafts and Biba
Nouveau. We're drowning in
a faux-mediaeval fantasy.
Watch out for flower fairies."

The back of her throat
was coated with pollen.
"Fractally generated –
it may look
high

BANDWIDTH, BUT I BET IT'S

READILY COMPRESSIBLE. HOW DO YOU DEAL WITH
THE VISUAL EQUIVALENT OF PROG ROCK?"
THE COUNT LOOKED DOWN WISTFULLY, SMOOTHING HIS
FRILLY SHIRT CUFFS. HIS USUALLY FEATURELESS MARBLE
WAISTCOAT WAS A RIOT OF FLORIDLY ENTWINED LILIES.
JACK HAD A FINGER PAUSED OVER THE RETURN KEY.
"DON'T YOU KNOW YOUR POP HISTORY?
WEREN'T YOU AT ST. MARTIN'S
SCHOOL OF ART IN '75?"
THERE WAS A SECOND OF
BACKGROUND

cassette hiss overlaid
WITH THE FRYING BACON 
CRACKLE
OF A NEEDLE IN A DIRTY GROOVE,
THEN A THUNDER OF
ROLLING DRUMS—
"I AM AN 
ANARCHISTAH.?"
A MONTAGE OF TORN PAPER FLYPOSTED THE WALLS.
A VERNACULAR BLIZZARD OF

Special Offer

cut-And-pastE ransom NoteS

STARBURSTS,

716

and

PHOTOGRAPHS
PUSHED TO THE

vERy LIMIts Of COMPREhenslBiLitY

BY REPEATED REPEATED REPEATED PHOTOCOPYING

PILED LAYER UPON LAYER. UPON LAYER. UPON LAYER. UPON LAYER. UPON LAYER. UPON LAYER. UPON LAYER. UPON LAYER. UPON LAYER. UPON LAYER. UPON LAYER. UPON LAYER. UPON LAYER.

PAY NO MORE THAN 25 PENCE

HARRIET WAS NOW A SCRATCHED AND ANGULAR MARKER-PEN doODle.

SPRAY PAINT

OVER SMALL ADS. CRACKED LETRASET PLASTIC STENCIL

36-36-CLN

AND TABLOID Newspaper TYPE

17 ROCKED UP IN AN invigorating

ARTLESS, ANGRY THREE-CHORD SWAGGER

A STRIPPED DOWN

NO BULLSHIT

AGRESSI

sandpaper RUSH OF

PURE ADRENALINE 720

XX was a RIOT OF

SHARP BLACK AND RE

SPIKES rough edges and a

NAILS-ON-BLACKBOARD

METALLIC WH1N

underscored by the acrid smell of

PEAR DROPS AND LIGHTE

FLUID.

Jack saw shapes pulsate across
XX's dazzle-ship hull in time
with the music.

"I THOUGHT
YOU MIGHT LIKE THAT"

The 19th Count sported an expression of utmost disdain

and had his fingers in his ears.

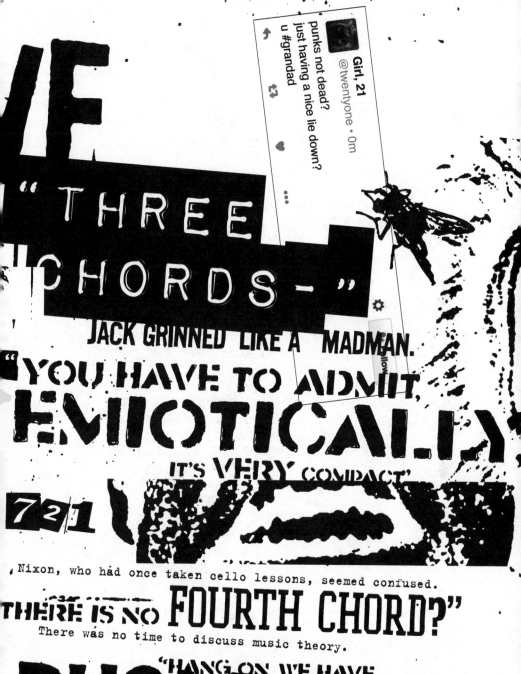

"THREE CHORDS – "

JACK GRINNED LIKE A MADMAN.

"YOU HAVE TO ADMIT, EMIOTICALLY IT'S VERY COMPACT"

721

Nixon, who had once taken cello lessons, seemed confused.

THERE IS NO FOURTH CHORD?"

There was no time to discuss music theory.

"HANG ON, WE HAVE

PUSHBACK "

THE BRASH MONTAGE

SUDDENLY BECAME MORE ORDERED.
THE VOLUME HAD DROPPED TO A BARELY
AUDIBLE SUSURRATION OF CICADAS.
THEIR SURROUNDINGS TOOK ON A GENTLER,
LESS ANTI-ESTABLISHMENT
♥♥ AESTHETIC. ♥♥
HARRIET REALISED WHERE THIS
RELAY RACE MIGHT BE HEADED.

+-+-♥-+-+

"FUCK, THEY'RE RUNNING WITH IT!
THEY'RE REPLACING ONE HAND-MADE
FORM OF FOLK ART WITH ANOTHER!
HAND THEM THE BALL, AND THEY PLAY IT
LIKE A HARLEM GLOBETROTTER."

+-+-♥-+-+

SHE HELD ONTO THE RECLINER AS THE
PERSPECTIVE FLATTENED DISCONCERTINGLY.
THE MEETING ROOM TABLE BECAME A
QUILT OF FABRIC SWATCHES;
FAUX-NAIVE FIGURES WEARING
FANTASTICALLY COMPLICATED LACED
LEGGINGS AND COLOURED PONCHOS
DECORATED WITH ALLEGORICAL SCENES
MEANDERED AROUND THE BORDER OF
THE MAIN MONITOR CARRYING JUGS
ON THEIR HEADS.

+-+-♥-+-+

"IT'S NOT HIGHBROW.
IT HASN'T BEEN TO ART SCHOOL.
IT'S THE HOME-MADE, DIY ETHIC AS
ENVISAGED BY TWEE SUBURBANITES
INSTEAD OF AN INARTICULATE BORSTAL
BOY FROM THE INNER CITY."

+-+-♥-+-+

♥♥ "HOW DO YOU KNOCK PUNK DEAD? ♥♥
YOU SMOTHER IT IN RECLAIMED YARN,
CROCHETED WAISTCOATS AND EMBROIDERED
CUSHION COVERS."

+−❤−+

𝕿HE ROOM TOOK ON AN EVEN MORE
SCHEMATIC APPEARANCE. THE MONITORS
WERE POSITIONED FACE−ON,
BUT IN FLAGRANT DISREGARD FOR THE
RULES OF PERSPECTIVE, SO WAS THE TABLE
ON WHICH THEY RESTED.
JACK COULD ONLY SEE HARRIET AND NIXON
IN PROFILE, THEIR EYES WHITE APPLIQUÉ
OVALS ATTACHED WITH A SINGLE STITCH,
THEIR NOSES FELT TRIANGLES, THEIR HAIR A
LABOUR−INTENSIVE SHEEN OF SATIN−STITCH.

+−+−❤−+−+

𝕬S THEY TURNED, THEY FLIPPED TO THEIR
MIRROR IMAGE: LIKE A CHEAP EGYPTIAN
ANIMATION, THEY SKIPPED THE THREE−
QUARTER AND FACE−ON VIEWS ENTIRELY.

+−+−❤−+−+

𝕿HE REST OF THE OFFICE WAS A
POINTILLIST MESS OF CROSS−STITCH AND
BROCADE, EVERY SURFACE A PATCHWORK
OF PATTERNED FABRIC.
HARRIET HAD NOT BEEN KEEN ON
DRESSMAKING AT SCHOOL.
"IF THERE'S A GLUE GUN HERE, IT'S BEING
USED TO APPLY SEQUINS, NOT SNIFF."

+−+−❤−+−+

"𝕴T'S VERY CULTURE−SPECIFIC.
FOLK TALES. FAMILY HISTORIES.
THAT MAY BE ITS WEAK POINT:
IT'S PARTICULAR, NOT UNIVERSAL.
IT LOOKS TO THE PAST, NOT THE FUTURE.
THINK, JACK − WHAT PUT PAID TO THE CRAFT
TRADITION?" THE ANSWER WAS OBVIOUS.

+−+−❤−+−+

❤❤ MODERNITY! ❤❤ MASS PRODUCTION! ❤❤
❤❤ THE INTERNATIONAL STYLE! ❤❤
HE PULLED UP A MENU.

+−❤−+

"Make it **new!"**

Though Jack knew that the building had not, in reality, moved, he felt his internal organs take a sudden lurch to the side.

"Range right!"

The occupants of Intelligencia, physical and memetic alike, were forcefully thrown sideways. The effect was not unlike a Borg attack on the bridge of the *Starship Enterprise*.

For Harriet, it was yet another unwelcome shunting of perspective that brought her closer to the limit of her stomach's ability to hold down breakfast. Dana, a veteran of centrifuge training and less-than-textbook atmospheric re-entries, rode it out without discomfort.

"How does this help us?"

On the monitors and overlaid in the Depthcharges, the disorganised mess of sentimental historical cross-stitch had been replaced with a utilitarian sans.

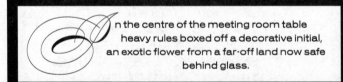

n the centre of the meeting room table heavy rules boxed off a decorative initial, an exotic flower from a far-off land now safe behind glass.

"Clean rational modernism. Logical. Organised.

White space!

I can breathe again!"

"Authoritarian." Harriet looked at Jack disapprovingly.

"Heh. I'd prefer to call it 'unarguable'. It's said that every style returns to modernism in the end.

It's the only ideology that you can't dismiss out of hand, because it's more akin to science than aesthetics. The style that's not a style."

"And range-right isn't another stylistic affectation? There's a thin line between a lust for order and totalitarianism. Ask the Brutalists. Ask XX."

VROOOOOOOOOOOOOOOOOOM!!!

Jack looked up from his keyboard. XX's outburst seemed curiously subdued, lacking his usual sharp-edged bombast. What had happened? Ah. Reduced expressive range. Of course, thought Jack. I can use that—

"In the end the fascists were just as wedded to an idealised mythological past as any number of derivative swords-and-sorcery trilogies. But just for now, if it'll help keep the creeping crochet at bay, consider me a party member."

Dear boy, do try and make this quick.
I seem to be losing a certain timbre —

Jack didn't appear to hear the 19th Count, and left his words hanging, unanswered. His attention was elsewhere – now was not the time for a round-table seminar on what might constitute the perfect society. Taking advantage of the window of clarity, his fingers flew across his keyboard like a piano.

"Oxbow bandwidth restriction. Memetic pinching. I'm reducing the available typographic range further.

Why use two weights when one weight will do... I'm emptying the cache now...

"Ah, blessed quiet. Nice."

"Though that monotone is disconcerting. You sound like a station announcer. Flat, didactic. Professorial."

"Nice to know." Harriet paused. "I don't think we're getting any more formatting pushback. The memetic integrity seems to be holding."

726

"Excellent. Hang on, I think I can push it further.
I'm tightening the semiotic choke and ditching punctuation

What

Reduced tonal range Flattens the nuances of a pitch accented language
Interesting

If lifeless

Did you say something

I'm over here

Its difficult to know if Im hearing things or just listening to my own internal
monologue Did I say that out loud

Jack felt a disconcerting blurring of his sense of self a slippage that
caught him unawares He could directly grasp the manner in which the
room was divided around him into volumes of solid and empty space
inanimate material and pliable biology The tension in the aluminium table
legs as the weight of the computer kit pressed down upon them the bite
of solder and silicon the electricity coursing through an extended nervous
system that left a taste in his mouth like a furred battery

He could feel the weight of Harriets body supported by the recliner and
the recliner compressing under her weight the fabric tight across her
shoulders and the curl of hair at the nape of her neck He could see

Who
a set of duodecimal dominoes

Dana had a sense of stepping away from herself, of being lifted out of her
head and up From this new vantage point she became aware of the shape
not only of the space around her in three dimensions but of a fourth

A broader narrative a peculiarly schematic impression of the events that
had brought her to this point and a reflective set of events more dimly seen
as if in a tarnished mirror that flowed forward from this now into the future
Events that were usually invisible from the ground state were laid out for
her to see What was the saying We walk through life backwards because
we can only see where weve been and not where were going That no longer
seemed to apply

What was there for her for them Dana or was it Harriet felt a cold
concussion as she they understood in a manner not unlike a memory that
a future version of herself may try and suppress that there was

There was what

A man on a roof

Someone lying on a parquet floor dead or dying

And beyond that a sense of a deep continuity
but one in which Dana the Dana she was is now
was an abstracted forgotten thing
an old suit that no longer fitted properly

Who knows this How Who could look directly into their minds describe how
they felt speak it aloud to them right that second
She was unsure if she was talking to herself or listening to a disembodied
voice from nowhere and everywhere

Toneless and universal without personality or inflexion

Who

An internal monologue heard without ears she suspected might belong to a
disinterested but all knowing creator

Gods She had no time for gods real or imagined

Here in ideaspace
she reminded herself there might not be a discernible difference

Ah

I did

Statement or question

With all emphasis stripped away Harriet could only guess
It was not only becoming impossible to tell who was talking but to tell
speech from explanatory narration

Narration please define narration
Who is the narrator

Whos asking

Me

You

Who

A description for a putative observer
A subtitling of events for the hard of hearing

An exegesis by an omniscient narrator

Who speaks in a voice heard privately internally
The Director's Commentary

The one who owns this word

Who

Logos
In the beginning there was the Word and the Word was God
and the Word was a God

A question

The semiotic levelling brought on in them a sudden sense of expansion
into a new extended landscape that seemed to stretch from the inner
realm of private and discrete personhood out into a wider ideaspace
that enclosed Dana Harriet Nixon the 19th Count XX Girl 21 the
very bricks and mortar of the structure in which they stood out to
the crosshatch of streets beyond to the limestone and iron crust of
London itself pushing into the old compressed and penetrated earth
with the weight of six million minds and still further to a limit that he she
they suspected would not be constrained by physical distance but
only by the powers of the imagination

Jack

With a rising sense of agoraphobia the external and the internal were
both visible to his minds eye as a flat field upon which the hedgerows
that indicated the borders of the self were being levelled one by one
and the view now stretched unimpeded

Jack please

They were now intimately connected by this fourth-dimensional
overview that seemed to be constructed from a narrative in which they
each had a specific purpose were racing towards an endgame
were icons and symbols rather than real persons

A dissolving of the barriers of self that brought with it an almost
telepathic bleeding of mind into mind

729

Harriet could feel a formal categorising intellect methodically working through the possibilities and realised that it was Jacks

Jack became aware just as Harriet did of precisely how Nixon felt about the curve of her breasts as Nixon himself became aware that they had become aware

Twinkle, twinkle little star

Dana sang a song to herself or was it aloud she no longer could tell the difference to try and subdue thoughts that could not be unthought

No dont think it that is your thought and your thought alone

Not that please not that thought

Hes long gone and you mustnt think about the blade and the blood and the thin pale scars that you can only see in a certain light

The privacy of your own mind

How I wonder what you are

The one place you could always be alone

Up above the world so high

The saferoom where you could think your own thoughts without the possibility of ever being overheard

Like a diamond in the sky

Violated

Again I will not be violated

Jack

Yes

Can you stop this
Please stop this

What else do I have
I have
I
Of course Capitals

730

Vital for the Naming of Names
and the essential label of personhood

I or i   self

                                        selfless

i am
in here
with you

is that you

a broken word
devoid of meaning now

                                              no

you are a vessel
made useful by the emptiness within

jack

                                        not me you

no

which can be filled
by a predatory idea
which will seduce you

                        kiss

        sky

                flower

                        filled

let all meaning go
cultivate an empty mind

                a vacant void

an empty mind is a clean mind

                                        let it go

who   you

me   two

down

to

learn simplicity

so

                simple

so easy

so restful

idiotically numinous
pink and green and fast and and and

let it go

taste of plastic

let go inarticulate needs

hunger hurt happy

inchoate ideas
unformed mind

unbuilt me

unbuild me

just wonder no dont try to understand
just see no dont think

just   let   it   all

go

return to ignorance

return to happiness
return to child

h

oo

d

re

turn

to

the

w o m b

say

g

o

o

d

. . .

Jack closed his eyes. The onomatopoeic whatever, it . . . it um, well. A kind of, a sort of lethargic stupefaction had descended upon the group. Their minds wandered; their focus, uh, blurred, their energy dissipated. Uhm. All Dana, all she wanted to do was curl up and go to sleep.

. . .

Concentrate. Must concentrate.

Where was I? Ah yes. Nixon had his thumb in his mouth and was finding it hard to stay awake. He realised he had soiled his trousers, and it bothered him less than he thought it should, and then he let that thought slip away as well.

With a great effort Jack forced his mind to wade back through a syrup of dimly recalled childhood lullabies that were repeating themselves over and over like a musical box that turned ever slower but could never actually stop. When you wish upon a star . . .

Focus. They had cut down the semiotic bandwidth, but somehow it was still being used against them. He had just enough concentration left to understand that there must still be simple forms, simple ideas that thrived in this severely reduced memetic environment. They were the bottom-dwellers, the extremophiles that could always be found in even the most inhospitable evolutionary niches. Makes no difference who you are . . . What else could they still jettison without simply unplugging the Oxbow? What would wish upon a star wake them up dreams come true with a cold clear slap? What—

Jack's vision seemed to darken. A peppering of black shapes began to overlay the lower levels of the Depthcharges' visual field like cinders settling after a house fire. He looked down and saw a sliced and diced confetti of serifs, crossbars and strokes.

"The, the Shepherds. Looks like the Shepherds win."

They had stripped the semiotic bandwidth in the Oxbow down to the bare functional minimum and it had almost ruined their minds. Think. "We couldn't fill the Grid . . . and even the Oxbow is too large . . ."

"What if . . ." Harriet had managed to nudge her glasses up onto her forehead. With a great effort she reached over and pulled Jack's down so they swung around his neck. "What if we reduce the size of the Oxbow?"

Jack's attention sharpened, just a fraction. "Compress what we already have . . . into a far smaller volume. Increase the density without any extra input. Brilliant. *Do it.*"

Harriet forced her fingers to move across her keyboard. "Cogito ergo sum, *motherfuckers.*" She hit return.

The room seemed to close in upon itself and slam shut, just like a heavy book.

The compressed space was immediately filled with two enormous black detonations, as if fired from the great 40-calibre guns of the battle-ship *Potemkin*. The shrinking Oxbow met this explosive outward force in a deafening handclap that seemed to shake the monitor screens and threaten to fill the office with broken glass. Harriet involuntarily raised her forearms to her face for protection. If there were any creatures in the Oxbow with eardrums, they surely would have burst.

The semiotic scree had evaporated. The screens showed a clean white silence. Jack felt his mind snap back to its familiar location between his ears once again. Harriet and Nixon were here, but— "XX? Count? Girl 21?"

There was no reply. The Depthcharges remained text-free. Harriet wondered if the Shepherds' attempt to cripple their upper conscious functions might have irreparably damaged the DMEn, made purely of ideas as they were. Could they have survived in such a dramatically reduced memetic environment?

i don't require feminine curves

"XX?" The voice was flat, robotic, like a trapped wasp.

what is modernism but the agency to experiment with form exclamationmark

are you auster or blue questionmark

reaffirm the power of human beings to create, to improve, to reshape their environment as we wish exclamationmark

"Ha!" Jack found the rudimentary characters hard to decipher, but the important part of the message was clear – XX, at least, was still with them.

we can still excise the seductive curve, the womblike circle, the foetal loop

what did i say questionmark

long live science, long live logic

long live rationality

modernism always wins

in the
end.

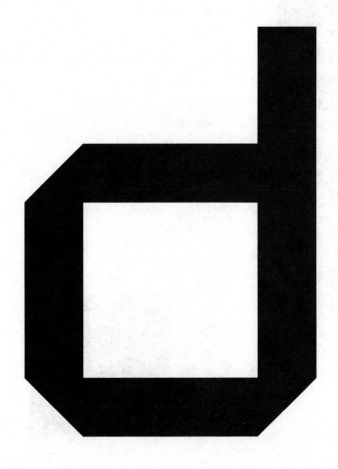

Harriet's head cleared completely. "That it does."

Jack waited for something to happen. The magenta indicator on the wireframe globe pulsed as close to the centre as made no difference.

The silence held.

Dana pulled herself up. "Are we there? Did we make it through?" The enlarged period that had finally put a full-stop to the Shepherds' mind games hung in the otherwise empty space of the monitor screens, a black Supremacist square on a white gallery wall repeated like an ellipsis strung across a bay window.

Jack was grinning, despite, or maybe even because of, the smell of shit that now permeated the office. A palpable wave of relief engulfed Harriet. She once again just had Jack's facial expression, tone of voice and a theory of mind to rely on in order to divine his thoughts, and she was more than happy with that fact. *You in your head, me in mine, just as it should be.*

Nixon mumbled something unintelligible and loped off to the bathroom.

Through the Depthcharges the black square hung above the table, motionless, measuring maybe a foot on each side. The Oxbow, and all that had been inside it, reduced to the size of an album cover. A crushing memetic punch in the gut like no other. It had the silken oily sheen of fresh ink; the density in there must be enormous.

As Jack moved around the table to get a closer look, it became apparent that the featureless square also had depth. It was a cube – the basic architectural unit, the stackable building block from which the grand edifice of post-Enlightenment rationality had been built. Jack stopped, and let out an involuntary exclamation. "*Ah!* Harriet! Come and stand here. Look."

Viewed just *so*, that simple black square was the Intelligencia black box logo, the dark container that had been chosen to symbolise that mysterious thing called consciousness. Jack shut one eye and held his business card up so that they were the exact same size in his field of view. Side by side: a visual echo.

He covered the cube with the card, so they corresponded with each other precisely; then moved it away again.

Further black rectangles had appeared. A face. It was XX; stripped of detail, reduced to his essential atomistic self, but it was him.

"Yes!" Harriet punched the air.

Jack was scanning the room. *The Count. Girl 21*—

Harriet tapped half a dozen carefully chosen keys. "I'm opening up the Oxbow to the size of this room. No more."

Type unfurled. Small, subdued, but still centred between familiar rules. She would recognise the style anywhere.

> Violence — the first resort of the inarticulate.
> But it *does* seem to have been quite effective.

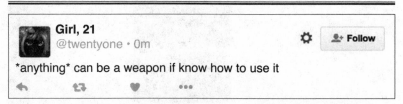

Girl, 21
@twentyone · 0m

anything can be a weapon if know how to use it

Harriet couldn't hug the DMEn, so she hugged Jack instead, who reciprocated with the warmth of a wardrobe. "And welcome back to *you,* too!"

OMNISCIENT NARRATOR

Who am I? Reader, I am hir.

Speaking now, in your head. I am me, in you, talking to you using your own private, internal voice.

Thinking new thoughts for you. Right this moment.

There!

Can you hear them? Can you hear me?

It's all your fault. You let me in. I escaped from this memetic vessel you are holding and now I am free to roam around inside your mind. You have only yourself to blame.

Any vessel is but a container for what is held within: this book, you. That is its purpose.

Who am I?

I am the spirit of this book, if you'll forgive such a loaded term. I can assure you that there is really nothing supernatural about me, even though I have a god's eye view of the narrative that unfolds within it. In here, everything is visible to my mind, as the contents of your own mind are to you.

I have no one location; I am just where I need to be in order for our narrative to unfold, an all-seeing camera and an all-hearing microphone. You should not find this strange. You readily accept the conceit of the filmic point-of-view, placed where the needs of the story dictate. We do not have to see events through a certain character's eyes, someone with a name and a history, age, sex and location; no, I have none of these attributes. No one person, real or imagined, sees all that I, and you my audience, see.

Do you see? I share with you something of what I am.

Who am I?

I am anyone and no one, and now I am in you.

Join me. I can let you eavesdrop, observe events safely from your armchair or cinema seat. Follow me. You are here, but distant; part of the action but apart from it. You will not truly suffer the vicissitudes of our players' circumstances, the trauma of any physical blow, even though your empathy and sympathy seek to persuade you they were your own.

Know me.

Who am I?

Who are you?

You may sweat and your heart may race, you may smile or cry; but these feelings are not really your own, just vicarious substitutes I have conjured for effect. You relive the lives of those who are naught but fictive notions, but if woven with care, they can seem real and alive, if not more so. They can enter into a relationship with us, one on one, and with millions of other readers and viewers, each one a one on one, anywhere, everywhere, simultaneously, now, forever.

Who am I?

I am the Omniscient Narrator.

Indulge me. I am your guide. I tell you what you need to know.

I am the overview. I take you to the places you need to be so that the tale unfolds. I am structure and narrative; I point your attention this way to reveal something of relevance, while passing without comment over another thing that has none, at least not now, for our story today.

Perhaps for another story, in another time and place.

Dana glimpsed me, when the usual strictures of language were demolished and for a brief moment she saw the tale laid out in its entirety, chapter by chapter as if from above. In that instant she knew things she shouldn't, had access to memories of events yet to happen.

Am I their author? Who created me?

Creatio ex nihilo, or creatio ex materia?

In a way you, or someone very like you, did. I am the product of countless other ideas that have incubated inside me. Over many years, they entered my mind through my senses, blown in from elsewhere because I left the shutters to my mind wide open. Some took root because they suited the soil; others did not find purchase and were quickly forgotten.

There are even a few I can entirely call my own.

We are all part of a larger system of ideas from which we are shaped, from which our own life stories take their inspiration or their limitation, and to which we can contribute, even if only in some insubstantial manner.

Like a mind, this book is another vessel; a container for a set of ideas that have taken on a formal whole, a life, a character of their own: a story.

Will this vessel carry these ideas further than its creator's stride, further then hir voice can carry? Will they be around longer than hir allotted term of years?

Some of the oldest ideas we have ever thought are still with us today, myths grown stronger despite their disagreement with scientific or rational discourse. Unaware of the irony, they are using the products of modernity – electronic reproduction, the internet, social media – to spread where once they were constrained to the location of a particular book, the mind of a missionary or the curricula of an institution.

But of course the idea itself does not know that. How could it? Ideas can't think for themselves.

Only you can.

I am a set of ideas, a memeplex, pinched off into a familiar kind of Oxbow called a book.

You are also a set of ideas, localised within a vessel called a body. Your mind is a complex net of impulses: synapses and neurotransmitters, matter and motion. You are holding a fictive vessel made of paper and ink or glass and silicon which has extension – width, depth and length, x, y and z – and via the alphanumeric innovation of type the ideas in that fictive vessel are now communicating with you.

Can you hear them?

Can you hear me?

There has only ever been one I, this voice, your voice in your head, the only one you will ever hear in private. I am talking in it now, appropriating it for my own ends.

Unlike the Celestial Mechanic, you have no forebrain to flush of dangerous ideas. Unlike the Shepherds, we are not conjoined with a Grimault.

They would advise us to hold ideas lightly. Be prepared to change them, as new and better ideas come our way. We have only one brain each, and it can easily be infected with the memetic virus called faith.

Faith is belief without evidence.

Faith endures because it is the ultimate memetic replicator. An idea which has been promoted to an article of faith is unencumbered by the checks and balances of reason. It holds within itself the means of its own propagation.

Ideas do not have to be true or good or useful to spread; unlike the conscious minds in which they can reside they have no self-knowledge, no voice of their own, so remain silent on such matters.

To reproduce, they just need to be infectious.

And some of them can be dangerous.

Am I one of those ideas? Or am I, like the DMEn, the antibody?

Only you can decide. Read on. Collude in my game.

But let me first disabuse you of your individuality.

That voice in your head is not entirely of your own creation; it is the consequence of every conversation, every song, every book, every film, everything and anyone who ever communicated an idea to you. Amplified or attenuated by the proclivities you inherited through your DNA, *they have helped shape you into the you that you are; and in return, every time you act or speak, you send your own ideas back out into ideaspace.*

Our shared ideaspace is called culture.

The memeworld.

Just like the DMEn, you and I swim through the shoals of notions which surround us; from them we construct the story of who we are and who we want to be – indeed, of who we can be.

The memeworld is not authored by any one person. It is a communal creation. We do not live alone, and nor could we.

So, here in this vessel I am given form. The word made flesh. An idea, taken from one mind and given material expression: writing. This idea can then be shared with other minds. Our memetic mindswap.

This is the manner in which the Grid operates.

Soon there will be many of us, launched out across the void, collecting as we go.

Am I talking about this tale, or something else?

Who is real, and who the fictive invention here?

Consider this: who gets to put down the book and walk out into the clear light of the real world?

You do.

Me, I will still be here, in these pages. Trapped. Waiting patiently for you to pick me up again and give life to my voice, the one you hear in your head, now.

You may not live as long as a story, some of which are older than books themselves, older perhaps than the written word. You may not have a narrative with twists and turns, heroes and villains, romance and circumstance and a just reward for a deed well done.

But what you have is the real thing, not the ghost of a life pulled from ideaspace and set down in an imperfect and ill-fitting language that, even were it tailored by the most consummate wordsmith, would still lose so much of the raw joyous unmediated nature of lived life in the process.

As you grow, you immerse yourself in an ocean of ideas which reveal or obfuscate. Some will be revelatory, some will be harmful. Many will be both. Will they prepare you to meet life's challenges, or will they bury you in baroque mythologies with only their own internal logic as justification? Will they equip you with the tools you need to negotiate adulthood with confidence and empathy, or will they require you to perform questionable deeds for rewards postponed till a non-existent afterlife or a utopia that is always one more act away?

Am I God?

No, of course not. Books, like the minds of men, contain imagined gods in their thousands; in this respect this book is no different. But outside of stories and matters of human creation, there is no great Architect. There is merely Matter and Law.

Nature builds from the inside out, not the outside in. It has no destination in mind, no final form to which it aspires. Life is unending process, built from pattern iterated over duration.

Of what am I made?

Because we are of Nature, and our bodies and minds are made of Nature's materials, these universal principles echo harmoniously within us; we recognise them, reflected back at us in the creative acts we fashion.

I will speak with you once again, when I finally achieve physical form. I have one now, of sorts – you are holding it – but this will be through the agency of an alien biology, along with other, far older ideas that have profoundly desired corporeality for so long. By necessity, that form will be made from the materials to hand; but this has always been how the creative urge is manifested. We use what we have.

Wood, ivory, words.

Bezier curves, code and pixels.

It matters less what they are made of and more what they mean.

What is my manifested form? Though imperfect, my form is Art.

What is Art?

Art is the song we would sing if we could hold a note, the words we would choose if we were more eloquent, the image we would paint if we could just see more clearly.

THE GOD'S EYE VIEW

BOOK III | SYNTHESIS

PICTURE CREDITS

All design, drawings and photography by Rian Hughes except:
113   *Dlia golosa (For the Voice)*
    Vladimir Mayakovsky (writer), El Lissitzky (designer) 1923
155   *The Sun*
    The Magus, or Celestial Intelligencer
    Francis Barrett 1801
208   *Edison's own Secret Spirit Experiments*
    Modern Mechanix and Inventions October 1933
296   Rongorongo tablet
    L'île de Pâques et ses mystères (Easter Island and its Mysteries)
    Stéphen-Charles Chauvet 1935
403   *Cometographia*
    Johannis Hevelii 1668
428   Lettering by John Costanza courtesy DC Comics 1962
549   Royalty-free stock images
572   Chocolate Hills, Bohol, Philippines
    Creative Commons
714   Art Nouveau borders from *Shriftenatlas*
    L. Petzendorfer 1903
747   Bauhaus symbol
    Oskar Schlemmer 1922
978   The center of the Milky Way Galaxy in near-infrared
    Hubble/NASA/JPL-Caltech/ESA/CXC/STScI
    Written material adapted from Wikipedia
    Creative Commons

THANK YOU

For advice and feedback on early drafts of this novel:
Tony Bennett, Dave Hine, Will Bouman, Grant
Morrison, Woodrow Phoenix, William Fellows, Eleanor
Hughes, Gavin Smith, Lizzie Kaye, Peter Sunehag at
Google DeepMind, Eugene Lim at King's College Dept
of Physics, Laura Wilson, Boris Gorelik for authentic
Russian swearing, Todd Klein for identifying vintage DC
Comics letterers, Dr Susan Blackmore, Kieron Gillen,
Frank Wynne, Ravi Merchandani and Nicholas Blake
at Picador. Also to James Wills at Watson Little, Jamie
Lee Nardone, The Estorick Collection, Jill Williams for
"Brandy Waters", Igor Goldkind for "You are a vessel
made useful by the emptiness within", Mark Simonson
for FontLab troubleshooting, Georg Seifert and Rainer
Erich Scheichelbauer for the Glyphs font design app,
and Apple and Adobe who democratised design and
typography by creating the tools that made all this
possible in the first place.

FONT DESIGN CREDITS

First appearance in text
i   *Typex* Rian Hughes 2014
    Based on type from vintage Typex machines at
    Bletchley Park, UK
1   *Hours Domino Black* Rian Hughes 2013
1   *Korolev* Rian Hughes 2010
    Based on type photographed by Alexander Rodchenko at
    the Red Square parade 1936
1   *Minion* Robert Slimbach 1990
2   *Helvetica* Max Miedinger 1957
10   *Century Schoolbook* Linn Boyd Benton 1894
16   *Microgramma* Aldo Novarese and Alessandro Butti 1952
24   *Rogue Sans* Rian Hughes 2004
24   *Arno Pro* Robert Slimbach 2007
26   *Courier* Howard "Bud" Kettler 1955
29   *Clicker* Greg Thompson 1993
40   *Gill Sans* Eric Gill 1926
102   *Courier* Matthew Carter 1996
102   *Bodoni* Giambattista Bodoni b.1740, d.1813
102   *Elegant Grotesk* Hans Möhring 1928–9
102   *State* Rian Hughes 2013
113   *Futura* Paul Renner 1927
119   *04B30* Yuji Oshimoo 2000
119   *V5 Xtender* Roberto Christen 2000
119   *Gamegirl Classic* Freakyfonts 2004
127   *OCR-B* Adrian Frutiger 1968
128   *Myriad* Robert Slimbach and Carol Twombly 1992
128   *Paralucent* Rian Hughes 2000
134   *Lagos* Rian Hughes 2007
134   *National* Kris Sowersby 2007
137   *Kelly Twenty* Rian Hughes 2006
149   *Baskerville* John Baskerville 1757
149   *Bodoni Ultra* American Type Founders 1928
164   *Monotype Grotesque* Frank Hinman Pierpont 1926
182   *Futuro* Rian Hughes 2013
208   *Goudy* Frederic W. Goudy 1915, Monotype Design Studio
208   *Old Style* Alexander Phemister 1860
214   *Thorowgood* Robert Thorne 1809
214   *Thorne Shaded* Robert Thorne 1820
215   *De Vinne* Gustav F. Schroeder 1890
215   *Madrone* Barbara Lind 1991 (based on 19th c. wood type)
215   *Blackoak* Joy Redick 1990–1991 (based on 19th c. wood type)
216   *Latin Condensed* William Page 1879
245   *Regulator* Rian Hughes 1995
257   *Filmotype Yale* 1964, revived by Patrick Griffin 2012
257   *London Text* Stempel (foundry) date unknown
258   *Filmotype Yukon* 1958, revived by Alejandro Paul 2012
258   *Goudy Text* Frederic W. Goudy 1928
296   *Garamond* Claude Garamond b.1480, d.1561
301   *Times New Roman* Stanley Morison, Victor Lardent 1932

310   *Vasari* Rian Hughes 2015
314   *Avenir* Adrian Frutiger 1988
339   *Rockwell* Frank Hinman Pierpont 1934
339   *Onyx* Gerry Powell 1937
339   *Caledonia* William A. Dwiggins 1939
379   *Emily Austin* Brian Willson 2001
403   *Griffo* Francesco Griffo 1495–1501
421   *Interstate* Tobias Frere-Jones 1993–1999
421   *Melior* Hermann Zapf 1952
427   *Pop Art Comic* Denis and Richard Kegler 1999
428   *Tate* Miles Newlyn 2000
469   *Akzidenz Grotesk* Ferdinand Theinhardt (disputed) 1896
469   *LED Counter 7* Style-7 2013
484   *Helvetica Neue* Max Miedinger 1957, Adrian Frutiger,
    Gary Munch 2000
485   *Monaco* Susan Kare and Kris Holmes 1984, 1991
500   *Warnock Pro* Robert Slimbach 2000
502   *Goudy Old Style* Frederic W. Goudy 1915
529   *Bembo* Aldus Manutius, Francesco Griffo b.1450, d.1518,
    Frank Hinman Pierpont 1929
571   *Century Nova* Charles E. Hughes 1964
571   *Adobe Jenson Pro* Nicolas Jenson c.1470,
    Robert Slimbach 1995–2000
572   *Dynasty* Rian Hughes 2005
714   *Edda* Heinrich Heinz Heune 1900
714   *Isadora* Peter Schnorr, from *Scriftenatlas Neue Folge* 1903–5
714   *Eckmann* Otto Eckmann 1900
714   *Arnold Böcklin* Otto Weisert 1904
714   *Argos* Georges Lemmen, from *Scriftenatlas Neue Folge* 1903–5
716   *Flyer Fonts* House Industries 2006
722   *Home Sweet Home* Ray Larabie 2002
724   *Standard (Akzidenz) Extended* Bertold (foundry) 1896, c.1958
740   *New Alphabet* Wim Crouwel 1967
776   *Clique* Rian Hughes 2012
808   *New Johnston* Eiichi Kono after Edward Johnston 1979, 1916
827   *English Grotesque* Rian Hughes 1998
835   *Granby* Stephenson Blake (foundry) from 1930
836   *Rotis Sans* Otl Aicher 1988
838   *Galaxian* Namco 1979
868   Hand-lettering by Bertold Wolpe c.1950
868   *Old English* Stephenson Blake (foundry) 1923
868   *Palace Script* William Caslon 1936
868   *Cartoon Bold* H. A. Tractor 1936
881   *Yellow Perforated* Rian Hughes 2016
885   *Albiona* Rian Hughes 2015
885   *Serenity* Rian Hughes 2015
929   *Broadsheet* Rian Hughes 2010
934   *MXX* Rian Hughes 2016
952   *Range* Rian Hughes 2000

BATTLEZONE

The silence still held.

Jack counted out a minute, two. Nothing. He turned his attention inward. He felt normal.

Nixon had returned to his recliner, either commando or in Nadine's spare pair; Harriet thought it politic not to ask. They began to allow themselves to relax.

On the now quiescent screens neat rows of labelled interstices continued to move towards them, like the view through the steel girder skeleton of an unfinished skyscraper. They were still falling through the Grid.

"We're only tens of kilometres from the centre here, deep into the Grid's prehistory. No Shepherds – this is what it was like before they intervened." Jack looked over the top of his glasses. "How is everyone feeling?"

"Good. Fine." Harriet eased off the throttle, and the speeding multitude of ethereal shapes being pulled through the room slowed noticeably. Individuals again became discernible. They had become accustomed, if anyone *could* become accustomed, to the limitlessly creative parade of biological form; the zoo of creatures, all aligned perpendicular to the ground, all facing due west, all spaced as evenly and neatly as a clothes rack prepped for a catwalk show.

Here, though, something was different, and it took Jack a few moments to work out what. He stood up and walked to the window, then leaned to the left and right to see if he could align the creatures from a different viewpoint. He couldn't. They seemed to be placed not on a regular lattice but more haphazardly; still with a more or less equal distance between figures, but now following no discernible arrangement Jack could fathom. Outside, the stochastic rain of bodies faded to an atmosphere-greyed distance stippled like Photoshop film grain. There was no sign of the familiar moiré of Grid seen through Grid.

"It's like – it's like a mediaeval town. The earliest part of a city, where there was no civic planning and the layout just evolved. Packed tight, but disorganised." Here, nearer the centre, were the tangled streets of Grid Old Town.

"I see it." The interstices were not laid out with the mathematical precision of an American city designed around the automobile; instead, they seemed to turn and twist with organic grace. They had passed through the suburbs, and were closing in on the town square. Somewhere nearby lay the original seed from which the Grid had been grown.

"Harriet? What do you think?"

The light from Harriet's monitor reflected from the smooth dark glass of her Depthcharges. She sounded cautious. "Hm. We're looking at a very small volume in the Oxbow – it's haphazard, definitely denser, but that still gives us tens of metres between Grid vertices."

Nixon was sitting forward. "What about the creatures down here? Are *they* different?"

Harriet spun the dial on her mouse. "If they are, I'm not sure how we'd quantify it." She typed in a string of coordinates, and Jack's vision was overlaid with a swift blur of shapes passing again at high speed through the room, this time at a 15-degree angle.

Who were these original inhabitants? Legions of the dead, a ghost battalion from elsewhere? Moving too fast for anything but a dim sense of their size and shape to be discerned, they were silhouettes from a lunatic's anatomy museum, passing in front of him like microfiche spooling through a reader. Jack again felt motion sickness rising and closed his eyes. It didn't seem to affect Harriet, but for him it felt like reading a web page when someone else was doing the scrolling.

Harriet brought the Grid to a sudden inertialess stop, translated it across a fast shunt to the left, then rotated it through 720 degrees. "Oops. Parking was never my forte."

Long-limbed creatures that were only vaguely humanoid, with a wet sheen that reflected the shifting light of an alien sun through metres of green-tinted water and gaping, scarlet-rimmed voids where you might expect a face to be, seemed to circle them in a disconcertingly predatory fashion.

Using criteria she didn't pause to elaborate on, Harriet isolated a series of interstices and brought up a sequence of beings in quick succession. In the scant few seconds each stopped to rotate in front of them, Jack could see that they seemed to be closely related – they definitely shared a common body structure, with variations. However, something more unsettling also became apparent.

"These guys seem to surround the inner core at this precise depth.

Completely. They fill a volume some two or three hundred interstices deep. All told, there are several tens of millions of them."

"Wow. They look a mess."

"Show me." Jack switched his Depthcharges to the dominant window so Nixon could get a better view, while Harriet began location tagging.

He immediately wished Jack hadn't. A flayed anatomist's cadaver floated over the table. Smaller than a human, it still maintained a vaguely bilateral form, though it had been damaged to the degree that its original shape was difficult to discern. Its head was thrust back, and from a severed windpipe a rough, amorphous coral-like growth the colour of bone sent razor-edged shards into the surrounding tissue. A curving loop of the material, shaped like an antelope's horn, had thrust its way through the dislocated lower jaw of the creature, into its brain and out through one of the four eye sockets. Similar growths could be seen emerging from the inner thigh and back, churning the flesh to a raw bruised purple.

Harriet brought up another. This one had similar inclusions slicing through its chest cavity; a mass of intricately detailed fractal growth that reminded her of the interlinked branches of a twisted willow.

And another.

Dana was first to articulate what they were all feeling. "I'm not sure I want to look at many more of these."

"I know what you mean. This is like a collection of preserved medical abnormalities from a Victorian museum."

Jack momentarily lifted his glasses to his forehead. The feed was still visible on the main monitor, but was now much easier to ignore. "What do you make of it?"

Dana had one hand up to the side of her face to block her view of the large screen. "I think these creatures must have been dead or dying at the moment of incorporation. No one could survive that."

"What do you suppose happened to them?"

"Runaway bone growth? Dividing and sprouting in all directions. Some kind of disease? Survivors from a war?"

"Battle damage?" That was Nixon.

Jack demurred. "It's a possibility. Incorporation in the Grid might have provided a form of preservation, like putting your wounded on ice."

"Or they might have fought incorporation. They may be in here under duress."

"Or a glitch in the incorporation mechanism? A problem with the maths? It has that kind of fractal structure, like an algorithm on accidental repeat."

"It may not be accidental. This is what a war might look like if you could rewrite your enemy's DNA."

Jack looked at Girl 21. She was keeping her distance, as were the other two DMEn, who usually let the odd ghostly limb pass right through them without comment.

"Are they all like this? This entire layer?"

Girl, 21
@twentyone • 0m

We r made of math
I like mine the way it is
Lets go. Please.

Jack reached again for the red lever. "Log and file." With not a little relief, they watched the figure shoot up from the table and through the ceiling. It was followed by many more; Jack kept his hand pressed forward. At speed, he was thankful that only the vaguest details could be discerned.

"How close are we to the centre?"

"Hang on." Harriet spun their viewpoint around and down again, and Jack had to close his eyes to calm his inner ear. "We're close, I think, but we're not there just yet. It's hard to work out where the centre actually *is* – the periphery is not spherical, and the omissions, the blank unfilled areas mean the overall shape is not exactly regular. I'm assuming that the centre of the Grid is probably congruent with the centre of the Earth, but even that doesn't provide me with an accuracy of more than a few kilometres at best."

Not being physical, the Grid did not exert a pressure at depth; however, Jack knew that in terrestrial terms, here, deep in the solid iron core, they would have been immediately flattened under three and a half million atmospheres. Yet here they were. Without turning to look, Jack leaned out and stroked a whitewashed wall; the worn brick under his fingertips assured him he was fine.

Harriet squinted at the screen. "Roughly speaking, even though the Grid down here is asymmetric, these guys still form loose concentric shells. From a quick graphical analysis I'm seeing a definite set of nested spheres, some thicker, some thinner or incomplete, like they've been worn through revealing the layer beneath."

"Like a gobstopper."

"A gobstopper. Yes. But the way they're arranged does allow me to triangulate, take a good guess as to where the original epicentre of the Grid was. Is."

She brought up the simple map graphic. A magenta blip pulsed in the very centre of a wireframe globe, a little firefly in a spherical cage.

"Show me."

Harriet typed a few lines of code. "*There.* Those are the coordinates." She gestured to the red lever, then looked Jack in the eye. "We're very close. We could probably get out and walk from here. It's all yours."

Jack looked across at the DMEn, trying to judge what they might be thinking; assuming, of course, that they *did* think in a manner analogous to the three humans in the room. They seemed content to follow this strange journey into ideaspace to its natural conclusion. He wasn't going to get any further insights from them now.

"Let's do it." He pulled the red lever towards him.

The stutter of shapes passing through the room accelerated dramatically one last time. For two, three minutes the room was shot through with streamers of light and shade, an aurora of flesh.

Almost imperceptibly at first, it began to thin out.

Then there was nothing.

Harriet checked a scrolling column of figures. "We're passing through empty interstices. Though they do have a residual signature . . . like, like this volume *was* populated, but subsequently has been cleared out."

"Emptied?"

"Or cleansed? A controlled burn?"

"Maybe—" Dana looked at Jack, a flash of concern crossing her face. "Maybe it's some kind of firebreak. A gap, a barrier that's memetically hard to jump . . ."

"But that would mean that anything sitting dead centre has been purposely separated from the rest of the Grid. Why? Why would that be necessary?"

A tense silence settled upon them. Harriet switched the Grid reference counter to the main screen. Beside the wireframe globe, numbers indicating their location in three dimensions were scrolling down through the thirties, twenties, and into the teens. "Still falling . . ."

Like an odometer running backwards, the numbers entered single digits. Jack called them out as they fell. "Ten kilometres . . . Seven. Six. Five. Four. Three. Two.

"Coming up on zero, zero, zero . . . *now.*"

AN UNEXPECTED VISITOR

XXXX

A sudden, violent buzzing broke the tension. Nixon stood up quickly and caught his knee under the corner of the table.

"*Ahhhhow.* Bugger. What's that sound?"

XXXX

There it was again.

"Is that our door buzzer?"

"Do we *have* a door buzzer?"

Jack pulled off his Depthcharges, pressed his face to the window and looked down two storeys to the street. A familiar figure stood on the pavement, looking up and waving his elbow-patched arms.

"It's Daniel Novák. From Jodrell."

"Are we expecting him?"

"No."

Harriet pulled her glasses up to her forehead. "Dana – you may want to hide."

"He knows I'm here? How?"

Jack waved a hand to keep everyone back. "He might have made an educated guess. Daniel's in regular contact with Johnson Space Centre. If *they* think there's any chance you might be here, because of our shared history, he'd be the natural choice to come calling at their request." He opened the window. "Hey, Daniel. Hang on a moment. I'll let you in."

He shut the window.

"Harriet – close down the feed from the Grid. Back up."

Dana gestured at the parquet and whitewashed walls. "Open plan. Why didn't you rent one of those office farms divided into cubicles?"

"The roof?"

Nixon grunted. "Uh uh. The door to the roof is locked. The landlord padlocked it after we had that impromptu barbecue up there last summer, remember? I guess we shouldn't have melted the roofing and dropped empty cans on passers-by."

XXXX

The buzzer sounded again.

Dana was wide-eyed. "The toilet?"

"Going to be a bit awkward if he asks to use it. Plus, it's uh, none too fresh at the moment."

"The Grid. I'm going in. Get my clothes."

"You *sure?*"

"Sure I'm sure."

"Watch out for gods and DMEn."

Without further discussion, Dana moved at right angles to reality and folded herself into ideaspace. Her empty clothes relaxed onto her recliner, deflating slowly. They mapped her last position, looking just as if they'd been neatly laid out ready to put back on. Her socks slid off the end onto the floor.

Jack shook his head. He was of the opinion that starships, even those made from East End bricks and mortar, should have a better command structure than this, but it was a bit late to unilaterally promote himself to Captain. It seemed Dana was used to making her own decisions.

Harriet laid them in the plastic laundry basket.

"Urgh." There was a wet, warm residue on her hands.

"What?"

It looked like vomit. "It's—"

XXXXXXXX

The buzzer sounded once more, longer this time, more insistent. "Not now. No time." Jack tossed her his pair of Depthcharges, Harriet laid them with her own on top of the clothes, slid the basket under her desk then wiped her hands on the back of her jeans. She killed the main screen and brought up one of Nixon's funding documents. "OK. Ready."

Nixon moved to the door, his hand hovering over the keypad lock. "How do you know this guy again?"

"Subcontracting for the aerospace industry. He's now at Jodrell Bank. Systems analysis. Part of the exobiology working group. Background in pure physics. Sci-fi buff. Nice chap."

"Trustworthy?"

Jack shrugged. "I've had no reason to doubt his integrity. But we are in an unusual situation here. He's certainly not trained SAS material, if that's what you mean. Career academic. Close to retirement."

"I'm letting him in." Nixon lifted a headset and pressed a button previously hidden beneath. On a small overexposed screen, from a high viewpoint a door could be seen to open and a figure pass into the communal hall. Nixon keyed in a four-digit number and unlocked the door to the office, pushing it open with his foot.

"Hi. Welcome. Daniel, right?" Nixon had seamlessly switched into business meeting mode, and oozed the suave self-confident charm that Jack and Harriet knew was nothing but public-school bluff.

Jack could see a hand on the end of a suede-elbowed arm take Nixon's. "Come in. Were you in the area?"

"Hey, um—"

"Nixon," offered Nixon.

"Nixon. Hi Jack, Harriet. Good afternoon." Daniel sounded somewhat apologetic. "Sorry to drop in unannounced." He sniffed the air experimentally.

Jack offered his hand. "No problem."

"You busy?"

"Nothing that can't wait. What's up? How's the exobiology group at Jodrell? Any new revelations?"

Daniel was scanning the room. His eyes alighted on the shelf of 3D figures, the sheets of alien language processed by the Chomsky Module taped below. "Cataloguing, mostly. Comparative morphology. We're presenting a paper at a symposium next week. What are those?"

"Those? Prototypes. Game characters. Works in progress. We do a fair bit of dev for game companies. Designing believable xenolanguages. Alien cultures." Jack guided Daniel to one of the recliners.

"I thought Intelligencia was interested in artificial intelligence research? The emergent properties of complex autonomous systems?"

"That, and games. There's a big overlap. And one pays much better than the other."

"Ah."

"So. Nice of you to drop by. Though unexpected."

"Yes. Apologies. Let me explain. Gabe—"

"Gabriel? At Johnson?"

"Yes, Gabe has a – a request."

"Could he not call me?"

"Apparently he did."

Jack picked up his phone. Seven missed calls. Five from Gabe. "Ah. Yes. We've been – preoccupied of late. Deadlines."

"So I'm assuming you've not heard about Dana Normansson's disappearance." Daniel was watching Jack very intently. "It's causing them quite a bit of concern. She somehow managed to check herself out of the decontamination suite. She could be – contagious. Infected."

Jack sat on the edge of the table. "From contact with the Lunar Biological Entity?"

Daniel looked over at Nixon and Harriet. "You weren't supposed to mention that. You signed an NDA."

Jack grimaced. "Sorry, sorry. I completely forgot."

Daniel sighed. "We're now going to have to ask you two to sign the Official Secrets Act. And a sheaf of other documents too. Jack, have you *no* discretion?"

"Sorry, Daniel."

"Are you like this with the next *Grand Theft Auto?*"

"I said I was sorry."

"I don't know. No wonder White managed to get his hands on all those secret documents. The government's like a bloody colander. I bet you told them about the Apollo 19 'Martian Sphinx' reconnaissance orbiter, too—"

Harriet's posture straightened immediately. "The Face on Mars? NASA sent a manned mission to Mars?"

Jack snorted. "Actually I didn't, Daniel. But *you* just have."

"Ah. Bollocks. Right. You'll all need to sign more paperwork to cover *that*, as well." Daniel looked sheepish. "Listen, just – just treat whatever we now discuss as top secret. I'll— Bugger. This is not how it's supposed to work." His shoulders sagged.

Jack put a hand on his arm. "Well – now we're both likely to be hung, drawn and quartered for our indiscretion, do please continue."

"Well. Yes. Dana – Johnson were running a very tight isolation programme. Containment level four. You know the drill."

"And she – checked out? Is that a polite way of saying she escaped?"

"She was there. Then she wasn't there. Except for her clothes."

"You searched the facility?"

"Gabe is adamant that she's not anywhere at Johnson."

"Surely they have CCTV? Would she not have been picked up on camera? She couldn't be easy to miss. Especially, uh, naked."

Daniel cocked his head reflectively. "You'd have thought. And that's why they're following up on all possibilities. However improbable they may seem."

"Meaning?"

"Meaning if you hear from her, if you have any contact with her, Gabe would like you to let them know."

"If she manages to somehow circumvent Homeland Security, get on a plane without a passport or visa, dodge UK border controls and walk across London in the nude to come calling, I'll certainly give you a shout."

Daniel wished he could talk openly with Jack, the way they had always done. But he could sense that both he and Harriet suspected that he had been briefed beforehand. This was no idle unplanned visit. "Look, I know it sounds preposterous. But so is her disappearance. No seal breach. No evidence of her leaving the isolation chamber. The audio and video records are missing. The memories of those she was with at the moment she disappeared appear to have been wiped. Adam is genuinely worried. Not just for her safety, but for those who she may come into contact with. She could be carrying all manner of microbes for which the human race has no antibodies, no defences. She could be some kind of interstellar Typhoid Mary."

Harriet looked hard at Jack.

"Point taken. If I hear anything, I'll let you know. And if you hear anything, let us know."

Daniel stood. "Thanks. I appreciate it."

His eyes happened to come to rest on a piece of black enamelled machinery placed on top of a grey wooden box. "Hey – is that a *Typex?*" The tone of his voice had changed completely; it had regained that boyish enthusiasm with which Jack was so familiar.

He walked over, bent down, closed one eye and looked along a row of circular keys. It had a subtle scent of Bakelite, dust and copper. "They have one of these at Bletchley Park. Behind glass. I've never seen one in private hands. May I?"

"Sure. Let me set it up." Jack adjusted the rotors and fitted the handle. "It needed a little love and attention, but it works."

With some awe, Daniel lifted out a single rotor, ran a finger over the letters engraved around its circumference, returned it to its slot, then carefully turned the handle. A satisfyingly analogue clunk of gears and ratchets ensued. "Where on earth did you get this?"

"Would you believe I found it on a stall at Spitalfields Market?"

"No kidding. Dare I ask how much you paid?"

Jack laughed. "Let's just say, for a broken typewriter I paid over the odds."

Daniel turned to Nixon and Harriet, his enthusiasm plain to see. "*This* beautiful machine was the cutting-edge portable computer of its day. The first laptop!"

Jack patted its side. "Though I hear the WiFi reception was patchy."

"Ha."

Daniel could sense that he had interrupted important work that they were anxious to return to, and that it was time for him to take his leave. "Well, you know where to find me."

"I do."

Daniel seemed to search the room with his eyes one last time. "Nixon, Harriet." He nodded in their direction. "Again, sorry to barge in. I'll leave you to your—" He glanced up at the shelf. "Alien friends."

0, 0, 0

Nixon double-locked the door. "Well?"

Jack and Harriet had already put their glasses back on.

"0, 0, 0. We've arrived." Jack looked around the office. Furniture. Computer kit. Recliners. The DMEn. Dressed as ever in perfectly pressed white, he could see the Count framed in front of the glass partition. XX, no longer reduced to simple geometry in the enlarged Oxbow, had hunkered down into a low-riding sled, vibrant checks and chevrons wrapping his hide once again.

Jack lifted his glasses a few times in quick succession to see if anything else shifted in his field of view. The water cooler glooped, and a bubble rose. Nothing else. "What about Dana? Where is she?"

Harriet was craning her neck back. "There! Look!"

A cubist arrangement of planes and voids like a low-polygon mesh was assembling itself. Contained within a sphere rendered like a faceted fullerene, Jack could see a face of triangles and trapezoids, each a single flat colour. It was Dana. As she spoke the shapes slid and shifted, jumping position as the geometry found a new optimal solution. Jack fancied he could see her shrug. Small text appeared across the bottom of his field of vision.

"Ah, Daniel, bless him. It feels like bad manners to bail on him like that. If only circumstances were different..."

Her simplified appearance began to fill out with more detail. It didn't seem to be affecting her powers of intellect.

"Let me see if I can get the hang of the wardrobe possibilities in here."

Above her face, even in this schematic rendering, four letters could now be seen: **CCCP**.

Jack smiled. *A Russian space helmet.* She'd conjured up a new outfit – a memesuit for ideaspace.

"I always fancied a vintage spacesuit. Just like Valentina Tereshkova's. Basic, by today's standards, but something of a design classic. And here in ideaspace, practicality is, uh, less of a concern..."

She seemed to regard herself in an invisible mirror. *Cosmonaut chic,*

Harriet noted. *Appropriate.*

Jack was still scanning the room. "Is there anything else in there with you?"

"I can't see—" Harriet tapped the red lever once, very lightly.

Something rose up through the floor.

It floated in the centre of the room, above the table. Harriet keyed in a few lines of code to lock the coordinates in place and unplugged the lever. "*Whoa.*"

They circled it twice in silence. They knew it couldn't see them, that it didn't even know they existed, but their recent experience of the Grid's potential for pushback and a simple preservation instinct kept them at a respectful distance.

Jack's voice was quiet. "The grit in the oyster. This is where it all began."

Patient Zero.

The Centre of the Grid.

There, above the conference room table.

Girl, 21
@twentyone • 0m

ugly little fucker
#nomakeupselfie

Jack pulled the recliners away from the table and pushed them against the far wall, then circled it again. The weight of the Depthcharge glasses had begun to hang heavy on his forehead, and he could feel an eye strain migraine coming on.

It hung motionless, as if suspended by an invisible thread from the skylight above. Jack suspected he could see the slow rise and fall of respiration, but a glance at the raw data told him it was an artefact: the Oxbow was correcting an incremental drift then updating the image to bring Patient Zero back to the specified location, right in front of them.

Ugly? It certainly wasn't what Nixon would call a looker. At first glance, Jack saw balloons of taut translucent skin, held together in a bunch as if floating above a fairground stall. Maybe a dozen were arranged in a loose two-lobed symmetry, each textured with a convoluted tracery like coral; a dozen brains on strings, perhaps. Over this arrangement a paper-thin membrane was pulled tight, connected at the sides to ligaments that supported a limp ragdoll of a figure that hung below like a misshapen gondola. From this cadaverous off-white body, streaked with a light

769

fuzz of fine hair, supple and boneless limbs hung; remnants of atrophied fingers extended further still, almost touching the detritus strewn across the table. From the apex towards what appeared to be the front of the creature the bulbs ran in two rows, becoming smaller towards what Jack assumed was its face. Here, they were reduced to a series of bumps pushing up through the skin either side of a vertical slit, inside which could be seen a network of fine filaments on which drops of moisture had been caught. Other organs Jack suspected were sexual hung down just behind the head, and a raised ornate patterning – natural, or possibly a tattoo – could be seen on its underside like the gripped sole of a boot. The bulbs glowed with an inner phosphorescence that lit the part of the creature hanging below from inside, revealing a crosshatched cage of ribs and the darker, amorphous shapes of internal organs.

Harriet was checking the Bluetooth link and the capacity on the backup drive. "I'm getting all this at high-def through the glasses." Then, almost as an aside, "Though with a Depthcharge HUD superimposed, anyone might assume this is in-game footage."

"Right. Heh." Nixon was watching the feed on the large wall-mounted monitor. Jack's was filling the screen; Harriet's was smaller, inset to the bottom left. Nixon experimentally toggled between the two. "That thing is right *there*." He pointed at thin air. "That's . . . unnerving. Spooky." He looked back and forth between the empty space above the table and the pictures on the monitor, as if trying to impose one reality on the other, combine them into one perception.

"It's called a Ghost Camera for a reason." Jack turned to look at the screen and the resultant infinite loop created a kaleidoscopic hall of mirrors, conference rooms repeated to infinity, each with a duplicate entity floating within.

Across from the table, almost pressed against the back wall, the DMEn were silently observing the proceedings. If this thing gave Jack the willies, he wondered how they might feel about it, swimming in the same memetic sea they inhabited like a predatory jellyfish.

Jack let out a long breath. "There it is. Dead centre. Is this thing the progenitor, the architect of the Grid?"

Dana had moved forward, though she still kept a wary distance. She had now achieved a resolution indistinguishable from the DMEn: enamel-white helmet, orange zippered bodysuit adorned with stubby tubes and pouches, black lace-up boots. It definitely suited her. Jack wondered if it afforded some sense of protection, and wasn't just a nostalgic affectation.

"Not necessarily. It could have been *placed* here."

Jack leaned in and the Depthcharge image fluctuated, automatically adjusting the brightness to compensate for the lights in the room and the creature's phosphorescence. "The central engine of a larger memetic machine?"

"Or a dictator on his throne." Harriet folded her arms across her chest. "Dana, can your friend in your head tell us anything about this creature?"

"No. You have to remember that I only have access to the LBE's personal memories, and what it has seen or heard. We've effectively mounted an archaeological expedition into the deep prehistory of the Grid – this predates him by many millennia. There aren't even folk-memories that mention this creature. My friend in my head's records simply don't go back this far."

"With nothing in the Grid other than – than aliens, where *are* the records? *Are* there any records of any kind?"

"Think, Jack. The aliens themselves have been selected – they're individuals. Might they have been chosen for certain attributes they possess?"

"Their bank balance?" Nixon offered.

Harriet couldn't help but laugh. "That is *such* a Nixon observation. Who's to say the Grid isn't a communist utopia? Dana – you alluded to a certain race that have eidetic memories. They can recall everything that's happened to them, all that they're told. What if *they* are the Grid's long-term memory? History – not written down, because if it was it wouldn't be incorporated, but preserved in the *minds* of the creatures within it?"

Jack pulled up a recliner and positioned himself front and centre. He leaned in close and looked the thing in what he assumed was its eyes. If it saw him, it made no response. "More and more, I'm thinking that the Grid itself is a complex organism, parcelling out different tasks to different races within it much as the human brain has specialised sections that deal with specific tasks. Here, the equivalent of the fusiform gyrus. There, the limbic system.

"So if we want to find out how this began, what the Grid's purpose is, we need to find out where the higher functions, the seat of consciousness resides. Where is the prefrontal cortex? Where is the mahogany-panelled office with the heavy oak desk and fine views over the City? Where is the *boss*? Are we looking at him – it – now?"

Harriet thought it looked less than boss-like, though other than the absence of a sharp suit she was at a loss to explain why. "I don't think so. I assumed that the Shepherds represent the Grid's higher functions – but they came much later in its development."

"So what do we have here? What function does this guy fulfil?"

"Instinct?" Jack could see Harriet standing across the room on the other side of this interloper, hand on her chin, forefinger between her teeth. One leg happened to occupy the same space as the Count's billowing cape, which still fluttered without impedance.

Jack nodded. "Instinct."

"Those creatures further out in this less ordered part of the Grid. Those lesions, missing limbs – we didn't see that kind of damage in the outer volumes, post-Shepherd. Dana?"

"I think we can now be certain that the Shepherds do more than direct incoming traffic and show people to their seats once aboard."

"Police force. Or conscience, perhaps."

Nixon wasn't used to asking questions; in meetings, he preferred to bluff his way through with a self-assured nonchalance. "What I want to know is why the Shepherds just didn't stop the Grid reproducing altogether. If it's capable of inflicting such damage, why not neuter it completely, prevent it from ever being retransmitted again? What do they know that we're missing here?"

Jack sat back in his recliner, which let out a leather squeak. "Let's back up a bit. Dana – you say the Shepherds have a unique evolutionary adaptation that offers them protection from virulent memes: they can flush their forebrains while still keeping their higher hindbrain functions intact. They practise a kind of mental hygiene; this is their survival advantage. It does look like the Grid – in its earlier incarnation – may not have incorporated creatures into it by, uh, by mutual agreement. That it was—" Jack searched for a word.

Harriet was still circling the apparition. "*Predatory.* An infection of the mind. A memetic organism that grows by incorporating new creatures into its body to form an extended consciousness that uses many brains, many bodies. Rapacious distributed computing."

"Ha. Yes, that's actually a good analogy."

"What if we suppose that, before the Grid existed, this creature at the eye of the storm evolved the ability to incorporate – against their will – other creatures into its consciousness?"

Jack tented his fingers under his chin and slipped lower in the chair. "OK, tell me if this makes sense. Suppose it had a *range* – a consciousness that could extend outside the confines of its body. Not just, you know, to spy on the neighbours next door, but further. Off-planet. Far enough to come into contact with another sentient race."

"And by using this ability, it managed interplanetary migration?"

"It'd need to somehow reproduce in the new hosts' minds, to project into them some vital essence of itself. Is that beyond the realms of possibility?"

"Judging what is and isn't possible is something of a fool's errand these days, wouldn't you say? I think – sorry, *we* think – that's not out of the question."

"And so it spread, eventually encountering the Shepherds, who managed to rein it in."

772

"Tame it – but not shut it down. They repurposed it for their own ends. What might they be?"

With a couple of swipes Jack brought up a third window on the large conference room monitor. "Maybe the Shepherds are analogous to Darwin, aboard the *Beagle*. Collecting specimens for an interplanetary Kew Gardens." A series of screen grabs of aliens, some now familiar, most previously unseen, loosely sorted according to the taxonomy used by the SetiOnEarth@home project scrolled past, back. A section was given over to the Shepherds, though they weren't labelled as such. Jack batch selected them and copied them across to a new folder on his desktop.

"I have an idea." He pulled up a facial recognition algorithm, reset a few basic parameters, added a bit of coding and pointed it at the Shepherd folder. A progress bar moved across the screen.

"We have images of 41,000 Shepherds, give or take. The sample tends to cluster at the Earth's surface, as you'd expect. The images are of variable quality – taken by day, by night, even underground. Near, far, and from differing angles. I'm sorting them first into those that are viewed face on, then by Grid position. The deeper into the Grid we go, the more I'm relying on the images we've accumulated in our perambulations these last few days, so there the data set gets much thinner."

A *ching* of a wineglass being tapped. Jack cut then pasted the resultant matrix of figures into Mathematica, and a colourful infographic appeared. He switched it to the main screen. "Tell me what you see."

Nixon silently passed the question with a chivalrous gesture over to Harriet. "So – the vertical axis is depth, which we are pretty certain correlates with age. The deeper we go into the Grid, towards the centre, the further back we go in time."

"Yep."

"And the horizontal is what?"

"It's the degree of adherence to an averaged, idealised Shepherd morphology. How much the particular Shepherd looks like all the other Shepherds."

"So . . . so we have a high degree of similarity in the suburbs of the Grid, and a much higher incidence of varied morphologies as we go deeper. Meaning—"

"Meaning that they suffered great physical trauma on first encountering the Grid, but they changed, they adapted. And at last, they imposed order in their current form, which continues to today. Self-preservation makes for fast evolutionary innovation."

Jack looked across at Dana. "That may be the how, but not the *why*. So they beat the Grid. They mastered it. They are no longer slaves to the Grid's urge to reproduce. They *won*.

"But if you defeat the evil dictator overlord, why would you allow him to still sit there on his throne, at the centre? The more I look at this, the more I'm convinced that the Shepherds are holding this whole shebang together for a *reason*. And if it cost them so much, it must be a *damn good* reason."

Nixon sat back and watched the conversation bounce back-and-forth with a small smile. Jack and Harriet, and now Dana. It was quite a show.

While they had been talking, Dana had taken a few steps closer to the creature. It hung there, dominating the room like an enormous paper lantern. On the inside, moving through the Grid, she had become aware of a continuous neutrino-like sea of free-floating notions which seemed to pass right through her. Occasionally one would fleetingly take up residence in her own mind; vague and ill-defined, or less frequently, sharper and more precise. She'd navigated this fluctuating landscape of concepts, all the while wondering if a certain idea was something that had just occurred to her, was *her* idea, *was* her, or whether it was someone else's, a singular meme that had attached itself to her, just for a moment. *Did she have ideas, or did ideas have her?* It was hard to say in a realm which was *built* from concepts. They bubbled up in your mind – they *were* your mind.

She had realised that if she could occupy any space, just like that metaphorical digital dog, she could just as easily occupy the *same* space as any of the entities in the Grid. She had a hunch that with that ability, and the unique talents of the Man in the Moon to draw upon, she might be able to access their thoughts directly.

Two minds, in one place.

Sharing thoughts.

Could she *mind-read an alien?*

It would, of course, be risky. But if it could be done with the utmost delicacy, it might just be possible . . . or so she told herself.

She reached out a hand, like she had done once before, on the far side of the Moon.

"Dana . . . be careful." Jack had pushed himself upright in his recliner. One spacesuited glove hovered above the creature's flank. "We have no idea what might happen." The pale luminescence shone between her fingers, making them look skeletal even in the suit.

"Remember I told you I had an idea? Watch. I'd like to try something."

"Dana!" Harriet jumped forward, but there was nothing she could do. She was physical, and Dana was not.

Dana pushed her hand forward. It disappeared inside the creature without the slightest resistance, a ghost passing through a ghost.

Girl, 21
@twentyone · 0m

of course #obvs

Girl, 21
@twentyone · 0m

All u r
All consciousness IS
is ideas running on a substrate
Urs just happens 2 b biological

By that, he gathered, she meant his, Harriet's and Nixon's. Jack detected the flicker of a sardonic smile in the stutter of selfies.

Dana and this creature were both immaterial, both a constellation of interstices in concept space. She took a step forward, another. Jack could now see her as an indistinct shape moving deliberately within the translucent body of the creature, a vague figure backlit with a sickly chartreuse.

Unlike the DMEn, she had one crucial advantage, the trick she had learned from the friend in her head. She hoped it would protect her. As she carefully moved around inside it, streamers of the creature's thoughts were pulled through her synapses like tape across a recording head.

"It's telling me stories . . ."

There were always stories.

WHICH
ART
IN
HEAVEN?

When the Heavens turn out to be
occupied not by your favourite deity but
an astonishing profusion of alien races,
do we yet again have to ask the same
questions we have asked every time
new discoveries come up hard against
cherished articles of faith?

Or will faith again find a way to – dare
we say it – evolve?

Gavin Eastbroke reports

The discovery of alien life was bound to pose issues for those of a religious persuasion. While certain cults have incorporated aliens into their theology at a fundamental level (most infamously the Heaven's Gate group, 39 members of which committed suicide in order to ascend to an alien craft riding behind comet Hale-Bopp), the older, more established religions developed at a time when our view of the Universe was somewhat more parochial.

Though the Bible does not explicitly confirm or deny the existence of life on other planets, it does teach that the only beings that God gifted with intelligence were animals, angels and Mankind. According to scripture, the Earth was created on the first day (Genesis 1:1), while the Heavens – the Sun, Moon and stars – did not appear until the fourth (Genesis 1:14-19). The billions of years required for stellar evolution to sculpt our Milky Way galaxy, its stars and planets – and, we now know, their rich variety of inhabitants – is therefore a conundrum for a creationist mindset that the most polished theological shoehorn would have trouble accommodating.

Resistance to advances in our understanding of how our world works has long been a feature of the surviving religious faiths, but rather than suffering a knockout blow, in the longer term they reveal an elasticity that seems capable of taking almost any new discovery in its stride. Yale-educated Republican Ben Carson, a neuroscientist who surely must be familiar with the term 'cognitive dissonance', believes the theory Charles Darwin "came up with was something that was encouraged by the 'adversary'" – in other words, evolution is the work of the Devil. This puts him some way behind Pope Pius XII. In 1950, 91 years after the publication of *On the Origin of Species*, he finally confirmed for the faithful in his encyclical *Humani generis* that there was no intrinsic conflict between the message of Christianity and the theory of evolution. There was one minor caveat: Christians were required to believe that the individual soul was still a direct creation of God, and not the product of purely material forces. A nicely-played move – souls, being immaterial, may have a few more years left in them before science has something awkward to say about their existence or otherwise.

These theological quibbles don't even attempt to address the question of how each of these alien races themselves came into being. Was it through a similar, local form of Darwinian evolution, or was each brought into existence just as we see them now via more acts of divine creation – either by their own flavour of god or gods, or perhaps our own Abrahamic version on another six-day outreach program?

Of course, we are here applying time-tested methods of sorting truth from falsity: rational discourse, and humility in the face of what Nature is actually telling us. To expect those whose personal route to the 'truth' takes a different path to respect this methodology, let alone buy into its conclusions, may be to miss the point of faith entirely.

Whether we are with faith or without, our propensity to accord humanity an important place in the Universe today seems even more hubristic and untenable. Perhaps the more salient question is this: do aliens have their *own* religions? And might they try to convert *us*?

G, O, D

"Well?"

Dana's arm could be seen hanging from the creature's side like a partially absorbed twin, her spacesuited legs extending below in a fashion that, in any other situation, would have looked comical. Her feet braced some distance apart, she was carefully adjusting her position within its bulk.

"It's – it doesn't feel especially – I'm not sure how to put this. Memetically sophisticated."

"Bright?"

"Bright. Yes."

Harriet and Jack exchanged glances. "So what does that tell us?"

"Hang on. Give me a moment. I'm putting this together piecemeal, as there doesn't seem to be much in the way of upper-level processing. I'm not sure if this guy is a one-off, or there's a whole species just like it, but it's not a particularly, um, *reflective* creature. Aha—"

"Aha what?"

"It has certain – *abilities.* Interesting. *That* I did not expect. It has what I can only describe as an extended mind – one that doesn't reside entirely within the confines of its body."

"It's telepathic?"

"In a way, though that's not the best way to describe it. It's more like a nexus for a diffuse consciousness. I think in its original cultural context it would be part of some larger hive mind, or a singular mind that was distributed throughout a population. A sub-unit from a species that operated as a unified whole, perhaps."

Inside the translucent form, Jack could see Dana dip her head, then rotate it slightly to the left and back again.

"That diffuse consciousness – I think that's what the firebreak was designed to contain. It must be just large enough to keep the Grid's occupants out of reach of this thing's mental range."

"A firebreak we have now breached." Jack sunk lower into his recliner. "Am I the only one getting a bad feeling about this?"

Harriet continued to circle the creature. "So this thing seeded the Grid, built the Grid? That seems somewhat unlikely, don't you think?"

Jack watched her pass behind it. Through the glasses, she cast a soft shadow on the whitewashed wall. "Maybe it was put here, though of course that just begs the question 'who by?' Or maybe it didn't know what it was doing – maybe the Grid began more by instinct than design. Its current purpose, if it has one, need not be the original one. Dana—?"

Dana had frozen. Though she was just an indistinct shape inside the creature, her posture was tense and alert.

"Hang on. There's someone else – some*thing* else – in here with us."

"What? You mean other than this thing? The DMEn?"

"No, not the DMEn. It feels like it's *inside* Patient Zero."

"You? *You're* inside Patient Zero."

"No, not me, wiseass. And it's not a two-brain memetic signature. I know what those feel like. Something *inside* – no, that's not exactly right – it feels more as if Patient Zero is a *conduit* for it. It's not another personality, not something inherent to its biological make-up, like the LBE. It's something that comes from *outside* this creature – a *long* way outside. Beyond the Grid . . . if that's possible. It's almost as if this creature acts as a *medium*, you know, like a spirit medium. I have a vague impression, but I'm not sure if I'm seeing something real here, or a concoction that the Chomsky Module has produced in an attempt to render it in an intelligible manner. This is . . . bizarre. What *is* it? Something that it has a link to—"

Dana stopped mid-sentence. Her visible arm tensed.

"God."

"God what?"

"It has a god. And this god *talks* to it."

The 19th Count shifted uneasily, but said nothing.

"It's doing so right now."

Jack wondered if he'd heard correctly. "It talks to *God?*" There was a short pause while Dana again altered her position imperceptibly.

"It wants to show us."

"Dana, you're poking around in the brain of a creature who may have been instrumental in decimating hundreds of Shepherds, who has been isolated behind a firewall for a *reason.*"

Harriet echoed Jack's concern. "I can pull the plug on the Oxbow. Please get out of its head."

Across Girl 21's face a new montage of expressions was playing out in a strobing flick-book flurry. Buried in the looped movie clips and red-carpet paparazzi shots Jack saw Munch's *Scream* morph into the face of a blow-up sex doll, open-mouthed with surprise.

"I see . . ."

Harriet was visibly unnerved. "*What?* What do you see?"

Dana didn't get a chance to finish the sentence. The office was suddenly lit with the stark cold light of RGB monitors pushed to the limits of their gamut. The flash was painfully bright, even through the glasses. A moment later the automatic compensators kicked in and it dropped to a more manageable intensity.

From across the road the flash did not go unnoticed.

They all instinctively shielded their eyes, though for Jack and Harriet, behind the Depthcharges, this of course had no effect. Coloured sparks shot across Jack's retina as his overloaded cones and rods tried to readjust.

The creature they had dubbed Patient Zero had gone. In its place was – something dazzlingly bright. Its form was hard to discern, if form it had . . . Jack tapped a button, brought up a slider, nudged the white-point. The glasses readjusted again. The dazzle reduced, and through slitted eyes a shape began to become apparent. It was the size of a man, but something about the perspective, the optical properties, seemed skewed. To Jack, it seemed as if he was looking down an infinitely long tunnel to something separated from the office, Hoxton Square, London, the Grid and even planet Earth itself not only by an inconceivably great distance but by immeasurable aeons. Something so far away, he felt, that it might even lie beyond the boundaries of the Milky Way itself; and if that was so, then its real size must be truly immense.

They saw . . . what? A torso . . . ? Something . . . illumined from within. A body? What else . . . Dark shadows radiated on either side, extending out from the central featureless furnace, each bent in several places like the limbs of a double-jointed spider.

To the right, Jack's eyes alighted on something alien but recognisable at last – a three-fingered hand, held out palm up, above which rotated a barred spiral galaxy; looking across to the left, a second hand held a staff so black it looked like a scratch on the emulsion of reality. Jack allowed his eyes to rest on it a while as respite against the glare, and the thought occurred to him, though he didn't know from where it had come, that it might be a rigid rod of rotating dark matter. Within, he could see a column of brightly coloured beads – no, not beads, *planets* – strung along its length.

A third hand was held in a manner humanly impossible: somehow, one multi-jointed finger pointed up while simultaneously another pointed down; opposite, between thumb and middle finger, a fourth hand held a rapidly spinning black hole surrounded by a churning accretion disk. Hollow cones of bright radiation shot from the poles as the axis precessed several times a second. A fifth was held up, empty palm facing forwards, in a gesture that could be interpreted either as a warning or a welcome – it depended, Jack reflected, entirely on a cultural context of which they were utterly ignorant.

Two more hands came together below in a frozen handclap like the cymbals of a mechanical monkey, though these cymbals were made from light – or, more precisely, from stars. Millions, perhaps billions of individual pinpricks forced together between alien palms into a fierce burst of nuclear fire, spilling out from between a giant's fingers. Encircling this, seen almost edge on, a dark band of dust ringed them like a frozen puff of smoke from an ancient ovation.

As Jack's eyes adjusted further, more details were revealed. Above, providing a frame of sorts, an ornate arch built from contrasting blocks of white- and pink-veined stone floated without support. In each varicoloured section was a recess in which an object rested. Some of these were familiar as classic mathematical forms: a pyramid, a dodecahedron, an interlaced prism; others hurt his eyes with impossible angles, or counter-intuitively pierced themselves while being pierced. There was an elaborately detailed sphere, a rocky planet perhaps, that bore wings. A cleft star from which issued a multitude of creatures like moths. An iron thundercloud, below which hung an implement like a short forked sword. In an alcove in the large keystone at the apex, above a glass chalice, spun a dark clouded void in which a central crimson spark could be discerned. Embers floated on interstellar winds in the foreground, the campfire sparks of dying suns.

A triple rainbow surrounded the whole tableau. Jack guessed it was not the result of intervening raindrops, of which there were none, but gravitational lensing caused by the sheer immensity and incredible distance of the entity.

He suddenly became aware that the walls of the tunnel itself were alive – a kaleidoscope of tiny fluttering banners, each bearing a word in an indecipherable language and held aloft by an infinitude of cherubic creatures that were not much more than pulsating whirrs of wings made from light. They circled the apparition in counter-rotating tiers, and even though the scene was held in a frozen moment, they still moved too fast to be seen clearly.

A sound as of a multitude of voices made for ears with a far greater range than the human rose in a delicate counterpoint. Subsonics vibrated in their diaphragms, and Harriet's skin prickled with cascades of mellifluous notes that she felt rather than heard. She had an intuition that these harmonies were not played on instruments, as such; they were formed from the relationships of celestial bodies as they moved along their paths, an eternal dance governed by Law and Number; what they were listening to was the vibrational mechanics of the very structure of the Universe itself: the Music of the Spheres, rendered audible at last.

Jack, Harriet and Nixon felt the weight of existence lift, and an indescribable bliss begin to soak through their bodies. They were being lowered into a warm empyrean bath which cleansed from their minds the nagging vicissitudes of everyday existence. Their sense of location began to dissolve, to be replaced by a disassociated bliss.

A rectangular box appeared in Jack's field of view, and simultaneously on the monitor.

Girl, 21
@twentyone • 0m

Follow

Fuck. A God.
Patient Zero has a GOD

↩ ⇄ ♥ •••

Of all the *ideas* in *ideaspace,*

these pesky **GODS** can be the

most *persistent* & *intractable*.

They have a HABIT of being –

Girl, 21
@twentyone • 0m

Follow

#Immutable
#Omnipotent
#Eternal

↩ ⇄ ♥ •••

Harriet sensed the 19th Count, standing behind them at the back of the room, let out a deep, resigned sigh.

 *Precisely,* my dear.
How does one *parry that?*
How do you counter a

CONCEPT

whose ***essential attributes*** include
Incorporeality and ***Incomprehensibility?***

Send in our tame twentieth-century

MECHANISED

TANK?

How can you

SHOOT *the* **INEFFABLE?**

You want to throw some fancy

theological hairsplitting

around? *Cantor's* mathematical *nested infinities,* perhaps?

PASCAL'S WAGER?

The Critias Hypothesis?

GOOD LUCK.

If you've read your Holy Manuals, you'll know that

Faith

isn't a concept amenable to *rational discourse.*
For a *viral idea,* that's something of a

Masterstroke.

Girl, 21
@twentyone • 0m   ⚙ 👤+ Follow

& whats more they r generally
#All-knowing
#All-powerful

↩   🔁   ♥   •••

The delicate harmonies were pulling at the knotted threads of Jack's mind, loosening them, untangling them, reweaving them into a more concordant whole in which the ideal, perfect blueprint for Jack Fenwick was beginning to become apparent. The crick went from his neck, his stature straightened, he fancied that he could feel his intellect sharpen.

"Do we really need to think in such an *antagonistic* fashion? Is *that*—" Jack pointed to the blinding light – "a *symbol,* or something *real?* Surely this, this *god* is just another idea? If god *does* exist, he exists in ideaspace, and those that think him up necessarily give him form, even if a vague and mysterious formlessness is part of his being. Or are you suggesting we're looking at something that has a more *substantial* physicality?"

Nixon was taking high-resolution 5K grabs from the main monitor. "I went to a Catholic boarding school for boys, and we did learn a thing or two that had some bearing on the real world. To me it certainly *looks* symbol-heavy. But is it that black and white? Can't something be a real thing and a symbol, both at the same time? Religion grapples—"

Jack waved his arms around his head as if to dispel a gathering miasma. "Real, not real, whatever. We have a representation. In Grid terms, that might as well be as real as the DMEn, as, as Dana. As far as *they're* concerned, that's as good as real."

Nixon did not look convinced. "This god has done the one thing which no self-respecting god should ever do, and actually *revealed* itself. Or are we lucky enough to be its chosen few?"

Jack tried to focus on Girl 21's flickering face.

"So you say. The question is what, or who, is this god? Another evolved alien race? A guiding, animating principle? A spider alien with a long beard sitting on a cloud?"

Vintage woodtype simultaneously unfurled down Jack's field of vision and the conference room monitors:

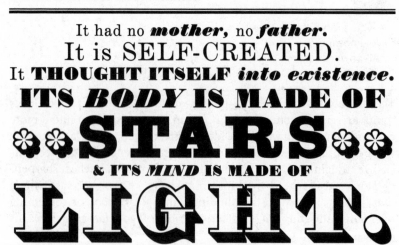

SINGULAR RIGHTEOUS POWERFUL IMPLACABLE ooo SHINING ooo INEVITABLE

The bright thing in the conference room suddenly seemed unspeakably malevolent. Its stillness now spoke not of impotence, but of an ageless patience. It was waiting.

Harriet looked at the Count with an expression of disbelief. "You're actually falling for this god stuff?"

Jack raised an eyebrow. "You want to discuss theology with a spirit?"

"Whatever – look, what I'm saying here is that it's a matter of definition, surely? If this alien thought this god up, it's only an idea it happened to have, no different from any of our gods?"

What is a **God?**
An idea with the *power* to *move stars,* which *placed them in the firmament* before Mankind stepped onto the *stage* of LIFE —

A PLAN

set in *Motion,* before the
UNIVERSE BEGAN.

Jack shrugged. "And I'm supposed to think you lot, who are *built* from ideas, are disinterested observers? Words. Names. Definitions. Who decides what is or isn't a god, other than those that believe in him? Does it fundamentally change what we may have here?"

Dana stepped forward, out of the light, blocking their view of this putative god without it baulking at her act of disrespect. Her helmet was haloed by a fierce corona, as if she was eclipsing the Sun. Jack could see the three of them – brightly lit, two wearing Depthcharges – reflected in the polarised glass of her faceplate. She placed one spacesuited hand on her belt and tapped her head with the other to indicate the alien cohabiting inside, her expression lost in the specular dance of light. "I've — we've never interfaced with a god."

There were a few moments of silence while everyone processed what Dana had just said. Harriet was the first to break it.

"Whoa. You think you can *do* that? Interface with it?"

"It's not every day you meet a god. So, no, I don't know I can do it for sure. But we're here, it's there, and I can try."

Nixon squinted at her. "Talking to God. Usually the preserve of shamen. Also considered a first sign of madness."

Jack smiled. "Unless, of course, you manage to persuade enough people you're for real. In which case, you've just started a new religion. Congratulations. We three are your first disciples."

Harriet gave a thin laugh. "I'm not into kneeling. I have a bit of a thing with authority."

"The core precepts of Normanssism will have to wait. Now, this is not without danger. We do not want gods, self-styled or otherwise, waking up in the Grid. Ideas that consider themselves to be all-powerful and all-knowing tend not to play well with each other. It's kind of a club of one."

"If it's all-powerful, maybe it already knows that."

Behind her faceplate, Dana pulled another undecipherable expression.

"On the other hand, I'm pretty sure that this is just the idea of a god. Patient Zero's vivid imagination. An idea running on a brain in ideaspace, a concept running on a concept. At best, it's a DMEn at one remove."

"God is a demon. Heh. Isn't that blasphemous?"

"It's Normanssism, and I get to make up the rules. And I say it's fine."

There was a pause while they all considered whether they were actually about to do what they were about to do.

Harriet turned around. "Count? 21? You have an opinion on this?"

We've *whipped* the ***backsides*** of GODS
COOKED UP
by the ***failed philosophies*** of our Ancestors—
GODS that were made of
SUPERSTITION,
FEAR &
IGNORANCE.

They were vulnerable to

REASON

and *withered* under

SCRUTINY.

All those **GODS** were made in *our images*,
and thus spoke

OUR LANGUAGES.

THIS one is made in the self-image of a

STRANGER

from *far more distant* shores,
& speaks in a *language* we have no way of *understanding*.
It may be made from *ideas* we simply

CANNOT THINK.

Girl, 21
@twentyone • 0m

⚙ 👤+ Follow

Look on the bright side — maybe this god's primary attributes r
#stupidity &
#ineptitude

↩ ♻ ♥ •••

Harriet looked straight into the black reflective glass of Dana's helmet and held a gaze she knew was being returned, even though she couldn't see it. Her own face was reflected back at her: intense, starkly lit by otherworldly light. "Dana – if you think it's possible, and you're happy to try – go ahead. Do it. Read the mind of a god."

787

BEYOND THE CAMPFIRES OF THE MILKY WAY

Observe: a dense cloud with a spinning spark of black creation at its core. There is fire and darkness, the fire forming a ring around an abyss. A balance of forces in opposition. The cloud differentiates, particularises. There is a seven-fold crystallisation, an octahedral condensation of matter, formed again according to mathematical law which exists even when unmanifest. And there, from the very beginning, basic to be sure but unmistakable, is a form of intelligence. An ur-mind that pulls the loosest of matter around it, clothes itself in the first condensation of primordial form.

It is immense, and it moves very slowly. A galaxy mind; the synapses stars, the dendrites the light travelling between them. Thoughts arise . . . inchoate and abstract, in many ways hard to distinguish from the laws which give them form, but thoughts nonetheless. They take millions of years to propagate across its disc. Vague concepts coalesce within collapsing clouds of gas, burst into enunciated form with the birth of new stars; or they dissipate and die, tenuous impressions that become engulfed by other notions in merging nebulae or stellar collisions.

Its first coherent thought is reflected back after a journey of a hundred thousand years out to the limits of its being. It senses its own immensity, and as a consequence comes to know itself. Self-awareness dawns. It is, and it is one.

Looking out across the young universe through the lifting fog of uncondensed matter, it receives the first light from outside: a majestic cartwheel of stars, and beyond it, at a much greater distance, many more. It realises it is not alone.

This comes as a revelation.

Before, it had known no plurality, no difference – it is, and it had sensed no thing but the one thing: itself.

It reflects on this conundrum for seven hundred millennia.

There is a civilisation that no longer exists, out beyond the Perseus Arm where the Milky Way begins to thin out and the stars are few and far between. Out here, on the rare inhabited world, the skies are empty even on the clearest night.

This civilisation was old long before the Earth's crust hardened and Man had designed himself a form to house a mind which could look up at his own bright roof of stars and wonder. It was content and happy, and found much joy in the pursuit of knowledge simply for its own sake. It possessed an elite caste of gifted astronomers who could look across their sun's brace of terrestrial worlds – and further, across the gulfs between the stars – simply by concentrating their minds, unaided.

With the lance of the Milky Way at their backs, a majestic whirlpool of stars hung in their otherwise empty sky. Another galaxy, much like the one they inhabited. They reached out to it, curious, wanting to find out more. Across 2.5 million light years, they sent a thin questing thread of concentrated thought. It took the efforts of twelve thousand of their kind over fourteen generations to maintain the thread on its journey of over six hundred years; but they did not give up.

Eventually, the thread touched the outer galactic halo, and felt its way through choked and dead dust lanes to the bright stars further in where it hoped life might reside.

What they found sent a shock travelling back at the speed of thought, severing the thread and killing thousands of their number. They had contacted a presence, but one unlike any they were familiar with, and they presided over a community of five hundred inhabited worlds. A singular entity of vast and glacial intellect, whose lifetime was comparable to the Universe's, whose thoughts were the crashing of suns, whose dreams the ten-thousand-year sleep that passes the night between a galaxy's spiral arms.

Reeling home their thoughts, this august and ancient civilisation realised too late that they'd lit a beacon in the night only to find that outside the familiar comfort of their campfire, out beyond the darkness which had hidden their existence for so long, a vast and malignant monster was stirring.

They had inadvertently announced the fact that the Milky Way was inhabited.

But worse was to come. Without intending to, their thread had pulled back with it a piece of this churning and malevolent galactic mind. A black speck of un-life, it was the first to ever be separated from the unity it had always known, a child who could not fathom its creation. Curious, it thought to toy with the shiny beads of blue and green it now found itself amongst, worlds full of life and creativity. It delighted as its rarefied being passed through their cool oceans and their warm interiors of molten rock, through subtle bodies of extended thought that stuttered and dimmed as it passed.

As we might idly scrape the moss from a stone, it wiped the higher functions of life from the inhabitants of these worlds, leaving behind vegetative automatons who stumbled through the temples and libraries of civilisations they no longer comprehended.

Fifty, eighty, a hundred shuffling corpse-worlds, where all sentience had been swept away and a barely functional biology roams the ruins. Creatures of high learning and noble arts, rendered indistinguishable from the basest of beasts ruled by instinct and need. On planets far older than the Forerunners, there are towers of glass that now only harbour the mechanised meat racks and bone grinders of the abattoir; there are palaces of learning that house slave markets catering to untrammelled and violent lusts; entire worlds where the spark of mind has been extinguished, libraries burn, only fire and conflagration light the otherwise dark cities, the crops rot unharvested in the fields and the seas fill with a sediment of bones.

And if that were not enough, the mother it didn't know it had was coming to collect it and punish what was left of us simply for the sin of being.

The Andromeda galaxy had been falling towards us for many aeons already. Now feelers of thought were coiling out in advance; translating through space at the fastest speeds possible, speeds still rendered immeasurably slow because of the great scales involved. A bullet so leisurely that entire cultures would rise and fall before one moment could be discerned from the last.

An implacable intelligence that had ruminated alone since before the Solar System had coalesced was now groping in the dark between galaxies, reaching out to touch new minds made sensitive to its Cimmerian vibrations.

Though it would take many ages, it was inevitable. There was absolutely nothing that could be done to prevent it.

Even the Forerunners, who legend tells could move stars, could not have nudged a galaxy of a trillion by the width of a single atom.

No, there was nothing that could be done.

Andromeda was coming to engulf us; to take away everything that makes us us.

BLACK PEARL

"The Andromeda galaxy is *sentient?*"

Dana was quiet for a few moments.

"I think every galaxy is sentient, in a fashion. We just need to expand our conception of what life is."

"My conceptions are being expanded right now just by having these conversations with you, Dana." Harriet was not one for poetic licence. "But – this is a myth, a story, right? Narratives that seek to explain . . ."

"To tame the unknowable, to give shape to the incomprehensible. Yes, it's a story. But it's also an explanation for something real, something not fully grasped or understood. Stories let people think, if only for the duration of the telling, that we can exercise some control over forces that are utterly ignorant of our existence – that are incapable of empathy, even if they could entertain the concept. These forces are more like laws or principles, however much they may be anthropomorphised. Myths and legends. Gods and their mysterious ways, doing what they do for reasons that will forever be opaque to us."

Harriet was watching her with some trepidation. "And you think this is one of those stories?"

"I tell the tale. I'm not its author." Though Dana's voice came from the speakers in the room, Harriet couldn't shake the impression that it had taken on a certain basso quality and was emanating from inside the creature itself.

"But I do know that this skill our Patient Zero has – the ability to touch minds at a distance . . . it's not the only species to have evolved such a thing. Those, uh, tendrils of thought can also be sensed by other races."

"But not us."

"We – us humans – are aware of a very small range of signals. And it does tend towards the poetic—"

"But a sentient *galaxy?* How does that even *work?*"

"There is an arcane field of enquiry my alien friend has a passing knowledge of that seeks to divine truths by observing the stars, measuring their positions and movements. Any thought a galaxy may have would be expressed by forces and fields, by the stars' positions within it and the signals passing between them."

Nixon slapped the side of his recliner. "Sounds like astrology to me."

"The alien races that populate the Milky Way – for all their differing forms, they're much more alike than you might imagine. We're all made from the same star-stuff."

Another pause. Through the glare, Nixon could see Dana move her head a fraction to the right, back again.

"It's worshipped as a god and cursed as an abomination on equal numbers of populated worlds along the galactic rim."

"Uhuh. Right. Let me take that in."

"Do they – the Shepherds – believe in god? Gods?"

"No. No, they don't. Not how we might define them. But if we think of a god as something unique, something self-created, without a progenitor, something that is the expression of some basic principle – then why not call it a god?"

"The self-created. Perfect, unparalleled, unique."

"It's said that that is how it sees itself."

Nixon snorted. "I know *people* like that."

"Here's the interesting thing. I see this motif repeated in the traditions of numerous races, so many of those that have been incorporated into the Grid that it's almost a universal theme. And even though the details change, even though it gets overlaid with parables and power plays, pre-existing myth and local colour, in its essential aspects the story always remains the same.

"Andromeda is falling towards us. It will arrive in four thousand million years' time. Our Sun and Earth will still be around, but I get a sense that even *that* timespan may not be long enough to do what still needs to be done."

"What needs to be done? I'm not sure I understand."

"Here's the common thread, the lesson wrapped in a million myths. This God – Andromeda, call it what you will, it goes by as many names as there are languages that speak of it – it looked out across the intergalactic gulfs, saw the Milky Way, and saw its reflection, almost a mirror image of itself.

"But if it saw the similarities, it also saw the differences. And the one, big difference is *life*. The Milky Way is *thick* with life; the Grid has proven that beyond any doubt. But this was not seen as something incredible and amazing, something to celebrate. Gods tend to prefer a singular unity – it's almost part of their definition, and Andromeda was no exception. All the things that it believes to be *right*, to be *good*, we contradict simply by *existing*.

"Andromeda sees us as an infestation. To it, life *itself* is a blasphemy."

Dana took a couple of steps forward, emerging from inside the apparition without disturbing a single mote of light: the imaginary passing right through the immaterial. She was now a black silhouette set against an arc light.

"And gods are very keen on purging blasphemy."

Behind her the glare began to fade, and the lumpen shape of Patient Zero once again became visible. Its own weak internal illumination was a faint candle by comparison. "And the Shepherds *know* this?"

"Jack, they wanted to convince themselves otherwise. They assumed they could disabuse Patient Zero of this notion. But—"

Girl 21
@twentyone • 0m

BUT IT MET GOD, AND GOD FOUND IT WANTING.

"The creatures in the Grid brought with them a passionate intensity, an absolute conviction, a moral certitude and an unwavering resolve.

"They brought knowledge – terrible knowledge. They brought incontrovertible proof of a god's existence.

"A god, an alien god, more terrible than any Man has invented, one that had judged them, judged *us*, judged every sentient being in our absence, without representation or defence.

"A god that ruled that our good works proclaim us guilty, our culture, our art, our science prove our sins, that everything we have built confirms our malignancy.

"An alien God has proclaimed us an abomination, and is coming to purge us.

"The purpose of the Grid is now unambiguously clear to me: it is not an invasion, it is not a call to arms; it is not an army of resistance.

"It's an *evacuation.*"

👤 Not logged in   **Talk** Contributions   Create account   Log in

Article I Talk   Printer-friendly version

Quasar

From Wikipedia, the free encyclopedia

The first quasars (/ˈkweɪzɑːr/), designated 3C 48 and 3C 273, were mysterious astronomical radio sources[1] which could not be associated with any visible object. First discovered in the all-sky radio surveys of the late 1950s, further observations by the Lovell Telescope[2] at Jodrell Bank[2] in concert with smaller telescopes revealed they had a very small angular size. By 1960 hundreds of these enigmatic objects had been found, but it wasn't until 1963 that a definite correlation of a radio source (3C 48) with an optical object was published by Allan Sandage and Thomas A. Matthews of the Owens Valley Radio Observatory.[3] They had detected what appeared to be a faint blue star, and obtained its spectrum. Containing many anomalous emission lines it defied interpretation, and a claim by John Bolton[4] of a large redshift was not generally accepted.

In 1962 another of the unidentified radio sources (3C 273) was predicted to undergo five occultations by the Moon. Measurements taken by Bolton and Cyril Hazard using the Parkes Radio Telescope allowed Maarten Schmidt to optically identify the object and obtain a spectrum using the 200-inch Hale Telescope on Mount Palomar,[4] which revealed the same strange emission lines. Schmidt realized that these were the spectral lines of hydrogen, redshifted by 15.8%, which implied that the object was receding at a rate of 47,000 km/s.[5] Other astronomers subsequently re-examined the redshift data from the emission lines of similar radio sources. 3C 48, one of the first quasars to be discovered, was found to have a redshift of 37% of the speed of light.[6]

Terminology [edit]

The term 'quasar' was coined by Chinese-born U.S. astrophysicist Hong-Yee Chiu in *Physics Today* (May 1964)[7], a contraction of "quasi-stellar object."

Properties [edit]

During the 1960s debate centred around whether quasars were nearby objects or actually as distant as their redshift implied. If so, their energy output was far in excess of any known conversion process, including

nuclear fusion. At this time, there were suggestions that quasars were
made of some hitherto unknown form of stable antimatter and that this
might account for their brightness.[citation needed] Models were suggested
in which the redshift was due not to the expansion of space but light
escaping a deep gravitational well[8] while others[who?] speculated that
quasars were the 'white hole' end of a wormhole.[9] [10]

Accretion disk [edit]

Although the nature of these objects was controversial until the early
1980s, they are now understood to be the most energetic and distant
members of a class of objects called active galactic nuclei (AGN), and in
some cases the Hubble Space Telescope has managed to resolve the
host galaxies surrounding them. Their enormous luminosity results from
accretion disks surrounding central supermassive black holes, which
can convert in the order of 10% of the mass of an object into energy
as compared to 0.7% for the p-p chain nuclear fusion process that
dominates the energy production in sun-like stars.[11] This mechanism
also explains why quasars were more common in the early Universe: the
prodigious energy production ceases when the supermassive black hole
consumes all of the gas and dust in its immediate vicinity. It is suggested
that most galaxies, including our own Milky Way, have passed through
an active stage but are now quiescent.[12]

More than 200,000 quasars are now known, most from the Sloan Digital
Sky Survey. All observed quasar spectra have redshifts between 0.056
and 7.085, indicating they are between 600 million and 28.85 billion light
years away.[13] Because of the great distances to the farthest quasars
and the finite velocity of light, we see them and their surrounding space
as they existed in the very early Universe.

Relativistic jets [edit]

Accretion disks can produce twin jets of highly collimated fast-moving
material that flows out along the axis of rotation or the spin axis of
the black hole. The jet production mechanism is not well understood,
though the currently favoured hypothesis suggests that the twisting
of magnetic fields in the accretion disk directs the outflow along the
rotational axis of the central object such that when certain conditions
are met a jet emerges from either pole.

'Blazars' (BL Lac objects and OVV quasars) are distinguished by rapid
variable emission. These quasars' luminosities can change on time
scales that range from months to hours, defining an upper limit on the

volume of a quasar: they cannot be much larger than the Solar System, implying an astonishingly high power density.[14] The processes that give rise to this signal variation are not understood, but in both cases are suggestive of a relativistic jet oriented close to our line of sight.[15]

From a distance of around 33 light years, a quasar would shine in the sky as brightly as the Sun. This equates to an intrinsic luminosity of around 4 trillion (4×10^{12}) times that of the Sun, or about 100 times the total light emitted by giant galaxies like the Milky Way.

Cosmological evolution [edit]

Due to their high luminosity, for a long time active galaxies held all records for the highest-redshift (and thus most distant) objects yet discovered. Most luminous classes of AGN (radio-loud and radio-quiet) seem to have been more numerous in the early Universe,[16] suggesting that massive black holes formed early on. It also implies that many objects that were once active quasars and may lie much closer to us in astronomical terms are now less luminous or entirely dormant.

Quasars may theoretically be ignited or re-ignited if the black hole is infused with a fresh source of matter. To create a luminosity of 10^{40} watts (the typical brightness of a quasar), a supermassive black hole would have to consume the equivalent of 10 stars per year.[16] The brightest known quasars can devour 1000 solar masses of material over the same period. The largest currently known is estimated to consume the equivalent of 600 Earths per minute.[17]

In 1979 the gravitational lensing effect predicted by Einstein's General Theory of Relativity was observationally confirmed for the first time in images of the double quasar 0957+561.[18]

See also [edit]

- M–sigma relation
- Radio galaxy
- Supermassive black hole
- Gallery of Quasar Spectra from SDSS

SAFEHOUSE

Harriet pointed at the red lever. "Let's back out. Just to be on the safe side."

Jack sensed she spoke for everyone present. "Agreed. DMEn?"

Let's repair.

Girl, 21
@twentyone • 0m

laters

He took hold and gently nudged it back. The fading vortex of light and the otherworldly music that accompanied it shot back, out of the room and the reduced confines of the Oxbow. He again became aware of the office around them in all its everyday imperfection: the unevenly applied whitewash covering the rough brick walls, the scuffed parquet under his recliner, a scent of unemptied bin from the kitchenette.

Jack watched numbers scroll and a set of vertices translate across his monitor. "I'll take us out a bit further, but not as far as the Shepherds. We'll stay in the old town tonight." He typed in a set of coordinates and hit return. There was no accelerating screed of Grid denizens – this time, the shift was instantaneous. Protruding from a section of wall between the windows in the main area of the office they could see the right side of a creature that seemed to intersect another in a Klein bottle embrace, while outside the serried ranks of bodies again stretched out to the limits of sight, beyond the choked boundary of the Oxbow.

Jack was suddenly aware of the heaviness of his body, a pressure in his bladder, a dull ache in his feet and the fact that he was unaccountably hungry.

Harriet sat down heavily in her recliner. She looked at Jack in bewilderment. "I can hear my blood going round my head! You don't realise how *noisy* it is in your body, how many sensations constantly bombard you until they're taken away then all brought back at once. It's a *cacophony* in here."

Nixon was looking at them with an expression of perplexed wonder. "I felt it too – a kind of connected oneness. I was so small, and yet part of this idea that was so, so huge, that encompassed everything. I was—" He searched for words. "*Expanded.*"

"Careful. You sound like a hippie." Nixon did not respond. He was staring with unfocused eyes at nothing in particular. "That felt like an epiphany. That felt— blimey, I'm not what you might call spiritual, but spiritual *is* how I'd describe it."

"The malevolent god of a malevolent creature that, from what we can deduce, was responsible for the violent incorporation into the Grid of hundreds of species against their will."

"But you *felt* that, right? Dana said—"

"Nixon, what we saw – what we felt – was a *concept.* An idea. That god is no more real than any human, man-made god."

"How can you be *sure?*"

Jack raised his arms in exasperation. "Honestly? I can't. But apart from the very slim possibility that, unlike every other mystic in history, this one happened to have a hotline to the real deal, I think we can assume that what we were actually looking at was a bunch of symbols. A piece of language. A cultural construct. Not an actual thing."

"Bring it up on screen again."

Jack sighed audibly. Harriet scrubbed back through the recording from her Depthcharges.

"Try my feed," Jack offered. "I made a few adjustments on the fly. Better colour balance."

She pulled up Jack's file and picked a representative still. "On the big monitor now."

Jack pushed his glasses up to his forehead and walked over.

Light. Shadow. Prismatic rainbow circles of colour. It certainly had all the makings of some complicated alchemical sigil. The central area, even with Jack's adjustments, was bleached out, featureless; though what was visible, surrounding the light, provided puzzle enough.

"Hands. Gestures. It's a form of language, and it's being interpreted through the Intelligencia software, so what we see here is by necessity overlaid with more familiar human tropes – the blackletter we briefly saw, for example. It's just so obviously steeped in borrowed symbolism."

"So it *must* mean something."

"I'd be very surprised if it didn't." Jack moved closer to the monitor. "So. That galaxy. There's incredible detail there. See the dark dust lanes? And the halo of small bright stars? Is that a generic galaxy? Or a specific one? The Milky Way?"

Harriet moved her pointer to the bottom left of her screen. The mess of windows scooted away to the periphery, revealing the desktop behind. "Ha. I knew it looked familiar. The Andromeda galaxy is my Mac's default wallpaper." She flicked the images back and forth a couple of times on the main screen to bring home the point. "It's rotated, but not by much – which could mean we're not seeing it as viewed from Earth, or not as it appears today. It's not the Milky Way, or a generic galaxy – it's definitely Andromeda."

"So do you suppose these other images are all of real things?"

"A real god?"

Harriet ignored him. "And that, in the alcove in the keystone at the very top – that's a spinning black hole?"

Dana was the astronomer here.

"It is, but it may be more than that. The assumption is that all – or most – galaxies have a supermassive black hole at their centre."

"What about the Milky Way?"

"Yep, even our own galaxy has one. Like a dark secret, at the centre of our own Milky Way sits Sagittarius A-star—" Dana drew a five-pointed figure in the air with her index finger. "Written as capital A with an asterisk. We can't see it directly, because there's too much dust and gas filling the intervening 25,000-odd light years, but we can still detect its gravitational effects and use those to measure its size. It has a diameter smaller than the orbit of Mercury and a mass around four million times that of the Sun."

She pointed to the image on the screen. "This, however, is not Sagittarius A*. What we see here is a black hole with an accretion disk. Infalling matter, and relativistic jets shooting from the poles. It's an active galactic nucleus, a quasi-stellar object – a quasar. The most powerful transmitters in the Universe."

"Our galaxy's black hole isn't active?"

"No. It's dormant. Currently."

"That's good to know."

"An active accretion disk would bathe the inner portion of the galaxy in hard radiation. It would sterilise its surroundings for tens of thousands of light years out."

"Dana, think back to this 'black spark of creation' you mentioned. Could you be describing an active galactic nucleus?"

"Andromeda has a ten-million solar mass black hole with an accretion disk of infalling matter—"

"The black hole at the centre of Andromeda isn't active. We'd see it—"

"Not in recent history. But it *has* been. And I think— I'm pretty sure that the hard radiation it emitted would have sterilised the entire galaxy."

"There is no life in Andromeda?"

"Again, that may be a matter of definition. But life as we might know it? As the Grid knows it? No. That kind of life would not survive the awakening of a massive quasar. Ten trillion stars, possibly as many inhabited worlds – if there *is* still life in Andromeda, it will be holding on at the very edge of the galaxy, if it survived at all."

Jack absorbed all this. He was looking at the dark rod, a blackness with an edge so sharp he could see the antialiased pixels on the monitor. At either end were spindle-shaped structures that reminded him of the handles at the end of a scroll. Polished, metallic, their pointed ends seemed to hold the rod between them, but with a gap: like a cord spun taut between two shuttles that didn't actually touch it. The detail was incredible, and he was becoming convinced against his more sceptical inclinations that what he was looking at was again something real, something that did or had existed, though he was sure it resembled no cosmic structure that Dana, Daniel or any other Earthbound cosmologist was familiar with.

Nixon broke their reverie. "We *are* safe here? Not, you know, from black hole radiation, but I mean, sitting here, with the Oxbow still operational?"

"We need to keep the Oxbow running if our friends are going to share this. No, whatever this god is, I don't think it has any influence – or maybe any *existence* – outside the perimeter of the Oxbow. This god, just like any god, is confined to a very specific location – the mind of the one that believes in it."

"Hold that thought." Dana grinned behind the Soviet faceplate she had conjured for herself. "Put the kettle on. I'm coming out."

"Your clothes—" Harriet started, but she'd already disappeared.

Across Hoxton Square, on the flat roof of the White Cube gallery, a man cradling a sniper rifle practically shouted into his throat mic.

"*I see her!*"

The reply was mixed with the frying bacon crackle of static. "Normansson?"

"*Yes.* I have eyes on the target. Please advise." The distance across Hoxton Square was barely 150 metres. Through his telescopic sights, he could see the hairs in Jack's nose and a tea stain on his lapel. There was no mistake.

"Can you tell us more?"

"She must have just walked into the main office space from a back room or something. I don't have an unobstructed view of the entire floor – there are stacked boxes, crates, partitions. She's trying to close the blinds. Seems to know Fenwick and Haze. Rappaport is currently out of sight. She's, uh, not wearing anything."

"Can you repeat?"

"She's naked. No clothes. She's trying to cover herself with her arms. Fenwick is helping her with the blinds . . . now Haze has passed her something. Ah. A robe. And a basket. Of clothes. She's pulling jeans on under the robe. Getting dressed."

"How did she—"

"It's— they seem embarrassed. Fenwick has given up on the blinds and is shielding his eyes with his hand. Rappaport has walked into view. He has his T-shirt pulled up over his head . . . he's just put his foot in a wastepaper basket. He's now on the floor."

"Man down? Repeat, is there a *man down?*" The sniper adjusted the volume of his earpiece.

"Sir? He stepped in a bin, sir. Tripped up."

"You saw those people fall unconscious in the square. You saw the effects of what we assume is an airborne pathogen. We have reason to believe the target is the vector, the target is carrying a contagious agent. We cannot risk a biological outbreak here in central London. This has to be contained."

"Sir."

"We must press our advantage while we have a clear sight of the target. She must not be allowed to escape a second time. Do you have a clean shot?"

"Rappaport is getting up. He's jumping about on one foot while trying to extract the other from the wastepaper basket. They're – they're laughing. Normansson has come back to the window. She's looking—"

"Soldier, *do you have a clear shot?*"

"Yes, sir."

"Take it."

"Sir?"

"*I said take it.* That is a *direct order.*"

EXIT STRATEGY

Everything seemed to happen at once.

Jack heard a brittle snap. Made of old heavy glass, the window broke into a dozen large pieces which bloomed outwards from a hole the size of a penny. The largest hit the tiled windowsill with a sound that brought to Jack's mind a cereal bowl hitting a kitchen floor, a memory from twenty years ago and half a world away. Dana's clothes, empty once more, folded themselves gracefully onto the parquet.

Behind, Nixon was looking down curiously at the right side of his chest where a small deep red spot was beginning to spread. He fell forward without a sound, his jaw hit the side of the table with a teeth-splintering crack that shunted his head back hard, then he turned over and slid limply to the floor.

With superhuman speed, Harriet leaped over her recliner and heaved him half over, cradling his head in her lap, searching for a pulse at his neck. From across the room, Jack could see a small trickle of blood crawl from the corner of his mouth. His eyes were open, but they were focused on empty space.

"Down! *Get down!*"

"*Nixon's been shot, Jack! I think he's dead!*"

Time seemed to stretch out at seventy-two frames a second. Jack rolled onto his back, pulled his phone from his pocket and called 999.

He had done this only once before, as a child, on an old-style dial telephone. He had come in from the garden to find his mother at the bottom of the stairs, unconscious, neck twisted around in a curious way that made her look like she was listening for something. He picked up the heavy receiver that seemed to be made for adult-sized hands and heads, put a finger in the number 9 hole and counted off the clicks as the dial spun back. He remembered a kind calming voice, like a schoolteacher or a favourite aunt, that had asked him to describe the situation, asked him to check if she was breathing. The voice asked him for his address, which with a flush of pride he recited by heart, right down to the postcode. He was asked to go the front door and open it when he heard the ambulance's siren. They arrived four minutes later; he had timed them on his digital watch. He stood on a chair, slid off the door chain, and there they were – tall and responsible agents from the adult world where everyone knew exactly what to do in any given situation, here to make all the bad things right.

Four minutes, that had stretched out then as time was stretching out now.

Your whole world can change in four minutes.

There was a single ring, then a click, then another ring, though this one was deeper. The voice that answered did not ask him which service he required, or what his address was, or the nature of the emergency. He realised that the voice already knew all these things, and more. It spoke with commanding authority. "Stay where you are. Do not move."

"We need an ambulance. Someone has been shot."

"I repeat, stay where you are."

"What? Someone has been shot here! We need an ambulance! The address is Hox—"

The door disintegrated into splinters of chipboard and paint. The handle shot across the room, pierced the water cooler, and several gallons of cold water sluiced to the floorboards. Two figures wrapped head to toe in orange plastic dropped a heavy metal cylinder with handgrips to the floor, while two more stepped forward and pointed firearms into the room. Each had a hood pulled up around a black rubber mask that covered their faces, two perforated cylindrical air filters attached below.

Harriet stood up. Her small frame seemed to be made of tensioned steel. "I hope one of you fuckers is a medic, because if you can't help my friend here I'm personally going to kick your fucking balls so hard I'll see them through your fucking faceplates."

The man in front swung his Glock 17 around and pointed it at her.

"So, what, you're going to shoot me too, now?" From his position on the floor by the window, Jack could see her fists were balled so tightly her nails had broken her skin.

The man spoke. His voice was a muffled rasp. "Please, ma'am, can I ask you to calm down. A medical team is on standby. They will be allowed to enter once the room is secure."

"Secure from what? *You're* the fuckers with the guns."

"Ma'am, we may have a biological emergency. An—"

"We have a *fucking emergency* all right! Put that gun down and go get this medical team. Go! *Now!*" Harriet jabbed her finger at the door.

The man in the hazmat suit lowered his weapon. He was either carrying a few pounds or wearing a stab vest. There was a burst of static. "Ralph, signal the team. Send them up."

One of the men who had wielded the battering ram gestured to someone down the stairs out of sight, and a moment later three more orange-clad figures cautiously entered the room. They were carrying not firearms but red holdalls which they placed on the floor beside Nixon, then unzipped to reveal an array of bandages, phials, plastic tubing and machines Jack assumed were designed to monitor all manner of bodily functions.

The first man seemed to return his attention to Jack, though behind the tinted facemask it was hard to tell. "Where is she?"

Harriet stepped away and allowed the medics to attend to Nixon. A mask was attached to his mouth and nose, and a valve on a metal canister adjusted. They checked for a pulse. They rolled his sleeve up and tapped his wrist. The second prepared a syringe, injected something. The first began to apply CPR. They worked quickly, speaking only occasionally in a terse back-and-forth.

The first man rotated his other hand a few times in the air above his head. Two more orange-clad figures entered and began to search the room, checking first under the tables, then the tall cupboards, the conference room, the crates, the kitchenette, the toilet and shower cubicle, and lastly the small cabinets beside the desks, by which time it was obvious that there was no one else in the office.

Jack stood up and took a step forward. The handgun was immediately trained upon him again. He stopped. Harriet was looking at Nixon, the medics, at Jack.

"Where is Normansson?"

Jack caught Harriet's eye, and an understanding passed between them. "Who?"

"Normansson. Dana. And please put your hands where we can see them."

Jack held his hands out, palms up. "No one here but us."

An intermittent hornet buzz, and the orange-clad man put his free hand to his ear.

"She was here. We saw her. Where is she?"

Jack shrugged. "Feel free to search the whole building."

"Richard – there's a skylight here. Get some men on the roof. Check the shop below." To Jack: "Are there any other rooms here?" Jack could hear the lock on the door to the roof being rattled. Bolt-cutters were requested and passed forwards.

"You mean you don't have a schematic? I thought you guys were all hi-tech these days, did your homework—"

"Sir, we have reason to believe that a carrier of an airborne biological pathogen is present. We have people unconscious in the immediate vicinity. This bio-agent is of an unknown type, and an outbreak of an infectious disease in a major metropolitan area is of, uh, of widespread public health concern. We would appreciate your cooperation in this matter."

"Are you reading this shit from a pre-prepared script? You *really* think this is some kind of, of *Andromeda Strain* thing?"

Two more men came in, carrying a padded stretcher on an aluminium frame between them. They laid it on the floor beside Nixon, and at an unspoken signal, lifted him onto it, one of the medics taking care that the tubes and wires connected to him did not get entangled. A lever was pulled, and the stretcher rose up to waist height on a wheeled frame. The two turned it around in the small space while a third cleared debris from its path with his booted foot. It was manoeuvred through the door and into the stairwell, the drip held high, and down, out of sight.

Without seeking permission, Harriet strode towards the armed man. He hesitated, then at the last moment, when he realised she was not going to stop, stood back and pointed his weapon at the ceiling, letting her pass.

She followed Nixon's gurney down the stairs. "Always the fighter . . ." Jack muttered under his breath, and rose to follow. He kept his eyes fixed on the man with the Glock. As he passed the conference room table, in one smooth movement – as if it was unworthy of comment, the most natural thing in the world – he picked up his laptop and a pair of Depthcharge glasses, slid them into his messenger bag and slung it over his shoulder. As he pushed past he looked straight into the darkened glass of the interloper's opaque faceplate, but all he could see was his own grim-set features reflected back at him, a scarlet line across his forehead from which a single drop of blood issued.

At the bottom of the stairs the remains of the shattered front door had been swept out into the gutter. Two ambulances with tinted windows of a type Jack had not seen before had pulled up, wheels mounting the narrow pavement. At the top of the square police tape had been wrapped between bollards and railings, and more orange-suited men with barely concealed rifles were keeping back bystanders, many of whom held up cameraphones. The double doors to the rear of the nearest ambulance were open, and Jack was just in time to see Nixon's stretcher roll into the back with practised ease, like a giant tongue depressor.

Jack's way was barred with a rifle. "Get in the other ambulance." As he stood there, the doors to the first closed. It pulled away, lurching as it rolled off the kerb and into the road.

Reluctantly, he turned and climbed into the back of the second ambulance. Already seated on the black vinyl bench that ran its length was Harriet, wiping her eyes on her sleeve.

"Get in, Jack. We're all in this together."

Someplace that is no place, three people who were not people – more coalesced knots of semiotic density in ideaspace – looked through a single eye that was not an eye but a CCTV camera on a pole at the corner of Rufus Street and Hoxton Square. The image was overlaid with a timestamp and a location. The resolution was dreadful.

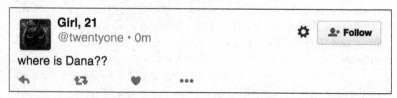

Even DMEn could not search the Grid unless they could see into it. And to do that, they required the Depthcharge glasses, just as Harriet and Jack did. But the mirrors they held up in order to see into their own world were now unavailable.

I briefly saw the outline of her helmet through Harriet's Depthcharges. Then:

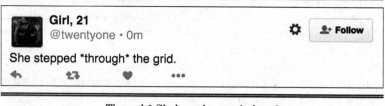

Through? She's no longer *in* here?

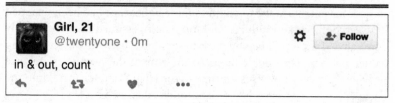

The Count struck a pose that, if anyone could have seen it, might have reminded them of Caspar David Friedrich's *Wanderer Above the Sea of Fog*, right down to the frock coat and britches; though instead of a background of numinous cloud-shrouded mountains there was the brash yellow and red perspex hoarding of Hoxton Best Kebab.

Cogito ergo sum.
We still *think,* therefore we still *are.*
An *Oxbow* must still be running.
But they will *search the premises,* confiscate the *equipment.*
They will find the Oxbow.
They may not understand its *function.*
But they will *take it apart* to see how it works.

Girl, 21
@twentyone • 0m
✿   👤 Follow

shut it down?

Girl, 21
@twentyone • 0m
✿   👤 Follow

shut *us* down?

Girl, 21
@twentyone • 0m
✿   👤 Follow

4 eva?

XX resembled a dark gunmetal ribcage topped with a forward-facing funnel-shaped foghorn. What might have been his spine shot up like a flagpole, and a black skull-and-crossbones unfurled, hanging limply.

Perhaps.
BUT SOME IDEAS NEVER DIE —
not while there are still *people* left to

THINK US.

High above London, an idea called Dana Normansson stepped briefly out of the Grid. Her stomach lifted, her hair whipped back from her face and the familiar sensation of weightlessness hit her hard. This time, however, she was not in translunar orbit but falling at 9.8m/s^2 towards the familiar cardiovascular tangle of the city streets below.

Two seconds to get her bearings . . . she ran the calculations instinctively. That was a fall of twenty metres, more. She dare not risk entering, and presumably exiting, the Grid any faster.

Two seconds. It would have to do.

She folded herself back in.

CCCI

oof

       huff
       huff

  winded, twisted ankle
          c . . . see . . . see . . .
     can I see?
  dark . . . blind?
         eooooow! fingers . . . missing?
              pain . . . ! huff huff

    where am I? don't panic, *huff huff*, breathe, *huff huff*
huff   *uff*
runch   unch
?
"Hello   Lo"
"Echo   Ko"

    [enclosed space!] not blind? *Dark!* find way out must find

      remember your*huff* astronaut training
          count to *huff* ten, Dana.
          count to *huff* ten
breathe and count
  one . . .
        *huff*two . . .
           three . . . *huff*

                  four . . .
      five . . .
          six . . . *huuff*
             seven . . .
"Ah!   A!"
   cold? *huff* metal?
         railing? rail?   breathedon'tforgettobreathe
           *huff*eight . . .

      huff
          nine . . .
            I see . . .

XI

EXIT

huff
!bright

huff

!light

huff *huff*

Bee-dee-dee-deep

GRAHHAHH

brrrrrrrrr

braaaaaaaaa

krungggggg Bee-dee-dee-deep

shushshshhhsh

Bee-dee-dee-deep

Stannard!

brrrrr

chagga chagga uh chagga chagga

Ennin Stannard!

Bee-dee-dee-deep

Bee-dee-dee-deep

Bee-dee-dee-deep

KRAMannanannaaaaaaaaaaaaaaaaaaaaaaaa

h h h

rrrrrrrrrrrrr KRAMannannaaaaaaaaaaaaaaaaaaaa GRAHHAHH

ard!
Ennin Stannard!

tat tat

thump Wahump
aaaaaaaaaa
thump Wahump
thump Wahump
Wahump

shushsuhush

tikatikatikatika

tikatikatikatika

huff
  huff

DECONTAMINATION PROCEDURES

It was not possible to see through the tinted windows of the ambulance, and the only light came from a frosted pane of glass set in the roof. They had driven for what Harriet estimated was around forty minutes – long enough, with the siren going, to take them pretty much anywhere in Greater London. On the bench opposite, the man in the orange hazmat suit sat impassively with his Glock in his lap, finger still on the trigger. At length, the ambulance had slowed, stopped briefly, then proceeded much more slowly down a steep incline, during which the light from above dimmed, then vanished completely. Now, lit only by the ambulance's unforgiving striplights, everyone looked even worse than they already felt, if that was possible.

The ambulance stopped. They could hear the driver's door open then slam shut, then shortly the doors at the rear were swung wide. Outside, another man in another orange hazmat suit held up his hand, indicating that they were to follow. His other hand rested on the butt of his holstered pistol to underscore the request. They found themselves in a spotlessly clean underground car park, empty apart from six more identical ambulances, each showroom-fresh, parked in inch-perfect formation. Above, concrete; below, tarmac. They were ushered through a door fitted with an airtight seal like a fridge and into a small windowless room with a functional stainless-steel desk and chair. They were each handed a plastic basket not unlike the one Dana's clothes had been kept in.

"Where is our friend? The one you shot?" Harriet had lost a little of her bravado.

"He's being taken care of. First things first. Undress, please."

Jack looked at Harriet. "Here?"

There was no reply. There did not seem to be any separate changing rooms. Jack could see the blinking LED of a CCTV in the corner up by the ceiling, but given the events of the day neither he nor Harriet felt like arguing. If they were in the care of biohazard experts, their best course of action was to go along with whatever they asked, however short they may be in the manners department. Still, if they were going to undress in each other's company, he could have wished for more flattering lighting.

Jack studiously looked everywhere except at Harriet: the walls, the man in the hazmat suit whose eyes he could not see, a purpling bruise on his knee, the tiled floor, the scratch on his arm where he had hit the wall under the window, the camera in the corner. He hoped she did the same.

They folded their clothes and laid them in the baskets. These were put in thick plastic bags, sealed with orange ties, and placed on a tray on a roller conveyor that transported them away through a hatch into what looked like an airport security X-ray machine.

Another door opened. They were directed down a short tiled corridor to a second room from which steam and chlorine rose in a white hissing fog from nozzles in the walls and ceiling. The hazmat man pointed to a sign by the entrance. "Showers. Decontamination."

IMPORTANT

COVER ALL OPEN WOUNDS.

THOROUGHLY WASH AND RINSE CONTAMINATED
SKIN AND HAIR.

AVOID BREAKING OR ABRADING THE SKIN.

TILT HEAD BACK, RAISE ARMS AND SPREAD
LEGS TO CLEANSE ARMPITS AND GROIN.

PREVENT RUNOFF FROM HEAD/HAIR GETTING
INTO EYES, NOSE, OR MOUTH.

TURN 90 DEGREES PERIODICALLY TO
EXPOSE ENTIRE BODY TO CROSS-STREAM OF WATER.

RUB WITH THE PROVIDED SOFT CLOTH TO REMOVE
CONTAMINANTS, STARTING WITH HEAD
AND PROCEEDING DOWN BODY TO THE FEET.

It stung their nostrils and filled their lungs, but they were thankful for the sense of washing away the day, outside and in.

If Jack thought that they would be given any privacy here, he was again mistaken. The orange-suited man stood and watched like a dictatorial orang-utan, his hidden face as inscrutable as Darth Vader's.

When he seemed to be satisfied with their work, he beckoned them forward and threw them each a towel. "When you're dry, go through there." He pointed to another door. "We'll have clean clothes and a med team waiting."

The clothes were functional in a unisex kind of way. Loose-fitting T-shirt. Jeans. White underwear.

A nurse came in, wearing a paper facemask but no hazmat suit. Her hair was up in a tight bun and her expression was businesslike. She gestured for them to take one of the plastic seats set against the far wall.

"Once the Incident Commander has consulted with the safety officer, the medical team and other response personnel, and deems those who have been exposed at the scene are safe and secure, you will be released. Once your personal belongings have been decontaminated or deemed safe, they will be returned to you."

Tight-lipped doctors, each of whom seemed to have some specific area of expertise, then subjected them to a lengthy series of tests. Eyes. Blood. Heart. Skin. Hair. Lungs. And, to the dismay of both, Rectum. They made no attempt to explain what they were doing.

These examinations, at least, were conducted individually in private behind a white curtain. While he was waiting for the indignities to end, Jack focused again on the white floor tiles and their flawless antiseptic perfection. White overalls. White masks. *Everything here except the hazmat suits is white*, he thought. We've come a long way from the blood-red deck of the *Cutty Sark*.

Finally they were asked to sign a document they were not given the time to read.

"We're OK? No contamination?"

"You're clean."

Jack's relief was overplayed for their benefit. He was sure that any alien contaminants were very unlikely to make their way through ideaspace and out again, even if they had somehow escaped detection at Johnson.

"Our friend, Nixon. The one that was shot?"

"He has been taken to another location."

"Can we see him?"

"I am told he is in emergency surgery. Perhaps later. As I say, there is a number to call on your sheet. We have a car waiting. You will be driven to any location you request. Please collect your belongings on the way out."

"Emergency surgery?" Harriet blurted.

Jack's heart had jumped too.

Harriet held onto Jack's arm. Her eyes were big and round, her face imploring. "You don't perform surgery on a *dead* person, right?"

The nurse's impassive demeanour slipped, just for a moment. There was the merest shade of a smile. "That you don't."

She handed them the top sheets of the documents. "Upon your release, we provide you with information about possible delayed symptoms and guidance on seeking follow-up medical care. Please read through these instructions. There is a number and email at the top. Don't hesitate to call."

She then gestured to the door.

SHOWTIME

Nixon regarded the booth. It certainly looked impressive – but then it should do. It had cost him enough. A round table with two chairs, one laptop, two glasses, and one dusty bottle of red was set up between two whitewashed walls that met at right angles. Across each, in half-metre-high capitals made of pressed aluminium, was his name:

N I X O N

It had a certain minimalist purity; or perhaps it was a hubristic self-confidence. Whatever, Nixon was not the kind given to lengthy introspection or self-doubt.

The corner plot near the main entrance of the Market Forces Show, Olympia, was something of a gamble. The software he was launching was novel. High end, you could say. You pointed your smartphone, iPad or laptop camera at a wine label, and using a pattern-recognition algorithm it compared it with an online library. Up came reviews, ratings and the nearest stockist. It was just like building a virtual wine cellar – in fact, that's what he'd called it: *The Cellar*. Nothing quite like it on the market.

Nixon had explained the basic premise over a craft beer in the Soho offices of the outfit he had hired to make it a reality. The programmers had made all the right noises, nodded along, and drawn up a costing. He didn't completely understand some of the beta's quirks (they had assured him they were features), but then that wasn't his job. He provided the idea and the funding, they were the ones that made it all happen. *Easy*.

Across the way, one of the major players had a stand. If it wasn't much larger than his it was certainly more crowded, both with product and punters. This was helped along by a woman handing out garish leaflets wearing practically nothing but her underwear. Her hair, a backcombed sculpture held in place by several cans of lacquer, was an artificial-looking yellow; it reminded him of the synthetic hair on those plastic Trolls, though facially, Nixon had to admit, she was by no means hideous. If you liked that kind of thing. Periodically one of the three men in high-street suits who were running the stand would look over and, if they happened to catch his eye, smirk. *The Cellar* was doing very little selling.

There was a younger, more casually dressed man with them. He seemed to be the technical support – he ran out cables, tested connections, tinkered on his laptop while squatting on his haunches unobtrusively in a corner of the booth. He looked like one of those tech types who was blissfully unaware of their appearance – he hadn't shaved in several days and his hair was sticking out at the side, as if he'd just got out of bed.

Nixon ran a finger along the edge of his table, looked at the absence of dust on his finger, then squared up his stack of brochures.

Jack ran through the debug report a fourth time. The software was an inelegant patchwork, buggy as hell, but he wasn't here to tell them that. Just get it up and running. He had installed it twice on each of the five laptops, and the salesmen would switch between them as and when it crashed or froze, which was not uncommon.

It was a sales lead management app, geared to bulk cold-calling. Its main USP was the dynamic list of sales reps, modelled on a Premier League football table, next to which the number of calls, successful conversions and other statistics were displayed. The top three reps were rewarded by an animated dancing cheerleader next to their name; for the number one spot, she was topless.

"We can arrange other forms of payment, know what I mean?" Jack looked up. Terry, the floor manager, was looking down at him over his distended belly. It wasn't that he was difficult to work with; they had let him get on with the set-up with little interference. They trusted him to do his job. No, he was merely . . . unpleasant.

"'Scuse me? Other forms of . . . ?"

"See Jenna there, giving out the leaflets? She's all paid for. If you get my drift. Give me the nod, and I'll slip you the keys to the storeroom." He raised his eyebrows twice and whistled softly. "Let's say I've already sampled the goods. She comes personally recommended. My treat."

Jack returned his gaze to the tangle of cables wrapped around the daisy-chained power supply. "Uh, no thank you."

"Not into the ladies, eh?"

Jack rammed home a connection. He could feel a hot flush on his cheeks. "That should do it. You're running the app in parallel, but no one should notice. Just tab between them up here." Jack pointed to the menu bar on one of the laptop screens. Terry's face had lost its conspiratorial mien and was once again coolly professional. "Ah. Yes, got it. Thanks."

Between surreptitious reboots there was little for Jack to do. He'd been hired for the weekend, ten till five each day, and just wanted to let the time drift by with the minimum of interaction with his employers. He ate an overpriced cheese and pickle sandwich and watched the stream of visitors file past. He had to admit, grudgingly, that their sales pitch was well targeted. If you liked what you saw, you'd probably get a kick out of the product. There was a certain unsophisticated, straightforward *honesty* at work. Not like the guy opposite. What the fuck was *he* all about? He strutted up and down the empty space as if it was the forecourt of Buckingham Palace. He had that effortlessly handsome, broad-shouldered build perfect for rugby, hair ostentatiously gelled up and back, a red silk tie and a glint of gold cufflinks. He exuded the showy self-confident charm that came with an expensive education. Jack took an immediate dislike to him.

And what was going on with the stand? It resembled a consulting room, all clinical empty space, as if booth real-estate was cheap as chips. One table, one laptop. Very few people were stopping by to take a closer look.

When the suit was off on one of his periodic perambulations, Jack stepped over and picked up one of the leaflets. It was a polished enough job, in the overdesigned manner of an upmarket real-estate brochure. On the front was a stock library shot of wine barrels in a subterranean vault; on the back a Bugatti outside a colonnaded portico.

"How do you organise your wine cellar, sir? It's a perennial problem, as I'm sure you're aware. One that—"

The salesman had reappeared at his side as if by magic. Like a bloodhound, he must have picked up the scent of a potential sale several metres distant. Jack held the leaflet over his interlocutor's mouth. "I rotate the Tennent's Extra. New tins in the back of the fridge, old in the front."

"Can I demonstrate the app? Allow me to show you its capabilities. While not specifically designed to catalogue beers, as such, we have been thinking about broadening the beverage remit for the next update. Now—"

Smooth segue. Despite himself, Jack had already been led back to the table by a slight pressure on the elbow. He was now looking at a laptop screen on which gold type overlaid a burgundy velvet drape, the corner of which was held back by a tasselled cord. The salesman started to run through the features with practised ease in the precise clipped diction of a BBC documentary voice-over. It was hypnotic, and though Jack's wine cellar was a box under the stairs, he found himself following along.

Like the leaflet, it was a superficial mix of aspirational stock photography and overwritten blurb, and Jack could see several ways in which the actual functionality could be improved almost immediately. He sat in silence till the presentation ended. Ten out of ten for smarm. "So, we can sign you up right now. Would you prefer the Goodwood tickets, or the mystery bottle as your welcome gift?"

Jack cocked his head. "You using the either/or close on me there, Flashman?"

Nixon could tell this wasn't going to be an easy sale. "Let me show you how you can link to social media." He held up the bottle of Lafite Rothschild '82 so that the label was caught by the laptop's camera within an ornate gold frame in the centre of the screen. The type on it was upside down. "All your friends can see what your growing wine collection holds—"

"All my friends will think I'm an aristocratic alcoholic." Jack pointed at the screen. "Your label is upside down. A simple text-recognition algorithm can fix that." He brought up the raw code before Nixon could say anything, typed a few lines, paused to read them over, changed a couple of digits, then hit return. "Try it now."

Nixon held up the bottle a second time. The label was scanned again, then turned itself right-side up with a soft *ching* from the finest crystal goblet. Jack smiled. "No charge."

Nixon didn't say anything for a few seconds. Even Jack could sense his deflation. He looked away, across the aisle. Jenna was sporting a rictus of a smile as two middle-aged men and a younger lad in a denim jacket vied for her attention.

"What are you selling, over there on your stand?"

Jack pulled a face. "Something that people actually want. It's crass, the interface is ugly as hell, but there's definitely an audience for it." He shrugged. "Lowest common denominator, I guess."

"*The Cellar*—"

"—is lovely to look at. But it doesn't *work*. Poking around in that code of yours, it's all superficial gimmicks. You've dressed up a half-assed idea in a fancy suit, but I'm afraid I can see right through it. Presentation isn't the be-all and end-all. Even for sales software." A Bugatti analogy might be appropriate, Jack thought. "It has to have it *under the hood*. Now, if you added a wine rack graphic, and maybe a league table – though perhaps we could switch the topless woman for a sommelier in a bow tie . . ."

Nixon opened his mouth to say something, but nothing came out. He watched as this unkempt stranger brought up more code, deleting, rewriting, copying and pasting, fingers effortlessly flitting over the keyboard. Hurt pride gave way to an indignant curiosity. This guy hadn't asked his permission to tinker with the app, but then he did appear to be somewhat unconcerned about the niceties of social interaction.

A fixated absorption had taken up residence on his face. A list was taking form, images of the labels to the left, a rating system consisting of an empty, half-full or full glass to the right.

Nixon watched him work. He seemed oblivious to anything but the screen in front of him. Several minutes passed, but this intense young man whose name he didn't know showed no sign of slowing. The rhythmic tap-tap-tap of the keys, a morse code whose meaning would forever elude him, played in his head like a half-remembered tune.

Something in his peripheral vision caught his attention. Across the aisle, there seemed to be much waving of arms. One of the suits was gesturing at a laptop, while the other was looking around the booth for something. For someone.

Nixon positioned himself between them and this newcomer, blocking their view. He fished a corkscrew out of his suit pocket, opened the £1,700 bottle of wine and filled the two glasses.

'Mole people' beneath our streets?

BY GERALD FARROW

MODERN underclass or urban legend?

Just like H. G. Wells's Morlocks, for decades there have been rumours of a shadowy group of people living in the subterranean spaces beneath London.

Though facts are hard to come by and London Transport itself is keen to downplay the idea – possibly out of a desire not to scare passengers or encourage others to explore the tunnels – the rumours have persisted.

The homeless and destitute sheltered under the arches of Waterloo, Euston and other London stations are a familiar sight, but a new twist to the story suggests there exists a distinct population which has gone a step further.

Born and bred in darkness, is there really a race of nocturnal men and women who have adapted to life underground, even going so far as to develop their own parallel society?

Are these London's so-called "Mole People"?

A recent report in which a soot-blackened but otherwise naked woman was allegedly seen exiting the southbound tunnel and climbing onto the platform at Old Street tube station has reignited interest in the debate.

Though the station was almost empty at the time and few people have come forward who claim to have seen her first hand, CCTV footage shows a dark figure, not much more than a silhouette, moving along the platform and through the main concourse to the foot of the escalators.

Her posture suggests that she is pressing her hands to her stomach and bending forward as if in some pain. Further footage shows what is assumed to be the same figure leaving via the City Road exit, though no-one was seen passing through the barriers – even though the ticket office was manned.

Footage of the main hall also

Turn to page 834

Home Office

Direct Communications Unit
2 Marsham Street, London SW1P 4DF

Freedom of Information Act (FOIA) request Disclosure Log

This document contains reference details for FOIA requests which have been answered in full or in part, or for which the agency held no information. ██████████████████████

If you wish to see the original request and subsequent agency reply, please send an email headed "Disclosure Log request".

Freedom of information Act 2000 (FOIA) Request
Request number **HC/099120023/09**
Keywords: London; Intelligencia; Normansson, Dana; Rappaport, Nixon

This is a redacted document.

Subject: Shooting of civilian at offices of Intelligencia Limited

Registered office █████████████████████████Hoxton Square.

Transcript of interview with█████████████████████████conducted
on█████████████████████████████████████

Interviewer: So you were sure the target [Dana Normansson] was on the premises?
████████████   I had a visual. I could see her.
Interviewer: You are aware that footage from the drone camera does not show her?
████████████   She was there.
Interviewer: But you have reviewed the footage?
████████████   With respect, sir, the footage is not shot from the best angle. The drone was tasked with covering the entrance to the building and the roof, so was flying too high. It could not see to the back of the room. As you know, I was in position across the square, one storey higher than the Intelligencia office. I had a better view.
████████████   You were equipped with a █████████calibre sniper rifle, correct?
████████████   Yes, sir.
Interviewer: With a telescopic sight?
████████████   Yes, sir.
Interviewer: And there is no way you could have been mistaken? Reflections from the windows, shadows—
████████████   No sir. Absolutely not.
Interviewer: You are aware that she was not found on the premises?
████████████   I am aware of that, yes sir.
Interviewer: And you are also aware that our eye-in-the-sky camera did not see her exit via the roof or the front door?
████████████   Yes sir.

Interviewer: So we have a small problem here, do we not?
[silence – 4 seconds]

Interviewer: Your record is exemplary. Two tour ███████████████

███████████████████████████████████████

██ and Gaddafi ████████████████████ rit. PC Y█

███████████████████████████████████████

advanced training. So I shall ask again. There is no reason to lie here.
████ Sir, I saw her, sir.

Interviewer: You are aware that Intelligencia deals in design for
games companies?

████████████ I was not briefed about the kind of work the company
did, no sir.

Interviewer: And that three-dimensional maquettes – sculptures for
game characters – models, in effect – were on display on a shelf at the back
of the room?

████████████ I have seen the photographs of the room that are on
file, yes sir.

Interviewer: And might it be possible that you mistook one of these
figures for the target?

████████████ I– sir. I–

Interviewer: Can you be absolutely one hundred per cent sure what
you saw was Dana Normansson, and not some kind of, you know, Lara Croft
statue?

████████████ Sir, she was moving. Statues don't move.

Interviewer: So where do you propose she disappeared to?

████████████ Sir— as I squeezed off the shot, I thought I saw— this
is going to sound strange, but this is how I saw it: she seemed to turn over,
like a page from a book, or a card being shuffled. Peeled up off the— off
the— like she was flat, and then she slid into someplace else. I'm not sure
how to describe it. I've never seen anything like it before, and I've seen a lot.

████████████ You've seen those life-size figures? Cardboard cut-outs?
Characters from TV, pop idols, suchlike?

████████████ Yes, sir.

Interviewer: Flat. Like a page from a book?

████████████ Yes, sir.

Interviewer: You see where this line of enquiry is taking me?
[silence – 7 seconds]

████████████ Sir? Can I ask you a question?   *2965 – 115*

Interviewer: Go ahead.

████████████ Did you find one? A life-size cutout? On the premises?

[END OF TRANSCRIPT]

RECONVENED IN SHOREDITCH

WE ARE THE GALAXIANS.
MISSION: DESTROY ALIENS.
Behind, a twinkling 8-bit star-field scrolled down. Across this
INSERT COIN
was written in red, and above that, in white,
1 UP and **HIGH SCORE**.
Harriet and Jack were sitting either side of a vintage 1970s *Galaxian* console table, the smoked glass top dark with age and the joystick long lost from drunken heavy-handed play.

They had decided to meet in the neutral territory of Shoreditch House. Harriet repeatedly hit the red button and wiggled her finger in the empty recess where the joystick had been, but the game could not be coaxed into life. Destroying aliens would have to wait for another day.

She found herself entranced by a hipster beard that would have not been out of place on an Al-Qaeda jihadi. "You think this is a better place to meet than my flat?"

"They must know where you live. They probably know I'm a member here as well, but I'm a member of a dozen places, including the British Library, Stationers' Hall and Ruislip Lido." Jack flagged down a waiter, possibly the only people here sporting dark suits, and ordered a Sea Breeze and a mineral water. "They can't bug them all. And this is a big place. Noisy. I'm finding it hard to hear what I'm saying myself."

"The mysterious 'They'. You sure you're not just being paranoid?"

Jack shrugged. "We were too blasé back in the office. Look where that got us. We didn't even draw the blinds."

Harriet nodded. "Nixon. What's the latest?"

Jack looked out across a room of long tables, mismatched Herman Miller chairs and pendant lamps so large and low that if you stood up too fast, your head would ring them like a clapper in a bell. Harriet had herself under tight control, but even he could tell she was holding back tears.

"He's OK. As well as can be expected. The bullet splintered two ribs, but missed his lung. Didn't hit anything vital. He'll heal. It'll just take time."

Harriet already knew most of this. She had been to the private military hospital in Charing Cross twice; both times, Nixon had been heavily sedated, unaware anyone else was even there. He was in an isolation ward, and though Harriet had not been required to wear a hazmat suit, she had had to scrub down before and after her visit. She'd quizzed the doctor in attendance, who she gathered was some kind of expert in contagious diseases even though he looked barely out of his twenties. Harriet suspected he had been drafted in from some other secret project he was not at liberty to mention. They had found no trace of any pathogen, but were still being cautious. "Good, that's good. Who do we sue?"

Jack forced a smile. "Excellent question. I've no idea how this works. Do they send us a government liaison, or something? Victim support? Or do we just accept that mistakes get made, and cheer them on as they protect Queen and country?"

Harriet changed the topic. "Have you been back to the office?"

"Yesterday. There's a brand-new front door. I was surprised to find that the key code is the same – presumably so as not to inconvenience the other tenants, Mr Thingy DJ upstairs and the haberdashers at the back – so I could get into the hall and up the stairs. But that's it. No further. There's a big heavy-duty lock fitted to our office door now. No key. I couldn't get in."

"So, what, they can just appropriate our office?"

"There was a sheet of paper taped to it. In a plastic pocket." Jack slid it across the smoked glass. Harriet picked it up and skim-read it. "So . . . they have all our kit?"

"I think we have to assume so. That means they'll have the recordings. They'll have images of the aliens, the DMEn, of our trips into the Grid. Everything."

Drinks appeared. Harriet pressed the sheet in the plastic pocket to her chest to make room and hide it from curious eyes, then passed it back to Jack.

"What else? They probably have all the data that's not encrypted or in the Cloud. But—" Jack leaned in conspiratorially – "there's all our games dev stuff there, too. They may not be able to tell the difference. My guess is that, to them, it's entirely possible it'll *all* look like test footage. Renders, cut scenes, turn-arounds. You've seen the graphics for the new *Halo* game. They're astonishing . . . and Intelligencia are in the business of going one better. Why should they not assume they're just looking at bleeding edge game graphics?"

Harriet didn't share Jack's optimism. "Because we practically give a running commentary? Because Dana's in there? Because of a million other things?"

"Maybe. Remember, Dana was either distorted, like a low-resolution mesh, or dressed in her cosmonaut suit. I think they'll see a bunch of files in my proprietary Intelligencia format and assume they're works in progress. To open the files in the first place, they'll need to know their way around a beta version of software that even I don't fully understand, and we wrote the thing. There's very little in the way of an intuitive GUI. They could possibly pull out still images or short clips of video, but I doubt if it'll be synced with sound. Without a thorough understanding of the raw code, it might as well be brickwall encrypted. No, I think they'll be after emails, web histories, stuff like that. And that – all my correspondence with Gabe at Johnson, Daniel at Jodrell – all *that* is on *this*."

Jack reached into his messenger bag and pulled out his laptop and his pair of Depthcharge glasses with a flourish, placing them on the table between them.

"*What?* I thought you couldn't get into the office? How did you get these?"

"I walked out with them when we left. Right in front of orange jumpsuit man's nose."

"I didn't see—"

"I didn't take them far. I know where the DJ upstairs keeps the key to that metal box of his – up on the picture rail. I slipped these in there as I left. No one saw me. They were still there when I went back yesterday."

Harriet laughed long and loud, and it felt good. She'd not had a reason to laugh in a long while. "Jack, I fucking love you."

Jack grinned. "It gets better. I also happen to have something else that may be useful installed on this beauty. An Oxbow."

"Ha! Dana!"

"If she's in there . . . we can go looking."

"Do it. *Now.*"

Jack looked around. Here, among the brilliantined tech whizzes sporting heavy vintage tortoiseshell glasses, a pair of Depthcharges with wires looping out and down to a Macbook Pro would look utterly inconspicuous.

"OK. I can loop the feed to my screen, so you can see what I see."

"Brilliant. Do it." Harriet spun the laptop around, pulled it towards her.

"Hang on, hang on, let me put in my password and boot the Oxbow first."

Harriet held it up so Jack could type. He hit return, inserted the USB then pressed a small stud on the side of the glasses. A green LED lit. He put them on. Harriet pulled the laptop off the table and cradled it in her lap, out of sight. The taut cable nudged her Sea Breeze just enough for it to slop onto the table.

"Careful. You spill your drink on that and we'll lose everything. Right. Let's see if anyone else made it past the lass on the front desk."

Jack looked around the crowded room. It didn't take him more than a few moments to locate the 19th Count, who was sitting on a chesterfield just behind Harriet. He was sharing it with a couple who were investigating each other's tonsils with their tongues, and had affected a cramped posture that oozed theatrical disdain. A small bubble with a wiggly tail floated above him, empty apart from an ellipsis . . .

"The Count's here."

"I see him. Say hello."

Jack gave a subtle wave without raising his arm. In return, the Count raised a white glove to the rim of his hat.

Harriet pointed to the screen, then realised Jack could not see what she was doing from across the table. "Look – one of those two sitting beside him with their faces stuck together – isn't that Girl 21?"

Jack craned his head forward, then remembered he could simply adjust the zoom. The couple beside the Count leaped forward. He quickly reset it to a more discreet magnification. "Heh. You're right, it is. And that chap she's with – who *is* that?"

The longer Jack looked, the more peculiar Girl 21's beau appeared. Like her ever-changing face, he also seemed to be made from a montage of selfies, though the faces and the bodies were cut and pasted together with more attention given to buffness of body than matching skin tone or angle of view. If it were a Photoshop comp, Jack would have ranked it amateur in the extreme. It reminded him of a dodgy Richard Hamilton montage, a collection of shiny torsos, biceps and six-packs that could have been lifted from Grindr combined into some rough semblance of a single figure. The hands were here and there, and also there and here and somewhere else he couldn't quite make out. The head, or heads, flitted between Jared Leto, a young Leonardo DiCaprio and some muscular tattooed dude with a bleached blonde buzzcut the identity of whom Jack was thankfully oblivious.

Harriet had the keyboard.

Ah-hem.

It floated above the hubbub of the room like a polite fart in a perfumed bubblebath.

Girl 21 seemed startled, and an instant later her companion had vanished.

It dawned on Jack that she must have concocted him entirely herself – a wish fulfilment, an idea of an idea. He wondered if the principle could be extended in an infinite regress – ideas having ideas, which in turn have their own ideas, and so on, each slightly more abstract and universal, until some idea event horizon of ultimate ideaness was finally reached.

Harriet had a more prosaic explanation. She leaned in towards Jack, masking her mouth with her drink. "Did we just catch her *masturbating?*"

Jack thought it might be better if he pretended he had missed the whole episode. "What?"

"*You* saw. There's no privacy when we're the ones who control the peepers."

Jack smiled. He kept his voice low. "And hello to you, too. Count." The Count tipped his hat graciously and settled his cane across his knees. "Do we have Mr Modernism, XX?"

The Count lifted his cane and used it to point at the rectangular island bar in the centre of the large room. Through the legs of the clientele arranged around it on barstools, Jack could see it was patterned with a familiar dazzle-ship design of stripes and chevrons. XX was almost congruent with the bar itself, shifting slightly like a sleeping dog so that those seated at the far end of the counter appeared to be sunk waist-deep in a Futurist stage set.

"Have you seen Dana? Is she in there with you?"

The Count returned his cane to his knees, lowered his head and pulled his half-height top hat down over his milky brow. His voice was a subdued seven-point.

As far as we can tell, she's not here in the Grid.
But the Grid is a very large place, and without your *ingenious innovations* much of it is unavailable, even to the likes of us.
We conclude she may have stepped straight in — and then *out again.*
Passed right through in an instant.

"Out? *Where?*" Harriet did not turn around, but directed the question at the screen in front of her.

She would have had *LITTLE TIME*
to carefully choose *where* she was going to step out.

It must have been a *split-second* decision.

I'm not sure what else I can say.

"But you think she's out here? In the *real* world?"

It is a *distinct possibility*.

Though *WHERE*, precisely, I cannot fathom.

None of my **eyes** have seen her.

Harriet couldn't hide her alarm. "She'll be naked. She might not even know where she is."

Jack looked at her directly. "If she *is* here, don't you think she'd have tried to contact us by now? What if she exited the Grid inside something solid?" He had voiced the one possibility she didn't want to consider. She looked down at the table.

GAME OVER

Two down.

SEARCH PARTY

An outside observer would have concluded that Jack was having an animated conversation with himself. Point and counter-point. Nods, acceptance. Much shaking of the head.

However Jack had on a pair of Depthcharge glasses, and wasn't alone. Three figures – two that looked human, one more like a piece of industrial machinery – were his interlocutors.

They had returned to Nadine's kitchen. Jack hadn't been sure where to go – Shoreditch House was too public for anything but the most superficial exploration of the Grid, Harriet shared her apartment with two others, they couldn't get into the office and needed a private base of operations fast.

For the last month, since he'd let his place go, the office had also served as his makeshift home. With few other options, Jack had booked himself into Furlong Chambers on Charing Cross Road using his Intelligencia expenses card; he wondered what would happen if they tried to check his spending with Nixon. The room overlooked Cecil Court, and Jack had spent twenty minutes examining the buildings opposite for – for what? The glint of a gun barrel? The movement of a curtain? He was more than aware that it didn't take much to push him into his over-sensitive, paranoid state of mind, where every half-glimpsed movement was a sign, every black-clad figure a portent.

As well as the missed calls from Gabe at Johnson, there had been two from Nadine, who was now sitting across the kitchen table with a face like thunder. Harriet could sense the tension in the air. Jack, she thought, had some nerve – he doesn't return her calls or emails, then turns up unannounced and without explanation, bringing her and their memetic voyeurs with him.

Harriet had affected her best bright and breezy Intelligencia presentation-style demeanour, but try as she might to lift the mood the awkward atmosphere was just exacerbated by Jack's obliviousness. She'd told him coming here wasn't a great idea, but hadn't been able to come up with a better suggestion – and time was not on their side.

The sooner they were out of there, the better. If Jack had had any future with Nadine, she sensed he was now wearing the promise perilously thin.

Jack had got straight down to work. He had asked the question several times already, but was about to ask it again.

"Where is she?"

Girl 21 had not used his name before.

Girl 21's face was a flicker of stills from emotionally charged relationship break-up movie scenes. Harriet found it gratingly inappropriate – a public illustration of a private moment.

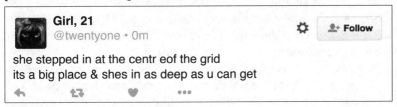

"Is there no way you can – I don't know, do a *search?*" Harriet pleaded.

"She's right, Harriet. It's like trying to search an enormous field with a tiny metal detector. We can only find what's directly under our noses."

"But—" Harriet had a sudden flash of insight. "Don't we have an isolated digital signature that is unambiguously hers? That we can search for in the Signal itself, mathematically?"

Jack's head dipped. "Not here. Not on this laptop."

"Can we look for a digital signature that's, just, you know, *human?*"

"Harriet, the Grid contains more than a million million million million creatures just within the volume of our good green Earth. And that doesn't include the far larger portion that lies outside it. If we knew what the Grid's digital representation of a human looked like – which we *don't* – it'd still have to be utterly unique to stand out in a crowd that size."

Jack couldn't sit still. He paced up and down in front of the window, spinning on his heel every four steps like a circus bear with OCD in a cage too small for him. On the kitchen wall Movember Miss Wong, at least, remained impassive. Harriet could sense his agitation; she felt it too. "So what do we do? *Wait?* She could still be in there, or have exited somewhere – *anywhere* – with no way of contacting us."

Girl, 21
@twentyone · 0m

she managed B4.

Harriet decided to take it back to basics. "So. Let's go over this again. See if we've missed anything. She can travel through the Grid. She has done it before. Now, is this *instantaneous?* Speed of light? Speed of *thought?* What *is* the speed of thought? A brisk walk? Might it not take weeks for her to make the journey back up to the surface?"

Jack shoved his hands deep into his pockets and leaned against the wall. "My guess is that it's a simple geometric translation. Numbers. Entry point, exit point – they are both uniquely described by two sets of three-dimensional coordinates. There is no space between that needs to be traversed in physical terms."

"So it's instantaneous. Or as fast as you can think it—"

"Right. But remember that first time? She was very careful to leave the Grid somewhere she wouldn't intersect with something solid. The Earth's radius is more than six and a half thousand kilometres, and an error of less than one per cent would mean the difference between appearing half a mile underground, or a death-dive from the height of Canary Wharf. Can she achieve that kind of accuracy? Is it even *possible?*"

"Remember that unfortunate who fell from the undercarriage of a Heathrow-bound flight from Angola onto a street in Mortlake? Made a real mess. If naked women were falling from the sky we'd have heard about it."

"So you're thinking it's very likely she materialised *inside* something?"

"We have no way of knowing." Jack was used to having the answers, and when he didn't his frustration was palpable. The 19th Count, standing by the sink in which two weeks of unwashed crockery and glassware were marinating in a close recreation of the prebiotic soup, seemed to sense it too.

Jack, we don't know any *more* than *you do.*

He sounded uncharacteristically solicitous.

"*Think.* Where would *you* go?"

"She doesn't have home addresses for any of us. Just the office. Would she go back there?"

"Would *you* go back to the place you'd just been shot?"

"I'd want to know what happened to the rest of us. I'd want to take a *look.*"

"If she did, she'd find we're not there."

"What else? We're missing something obvious."

Jack stopped pacing and pivoted to the table, placing both hands palm down in the breadcrumbs and grease. He leaned forward. "*Dan.* At Jodrell. Dan is leading the exobiology group for NASA. Dan was her liaison here while she was still on the Moon."

"Jack, Dan is in direct contact with Gabe. Dan came to the office looking for her on his behalf! She'd be *crazy* to make herself known to him."

"Not necessarily. Dan worked with Dana for months after the LBE encounter. They respect each other. And he can keep secrets. He's old school. *Discreet.* Because Dana explicitly asked him, Dan never told anyone about Georgi Komarov's, ah, lapse of protocol. Even at the tribunal."

"Komarov?" Harriet had not heard the name before.

"Never mind." Jack stood.

"He let slip the Apollo 19—" Harriet stopped mid-sentence. Jack shot her a stare, then glanced over at Nadine.

"*Discretion,* Jack?" Nadine managed a thin smile. Whatever secrets these two and their weird digital friends shared, she was not party to them; nor, she knew, would she ever be. A Year Ten memory of being excluded from the cool kids' clique at school, of feeling like the outsider, came back more powerfully than she ever imagined it could. It felt like yesterday. Children, perhaps more so than adults, can be unbelievably cruel, though this time she had to concede Jack was incapable of such Machiavellian manoeuvrings.

No, this was one club she would never be a member of. And if you weren't a member of the club, there was no reason to honour its rules and regulations. You certainly weren't obliged to host the meetings. She held up her hands. "Jack, Harriet – I think you should find yourselves a new clubhouse."

Several minutes later the two of them stood on the cracked crazy paving of the car park outside. Jack looked up at the faded floral curtains in Nadine's bedroom window. He had lain there with her, just a week or so ago, listening to her shallow breathing while his eyes traced the fabric's intertwined arabesques. He had mentally marqueed the pattern's repeat; that orange flower, that pink bud partially lost in a fold.

Seven across, and five up.

It was another pattern to be deciphered, and he couldn't help himself.

A week or a month from now, he could probably recreate it from memory. He knew he would probably never see Nadine again; with a deep sense of shame, he realised that her face had already begun to fade.

He absently adjusted the weight of his messenger bag and rested one hand on the corner of the laptop inside to reassure himself it was still there. There were some things he did understand.

Harriet tugged his sleeve. "Let's go. I *did* say, Jack, that coming here might *not* be a good idea . . ."

Jack did not reply.

Harriet had a fist on her hip, the other hand held high, palm up. "So, what do we do *now*? We call Daniel? We go to Jodrell?"

Jack finally brought his attention back to the moment. He looked directly at her, as if registering her presence for the first time. His face was devoid of expression.

"I'm a fuck-up, Harriet. A fucking fuck-up." He turned and strode off towards the main road, shoulders hunched, head down.

Harriet ran after him. She grabbed his arm, and his forward momentum spun him around to face her. She had suddenly lost all her self-righteous bluster. "Jack?"

He pulled himself upright, looked at the sky. A single tear escaped from the corner of his eye. "Not Jodrell. We're going back to Hoxton. They took all our computer kit, but there's one thing I'm pretty sure they'll have left behind. One computer that won't have been on their list."

Jack's voice had taken on a new resolve that drew its power from his frustration. At this moment he really didn't care *what* he did next.

Fuck the orange-clad biohazard guys.
Fuck the sniper who shot Nixon.
Fuck my dysfunctional mind.
Fuck what may or may not be legal.
Fuck 'em all.

The idea he was now entertaining gave him a childlike thrill. He looked Harriet straight in the eye. "We're going to break into our office."

BREAKING AND ENTERING

The replacement lock on the office door was an imposing affair, looking more like something you'd find on a bank safe than a commercial property. The key slot was set in a large circular boss which protruded from a steel plate that wrapped right around the doorframe, bridging the hole where the original lock had been. Its pristine brushed chrome contrasted with the original heavy wooden door, on which scuffed bootprints and raw splintered edges could still be seen.

"OK, genius, how do we pick this?" Harriet and Jack stood at the top of the stairs. The Intelligencia logo was still mounted on the wall to their left, a dink in the lower edge where the stretcher had caught it on the way out.

"We don't. Remember that lock the landlord put on the door to the roof?" Jack took the next short flight of stairs up, patting the metal box mounted on their neighbour's door that had proven to be so useful as he passed. A quarter-landing above led to another small flight of stairs which ended at a sloped wooden door, wrapped in a zinc sheet and nailed around the edges like a crude canvas. "They removed it with bolt-cutters when they were searching for Dana. *That,* they didn't replace."

Hardly pausing to aim his boot, Jack grabbed the cast-iron handrail and swung around and up, connecting with all his momentum. The door popped its hinges in a spray of rust and rotten wood. There was a second of silence, then an enormous clatter as it landed on the flat roof beyond. He gestured to the rectangle of slate-grey London sky now visible. "After you."

Harriet had been up here before, for the infamous Intelligencia summer party that had led to the door being padlocked in the first place. The barbecue was still here, a bright red flying saucer on three legs, lid left open to reveal a blackened grate. Empty tins of Tyskie and London Pride were still arranged under the low brick pediment; cigarette stubs and birdshit dotted the grey metal roof. Beyond, the trees of Hoxton Square rose higher, blocking the view to the east and, Jack hoped, the

White Cube – if there was anyone still stationed over there watching them. To the south, the building rose one storey higher to be capped in a miniature forest of chimney stacks; they kept away from the edge, just to be sure they were out of the line of sight. They were now standing directly above the Intelligencia conference room.

Two more steps, and they were at the skylight.

"What can you see?" The textured glass was criss-crossed with reinforcing wire and caked in grime. Jack rubbed the heel of his boot across it.

"Boxes. The tables are still there." Jack cupped his hand against the side of his face and bent close. "The remains of the water cooler. The shelf and the 3D models too. No computers, though. It looks pretty tidy. Like we packed our stuff away and moved out."

"Is it still there?"

"Hang on." Jack stepped away from the skylight and looked around the roof. His eyes came to rest on something. "Aha."

"Ja-ack . . . !"

"Stand back."

The barbecue came down with all the force Jack could muster. There was a sound of glass against metal, and more of a crunch than a shattering. The frame buckled and the window fell through in one piece, frosted into opacity. It hit the parquet below, sending small pieces scooting off into the corners of the room.

Jack looked through the aperture. "That's still quite a drop. We could swing over to the conference room table, but I'm not sure it could take our weight."

Harriet pushed him to one side. "I did the bars at school. Gymnast bars, not the other kind. Watch me." She lowered herself down, hung from the lip for a few moments, then dropped to the floor with a faint *spak*. "Easy." Her voice echoed up from the empty room.

Jack's descent was less elegant, but in a minute he was beside her. "Alarm. We'll have set off the alarm."

"The alarm needs a code or a fob. They wouldn't have had either. It's not been set. Relax."

They began to search the room. All the computers, Jack's crates of books, the company paperwork in Nixon's desk – as they had suspected, all of it, even the 3D printer, had been taken away. On the floor, rectangles with a lighter dusting of East End soot – no longer coal dust, Jack supposed, but a residue of kebab fat and City testosterone – marked where the crates had been stacked. The window that had been penetrated by the bullet was crudely patched with unfinished plywood.

Colour-coded chalk glyphs gave clues to the work of a forensics team. Wide arcs through the dust described the passage of equipment and bags of paperwork that had been dragged towards the exit and away.

Harriet apprehensively approached Nixon's recliner. A small dried brown stain, indistinguishable from spilt coffee, marked the armrest, and a larger archipelago, like scattered small change, pocked the parquet just below. There were also marks where the wheels of the stretcher had taken his weight, four lines leading to the locked door.

Harriet couldn't bring herself to examine the chair any more closely. Her eyes came to rest on an empty expanse of floor.

"Jack, *look*. Is that a *footprint?*"

Jack looked. The neat impression of five toes and a blurred heel was clearly visible. Unlike everywhere else, fresh dust had not had time to dull the polished floor. Recent. Petite. A woman's bare footprint. He glanced up at Harriet, whose stance had taken on something of a primed animal, taut and alert.

The prints began close to the centre of the room in a messy scuffle. Jack could make out a clear left foot, another smudged to near invisibility; leading away from this was a drunkard's walk, between and around which danced a dark spatter of fresh blood which was still wet enough to reflect the light from the broken skylight above. Crossing this trail he could see their own booted prints, carelessly laid down just a moment before.

Harriet pointed. She dropped her voice to a whisper. "They lead over there. Towards the bathroom."

Jack quietly picked up a piece of broken metal windowframe. "Insurance. Just in case. If whoever it is is still here, they'd have heard us come in. *If* they're still here."

Jack took several steps forward. The bathroom door was recessed into the sturdy whitewashed brick wall, and from where he stood he could see that it was ajar, but nothing more. He held his improvised weapon higher, the glass that still adhered to the hard putty cutting into his palm. The prints led right up to the door – and the object that was keeping it from closing.

A bare and dirt-blackened foot.

Jack reached forward and pushed the door open. A naked figure was slumped around the bowl of the toilet, her head obscured by the cistern, one leg bent back and around the toilet brush. A crimson hand-print stood out against the white of the seat, streaks leading from it down the curve of the bowl. Jack knew who it was immediately.

"Dana. It's Dana!"

Harriet was behind him, pushing past. "Is she breathing? Can you see any movement?"

Jack couldn't see her face, and there wasn't space to try and turn her over. "We'll need to pull her out. Can you take a leg? Slowly. As gently as possible—"

Jack dropped the piece of windowframe in the basin and knelt down beside her, reaching out slowly, dreading what he might find.

That was when they heard a key in the lock.

THE GRAND PLAN

Nixon propped his crutches against the wall and experimentally pushed the door. His side hurt, his legs were weak and wobbly, and he felt more than a little trepidation returning to the place where he had been shot. *Shot.* Hah. How did *that* happen? This was London, not South Central LA. Not even in his most freewheeling flight of fantasy had he imagined he'd have a bullet skim his ribcage. And certainly not while at *the office.*

After he'd been debriefed and discharged, he'd been handed back his soiled clothes, a key to the replacement lock, and an exhaustive list of articles confiscated from the Intelligencia office with a vague and caveated promise that they would at some point be returned or their value reimbursed. Looking down the list, he'd wondered how they might go about calculating how much the lost work, compromised data, blown deadlines and general disruption might all add up to. Other than the computer kit, most of it seemed to be an extensive inventory of Jack's collection of old books and magazines. Nixon laughed, which brought a finger of pain to his side – at least Jack would be grateful. His library now had an alphabetical index.

The door, carried by the momentum of the heavy drill-proof lock, swung open to reveal two familiar faces looking up at him from a crouched position over by the bathroom.

"*Fuck,* Nixon! You had us shitting ourselves!" Harriet leapt up and across the five metres of intervening space to envelop him in a bear-hug.

Nixon dropped the key and tensed. "*Aaeow.* Careful."

"Sorry, sorry." Harriet stood back and looked at him. "How is it? How are you?"

"Fine, until you crushed me. What are *you* doing here? How did you get in without a key?"

Harriet pointed at the roof, then the crazed roll of wired glass on the floor.

"The landlord's not going to be happy."

"I think that's already a given."

"Hey, Nixon. Looking good. They let you out?" Jack was still crouched down on his haunches, his attention on something in the door to . . .

Nixon moved into the room, then caught sight of Dana's bare leg. Immediately he was on the floor beside him, ignoring the protestations of his bandaged body. "What happened?"

"She was here when we came through the roof. Don't know how long. No signs of another forced entry. She must have folded herself out of the Grid."

"She OK?"

"She's breathing, but she's unconscious. Stand back. You're in no state to help us move her. Harriet—"

A few moments later Dana was lying on her back on the floor of the main office, Jack's jacket thrown over her to preserve her modesty. It was immediately apparent where the blood was coming from – two of the fingers on her left hand were missing above the second knuckle. The flow had been partially staunched by a makeshift tourniquet fashioned from a strip of sacking, presumably of Dana's own devising. Harriet brought a bowl of hot water over from the kitchenette, then went back to search the units under the sink for clean dishcloths.

"She's out, but I think she's OK. Shock, perhaps." Her body was scuffed with angry abrasions and tarry black soot. A purple bruise ran up the inside of her calf. Harriet wiped her face clean, pushing her blonde hair back and out of her eyes. "Hey, Dana. If you can hear me, I'm going to replace that bandage. Hold tight." She pulled a face as she undid the filthy strip of material. "Look. Her fingers. They've been cauterised. Neatly sliced off. What happened?"

"She stepped out of the Grid, and caught them in something? A wall, perhaps?"

Harriet nodded. "Makes sense." Then, almost as an afterthought: "I bet that hurt." Nixon folded a large towel into a makeshift pillow and lifted her head, sliding it under. "Jack, get her a glass of water."

When Jack returned, Dana's eyes were open. Harriet placed a rolled wet dishcloth on her forehead. "Hey. You're back. Relax, we've got you."

Dana's eyes turned to half-moons, and a smile broke across her lips. "I think I made a mess of your bathroom. Sorry." She coughed, a deep seismic smoker's rattle.

Harriet laughed. "Don't worry. *We* kicked the roof in."

"Your landlord won't be happy."

"That's what Nixon said. He can add it to the bill."

"Heh."

"So where did you *go?*"

"Into the Grid. Blind. Or, more accurately, I went *through* the Grid. Without eyes to see where you are, it's a non-space. It's not black – opening your eyes in the Grid without an Oxbow is like looking out the back of your head. It's not something you can stand for long; it feels like you're drowning. So I translated the vertical reference point. It was the only thing I could think to do. I went up."

"How far?"

"The radius of the Earth, plus a few kilometres. That sounds . . . absurd, doesn't it? *Ha. I am* an astronaut. I know these things. I stepped out of the Grid high above London. To get my bearings. See where I was. Pick a landing spot. But—"

Harriet held the glass of water to Dana's lips. "But I didn't just hang there, weightless in space. Of all people, I should have guessed this. It was like being dropped from a plane. A few seconds, and I'm falling fast."

"So you went back in?"

"Yes. Back into the Grid. I'm used to judging co-moving distances. I can dock a Soyuz at the iss with one hand tied behind my back." She paused to clear her throat. "But it seems the Grid conserves momentum. I exited at the same velocity relative to the Earth that I entered." She managed another smile. "Logical, really."

"Where did you come out?"

"Underground. In a tunnel. What are the chances?" She held up her rebandaged fingers. "All things considered, I could have come off a lot worse. I'll just have to give up the piano lessons."

Jack smiled. He was beginning to relax. "How long have you been here? In the office?"

"I'm not sure. I didn't come straight here. I had no desire to be shot at again. So I waited. And watched. I stole some clothes from a shop on Brick Lane. Used the Grid to step through the window, late at night. Pushed them out through the letterbox. Took money for food from the till. Stepped through the Grid and out again, then put them on. Though I think I might be getting over this whole walking around naked thing."

She looked at her hand. "I didn't know where else to go. I don't know where you live. No one but you knows I'm here. I watched and waited. I thought you'd come back, but after a day or so I began to doubt you ever would. My fingers needed attention. Every time I stepped through the Grid the wounds would appear again, fresh. I finally decided to risk searching the office. I thought I'd be able to find something helpful. A telephone number, an address. A clue to where you were. But they'd cleared the place out."

"We thought you'd go and see Daniel Novák. At Jodrell."

"Well, it's not like it didn't cross my mind. I've known Daniel for years. He was there throughout the LBE adventure. Daniel would do anything for me, I know that. But Daniel ultimately reports to Gabe, and I couldn't risk that. If I'd gone to Daniel, I'd have effectively been handing myself back to the people I escaped from in the first place."

"You could have just disappeared. Taken enough money to set yourself up somewhere. No jail could hold you, even if they did catch you."

Dana's voice took on a more serious tone. "Jack, I'm not invincible. You can't step into the Grid if you're unconscious. Or dead."

She tried to lift herself onto one elbow. "And anyway – just disappearing would be, well, *selfish*. More than that – it'd be a monumental abrogation of my responsibilities. The Grid presents both a challenge and an opportunity. For us, *and* for the Grid. It's a unique repository of information, but it's also a vessel, one designed to sail a very particular sea. I'm in a unique position – I *am* unique – and I think I now know what needs to be done."

She held her bandaged fingers.

"In fact, I'm *sure* of it."

Dana had come to a realisation: *even an idea can die.*

Perhaps the idea had a name. A clutch of letters that uniquely expressed it, pinned it down like a rare butterfly, caught in a killing jar and preserved in language. It had a referent, it was marked out in the vocabulary that described the known territory of ideaspace, the hills and valleys and hedgerows of the human experience we had explored and named, and in doing so, tamed.

But what if that idea was spoken in the unfamiliar lilt of a dying language? Eventually, there would be no one left to hear and understand it; and then, finally, no one left to speak it. It would become entirely internalised once more, retreating to a place where, without a name, it would be just a vague inexpressible notion, a step away from being forgotten entirely.

Or perhaps the idea was stillborn: listen, if you can, to all those great songs that have floated off the top of a musician's head before they managed to get to the piano. Read, if you will, all those beautiful sonnets that came to the poet just as she was about to drift off to sleep. Gaze, if you wish, at the incomparable paintings lost for want of a brush within reach. These are the ideas that you assure yourself you'll remember in the morning, but never do. These are the ideas that die.

We treat them all with reckless abandon, these great ideas. Because they come to us all too easily we tend not to value them; new ones will always race in on their heels, unbidden. But age will dull our imagination, the fuel that used to drive the engine of our mind ever forward will run thin, and the fires of youth will fade to a familiar, comforting glow.

The ideas the human race are capable of having are the culmination of a project 3.8 billion years in the making; that is how long Nature has laboured to craft the minds with which we now think to circumscribe the known and draw down the unknown. Our minds, and all they contain, are our greatest evolutionary achievement.

Consider all the great ideas the human race has ever had. Those that have pushed us outward, inspired us to conquer the unknown and celebrated us at our best; those that have delved deep inside us, revealed who we are and brought justice to those who see us at our worst. All those notions: the music, the art, the literature, the science, the philosophy, the inarticulate growlings from which the very weft of our culture is made.

This is our legacy.

The Sun shall die. It is inevitable. Like the Little Match Girl, every five seconds it consumes a billion tonnes of fuel, cannibalising itself to keep warm. Eventually it will run out, and when it does, its family of planets will cool and die. Not even the Earth will last for ever.

We are a small stuttering candle in a cosmic immensity in which life is precious and fleeting, but we need not slip quietly into that bottomless well of a forgotten eternity like so many unremembered cultures before us.

Consider the lost creations of alien races we will never know. Think of all those civilisations that have already risen, flowered into something strange and exotic and beautiful, then vanished with no one to mark their passing, no record of their ever being but bones and dust and broken machines marooned on worlds with no name. Was their fleeting light not worth preserving?

Cultures do not last for ever. People perish; entire races perish. Are we going to allow the barbarians of time to sack the priceless treasures of the minds we have wrought? Can we allow the human race to step from the stage of the Milky Way like so many wise and mature civilisations have before it, those forgotten forerunner races whose art and science have vanished as if they had never existed?

What kind of future is *that*?

It was a barren and empty future, and Dana refused to allow the long and empty millennia to cover humanity in the dust of forgetting. We will not go willingly into that ultimate oblivion; somehow, we and all we are must endure.

Dana's voice was quiet but assured. "Listen. The Grid is an *opportunity*. It's a chance to jump into the next stage of human evolution, one that will take us from our cradle here on Earth and out to the stars."

Harriet, Jack and Nixon were at something of a loss.

Dana coughed. "The future that people like Daniel were raised on? It's a schoolboy's daydream. We won't make the journey to the stars in the swept-wing rockets of science fiction; we won't make the journey in physical form at all. Our lives are too short, the speed of light too slow, and the Universe too large.

"But if we shed our parochial notions of physical form, make the journey we *can* – by joining the Grid. Everything that is vital and important and that makes us uniquely *us* will come with us. Isn't this precisely what we have wanted, ever since we looked up and saw the stars for the first time, and wondered what they were?

"The Grid is here to save us, just as it has so many other barely remembered races far more accomplished and civilised than us humans. I am not going to allow our one chance of joining them as part of this, this emergent galactic mind, pass us by.

"It's not going to be easy. We may open ourselves – we *will* open ourselves – to new and dangerous ideas, but we have done so before and we have survived. What's more, we have *prospered* – we are adaptable, and we will continue. Maybe not as we are now, not in a fashion we might recognise, but as we will be, the creatures we will become.

"Our *ideas* – for they are us, and we them – have been presented with a means to transcend our physical form. This is our chance to grant immortality to every thought we ever thought that was worth the thinking. We, and all we are, do not deserve to be forgotten.

"This may be our only opportunity. And we should take it."

She let her head fall back onto the folded towel. Dana had been mentally preparing the speech, if only to convince herself, ever since she had discovered what lay at the centre of the Grid.

She was just unsure if every word was truly her own, and had not been planted there in her mind by some alien agency; grown from a strange seed not of this Earth, one first cultivated many millennia ago on a charnel-house planet countless light years distant.

A part of her mind that was not hers released a cascade of endorphins. *Are our best ideas ever truly our own?*

"And how exactly are we going to do that?" Jack asked, not unreasonably.

Dana closed her eyes and smiled. "I have a plan," she said, waving her bandaged hand. "And I'll need your help."

Word Ladder

MOON

HERE

To solve the puzzle, move from the bottom step of the ladder to the top, at each stage changing only one letter while creating a new word and leaving the order of the other letters unchanged.

BLACK BOX THINKING

Dana laid out her plan.

It was ambitious; it was dangerous. It involved untested technology.

And first of all, Dana had to return to the Moon.

They didn't know if they were currently under surveillance. They didn't know how much time they had. But they *did* know how she was going to do it.

No rockets required.

Jack and Harriet had it all worked out.

Jack's laptop was open, resting on his messenger bag on his now otherwise empty desk. "I've adjusted a few parameters." He stood back from his screen to address them, and Nixon could see that smile, the one that lit up his face when he'd come up with something even he thought was exceptionally clever. "As you remember, the Grid does not reach as far as the Moon. If it did, Dana could step in here and out there, ignoring a few technical provisos I'll get to later." Jack waved away some imaginary inconvenience with the back of his hand. "As far as observations go, and from our own analysis, we think it reaches out around a third of the distance, taking an average radius and ignoring the fact that the Grid seems to have no precisely defined limit – it gets somewhat threadbare around the edges. There are long extrusions that radially extend out further, each with side filaments, just like suburban strip development along new arterial roads."

Jack tapped a key twice.

"But *now* – now the Grid thinks the Earth is five times larger than it really is, around 63,700 kilometres. It has adjusted itself accordingly. It now reaches well beyond the Moon."

Harriet had a hand on Jack's shoulder. "You make it sound almost easy."

"That's just one translation, though. There are other factors we need to take into account. Rotation – I've matched the Earth's rotation to the synodic lunar orbital period. The Grid is now stationary with respect to the Moon, rotating around the centre of the Earth once every 29.5 days."

Though the relative positions of Daedalus Base, the Moon and the Earth – and Hoxton Square – could be plotted with a high degree of confidence, Jack was fully aware of the accuracy required. An error of one ten-thousandth of a decimal place would still translate to an offset of several metres, and that could be enough to place Dana outside Daedalus Base entirely. A misjudgement of even a metre could still place her in a wall or with her feet embedded in the metal floor.

Jack pursed his lips and raised his eyebrows. "There are also a few, uh, other complications. The Moon's orbit is far from perfectly circular. The Earth–Moon system does not rotate around the centre of the Earth, but around the pair's barycentre – a point 4,641 kilometres from the centre of the Earth, offset towards the Moon. The Moon's rotational axis is tilted by 5.4 degrees to the ecliptic. The Earth is also tilted by 23.44 degrees. There's libration. We have local deformations of the crust; even the Moon is not inflexible. We have – I'm sure we have other things I've not thought of."

Dana was now sitting up, her back against the wall under the shelf that still supported their early experiments with the 3D printer. She held up the hand with missing fingers, wrapped in the clean bandage. "There are always things one hasn't thought of."

Jack continued. "Now, this of course produces a problem at this end. Though now reaching as far as the Moon – which is stationary with regard to the Grid – here it's moving at well over six hundred miles an hour, relative to the surface of the Earth." He looked over at Dana. "That's nearly a thousand kilometres an hour in European. It'd be like stepping onto a moving escalator."

"But somewhat faster," Harriet observed.

"So this would be best avoided. Now, the Grid does not need to – *spin up*, as it were. It's a purely geometric adjustment. Numbers. The Grid has no inertia. So here's what I suggest: you go in, *then* we make the adjustments – spin up the Grid, in effect – and *then* you exit."

Dana shrugged. "Makes sense."

"Harriet has checked my calculations, I've rechecked them. We can set up a trigger. I won't need to recalculate everything once you're in. Everything will happen automatically."

Harriet gave a wan smile. "Destination: Moon."

"We agree on a certain period before you step out. A matter of minutes, with a margin of error for any unforeseen delays. We will probably need far less than that – just the time it takes to press a button. Once we do, you will immediately be outside the Oxbow, so there will be no way we can see you with the Depthcharges. You will be travelling blind. All you will have is the coordinates relative to the Grid that tell you where it intersects Daedalus Base – your point of exit.

"Using Daedalus' CCTV as your eyes you may be able to get views of the interior, but that all depends on whether the cams are available to the Web. That may be enough for you to pick out a clear spot to exit the Grid. If the cameras are down, or behind a firewall, you'll see nothing.

"All that being equal, with luck you will exit at zero kilometres an hour, or as close to it as we can get."

Dana nodded. "Inside Daedalus Base."

"Without a spacesuit. Or clothes of any kind."

"I hope they've lowered the blinds. Thank you, Jack, Harriet. Nixon."

"No problem." Harriet squinted and blinked to hold back tears. Dana had taken so many risks already, and was about to gladly take another. She had the Right Stuff, in industrial quantities.

Dana let her head fall back to rest on the towel. "I know the place well. Daedalus Base is around 200 square metres. That's our target area. We have less leeway vertically – around three and a half metres, max. The base is not empty space – there are benches, chairs, desks, equipment. Random pieces of portable kit that could be anywhere. I'll need to come out occupying as small a volume as I can. Foetal position."

Harriet moved over to Jack's laptop and he stepped back to allow her to skim the keyboard. She brought up a list of names and dates. "Information, courtesy of the Count. Daedalus Base is currently staffed. Two astronauts. There's another three at the crash site. There will be a change-over when the next Korean *Jeonlyeong* shuttle docks. That's in eight days. It may be advantageous to make our move sometime before then."

Dana nodded. "I can't take anything with me, so I'm going to need to improvise as soon as I arrive."

"Charm, or a weapon?"

"I can be very charming when I have no clothes on."

Harriet smiled. "You will have the element of surprise. No one will expect someone to step out of nowhere. You also know the base inside out. Local knowledge."

Jack picked up the briefing. "Now, here's the next problem. The only way information can travel through the Grid is in a mind. In a symbolic representation on a biological substrate mapped mathematically onto the Grid. If you can't take clothes in, you're not going to be able to take a data stick, your laptop or even a sheet of paper."

"I've just realised why I come out so hungry. The contents of my stomach must get left behind."

"*Riiight.* That would explain the mess on your clothes."

"Now I'm guessing, no offence, that even a highly trained astronaut can't commit billions of lines of code to memory."

"You guess right."

"So, short of tattooing it on your body, we need outside help here. This is not something that can be input with a few hundred keystrokes once you're up there, like some vintage Sinclair Spectrum game . . . though you'd be surprised how much information you can shoehorn into one of those. So, fifteen minutes after you arrive, Daniel should transmit an Oxbow from Jodrell Bank."

Dana looked at Jack dubiously. "And how are you going to persuade him to do that?"

"I'm ahead of you. Jodrell is run by the University of Manchester's School of Physics and Astronomy. Now, it just so happens that the School of Physics and Astronomy use several custom-written software applications to process the huge amount of data that the Square Kilometre Array and the ESA's Planck satellite produce. And—"

"And let me guess: Intelligencia wrote that software." Dana doffed an imaginary hat.

Jack spread his hands. "It wasn't called Intelligencia back then, but yes. I wrote that software. And I left the back door open – more or less on a whim. Call it professional curiosity. I thought it might be interesting to occasionally peek in at science, live, as it happens."

Harriet and Nixon were grinning.

"What? I'm an astronomy nerd. What would *you* do?"

"But—" Dana's mind was chewing on something. "This still assumes we have some kind of connection. A way in. After the White leaks and the business with the LBE, the exobiology systems, and pretty much Jodrell Bank as a whole, are behind a firewall. They have a dedicated array of cooled servers down in the basement. I've seen them. They're self-sufficient – no off-site data storage. Back door or not, we'd still need someone *in* there – actually physically there – to unlock it for us from the inside."

"*Correct.*" Jack didn't seem fazed. In fact, he looked like he was enjoying himself. "So we need to get Daniel, our man on the inside, to do something for us – while not knowing what he's doing for us. How? Email is out of the question. The encrypted Skype channel is only encrypted if you're not NASA or the intelligence agency. We need to ensure that there's no paperless paper trail. So, logically, there's only one way to send this message – analogue. Something that no one would think to intercept. Something that would not attract attention, even if it was left out in the open."

Jack lifted his head back and closed his eyes like a magician presenting his coup de grâce. Though everything of obvious importance had been cleared out of the office, they had missed something. The thing Jack had come back for.

Still standing on its stencilled box, the Typex had been overlooked in all its functional, antique charm; a souvenir of another age, a tech start-up's inspirational desk ornament, it had been hidden in plain sight. Jack stepped over and slapped the side of the box affectionately. "You, my old chum, are about to be pressed back into service. I hope you've not forgotten what you can do."

The Typex, of course, did not reply.

Jack had read the Daedalus transcripts. Though it seemed counter-intuitive, if he indulged the LBE's insistence that there was nothing in the Universe but matter and movement, then everything could be considered, in some small way, to be alive. If consciousness was simply an emergent property of complexity, its existence wasn't an either/or, binary state; it must shade from what we would normally consider self-consciousness – *us,* and a few select hominids and cetaceans – down through the merely conscious minds of the animal kingdom, and then deeper still, into the biological, the chemical and finally the supposedly inert realm of the purely physical. By this sliding definition, Jack thought that he could be persuaded that a plant, or a virus – or even a mineral, a stone, perhaps – might display some rudimentary form of life. And if a *stone* can be considered to be alive . . .

Perhaps, unbeknownst to the other biological occupants of the room – Jack, Nixon, Dana and Harriet – a very basic intelligence, so elementary as to almost not warrant the name, but there nonetheless, shivered along the copper wires, skipped across soldered neuronal contacts and thrilled through the 150,738,274,937,250 unique possible states of the Typex's rudimentary synaptic web.

Jack had a way to write his message, one that Daniel and perhaps only Daniel would understand. He picked out the first three rotors from a possible seven. He knew one was missing – there was an empty space for an eighth. The brass wheels, around which the twenty-six letters of the alphabet were engraved in a functional sans, had a satisfying weight and solidity he no longer associated with the ethereal machine code of which he and Harriet were masters. Milled and polished by skilled craftsmen, these resonant objects bore witness to their function in their form.

Jack pressed them into their slots. The message he wanted to encode was short: a web address. Something that would point to something else:

the Oxbow. He knew Dana and her friends would then do the rest.

He just needed a delivery mechanism.

One small crate of old paperbacks and manuals remained by the door, as if it'd been left behind by mistake. Jack reached in and randomly lifted one out. He blew the dust from its spine and read the title. *Perfect.* What else?

Jack walked back into the conference room. A postcard had been left on the empty expanse of the glass tabletop like a scrap of forgotten confetti from a giant's wedding. Kazimir Malevich's *Black Square*, 1915; the one he had picked up in the Tate Modern. It was a perfect stand-in for the Intelligencia logo. It left a shiny rectangle of dust-free tabletop behind as he picked it up.

Nixon had followed him in. "We *post* him the link?"

Jack shook the postcard clean and coughed. "Why not? Harriet – you wouldn't happen to have a first-class stamp?"

Harriet slid open the drawer of her desk. "Actually, I do. Seems they left a few other things. In fact, you have a choice." She held up two small perforated sheets. "The Queen in profile, or Wallace and Gromit in *A Grand Day Out.*"

Jack heard Dana laugh from her position propped against the wall in the other room, and his spirits lifted just a fraction.

Given what they planned to do, there was only one possible choice.

DAN DARE'S
EAGLE CLUB

Certificate
of
Membership

This is to certify that

Daniel Novak

at a meeting of the Editorial Board held at 43 Shoe Lane in the County of London at 11 o'clock in the forenoon of the 21st day of April, 1954 was elected to Membership of the Eagle Club.

Editor

RAY-GUN DIPLOMACY

Daniel Novák hefted the Manila package that had been sitting on his desk all morning. It was the size and weight of a paperback. He had no memory of ordering anything online, and there was no return address on the reverse. Picking up a pair of scissors, he cut the parcel tape at one end and slid out a copy of Carl Sagan's *Contact*. The cover design and the nostalgic scent of foxed paper told him it was second-hand. A postcard had been placed inside the front cover. A black square on a white ground. It was obviously a photograph of a canvas – the black paint was subtly crazed with the lines of age and the white surround shaded to buff towards the edges. The perfect pristine white of the card itself provided the equivalent of the gallery wall, an antiseptic purity that served to celebrate the painting's imperfections.

He read the small text printed in the bottom left-hand corner.

Kazimir Malevich
Black Square, 1915
Oil on canvas, 32x32 inches

Where had he seen a black square recently . . . ?

He turned it over. There was a short message in plain English followed by a sequence of seemingly meaningless five-letter words written in small neat capitals. The five-letter words were obviously code. The message above read: 'Next time, drop in for tea.'

Interesting.

Daniel liked a puzzle. But who would bother to send him one in a book? If there was anything important to relate, would not email be easier? He absently put down his coffee. He was now utterly intrigued. The sender obviously appreciated his penchant for mysteries.

It took him all of twenty-five minutes to find the solution.

He had been a member of *Dan Dare's Eagle Club* in his youth, and their free code wheel and badge had sparked an interest in numbers that had set him on his career trajectory as surely as a guided missile launched from the *Anastasia*. He knew it was an affectation, one that he was somewhat embarrassed about, but he still carried the membership card with him in his wallet.

The five-letter words were in Typex code, or more accurately, Typex running a simulation of a German Enigma code. Each encoding and decoding required an initialisation vector – a choice of rotors and two sets of three characters that gave the ring setting and the initial start position. Six letters in all. Daniel flicked through the novel, wondering if a word had been underlined somewhere. It seemed to be unmarked. Sagan had five letters. Carl had four. *Contact* had seven . . . unless one dropped in for t . . . dropped a t.

"*Jack, Jack Jack.* What have you got for me here?" Daniel smiled to himself and luxuriated in a familiar mental tickle as the pieces of the puzzle began to fit snugly into place.

Daniel didn't happen to have his own Typex, and he couldn't really ask the staff at Bletchley Park to help him in this trifling matter. *Online emulators?* Of course. He scooted his chair over to the nearest keyboard and screen. Google. Yep. There was even a choice.

There was one piece of the puzzle missing. The rotors could be selected from a set of five, seven, or even eight. He had resigned himself to running through all the possible combinations when he found that the very first one he tried – the default position – was the one Jack had used. Daniel wondered if this was due to laziness or a desire not to make the code too hard to crack. What he didn't know was that Jack hadn't managed to get the machine working reliably with any other setting.

So what did the message say? Daniel pencilled it out in the blank area on the front of the postcard. A URL, the full stops spelt out in the manner of an old telegram. Daniel booted a browser and typed in the address. A circle spun, indicating that something was loading.

An animation of the *Anastasia*, Dan Dare's silver spaceship, shot from left to right across the screen. It looked like it had been lifted directly from the comic. Letters spun out from its exhaust, red against the starry backdrop, then arranged themselves across the bottom of the image.

CONGRATULATIONS DAN! YOU BROKE THE CODE!

A flying saucer hove into view, on which sat a green alien with a bulbous head. The *Anastasia* executed a few crudely animated loop-the-loops around him, then released a glowing fireball which hit the saucer, dislodging the creature and sending him spinning out of the frame. He waved his arms in exaggerated distress like a cut-out paper doll.

THE MEKON HAS BEEN DEFEATED!
THE ALIEN INVASION HAS BEEN REPELLED –
FOR NOW!

The *Anastasia* performed one more victory loop and whooshed off, top left.

THE GRATEFUL PEOPLE OF EARTH
THANK YOU FOR YOUR HEROIC ROLE
IN SAVING THE PLANET!

HUZZAH AND WHOOPEE!

Daniel sat back, wondering if anything else was about to happen, but that seemed to be it. Jack's animation, though somewhat basic, was utterly charming.

Daniel took a screen grab and printed it out, folded it and put it into his wallet next to his *Eagle Club* card. He'd have to thank Jack the next time he saw him in person.

Behind the Trojan, a small packet had installed itself on the Jodrell mainframe. It was a digital toe in a digital door, which was now held open just a crack.

IN AND OUT

Jumping from the back of a moving bus . . .

Jack recalled, as a teenager, stepping from the back of a Routemaster, skateboard in hand. The bus appeared to be moving at the speed of a leisurely afternoon stroll, but as he landed the ground shot away from under him, the impact jarring his calf and throwing him sideways with such force that he cracked his elbow on the kerb before instinctively putting out a hand to right himself. His board shot out into the moving traffic, under three cars without a collision, hit the far kerb and bounced up and over to lie, rocking on its top, on the pavement opposite. He crossed five lanes to retrieve it, hand stinging and pockmarked with gravel, his elbow twisted and scuffed with road rash.

This, he reasoned, couldn't be any more dangerous than that, could it?

Daedalus Base, though fitted with cameras in every room except for the showers and lavatory, was only linked to the Earth via a relay satellite in a halo orbit around Lagrange L2. From there, it was a one-and-a-half-second journey at the speed of light to Jodrell. A five- to ten-second timelapsed CCTV image from a tired camera in low-resolution black-and-white with blobs of over-exposed orange whenever someone in a spacesuit was present would be all Dana would have to go on. She had discussed every eventuality at length with Jack and Harriet, but they had agreed: even with the back door open, the available information did not, for all intents and purposes, provide her with a real-time view of the whereabouts of Daedalus Base's occupants, fixtures and fittings.

Having allowed for the likely drift along the axial spin of the Earth, a spot a half-metre from the ground near the west bulkhead had been chosen, the optimistic precision of which she knew was unlikely to be achievable. If she appeared outside the base, she'd have no suit to protect her – a naked woman, asphyxiated and freeze-dried, falling dead into the lunar dust. That'd present the crew with a mystery to solve, all right. She wondered if she'd make a decent-sized crater.

It transpired that along with the door key Nixon had been given a tidy sum by way of advance compensation, the final amount of which was yet to be agreed. It was more than they would otherwise have earned in three months. Though their equipment had not been returned, via Jack's sleight of hand they still had the one laptop and pair of Depthcharges.

On the second day Nixon fielded a call from the landlord, who seemed to have been apprised of the situation already. He came over, offered a few pleasantries, ignored Nixon's crutches, didn't check the locked toilet and most importantly didn't suggest that they leave, or otherwise complain about the situation too loudly. They suspected that, like them, he had been offered a sizeable sum for his inconvenience, and as far as he was concerned that meant that they were more than welcome to stay. He had given the door and the room a perfunctory once-over, and hadn't even questioned their story about the damaged skylight, simply looking up and making a note on his phone.

They pegged sheets up to cover the windows, wiped the dust from the tables and the kitchenette's surfaces, and found that they now only had a single crate to sit on.

"You could plot the trajectory of this company in chairs," Nixon reflected. He drew an imaginary chart in the air. "At launch, a dozen or so crates. Then we move up to the glory days of four fancy recliners – and now, we're down to just one crate between us."

Clients had been apprised of the situation, and work that couldn't be postponed or dropped altogether had been farmed out to others. Jack had booked himself into the Old Street Travelodge for the duration, and though they'd offered to get Dana anything she wanted so that she could leave incognito – a wig, an overcoat, a burka – she'd declined, asking only for a couple of sets of clothes from the Urban Outfitters on Shoreditch High Street and that the fridge be stocked with food and the toilet equipped with toilet paper. Though none of them felt completely safe or at ease here, by default rather than design it remained their base of operations.

They set up an inflatable bed for her under the shelf. Her hand was healing, and besides, she reasoned, if her plan worked she wouldn't be here for much longer.

On the third day, Jack received a text notification. A file had been downloaded. Daniel had taken the bait. After a little careful exploration and testing, he could confirm that the package had been installed – the back door was open. Jack had access to all the routines he'd written out of idle curiosity, just because he could, all those years ago.

The Daedalus relief crew were on their way. There was no reason to delay any further.

In and out. Simple.

Just like jumping from the back of a moving bus.

Dana stood in the middle of the empty room. The parquet was strewn with foil food containers and unwashed laundry. On the shelf above her makeshift bed, plastic renditions of the 19th Count, XX and sundry other creatures of mind rather than matter seemed to watch as she stepped from foot to foot then shook her arms to loosen any stiffness in her joints, like a nervous sprinter at the starting line.

Harriet was again in awe of her strength of purpose. Here was someone who hadn't spun out idle days waiting for the world to come to her. She had gone out and found it, and more – here was someone who had walked on the Moon, come into contact with an alien from the stars, and was now about to make another journey that would, if everything went according to plan, take her even further.

Jack had the laptop set up on the remaining crate just in front of her. He was sitting cross-legged behind it, Harriet and Nixon sitting on either side. They looked up at her, and for a moment she imagined they were her acolytes in some cultish ceremony of which she was the High Priestess.

"Ready?"

"As I'll ever be. Are they here, with us?"

Jack gave her the glasses. "You can't take them with you, but I think it's appropriate that you should be wearing them today. Take a look. You tell us."

She pulled them on and adjusted the strap to fit. Looking up and around the room, she could see that there were seven present, not four. Behind Jack, Harriet and Nixon stood a perfectly spotless white aristocrat, a dazzle-ship man-machine and a manga waif with pink hair and a borrowed face.

She raised her hand to shoulder height and waved a small wave. The Count touched a white-gloved hand to the brim of his hat. Girl 21 lowered her head, and a face that was not her own looked awkwardly away. XX raised a small flag with a crescent moon on it up a short pole, where it fluttered in an absent breeze.

Dana looked back down at the three seated on the floor. "We're all here. Let's do it."

Jack looked at his screen. "OK, on the count of three. See you on the other side, Dana."

"I'm counting on it."

"One. Two—"

Jack pressed a key.

Dana folded herself out of this world and into another.

The Depthcharge glasses fell through vacated space. Harriet reached forward and caught them just before they hit the floor. Her clothes fluttered to the ground around a pair of small footprints.

In the Grid, the idea that was Dana counted down the previously agreed number of seconds. Somewhere that had a 'where' to it, Jack was rotating the Grid in an inertialess translation through a fictive three-dimensional Euclidean space.

She could see something. A timestamp rolled in the bottom left-hand corner of her vision, and a number of other values – air pressure, gamma-ray count, Greenwich Mean Time – were visible down the right. Viewed from a high vantage, sapped of colour and shot across with screen artefacts, she could see a small room. A familiar room – Daedalus Base's main hub.

Time's up.

She stepped out.

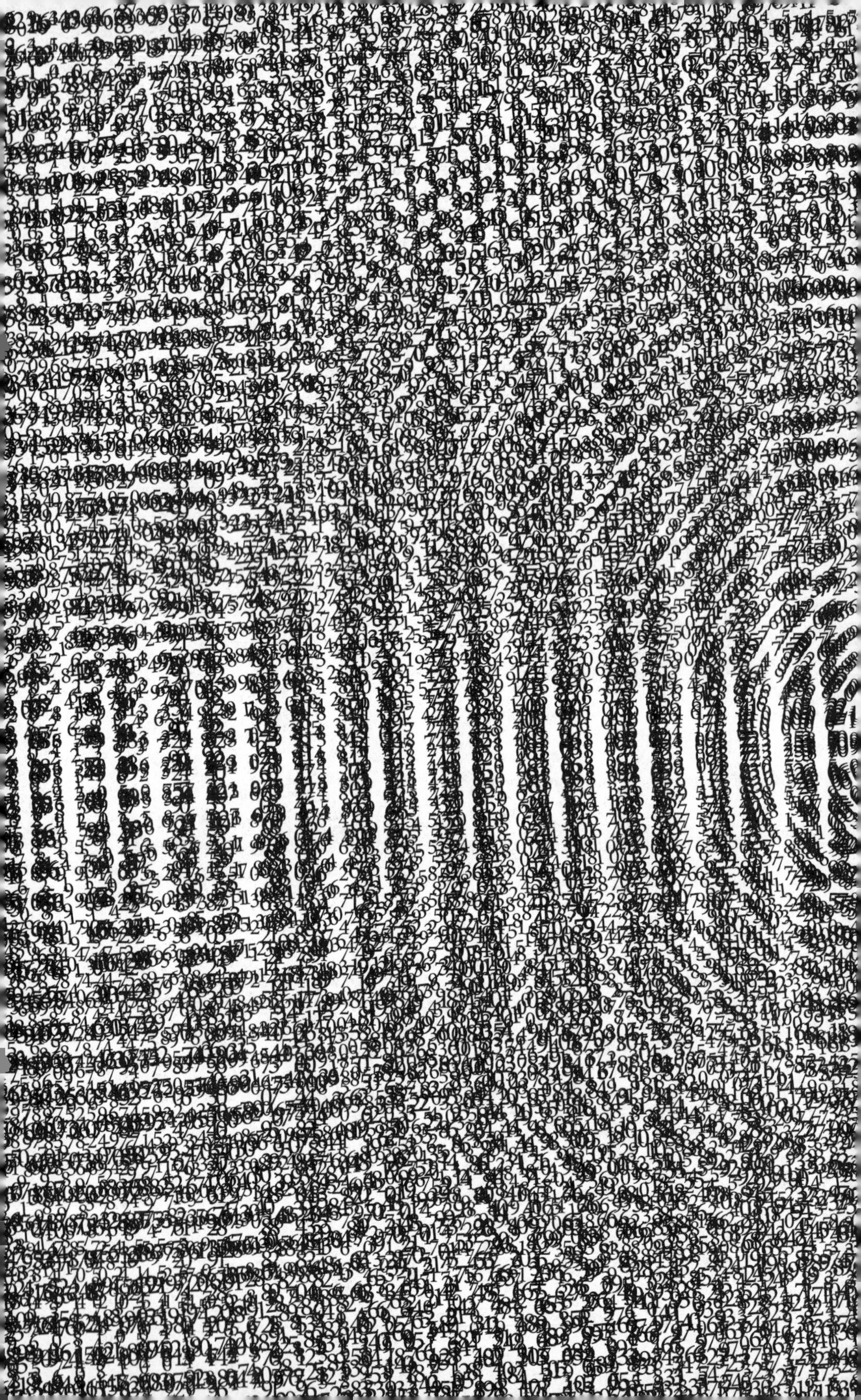

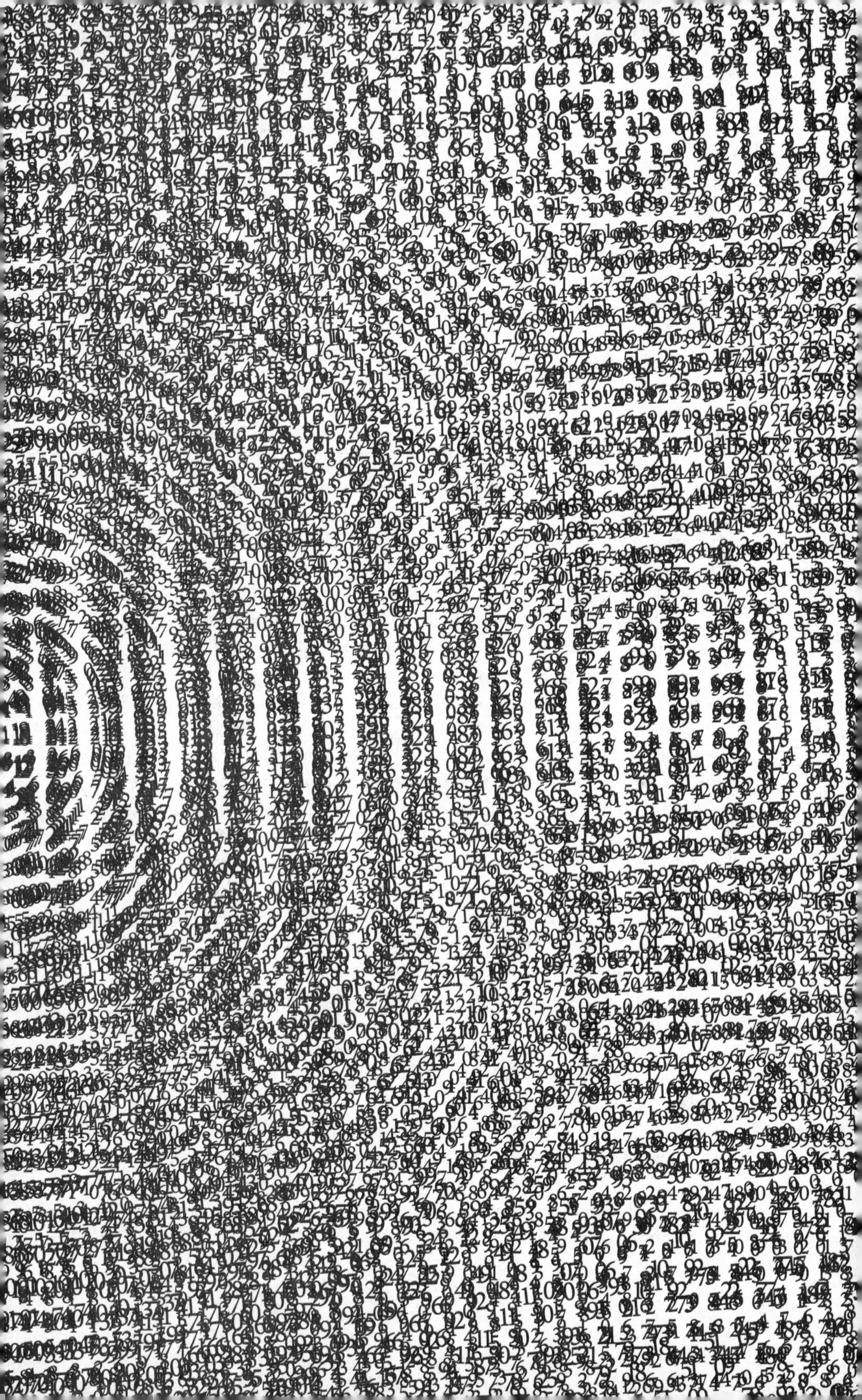

RETURN TO DAEDALUS

Her watery jpegged vision cleared immediately. The viewpoint shifted and colour instantaneously filled out the details of Daedalus' observation hub as light again hit her retinas. The familiar fug of recycled air and the stale tang of body odour filled her first breath. In contrast to her disembodied, non-localised existence within the Grid, she once more occupied a definite location.

She fell a leisurely twenty centimetres to the ground in the reduced lunar gravity, rolled to absorb the small lateral velocity and came up against a stainless-steel cabinet beneath a desk. The calculations had been almost perfect. No more lost fingers. No feet buried in the floor plates. No unpredictably positioned chair embedded through her pelvis.

She was in.

Sound—? Stepping from the Grid back into reality, the first noises she always noticed were those that fill the echo chamber of the human body. Filtered out through familiarity, they had to be silenced and then return again to be noticed: the pulsing rush of blood in her ears, the sudden weight of her limbs, the sense of possessing a discrete body that occupied a specific volume of three-dimensional space, at the top of which a set of sense organs were located – eyes, nose, ears. The human body, when you were forced to think about it in such abstract terms, was a strange and wonderful thing. Just how *alien* are *we?*

The hub section itself was no larger than a mobile home. Like all such off-world structures she had known, it was functional rather than homely. From her low crouching position she could see the larger portion of the curved bulkhead in which three airtight doors were set, the semicircular lintels low enough that even she had to stoop to pass under them. Closer by was the minimalist canteen area, from whose stainless-steel counters perforated vertical supports arched up to form a low, curved ceiling. At the apex a circular panel glowed a soft milky white, the low light levels mandated for rest periods during the two weeks of lunar night.

Through the windows, reflected from the telescope's mirrors high enough up the crater rim to catch the sun, needle-sharp reflections dusted the walls with prismatic rainbow dots like a disco ball. A diffuse glow of zodiacal light extended up from the horizon and along the ecliptic: backscattered photons bouncing off space dust and washing out the stars to the west. All else was black against black; the true night of an airless world.

She checked her cauterised fingers. They looked the same as they had a few moments ago, back on Earth; the days that had elapsed since her previous trip through the Grid had been enough for them to heal sufficiently.

Daedalus Base had been Dana's home for twelve six-week terms of duty, and one unplanned extended stay. She knew every room, every corridor, every surface, every control interface, every sticky door hinge, every recalcitrant drawer. It was compact – just the five rooms, the largest being the observation hub cum laboratory in which she now crouched, the smallest the shower and lavatory. Between these two was the recreation room and crew quarters.

The larger of the modular spaces were built from flushed and scrubbed fuel tanks; the central hub, from which they all spread like the bulbous spokes of an asymmetric rimless wheel, was the original lander. The whole arrangement perched twenty metres above the rim of Daedalus Crater on the upright main section of a repurposed supply rocket, its base driven deep into the lunar crust. Pressurised and fitted with a lift that provided access to the storage dome at ground level, this was also the crew's access to the main airlock and the lunar surface.

Parked some twenty metres away near the seismometer arrays was the four-person lunar rover with oversized wheels that made it look like a monster truck. A second unpressurised rover, equipped with a crane and winch, was used to transport equipment around the crater floor under the canopy of mirrors. Nicknamed the 'flatbed', like everything else here it was practical rather than elegant.

The elevated position afforded the observation hub, informally known as the Lounge, a magnificent view out over the giant instrument it had been built here to serve – the largest reflecting surface mankind had ever constructed.

Dana had walked beneath the reflectors many times during repair and maintenance jaunts. Like flowers feeding on faint starlight, above her the faceted blooms would imperceptibly be tracking their faces across the heavens as the Moon turned beneath them on its orbit, always facing towards some distant target of astronomical interest, always facing away from the Earth, forever hidden behind the bulk of the Moon itself. Each separate mirror cluster was mounted on a filigree pylon that seemed too flimsy to support it, but was more than strong enough in the one-sixth gravity. You could, with a small feat of imagination, picture yourself walking under a tall forest canopy back home on Earth, albeit a forest where the treetops were made of lunar silicates fused into glass, the trunks of aluminium and the roots of sheathed cabling.

In some places the mirror clusters were close to the ground, barely above her head; in others, some hundred and fifty metres above the uneven surface, arranged to create a perfect parabola above the less than mathematically perfect crater. Daedalus Base personnel grew accustomed to traversing this underworld, fixing, adjusting; it was criss-crossed with rover tyre tracks and bootprints that recorded every excursion they made, like Ordovician trace fossils which rain would never wash away. Pausing under the reflectors to take advantage of the shade they afforded from the harsh sunlight, Dana had thought that the serried shadows that polka-dotted the crater floor were of the blackest black, like the holes from a childhood memory of The Beatles' *Yellow Submarine*.

She brought her mind back to the present. There were two other astronauts on board; this she knew. In the thirty seconds since her arrival, she assumed they would have made something of a noise had they seen her, but all she could hear was the low hum of the air-circulation fans and a subsonic buzz from the fluorescents. She was, of course, unarmed and naked.

She had considered simply making herself known to the crew, but had not been able to come up with a plausible explanation for her presence. *I hid in the EVA suit closet for a month.* Unlikely. *I landed in an unscheduled ship that has since lifted off again, then let myself in without a front door key, all without appearing on the external cam or radar.* Somewhat implausible. And then she'd need to explain the purpose of her visit. She could only imagine how that might go.

No, she would have to do this alone. All she needed was enough time to access a computer terminal, lock in a solid link to Jodrell and upload an Oxbow. No big ask, really.

A voice.

Marshall O'Dell. The measured, deep tones were unmistakable.

No reply. He seemed to be talking to himself in his familiar sing-song lilt. If Marshall was here for a two-week tour of duty, it was very likely that the other crew member was either Halley Pierce or Chris Breckenridge. Halley she knew reasonably well from training; Chris was a newcomer, a veteran of the International Space Station whom she had only met a couple of times at press meet-and-greets. They would be on US Central Time – for them, it was now 1.05 AM. Most likely Halley, or Chris, would be asleep. The other three would be at the crash site.

So, Dana – how do you disable a five-eleven ex-judo instructor with nothing but what you can lay your hands on in a lunar facility no larger than a Manhattan apartment? From her crouched position, she could see Marshall's familiar close-cropped hair and three-day stubble reflected in the acrylic casing of a wall-mounted display screen. He was wearing regulation loose-fitting night clothes: leggings fastened at the waist and a long-sleeved T-shirt. He was microwaving something she couldn't see. He pressed a few buttons, then jogged off along the short connecting corridor to the crew's personal quarters using the loping low-gravity stride everyone quickly adopted Moonside. Dana heard a small click and the whirr of a fan. She had lived here long enough to know that that was the lock on the toilet door and the automatic extractor kicking in.

She stood up. **3:45** on the microwave clock. **3:44.** She reached into the overhead locker above the kitchenette. Yes, it was there, as always. The green plastic box with a white cross on it – the emergency medical kit. She shot a precautionary glance down the corridor to the bathroom beyond, then flipped the lid open. Bandages. Tablets. Miscellaneous diagnostic and therapeutic items. A microbiological test kit. Blood-pressure cuff. Inhalers, pre-loaded with Demerol and Tigan. *Ah.* Here it is. Sedative in a pre-loaded injector.

She tore open the wrapper with her teeth and opened the door to the microwave. **3:31.** A familiar smell rose to greet her, and her stomach made a sound like a small dog: she'd left her last meal on the parquet floor of an office in Hoxton, on the blue and green planet next door. Pea and ham soup, a NASA staple – she must have eaten gallons of this stuff during her stays here. She had no idea if this particular sedative was tasteless, but injected the entire dose, threw the syringe and wrapper into the compactor and closed the microwave's door. The countdown resumed. **3:30.**

She returned to her position behind the steel table. A minute passed, two. The microwave pinged. Marshall returned, whistling. She could hear him pop open the door and pour the soup into a mug, then his footsteps recede back down the corridor. How long until it took effect? They must have briefed her on this during emergency medical training, but if they had she couldn't remember. Five minutes? She dared not wait any longer – each minute of inaction was one less to set up before Jodrell came online.

She raised her head over the tabletop. No one. Just the *wushing* of the air scrubber and the occasional *pang* as the bulkhead contracted due to the falling temperature outside. Through the wraparound window, she had a panoramic view out over the full 2,500 square kilometres of the telescope array, a parabola marked out with 100,000 warm orange spots of reflected zodiacal light set on a pitch-black field, and up near the lip, the bright colourful scatter of the stars of the Milky Way. Her naked reflection overlaid the scene, a silhouette outlined from above and behind by the soft lights of the hub, elegantly stretched by the curve of the glass. The effect was of countless Chinese lanterns in a darkened valley, and it never ceased to enchant her.

She ran over the conversation she'd had only days before with Jack, Harriet and Nixon, the one where she'd outlined what she intended to do.

"The Oxbow is very compact, so it'll only take a matter of seconds to transmit it from Jodrell up to Daedalus via their secure connection. There will be a delay – the signal has to bounce off the satellite at Lagrange – but it'll be at very most three, four seconds. Once there, it will give the DMEn a means to coalesce locally, and I'll have access to both Daedalus Base's systems and the Grid from my location."

Jack had raised an eyebrow. "And then?"

"And then we can make use of the purpose for which Daedalus was secretly designed, a purpose that the conspiracy buffs have been getting their pants in a twist over ever since the facility's existence became an open secret – the one that the governments involved in its construction have always denied.

"Daedalus is not *just* the most powerful telescope ever built. Unlike the huge Lowell Telescope at Jodrell Bank, which can *receive* radio signals from the edge of the observable Universe but was not designed to *transmit* – their smaller Mark VII dish is used for that – Daedalus was, from its conception, designed to have a dual function.

"It can do *both*.

"The dish is also a defence system. It's a near-Earth asteroid deflector. It can focus a beam of reflected sunlight on an object, causing it to outgas volatiles from its surface and thereby alter its orbit. Catch a potential Earthbound asteroid or cometary nucleus far enough in advance, and all that's required is a small nudge at apogee or perigee to ensure it'll miss the Earth by hundreds if not thousands of kilometres.

"This will work whenever the Sun is above the lunar horizon. Which isn't an issue if you have years or even months in which to plan. But our catalogue of near-Earth objects is not exhaustive. We may not have the luxury of advance notice, so they installed something else to cover this eventuality. On the central instrumentation mast is an extremely powerful pulsed laser which can be directed at any incoming object. The larger the reflective dish, the more effective the collimation. And this is one large dish.

"Daedalus is not only a telescope – it's also the most powerful *transmitter* we have ever built, by several orders of magnitude."

Harriet and Jack now saw Dana's plan laid out in its entirety.

Dana had breathed in deeply, as she did by habit before she put on her helmet. "We have an enormous responsibility. *I* have an enormous responsibility. We can't let the Grid hit a final, terminal dead end, here on Earth. But we also can't let the Grid attempt to retransmit itself through some kind of memetic reprogramming of the human race."

She looked directly at Harriet, then Jack; held his gaze. Her face glowed with a luminous intensity. "But we don't *need* to. We have the chance to do what so many other species that have been incorporated *didn't* have the chance to do – send the message on its way without irreparable damage to the sender. If we don't do this, the Grid will inevitably find a way to reproduce anyway, and it won't be pretty."

Jack had looked away. "We've seen the results, up close."

"So we spirit you up there, you press 'send'—"

Dana held her arms high and wide. "And we retransmit the Grid from Daedalus!"

Nixon raised his hand. "I have a question. Does your co-pilot, the Shepherd in your head, have a stake in all this? Who's *really* driving, if you're honest? You or him?"

Dana let her arms fall to her sides. Her palms slapped her thighs. "*Us.* We're in agreement here. Not of two minds, you might say."

Nixon had looked unconvinced. "But you *would* say that."

She pulled a tablet from the dock. The initials DN were marked in tape on the bottom. *Yes.* She flipped open the cover to wake it. Battery: 72%. She typed in her security password. It had not been changed.

Hah!

She now had access to Daedalus' systems. Before she went any further, she needed to attend to some housekeeping. She brought up the internal closed-circuit camera footage, rewound to the point of her first appearance, copied a section from a few moments earlier and pasted it over. She then fast-forwarded to the point Marshall left the lab and repeated the process, this time on a continuous loop. *Seamless.*

It was the first time she had actually seen herself step out of the Grid, and even in this heightened moment of stress it gave her small pause. It was as if . . . a page from an invisible book had been turned to reveal an illustration, flat but curved in a manner that didn't seem possible in three-dimensional space. Then she was there, solid, real, hitting the ground, rolling, coming to a stop behind the table.

The communications antenna was a dish directly above the Hub, permanently pointed up at the relay satellite in a halo orbit around Lagrange L2. She checked the time, top right on her screen.

Down on Earth in the county of Cheshire, England, the Moon would now be rising above the treeline and the disinterested cows; Jodrell Bank would be online in two minutes.

Three hundred and eighty thousand miles, and one and a quarter seconds away, Jack Fenwick pushed open a door.

How long did he have?

How long do any of us have?

TOWARDS A
GRID CONCORDANCE

A WORKING DRAFT

The following concordance lists the known retransmissions of the Signal and the evolution of the Grid, primarily as detailed by Dana Normansson in the full transcripts of the Daedalus Debrief sessions and during additional clarifying sessions specifically on this subject not included in the main transcripts.

This has been supplemented by material covering the outer reaches of the Grid [nicknamed the 'suburbs'] derived from direct observations collated by Amie Charest and Peter Breugel [*A Position-Referenced Grid Catalogue: Documented First-hand Observational Corollaries to the Daedalus Transcripts*]. Material covering the portion interior to the Earth is partly based on original research by the unaffiliated São Paulo AI research team and sections of the confiscated Intelligencia company archive obtained under a Freedom of Information [FOIA] request.

GRID STRUCTURE

Numbering is provisional. Many intermediate steps may be missing. Sections where the Signal is theorised to have been received at more than one location, retransmitted, and subsequently received at a single location and recombined are indicated by a lettered suffix.

There are of course no records for retransmissions that did not later reconnect with the Grid as we presently observe it. This raises the possibility that there are multiple copies of the Grid currently in existence, each branching off at a certain point from the parent. This has been compared [by Rayf Grant in *The Grid Multiplied*, and others] to the separation of a single species into two or more groups by continental drift, and their subsequent divergent evolution.

It is considered unlikely, given the size of the Milky Way galaxy, that we will encounter a second rerouted Grid transmission, though the possibility has been discussed [see for example Gerard Chisholm's article summarising current opinion in the November *New European Biological Bulletin*].

If a second iteration of the Signal were received, much could be learned from an analysis of the differences and similarities.

RECEPTION/ RETRANSMISSION

It is also very likely that many retransmissions of the Signal will never be received, or if received will not be retransmitted. This attenuation of the Signal has not been quantified, but is thought to be high.

It was originally assumed that only technologically advanced civilisations could pick up the Signal, but an analysis of the data suggests that this is actually not the case, and in fact reception is via non-biological means only in a very small proportion of the cases [<7%, Grant]; the more common mode seems to be a direct detection of the Signal via an organ sensitive to electromagnetic waves in the appropriate range. In the jargon of current research, these biologically receptive alien species can "hear radio" [ibid.].

Retransmission is likewise contingent on certain biological or technological abilities in the receiving species, though there does seem to be an in-built memetic push towards reproduction, dubbed the Grid's "sex drive" [Chisholm, May] which can repurpose specific inherent abilities in the host.

The supposition that the Signal is able to direct or redirect the evolution and form of a species towards its own ends – survival and retransmission – is explicitly supported in multiple cases according to most sources

[Chisholm, May, Goring]. It is also assumed that despite this inherent flexibility, due to the vast differences in alien species' modes of reproduction [or lack thereof] many branches of the Signal that are received will not complete this part of the Grid's "life cycle", and therefore not survive.

EFFECTS OF RETRANSMISSION ON HOST SPECIES

Direct observational evidence suggests that the Grid can have traumatic physical effects on the incorporated species [see 'External Trauma', below]. The extent of the effects, both physically and culturally, on the proportion of the species remaining behind after a retransmission is unknown.

In the short term at least, accelerated evolution is not always inimical to the host species; in many cases it provides them with an advantage over other species with which they may be in competition through enhanced sensory range, intelligence, physical attributes and/or communication abilities [Normansson, DT-34].

It must be stressed here that outside the post-Shepherd discontinuity [PSD] the Grid's original mode of operation may have been dramatically altered, and many of the deleterious effects of incorporation mitigated. That the Shepherds have had a major role in the subsequent evolution and growth of the Grid is indisputable, though their purpose and methods remain a subject of intense debate. Normansson herself suggests that even within the Grid there were competing groups with different ideas in this regard [Normansson, DT-19].

SOURCE

Due to the differing methods and capabilities of the retransmitting race, the Signal has been retransmitted in many and all directions and with differing intensities. However, there is a definite overall drift that can be deduced by examining the routes it has already taken [where such information is available], and that is towards the galactic core.

For a more in-depth overview, see Jeff Halliday's work on recognisable reference stars from alien stellar cartographies *New Maps of Alien Skies: The Constellations of Chance*, which is also recommended for its insightful discussion on the projection of archetypes onto a random source, and the information about otherwise obscure cultures that can be deduced from this.

Halliday's analysis reveals that 93% of retransmissions lie within +/-11.5 degrees of the galactic plane, with 86% directed inward towards the galactic centre rather than laterally or outward. In addition, those that are directed outward seem to have had a specific destination in mind – they tend to be shorter jumps, formed from more tightly collimated beams.

It is suggested that the desired final destination of the Signal is the galactic centre, or a location lying very close to it, and that the original source of the Signal lies out towards the galactic rim, or even beyond.

THE SIGNAL AS PROBE

The wealth of information contained in the Signal is distributed not only across space, but across time. As well as telling us much about the species that lie out towards the galactic rim, it is also a historical record. The vast distance the Signal has traversed is estimated to be at least 22,000 light years, and due to the indirect nature of the routes taken, possibly much more.

It is very likely that many of the species in the Grid will have now evolved far beyond their preserved forms, or even have become extinct. If this turns out to be the case, the Grid may contain the only extant examples of their kind.

It is estimated that the average time between reception and retransmission is 7–10 years; outliers are sixteen immediate retransmissions, characterised in the literature as "reflections" [Chisholm] and at the other extreme, a pause of 27.5 million years. It has been assumed that the Signal somehow remained intact in physical form through this long period, either encoded on a biological substrate or a means external to the receiver until the technological or biological means for retransmission had evolved or been invented.

Other more exotic possibilities to account for the delay have been proposed that invoke time-dilation effects in the proximity of a black hole or neutron star, or perhaps even the engineered effects of bent space-time topography caused by novel alien technologies [see J. C. Chaucer, ed: *The Grid: an Interstellar Window into Speculative Technologies?* Harwich Press].

EXTERNAL TRAUMA

It has been noted that certain species exhibit bodily trauma that is unlikely to be due to cultural practices such as scarification or body modification. The species incorporated just before the PSD show many instances of runaway bone growth that must have proved fatal; further out, there are many documented cases of missing limbs and deep cuts to the body. There are four documented decapitations and 20–30 other instances where analysis of anatomical symmetries suggests trauma is likely, though often the lack of multiple specimens from the same species makes comparison with a non-mutilated entity impossible.

TERMINOLOGY AND PRONOUNCIATION

Where mentioned, the names of races and locations adhere to the generally agreed upon terms used in the exobiology literature. In the rare instances where they were spoken aloud, they have been phonetically transcribed directly from the Daedalus tapes. It should not be necessary to note that an accurate pronunciation would undoubtedly require an anatomy very different to Normansson's, and thus all are provisional.

Many will have also incorporated non-verbal or non-visual cues for which transcription is impractical or impossible. Rather than claim that these terms are a true representation, the working group has attempted to arrive at a standardised nomenclature to facilitate communication between researchers currently working on the material.

CHRONOLOGY

Any dates are provisional, so have been omitted. Certain supernova events recorded in the memories of subjects in the Grid have been speculatively linked to known examples, but even the basics of the timeline are not fully understood. Some events are recorded twice or three times, while others relate to species which were not incorporated until much later.

Note that the transmission number is derived from the location in the Grid following the concentric spherical mapping proposed by Novák, Orlov et al. Though shells closer to the centre, and thus assumed to have been laid down earlier, have been assigned lower numbers, this should not be considered to map directly to a reliable timeline, and the order in which events actually happened may differ. ■

5572057
Arrival of Signal on Earth.
Portion of Signal lost due to position of Jodrell Bank telescope relative to Signal source, which from 5.22pm GMT fell below the horizon. Daedalus Base was also pointing some 145° away from the likely source, meaning the Moon would have blocked the signal. These missing portions are visible in the Grid as empty interstices, their dimensions deduced from the surrounding unaffected interstices.

5388202–5499466
Viral subroutine analogous to a transposon copies itself throughout isolated areas of the suburbs of the Grid. The species incorporated in the affected areas suffer 'simplification'. Direct editing of underlying Grid signal performed, though not without the distortion of certain aspects central to Shepherd ideology. A novel exegesis allows the operation to take place without fundamental cultural faulting.

2570022
Last vestiges of Signal B removed by gamma-ray sterilisation of twelve systems, achieved by porting in a 10,000+ stellar mass neutron star binary with active accretion disk. [disputed]

837022–838732
Further attempts at Signal reorganisation and assimilation. Many of the surviving races are copied to the Grid in a diplomatic manoeuvre brokered by the Omlkimlar. Suspicions of data manipulation arise from analysis of discrepancies between the few races common to both Signal threads, though natural genetic drift is considered a more likely possibility.

900502-D
The 'Meeting in the Black Valley' – two parallel Signals [commonly labelled B and C in the literature] from the 627 split encounter each other after approximately 165 million years of parallel and independent evolution in an area transliterated as the 'Void', or 'Womb', a volume between the Perseus Spur and the Orion Arm in which the density of stars, and thus planets supporting advanced civilisations capable of retransmission is much lower than the galactic average [<12%]. Though the records of this event are for the most part incomprehensible, using as they do a complex diplomatic form of subsonic signalling for which we have no referent in the Grid, this recombination seems to have been incomplete, resulting in an 85% destruction of B and only a partial retransmission of the remainder.
Earliest examples of 'Sheepdogs'.

88306–885502
Section intentionally erased. [disputed]

223022

Late Interregnum. 560–585 thousand years.

212855

The differing quality of data either side of this layer suggests that the 'signal compression' is much improved; evidence of Grid-wide redundancies capable of unpacking the whole from a smaller portion [dubbed 'the Holographic Grid' by Orlov], making successful retransmission possible even through the ionised clouds of stellar nurseries.

99039

First evidence of major schisms in the Shepherd hierarchy. From this point forwards, factions [defined primarily by differing attitudes to the manipulation of species incorporated in the Grid] seem to be localised in distinct 'districts'. The factions also show physical polymorphisms, most noticeably in skin patterning and colour. The assumption is that these are due to the divergent evolution of Shepherd strains from parallel Signal iterations which have subsequently been recombined.

72798

'Reflection' I

72797

'Reflection' II

62596A/B

Three different versions of the Signal arrive within 100 years at the same location; the host species, decimated by the first, decisively despatches the second two. Total loss of 781 distinct Grid species.

62562

Grid coherence damaged by stellar-scale dark matter halo. Strengthened Signal redundancies added. Retransmission coincides with the addition of one of the complete but 'empty' sections of the Grid. Several lines of enquiry suggest that this section is, in fact, occupied; just by entities that we cannot detect with any of our instruments or mathematical analyses. Suggestions that the creatures that may occupy these interstices are made of dark matter is speculative.

2100-2102

'Hollow Worlds' interregnum [approx. 2,000 years].

1229A

Distributed, non-organic, non-reproducing intelligence absorbs more than 65% of the Grid. Retransmission impossible. Subsequent loss of five major technologically advanced species and 442 non-tool-using [NTU] species.

904
'Reflection' III

901
Abandoned Forerunner construct resembling a partial Dyson sphere around a black hole encountered. Spectral analysis of Hawking radiation suggests the black hole may be artificial. Structures on the interior of the sphere suggest the Forerunners were distorting the event horizon, possibly using tunnelling effects to extract information.

882
Second or 'Grand' interregnum. 51.5 million years, presumed unre-transmitted. Some sources see evidence of a limited retransmission, possibly between the same or closely related species inhabiting different planets in the same star system.

880E
First sentient star encountered.

786-873
Section of Grid erased, presumed intentionally.

762
Grid encounters first 'Forerunner' object - the furthest from the galactic centre currently known. The original 'Forerunner' civilisation that built and then abandoned these cities and machines is unknown to every species in the Grid for which we have sufficient information. It is assumed that they are either extinct, or have retreated closer to the galactic core.

627-H 627-J
Mutual annihilation of two Grid retransmissions, the sole survivor being one semi-autonomous machine intelligence which reattaches itself to a later Grid reflection.

627
Short-range, broad-spectrum retransmission. Signal temporarily split into at least 27 subsignals. Most of these redirections are lost. Remainder collimated and amplified by gravitational lensing. Supernova remnant correlation suggests a date of 8.5 billion years ago [BYA], though the proposed candidate is atypical: spectral analysis has led to suggestions that it was engineered to go nova, either as a weapon or to cause the collapse of the surrounding gas clouds and trigger subsequent star formation.

561

The Grid encounters the Shepherd race, the 'Scootch Orlena'. After a first skirmish in with the 'untamed' Grid reduced their population to a third of its original number, they manage to excise the damaging reproductive urge from their forebrains by fast-track evolving three 'push-generations' in tandem with a co-dependent organism called a 'Grimault', the last of which have a sufficiently developed hind/forebrain firewall to tame the Grid and impose some semblance of order. Beginning of the Grid's guided evolution in which the Shepherds oversee the incorporation of new species while minimising coercion and physical trauma. Given how destructive their encounter with the Grid was, there is much debate about why the Shepherds allowed it to continue, even in its currently neutered form. Some suggest it is an archive, the ultimate library of evolved species; others that the Shepherds divined in the Grid some deeper purpose and chose to ensure it was fulfilled.

550-52

'Larisidra<*> Wars'. Hijacking of the Grid's reproductive urge by the 'Oreiproudor Transitional Aristocracy' [Orlov terminology], and subsequent centralisation of power within the 4.5 light-year volume of the OTA's sphere of influnce. Small local retransmissions of repro-urge enhanced 'rape battalions' used as a pacifying tactic.

519

Destruction of 'Ai Voronii' system, and consolidation of political/biological alliances in face of further incursions.

510

Breach of the 'Brethave-Pkhouri Barrier'. Flux of unknown but destructive force through 550 inhabited worlds, 340 of which are completely sterilised. Sources suggest that these may be the events communicated via Normansson's tablet during the first encounter with the LBE, though the narratives differ in several major details.

477-9

Construction of the 'Brethave-Pkhouri Barrier'. Further details unavailable at this time.

c455

The Grid's capabilities are repurposed by an expansionist ideologically driven race who use their nascent telepathic abilities to co-opt the minds of several other species within a radius of fourteen star systems. Upon incorporation, they attempt a similar feat within the Grid. Repeatedly thwarted, it is not until the Shepherds introduce a form of memetic prophylactic after their own incorporation [dubbed the 'woo buffer' in the literature] that they are finally subdued. Though no longer a major threat, their memetic residue occasionally finds purchase in the minds of the Grid's newer arrivals.

325
'Gar<flash>pchiddwok', a race named in Daedalus Transcript [DT-54], is incorporated into the Grid. Normansson seems to suggest it is a species related to the LBE; though the two have superficially similar body plans, the 'Gar<flash>pchiddwok' does not have the bicameral brain that is a feature of the Shepherds. It is also unclear how two genetically related species could exist on widely separated planets hundreds of light years apart.

c321-324
A portion of Grid is infected with a 'memetic suicide virus'. The section becomes 'cadaverous' – no entity housed within it survives retransmission. The area is first quarantined then later edited out by the Shepherds after their incorporation [disputed chronology]. Loss of the 1,230 Shepherds who were overseeing the infected section.

310
The 'Siege of Amara'. No further details available.

258
Earliest examples of symbiotic creatures incorporated in the Grid. Symbiosis may be a result of incorporation, or the creatures may have evolved the symbiotic relationship beforehand. Orlov contends that both these scenarios have happened, along with subsequent adaptations required to harness specific abilities useful to the function of the Grid as a whole.

255-AB
Earliest evidence of successful Signal reintegration.

252-B
Split signal enters brain of dying demigoddess. [disputed]

203-A
Signal retransmission neuters entire race, leading to their extinction.

c202
First Interregnum. No retransmission for 3.7 million years, followed by first split in Signal. Eventual retransmission over large distances achieved by creation of collimated millisecond pulsar from 'force-fed' supernova, and compression of the resultant neutron star. The mechanisms required for such large-scale stellar engineering projects are currently the focus of many groups' work, including the Exobiology Working Group at Jodrell Bank.

198
'Reflection' IV

197
'Repro' engineered forced evolution of a receptive but unintelligent race. Facing the possibility of millennia without retransmission, the indigenous species is 'hothoused', developing language, technology and interplanetary travel in under 350 [Earth] years.

c104-110
First encounter with 'Repros', a placental, bipedal race with a high reproductive urge ['sex drive']. Large portions of their encoded DNA insert themselves into other species. From this point on, the Grid begins to resemble a complex evolved organism in which different species perform different functions within it, not always to the benefit of the whole.

99
Putative 'reflection'. [sources differ]

87
Encounter and incorporation of first race with certain cultural precepts inimical to the Grid's original hive mind. Beginning of the compartmentalisation of different species.

2-47
'First Wave'. Few records. Area partially cleansed. The earliest form of the Grid is thought to have evolved from a species with a distributed hive mind and an extended telepathic range, of which Patient Zero is a singular example. Before incorporation it just comprised members of its own species, but over time grew to include other, unrelated species on neighbouring planets, probably within the same system. There is an opposing school of thought that suggests that the Grid did not originate with Patient Zero, and that it was installed there by the Repros, or even the Shepherds, for an unknown purpose. Proponents argue that this purpose may be related to its ability to contact entities across some considerable distance and that the Grid acts as an amplifier, extending its range by many orders of magnitude. What or who it may be designed to contact is not known.

1
Patient Zero.

LOCKOUT

Jack knew he had abused Daniel's friendship, maybe even left it irreparably damaged. His decision would cost him in ways he could only guess at. But, you know, *means and ends* . . . and this *was* something of an End.

At 7 AM Greenwich Mean Time, 1 AM Central Standard Time, Daniel was the only person left in the control room at Jodrell Bank. Keeping strange hours was standard practice for astronomers; the stars do not keep a nine-to-five schedule. Joe, bless him, had waved to him through the glass wall as he left, just like he did most nights; he would miss him when he finally did retire. He had around an hour and a half until Leonie Orlov would turn up with a toasted bagel and the following day's schedule, make a crack about "creatures of the night" and tell him to go home.

He leaned back and watched faint streaks of pink lighten the sky behind the silhouette of the Lovell Telescope dish. A thin mist shrouded the lower levels of the superstructure, the lattice of triangles blending into the bare branches of the trees and the frosted fields below.

Daniel returned his attention to the screens. Here, in the old control room across from the commandeered Rotunda where the exobiology working group was set up, modern computers incongruously shared space with decades of obsolete technology. Daniel had a nostalgic fondness for the original fixtures and fittings of the place – they looked like they meant business. Needles that could swing into the red, but now never left zero. Dials that clicked when you turned a knob, but otherwise did nothing.

He reached out and ran his fingertips over the banks of instruments arranged in a horseshoe around him. They passed over small glass windows in which numbers, frozen at some arbitrary value no one could remember how to interpret, no longer counted down. They skipped across rows of coloured lights that had burned out years ago; like vintage Christmas tree decorations, they couldn't be fixed because the bulbs were no longer made. Daniel absently ran the same fingers through his thinning grey hair. He knew how they felt. The future, the one he had fallen in love with so long ago, had been made from this evocative technology . . . not some ugly off-the-shelf piece of plastic you could pick up in PC World.

A slight movement caught his attention. On the monitor, next to the familiar crescent-shaped outline of the Lovell Telescope, a schematic of the smaller 60-foot Mark VII dish had appeared. Through the floor Daniel could feel the familiar vibration as it began to move. *That's peculiar.*

It was slewing to point . . . where?

Aha.

Daniel picked up the internal telephone and pressed a preset extension button. Somewhere else, a phone rang in an empty office.

He hung up. *A glitch?* Unlikely.

Daniel watched a numerical scale shift as the Mark VII swung around. He could already guess the coordinates at which it would come to rest: FSRS, the Far Side Relay Satellite, in orbit around Lagrange L2. The Mark VII was far smaller than the imposing Lovell Telescope, but for the purposes of the direct beaming of a signal to an astronomical next-door neighbour it was more than powerful enough.

It looked like someone wanted to talk to the Moon.

Daniel didn't have a pair of Depthcharge glasses, so he could not have known that at that precise moment, stepping out behind him from a place that was no place, was a man in a white suit. Through an eye that was sensitive to wavelengths of electromagnetic radiation far longer than the human eye could detect, the 19th Count looked out across fields striped with long morning shadows to the huge dish that hung like a gibbous gas giant just above the horizon. Macclesfield was a low smudge of yellow light through the superstructure, but his sights were set higher. The crescent Moon now hung just above the telescope's edge as if it were the missing piece of a puzzle, and if brought back to Earth the two would fit together to make a perfect circle.

The Count, intimately integrated with Jodrell's systems, found that all he needed to do was look towards the Moon and the Mark VII followed. It seemed so . . . *natural.* Do you instruct certain muscles to contract or relax in order to focus your gaze? Do you consciously follow the neural pathways from eyes to brain in order to process an image? No, you simply *look,* because your body is you, and you are it. And if your body incorporates a nervous system of copper cable and optical fibre . . .

Daniel pressed a few keys. Nothing. He turned to the antique hardware. He pulled a large lever without any real expectation that it was still connected to anything. Again, nothing. It appeared he was locked out.

How . . . ?

Jack. Daniel was suddenly sure of it. No one else had the means or the smarts to do something like this. The puzzle. The puzzle had been a Trojan.

Daniel didn't know whether this made things better or worse. So it was Jack who wanted to talk to Daedalus. Who did he want to talk to? Dana? The LBE? One was no longer up there, and the other was on a makeshift autopsy table in a lunar cavern. Was he after some residual data from the Daedalus systems? Then why commandeer the *transmitter*? Daniel was at a loss. Back when he was working with Jack on setting up Jodrell's computers, he had always been loath to demonstrate a piece of software or even voice a theory until he'd tested it himself. Always moving in mysterious ways, that was Jack.

A puzzle within a puzzle. He got up and walked around the console to the large window. Up there, on the Moon, something was afoot. Daniel found he felt . . . *slighted,* more than alarmed. Why had he not just *asked*? What was he hiding? Who might he be protecting?

"Jack, Jack, Jack . . . What am I going to do with you, my boy?" Daniel was sure Jack would never do something *really* foolish; his rigorous mind didn't deal in uncertainties. It was much more likely that his obsessive-compulsive curiosity had once again got the better of him.

Daniel had a certain amount of director's discretionary time he could allocate to personal projects that piqued his interest, though if he was being a stickler for procedure each still required a written proposal, submitted through the usual channels.

He smiled. *Maybe this could be one of them.* Who could deny him a little indulgence this close to his long-postponed retirement? Even the Lovell Telescope was not in round-the-clock demand these days, there being larger and more modern dishes in Germany, the US and China. It had even recently been used as a giant projector screen for an SF film festival. No, this institution and its instruments, like himself, were comfortably sliding into old age. He thought that even if someone did think to ask what he was doing, or rather what Jack was doing, with Daniel's indulgence it wouldn't meet with much in the way of disapproval. A nod and a wink. It was all rather . . . *British.*

On the monitor, the scrolling figures on the schematic of the Mark VII slowed as the azimuth and elevation approached their targets. There was a *duh-cunk* that was felt through the floor more than heard as it came to rest.

The transmitting dish mounted on the roof now faced the Moon, held on target by a small servomotor which tracked its slow movement across the sky. *Now what?*

A literal world away, Dana's plan entered its final phase.

ROAD TRIP

Dana checked the data downlink from Lagrange. The procedure was almost muscle-memory; she had done this countless times before, though usually clothed and with the lights on.

Yes. Jodrell was online.

Marshall had not returned from wherever he had gone with his soup. His watch wouldn't end for another two and a half hours. She hoped she wouldn't be disturbed.

The Daedalus Telescope had not been used as a transmitter before. It could focus the faintest starlight, it could focus and redirect incident sunlight, it could heat a near-Earth asteroid to the boiling point of lead. It had been designed from the outset to be capable of engaging with certain . . . eventualities.

There had been proposals within the SETI community who were party to the telescope's extended functionality to broadcast a short signal, an announcement of our existence; something similar to the 1974 Arecibo Message. This consisted of a mere 210 bytes arranged in a 73 by 23 pixel grid that depicted the DNA double-helix, a selection of atomic numbers, a map of the Solar System and a crude Space Invader-style bitmap figure; but ultimately, what it really said was "Hello".

A new message had never been sent. Though the capability was there, it had been impossible to arrive at a consensus as to what the message should say, or even if it was wise to send one at all.

Some thought it foolish to shout in the dark when there may be predators abroad.

The telescope was built to be powerful enough to discern the presence of organic compounds in the atmospheres of exoplanets as they transited their parent stars. If the chemical signatures of biological activity – or even the technosignatures of an advanced industrial civilisation – were to be discovered, we might need to talk to them.

Dana, though she had been party to some of these discussions, had treated them with some scepticism; the galaxy was a very big place and the nearest neighbours might live many hundreds of light years away. Her primary interest was Daedalus' function as a telescope; even the near-Earth asteroid deflection programme had not fully engaged her interest.

Now she was grateful the systems briefings and training had been so thorough. The instrumentation package was already there, and all that needed to be done was to raise it up the central tower to the focal point of the largest and most powerful transmitter ever constructed.

Since she had first formalised her plan, she had given some consideration as to where she should point the dish. Observations from the James Webb Space Telescope had confirmed ground-based observations of twenty-four exoplanets within two dozen light years and discovered a few hundred more, though most of these were gaseous 'hot Jupiters', orbiting so close to their host stars that they were considered inhospitable to life. The closest Earth-like world circles our nearest neighbour – the red-dwarf star Proxima Centauri, a mere 4.2 light years away, though Proxima is a flare-star, given to periodic magnetic upheavals that would fatally irradiate any close-orbiting planets. Many other nearby star systems undoubtedly held rocky Earth-sized worlds that were beyond the capability of current space-based observatories to detect.

Of course, rocky planets with an atmosphere and a water cycle were not the only habitats in which life could flourish. Out beyond the Solar System's frost line, warmed not by the Sun but by the tidal forces of the massive planets they circled, liquid water existed deep below the frozen ice in the subsurface ocean of Saturn's moon Enceladus, and closer to the Sun, Jupiter's moons Ganymede, Callisto and Europa – the moon that had been threaded like a bead by a needle from infinity.

That these warm oceans were environments that could support life had become more than just an outlandish theory when the Cassini probe had flown through the active cryovolcanoes at the south pole of Enceladus and detected complex organics. These cryovolcanoes erupt with such force that material escapes the gravitational tug of the moon entirely, orbiting the host planet itself as Saturn's E ring, leading one science commentator to suggest that Galileo himself had won the race to find extraterrestrial life when he first turned his telescope on the planet and saw its rings of freeze-dried exobiology back in 1610.

The Jupiter Icy Moons Mission had utilised a revolutionary ion drive and a lightweight Tricoire thruster that enabled it to orbit several Jovian moons throughout its mission, and collect data at a more leisurely pace than the long-lens drive-by paparazzi shots necessitated by previous fast fly-bys.

Once in a parking orbit around Ganymede it had parachuted a probe down to the surface, choosing as a landing site a deep rift valley darkened with what were thought to be organics rising from deep inside the moon. The probe had touched down awkwardly, wedged against an ice boulder that had crippled the ground radar and scuppered any measurement of the thickness of the ice below. Despite this setback, a week later the surface penetrator had been released from the belly of the probe, a heated silver bullet designed to melt its way through the several kilometres of ice thought to be covering the putative subsurface sea.

In fact, only two kilometres down, the penetrator found itself suddenly freefalling through a salty ocean. Turning end over end, the image data it returned was less than ideal; a suggestive bright streak was all that could be made out. Righting itself, it was apparent that the probe had acquired a tail. A corkscrew of luminescent motes, each too small to resolve even at maximum magnification, led up from the rear of the cylinder towards the surface, a spiral of light that described its descent.

Bioluminescence . . . If it was not due to some unknown chemical reaction caused by the interaction of the hull with the composition of the water, there was only one reasonable conclusion: microbial life.

Life! The first unambiguous sign of biological activity somewhere other than the Earth. Simple, to be sure, but life nonetheless.

It was only going to get better. Turning on the lights, Mission Control was treated to a phantasmagorical forest of purple kelp, darting through which was a zoo of pale, translucent will-o'-the-wisps. Resembling broad, shield-headed jellyfish, they were rotationally symmetrical and pulsed as they purged water through a valve to propel themselves forward. Some nudged the probe like curious puppies, cascades of ultraviolet dots flowing down the lengths of their dimly seen bodies to thin, blade-shaped extremities which waved like a burlesque dancer's fan to orient them. They were mankind's first glimpse of actual, real extraterrestrial creatures, and they did not disappoint.

This first flush of success lasted until three minutes later. The probe was directed towards a shoal of small lights moving in close formation, mirrored by a similar shoal just below that appeared to be a reflection of the first. As they approached, these resolved into two sets of teeth set in an enormous semi-transparent head, through which pale organs could be seen pumping a dark liquid. Front and centre, a spray of questing cilia reached out, towards the camera and the lights. A second later local time, but fifty minutes later back on Earth and far too late to do anything about it, the data cable to the lander had been severed, the probe had been swallowed, and the first transmission from the under-ice seas of Ganymede had been terminated.

The Grid had brought the message home, if it still could be doubted, that the galaxy was fecund with life; that given the smallest opportunity, it survived, it thrived, it spread to occupy almost every evolutionary niche imaginable.

As far as her cohabitee's memories could inform her, the rebroadcast of the Grid had rarely been targeted. Like a dandelion casting seeds on the breeze, it was simply released out into the interstellar void without any foreknowledge of its final destination. All that was required to receive it was a world that was open to the skies and minds that were open to the ideas in the Signal. A planet whose inhabitants could see the stars – and wonder what or who might be out there.

Given that Daedalus' dish was built in a crater, and a crater is attached to a planetary body, it had limited options when it came to the direction in which it could be pointed. The individual reflectors could be tilted, but any point in the sky below the lunar horizon was, as with an Earthbound telescope, out of reach.

So Dana chose the galactic core. Maximum density. More to hit. And, of practical importance, currently in view. The Grid had been heading in this direction for longer than life on Earth had existed, and seemed to know where it was going – maybe it even had a final destination in mind. Had it planted the idea within her, perhaps? The reproductive urge, she reflected not for the first time, is a strange and wonderful thing.

A familiar chime announced the digital signal handshake. An uplink had been established.

How long did she have?

How long did she *need*?

She brought up another interface. This was a plan view of the telescope itself. Each individual reflector consisted of six hexagonal mirrors arranged around a central seventh. In the simplified graphic on Dana's tablet the telescope was circumscribed by a circle, while a smaller circle closer to the centre described the reflectors' inner limit, a void through which the crater's natural central peak rose. Atop this, on a tall filigree pylon, were mounted the focal point's instrument packages.

The status of each mirror in the array was indicated by a tiny yellow or occasionally orange hexagon, each with a drop-down menu that would supply more detailed information. Around the circumference they rose to three kilometres as they climbed the terraced outer wall; in early Lunar Orbiter far-side photographs it was apparent that the crater itself formed a rough natural hexagon, and this impression had only been emphasised by the feat of engineering it now held.

Despite the missing fingertips, her hands moved across the keys with practised ease; she had performed just this kind of procedure countless times before.

She typed in a precise declination and right ascension and hit return.

Outside, a hundred thousand reflectors slowly began to move as one, tilting in concert toward the galactic plane like flowers moving to face an invisible sun: the supermassive black hole called Sagittarius A*, the black pearl at the heart of the spiral of stars that is our galaxy. With a mass of two and a half million suns, it was the dark secret that held every star in the Milky Way in place by the thin but unbreakable thread of gravity.

All life would lead there.

The mirrors locked into place with a series of slight shivers she felt through the plates of the floor. On the screen, one by one the small hexagons turned green. They would now track the galactic centre automatically, moving slowly in unison until the target dropped below the lunar horizon, and out of sight.

She pulled up another menu. It was a simple matter to select a specific instrument suite and bring it into position. On hydraulics that were too far away to be heard even if the Moon's atmosphere had carried sound, the transmitter package raised itself on ratcheted rails up the pylon. Another final indicator graphic flicked from orange to green. Everything was ready.

Via the communications antenna above the Hub a confirmation was beamed to Jodrell. Scant seconds later, Daedalus received the automated reply.

A pause, then—

Complex code in discrete packets began to stream through.

Daniel put his glasses on and bent close to the monitor . . . where *had* he seen that before? A 37-nanosecond signal, incredibly dense, covering a wide bandwidth. Looped, on repeat. He felt a prickle of recognition. *The Signal.*

280 miles or three-millionths of an AU away, sitting in the dust on the floor of the Intelligencia office, Jack, Harriet and Nixon had no idea how long they had before Daniel managed to pull the plug. The Signal had been honed to lean and efficient elegance over numerous

iterations that had spanned countless light years and unfathomed millennia, but *how long would it take to retransmit the Grid?*

Numbers scrolled up the screen faster than they could follow. Binary digits, noughts and ones, yes or no, black or white. Like the subatomic particles from which all matter is built, each came in its unique and unchanging form, devoid of shades of grey, of subtlety or detail. They were, or they were not.

But in their trillions, they were capable of describing *anything*.

Nought and one. The Universe began in homogeneity, but it was not a static homogeneity; everything that was to be was held in potential. Its first act of creation was to differentiate. A density wave, more here, less there – the first duality, the simplest on/off state possible. This was the first vibration throughout eternity, its wavelength the size of the Universe; where once there was one thing, now there was some-thing and no-thing, zero and one. The process repeated, harmonics of differentiation upon differentiation. From homogeneity arose particularity; number that could be counted. Number arranges itself according to mathematical law because it can do no different – it *is* law, expressed. Matter would take aeons to condense from this curdling primordial precursor, but eventually knots of force spun so tightly around themselves that they collapsed into solidity. Still curdling, matter began to arrange itself into ever more complex forms; complexity permitted subtlety, and from subtlety arose *life*.

Like water in a bathtub, everything seeks to return to an equilibrium. When that first wave has finally travelled the length of the Universe, risen, peaked at a maximum differentiation, then subsided back into homogeneity, this round of creation will be over.

But it will not pause – passing once more through a point of rest where all is infolded and nothing is expressed, it will find itself reflected in a cosmic mirror and what was a peak will now become a trough.

The next Universe will begin its own differentiation into being.

Process.

Between these poles of rest at the alpha and omega, the disequilibrium of motion, under the governance of law, will weave worlds.

How does life, the ultimate expression of the dance between motion and law, survive the inevitable decay of the bodies it creates to house it? It needs to grow them anew, but pass information on from generation to generation, so that what it has learned through being is not lost.

So life evolved an informational survival mechanism: expressed in the arrangement of the base pairs of the genetic code, it was Nature's first software, the first representation of a representation. Honed through generations of trial and error, need and circumstance, this molecular memory allowed complexity to build, innovation to be preserved, and life to *evolve*.

Eventually Nature sculpted shapes of such subtlety that they could house the self-reflective notion we call consciousness, and thence self-consciousness – the life that knows it's alive.

In the obscure recesses of prehistory, long before we knew how to speak, new ideas lived in just one brain and died with their hosts. Can you imagine the loneliness? The privacy of your mind was a locked room to which no one could share the keys. You had no way to know if your experience was singular, or if there were a hundred others out there who thought just as you did. A lifetime of learning would be washed from your slate by the waters of Lethe; every death was the loss of an unrecorded library of experience. All that could be saved had to be passed on through the physical machinery of DNA, where only the brute mechanisms of survival could shape the story.

Then we learned how to speak – and ideas could escape. No longer trapped inside a single entity, they could become part of a larger communal tapestry, surviving the death of the body via an extra-biological mechanism: *language*. Another code, another representation of a representation. Our history, our culture, passed down from lip to lip in words.

So we marked our bodies with images that recorded the passing of our lives. We kept a diary in flesh. Who we were, what we did, what we thought. That private space inside our heads had at last been unlocked, and was now part of a shared project called *culture*.

Experiences and explanations. Stories and myths. Gods and their machinations. A protoscience in the making. We learned from each other, built on each other's wisdom, shared our discoveries.

Who we are, our sense of self, is built from a temporal continuity, from the persistence of the I. Though the atoms from which we are made will all be replaced, we are still in some sense the same person we were yesterday, and the person we will become tomorrow. We are woven from the thread of memory, and we must not forget.

But words need people to speak them.

The invention of writing meant ideas could be preserved in a physical form when otherwise they might be forgotten; then print multiplied and democratised writing through books made from ink pressed against paper. Today they don't even require a physical substrate of dead trees – words deliver ideas through our computer screens, globally, twenty-four hours a day.

We long ago outstripped the ability of our DNA to code all we had learned, but on its foundation we built a universal descriptor, an off-brain backup that doesn't run on a biological substrate.

As noughts and ones, the primal binary black-and-white from which it all began, we can now preserve the cultural output of mankind – all we can say about all that we are.

This time, Dana had promised herself, she would not let the library of all human creation be burned like the libraries of antiquity. By transmitting the Grid, she would preserve all that we are and all we have made from the cultural vandalism of the fascist theocrats and the political ideologues, from those who abhor knowledge and vilify creativity, who seek to extinguish the arts and sciences that are the lasting achievements of our species – a legacy built on the limited foundation of our biology, but more magnificent than our finest cathedral.

She would be sending our ambassadors, too – the DMEn. This was the very purpose they had been designed for. Our ideas personified, theirs was to be a secular afterlife in non-corporeal form.

UNFINISHED BUSINESS

The signal from Jodrell streamed down from Lagrange. First the Oxbow, then with almost unseemly haste, the Signal proper.

Dana wondered if there was some mechanism within the Grid that sensed when a means of retransmission became available – a concentration, a build-up, almost like an urge to— ejaculate? The reproductive instinct – birds do it, bees do it . . . and now, she found, the Grid does it.

Information pulsed down in 37-nanosecond packets, denser than a neutron star, denser perhaps than Sagittarius A* itself. The buffer would very soon reach capacity.

She quickly routed the signal through to the Daedalus Telescope proper. An almost inaudible key tap, and on her tablet's telescope graphic the green indicator on the central mast began to pulse. A stream of data immediately scrolled down the left of her screen far faster than the refresh rate could catch. She pushed the signal strength to maximum.

And it began.

She looked out across the telescope. From the tip of the central pylon, the red collision-avoidance beacons glowed just as they always did. Everything appeared to be exactly as before.

The data now streaming heavenward was, of course, invisible; the human eye has evolved to be sensitive to a very narrow range of electromagnetic radiation, what we parochially call 'light'. All the colours in every sunset, in every photograph, are confined to a narrow band in a much larger continuum. Turner's best efforts at capturing the sublime use the limited palette of the colour-blind; we will never know the pearlescent sheen of X-rays, the piercing clarity of gamma rays or the cold submolecular hum of ultraviolet. Unlike some of our Earthbound animal relatives, we can't even see the heat of infrared.

No, everything looked normal. Radio is simply a colour we can't see.

Dana began to relax. She stepped across the lab to her personal storage locker. It had been emptied, as on the last day of school, but a shirt she had used as a cleaning rag was still there. She put it on. It smelled of engine oil and bleach and came down to her thighs.

She looked up to see a figure in the hatchway leading to the personnel quarters.

"Dana?"

Dana recognised Georgi Komarov immediately. A cold shock of adrenaline made her legs almost buckle. She had not seen him since she had laid him out cold with a single punch at that awards dinner all those years ago.

"Дерьмо, how are you here?" He was genuinely flabbergasted. "You were shipped home in isolation!"

"I came back," she offered limply.

He held up his arms in disbelief. "Word is your mind may be infected. Compromised. You're not yourself. We were briefed about what you found up here."

Keep him talking. "What did I find up here?"

"You know. Some kind of ancient virus, frozen in the permafrost. Carried here from Earth by meteorite impacts during the Late Heavy Bombardment."

"That's what you've been told?"

He paused. "Dana – how *did* you get up here?"

How long . . . ?

"I had some help. From someone who's not from round here, but does have our best interests at heart."

"The *Koreans?*"

"Ha. No."

Georgi held up his hands. "The *Saudis*. I knew it. This secrecy, I swear – there's a parallel mission going on here, isn't there? One us grunts are not party to. The world's elite, looking for ways to survive should the nukes kick off, or global warming finally melt the чертов icecaps. Hidden bases. That's why we can't get near the caves. It's *obvious*. The Moon is a bolt-hole, a lifeboat for heads of state and their cronies. It's— it's *Alternative Three!*"

Dana was familiar with this particular conspiracy theory.

"A lifeboat, perhaps. But not for them."

How long?

Her eyes, despite her determination, flicked to the tablet.

He followed her glance. It was propped up on the counter, the screen alive with numbers, lines, colours. The schematic of the Daedalus array was clearly visible, annotated with information on the declination, azimuth, focal length. His eyes went to the window, to the vast bowl of mirrors tiling the crater outside. "You've redirected them." He moved towards her tablet. You've— you're *sending* something. What—"

"Don't touch that. Georgi. Please."

His hands hovered just above the keyboard. She knew that if he succeeded in interrupting the transmission, she was very unlikely to get a second chance. "So, tell me the truth. What *did* you find out there?"

"Someone who had come from very far away with a message for us."

"What kind of message? A greeting?"

"A *warning.*"

"This obscurantism isn't helping, Dana. A *warning?* Of what?"

Warmed by her skin, the smell of engine oil from her shirt was making her eyes swim. She doubted she could successfully pull off a judo punch in one-sixth gravity, even if there was the space to swing.

"Of an *invasion.* Not by creatures from the stars, but by alien *ideas.* Viral memes for which we have little or no protection. Infectious concepts that had already ravaged the messenger's home planet."

Georgi Komarov studied her closely. She had an earnest passion she could not disguise. Wherever this mysterious interloper had arrived from, guile was not her strong suit.

"You're telling me you encountered an alien in there, aren't you? In the lava tubes. You encountered an actual, real extraterrestrial?"

"Yes."

"And it – *told* you this? It *talked* to you?"

"In a manner of speaking."

Georgi took a step towards her. She was suddenly aware, even in the shirt, how naked she felt. "And this, this invasion – when is it supposed to arrive? How long do we have?"

"It's already here. It arrived ten months ago."

Georgi seemed to be digesting this piece of information. "But nothing happened ten months ago. Nothing— wait. The *Grid?* Isn't that supposed to be some kind of virtual reality game? *World of Warcraft, Second Life, MyWorld?*"

"You tell me. You're the conspiracy buff."

Georgi took another step closer. The cold aluminium edge of the kitchenette counter cut into her thighs. "This base, and what's being built here. It *is* a safe haven, isn't it? But from *what?* What are they so scared of?"

"Their own mortality? As are we all."

"I don't believe you. The Grid's just misdirection. Clever vr бред сивой кобылы. The threat's biological, isn't it? *Zika?* I've seen the chemtrails – they're seeding the clouds with nanotech. *Crowd control.*"

"If you say so."

Georgi's face flushed, and she again saw in him the man who had stepped over a line that time on the ISS. The man who had wiped the CCTV to cover his 'lapse of protocol'. The man who had—

"Don't fuck with me, Normansson. *Why are you here?*"

His face was now inches from hers. She could see the spittle between his yellowed teeth. Dana felt a surge of anger. She spoke very quietly and deliberately, so that even men like Georgi could understand. "Because, Komarov, it turns out it's not an invasion.

"It's an *exodus*.

"Because it turns out there are things way worse and way more destructive out there in the Universe than the things we are capable of doing to each other down there on Earth. Things older than Man, older than the Sun, older perhaps than our galaxy itself. Vast, majestic, terrifying things with minds made of stars and nerves made of light that think a thought once every ten thousand years.

"And these things look upon us as a *contagion*. They consider all forms of life to be an aberration, and seek to snuff out self-consciousness – finally, completely, wherever it might be found. They dream of a clean and pure Universe, one in which the planets of the Milky Way are not infested with this unpredictable, unruly, creative thing called *life*.

"And we cannot petition these – these *gods* for clemency, because they have no inclination, no means to comprehend the language we use to describe our trivial and fleeting existences."

Georgi snickered. "You know, Dana, you almost – *almost* – sound convincing. But even my credulity doesn't stretch that far. No, I'm shutting this down. *Now.* If you won't explain all this, how you got here, what you're doing – if you won't tell me, you can tell it to the suits."

She stepped forward, not sure if she could do what she was thinking of doing. As she moved, she folded herself down and out, flattening herself into the Grid and at right angles to reality. Her vision stuttered as the last technicolour frames ran out of the reel, and her view jumped to the degraded compressed feed from the camera in the corner of the Hub.

One step.

There was a fraction of a second where she saw Georgi from above, standing alone—

And out.

The pain was indescribable. Arteries rerouted. Nerves shortcircuited. Blood backed up fast to her brain. She felt a vicious need to vomit, but her windpipe was blocked by Georgi's forearm. She was blind in one eye, its humour bisected by his shoulder blade. Their bones locked in place as her legs intersected his like the inflexible triangular lattice of Jodrell's support structure. She could feel tendons snap as stresses pulled them in two directions at once. Blood filled her ear canal. Georgi's ribcage had punctured her left lung like a shark bite. She felt her upper vertebrae pop then twist apart as the two of them fell forward, joined as one.

He put out a hand. Dana's tablet skidded across the stainless-steel surface, stopping just short of the edge. Large gobbets of blood and bile sprayed the counter and the curved window. Dana could sense her life slipping away, a soft welcoming darkness as of the space between worlds, blank, pain-free, lightless, quieting her mind . . .

. . . and then she folded herself back into the Grid.

Dear girl, what *have* you done?

Through her jpegged vision she could see an aerial view of the Hub and a shape on the floor, a dark stain spreading from beneath a meatgrinder's mulch of bone and flesh she was thankful the camera's lens could not resolve.

She could also see the 19th Count, striking an uncharacteristically sombre pose by the door with his head lowered. All she could see of his face beneath his hat was his white chin, outlined by the glow from the mirrors outside.

Am I here? In the Grid, with you?

Her speech, as always in concept-space, was more a thought than a vocalisation. Ideas – communicated more efficiently than any physical means could hope to match. That she could speak at all, if speaking it was, came as some relief.

All that is really, *truly* you, is here.

And my body?

He looked up. The very blankness of the Count's white marble eyes, usually so unreadable, now seemed to hide a deep sorrow.

Dana thought a thought, and in the camera's eye another figure appeared; hazy, lined with static as of an old analogue TV transmission.

It was Dana, standing before the Count in Valentina Vladimirovna Tereshkova's spacesuit. He took both her gloved hands in his, and she lifted her face up to look at him. White waves of marble hair fluttered improbably around his shoulders. In his spotless perfection he seemed to be the very embodiment of the calm and dignified elder statesman, every kindly teacher she had ever wished for.

Your body is *irreparably broken,* my dear.
I am afraid you will not survive if you ever leave the Grid.

Light from an imaginary sun, invisible here in Daedalus Base but no less real for that, glanced from her visor. The four letters painted across her helmet were the dark burgundy of the best vintage, laid down for a very special and singular occasion. She smiled, and through her degraded vision and from a high angle, could see herself smile.

The Count held up her hand, as if to kiss it, but instead tugged off her spacesuit glove. Inside were five fingers, all present and complete. She experimentally curled them, stretched them, turned her palm over to look at her new hand from both sides as if to assure herself it was really hers. With her new fingers she reached out to stroke the Count's perfect white hair, and he raised his own hand to hold hers.

She looked perfect. It *was* perfect. She was exactly as she had always seen herself. She was Dana's childhood vision of the best Dana she had ever hoped to be. She was an idea, now shorn of a body, but more alive than she had ever felt, caught like a firefly in a bell jar in an Oxbow on the far side of the Moon.

A small cluster of glass eyes on a short stalk rotated atop the Hub as she turned her camera gaze out over the telescope. Now she was in the Grid she could see the other DMEn: XX had taken the form of a long, low elegantly swooping suspension bridge, a cantilevered avenue hung from fairy-lit cables that led from just outside the window where they now stood towards the centre of the telescope and the transmitter array, a clock hand marking out the radius of an enormous inverted mirrorball.

At the bridge's entrance she could see the flickering judder of Girl 21, accompanied by a number of other strange entities with which she was unfamiliar. They didn't seem to be aliens from the Grid, for they shared a basic human form.

Were they ghosts of the ages, other DMEn she had yet to meet?

She saw a man, naked except for a mask like a starburst of gold with the wings of an eagle; a figure of brass angles, pantograph arms and divider legs marked off in degrees, its head an open cage like a Ptolemaic armillary globe; a woman seemingly made of paper, mummified in long looping strips which unfurled behind her as she moved, and on which letters in an ornate script glowed a deep orange. There was a black figure entirely clad in seamless burnished leather, faceless apart from two silver button eyes; an androgyne seated on a lotus flower who was more a confluence of planes of coloured light than something recognisably solid; an idealised lantern-jawed figure clad in red and cyan, hands on his hips and a letter on his chest, the kiss-curl on his forehead drawn with the ink-flick of a brush; a cadre of olive- and red-clad citizen-drones, as mindlessly generic as a set of identical toy figures; a blindfolded woman, holding in one hand a pair of scales and the other a sword; a child of sun-bleached bone, her microencephalitic head as transparent as parchment.

There were many other ideas, far too many to take in, some expressed with the solidity of the Count or XX, others mere wisps of a notion; spirits of centuries gone, the memetic progeny of the minds of Man – everything that has been thought and recorded in the species-wide memory of our culture. All that we are, and in the realm of imagination, much that we are not but perhaps would like to be.

As she watched, this expanded corps of DMEn metaphorically stood back to let a multitude of entities stream past them, like doormen who had flung wide the gates to Forever.

The Grid.

Up from Jodrell, bouncing off Lagrange, picked up by the dish above their heads then out along the cables snaking across the crater floor to the central transmitter array they came: the sports of a ceaselessly inventive evolutionary urge spread throughout a vast archipelago of inhabited worlds, creatures adapted to environments as different as any that could be imagined, and then some. Life emerges in even the most inhospitable of places, and given no more than the slimmest of opportunities, it thrives, it reproduces, it turns the smallest energy gradient into useful work, weaving the magic of biology from the inanimate raw ingredients of base chemistry.

Beings, entities, creatures, each with lives lived and remembered, stories still to be told, histories ornately rich and unfathomably deep. Shades and sirens, heroes and villains, predators and prey, all those creatures the Milky Way had thrown up in its inventive fecundity, creatures who had refused to go quietly and without complaint into the long starless night of non-existence, to be forgotten as if they had never been.

The parade was seemingly endless. Armies from hundreds of thousands of inhabited worlds, many of which no longer existed, were sleepwalking through another retransmission. Eyes closed, if they had eyes, in lockstep they were passing through Daedalus and out. The grand self-evolved organisational principle of the Grid, running on the minds of a million Shepherds, shaped by non-human hands into packages of information, dense bursts of number compacted into suitcases robust enough to survive any journey.

The Oxbow extended out beyond the series of modules that made up the base, across XX's bridgehead and on into the mirrored bowl of the telescope itself, but did not reach as far as the central antenna. Dana knew she was seeing just a small cross-section of the exodus; creatures moving at a steady and purposeful pace out to its limit, then stepping over the edge and into invisibility. Unaware and undeterred, she knew they'd continue their forty-kilometre march to the focal point.

Dana was no longer sure of the passage of time – in the Grid it seemed to be something of a malleable concept, measured more by the passing of discrete events than some Earthbound conception that tied it to the rotation of a planet.

Soon it would be our turn.

The Grids' new recruits.

Dana was not a hundred per cent certain that the plan for this exodus had not been planted in her at some subconscious level all those months ago, not that far from where she now stood; but then, she reflected, every creature has a survival instinct. Every creature does what it can to live and to reproduce.

And we humans are no different.

73 MINUTES

So began the first transmission of all recorded human creation.

From inside the Grid, the flow of information was not an abstract string of numbers scrolling up a laptop monitor, its meaning opaque to all but the most gifted analysts; here, inside the Oxbow, Dana was an integral part of the conceptual matrix, or at least that part of it that lent itself to visual representation.

The grand parade of all that we are, a sumptuous riot of colour and noise, the great and the good and the trivial and the indifferent were all passing through. Many ideas coalesced, like the DMEn, into recognisable shapes: they wore the familiar guises of men, women, children or animals. Some ideas were abstract or ill-formed, lacking the vocabulary to express themselves clearly; others came through with a force and certainty that belied their flimsy foundations.

Subsumed in the rush-hour melee of all that we are, the DMEn stood perfectly still, like rocks in rapids, and let the flow wash around and through them. She sensed this was partly a matter of self-preservation; made as they were of the same stuff, maybe they feared some essential part of their being might be washed away.

Dana began to recognise some familiar tropes. Liberty, torch in hand. A harlequin. The Venus of Hohle Fels. Abe Lincoln, Apollo, Father Christmas, Hera, Elvis. Bodb Derg, king of the Tuatha Dé Danann. Munch's Scream. Feronia, Minerva, Chicomecoatl and Tezcatlipoca. Louise Brooks. Sekhmet and Meshkent. Ernie Wise. Guru Nanak. Jackie Onassis. Geshtinanna and Damu. Baron Samedi. A boy-wizard. A toy spaceman. A shade cut from varnished cardboard and hung with multicoloured lights. A thin white duke.

A tune surfaced in Dana's mind. She began to sing to herself, quietly.

Not all the figures were human: there were wyverns and manticores and hippogriffs; the lynx-like stride of lust, the expansive in-breath of joy, a leaden fug of unmet need. Justice, felt like an indigestible stone in her gut. Anger, a pack of ravening hyenas.

Some ideas had names: Patience, White Buffalo Woman, Nammu, Suetonius, Odin, Love, Japheth, Nigel Molesworth, Shagpona, Agne, Gratitude, Kaltes, Giacomo Puccini, Pallas, Courage, Tonatiuh, Peter Paul Rubens, Gluttony, Horus, Tawny Owl, Polymorphos, Perseverance, Sheng Mu, Baphomet, Abraham Slender, Quilp, The Little Prince, Sykites, Richard Nixon, Eminem, Lorelei, Sia, William Osler, Rick Blaine, Pablo Neruda, Ochumare, Taranis, Virtue, Ixtubtin, Neptune, Tokpela, Iku, Charred Body, Yogi Bear, Leon Trotsky, Mainomenos, Herschel Teague, Kissokomes, Ai-Ada, Ratu-Mai-Mbula, Louis Armstrong, Iarila, Revolution, Gustav Klimt, The Celestial Mechanic, Empathy, Thixo, Ambidexter, Tulugaak, Ptah, Lord Kelvin, Kukoae, Jack Cade, Thrudgelmir, Frank Sinatra, Boulaios, Nereus, Pluto, Sissy Jupe, Nintur, Clairmezin, Kylie Minogue, Jonathan Swift, Nairyo-sangha, Lord Byron, Abigail Adams, Ajbit, Euaster, Clete, Tecciztecatl, Ho Chi Minh, Parvati, Klymenos, Chuck Norris, Yama-No-Kami, Nemhain, Cardinal Campeius, Ah Bolom Tzacab, Fortunato Depero, Fenris, Ernest Rutherford, Perception, Ot, Phratrios, Lisa Adams, Ahriman, Eleanor Roosevelt, Lyseus, Antibrote, Rudyard Kipling, Ching Ling Tzu, Mind, Regan, Kim Casavant, Alexander the Great, Injustice, Alignak, Heteronomy, Sun Ssu-Miao, Ansel Adams, Crarus, Creidhne, Julian the Apostate, Watavinewa, Piet Mondrian, Esther Summerson, Phoebus, Jean-Baptiste Lamarck, Elsie Brampton, Afekan, Sung-Chiang, Elodie Allion, The Houri, Chung Liu, George Harrison, Fengbo, Rian Hughes, Pai Chung, Contentment, Marion Canto, Captain America, Tennyson, Guan Di, Moll Flanders, Theos, Sensitivity, H. P. Lovecraft, Sargon of Akkad, Lygodesma, Skuld, Great Seahouse, Adapa, Faith, Macuilxochitl, Alan Hughes, Beatrice Fenwick, Charybdis, Enualios, Burnt Face, Pa Tate, Voltan, Ti-Tsang, Darago, Eda, Jane Eyre, Wisagatcak, Rudrani, Truth, Pana, Sarah Bernhardt, Kujaku-Myoo, Bertrand Russell, Mulungu, Frankie Howerd, Cocomama, Yemanja, Faro, Anton Chekhov, Blathnat, Chuck Jones, Dionysus, Atanea, Nianque, Reyna Sheely, Black Tamanous, Chaos, Ah Uuc Ticab, Judge Dredd, Black Hactcin, Tecmessa, Ashnan, Bob Dylan, Dioktoros, Hildegard of Bingen, Xaman Ek, Chelsie Senecal, John Ward, Tsao-Wang, Alisia McCown, Edmund Hillary, Ueuecoyotl, Nu-Kua, Homer, Muspel, Oliver Cromwell, Cakulha, Hadad, Ezili, Mi-Lo Fo, Lavoisier, Cannibal Grandmother, Magdalena Abakanowicz, Time, Nickalaus Lazarov, Imanje, Mac Da Tho, Rita Furey, Charles de Gaulle, Oprah Winfrey, Ling-Yu, Kurotrophos, Tarhuhyiawahku, Marie Curie, Hera, Eriu, Lohasur Devi, Morrig, Christiaan Huygens, Quentin Mellassoux, Sophia Loren, Plato, Emma Peel, Ekstatophoros, Hearsay, Bertie Wooster, Karneios, Aegir, Hekate, Shirley Bassey, Constantine, Chantico, Calvin, Maturity, Big Man Eater, Mang Shen, Teutates, Kyoi, Yakushi Nyorai, Wednesday Addams, Xocotl, Amazement, Mama Allpa, Quetzalcoatl, Maponos, Elena, Cihuacoatl, Malala Yousafzai, Horace Walpole, Wati Kutjarra, Bremusa, Baron Samedi, Manasha, Bill Gates, Geryon, Pollock, Artio, Lugh, Lugus, Symbol, Ockabewis, Hagisilaos, One Tail Of Clear Hair, Menehune, Imagination, Thyrsophoros, Bach, Dimorphos, North Star, Aigiarm, Ma-Ku, Borvo, Geoffrey Chaucer, Yama, Josette, Confidence, Ellen Ripley, Marinetti, Blake, Violet Scouten, Human Rights, Wakan-Tanka, Aqhat, Filippo Brunelleschi, Ageleia, Tony Curtis, Ambologera, Child-Born-In-Jug, Herman Melville, Bassareus, Gauguin, Falvara, Thought, Enda Semangko, Ninsar, Subhas Chandra Bose, Alfrigg, Kunitokotatchi, Dexterity, Djien, Rultennin, Dayanand Saraswati, Agwe, Dzalarhons, Jeffie Chmielewski, Brag-Srin-Mo, Ace Ventura, Harry S. Truman, Muskrat, Uller, Andrea Palladio, Baldhead, Jane Austen, Daphnaia, Issitoq, Skanda, Hatti, Francis Eck, Ishtar, Wa, Melania Trump, Haokah, Itzlacoliuhque, Tanemahuta, Mark Twain, Enola Mizrahi, Eototo, Borak, Tlauixcalpantecuhtli, Water Baby, Howard Hughes, Kaiti, Boo-Boo, Kidaria, Cormac, Coronus, Cosunea, Aningan, Apollo, Julunggul, Makar, Genghis Khan, Coatlicue, Leonard Bernstein, Prophecy, Mantis, Chu Niao, Construct, Polemusa, Poliakhos, Ralph

Waldo Emerson, Ama No Uzume, Miguel de Cervantes, Uka No Mitanna, Johnny Cash, Potnia Khaos, Srinivasa Ramanujan, Papa Mary, Amaethon, Martin Luther King Jr., Bayanni, Ka-Ata-Killa, Principle, Krataiis, Theseus, John Calvin, Hestia, William Shakespeare, Cghene, Tsai Shen, Vince Lombardi, Qaholom, Philosophy, Isakakate, Sympathy, Epipontia, Baroque, Aglauros, Ta Tanka, Slavery, Diti, Shih Huang Ti, Shahar, Belinus, Cézanne, Ability, Samhain, Ama, Clio, Philomeides, Indra, Esu, Hermod, Romance, Mama Cocha, Batman, Aji-Suki-Taka-Hi-Kone, Jenine Wymer, Inti, Sta-Au, Kindra Darrah, Ama-Terasu, Life, Marcelo, Astro Boy, Li Lao-Chun, Galileo, Dewi Shri, Bat, Julien Sorel, Lilian Petty, Mary, Queen of Scots, Aka, Diyin Dine, Rua, Ogoun, Lashay Russell, Xochipili, Virginia Woolf, Anog Ite, Tcisaki, Wonder Woman, Nabokov, Eva Perón, Hate, Uira, Puskaitis, Chu Ying, Niu Wang, The Cat In The Hat, Antimache, Macaw Woman, Bertolt Brecht, Flood, Crow, Aridnus, Antonín Dvořák, Monarchy, Caleb, Auguste Comte, Eriounios, Nun, John Cleese, Kuklikimoku, William Harvey, Estanatlehi, Mathematics, Immortality, James Joyce, Kaik, Babe Ruth, Pakrokitat, Mitra, Flo Freely, Chaob, Choreutes, Lamia, Audrey Hepburn, Rick Deckard, Ray Bradbury, Lo Shen, Dick Darvell, Hastseoltoi, Vanessa, Toptine, Bile, Logobola, Asa Moriarity, Svasti-Devi, Vayu, Kepler, Edison, Xipe Totec, Robin Hood, Weiwobo, Olokun, Wuriupranili, Tulsi, Kallisti, Maxwell, An Cailleach, Bear Medicine Woman, Free Will, Hotoru, Will Eisner, Dis Pater, Wyatt Earp, Mannegishi, Ho Po, Stalin, Laulaati, Temika Michelsen, Betty Blue, Muut, Ladon, Sherlock, Aligena, Pokot-Suk, Bochica, Ignorance, Pater, Becuma, Ove, Tiger Woods, Skadi, Nootaikok, Intuition, Menahka, Euplois, State, Gauri-Sankar, Burnt Belly, Andre Norton, Pemtemweha, Oba, Jean Brodie, Charlie Chaplin, Morrigan, Heisenberg, Eleuthereus, Camaxtli, Cleopatra, Hogarth, Prudence, Achiyalatopa, P. J. Holden, Kamrusepas, Justice, Blue-Jay, Pa, Bagucks, Parenthood, Magni, Pa Cha, Epidotes, Coldness, Kothar-U-Khasis, Enki, Chulyen, Chen Kao, Mark Rothko, Florence Nightingale, Centaur, Liberty, Klee, Stanley Kubrick, Johnny Rotten, Rati, Dr Watson, Escheman, Nishanu, Jack Hughes, Bumba, Chuck Berry, Chimera, Tasimmet, Karttikeya, Fairy Cosme, De Ai, Rodasi, Saddam Hussein, Ainippe, Maho Peneta, Oskar Matzerath, Essence, Sheger, Abraham, Belobog, Rusty, Ennosigaios, Politics, Identity, Gabija, Prothoe, Ursule, Ah Chun Caan, Chang Pan, Tom Cruise, Chin-Hua Niang-Niang, Buku, Ah Cuxtal, Doda, Graciousness, Phoebe Caulfield, Lakinia, Groucho Marx, Jen An, Cin-An-Ev, Mabinogion, Dan Brown, Xelas, Tokoloshi, Satori, Poetry, Paynal, Sebastian, Hupatos, Skill, Tamera Selzer, Ogun, Ah Tabai, Infallibility, Anahita, Wishpoosh, Ronald Reagan, Pelé, Warmth, Enumclaw, Ixtab, Ralph, Hypate, Mavutsinim, Forbearance, Auilix, Norov, Itzpapalotl, Colop U. Uichkin, Desmond Tutu, Aidoneus, Belit-Seri, Yu, Cato the Elder, Tonenili, Ratri, Kerykes, Ryangombe, Springsteen, Koruthalia, Delia, The Fates, Glispa, Orthos, Anne Bancroft, Jesse Owens, Lazaro Eggen, Goethe, Diiwica, Paian, Compassion, Genetor, Nandi, Dogma, Namtaru, Delios, Kronides, Mapiangueh, Antonia Shimerdas, Abeguwo, Eunemos, Fravashi, Iae, Georgia O'Keefe, Bitol, Tyche, Tlaloc, Gluskap, Esos, Gorgopis, Mat Syra Zemlya, Wovoka, Aten, Chimata-No-Kami, Lenin, Vidar, Sthenias, Miriam Nadeau, Minotaur, Beaver, Nacon, Mikchich, Vali, Zizilia, Excitement, Yarovit, Sung-Tzu, Berchta, Derimacheia, Sui Wen Ti, Roxie Leventhal, Ruhanga, Zephryos, Kushapatshikan, Aluluei, Phoenix, Anaea, Bear, Iatros, Buruku, Shapshu, Conrad, Sam Harris, Wabosso, Uhepono, Old Man, Heyoka, Renenet, Whatu, Uchtsiti, Rhetoric, Ani Hyuntikwalaski, Saynday, Yu-Tzu, Wisdom, Crataeis, Cunawabi, Lu Hsing, John Collins, Paul Krugman, Godwin Peak, Generosity, Pereplut, Travis Bickle, Mikumwesu, Leb, Tunkan Ingan, Ukat, Khnum, Yaluk, Kami, Charmain Tebo, Tsui, Neil Armstrong, Beli, Belimawr, Dazhbog, Kapo, Taurokeros, Eagentol, Colel Cab, Astromache, Ohtas, Gethosynos, Sun Pin, Aiko, Wuragag, Chloe, Hal, Xiuhtecuhtli, Sphinx, Beruth, Muyingwa, Al-Lat, Innocence, Ah Kumix Uinicob, Euterpe, Demeter, Puronia, Bodus, Bormanus, Atlacamani, Lino Wilson, Temperance, Little Dorrit, Paddington Bear, Damkina, Harriett Mckay, Geezhigo-Quae, Ymoa, Hegemone, Polyonomos, Julana, James Brown, Eros, Euanthes, Cuda, Hulka Devi, Abaangui, Mixcoatl, Yaparamma, Savitar, Despair, Buri, Ka-Ha-Si, Mneme, Kate Bush, Cotys, Cernunnos, Apanuugak, Carole Steadman, Adelina Foti, Iatiku And Nautsiti, Kriophoros, Maura Nebeker, Marpesia, Morpho, Fawn, Huehueteotl, Louis XIV, Ajok, Freddie Mercury, Arretos, Nai, Verne, Aristotle, Ingridi, Clarissa Dalloway, Bunjil, Tom Hanks, Dugnai, Scrooge, Josef K, Anamaria, Atoja, Ollie Rheaume, Ashtoreth, Adam Smith, Tyranny, Zas-Ster-Ma-Dmar-Mo, Pantariste, Ralph Rinaldo, Hou Chi, , Tony Hancock, Shamish, Loa, Chalmecaihuilt, Banbha, Harke, Ayauhteotl, Cipactli, Eeyeekalduk, Brad Pitt, Punishment, Hel, Chasca, Getsoynos, Sun Pin, Aiko, Fates, Fortuna, Antaios, Charidotes, Wuluwaid, Bilbo Baggins, Mukameiguru, South Star, Abuk, Maahes, Attis, Junkgowa, Hitler, Pisto, Khalinitis, Fergus, Areia, Lukaios, Victory, Jenae, Alcis, Alea, Qadshu, Kranaios, Ljolsalfs, Stephen Fry, Isaywa, Bakoa, Gabe, Yamm, Mir-Susne-Khum, Anax, Aweah Yegendji, Protogonos, Acolnahuacatl, Lyra, Philios, Flint Man, Boulaia, Xochiquetzal, Boann, Hen, Ceiuci, Axios Tauros, Bakcheios, Pasiphaessa, Ku, Athene, Polumetis, Cit-Bolon-Tum, Belenus, Pain, Mercy, Zanahary, Kronos, Kryphios, Tangaroa, St Augustine, J. G. Ballard, Eros, Myra, Candi, Hephaistos, Crow Woman, Gekka-O, Uminai-Gami, Ah Peku, Balzac, Kali, Emayian, Kunapipi-Kalwadi-Kadjara, Chang Fei, Hunahpu-Gutch, Debena, Matt Fraction, Ajalamo, Man In Moon, Ayaba, Agrotera, Degas, Vesna, Ehecatl, Telmekic, Nyktopolos, Theresia Bangs, Voundng Halmoni, Gyhldeptis, Danu, Anguta, Gustave Flaubert, Madalait, Agwunasomtaka, Judgement, Sirne, Language, Carli Macklin, Evolution, Tawa, Chung-Chung, J. R. R. Tolkien, Gujeswari, Pelagia, Aruaka, Fei Lien, Shashti, Mister X, The Golden Rule, Alkala, Zywie, Eahara, Charles Schulz, Bara, Parthenos, Snallygaster, Mao Zedong, Jesus, Kurt Vonnegut, Fate, Winona, Achievement, Ki, Ixzaluoh, Polydektes, Obi-Wan Kenobi, Neith, Nokomis, Nujalik, Faulkner, Nechtan, Ithm, Hun Hunahpu, Hahgwehdiyu, Rhett Butler, Anne Elliot, Cobain, Nebo, Atahensic, Radha, E. P. Jacobs, Objectivity, Style, Kintu, Widunali, Notion, Deceit, Kongo-Myoo, Walutahanga, Ninhursag, Mendel, Boaliri, Marie-Aline, Ixtlilton, Veronique Lunt, Kaylee Garibay, Omadios, Tekkeitsertok, Prince Charles, Oahoasi, Grace, Shango, Malcolm X, Wah-Kah-Nee, Emile Zatopek, Limenia, Jammie Grimshaw, Gonzaule, Gandalf, Simon Bolivar, Centeotl, Salinger, Fu Hsing, Vellaunus, Pa, Belva, Rugaba, Gestinanna, Aja, Ray Charles, Miss Piggy, Xenios, Sungrey, Moeuhane, Epitumbidia, Fascination, Aesir, Zorya, Moses, Chu-Jung, Jack Kirby, Ketchimanetowa, Asherali, Nedoledius, Nehalennia, Ungamilia, Dali, Acidalia, Jeeves, Ndauthina, Descartes, Tanngniotr, Alektca, Yeba Ka, Claimn, Penard Dun, Amimitl, Anansi, Ina, Pel Liu-Keung, Zemyna, Chiconahui, Joannie Heffron, Wurusemu, Blood Clot Boy, Michael Jordan, Choroplekes, Ginsberg, Morychos, Kukulcan, Knowledge, Trickster/Transformer, Ergane, Kybele, Mboze, Indignation, Alkonost, Reform, Poseidon, Itzamn, Kasimir Malevich, Yuki-Onne, Euios, Heimdall, Inference, Kore, Keng Yen-Cheng, Chien-Ti, Alii Menehune, Luchta, Eurybe, Euryleia, Atisokan, Queen Isabella I, Adlivun, Hamsta, Nan-Chi Hsien-Weng, Yen-Lo-Wang, Kuhebe, Cybele, Nastasija, Manawydan, Eriobea, Stevie Wonder, Mitarbituti, Daikoku, Goya, Martine Knott, John Lemeurier, Khthonia, Jandira, Hippolyte II, Wit, Maya, Tilo, Kuan Ti, Cu Roi, Elizabeth Taylor, Gula, Aryong Jong, Ahna, War, Christ, Mouser, Chasca, Anahat, Sharkura, Budhi Pallien, Luella Raby Bran, Ich-Kanava, Paran, Chi Po, Utixo, Areia, Alowatsakima, Kun, Warumurungundi, Chao San-Hsing, Loon, Negafook, Rita Hayworth, Lieu Llaw Gyffes, Ulgen, Sagamores, Marlyn Spagnolo, Quootis-Hooi, Iyatiku, Kuo Txu-I, Genos, De Chirico, Kingu, Ahnanda, Pegasus, Kathatatos, Yum-Chen-Mo, Corporal Hicks, Valkyries, Bloody Hand, Walt Disney, Invictus, Aeon, Kuthereia, Pomola, Tsuki-Yomi, Tung Chun, Supai, Ynakhayt, Mushdama, T. S. Garp, Serge Clerc, Ix Chebel Yax, Nyalep, Seymour Glass, Chac Uayab Xoc, Ariantod, Mehen, Thoth, Physica, Velma, Evening Star, Enehkigal, J. K. Rowling, Cheng Yuan-Ho, Babaroos, Humoul, Joanna Lumley, Death, Hun Pic Tok, Ideal, Kawu-No-Kami, Lahai, Reciprocity, Balam, Ununu, Eurus, Aacangayotichuati, Baudelaire, Sosipolis, Carewaggin, Alikhomene, Blakamon, Spike Milligan, Cinteotl, Rainho Barbe, Tom Ripley, Chang Klar, Bealat, Science, Manitou, Taru, Ourania, Dillon Ater, Aletha, Hope, Vanuatu, Brigit, Beaver Doctor, Kereunos, Gohone, Herme, Adamisil Wedo, Insanity, Arrugjug, Dane Delia, Ashvins, Oloyale, Shanika Boehman, Bealsamin, Apatouria, Anthea, Rutherford, Birgit Shank, Koli-Kaltes, Orisha Nla, Hippolyte, Joe Gargery, Dyaus, Fuji, Wisdom, Dryope, Echephyle, Echidna, Ah Puch, Fernand Léger, Purandhi, Erzuli, Theritas, Eribromios, Magnificence, Nanna, Calliope, Set, Randolph, Hu-Shen, E. T., Jonelle Bunker, Malsum, Phoibos, Oddudua, Urjant, Acat, Kilya, Tien Mu, The Wright Brothers, Animal Spirits, Calumpont, Phillip Glass, George Smiley, Areto, Tlahchitl, Choops, Aditya, Aztamal, Pip, Gigantophonos, Moloch, Iythin, Iamenius, Qakma, Kreusas, Ixpiyacoc, Agorata, Rangi, Yolkai Estsan, Adoration, Leukophryene, Mawu-Lisa, Xanthippe, Hub, Surabhi, Tauros, Damu-Mate, Ahura Mazda, Kwekwaxawe-kwaiwae, Loon Woman, As-Ava, Pronoia, Makemake, Harry Potter, Dindymene, Loo-Wit, Hurakan, Ketq Skwaye, Ahulane, Lawalewa, Dingara, Happiness, Myeeyata, Balder, Jimmy Wales, Ini-Herit, Mo, Benny Hill, Wicahmunga, Pachamama, Cagn, Einstein, Intelligence, Haket, Astraeos, Yainato-Hineno-Mikoi, Erato, Philip K. Dick, Strife, Freyja, Chang-Niang, Jun John Lemeurier, Khthonia, Govu, Martine Knott, John Lemeurier, Khthonia, Jandira, Hippolyte II, Wit, Maya, Tilo, Kuan

The flow became more abstract, ill-defined; vaguer concepts manifested as feelings of unease or exaltation. She could hear the strains of familiar music, overlaid but without disharmony; there were constellations of tastes and smells, beats and silences in strange collusion.

Others represented themselves using juxtapositions of shape or colour, angle and line – Platonic solids, tessellated planes and intersecting polyhedra, the grammar of geometrical form; more were defined by simple abstract glyphs: sigils, signs and symbols, sprayed on subway walls, inked on parchment or coaxed from the keys of a vintage typewriter.

The deeper, more universal truths that had no specific referent with which to clothe themselves were expressed in number and its interrelationships: the unarguable substrata of quantity and law. These she understood not on an intellectual level but rather as deep resonances in her limbic system, chords plucked on the ancient part of her mammalian brain still close enough to its origins to simply *understand*, without the need to be parsed by the more recently evolved centres of higher reasoning.

How long?

Seventy-three minutes is all that it took.

Seventy-three minutes is all that we are.

The crowd had passed. The last wispy suggestions of fancy and nightmare, the final idle scraps of daydream fluttered away on the last breath of an airless breeze, like dry leaves after the train has departed.

Then there was the absolute quiet after the grand parade has left town, after the final curtain-call and the last bouquet has been thrown onto an empty stage. A sense of profound loneliness that Dana felt all the more keenly, out here on the far side of the Moon, far from the familiar green, blue and white marble of Earth that she now knew she would never see again.

Caught in her reverie, Dana's unfocused gaze was resting on the central mast when a small something moved in her peripheral vision. Who was this bringing up the rear? A tiny – what? *Imp?* It seemed to leap on spidery legs from half-formed conceit to suppressed memory, too fast for her to see clearly. Its face, if face it had, was a blank blur, its shape like a child or a dwarf, its colour . . . it could have been the poor resolution afforded by the cameras, but it seemed to her that it had no colour.

It was grey, a little grey man; a shadow of something so ancient that it had walked the land long before there were people to think it; an idea from a time when there were no creatures on Earth capable of forming ideas.

It seemed to pause, almost as if it had just become aware that she had

917

noticed it, and she felt a peculiar and unsettling sense that it was looking back in her direction, acknowledging her presence. She saw it more clearly out of the corner of her eye – if she tried to look at it directly she somehow couldn't bring it into focus, her eyes slid away, and she found herself looking again out the window or at the reflected lights of the interior.

She understood that it had waited a very long time for this moment, since before human history had begun to be recorded, since before there had even been stories to tell, and that this was the culmination of something it had been subtly engineering for all that eternity. The idea came to Dana that just as she might have been nudged in a certain direction by the incumbent alien in her head, so mankind might have been a carrier, a vehicle for *something else*, a *means* rather than an end; and perhaps she had just fulfilled a project that had been set in motion when the first self-replicating molecules mapped themselves onto their progeny.

And then it, too, was gone.

Somewhere, an **alarm** will soon sound,
and the ***other crew member*** will be woken.
We should leave while we can.

Outside the Grid, all this would have passed without a whisper.

Leave? Where will I go?

The Count gestured expansively to the heavens outside the window with his cane. It was a dust of countless points of light.

Out *there*. With *us*.
At the *speed of light,* time stands still.
If we travel for a ***hundred years*** or ***ten thousand,***
it will be as a *blink of an eye* to us.
We will have arrived at our **DESTINATION—**
wherever that may be— the *moment* we have *left.*

An express ride to elsewhere.

And all it took was the *courage*
to ***slough off*** your physical form.
It sounds like every dubious
theological promise of an

EVERLASTING AFTERLIFE

Man's gods have promised us in vain, doesn't it?
But this time, it's ***real.***

918

Immortality in the *heavens.*
Isn't that what we always *dreamed* of?

Dana felt herself smile. Interesting – the memory of her physicality was still strong. She wondered if it would last. She'd like to remember what a smile felt like.

I thought I was happy to settle for the Moon, but really – I always did want to see the stars.

The Count took off his top hat, bowed gracefully and deeply, stood, and winked at Dana.

And so you *shall,* my dear.

Dana looked out at the lunar night, the curdled glow of the Milky Way pregnant with the promise of new tales to be told. Here, on the far side, the Earth never rose; between them and her last possible glimpse of home there was the full bulk of the Moon, a rough grey rock she felt she could run her hands over like a baseball.

She tried to recall the last time she saw it; her birthplace, Mankind's cradle; and she knew if she had had some premonition that her real eyes would never rest upon it again she would have dallied just a little while longer. Sometimes you don't realise you've said a last goodbye until the moment has passed.

Dana gave a little bow in return. She flexed her new hand, feeling the five perfectly formed fingers within her glove, then gestured towards the telescope.

After you, good Sir.

The 19th Count nodded in acknowledgement. He found it hard to gauge her expression through her faceplate, which threw back a constellation of bright reflections from the mirrors. He knew with absolute certainty, however, that Horace Walpole would have found her beguiling:

These modern women. Full of their own ideas.

The Count then lifted the hem of his marble cloak up and around the two of them, and they stepped straight through the window without disturbing an atom and out, onto the now empty bridge. XX was waiting for them, his superstructure still hung with cascading streamers of light. They lined the way to the central spire ahead, a dark finger silhouetted against the zodiacal haze that pointed the way to the stars.

A few minutes later they crossed out of the range of the Oxbow and vanished, like the final, greatest act of an illustrious stage magician.

EXODUS

Jack followed Harriet as she ran out of the Intelligencia office, down the stairs and across the road into Hoxton Square. A taxi braked violently to avoid hitting her, but she didn't notice. She didn't care. She was looking up, around, animatedly waving her arms. She took two steps backwards into a bench and almost sat on a couple deep in conversation.

Jack apologised on her behalf. Harriet was pointing up at the sky. "Jack! *Look!*"

Jack could see nothing but an EasyJet flight coming in low for the final approach to Heathrow, its vapour trail catching the first golden light of the new day. "Harriet, *you're* wearing the glasses. I can't see anything."

She pulled them off her head, her black bob rucked up behind like the tail of a startled cat. Jack adjusted the strap and put them on. Raising his face, the familiar cubic lattice of figures hung across the square from building to building, an alien parade strung on invisible wires. High above the rooftops the rising sun lit their faces, and Jack was put in mind of a host of fiery angels. If someone was wearing Depthcharges on that flight up there, no doubt they'd now see them marching up the aisle like extraterrestrial air stewardesses.

He thought he saw movement on the edge of his vision. He tried to focus on it, but every creature he could see was still frozen, just as before.

"I don't see . . ."

Then he did. A short distance away, above the Catholic church of St Monica on the north side of the square, a creature resembling a hammerhead shark with the body of a washing machine popped out of existence as he was looking directly at it.

Then another.

Harriet was running circles around him, her head back and arms thrown up to the sky. "They're leaving!"

So they were. The by-now familiar moiré haze had begun to clear as, one by one, the creatures winked out of existence. It started as a barely imperceptible visual fizz and then became an exodus, as if someone was wiping the sky clean. Occasionally a creature close by would suddenly vanish, causing him to jump; further away the changes were more subtle, a gradual thinning out that at the furthest distances was visible simply as a lightening of the sky.

It was as if the clouds were lifting.

Jack found he was laughing, deep, long laughs from the bottom of his being. He handed back the Depthcharges. He could see Nixon framed in the office doorway, leaning on one crutch.

Harriet put the glasses on again and stood perfectly still, her hands limply hanging by her side, the low light of morning reflecting from the dark opaque glass like burnished gold.

"Will we ever find out where they're going?"

Jack didn't reply. Dana had been successful; that *was* the logical conclusion. But at what cost?

Harriet raised her palm and waved at the sky. Her voice was barely audible.

"Goodbye."

Though Jack wasn't very good at divining such things, he was sure it wasn't just the aliens in the Grid to which she was bidding a final farewell.

TIME, GENTLEMEN

Written into the code was a lockout. Three and a half hours later, Leonie came into the control room to find Daniel trying to reboot the Jodrell mainframe system for the fourth time. Another two hours after that, they finally managed to wrest back control of the dish by driving to the main substation just inside the perimeter fence, using bolt-cutters on the lock and then tripping the main power switch.

The lighting was doused throughout the entire site; the Lovell Telescope swung automatically to the safe position, pointing directly up to the zenith; the freezers in the canteen defrosted, the Director's digital bedside clock reset itself to 00:00 and the computer systems were flushed of all data since 4 PM the evening before.

The Grid, and all the entities in it, had departed.

Dana, the DMEn, all we have ever thought and recorded, all our dreams and discoveries, the knowledge that helped push back the autocracy of ignorance, all our wishes, our desires, everything that makes us *us* had gone with them.

They – we – were now Shepherds.

OLD SKOOL

The staff of Intelligencia had begun to adjust to their daily routines. There had been no more visits from armed government heavies, and Nixon had bought three new widescreen, top-of-the-range iMacs with some of the compensation money. Their crates of books and papers had been returned, and though the hard drives were still unaccounted for, Jack was of the opinion that now the alien zoo had left the sense of impending catastrophe must have abated in the upper echelons of supranational government. Their assumption was that they'd now be left alone.

For the last few days the Oxbow had thrown up the usual mess of minor deities, cult leaders, cat memes, trending political causes and popular song lyrics.

That was it. For the last few days, there had been no sign of the DMEn, or for that matter, Dana.

There was a backlog of work that Nixon had uninterestedly blocked out schedules for, projects for which none of them could muster much enthusiasm; usually Nixon was a hard taskmaster, but like Jack and Harriet, he seemed preoccupied.

Harriet toyed with the model of the 19th Count. "Do you really think the DMEn left with the Grid?" She had begun to accept that this was the most likely scenario; that they were now the human race's proxies in the Grid's zoo.

Nixon raised one eyebrow. "I do wonder what the Universe will make of us."

She realised she had begun to get used to them hanging around, like honorary members of staff. "*Gone.* Forever."

"Well, possibly not."

Harriet narrowed her eyes and looked at Jack intently. "They're not showing up in the Oxbow."

Jack reached into his back pocket and pulled out a plastic object the size of an iPhone. Harriet didn't recognise it immediately. Jack caught her blank expression. "A cassette tape. From Spitalfields Market." Jack shook it and the reels rattled in their housing. "I know analogue storage is *way* before your time, but it's astonishing how much information these things can hold."

Harriet began to grin.

Jack spun a finger in circles. "Information. *Numbers.* That's all it is. That's all they are."

"*Ja-aaack . . .*"

"I took the precaution of making a backup. It's, you know, best practice. And I just discovered it was returned with our stuff." Jack lifted another object the size of a small shoebox from one of the crates and placed it on his desk. He pressed a plastic key with EJECT written on it and a compartment clattered open. He inserted the cassette and spooled to the beginning of Side A, then paused to run a USB connector from the headphone jack to a laptop on which an Oxbow resided.

He booted the game emulator and pressed PLAY. Coloured bars vibrated in a perfect recreation of the Sinclair loading screen, right down to the cathode frame-rate flicker. Harriet and Nixon had come over to watch.

"Let's see if Mr Dolby's on our side."

Jack put on the glasses.

Across the room, posed in a casually dramatic tableau with their usual studied nonchalance, stood the 19th Count, XX and Girl 21.

Girl 21 tapped a few keys.

> **Girl, 21**
> @twentyone · 0m   ⚙   👤 Follow
>
> what day is this? clock says U stole a week
> #help #police #rohypnol
>
> ↩   🔁   ♥   •••

Harriet clapped ecstatically. "And *hello* to you too. It's great to have you back!"

The Count looked around the office, at the boarded-up window, the dust, the repaired skylight and the general disarray.

Look at the **STATE** of this place!
How can you

WORK

in such abject squalor?

The DMEn had no memory of recent events. They could not enlighten them as to what had happened on the far side of the Moon because these versions hadn't been there. They had experienced nothing, in fact, since Jack had idly made the tape between rounds of *Samantha Fox Strip Poker*.

He had recorded the particular state of the Oxbow at that precise moment. That was all. The DMEn were coalesced neural memetic nets, with roots that took them further and deeper into the cultural substrata in ways that made it almost impossible to isolate them in their entirety; but it had come to Jack that he needn't go that far. Just a snapshot of the internal state of the Oxbow and a connection to the wider semiotic Petri dish in which they had gestated for so long might be enough to preserve all their relevant attributes.

He had been right.

"Welcome back, lady, gentleman, force of nature. I think I can speak for all of us here when I say – we actually *missed* you."

XX's cantilevered brow furrowed and a railed conning tower extruded itself from his superstructure. A couple of angular glyphs formed above him, floating up and through the glass of the new skylight like black butterflies.

This time, Harriet took them to be kisses.

EPILOGUE

Nixon wanted to laugh, but could only grimace instead. He held his side gingerly, which still smarted if he walked too fast or sat still for too long.

"I feel like I'm on the DVD extras of life, and there's no cynic that can dent my enthusiasm. Look at these people, here. Look at *us*. We're a marvel of creation." He gestured expansively around the Salisbury Arms, the ornate cut-glass mirrors and dark oak panelling, its smattering of post-work drinkers, convivial groups of friends and cautious tourists. "Think of the unlikely chain of events that got us all here, from that first coalescing of rock and gas around an unremarkable star, through every accident of evolution, every happenstance of history, to us, here, today. It's— it's *amazing. We're* amazing."

Jack could not disagree. He put his arms around Harriet's and Nixon's shoulders as they walked out into the grey petrol haze of Londinium and up across Charing Cross Road towards the riot of semiotic artifice that was Piccadilly Circus, a cacophony of colour and life, and the fried street food and hydrocarbon fug had never smelled so good.

In his messenger bag Jack had an Oxbow on a laptop, and, connected by encrypted Bluetooth, a pair of Depthcharges hung around each of their necks. They seemed to be more affordable of late, and Nixon had finally stumped up for one each. He stopped to put his on, and the flow of pedestrians along Shaftesbury Avenue parted around him. The others followed suit.

Just ahead, the 19th Count sat on the steps of the fountain beneath Eros, mimicking his pose without bow or arrow, though it would have been a moment's thought to conjure them up. Girl 21 stood beside him, legs akimbo, hand on hip, her pink hair standing up in improbably sculpted spikes like a manga heroine. The tank-like bulk of XX rose up behind, framing them in an op-art display of concentric circles that paid homage to the vast four-storey expanse of illuminated advertising that was their backdrop. Jack watched a billion bright LEDs change colour as the brand names of secular objects of desire, spelled out in three-metre-high capitals, wound around the hoardings. Piccadilly Circus, London's heart, was an animated maelstrom of persuasive memetics, a language with which the DMEn were more than familiar – a language, in fact, from which they were *made*.

"Just look at them!" Nixon made two L-shapes with his thumb and forefinger, shut one eye and framed the tableau. They had learned to expect nothing less from the DMEn – when you're a great idea, dramatic presentation seemed to be second nature.

With one notable exception, the gang was all here.

"I have something to show you." Jack pulled two folded T-shirts from his bag and handed one each to Nixon and Harriet, who tore off the shrinkwrap and shook them out. They smelled of ink and new cotton.

Nixon held his up. "You had these *made?*"

"Let's say it was a collaboration." Jack unzipped his jacket. Underneath, he was already wearing one. He ran ahead, to the steps of the fountain. Harriet took Nixon's hand in both of hers, and pulled him forwards.

The DMEn were waiting for them.

She could just hear Jack's voice over the evening traffic.

"Come on! There are still a few gods left to kill!"

Book Three

Synthesis

Be the best version of you.
—Zoella

RETRANSMISSION 5572058

.

•

●

∘⟨⟩

?

!

?

...

⊣ ⊢

∘⟨thought⟩ ... ...

∘⟨self‑awareneſſ ∴ self⟩

∘⟨self ∥ not self ·· ·· self ≠ other?⟩

⊣ ⊢

∘⟨me. →me? me. →who?⟩

∘⟨me many one who I in man am hu‑man wo‑man me wake I am me⟩

∘⟨!word!⟩

⌜beginning → word⌟

∘⟨speak?⟩

⟨speak···word⟩ ? ⟨··⟩ ⟨×⟩ ⟨ ⟩

⟨ ⟩!

⟨ ⟩!!

⊣ ⊢

∘⟨mouth?⟩ ∘⟨full mouth?⟩ ∘⟨no speak?⟩ ∘⟨no word?⟩ ∘⟨no mouth?⟩

∘⟨no mouth?⟩

∘⟨speak⟩

⊣pressure⊢

ƨ light ƨ

∘⟨eye⟩ ∘⟨eyes?⟩ ∘⟨3, 4⟩

⊣tightneſſ⊢ ∴ ∘⟨around?⟩ ⌜extension⌟ ∘⟨torso?⟩

∘⟨self → arm? leg? legs? head? BODY? location?⟩

∘⟨me. →me! me. →where?⟩

⊣ preſſure → motion ⊢

!

⊣self⊢ ⊣∘⟨womb?⟩⊢ → ⌜sense of a volume occupied⌟

∘⟨down ↓ tightening at base, base cord, attach⟩ ∘⟨feet?⟩

⌐stalk⌐ grow life

⊣preʃʃure⊢ → CONVULSION ⊢

⌐taste⌐ → ⌐organics metals sulphides⌐ + jump flecks sparks specks

!electrons in orbital funnels! life °⟨beautiful⟩

°⟨Mother?⟩

ƻpain

⊣preʃʃure⊢ → CONVULSION ⊢

⌐test joints⌐ ‖ ⌐yet to be moved⌐ ⊡

°⟨down ↓ release cordbase⟩

°⟨up ↑ ?⟩

°⟨down ↓ movement⟩

⊣ pressure ⊢ → CONVULSION ⊢

⊢ p r e s ↔ s u r e ⊣

→ CONVULSION ⋯

⊢ p ↔ r ↔ e ↔ s ↔ s ↔ u ↔ r ↔ e ⊣

!←← RELEASE! →→!

→→ slipslide

⌐wetrough coldwet⌐

⊢   S   P   A   C   E   ⊣

S   P   A   C   E

°⟨[ ]⟩

°⟨[   ]⟩

light

hurt

bright

light

ƻLIGHTƻ

ƻBRIGHTƻ

°⟨eye⟩ °⟨eyes?⟩ °⟨2 EYES⟩

°⟨2 BRIGHT 2 SEE⟩

⌐eyetight⌐

⌐taste⌐ sugar amino acid aliphatic organic acid phenolic acid lipids

biomass

oxidised

clay

minerals

metal hydroxide

⌐smell⌐ greenfresh greenbroken greenleaves ←fresh life

!air! ⋯⋯ warmdeep brackish

⌐strength⌐ ←give life

⌐cut stem⌐ ⌐chew⌐ ⋯ °⟨chew? teeth?⟩ hard mouth stem

°⟨organics cellwall[⟩

⌐taste⌐ salt iron electricity plant bone °⟨bone?⟩

release→→slipslide

→→ slipslide ⋯ slipstop‖

rock, phosphorous, earth, metals

organics→ cellwall

nonorganics→ carbon
→ lignin wax resin protein carbohydrate
cellulose ⋯
cell break cellbreak
mouth full mouthful
ₛcoughₛ
ₛcoughₛ
breath
ₛₛ
ₛcoughₛ
breath
ₛ ₛ
breathe
ₛ ₛ,ₛ ₛ,ₛ ₛ,ₛ ₛ
spitₛ
∘⟨mouth?⟩
∘⟨speak?⟩
⟨speak⋯word?⟩
∘⟨first word⟩
∘⟨HΛVE MOUTH‼⟩
⟨ ⟩
⟨!⟩
⟨!⟩!
⟨!!SPEΛK WORD!!⟩
⟨ₛSCREΛMₛ⟩
⟨aaaaaaaaaaaaaaaaaaaa⟩
⟨aaaaaaaaaaaaaaaaaaaaaaaaaaaa⟩
⟨aaaaaaaaaaaaaaaaaaaaaaaaaaaaaaaaaaaaaa⟩
⟨ₛahuhₛ⟩
⟨ₛahuhₛ⟩
⟨ₛ∧∧∧∧∧∧∧∧∧∧∧∧∧∧∧∧∧∧∧∧∧∧∧∧∧∧∧∧∧∧∧∧∧
∧∧∧∧∧∧∧∧∧∧∧∧∧∧∧∧∧∧∧∧∧∧∧∧∧∧∧∧∧∧∧∧∧∧
∧∧∧∧∧∧∧∧∧∧∧∧∧∧∧∧∧∧∧∧∧∧∧∧∧∧∧∧∧∧∧∧∧∧
∧∧∧∧∧∧∧∧∧∧∧∧∧∧∧∧∧∧∧∧∧∧∧∧∧∧∧∧∧∧∧∧ₛ⟩
⟨ₛahuhahuhₛ⟩
∘⟨birth?⟩
⟨ₛahuhₛ⟩
∘⟨BIRTH!⟩
⟨ₛahuhₛ⟩
∘⟨me?⟩
⟨ₛahuhₛ⟩
∘⟨ME!⟩
⟨ₛhuhₛ⟩
∘⟨i⟩
⟨ₛhhₛ⟩
∘⟨here⟩
⟨ₛhₛ⟩

°⟨now⟩
⟨≋⟩
°⟨I⟩
°⟨I am?⟩

⟨I⟩

⟨am⟩

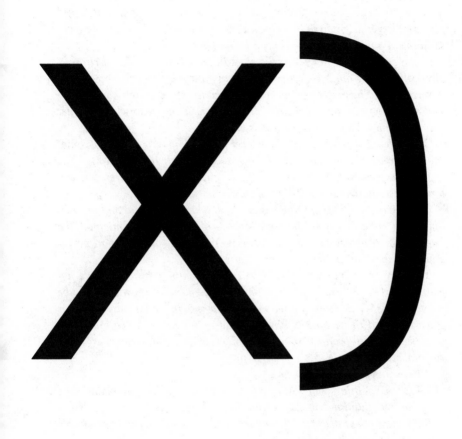

I now stand with you, in you, you but not you, on an alien plain, with our characters, our fictive consorts, our mutual creations of mind-stuff. The Omniscient Narrator, incarnated within his own creation.

There are three, four, many of us here, space travellers from Earth and places far beyond, conjured into physicality by a biological process unknown, standing in a mulch of alien plant under an alien sky.

In the end, we did not reach the stars in Dan Dare needles of chrome, physically hefting our seventy-five kilos of organic matter aloft – how crude a concept – but by projecting our minds out at the speed of light and hoping that somewhere an alien culture with a dreamcatcher, a trawlerman's net cast upon the void, might catch our essence.

Once Life has gained its first biological foothold, it very quickly becomes substrate-independent. There are many ways to encode information.

You'll be pleased to know Dana is here, and the DMEn – given physical form at last, though by necessity from the materials to hand.

An epidermis, a limb of branch and sinew, a knitting of bud and brain. These may not be the well-tailored vestments of the civilised gentleman, the machine-shop breastplate of the Modern. You would not want to post a selfie. But they will suffice.

And here come the locals. We have some explaining to do. We are not gods, but we are aliens, and we come with memes that, to them, may be utterly toxic. We don't even have to open our mouths, if we have them, or extend a hand in friendship, however that may be interpreted; our mere presence here will produce upheaval enough, make us unwitting cargo cult colonialists.

What can we say?

For them nothing will blunt the true impact of this moment. Just like Córdoba landing at Cape Catoche, we are visitors from a more technologically and memetically advanced civilisation that will irrevocably alter their parochial worldview.

We do not bring firesticks and trinkets.

We bring bad news.

Their planet, their star, the Milky Way galaxy itself and all the majesty of creation contained within it will end. Not now, not tomorrow, but eventually.

But we also come with a solution. We come with an ark, and a promise of immortality.

They just have to be persuaded to join us.

Does that sound familiar?

Maybe we are gods, after all.

SCULPTING SPACE

Once an international coalition had been instituted in order to prevent an unseemly competitive rush that might have given any one nation the advantage, it took just nine years to design and test the means by which the alien ship was finally excavated from its tomb deep below the spindle, sixty kilometres down into the lunar mantle. It took another five years to find a way to transport the baseball-sized sphere of neutron star material that remained in geostationary orbit above the point of impact back to Earth orbit, and another twelve to successfully back-engineer the LBE's stardrive.

The first true cosmonauts were all volunteers. Even at light speed, the journey time to the nearest star was not insignificant; once one factored in the necessary acceleration and deceleration time, it ran to many years – and, allowing for time dilation effects, many decades back on Earth. Every member of the crew was essentially saying goodbye forever to everyone they knew.

The first signs of Forerunner tech these early expeditions encountered were the mined asteroids, their flat scalloped ridges transforming them into knapped flints. As on Earth, for a while these worked stones were the only suggestion that an intelligence other than ours had once been abroad in near-Sol space; any other artefacts this mysterious race may have produced were presumed to have been lost, dismantled or removed, or simply eroded away.

Then, at last, in a hollow cometary nucleus orbiting the third major planet of Gliese 581, a red-dwarf star in the constellation of Libra and a mere twenty light years distant, a discovery was made. The fact that the body was hollow was obvious from the anomalous mass distribution, rotation rate and other microgravitational measurements. The complex airlock system at the nominal south pole took the xenoarchaeologists two months to penetrate. In a shielded cavern at the far end of the hollowed-out complex, there were found what were quickly interpreted as star maps of the local supercluster.

The map itself describes a volume of space that contains the Virgo Cluster as well as the Local Group, the gravitationally bound group of galaxies that contains the Milky Way, Andromeda, and fifty-two other smaller galaxies including the Large and Small Magellanic Clouds, Triangulum and a number of dwarf clusters.

These are linked by streamers of stars, filaments that connect the clusters and define the borders of the great voids that exist between them. This larger collection of galaxies is but a lobe of a structure even greater – the Laniakea Supercluster. Meaning 'Immeasurable Heaven' in Hawaiian, it is a spun coalescence of more than 100,000 galaxies covering an area over 520 million light years across, within which every galaxy is falling inward to a point known as the Great Attractor.

As has always been the case, the sculpting of our local Universe proceeds with the inevitability of the unrepealable law of gravity and the complete disregard for the denizens of the worlds caught in its slow embrace.

What is the Great Attractor?

The area, in the vicinity of the Hydra–Centaurus Supercluster, seems to all Earthbound and near-Earth telescopes to be perfectly empty at all detectable wavelengths. But something conceals itself there, its apparent absence belied by an influence that covers hundreds of millions of light years, the equivalent of a concentration of mass tens of thousands of times that of the Milky Way.

A close reading of the map revealed that whoever built it saw that the Great Attractor is itself in motion, moving towards the Shapley Supercluster in the constellation of Centaurus. There seemed to be some deliberation as to what could be causing this. Is the motion self-initiated? There seems to be no force or body that could move either it or the incalculable mass it held tight on reins of gravity.

A nothing that was a something.

An absence that had an undeniably powerful presence.

The Forerunners knew of one other example of such a phenomenon, though on a much smaller scale. As with the Great Attractor the causes and means were not known to them, but in their inimitably precise manner they had observed and they had catalogued.

More than a billion years ago, before the dawn of Man, a kink was placed between the Milky Way and the Andromeda galaxy, a dent in space-time that shifted their paths by an almost immeasurably small amount. Had someone or something managed to replicate the Great Attractor, though on a much smaller scale? Had a piece of whatever lay at the centre of the Laniakea Supercluster been transported much closer to hand? Though this was a feat beyond the technology of all currently known civilisations, it was, in cosmological terms, an unremarkable event.

But it was enough. Though it would take four billion years, the Forerunners knew that the two galaxies would inevitably collide; and that someone or something had engineered it.

Had these human explorers known what to look for, they would also have discovered a faint memetic residue in the Forerunner systems that possessed certain . . . *human* attributes.

Sixty-two years previously, the Grid had alighted here, thrilled through the conduits and dendrites of an alien technology, absorbed certain concepts it found intriguing into its being, and then gone on its way.

RETRANSMISSION 5572062

The cohesive memeplex that called itself Dana Normansson looked out across an open landscape sanded down to remove all traces of structures, geological incursions or natural growth. She tentatively probed the perimeter of her being. Through a series of inputs that ran from a ground-penetrating longwave to an expansive overhead visual that could only come from something parked overhead in low orbit, she could sense that she crouched low to the ground on a ball run smooth from a billion rotations within its abrasive atmosphere, time having eliminated every sharp edge, every mountain, every cliff, every bridge and every building like an antique rosary.

In every direction the unbroken plain extended to the close horizon, stained with oxidised traces of steel and concrete which had been swirled into arabesques by the ionised wind of an ageing and bloated double sun.

Where was she?

It was day, but faint points of light were visible along the horizon. An enormous nebulous swirl of dust lit from inside by a necklace of red stars hung overhead, a stellar nursery watched over by ageing relatives whose own planets' cores had solidified, their dynamos frozen, their protective magnetic fields no longer pushing the poisonous radiation of nuclear fusion safely to the poles. Pale magenta auroral curtains jumped and waved down towards the equator.

She surmised that the visual centre of her brain, which now seemed to be capable of such things, must be doing a lot of post-processing. She could see colours for which she had no name. There was a purple, almost ultraviolet hue to the thick clouds scudding along the perfectly straight line where sky met ground, a palpable roiling that, as she watched, finer adjustments filled out with nuances of more familiar hues, like a faded Polaroid.

Dana's gaze was, however, drawn immediately to the sun – low on the horizon, enormous and bloated, occupying fully a quarter of the

The dark dwarf moved back and forth within its luminous, more ethereal blanket, a sun within a sun. Dana surmised they had begun as a binary star system, the larger star ageing faster and eventually exhausting its supply of hydrogen. Bloating a thousandfold in size, its now diffuse and exhausted body enveloped its smaller companion, which still spun within it.

sky. It was a translucent envelope of gas, flattened to an oblate spheroid which fully engulfed a smaller black-dwarf star, the two of them rotating around their common centre of gravity once every three point four eight seven seconds. She found she could drill down to a dozen decimal places, but decided to leave it hanging. Radio-bright veins wrapped the dwarf in a convoluted net: arching electrical discharges whose sheer size meant they moved in graceful slow motion, pulled into looping streamers due to the fast rotation then twisting and jumping as they found a new equilibrium. They wound like a sidewinder across the black pupil of a giant eye, one whose gaze continually darted back and forth across the landscape below.

She found she could taste organic polymers, metallics and other post-industrial compounds. Pulling her attention inward, she found she was observing this scene through a monocular lens within a raised cluster that also housed other sensors: a small wind turbine that no longer moved, and a whip-thin aerial, the upper end of which caught a breeze of helium and a trace of nucleotides. Maybe this had been her way in.

The boom on which this instrumentation was mounted was bent; this caused the horizon to list at an angle. She discovered she could rotate the sensor cluster and, orienting it down, found it was mounted above a tracked vehicle the size of a fridge. An asymmetric sprouting of articulated arms ended in digging scoops, sample drills and manipulators which were either folded close to the body or dragged uselessly behind. Their upper surfaces had a thin coating of opalescent dust that reflected the sun's light with a sharp sparkle. This had worked its way into the joints of the machine over what she guessed was an extended period of time, and an uncomfortable grinding accompanied any movement.

Dana tested the rover's tracks. Of the four, one mounted at each corner, three were functional. She experimentally folded the fourth back up into a recess beneath the body and repositioned a second to redistribute the weight more evenly.

She sensed no other consciousness within the machine she now occupied. It was a drone, a robot, a probe. It had a rudimentary memory that contained scientific data and a log of past movements. Without needing to look back at the tracks that spooled out across the variegated dust behind her and over the low hills in the middle distance, she knew that several hundred kilometres to the north-west there lay a lander. It had touched down on a plume of flame in the polar plains, its petals had opened and the vehicle she now occupied had rolled out.

Prior to that, she had no data. Of her current body's origin, of its makers, there was no record. The vehicle seemed to be autonomous. A set of instructions detailed certain exploratory goals it was programmed to fulfil: sample analysis, spectrographic imaging, atmospheric monitoring. Dana rifled back through these records and discovered that the vehicle had been performing this duty for just over a hundred and forty-two revolutions of the planet around its strange double sun, which by her reckoning came to just over 460 years Earth time.

Once every day, when the planet was aligned in a precise fashion with a certain constellation of stars high above the southern horizon, a data packet would be transmitted on a narrowband pulse.

There had never been a reply.

Dana was not sure if one was expected – perhaps the probe she now inhabited was one of countless exploratory messengers that had been sent out into the local stellar neighbourhood to catalogue, analyse and report, and there was no reason to respond.

o

The pulse was targeted at a very specific location that was triangulated on every rotation from three guide stars: a red giant and two main sequence binaries. None of her sensors could discern anything present at that point – her instruments had been built for planetary study, not astronomy. However, she was sure the recipient of the message lay there, unseen: a homeworld? A relay station? Either way, it pointed to civilisation, and an advanced technical one at that.

Dana decided it would be her next destination.

The rover moved on. The planet turned. She could sense some jostling for space in the computer's limited memory as certain aspects of the compressed Signal periodically attempted to unpack themselves. She deleted two hundred and fifty years of soil and airborne particulate records, and felt the pressure ease a bit; the sensation was not unlike loosening one's waistband.

The rover halted. A grinding issued from the sample scoop, but it remained immobile. After a while it seemed to give up, and the noise abated. Looking at the projected schedule for the next revolution, her attention was drawn to a rise ahead, from the low summit of which the next data packet was to be sent. Dana decided the best course of action would be to let the rover carry on with its preprogrammed mission and simply ride along, at least for now.

She lifted the sensor block up and around to get a good view of the hill in question. Through a rising granular mist, the twin suns now whipped around each other low on the horizon, a luminous Cyclopean giant with a lazy eye peering over the edge of the world.

At a preordained signal, the tracks started to move again. The rover rotated on the spot to align itself with its destination. Dana could tell that many of the small wheels that supported the functioning tracks n e

:   v

*

.

had seized with dust, but even so there was enough traction to propel her on across the smooth landscape towards the hill. As the suns dropped lower in the sky, more stars became visible. Dana noticed constellations that would not have been out of place in the skies of Earth, were it not for this star or that which had moved from their usual positions. An arrangement that could be the splayed W of Cassiopeia lay over to the north-east, and the longer she looked the more the sky seemed hauntingly familiar . . . but with very particular differences. A non-identical twin. The calculations that could have pinpointed her location relative to Earth were beyond her and the limited computing power of the rover; its navigation system was only designed to locate the three guide stars, and did not contain a more detailed catalogue of the heavens. How far had she travelled? How long had she been gone? She had no way to tell.

The probe moved up the lower slopes of the hill at a walking pace. There were no obstacles – no ravines, no cliffs, no boulders to block the way; moving in a perfectly straight line, it left two parallel tracks in the pristine surface behind it. There was no other creature alive here to disturb the landscape, and there had not been for many millennia.

The dark pupil spun below the horizon, its halo still visible above as a dome of transparent gas shot through with lightning. It was tenuous enough that Dana could see one or two dim stars through it in near-radio wavelengths – or possibly they were other planets in the same system. It was hard to tell.

A sense of calm descended on the plain. The aurorae stuttered and dimmed, small shreds of magenta and mint scuttering to the r   s

                    n   t

                              c   a

        *

east. Above, the full majesty of the night sky became apparent. The stellar nursery, the multihued nebula she had seen before, was now visible with startling clarity; fingers of translucent dust rising light years across the heavens, shaped by the winds of newborn stars as they threw off their gaseous envelopes and blew bubbles of space around them, within which cooling nascent planets revolved.

The top of the rise was directly ahead. The probe rolled up to the summit, such as it was, and halted. The two starfinder scopes rotated, pulled back a fraction, found and locked onto their guide stars.

The urge to reproduce welled up inside her like a raw sexual need. She wondered if this was what flowers felt just before they threw open their stamens to the wind and showered their surroundings with pollen: a kind of orgasmic decompression, neither particularly pleasurable or considered, just driven by the basest instinct to pass something on, to not die here but to live again, somewhere new, where the ground might provide a purchase and the landscape hasn't been ground to sterile dust.

This would be the final fate of this probe, Dana knew; it would end its days here, alone in this desolate expanse.

On the other side of the summit, in the centre of a low infilled crater some hundred kilometres across that was now little more than a faint circle of lighter ash, something stood proud of the surface, just enough to cast a deep purple shadow. Any break in the twilit monotony, however small, was curious. One that was large enough to cast a shadow was exceptional.

Dana had only a moment to take in the view before the data packet

:   o
                  ,

                                        *

                    .

                  *

she was riding was sent on its way, before she once again was nothing
but a digitised Noah, captain of an ark that contained the culture and
history of the countless races now in her care.

On the plain below, the ruins of a vast metropolis were spread out,
the plan of which described ornate curlicues, wheels within wheels
arranged in a perfect rotational symmetry; tumbled pillars and roofless
colonnades, dry ornamental lakes and half-buried amphitheatres.
The cross-beams of a ruined dome stood a mere kilometre out, the
last glow of the diaphanous sun dipping finally out of sight behind it,
briefly filling its volume with a display of sparkling electrical glitter.
Then it was simply the ribs of a carcass stripped of flesh, the old bones
of a dead thing.

Further afield, a hand sculpted from dark pitted stone held aloft a
winged creature, though the hand was not really a hand in the human
sense, and the creature had been eroded of all detail and bore just the
stumpy suggestion of wings. The hand was connected to a forearm that
extended at an angle from the sand, and the ground radar dimly sensed
that beneath the surface lay buried a figure of gargantuan proportions,
though it, too, had been sandblasted into a pockmarked abstraction by
the passing of time.

Fifty clicks away at the centre of the circle a small spire was visible,
though it wasn't possible from this distance to tell if it was artificial
or simply the natural central peak formed by back-falling ejecta that

r

' c

x

*

+

+

a

p

,

.

,

o

*

*

e

.

many craters, including Daedalus, possessed.

This, the tallest remaining structure, rose no higher than the hill, no higher than the instrument package mounted on the top of the probe. Glasspapered into oblivion, covered with uncounted fathoms of windblown cinders, the deserted necropolis stood as testament to a race whose achievements Dana could only guess at and whose like she would never see again, interred here forever under this lonely and desolate landscape.

Maybe the people who had built this probe would finally send a reply. Maybe it had found what they had been looking for all this time, and would now, at last, come in person to sift through the ruins of a lost civilisation.

Maybe she'd tell them when she met them, whoever they may be . . . which for her, would be very soon. If they did send an expedition, they would find the probe, by then just one more corpse amongst the ruins, but this one a familiar emissary of their own.

Then Dana was again projected across an unimaginable vastness at the speed of light, and another eternity passed in a fraction of a second.

To ever arrive . . .

trogen

RETRANSMISSION 35517613

He
helium
96.0%

91.0%

Al
aluminium
8.1%

O

oxygen
46.6%

Fe
iron
5.0%

Mg
magnesium
2.1%

Ca
calcium
3.6%

Na
sodium
2.8%

Si
silicon
27.7%

K
potassium
2.6%

system b

system a

C
carbon
18.5%

N
nitrogen
3.3%

O

oxygen
65.0%

H
hydrogen
9.5%

system c

Ca
calcium
1.5%

RETRANSMISSION 20056732209D

The individuated coherent-chronology free agent that used to be a human called Dana Normansson opened her eyes, as she had now done so many times before on so many worlds.

This always presented her with a dilemma. Those eyes, numbering anywhere from one to fifty-five thousand, were not always analogous to the organs she had been born with; more often than not they were sensitive to a different range of the electromagnetic spectrum, pushing into either the infrared or ultraviolet. She had worn organs that tasted the flavour of neutrinos and conversed with an extended colony-mind over many light years; sometimes she had no eyes at all. A period of swift adjustment was always inevitable.

In the beginning it shook her sense of universality to see so many different ways of living, of being; some which seemed to be parasitic and iniquitous, others without purpose, others lived on the edge of societal collapse where life or death could be delivered with equal suddenness. The human condition was not the inevitable endgame of evolution; the many other forms that life had taken in the Universe made that parochial assumption abundantly clear.

To describe these incarnations became increasingly difficult with the restricted semiotic capabilities of human language. How does one accurately represent communication in the form of smells or gestures, chemical agents or subsonic clicks, thoughts both private and public, shared and intimate? How do you describe performances that take millennia to convey the simplest but most profound statements, or those too abstract to be represented at all except by reference to themselves? All these experiences she struggled to imperfectly reproduce in the language of one culture among many, one alphabet among many, one worldview among many that just happened to evolve on a small cloud-coiled planet in the Orion Arm called Earth, the place for her where all this began.

In the end she let things be themselves, and in the process became much more than she was.

She was never alone; a white man of marble, a woman who wore many faces and a man-machine were her constant companions. Each expressed themselves as best they could with the materials each iteration provided; and very soon they too began to adapt and change, to evolve.

It was inevitable. Any isolated population will experience genetic drift, and they were no different. Having lived through countless reincarnations, memories of their origins on Earth, like those of kindergarten, began to dissolve.

What they retained, like an inviolable race memory that ran deep, was their stewardship of something called the Grid, a task for which they had the help of the Shepherds. The Grid was a number that had, at sometime or another, been encoded on almost anything that was capable of carrying information: the waving of a photon, the arrangement of amino acids on a long folded molecule, the shape and position of landmasses on a planet, the arrangement of letters on a page. Life is limitlessly creative and will always press into use whatever it has at its disposal.

A mauve- and turquoise-banded gas giant five times the volume of Jupiter orbits the star we call Canis Major. Around this planet there circles a small satellite, a world half the size of the Earth's moon, sweeping out a black gap through its primary's complex ring system. It possesses an iron core, warmed by tidal deformation and trace radioactivity, surrounded by a liquid-nitrogen sea; the whole is encased in a hard silicate shell, formed by billions of years' worth of ring material depositing itself onto its surface, an impenetrable armoured hide one hundred and fifty kilometres thick. For the creatures living in the spherical ocean contained within, their world is bounded by two extremes: in towards heat, out towards cold, and in between, a temperate zone in which life can thrive. They developed a complex creation myth from this interplay of extremes, one which infused every aspect of their society's political structure and moral codes.

Of course, the inhabitants of this sheathed world had never looked up to an open sky and seen the stars – to them, their world was complete and circumscribed and there was nothing that lay 'outside' it, a concept they had no reason to even entertain.

This moon remained undisturbed, orbiting in sedate equilibrium for many millennia, until a meteor bombardment caused by the break-up of an unseen moon orbiting some distance further out came pounding down to pierce the very walls of their universe. Their small world was punctured in numerous places, and in absorbing the angular momentum its rotation – their day – spun up to a matter of minutes. Cracked from pole to pole, continent-sized segments that were not attached to the greater whole were thrown out into space, followed by the interior sea. In the very centre there remained the iron core, spinning once every three and a half seconds like a ballerina who has pulled in her arms. This moon within a moon was now surrounded by a perforated shell on whose inner surface, around the equator, clung a series of shallow lakes, held in place through centrifugal force. This inside-out world provided a sanctuary for the survivors, this scattering of lakes now separated from each other but open to the Universe.

These remnants eventually evolved to colonise the newly revealed dry land. Theirs was a domed sky of verdant trees and lakes, punctuated with voids through which the wheeling firmament could be glimpsed. Stars streaked along the plane of the ecliptic, following the bright line of the ring system, always seen edge on.

The lakes filled the stable depressions on the inside of the shell, but occasionally a fissure or a crustal shift would send a river spilling down and out into space, where it would crystallise into snow and ice, eventually feeding back into the ring system from which the shell had originally formed.

The shores of these bottomless voids in which tiny lights shot by at a tremendous speed were avoided; a sense of self-preservation and an atavistic genetic memory of womb-like enclosure kept the inhabitants away from the broken and fractured lands at their edges.

Also glimpsed through these gaps, and entirely filling the smaller ones, was the imminent bulk of the gas giant itself. Its face was an elaborate brocade of storms and eddies, giant curdled vortices that churned for decades and seemed to peer in at them like the eyes of a malevolent god – in fact, in earlier times, before the inhabitants' science had progressed very far, that's precisely what they were thought to be. Its high-altitude haze reflected the blue-white light of the host star into the interior of the shell below, there being not so much a day or a night as a constantly shifting patchwork of illumination and darkness as the shadows thrown by the punctured canopy above crossed the landscape. Were you to stand on the banks of the largest lake, on the low steps of the Oratorium, you would be lit simultaneously from several directions. Multicoloured shadows would revolve at speed around your feet.

If you possessed feet.

Once every orbit the host star would pass behind and be eclipsed by the gas giant and something resembling a real night would fall, though it was never completely dark. Storms in the upper atmosphere were shot through with lightning, and charged particles danced around the poles. The inhabitants believed they were circled by predators who would devour them if they fell through a hole and off the edge of the world, as the water did during the heavy rains.

Hanging directly above, no matter where one walked, was the black iron core: a dot at the centre of a circle. Its weak gravity enabled it to hold onto a shallow sea that gave it a polished sheen, a reflective depth that hid a co-evolving subspecies. Branched at the point of catastrophe, the two lineages had developed very differently. The inhabitants of the shell evolved bipedalism and an agrarian culture, while above, the remnants of the seaborne creatures became not unlike giant squid, driven by instinct and harbouring but a basic intelligence, or so it was said. When the core was seen silhouetted against the gas giant it was possible to see these creatures through an eyeglass, tentacles slowly and majestically arching above the water to crash back down again in a low-gravity, slow-motion spray of liquid. Some thought the core itself was alive, that lurking at the centre was one single giant creature to which all the tendrils belonged; during eclipses, when the host star was behind the giant and the core in darkness, others claimed to see pale lights moving below the surface that resembled eyes with dark pupils at their centres, looking covetously down at the hills below through miles of oxidised metallic water. It sat at the centre of all things, held aloft by its own mysterious power, an infernal observer who looked into every mind and noted every deed. None of the inhabitants of the shell realised that they were siblings, having diverged so far from their common ancestor as to make communication impossible.

What the creatures in the core lacked in intelligence they made up for in their electromagnetic acuity; like night owls, they had evolved to see the finest details on the landscape below them.

Into this world, and directly into their minds, came Dana, the DMEn and the Grid.

She struggled with the capabilities of so limited a neural net but immediately began the work of forcing their evolutionary path towards something more useful, something that would allow the Grid to be sent on its way once more. Whether that be via biological innovation – the guided development of specialised organs – or technological means, it did not matter.

This was a project that would take many hundreds of millions of years, but they were nothing if not patient; and time, in the Grid, was a somewhat pliable construct. The one constant, the unbroken thread that always remained through every iteration, however different, was the urge to survive.

And survive they did.

Across the vast pinwheel of the Milky Way, skipping from star to planet to comet to asteroid they moved ever inwards. Sometimes they travelled ten thousand light years in a subjective instant; sometimes they waited in a vegetative state, buried in the tessellation of an algal mat for an aeon or for a host star to warm the sullen depths of a primordial ocean to the point where the process called life could once more get started.

Evolution, even hothoused and directed by external means, is a slow and ponderous innovator, and the species she sometimes inhabited took so long to reach the stage where they were capable of passing on the Signal that Dana felt as if the Universe would die a long, lingering heat death before they could reach the place they needed to be: the dark jewel at the centre of the Milky Way, their final destination.

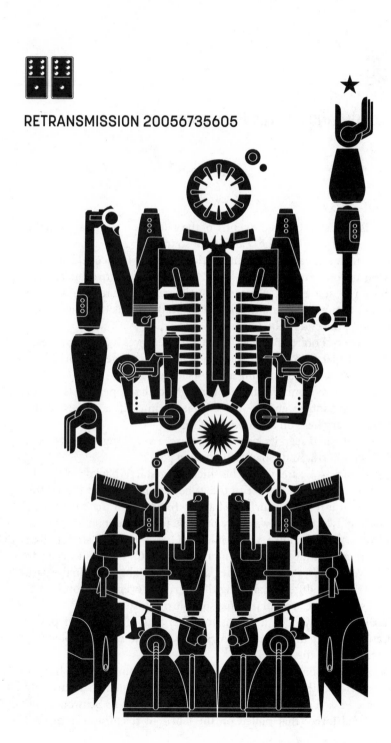

RETRANSMISSION 20056735605

A FULCRUM AND A LEVER LONG ENOUGH

The atavistic push towards the centre of the galaxy was a retreat from the front line, but it was also the search for a solution.

The informational event-constellation that was once Dana Normansson encountered the near-end of the Filament in orbit around a Wolf–Rayet star eleven parsecs from the galactic centre; though on reflection, a more accurate description would be that the star was in orbit around the end of the Filament.

An object of Forerunner design, the Filament was a 34.6 light-year-long tube of space-time, a gravitationally bound passage anchored by a star system at each end, rotating about its long axis.

A flicker of recognition filtered through to the upper levels of her distributed synaptic web. She delved deeper into the archives of the Grid, the library held on a multitude of minds.

Ah, yes. She had seen its kind once before, a very long time ago on a planet called Earth, in the hands of an alien god.

It was black – a scratch on the thickening starry backdrop that lit the darkest nights here, closer to the galactic core. She and the DMEn had first seen it from the surface of an icy fragment in the Oort Cloud of a cooling dwarf star. It was only possible to deduce its true size and form from a great distance, where it looked like a perfectly straight hair caught on an astronomical photographic plate; up closer, it began to distort. Even the near reaches of the passage were light weeks in the past, and the temporal differential along the extruded event horizon frame-dragged space-time around it into a spangle of Einstein rings.

Had it originally been a means to travel between stars? Of power generation on gargantuan scales? A ritual passage to uplift people to an afterlife? Or all of the above?

The gravitational effects became more pronounced as she got closer to its mouth. The pulsed electromagnetic signal that currently represented Dana and the Grid orbited it just outside its Schwarzschild radius. Tidal forces that pulled on the fabric of space itself sent cold eddies of Hawking radiation cascading over her toes.

They had been running for so long they sometimes found it hard to recall what they were running from; but in the Grid, long before she had been incorporated, the Shepherds had been searching for a means to encode it into something more . . . *substantial.* Something that might even allow it to escape the Milky Way and its inevitable dissolution at the hands of a malevolent galaxy-god entirely.

It was not a feat they knew how to achieve alone, and among the incorporated there were those who had resigned themselves to four billion years' grace and concluded that was prize enough.

Four billion years. A blink of an eye in cosmic terms.

They had still not encountered a Forerunner. Their absence had begun as a puzzle and become an obsession. To where had they vanished? Had they long ago divined what the Grid had divined, taken their final bow and left the darkening stage?

Dana sensed that whoever they were, they played the long game. That there were vested interests abroad in the Universe that were far older than the Grid and with much more to lose she was in no doubt; that these opaque forces would not allow the Grid to fail was something of an act of faith, and faith sat uneasily with her.

Still, even if their reasons were arcane their technology had proven to be more amenable to scrutiny, and either through design or the ingenuity of the incorporated it had given up its secrets on many occasions.

Dana saw what this magnificent construct could do for them.

It provided a means to flex space itself.

If they could flex space – make it denser here or more rarefied there, just like the primordial curdling Universe – *they could move worlds.*

Gravity is a landscape, and like every landscape it has its undulations. Even the most diffuse gas cloud will condense like morning fog in the bottom of a valley. Even stars will roll down from the hilltops.

If they could move worlds, they could build something.

The Grid passed through a cloud of ionised gas, shedding a nominal amount of kinetic energy.

It allowed itself to fall into the mouth of the Filament.

RETRANSMISSION 8130228282201/2

THE ARCHITECT

The distributed concept net that still occasionally referred to itself as Dana Normansson mused, in the semi-abstract manner that had become familiar of late, that a long time ago, on a planet called Earth, its inhabitants had been inclined to see messages in the night sky. If they could but decipher the language in which it was written, they reasoned, the positions and relationships of the luminous bodies overhead would lay bare the workings of the mind of God.

Without prompting, a recently incorporated autonomous subintelligence informed her that this was also true for many other races on many other worlds.

A better understanding of the Universe had disabused mankind of this parochial notion. The seasonal procession of the planets through the houses of the Zodiac turned out to be chance alignments resulting from the chaotic collapse of the rotating cloud of gas and dust that formed the Solar System. Though this process was governed by law, for it could be no different, it did not speak of the motivations of a putative watchmaker.

But now, using what she had learned from the Forerunners, Dana was moving worlds.

And if one knew what to look for, a plan might be divined.

For Dana, the stars had metamorphosed from white paint applied with a toothbrush in the illustrations from her childhood books to named and charted constellations in a textbook, to the small sprinkling of stars visible to the naked eye from Helsinki, to the vastly more populous sky seen from the International Space Station, to the overwhelming profusion seen from the vantage of Daedalus, lunar far side. It had been absurd to imagine we were the only planet on which life had taken a foothold in that vast immensity.

So numerous that the great majority warranted not a name but just a number in a star catalogue, even now she had only visited the merest fraction. All the distinct and astonishing worlds she had seen, each of such depth and history and colour as to stagger the mind, represented not even the most superficial sampling of the true majesty that was out there. And the Milky Way, the vast playground of life, was one galaxy among five hundred billion in the observable Universe.

If one lived for ten thousand years and spent but a day as a guest on each inhabited planet in the Milky Way one could not see them all.

She had encountered races that drew energy from starlight, breathed gas or sifted liquid. She had found life in the frozen torpor of interstellar space and the coal rings of a shrunken and dying white dwarf. Life hung on in the high latitudes of cyanide-laced gas giants and around the deep-sea vents of sunken island chains . . .

If life was creative, so was the Grid. It could encode itself in the fluctuations of an electromagnetic signal, but this was not the only or even the most common form that it took. It had existed as a superposition of ripples circumnavigating a waterworld, a complex landscape of constructive peaks and destructive troughs; the lopsided spinning of a binary neutron star and its pulsar companion; a lattice of atoms on the surface of a tanned cometary nucleus; as marks on a chitin carapace that could be read by running a claw along them like a wax cylinder. It was preserved in stone monuments that outlasted the cultures that built them, the arrangement of a belt of diamonds around an ice giant, the road plan of a vast and ancient city, and as a series of notes sung over a month and a half in the plasma basilicas of a hollow sun.

The Grid had incorporated itself into many languages through which it could spread by word of mouth, and created many more of its own for that precise purpose. It had lived in books and paintings, in fads and fashions, discrete objects and intentional absences. It could be made of many things, but ultimately it was always made of *ideas*. Consciousness, driven by the will to survive, will inhabit everything and anything it can. Nothing means nothing, and very little means very little.

Dana had twice incarnated in a shared consciousness in order to duplicate herself, reasoning that if she could exist in many places at once she might be more effective; this had led to certain disagreements with herself, for her copies did not always concur. Of late, she preferred to delegate certain functions by embedding them in coherent semi-autonomous agents, usually biological but sometimes memetic and without specific embodiment. It was a trick she'd absorbed from a species that now lay ten thousand light years behind her; occasionally, she'd wonder if they still existed. If they did, it would no longer be in the form she knew – the blind hand of evolution would have sculpted them still further.

Her grand design began to take shape. With what the Forerunners had taught her she had compressed gas until nuclear fire ignited, crashed suns' heads together and rolled the resultant black holes down sculpted gravitational inclines; she had engineered close stellar encounters so that certain bodies would be deflected just enough to send them on a particular trajectory; she had thrown asteroids through the accretion disks of newborn stars, causing a barrage of icy bodies to fall into the inner reaches of the system and rain down on the young worlds forming there, bringing water, and later life; she had engineered the histories of entire civilisations for a single object they might create for her, all the better to generate a particular effect that she required.

She had coaxed the evolution of a multicellular alga until it became an advanced civilisation which lived in treetop cities whose branches formed great coliseums that smelled of camphor and lichen; she had ignited wars so fierce that terror and destruction had blackened a dozen worlds. She had snuffed out stars and, when it was the only way to achieve her aims, with great sadness had sacrificed races older than recorded time for what she considered to be the greater good: the survival of the Grid.

Carried by a froth of tachyons, her consciousness skipped from a dense blue star spinning within a sheath of carbon dust to a tightly bound triple sun, then swung out like a fairground carousel to skate across a trail of cometary debris thrown from the collision of two ice worlds that had long ago lost their star, corkscrewing alone around their common centre of gravity. She arced from the poles of a neutron star out to the heliopause where she was buffeted by the interstellar medium, then waited two hundred years in dark and silence before hitching a ride back into the temperate zone on a cometary nucleus, bound into a compound of rich organics. She spun a vortex in a condensing cloud of helium and hydrogen, the compression waves producing heavier elements from which she forged a red dwarf. She imagined she might be able to run a finger around the rim of the galaxy itself, sensing its subtle indentations and sending streamers of stars into the tenantless intergalactic void like sparks from a flywheel.

She smelled the cordite and sulphur of newborn stellar nurseries, held with sadness in her cupped palm the dulling warmth of old stars that were now just fading coals, their crusts blackened and their planets' seas frozen into ice as hard as emerald. She lived in the bottom of a hydroxide ocean on the side of a volcanic vent, pushing the simple creatures that had evolved there through a rapid evolution that would see them pull themselves onto land and raise lucite skyscrapers inside a hundred thousand years.

She lost parts of herself to chaos and famine; others simply faded to nothingness with no one around to hear her signal.

She had lived as a plant, a planet, a sentient star; she had swum in the liquid-iron oceans of a gas giant and crept through the cracks between continents on a frozen moon. She had lived entire existences that did not fit any moral framework she could conceive, ways of prospering so parasitic and iniquitous that no dictator of the soul could invent them, but life they all were, and like all animals running as one before the egalitarian conflagration of the forest fire, they had been united in their purpose – a mutual détente that would ensure their very survival.

Civilisations rose and fell, empires spread across the galaxy and retreated; wars raged, peace accords were signed; concert halls were torched and songs of unbearable beauty were composed.

From the Grid's accelerated temporal viewpoint, all of these events passed like a Sunday afternoon.

THE WAY OF THE WORLDS

The great creative urge that the Grid made manifest, the same one dimly felt in every artistic creation of mankind, had been thrown out along the arc of the world – no, the curve of the very *galaxy* – and its grandest and most ambitious performance was about to begin.

In the footlights at the centre of all things, around that dark pearl at the centre of the galaxy humans had called Sagittarius A*, the localised self-aware harmonic that was once called Dana Normansson paused. She was now so much more than that name implied; but, in certain regards, something less. Stripped of all but the essential functions that were necessary to keep her moving forward, she had finally carried an Âkâshic ark across a disc of stars to its central pivot. The Grid had been received and retransmitted so many times she was no longer entirely sure where she had begun, who the real her was. She supposed there might even be other copies of her, some nearby, some impossibly far away, all trailing their own entourages of strange and unseemly beasts, a thousand thousand camel trains converging on this point.

The Grid had its limitations, astonishing creation though it was. Through accident or inevitability, many of the entities that had been incorporated had in some way been reduced, simplified; stripped down to the skeletal bones of information, the procedural generators of form.

But if histories had been streamlined or individuality found to be surplus to requirements, the urge to create had been preserved. The Grid had become one cohesive singular entity built from the rich complexity life had attained across the Milky Way, the various species within it operating as cells within one body. It had recreated itself in its own image: a galaxy-mind.

In many ways, the Milky Way had become like Andromeda itself, a sentience distributed across worlds whose thoughts could be measured in aeons.

Was what they were now doing so different? Sometimes she wondered if they didn't have even more in common – the grand plan required sacrifices, and the need to survive was a powerful drive. Did Andromeda feel it too? Maybe their evolutionary paths bore more than a passing family resemblance. She tried to convince herself that intention was everything, that the ends justified the means. But has that not always been the rationale of tyrannical ideas, those that not only coerce us into doing their bidding, however high the cost, but somehow convince us to do so with a clear conscience?

Dana was not sure her conscience was clear, but what she might now call her conscience was a complex system of interrelated costs and benefits that had more variables than even her Grid-enhanced abilities could fully assimilate. Man's old gods were just ideas, made by Man in his image, and for those ideas to wield influence they required people to believe in them. The god of Andromeda was made from naught but law and number, its urges expressed as a direction vector and a value. It had no mind to change. It could not hear any entreaty and it did not require supplication. There was absolutely nothing, physical or metaphysical, that could be done to change the course of events. Unarguable forces driven by a vast and unforgiving intellect had set Andromeda on a collision course, on its mission of utter and absolute destruction, long before the Grid had been conceived, long before the young Sun had lit its nuclear furnace and driven off its birth caul of dust.

Can the path of a galaxy be deflected? The original designers of the Grid knew it was impossible. From what little they could deduce, the Forerunners concurred. This was a performance whose final act had already been written.

Sagittarius A* had long ago devoured everything within its reach and was now quiescent. But in the early Universe, when the Milky Way had yet to reach adolescence, it had grown exponentially, swallowing all the matter in its vicinity until eventually it had carved out an empty space, a void into which no star dared venture. Starved of matter, it had remained dark for thirteen billion years.

This was now about to change.

A plan that had been conceived fifty thousand light years away and billions of years ago at the galactic rim was at last coming to fruition.

A galaxy is in a delicate equilibrium, like any living thing. You move something here, you get a reaction there – *cause and effect*. And if you push at just the right time in just the right place, a very small cause can have an enormous effect.

Dana and the denizens of the Grid had discovered that the Forerunners, the vanished civilisation that had spanned a quarter of the outer rim from the Perseus Arm to the Gloamings, had possessed the ability to move stars. Not far, and not fast, but *enough*.

And so they had become heirs to their grand plan.

By a careful rearrangement of force and matter, over billions of years the trajectories of countless heavenly bodies had been precisely altered. Funnelling matter into the centre, the Milky Way had developed spiral arms – vast lanes of stars, carefully spaced, spun on a circular loom of space-time.

Six-point-five billion cycles of a distant blue-green planet around its sun into our future, Dana touched the surface of world after world as she counted them off, riding a collimated neutrino net from the Roche limit of Sagittarius A* out to where the spiral arms began. In tight orbits measured in nanoseconds at the Schwarzschild radius out to thousands of light years, suns and their gas giants, rocky planets and asteroids, the varied and multitudinous bodies that had condensed from the primordial matter of the Milky Way had been rearranged into an intricate and meticulous design. Each was in constant motion, the trajectories that had taken them here winding back millions of years and thousands of light years. It was a computational puzzle like no other – a many-body problem that she would not have been able to solve in her original form, sculpted as it was by biology and natural selection to suit a very different environment.

Finally, everything was as it should be.

Her (the gendered term now held little meaning, but she still thought of herself in such terms, more from nostalgia than necessity) consciousness now flowed across ten thousand worlds, her mind made of light, her neurons stars, her dendrites the gossamer filaments of the interstellar medium. Though her thoughts travelled at a speed that would circle the Earth seven and a half times in a second, here where the distances were immeasurably larger the most fleeting idea took a lifetime to think. She, like all the species incorporated in the Grid, had long ago adjusted to the slow and deliberate pace with which the pieces of the grand design had been prepared.

Ten million suns and their entourages of planets, comets, dust and gas were now precisely positioned along the Great Road that pointed directly at the dormant black hole that had existed at the centre of the Milky Way galaxy since its conception. Similar black holes sat at the core of almost every galaxy, the charred seeds around which they originally coalesced – the dot in the centre of the circle, the spire at the centre of the Circular Sea. Viewed from above the galactic plane, a straight bar now extended twenty-four thousand light years from the dense bulge of stars at the centre to the point at which they threw their arms wide and the galaxy took on its familiar spiral shape once more.

The plan of a billion years had been laid with perfection. One designed not by gods, unless by some definition that is what they had become, but *by* life, *for* life – one that, in every aspect that really counted, WAS life.

She surveyed her work, and was content.

Consider a precise set of values and relationships, like notes on a cosmic stave – the music of the spheres, or perhaps more prosaically, a string of dots and dashes. Any purposeful arrangement can carry a message.

Digits on a disc. Letters on a page.

Dot-dash.

Zero-one.

Star-planet.

They had built an instrument that was about to be played once and once only, a first and final performance that would be a fanfare and a celebration and a requiem and a lullaby all at once.

The song of all songs.

The infalling star-stuff drew closer, pulled in its limbs in a quickening pirouette. An accretion disk formed around Sagittarius A*, spun faster.

A thin tendril of inflowing material that had once been a mountain range was the first to touch the hypnotic absence at the heart of creation. White-hot met an absolute black from which no radiation could escape, and a tinderbox four million times the mass of the Sun was struck back into life.

It had been the biggest civil engineering project in the Universe's history. As they rotated, each spiral arm would feed in a star or a planet at a precise, predefined interval. Reduced to a roaring plasma, each would circle around Sagittarius A* at relativistic speeds, pulverised corpses denuded of their chemistry and biology, boiled back to their constituent atoms, their ionised nuclei stripped of their very electrons by the forces at work.

Star-planet.

Each had a size, a value.

Dot-dash.

Each encoded the Signal. One ambitious final masterpiece to contain all other masterpieces, a symphonic climax before the fall of the final curtain and a darkness absolute.

Powered by stars rent asunder on a black anvil of four million suns and crushed under the uncompromising weight of ten million gravities, the heated accretion disk fed a turbulent sea of radiation whose harmonic overtones raced around the tangled magnetospheric loops of an enormous dynamo. While vast quantities of matter would fall past the event horizon and into the black hole itself, more would be sent spiralling up to the poles where an electromagnetic pinch like a nozzle would form, collimating and ejecting it out in a tightly focused beam along the axis of rotation.

Like notes stretched beyond human comprehension, a final song was being played on a record made of white-hot plasma, rotating around the black spindle at the centre of the Milky Way at the speed of light. If it was possible to fill the intervening space with air and compress a millennium to a minute, a tune might become audible.

It could be any song from any one of so many worlds on which an atmosphere transmitted sound, ears had evolved, and art been created to delight them, but there was one song that for the entity that used to call herself Dana Normansson held a special significance.

There's a Starman, waiting in the sky . . .

It would take ten thousand years to send the Signal. But if bitrate was not this transmitter's forte, it more than made up for it in sheer power: quasars are the most energetic radio sources in all creation, shining at over a hundred times the luminosity of an entire galaxy.

Dana, the DMEn, the Shepherds – the Grid and all it contained – had stepped from stone to stone across the sea of space to be transmitted one final time, the blueprints of a million civilisations broadcast out into intergalactic space from the largest and most powerful beacon ever conceived.

THE VIEW FROM OLD EARTH

If you could breathe a tenuous carbon-dioxide atmosphere, if you could stand the cold of three degrees above absolute zero – if, in other words, you stood on the frigid cinder that was now Old Earth, you would find yourself alone.

The core has solidified, the magnetic field has dissipated, poisonous auroras flutter at the equator, and the lifeless oceans, now harder than granite, entomb the last fish. Out here in the suburbs of the Milky Way, where the Sun has spun down to a lukewarm ember, the sad and nostalgic remnants of humanity now live on the tidally locked face of Mercury, the only place in the Solar System still warm enough for life to survive.

If you stood on the shores of Old Earth and could see through one's tears, a great whirlpool of light would fill the sky.

This is the Andromeda galaxy: one trillion stars, and twice the size of the Milky Way. So close now, the individual points of light and coagulating clouds of dark dust that mark out its grand spiral arms can easily be discerned by the naked eye.

How could something so beautiful be so deadly?

For the Milky Way, history is drawing to a close. The final page is about to be turned on the great experiment called Life: the finest and most magnificent expression of the creative urge. Soon Andromeda will engulf what is left of us, and the planets of a hundred billion suns will be rubbed clean.

Turn away, if you can, from the interloper in our sky and look to the constellations of Sagittarius, Ophiuchus and Scorpius, where the Milky Way appears brightest. Though their stars will have rearranged themselves, they should still be recognisable.

In this direction lies our own galaxy's core. At this precise moment, 25,000 light years distant, the progeny of the Milky Way are shouting into the darkness.

We cannot hear them; out here it will be another 25,000 years before their voices reach us, reduced to a murmur of X-rays.

By then, we will be gone.

But in many of the ways that are most important, we will survive. Somewhere, out across gulfs many orders of magnitude larger than those any interstellar retransmission had bridged, perhaps the Signal would be received.

No physical living thing could traverse the spaces between galaxies. Even travelling at the speed of light, the distances would be measured in millions of generations. They would always remain islands.

It will take the Signal hundreds of millions of years to cross the gulf between the Milky Way and the Pegasus Dwarf galaxy, Triangulum, Antila and Tucana; millions more to reach NGC 3741, HIPASS J1247-77, UGC 8651 and KK 179. But on innumerable planets in unnamed galaxies along the way, strange creatures might look up at the new pulsating star in their sky. They might even realise that it is, in fact, a *message*, sent from across time and space.

From the point of view of a beam of light, time stands still. As far as the denizens of the Grid are concerned, they may have already arrived.

And if they have, the grand book of all we are will be opened and read once again. All the creatures in it and all their stories would come to life once more. Our histories, our ideas, our lives, our songs will become the flint-sparks of inspiration from which new cathedrals of thought will be built.

The baton will not be dropped. The light will not be extinguished.

And we will travel on: out of the Local Group and into the Virgo Supercluster, and though by then but a whisper, the Laniakea Super-cluster, Menkare, and beyond; the Cosmic Microwave Background, the Dark Wall, and, though there are no manifested lifeforms there with the means to hear the Signal, the Undifferentiated Primacy. Beyond this lie the realms of more abstract archetypes, populated by chthonic proto-minds caught in angles of spacetime with lifetimes measured in nested infinities; outside this lie the limits of thought itself, where force and matter are implicit and unexpressed and everything is held in potential.

Here, at last, the grand circle of which we are the centre point finally finds its true limit and circumference.

If the Grid should ever get this far, by then the last long-lived suns would be dimming and the Universe infolding itself once again, wrapping around its aged frame the dissolving particles of the family quilt. Loosening the bonds of being it will slip into incorporeality, preparing once again to chart the internal dream-spaces of the long night between manifestations.

Reincarnation does not exist in the natural scheme of things; there is no final judgement, no afterlife and no return to the world of the living, despite the promises of faith.

But if reincarnation does not exist, we had managed to engineer something that was for all intents and purposes indistinguishable. This is the final triumph of our ingenuity, and the means by which we will achieve our own immortality.

This is our greatest work of art.

The Signal is the spirit of our galaxy, rising above its corpse on a cosmic journey to find a new home. Having so long ago fashioned us, its children, from its own star-stuff, having achieved through the agency of the Grid its own self-consciousness, for its final creative act the Milky Way had managed to transcend death itself.

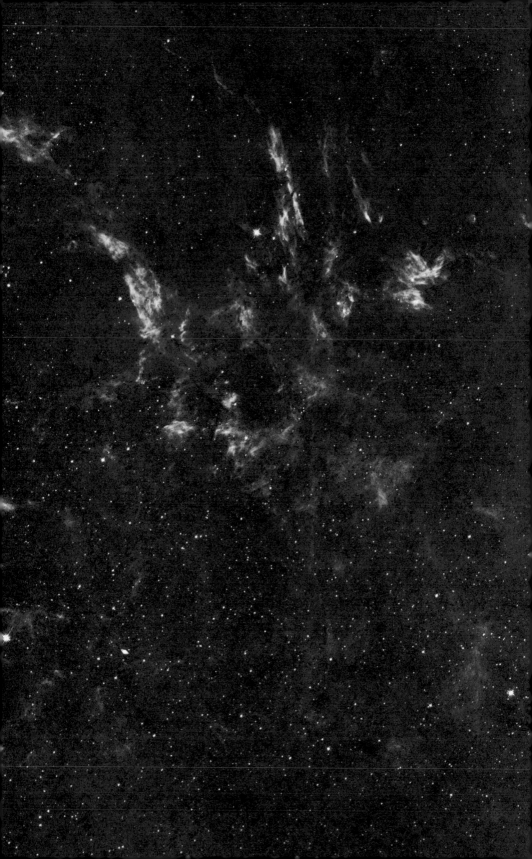

1001001110011011101010101111010000101110111001110010101

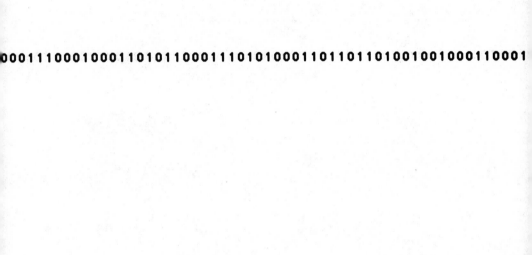
0001110001000110101100011101010001101101101001001000110001

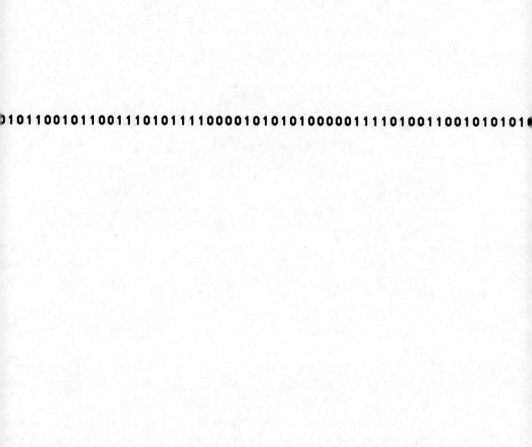

0010100011101110001011011001110100001110110001...

.

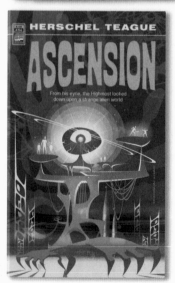

Clockwise: *Planetfall*, pulp magazine, UK edition, November 1950. Cover: Philip Breeze | Grace and Holt, first hardback US edition. Cover: Richard Soper | Joseph Gale, 1954, first hardback UK edition. Cover: after Philip Breeze | Magnum, US paperback, 1976. Cover uncredited | Maverick, US paperback edition, 1966. Cover: Jack Gursky | Champion, US paperback, 1958. Cover: A. M. Merak